The Best of *Best Short Stories* 1986–1995

Giles Gordon was born in Edinburgh in 1940. He
has published ten novels and collections of stories.
He has also edited and co-edited twenty
collections of short stories and compiled for the
British Council a bibliography of *The British
Twentieth-Century Short Story*. Like David
Hughes, he is a Fellow of the Royal Society of
Literature. His memoirs, *Aren't We Due a Royalty
Statement?*, were published in 1993.

David Hughes was born in Hampshire in 1930.
He was educated at KCS Wimbledon and Christ
Church, Oxford, where he read English. He is
fiction reviewer for the *Mail on Sunday*. His
better-known novels include *The Pork Butcher*, for
which he won the W.H. Smith Award, and *But
For Bunter*. His latest work, *The Little Book*, is to
be published soon.

The Best of *Best Short Stories* 1986–1995

EDITED BY
GILES GORDON
AND DAVID HUGHES

Minerva

A Minerva Paperback
THE BEST OF BEST SHORT STORIES 1986–1995

First published in Great Britain 1995
as a Minerva Paperback Original
by Mandarin Paperbacks
an imprint of Reed Books Ltd
Michelin House, 81 Fulham Road, London SW3 6RB
and Auckland, Melbourne, Singapore and Toronto

A CIP catalogue record for this title
is available from the British Library
ISBN 0 7493 9562 1

Printed and bound in Great Britain

Contents

Introduction

Best Short Stories has appeared under our editorship each year since 1986 to, on the whole, an ever warmer annual welcome. In this its tenth year we have, at the request of our publisher, picked in celebration our thirty-five favourites from those yearly volumes, our only rule being not more than one story by any author.

As we have chosen from hundreds of stories, scores of writers, we have had to leave out dozens of good ones. But we hope that this sampling will encourage newcomers to our anthology to seek out the original volumes, in hardback or paperback, library or bookshop. In these pages we offer a glimpse of the range of the exciting short stories produced in the United Kingdom, the Commonwealth and the Republic of Ireland during a decade in which this entertaining art has shown its vigour and mettle, its social awareness and literary acumen.

Giles Gordon and David Hughes

Career Move

MARTIN AMIS

WHEN ALISTAIR FINISHED his new screenplay, 'Offensive from Quasar 13', he submitted it to the *LM*, and waited. Over the past year, he had had more than a dozen screenplays rejected by the *Little Magazine*. On the other hand, his most recent submission, a batch of five, had been returned not with the standard rejection slip but with a handwritten note from the screenplay editor, Hugh Sixsmith. The note said:

> I was really rather taken with two or three of these, and seriously tempted by Hotwire, which I thought close to being fully achieved. Do please go on sending me your stuff.

Hugh Sixsmith was himself a screenplay writer of considerable, though uncertain, reputation. His note of encouragement *was* encouraging. It made Alistair brave.

Boldly he prepared 'Offensive from Quasar 13' for submission. He justified the pages of the typescript with fondly lingering fingertips. Alistair did not address the envelope to the Screenplay Editor. No. He addressed it to Mr Hugh Sixsmith. Nor, for once, did he enclose his curriculum vitae, which he now contemplated with some discomfort. It told, in a pitiless staccato, of the screenplays he had published in various laptop broadsheets and comically obscure pamphlets; it even told of screenplays published in his university magazine. The truly disgraceful bit came at the end, where it said 'Rights Offered: First British Serial *only*.'

1

Alistair spent a long time on the covering note to Sixsmith – almost as long as he had spent on 'Offensive from Quasar 13'. The note got shorter and shorter the more he worked on it. At last he was satisfied. There in the dawn he grasped the envelope and ran his tongue across its darkly luminous cuff.

That Friday, on his way to work, and suddenly feeling completely hopeless, Alistair surrendered his parcel to the sub post office in Calchalk Street, off the Euston Road. Deliberately – very deliberately – he had enclosed no stamped, addressed envelope. The accompanying letter, in its entirety, read as follows: 'Any use? If not – w.p.b.'

'W.p.b.' stood, of course, for 'wastepaper basket' – a receptacle that loomed forbiddingly large in the life of a practising screenplay writer. With a hand on his brow, Alistair sidled his way out of there – past the birthday cards, the tensed pensioners, the envelopes, and the balls of string.

When Luke finished the new poem – entitled, simply, 'Sonnet' – he Xeroxed the printout and faxed it to his agent. Ninety minutes later he returned from the gym downstairs and prepared his special fruit juice while the answering machine told him, among many other things, to get back to Mike. Reaching for another lime, Luke touched the preselect for Talent International.

'Ah. Luke,' said Mike. 'It's moving. We've already had a response.'

'Yeah, how come? It's four in the morning where he is.'

'No, it's eight in the evening where he is. He's in Australia. Developing a poem with Peter Barry.'

Luke didn't want to hear about Peter Barry. He bent, and tugged off his tank top. Walls and windows maintained a respectful distance – the room was a broad seam of sun haze and river light. Luke sipped his juice: its extreme astringency caused him to lift both elbows and give a single, embittered nod. He said, 'What did he think?'

'Joe? He did backflips. It's "Tell Luke I'm blown away by the new poem. I just know that 'Sonnet' is really going to happen." '

Luke took this coolly. He wasn't at all old but he had been in poetry long enough to take these things coolly. He turned. Suki, who had been shopping, was now letting herself into the apartment, not without difficulty. She was indeed cruelly encumbered. Luke said, 'You haven't talked numbers yet. I mean like a ballpark figure.'

Mike said, 'We understand each other. Joe knows about Monad's interest. And Tim at TCT.'

'Good,' said Luke. Suki was wandering slenderly towards him, shedding various purchases as she approached – creels and caskets, shining satchels.

'They'll want you to go out there at least twice,' said Mike. 'Initially to discuss . . . They can't get over it that you don't live there.'

Luke could tell that Suki had spent much more than she intended. He could tell by the quality of patience in her sigh as she began to lick the sweat from his shoulder blades. He said, 'Come on, Mike. They know I hate all that LA crap.'

On his way to work that Monday, Alistair sat slumped in his bus seat, limp with ambition and neglect. One fantasy was proving especially obdurate: as he entered his office, the telephone on his desk would actually be *bouncing* on its console – Hugh Sixsmith, from the *Little Magazine*, his voice urgent but grave, with the news that he was going to rush Alistair's screenplay into the very next issue. (To be frank, Alistair had had the same fantasy the previous Friday, at which time, presumably, 'Offensive from Quasar 13' was still being booted round the floor of the sub post office.) His girlfriend, Hazel, had come down from Leeds for the weekend. They were so small, he and Hazel, that they could share his single bed quite comfortably – could sprawl and stretch without constraint. On the Saturday evening, they attended a screenplay reading at a bookshop on Camden High Street. Alistair hoped to impress Hazel with his growing ease in this milieu (and managed to exchange wary leers with a few shambling, half-familiar figures – fellow screenplay writers, seekers, knowers). But these days Hazel seemed sufficiently impressed by him anyway, whatever he did. Alistair lay there the next morning (her turn to make tea), wondering about this business of being impressed. Hazel had impressed him mightily, seven years ago, in bed: by not getting out of it when he got into it. The office telephone rang many times that Monday, but none of the callers had anything to say about 'Offensive from Quasar 13'. Alistair sold advertising space for an agricultural newsletter, so his callers wanted to talk about creosote admixes and offal reprocessors.

He heard nothing for four months. This would normally have been a fairly good sign. It meant, or it might mean, that your screenplay was receiving serious, even agonised, consideration. It was better than having your screenplay flopping back on the mat by return post. On the other hand, Hugh Sixsmith might have responded to the spirit and the letter of Alistair's accompanying note and dropped 'Offensive from Quasar 13' into his wastepaper basket within minutes of its arrival: four months ago. Rereading his fading carbon of the screenplay, Alistair now cursed his own (highly calibrated) insouciance. He shouldn't have said, 'Any use? If not – w.p.b.' He should have said, 'Any use? If not – s.a.e.'! Every morning he went down the three flights of stairs – the mail was there to be shuffled and dealt. And every fourth Friday, or thereabouts, he still wrenched open his *LM*, in case Sixsmith had run the screenplay without letting him know. As a surprise.

'Dear Mr Sixsmith,' thought Alistair as he rode the train to Leeds. 'I am thinking of placing the screenplay I sent you elsewhere. I trust that . . . I thought it only fair to . . .' Alistair retracted his feet to accommodate another passenger. 'My dear Mr Sixsmith: In response to an inquiry from . . . In response to a most generous inquiry, I am putting together a selection of my screenplays for . . .' Alistair tipped his head back and stared at the smeared window. 'For Mudlark Books. It seems that the Ostler Press is also interested. This involves me in some paperwork, which, however tedious . . . For the record . . . Matters would be considerably eased . . . Of course if you . . .'

Luke sat on a Bauhaus love seat in Club World at Heathrow, drinking Evian and availing himself of a complimentary fax machine – clearing up the initial paperwork on the poem with Mike.

Everyone in Club World looked hushed and grateful to be there, but not Luke, who looked exhaustively displeased. He was flying first class to LAX, where he would be met by a uniformed chauffeur who would convey him by limousine or courtesy car to the Pinnacle Trumont on the Avenue of the Stars. First class was no big thing. In poetry, first class was something you didn't need to think about. It wasn't discussed. It was statutory.

Luke was tense: under pressure. A lot – maybe too much – was riding on 'Sonnet'. If 'Sonnet' didn't happen, he would soon be able to afford neither his apartment nor his girlfriend. He would recover from Suki before very long. But he would never recover from not being able to afford her, or his apartment. If you wanted the truth, his deal on 'Sonnet' was not that great. Luke was furious with Mike except about the new merchandizing clause (potential accessories on the poem – like toys or T-shirts) and the improved cut he got on tertiaries and sequels. Then there was Joe.

Joe calls, and he's like 'We really think "Sonnet"'s going to work, Luke. Jeff thinks so, too. Jeff's just come in. Jeff? It's Luke. Do you want to say something to him? Luke. Luke, Jeff's coming over. He wants to say something about "Sonnet".'

'Luke?' said Jeff. 'Jeff. Luke? You're a very talented writer. It's great to be working on "Sonnet" with you. Here's Joe.'

'That was Jeff,' said Joe. 'He's crazy about "Sonnet".'

'So what are we going to be talking about?' said Luke. 'Roughly.'

'On "Sonnet"? Well, the only thing we have a problem on "Sonnet" with, Luke, so far as I can see, anyway, and I know Jeff agrees with me on this – right, Jeff? – and so does Jim, incidentally, Luke,' said Joe, 'is the form.'

Luke hesitated. Then he said, 'You mean the form "Sonnet"'s written in.'

'Yes, that's right, Luke. The sonnet form.'

Luke waited for the last last call and was then guided, with much unreturned civility, into the plane's nose.

'Dear Mr Sixsmith,' wrote Alistair,

> Going through my files the other day, I vaguely remembered sending you a little effort called 'Offensive from Quasar 13' – just over seven months ago, it must have been. Am I right in assuming that you have no use for it? I might bother you with another one (or two!) that I have completed since then. I hope you are well. Thank you so much for your encouragement in the past.
>
> Need I say how much I admire your own work? The austerity, the depth. When, may I ask, can we expect another 'slim vol.'?

He sadly posted this letter on a wet Sunday afternoon in Leeds. He hoped that the postmark might testify to his mobility and grit.

Yet, really, he felt much steadier now. There had been a recent period of about five weeks during which, Alistair came to realise, he had gone clinically insane. That letter to Sixsmith was but one of the many dozens he had penned. He had also taken to haunting the Holborn offices of the *Little Magazine*: for hours he sat crouched in the coffee bars and sandwich nooks opposite, with the unsettled intention of springing out at Sixsmith – if he ever saw him, which he never did. Alistair began to wonder whether Sixsmith actually existed. Was he, perhaps, an actor, a ghost, a shrewd fiction? Alistair telephoned the *LM* from selected phone booths. Various people answered, and no one knew where anyone was, and only three or four times was Alistair successfully connected to the apparently permanent coughing fit that crackled away at the other end of Sixsmith's extension. Then he hung up. He couldn't sleep, or he thought he couldn't, for Hazel said that all night long he whimpered and gnashed.

Alistair waited for nearly two months. Then he sent in three more screenplays. One was about a Machine hit man who emerges from early retirement when his wife is slain by a serial murderer. Another dealt with the infiltration by the three Gorgons of an escort agency in present-day New York. The third was a heavy-metal musical set on the Isle of Skye. He enclosed a stamped, addressed envelope the size of a small knapsack.

Winter was unusually mild.

'May I get you something to drink before your meal? A cappuccino? A mineral water? A glass of sauvignon blanc?'

'Double decaf espresso,' said Luke. 'Thanks.'

'You're more than welcome.'

'Hey,' said Luke when everyone had ordered. 'I'm not just welcome anymore. I'm more than welcome.'

The others smiled patiently. Such remarks were the down-side of the classy fact that Luke, despite his appearance and his accent, was English. There they all sat on the terrace at Bubo's: Joe, Jeff, Jim.

Luke said, 'How did "Eclogue by a Five-Barred Gate" do?'

Joe said, 'Domestically?' He looked at Jim, at Jeff. 'Like – *fifteen*?'

Luke said, 'And worldwide?'

'It isn't *going* worldwide.'

'How about "Black Rook in Rainy Weather"?' asked Luke.

Joe shook his head. 'It didn't even do what "Sheep in Fog" did.'

'It's all remakes,' said Jim. 'Period shit.'

'How about "Bog Oak"?'

'"Bog Oak"? Ooh, maybe twenty-five?'

Luke said sourly, 'I hear nice things about "The Old Botanical Gardens".'

They talked about other Christmas flops and bombs, delaying for as long as they could any mention of TCT's ''Tis he whose yester-evening's high disdain', which had cost practically nothing to make and had already done a hundred and twenty million in its first three weeks.

'What happened?' Luke eventually asked. 'Jesus, what was the publicity budget?'

'On "'Tis"?' said Joe. 'Nothing. Two, three.'

They all shook their heads. Jim was philosophical. 'That's poetry,' he said.

'There aren't any other sonnets being made, are there?' said Luke.

Jeff said, 'Binary is in post-production with a sonnet. "Composed at – Castle". *More* period shit.'

Their soups and salads arrived. Luke thought that it was probably a mistake, at this stage, to go on about sonnets. After a while he said, 'How did "For Sophonisba Anguisciola" do?'

Joe said, "For Sophonisba Anguisciola"? Don't talk to me about "For Sophonisba Anguisciola".'

It was late at night and Alistair was in his room working on a screenplay about a high-I.Q. homeless black man who is transformed into a white female junk-bond dealer by a South Moluccan terrorist witch doctor. Suddenly he shoved this aside with a groan, snatched up a clean sheet of paper, and wrote:

Dear Mr Sixsmith,

It is now well over a year since I sent you 'Offensive from Quasar 13'. Not content with that dereliction, you have allowed five months to pass without responding to three more recent submissions. A prompt reply I would have deemed common decency, you being a fellow-screenplay writer, though I must say I have never cared for your work, finding it, at once, both florid and superficial. (I read Matthew Sura's piece last month and I thought he got you *bang to rights*.) Please return the more recent screenplays, namely 'Decimator', 'Medusa Takes Manhattan' and 'Valley of the Stratocasters', immediately.

He signed it and sealed it. He stalked out and posted it. On his return he haughtily threw off his drenched clothes. The single bed felt enormous, like an orgiast's fourposter. He curled up tight and slept better than he had done all year.

So it was a quietly defiant Alistair who the next morning came plodding down the stairs and glanced at the splayed mail on the shelf as he headed for the door. He recognised the envelope as a lover would. He bent low as he opened it.

Do please forgive this very tardy reply. Profound apologies. But allow me to move straight on to a verdict on your work. I won't bore you with all my personal and professional distractions.

Bore me? thought Alistair, as his hand sought his heart.

I think I can at once give the assurance that your screenplays are unusually promising. No: that promise has already been honoured. They have both feeling and burnish.

I will content myself, for now, by taking 'Offensive from Quasar 13'. (Allow me to muse a little longer on 'Decimator'.) I have one or two very minor emendations to suggest. Why not telephone me here to arrange a chat?

Thank you for your generous remarks about my own work. Increasingly I find that this kind of exchange – this candour, this reciprocity – is one of the things that keep me trundling along. Your works helped sustain my defences in the aftermath of Matthew Sura's vicious and slovenly attack, from which, I fear, I am still rather reeling. Take excellent care.

'Go with the lyric,' said Jim.

'Or how about a ballad?' said Jeff.

Jack was swayable. 'Ballads are big,' he allowed.

It seemed to Luke, towards the end of the second day, that he was winning the sonnet battle. The clue lay in the flavour of Joe's taciturnity: torpid but unmorose.

'Let's face it,' said Jeff. 'Sonnets are essentially hieratic. They're strictly period. They answer to a formalised consciousness. Today, we're talking consciousnesses that are in *search* of form.'

'Plus,' said Jack, 'the lyric has always been the natural medium for the untrammelled expression of feeling.'

'Yeah,' said Jeff. 'With the sonnet you're stuck in this thesis-antithesis–synthesis routine.'

Joan said, 'I mean what are we doing here? Reflecting the world or illuminating it?'

It was time for Joe to speak. 'Please,' he said. 'Are we forgetting that "'Tis" was a sonnet, before the rewrites? Were we on coke when we said, in the summer, that we were going to go for the *sonnet*?'

The answer to Joe's last question, incidentally, was yes; but Luke looked carefully round the room. The Chinese lunch they'd had the secretary phone out for lay on the coffee table like a child's experiments with putty and paint and designer ooze. It was four o'clock and Luke wanted to get away soon. To swim and lie in the sun. To make himself especially lean and bronzed for his meeting with the young actress Henna Mickiewicz. He faked a yawn.

'Luke's lagged,' said Joe. 'Tomorrow we'll talk some more, but I'm pretty sure I'm recommitted to the sonnet.'

'Sorry, said Alistair. 'Me yet again. Sorry.'

'Oh yes,' said the woman's voice. 'He *was* here a minute ago . . . No, he's there. He's there. Just a second.'

Alistair jerked the receiver away from his ear and stared at it. He started listening again. It seemed as if the phone itself were in paroxysm, all squawk and splat like a cabby's radio. Then the fit passed, or paused, and a voice said tightly but proudly, 'Hugh Sixsmith?'

It took Alistair a little while to explain who he was. Sixsmith sounded surprised but, on the whole, rather intrigued to hear from him. They moved on smoothly enough to arrange a meeting (after work, the following Monday), before Alistair contrived to put in: 'Mr Sixsmith, there's just one thing. This is very embarrassing, but last night I got into a bit of a state about not hearing from you for so long and I'm afraid I sent you a completely mad letter which I . . .' Alistair waited. 'Oh, you know how it is. For these screenplays, you know, you reach into yourself, and then time goes by and . . .'

'My dear boy, don't say another word. I'll ignore it. I'll throw it away. After a line or two I shall simply avert my unpained eye,' said Sixsmith, and started coughing again.

Hazel did not come down to London for the weekend. Alistair did not go up to Leeds for the weekend. He spent the time thinking about that place in Earl's Court Square where screenplay writers read from their screenplays and drank biting Spanish red wine and got stared at by tousled girls who wore thick overcoats and no makeup and blinked incessantly or not at all.

★

Luke parked his Chevrolet Celebrity on the fifth floor of the studio car park and rode down in the elevator with two minor executives in tracksuits who were discussing the latest records broken by ''Tis he whose yester-evening's high disdain'. He put on his dark glasses as he crossed the other car park, the one reserved for major executives. Each bay had a name on it. It reassured Luke to see Joe's name there, partly obscured by his Range Rover. Poets, of course, seldom had that kind of clout. Or any clout at all. He was glad that Henna Mickiewicz didn't seem to realise this.

Joe's office: Jim, Jack, Joan, but no Jeff. Two new guys were there. Luke was introduced to the two new guys. Ron said he spoke for Don when he told Luke that he was a great admirer of his material. Huddled over the coffee percolator with Joe, Luke asked after Jeff, and Joe said, 'Jeff's off the poem,' and Luke just nodded.

They settled in their low armchairs.

Luke said, 'What's "A Welshman to Any Tourist" doing?'

Don said, 'It's doing good but not great.'

Ron said, 'It won't do what "The Gap in the Hedge" did.'

Jim said, 'What did "Hedge" do?'

They talked about what 'Hedge' did. Then Joe said, 'OK. We're going with the sonnet. Now. Don has a problem with the octet's first quatrain, Ron has a problem with the second quatrain, Jack and Jim have a problem with the first quatrain of the sestet, and I think we *all* have a problem with the final couplet.'

Alistair presented himself at the offices of the *LM* in an unblinking trance of punctuality. He had been in the area for hours, and had spent about fifteen quid on teas and coffees. There wasn't much welcome to overstay in the various snack parlours where he lingered (and where he moreover imagined himself unfavourably recollected from his previous *LM* vigils), holding with both hands the creaky foam container, and watching the light pour past the office windows.

As Big Ben struck two, Alistair mounted the stairs. He took a breath so deep that he almost fell over backward – and then knocked. An elderly office boy wordlessly showed him into a narrow, rubbish-heaped office that contained, with difficulty, seven people. At first Alistair took them for other screenplay writers and wedged himself behind the door, at the back of the queue. But they didn't look like screenplay writers. Not much was said over the next four hours, and the identities of Sixsmith's supplicants emerged only partially and piecemeal. One or two, like his solicitor and his second wife's psychiatrist, took their leave after no more than ninety minutes. Others, like the VAT man and the probation officer, stayed almost as long as Alistair. But by six-forty-five he was alone.

He approached the impossible haystack of Sixsmith's desk. Very hurriedly, he started searching through the unopened mail. It was in Alistair's mind that he might locate and intercept his own letter. But all the envelopes, of which there were a great many, proved to be brown, windowed, and registered. Turning to leave, he saw a jiffy bag of formidable bulk addressed to himself in Sixsmith's tremulous hand. There seemed no reason not to take it. The old office boy, Alistair soon saw, was curled up in a sleeping bag under a worktable in the outer room.

On the street he unseamed his package in a ferment of grey fluff. It contained two of his screenplays, 'Valley of the Stratocasters' and, confusingly, 'Decimator'. There was also a note:

> I have been called away, as they say. Personal ups and downs.
> I shall ring you this week and we'll have – what? Lunch?

Enclosed, too, was Alistair's aggrieved letter – unopened. He moved on. The traffic, human and mechanical, lurched past his quickened face. He felt his eyes widen to an obvious and solving truth: Hugh Sixsmith was a screenplay writer. He understood.

After an inconclusive day spent discussing the caesura of 'Sonnet''s opening line, Luke and his colleagues went for cocktails at Strabismus. They were given the big round table near the piano.

Jane said, 'TCT is doing a sequel to "'Tis".'

Joan said, 'Actually it's a prequel.'

'Title?' said Joe.

'Undecided. At TCT they're calling it "'Twas".'

'My son,' said Joe thoughtfully, after the waiter had delivered their drinks, 'called me an asshole this morning. For the first time.'

'That's incredible,' said Bo. '*My* son called me an asshole this morning. For the first time.'

'So?' said Mo.

11

Joe said, 'He's six years old, for Christ's sake.'

Phil said, 'My son called me an asshole when he was five.'

'My son hasn't called me an asshole yet,' said Jim. 'And he's nine.'

Luke sipped his Bloody Mary. Its hue and texture made him wonder whether he could risk blowing his nose without making yet another visit to the bathroom. He hadn't called Suki for three days. Things were getting compellingly out of hand with Henna Mickiewicz. He hadn't actually promised her a part in the poem, not on paper. Henna was great, except you kept thinking she was going to suddenly sue you anyway.

Mo was saying that each child progresses at his own rate, and that later lulls regularly offset the apparent advances of the early years.

Mo said, 'My son's three. And he calls me an asshole all the time.'

Everybody looked suitably impressed.

The trees were in leaf, and the rumps of the tourist buses were thick and fat in the traffic, and all the farmers wanted fertilizer admixes rather than storehouse insulation when Sixsmith finally made his call. In the interim, Alistair had convinced himself of the following: before returning his aggrieved letter, Sixsmith had *steamed it open and then resealed it*. During this period, also, Alistair had grimly got engaged to Hazel. But the call came.

He was pretty sure he had come to the right restaurant. Except that it wasn't a restaurant, not quite. The place took no bookings, and knew of no Mr Sixsmith, and was serving many midday breakfasts to swearing persons whose eyes bulged over mugs of flesh-coloured tea. On the other hand, there was alcohol. All kinds of people were drinking it. Fine, thought Alistair. Fine. What better place, really, for a couple of screenplay writers to . . .

'Alistair?'

Confidently, Sixsmith bent his long body into the booth. As he settled, he looked well pleased with the manoeuvre. He contemplated Alistair with peculiar neutrality, but there was then something boyish, something consciously remiss, in the face he turned to the waiter. As Sixsmith ordered a gin-and-tonic, and as he amusingly expatiated on his weakness for prawn cocktails, Alistair found himself wryly but powerfully drawn to this man, to this rumpled screenplay writer with his dreamy gaze, the curious elisions of his somewhat slurred voice, and the great dents and bone shadows of his face, all the faulty fontanels of vocational care. He knew how old Sixsmith was. But maybe time moved strangely for screenplay writers, whose flames burnt so bright . . .

'And as for my fellow-artisan in the scrivener's trade, Alistair. What will *you* have?'

At once Sixsmith showed himself to be a person of some candour. Or it might have been that he saw in the younger screenplay writer someone before whom all false reticence could be cast aside. Sixsmith's estranged second wife, it emerged, herself the daughter of two alcoholics, was an alcoholic. Her current lover (ah, how these lovers came and went!) was an alcoholic. To complicate matters, Sixsmith explained as he rattled his glass at the waiter, his daughter, the product of his first marriage, was an alcoholic. How did Sixsmith keep going? Despite his years, he had, thank God, found love, in the arms of a woman young enough (and, by the sound of it, alcoholic enough) to be his daughter. Their prawn cocktails arrived, together with a carafe of hearty red wine. Sixsmith lit a cigarette and held up his palm towards Alistair for the duration of a coughing fit that turned every head in the room. Then, for a moment, understandably disoriented, he stared at Alistair as if uncertain of his intentions, or even his identity. But their bond quickly re-established itself. Soon they were talking away like hardened equals – of Trumbo, of Chayevsky, of Towne, of Eszterhas.

Around two-thirty, when, after several attempts, the waiter succeeded in removing Sixsmith's untouched prawn cocktail, and now prepared to serve them their braised chops with a third carafe, the two men were arguing loudly about early Puzo.

Joe yawned and shrugged and said languidly, 'You know something? I was never that crazy about the Petrarchan rhyme scheme anyway.'

Jan said, '"Composed at – Castle" is ABBA ABBA.'

'Jen said, 'So was "'Tis". Right up until the final polish.'

Jon said, 'Here's some news. They say "Composed at – Castle" is in turnaround.'

'You're not serious,' said Bo. 'It's released this month. I heard they were getting great preview reaction.'

Joe looked doubtful. '"'Tis" has made the suits kind of antsy about sonnets. They figure lightning can't strike twice.'

'ABBA ABBA,' said Bo with distaste.

'Or,' said Joe. '*Or* . . . *or* we go unrhymed.'

'*Un*rhymed?' said Phil.

'We go blank,' said Joe.

There was a silence. Bill looked at Gil, who looked at Will.

'What do you think, Luke?' said Jim. 'You're the poet.'

Luke had never felt very protective about 'Sonnet'. Even its original version he had regarded as no more than a bargaining chip. Nowadays he rewrote 'Sonnet' every night at the Pinnacle Trumont before Henna arrived and they called room service. 'Blank,' said Luke. 'Blank. I don't know, Joe. I could go ABAB ABAB or even ABAB CDCD. Christ, I'd go AABB if I didn't think it'd tank the final couplet. But blank. I never thought I'd go *blank*.'

'Well, it needs something,' said Joe.

'Maybe it's the pentameter,' said Luke. 'Maybe it's the iamb. Hey, here's one from left field. How about syllabics?'

At five-forty-five Hugh Sixsmith ordered a gin-and-tonic and said, 'We've talked. We've broken bread. Wine. Truth. Screenplay writing. I want to talk about your work, Alistair. Yes, I do. I want to talk about "Offensive from Quasar 13".'

Alistair blushed.

'It's not often that . . . But one always knows. That sense of pregnant arrest. Of felt life in its full . . . Thank you, Alistair. Thank you. I have to say that it rather reminded me of my own early work.'

Alistair nodded.

Having talked for quite some time about his own maturation as a screenplay writer, Sixsmith said, 'Now. Just tell me to shut up any time you like. And I'm going to print it anyway. But I want to make one *tiny* suggestion about "Offensive from Quasar 13".'

Alistair waved a hand in the air.

'Now,' said Sixsmith. He broke off and ordered a prawn cocktail. The waiter looked at him defeatedly. 'Now,' said Sixsmith. 'When Brad escapes from the Nebulan experiment lab and sets off with Cord and Tara to immobilise the directed-energy scythe on the Xerxian attack ship – where's Chelsi?'

Alistair frowned.

'Where's Chelsi? She's still in the lab with the Nebulans. On the point of being injected with a Phobian viper venom, moreover. What of the happy ending? What of Brad's heroic centrality? What of his avowed love for Chelsi? Or am I just being a bore?'

The Secretary, Victoria, stuck her head into the room and said, 'He's coming down.'

Luke listened to the sound of twenty-three pairs of legs uncrossing and recrossing. Meanwhile he readied himself for a sixteen-tooth smile. He glanced at Joe, who said, 'He's fine. He's just coming down to say hi.'

And down he came: Jake Endo, exquisitely Westernised and gorgeously tricked out and perhaps thirty-five. Of the luxury items that pargetted his slender form, none was as breathtaking as his hair, with its layers of pampered light.

Jake Endo shook Luke's hand and said, 'It's a great pleasure to meet you. I haven't read the basic material on the poem, but I'm familiar with the background.'

Luke surmised that Jake Endo had had his voice fixed. He could do the bits of the words that Japanese people were supposed to find difficult.

'I understand it's a love poem,' he continued. 'Addressed to your girlfriend. Is she here with you in LA?'

'No. She's in London.' Luke found he was staring at Jake Endo's sandals, wondering how much they could possibly have cost.

A silence began its crescendo. This silence had long been intolerable when Jim broke it, saying to Jake Endo, 'Oh, how did "Lines Left Upon a Seat in a Yew-Tree, Which Stands Near the Lake of Easthwaite, on a Desolate Part of the Shore, Commanding a Beautiful Prospect" do?'

' "Lines"?' said Jake Endo. 'Rather well.'

'I was thinking about "Composed at – Castle",' said Jim weakly.

The silence began again. As it neared its climax Joe was suddenly reminded of all this energy he was supposed to have. He got to his feet saying, 'Jake? I guess we're nearing our tiredness peak. You've caught us at kind of a low point. We can't agree on the first line. First line? We can't see our way to the end of the first *foot*.'

Jake Endo was undismayed. 'There always are these low points. I'm sure you'll get there, with so much talent in the room. Upstairs we're very confident. We think it's going to be a big summer poem.'

'No, we're very confident, too,' said Joe. 'There's a lot of belief here. A lot of belief. We're behind "Sonnet" all the way.'

'Sonnet?' said Jake Endo.

'Yeah, sonnet. "Sonnet".'

'"Sonnet"?' said Jake Endo.

'It's a sonnet. It's called "Sonnet".'

In waves the West fell away from Jake Endo's face. After a few seconds he looked like a dark-age warlord in mid-campaign, taking a glazed breather before moving on to the women and the children.

'Nobody told me,' he said as he went toward the telephone, 'about any *sonnet*.'

The place was closing. Its tea trade and its after-office trade had come and gone. Outside, the streets glimmered morbidly. Members of the staff were donning macs and overcoats. An important light went out. A fridge door slammed.

'Hardly the most resounding felicity, is it?' said Sixsmith.

Absent or unavailable for over an hour, the gift of speech had been restored to Alistair – speech, that prince of all the faculties. 'Or what if . . .' he said. 'What if Chelsi just leaves the experiment lab earlier?'

'Not hugely dramatic,' said Sixsmith. He ordered a carafe of wine and inquired as to the whereabouts of his braised chop.

'Or what if she just gets wounded? During the escape. In the leg.'

'So long as one could avoid the wretched cliché: girl impeded, hero dangerously tarrying. Also, she's supernumerary to the raid on the Xerxian attack ship. We really want her out of the way for that.'

Alistair said, 'Then let's kill her.'

'Very well. Slight pall over the happy ending. No, no.'

A waiter stood over them, sadly staring at the bill in its saucer.

'All right,' said Sixsmith. 'Chelsi gets wounded. Quite badly. In the arm. *Now* what does Brad do with her?'

'Drops her off at the hospital.'

'Mm. Rather hollow modulation.'

The waiter was joined by another waiter, equally stoic; their faces were grained by evening shadow. Now Sixsmith was gently frisking himself with a deepening frown.

'What if,' said Alistair, 'what if there's somebody passing who can take her to the hospital?'

'Possibly,' said Sixsmith, who was half standing, with one hand awkwardly dipped into his inside pocket.

'Or what if,' said Alistair, 'or what if Brad just gives her *directions* to the hospital?'

Back in London the next day, Luke met with Mike to straighten this shit out. Actually it looked OK. Mike called Mal at Monad, who had a thing about Tim at TCT. As a potential finesse on Mal, Mike also called Bob at Binary with a view to repossessing the option on 'Sonnet', plus development money at rolling compound, and redeveloping it somewhere else entirely – say, at Red Giant, where Rodge was known to be very interested. 'They'll want you to go out there,' said Mike. 'To kick it around.'

'I can't believe Joe,' said Luke. 'I can't believe I knocked myself out for that flake.'

'Happens. Joe forgot about Jake Endo and sonnets. Endo's first big poem was a sonnet. Before your time. "Bright star, would I were steadfast as thou art". It opened for like one day. It practically bankrupted Japan.'

'I feel used, Mike. My sense of trust. I've got to get wised up around here.'

'A lot will depend on how "Composed at – Castle" does and what the feeling is on the "'Tis" prequel.'

'I'm going to go away with Suki for a while. Do you know anywhere where there aren't any shops? Jesus, I need a holiday. Mike, this is bullshit. You know what I *really* want to do, don't you?'

'Of course I do.'

Luke looked at Mike until he said, 'You want to direct.'

When Alistair had convalesced from the lunch, he revised 'Offensive from Quasar 13' in a rough accordance with Sixsmith's suggestions. He solved the Chelsi problem by having her noisily eaten by a Stygian panther in the lab menagerie. The charge of gratuitousness was, in Alistair's view, safely anticipated by Brad's valediction to her remains, in which sanguinary revenge on the Nebulans was both prefigured and legitimised. He also took out the bit where Brad declared his love for Chelsi, and put in a bit where Brad declared his love for Tara.

He sent in the new pages, which three months later Sixsmith

acknowledged and applauded in a hand quite incompatible with that of his earlier communications. Nor did he reimburse Alistair for the lunch. His wallet, he had explained, had been emptied that morning – by which alcoholic, Sixsmith never established. Alistair kept the bill as a memento. This startling document showed that during the course of the meal Sixsmith had smoked, or at any rate bought, nearly a carton of cigarettes.

Three months later he was sent a proof of 'Offensive from Quasar 13'. Three months after that, the screenplay appeared in the *LM*. Three months after that, Alistair received a cheque for £12.50, which bounced.

Curiously, although the proof had incorporated Alistair's corrections, the published version reverted to the typescript, in which Brad escaped from the Neulan lab seemingly without concern for a Chelsi last glimpsed on an operating table with a syringe full of Phobian viper venom being eased into her neck. Later that month, Alistair went along to a reading at the Screenplay Society in Earl's Court. There he got talking to a gaunt girl in an ash-stained black smock who claimed to have read his screenplay and who, over glasses of red wine and, later, in the terrible pub, told him he was a weakling and a hypocrite with no notion of the ways of men and women. Alistair had not been a published screenplay writer long enough to respond to, or even recognise, this graphic proposition (though he did keep the telephone number she threw at his feet). It is anyway doubtful whether he would have dared to take things further. He was marrying Hazel the following weekend.

In the new year he sent Sixsmith a series – one might almost say a sequence – of screenplays on group-jeopardy themes. His follow-up letter in the summer was answered by a brief note stating that Sixsmith was no longer employed by the *LM*. Alistair telephoned. He then discussed the matter with Hazel and decided to take the next day off work.

It was a September morning. The hospice in Cricklewood was of recent design and construction; from the road it resembled a clutch of igloos against the sheenless tundra of the sky. When he asked for Hugh Sixsmith at the desk, two men in suits climbed quickly from their chairs. One was a writ-server. One was a cost-adjuster. Alistair waved away their complex requests.

The warm room contained clogged, regretful murmurs, and defiance in the form of bottles and paper cups and cigarette smoke, and the many peeping eyes of female grief. A young woman faced him proudly. Alistair started explaining who he was, a young screenplay writer come to . . . On the bed in the corner the spavined figure of Sixsmith was gawkily arranged. Alistair moved toward it. At first he was sure the eyes were gone, like holes cut out of pumpkin or blood orange. But then the faint brows began to lift, and Alistair thought he saw the light of recognition.

As the tears began, he felt the shiver of approval of consensus, on his back. He took the old screenplay writer's hand and said, 'Goodbye. And thank you. Thank you. Thank you.'

Opening in four hundred and thirty-seven theatres, the Binary sonnet 'Composed at – Castle' did seventeen million in its first weekend. At this time Luke was living in a two-bedroom apartment on Yokum Drive. Suki was with him. He hoped it wouldn't take her too long to find out about Henna Mickiewicz. When the smoke cleared he would switch to the more mature Anita, who produced.

He had taken his sonnet to Rodge at Red Giant and turned it into an ode. When that didn't work out he went to Mal at Monad, where they'd gone for the villanelle. The villanelle had become a triolet, briefly, with Tim at TCT, before Bob at Binary had him rethink it as a rondeau. When the rondeau didn't take, Luke lyricised it and got Mike to send it to Joe. Everyone, including Jake Endo, thought that now was surely the time to turn it back into a sonnet.

Luke had dinner at Rales with Joe and Mike.

'I always thought of "Sonnet" as an art poem,' said Joe. 'But things are so hot now, I've started thinking more commercially.'

Mike said, 'TCT is doing a sequel *and* a prequel to "'Tis" and bringing them out at the same time.'

'A sequel?' said Joe.

'Yeah. They're calling it "'Twill".'

Mike was a little fucked up. So was Joe. Luke was a little fucked up, too. They'd done some lines at the office. Then drinks here at the bar. They'd meant to get a little fucked up. It was OK. It was good, once in a while, to get a little fucked up. The thing was not to get fucked up too often. The thing was not to get fucked up to excess.

'I mean it, Luke,' said Joe. He glittered potently. 'I think "Sonnet" could be as big as "–".'

'You think?' said Luke.

19

'I mean it. I think "Sonnet" could be another "–".'

' "–"?'

' "–" .'

Luke thought for a moment, taking this in. ' "–" . . .' he repeated wonderingly.

The Age of Lead

MARGARET ATWOOD

THE MAN HAS been buried for a hundred and fifty years. They dug a hole in the frozen gravel, deep into the permafrost, and put him down there so the wolves couldn't get to him. Or that is the speculation.

When they dug the hole the permafrost was exposed to the air, which was warmer. This made the permafrost melt. But it froze again after the man was covered up, so that when he was brought to the surface he was completely enclosed in ice. They took the lid off the coffin and it was like those maraschino cherries you used to freeze in ice-cube trays for fancy tropical drinks: a vague shape, looming through a solid cloud.

Then they melted the ice and he came to light. He is almost the same as when he was buried. The freezing water has pushed his lips away from his teeth into an astonished snarl, and he's a beige colour, like a gravy stain on linen, instead of pink, but everything is still there. He even has eyeballs, except that they aren't white but the light brown of milky tea. With these tea-stained eyes he regards Jane: an indecipherable gaze, innocent, ferocious, amazed, but contemplative, like a werewolf meditating, caught in a flash of lightning at the exact split-second of his tumultuous change.

Jane doesn't watch very much television. She used to watch it more. She used to watch comedy series, in the evenings, and when she was a student at university she would watch

21

afternoon soaps about hospitals and rich people, as a way of procrastinating. For a while, not so long ago, she would watch the evening news, taking in the disasters with her feet tucked up on the chesterfield, a throw rug over her legs, drinking a hot milk and rum to relax·before bed. It was all a form of escape.

But what you can see on the television, at whatever time of day, is edging too close to her own life; though in her life, nothing stays put in those tidy compartments, comedy here, seedy romance and sentimental tears there, accidents and violent deaths in thirty-second clips they call *bites*, as if they are chocolate bars. In her life, everything is mixed together. *Laugh, I thought I'd die*, Vincent used to say, a very long time ago, in a voice imitating the banality of mothers; and that's how it's getting to be. So when she flicks on the television these days, she flicks it off again soon enough. Even the commercials, with their surreal dailiness, are beginning to look sinister, to suggest meanings behind themselves, behind their façade of cleanliness, lusciousness, health, power and speed.

Tonight she leaves the television on, because what she is seeing is so unlike what she usually sees. There is nothing sinister behind this image of the frozen man. It is entirely itself. *What you see is what you gets*, as Vincent also used to say, crossing his eyes, baring his teeth at one side, pushing his nose into a horror-movie snout. Although it never was, with him.

The man they've dug up and melted was a young man. Or still is: it's difficult to know what tense should be applied to him, he is so insistently present. Despite the distortions caused by the ice and the emaciation of his illness, you can see his youthfulness, the absence of toughening, of wear. According to the dates painted carefully onto his name-plate, he was only twenty years old. His name was John Torrington. He was, or is, a sailor, a seaman. He wasn't an able-bodied seaman though; he was a petty officer, one of those marginally in command. Being in command has little to do with the ableness of the body.

He was one of the first to die. That is why he got a coffin and a metal name-plate, and a deep hole in the permafrost – because they still had the energy, and the piety, for such things, that early. There would have been a burial service read over him, and prayers. As time went on and became nebulous and things did not get better, they must have kept the energy for themselves; and also the prayers. The prayers would have ceased to be routine and become desperate, and then hopeless. The later dead ones got cairns of piled stones, and the much later ones not even that. They ended up as bones, and as the soles of boots and the occasional button, sprinkled over the frozen stony treeless relentless ground in a trail heading south. It was like the trails in fairy tales, of breadcrumbs or seeds or white stones. But in this case nothing had sprouted or lit up in the moonlight, forming a miraculous pathway to life; no rescuers had followed. It took ten years before anyone knew even the barest beginnings of what had been happening to them.

All of them together were the Franklin Expedition. Jane has seldom paid much attention to history except when it has overlapped with her knowledge of antique furniture and real estate – '19th C. pine harvest table', or 'prime location Georgian centre hall, impeccable reno' – but she knows what the Franklin Expedition was. The two ships with their bad-luck names have been on stamps – the *Terror*, the *Erebus*. Also she took it in school, along with a lot of other doomed expeditions. Not many of those explorers seemed to have come out of it very well. They were always getting scurvy or lost.

What the Franklin Expedition was looking for was the Northwest Passage, an open seaway across the top of the Arctic, so people, merchants, could get to India from England without going all the way around South America. They wanted to go that way because it would cost less, and increase their profits. This was much less exotic than Marco Polo or the headwaters of the Nile; nevertheless, the idea of exploration appealed to her then: to get onto a boat and just go somewhere, somewhere mapless, off into the unknown. To launch yourself into fright; to find things out. There was something daring and noble about it, despite all of the losses and failures, or perhaps because of them. It was like having sex in high school, in those days before the Pill, even if you took precautions. If you were a girl, that is. If you were a boy, for whom such a risk was fairly minimal, you had to do other things: things with weapons or large amounts of alcohol, or high-speed vehicles, which at her suburban Toronto high school, back then at the beginning of the sixties, meant switchblades, beer, and drag races down the main streets on Saturday nights.

Now, gazing at the television as the lozenge of ice gradually melts and the outline of the young sailor's body clears and sharpens, Jane remembers Vincent, sixteen and with more hair then, quirking one eyebrow and lifting his lip in a mock sneer and saying, 'Franklin, my dear, I don't give a damn.' He said it loud enough to be heard, but the history teacher ignored him, not knowing what else to do. It was hard for the teachers to keep Vincent in line, because he never seemed to be afraid of anything that might happen to him.

He was hollow-eyed even then; he frequently looked as if he'd been up all night. Even then he resembled a very young old man, or else a dissipated child. The dark circles under his eyes were the ancient part, but when he smiled he had lovely small white teeth, like the magazine ads for baby foods. He made fun of everything, and was adored. He wasn't adored the way other boys were adored, those boys with surly lower lips and greased hair and a studied air of smouldering menace. He was adored like a pet. Not a dog, but a cat. He went where he liked, and nobody owned him. Nobody called him *Vince*.

Strangely enough, Jane's mother approved of him. She didn't usually approve of the boys Jane went out with. Maybe she approved of him because it was obvious to her that no bad results would follow from Jane's going out with him; no heartaches, no heaviness, nothing burdensome. None of what she called *consequences*. Consequences: the weightiness of the body, the growing flesh hauled around like a bundle, the tiny frill-framed goblin head in the carriage. Babies and marriage, in that order. This was how she understood men and their furtive, fumbling, threatening desires, because Jane herself had been a consequence. She had been a mistake, she had been a war baby. She had been a crime that had needed to be paid for, over and over.

By the time she was sixteen, Jane had heard enough about this to last her several lifetimes. In her mother's account of the way things were, you were young briefly and then you fell. You plummeted downwards like a ripe apple and hit the ground with a squash; you fell, and everything about you fell too. You got fallen arches and a fallen womb, and your hair and teeth fell out. That's what having a baby did to you. It subjected you to the force of gravity.

This is how she remembers her mother, still: in terms of a pendulous, drooping, wilting motion. Her sagging breasts, the downturned lines around her mouth. Jane conjures her up: there she is, as usual, sitting at the kitchen table with a cup of cooling tea, exhausted after her job clerking at Eaton's department store, standing upright all day behind the jewellery counter with her bum stuffed into a girdle, and her swelling feet crammed into the mandatory medium-heeled shoes, smiling her envious, disapproving smile at the spoiled customers who turned up their noses at pieces of glittering junk she herself could never afford to buy. Jane's mother sighs, picks at the canned spaghetti Jane has heated up for her. Silent words waft out of her like stale talcum powder: *What can you expect*, always a statement, never a question. Jane tries at this distance for pity, but comes up with none.

As for Jane's father, he'd run away from home when Jane was five, leaving her mother in the lurch. That's what her mother called it – 'running away from home', as if he'd been an irresponsible child. Money arrived from time to time, but that was the sum total of his contribution to family life. Jane resented him for it, but she didn't blame him. Her mother inspired in almost everyone who encountered her a vicious desire for escape.

Jane and Vincent would sit out in the cramped backyard of Jane's house, which was one of the squinty-windowed little stuccoed wartime bungalows at the bottom of the hill. At the top of the hill were the richer houses, and the richer people: the girls who owned cashmere sweaters, at least one of them, instead of the orlon and lambswool so familiar to Jane. Vincent lived about halfway up the hill. He still had a father, in theory. They would sit against the back fence, near the spindly cosmos flowers that passed for a garden, as far away from the house itself as they could get. They would drink gin, decanted by Vincent from his father's liquor hoard and smuggled in an old military pocket flask he'd picked up somewhere. They would imitate their mothers.

'I pinch and scrape and I work my fingers to the bone, and what thanks do I get?' Vincent would say peevishly. 'No help from you, Sonny Boy. You're just like your father. Free as the birds, out all night, do as you like and you don't care one pin about anyone else's feelings. Now take out that garbage.'

'It's love that does it to you,' Jane would reply, in the resigned ponderous voice of her mother. 'You wait and see, my girl. One of these days you'll come down off your devil-may-care high horse.' As Jane said this, and even though she was making fun, she could picture Love, with a capital L, descending out of the sky towards her like a huge foot. Her mother's life had been a disaster, but in her own view an inevitable disaster, as in songs and movies. It was Love that was responsible, and in the face of Love, what could be done? Love was like a steamroller. There was no avoiding it, it went over you and you came out flat.

Jane's mother waited, fearfully and uttering warnings, but with a sort of gloating relish for the same thing to happen to Jane. Every time Jane went out with a new boy her mother inspected him as a potential agent of downfall. She distrusted most of these boys; she distrusted their sulky, pulpy mouths, their eyes half-closed in the updrifting smoke of their cigarettes, their slow, sauntering manner of walking, their clothing that was too tight, too full, too full of their bodies. They looked this way even when they weren't putting on the sulks and swaggers, when they were trying to appear bright-eyed and industrious and polite for Jane's mother's benefit, saying goodbye at the front door, dressed in their shirts and ties and their pressed heavy-date suits. They couldn't help the way they looked, the way they were. They were helpless; one kiss in a dark corner would reduce them to speechlessness, they were sleep-walkers in their own liquid bodies. Jane on the other hand was wide awake.

Jane and Vincent did not exactly go out together. Instead they made fun of going out. When the coast was clear and Jane's mother wasn't home, Vincent would appear at the door with his face painted bright yellow, and Jane would put her bathrobe on back to front and they would order Chinese food and alarm the delivery boy and eat sitting cross-legged on the floor, clumsily, with chopsticks. Or Vincent would turn up in a threadbare thirty-year-old suit and a bowler hat and a cane, and Jane would rummage around in the cupboard for a discarded church-going hat of her mother's, with smashed cloth violets and a veil, and they would go downtown and walk around, making loud remarks about the passers-by, pretending to be old, or poor, or crazy. It was thoughtless and in bad taste, which was what they both liked about it.

Vincent took Jane to the graduation formal, and they picked out her dress together at one of the second-hand clothing shops Vincent frequented, giggling at the shock and admiration they hoped to cause. They hesitated between a flame-red with falling-off sequins and a backless hip-hugging black with a plunge front, and chose the black, to go with Jane's hair.

Vincent sent a poisonous-looking lime-green orchid, the colour of her eyes he said, and Jane painted her eyelids and fingernails to match. Vincent wore white tie and tails, and a top hat, all-frayed Sally-Ann issue, and ludicrously too large for him. They tangoed around the gymnasium, even though the music was not a tango, under the tissue-paper flowers, cutting a black swathe through the sea of pastel tulle, unsmiling, projecting a corny sexual menace, Vincent with Jane's long pearl necklace clenched between his teeth.

The applause was mostly for him, because of the way he was adored. Though mostly by the girls, thinks Jane. But he seemed to be popular enough among the boys as well. Probably he told them dirty jokes, in the proverbial locker room. He knew enough of them. As he dipped Jane backwards, he dropped the pearls and whispered into her ear, 'No belts, no pins, no pads, no chafing.' It was from an ad for tampons, but it was also their leitmotif. It was what they both wanted: freedom from the world of mothers, the world of precautions, the world of burdens and fate and heavy female constraints upon the flesh. They wanted a life without consequences. Until recently, they'd managed it.

The scientists have melted the entire length of the young sailor now, at least the upper layer of him. They've been pouring warm water over him, gently and patiently; they don't want to thaw him too abruptly. It's as if John Torrington is asleep and they don't want to startle him.

Now his feet have been revealed. They're bare, and white rather than beige; they look like the feet of someone who's been walking on a cold floor, on a winter's day. That is the quality of the light they reflect: winter sunlight, in early morning. There is something intensely painful to Jane about the absence of socks. They could have left him his socks. But maybe the others needed them. His big toes are tied together; the man talking says this was to keep the body tidily packaged for burial, but Jane is not convinced. His arms are tied to his body, his ankles are tied together. You do that when you don't want a person walking around.

This part is almost too much for Jane, it is too reminiscent. She reaches for the channel switcher, but luckily the show (it is only a show, it's only another show) changes to two of the historical experts, analysing the clothing. There's a close-up of

John Torrington's shirt, a simple high-collared pinstriped white and blue cotton, with mother of pearl buttons. The stripes are a printed pattern, rather than a woven one; woven would have been more expensive. The trousers are grey linen. Ah, thinks Jane. Wardrobe. She feels better: this is something she knows about. She loves the solemnity, the reverence, with which the stripes and buttons are discussed. An interest in the clothing of the present is frivolity, an interest in the clothing of the past is archaeology; a point Vincent would have appreciated.

After high school, Jane and Vincent both got scholarships to university, although Vincent had appeared to study less, and did better. That summer they did everything together. They got summer jobs at the same hamburger heaven, they went to movies together after work, although Vincent never paid for Jane. They still occasionally dressed up in old clothes and went downtown and pretended to be a weird couple, but it no longer felt careless and filled with absurd invention. It was beginning to occur to them that they might conceivably end up looking like that.

In her first year at university Jane stopped going out with other boys: she needed a part-time job to help pay her way, and that and the schoolwork and Vincent took up all her time. She thought she might be in love with Vincent. She thought that maybe they should make love, to find out. She had never done such a thing, entirely; she had been too afraid of the untrustworthiness of men, of the gravity of love, too afraid of consequences. She thought however, that she might trust Vincent.

But things didn't go that way. They held hands, but they didn't hug; they hugged, but they didn't pet; they kissed, but they didn't neck. Vincent liked looking at her, but he liked it so much he would never close his eyes. She would close hers and then open them, and there would be Vincent, his own eyes shining in the light from the streetlamp or the moon, peering at her inquisitively as if waiting to see what odd female thing she would do next, for his delighted amusement. Making love with Vincent did not seem altogether possible.

(Later, after she had flung herself into the current of opinion that had swollen to a river by the late sixties, she no longer said 'making love', she said 'having sex'. But it amounted to the same thing. You had sex, and love got made out of it whether you liked it or not. You woke up in bed or more likely on a mattress, with an arm around you, and found yourself wondering what it might be like to keep on doing it. At that point Jane would start looking at her watch. She had no intention of being left in any lurches. She would do the leaving herself. And she did.)

Jane and Vincent wandered off to different cities. They wrote each other postcards. Jane did this and that. She ran a co-op food store in Vancouver, did the financial stuff for a diminutive theatre in Montreal, acted as managing editor for a small publisher, ran the publicity for a dance company. She had a head for details and for adding up small sums – having to scrape her way through university had been instructive – and such jobs were often available if you didn't demand much money for doing them. Jane could see no reason to tie herself down, to make any sort of soul-stunting commitment, to anything or anyone. It was the early seventies; the old heavy women's world of girdles and precautions and consequences had been swept away. There were a lot of windows opening, a lot of doors; you could look in, then you could go in, then you could come out again.

She lived with several men, but in each of the apartments there were always cardboard boxes, belonging to her, that she never got around to unpacking; just as well, because it was that much easier to move out. When she got past thirty she decided it might be nice to have a child, sometime, later. She tried to figure out a way of doing this without becoming a mother. Her own mother had moved to Florida, and sent rambling, grumbling letters, to which Jane did not often reply.

Jane moved back to Toronto, and found it ten times more interesting than when she'd left it. Vincent was already there. He'd come back from Europe, where he'd been studying film; he'd opened a design studio. He and Jane met for lunch, and it was the same: the same air of conspiracy between them, the same sense of their own potential for outrageousness. They might still have been sitting in Jane's garden, beside the cosmos flowers, drinking forbidden gin and making fun.

Jane found herself moving in Vincent's circles, or were they orbits? Vincent knew a great many people, people of all kinds; some were artists and some wanted to be, and some wanted to know the ones who were. Some had money to begin with, some made money; they all spent it. There was a lot more talk about money, these days, or among these people. Few of them knew how to manage it, and Jane found herself helping them out. She developed a small business among them, handling their money. She would gather it in, put it away safely for them, tell them what they could spend, dole out an allowance. She would note with interest the things they bought, filing their receipted bills: what furniture, what clothing, which *objets*. They were delighted with their money, enchanted with it. It was like milk and cookies for them after school. Watching them play with their money, Jane felt responsible and indulgent, and a little matronly. She stored her own money carefully away, and eventually bought a townhouse with it.

All this time she was with Vincent, more or less. They'd tried being lovers but had not made a success of it. Vincent had gone along with this scheme because Jane had wanted it, but he was elusive, he would not make declarations. What worked with other men did not work with him: appeals to his protective instincts, pretences at jealousy, requests to remove stuck lids from jars. Sex with him was more like a musical work-out. He couldn't take it seriously, and accused her of being too solemn about it. She thought he might be gay, but was afraid to ask him; she dreaded feeling irrelevant to him, excluded. It took them months to get back to normal.

He was older now, they both were. He had thinning temples and a widow's peak, and his bright inquisitive eyes had receded even further into his head. What went on between them continued to look like a courtship, but was not one. He was always bringing her things: a new, peculiar food to eat, a new grotesquerie to see, a new piece of gossip, which he would present to her with a sense of occasion, like a flower. She in her turn appreciated him. It was like a yogic exercise, appreciating Vincent; it was like appreciating an anchovy, or a stone. He was not everyone's taste.

There's a black and white print on the television, then another: the nineteenth century's vision of itself, in etchings. Sir John Franklin, older and fatter than Jane had supposed; the *Terror* and the *Erebus*, locked fast in the crush of the ice. In the high arctic, a hundred and fifty years ago, it's the dead of winter. There is no sun at all, no moon; only the rustling northern lights, like electronic music, and the hard little stars.

What did they do for love, on such a ship, at such a time? Furtive solitary gropings, confused and mournful dreams, the sublimation of novels. The usual, among those who have become solitary.

Down in the hold, surrounded by the creaking of the wooden hull and the stale odours of men far too long enclosed, John Torrington lies dying. He must have known it; you can see it on his face. He turns towards Jane his tea-coloured look of puzzled reproach.

Who held his hand, who read to him, who brought him water? Who if anyone loved him? And what did they tell him, about whatever it was that was killing him? Consumption, brain fever, Original Sin. All these Victorian reasons, which meant nothing and were the wrong ones. But they must have been comforting. If you are dying, you want to know why.

In the eighties, things started to slide. Toronto was not so much fun any more. There were too many people, too many poor people. You could see them begging on the streets, which were clogged with fumes and cars. The cheap artists' studios were torn down or converted to coy and upscale office space, the artists had migrated elsewhere. Whole streets were torn up or knocked down. The air was full of wind-blown grit.

People were dying. They were dying too early. One of Jane's clients, a man who owned an antique store, died almost overnight of bone cancer. Another, a woman who was an entertainment lawyer, was trying on a dress in a boutique and had a heart attack. She fell over and they called the ambulance, and she was dead on arrival. A theatrical producer died of Aids, and a photographer; the lover of the photographer shot himself, either out of grief or because he knew he was next. A friend of a friend died of emphysema, another of viral pneumonia, another of hepatitis picked up on a tropical vacation, another of spinal meningitis. It was as if they had been weakened by some mysterious agent, a thing like a colourless gas, scentless and invisible, so that any germ that happened along could invade their bodies, take them over.

Jane began to notice news items of the kind she'd once skimmed over. Maple groves dying of acid rain, hormones in the beef, mercury in the fish, pesticides in the vegetables, poison sprayed on the fruit, God knows what in the drinking water. She subscribed to a bottled springwater service and felt better for a few weeks, then read in the paper that it wouldn't do her much good, because whatever it was had been seeping into everything. Each time you took a breath, you breathed some of it in. She thought about moving out of the city, then read about the toxic dumps, radioactive waste, concealed here and there in the countryside and masked by the lush, deceitful green of wavering trees.

Vincent had been dead for less than a year. He was not put into the permafrost or frozen in ice. He went into the Necropolis, the only Toronto cemetery of whose general ambience he approved; he got flower bulbs planted on top of him, by Jane and others. Mostly by Jane. Right now John Torrington, recently thawed after a hundred and fifty years, probably looks better than Vincent.

A week before Vincent's forty-third birthday, Jane went to see him in the hospital. He was in for tests. Like fun he was. He was in for the unspeakable, the unknown. He was in for a mutated virus that didn't even have a name yet. It was creeping up his spine, and when it reached his brain it would kill him. It was not, as they said, responding to treatment. He was in for the duration.

It was white in his room, wintry. He lay packed in ice, for the pain. A white sheet wrapped him, his white thin feet poked out the bottom of it. They were so pale and cold, Jane took one look at him, laid out on ice like a salmon, and began to cry.

'Oh Vincent,' she said. 'What will I do without you?' This sounded awful. It sounded like Jane and Vincent making fun, of obsolete books, obsolete movies, their obsolete mothers. It also sounded selfish: here she was, worrying about herself and her future, when Vincent was the one who was sick. But it was true. There would be a lot less to do, altogether, without Vincent.

Vincent gazed up at her; the shadows under his eyes were cavernous. 'Lighten up,' he said, not very loudly, because he could not speak very loudly now. By this time she was sitting down, leaning forward; she was holding one of his hands. It was as thin as the claw of a bird. 'Who says I'm going to die?' He spent a moment considering this, revised it. 'You're right,' he said, 'They got me. It was the Pod People from outer space. They said, "All I want is your poddy."'

Jane cried more. It was worse because he was trying to be funny. 'But what is it?' she said. 'Have they found out yet?'

Vincent smiled his ancient, jaunty smile, his smile of detachment, of amusement. There were his beautiful teeth, juvenile as ever. 'Who knows?' he said. 'It must have been something I ate.'

Jane sat with the tears running down her face. She felt desolate: left behind, stranded. Their mothers had finally caught up to them and been proven right. There were consequences after all; but they were the consequences to things you didn't even know you'd done.

The scientists were back on the screen. They are excited, their earnest mouths are twitching, you could almost call them joyful. They know why John Torrington died; they know, at last, why the Franklin Expedition went so terribly wrong. They've snipped off pieces of John Torrington, a fingernail, a lock of hair, they've run them through machines and come out with the answers.

There is a shot of an old tin can, pulled open to show the seam. It looks like a bomb casing. A finger points: it was the tin cans that did it, a new invention back then, a new technology, the ultimate defence against starvation and scurvy. The Franklin Expedition was excellently provisioned with tin cans, stuffed full of meat and soup and soldered together with lead. The whole expedition got lead poisoning. Nobody knew it. Nobody could taste it. It invaded their bones, their lungs, their brains, weakening them and confusing their thinking, so that at the end those that had not yet died in the ships set out in an idiotic trek across the stony, icy ground, pulling a lifeboat laden down with toothbrushes, soap, handkerchiefs and slippers, useless pieces of junk. When they were found (ten years later, skeletons in tattered coats, lying where they'd collapsed) they were headed back towards the ships. It was what they'd been eating that had killed them.

Jane switches off the television and goes into her kitchen – all white, done over the year before last, the outmoded butcher-block counters from the seventies torn out and carted away – to make herself some hot milk and rum. Then she decides against it; she won't sleep anyway. Everything in here looks ownerless. Her toaster oven, so perfect for solo dining, her microwave for the vegetables, her espresso maker – they're sitting around waiting for her departure, for this evening or forever, in order to assume their final, real appearance of purposeless objects adrift in the physical world. They might as well be pieces of an exploded spaceship orbiting the moon.

She thinks about Vincent's apartment, so carefully arranged, filled with the beautiful or deliberately-ugly possessions he once loved. She thinks about his closet, with its quirky particular outfits, empty now of his arms and legs. It has all been broken up now, sold, given away.

Increasingly the sidewalk that runs past her house is cluttered with plastic drinking cups, crumpled soft-drink cans, used take-out plates. She picks them up, clears them away, but they appear again overnight, like a trail left by an army on the march or by the fleeing residents of a city under bombardment, discarding the objects that were once thought essential but are now too heavy to carry.

Answers to a Questionnaire

J. G. BALLARD

1) Yes.
2) Male (?)
3) c/o Terminal 3, London Airport, Heathrow.
4) 27.
5) Unknown.
6) Dr Barnardo's Primary, Kingston-on-Thames; HM Borstal, Send, Sussex; Brunel University Computer Sciences Department.
7) Floor cleaner, Mecca Amusement Arcades, Leicester Square.
8) If I can avoid it.
9) System Analyst, Sperry-Univac, 1979–83.
10) Manchester Crown Court, 1984.
11) Credit card and computer fraud.
12) Guilty.
13) Two years, HM Prisons, Parkhurst.
14) Stockhausen, De Kooning, Jack Kerouac.
15) Whenever possible.
16) Twice a day.
17) NUS, herpes, gonorrhoea.
18) Husbands.
19) My greatest ambition is to turn into a TV programme.
20) I first saw the deceased on 17 February 1986, in the chapel at London Airport. He was praying in the front pew.

21) At the time I was living in an out-of-order cubicle in the air traffic controllers' washroom in Terminal 3.

22) Approx. 5 ft 7 in, aged 33, slim build, albino skin and thin black beard, some kind of crash injuries to both hands. At first I thought he was a Palestinian terrorist.

23) He was wearing the stolen uniform trousers of an El Al flight engineer.

24) With my last money I bought him a prawnburger in the mezzanine cafeteria. He thanked me and, although not carrying a bank-card, extracted £100 from a service till on the main concourse.

25) Already I was convinced that I was in the presence of a messianic figure who would help me to penetrate the Nat West deposit account computer codes.

26) No sexual activity occurred.

27) I took him to Richmond Ice Rink where he immediately performed six triple salchows. I urged him to take up ice-dancing with an eye to the European Championships and eventual gold at Seoul, but he began to trace out huge double spirals on the ice. I tried to convince him that these did not feature in the compulsory figures, but he told me that the spirals represented a model of synthetic DNA.

28) No.

29) He gave me to understand that he had important connections at the highest levels of government.

30) Suite 17B, London Penta Hotel. I slept on the floor in the bathroom.

31) Service tills in Oxford Street, Knightsbridge and Earl's Court.

32) Approx. £275,000 in three weeks.

33) Porno videos. He took a particular interest in Kamera Klimax and Electric Blue.

34) Almost every day.

35) When he was drunk. He claimed that he brought the gift of eternal life.

36) At the Penta Hotel I tried to introduce him to Torvill and Dean. He was interested in meeting only members of the Stock Exchange and Fellows of the Royal Society.

37) Females of all ages.

38) Group sex.

39) Marie Drummond, 22, sales assistant, HMV Records;

Denise Attwell, research supervisor, Geigy Pharmaceuticals; Florence Burgess, 55, deaconess, Bible Society Bookshop; Angelina Gomez, 23, air hostess, Iberian Airways; Phoebe Adams, 43, cruise protestor, Camp Orange, Greenham Common.

40) Sometimes, at his suggestion.

41) Unsatisfactory.

42) Premature ejaculation; impotence.

43) He urged me to have a sex–change operation.

44) National Gallery, Wallace Collection, British Museum. He was much intrigued by representations of Jesus, Zoroaster and the Gautama Buddha, and commented on the likenesses.

45) With the permission of the manager, NE District, British Telecom.

46) We erected the antenna on the roof of the Post Office Tower.

47) 2500 KHz.

48) Towards the constellation Orion.

49) I heard his voice, apparently transmitted from the star Betelgeuse 2000 years ago.

50) Interference to TV reception all over London and the South-East.

51) No. 1 in the Jictar Ratings, exceeding the combined audiences for Coronation Street, Dallas and Dynasty.

52) Regular visitors included Princess Diana, Prince Charles and Dr Billy Graham.

53) He hired the Wembley Conference Centre.

54) 'Immortality in the Service of Mankind'.

55) Guests were drawn from the worlds of science and politics, the church, armed forces and the Inland Revenue.

56) Generous fees.

57) Service tills in Mayfair and Regent Street.

58) He had a keen appreciation of money, but was not impressed when I told him of Torvill and Dean's earnings.

59) He was obsessed by the nature of the chemical bond.

60) Sitting beside him at the top table were: (1) The Leader of Her Majesty's Opposition, (2) The President of the Royal Society, (3) The Archbishop of Canterbury, (4) The Chief Rabbi, (5) The Chairman of the Diners Club, (6) The Chairman of the Bank of England, (7) The General Secretary of the Inland Revenue Staff Federation, (8) The President

of Hertz Rent-a-Car, (9) The President of IBM, (10) The Chief of the General Staff, (11) Mr Henry Kissinger, (12) Myself.

61) He stated that synthetic DNA introduced into the human germ plasm would arrest the process of ageing and extend human life almost indefinitely.

62) Perhaps 1 million years.

63) He announced that Princess Diana was immortal.

64) Astonishment/disbelief.

65) He advised the audience to invest heavily in leisure industries.

66) The value of the pound sterling rose to $8.75.

67) American TV networks, *Time Magazine, Newsweek.*

68) The Second Coming.

69) He expressed strong disappointment at the negative attitude of the Third World.

70) The Kremlin.

71) He wanted me to become the warhead of a cruise missile.

72) My growing disenchantment.

73) Sexual malaise.

74) He complained that I was spending too much time at Richmond Ice Rink.

75) The Royal Proclamation.

76) The pound sterling rose to $75.50.

77) Prince Andrew. Repeatedly.

78) Injection into the testicles.

79) The side-effects were permanent impotence and sterility. However, as immortality was ensured, no further offspring would be needed and the procreative urge would atrophy.

80) I seriously considered a sex-change operation.

81) Government White Paper on Immortality.

82) Compulsory injection into the testicles of the entire male population over 11 years.

83) Smith & Weston short-barrel 38.

84) Entirely my own idea.

85) Many hours at Richmond Ice Rink trying unsuccessfully to erase the patterns of DNA.

86) Westminster Hall.

87) Premeditated. I questioned his real motives.

88) Assassination.

89) I was neither paid nor incited by agents of a foreign power.

90) Despair. I wish to go back to my cubicle at London Airport.

91) Between Princess Diana and the Governor of Nevada.
92) At the climax of Thus Spake Zarathustra.
93) 7 feet.
94) Three shots.
95) Blood Group O.
96) I did not wish to spend the rest of eternity in my own company.
97) I was visited in the death cell by Mr Terry Waite, special envoy of the Archbishop of Canterbury.
98) That I had killed the Son of God.
99) He walked with a slight limp. He told me that, as a condemned prisoner, I alone had been spared the sterilising injections, and that the restoration of the national birthrate was now my sole duty.
100) Yes.

Dragons

JULIAN BARNES

PIERRE CHAIGNE, CARPENTER, widower, was making a lantern. Standing with his back to the door of his workshed, he eased the four oblongs of glass into the runners he had cut and greased with mutton fat. They moved smoothly and fitted well: the flame would be secure, and the lantern would cast its light in all directions, when this was required. But Pierre Chaigne, carpenter, widower, had also cut three pieces of beechwood the exact size of the panels of glass. When these were inserted, the flame would be cast in a single direction only, and the lantern would be invisible from three of the four compass points. Pierre Chaigne trimmed each piece of beechwood carefully, and when satisfied that they slid easily within the greased runners, he took them to a place of concealment among the discarded lumber at one end of the workshed.

Everything bad came from the north. Whatever else they believed, the whole town, both parts of it, knew that. It was the north wind, arching over the Montagne Noire, that made the ewes give birth to dead lambs; it was the north wind which put the devil into the widow Gibault and made her cry out, even at her age, for such things that she had to be stopped in the mouth with a cloth by her daughter, lest children or the priest hear what she wanted. It was to the north, in the forest on the other side of the Montagne Noire, that the Beast of Gruissan lived. Those who had seen it described a dog the size of a horse with the spots of a leopard, and many was the time, in the fields around Gruissan, that the Beast had taken livestock, even up to a small calf. Dogs sent by their masters to confront the Beast had had their heads bitten off. The town had petitioned the King, and the King sent his principal arquebusier. After much prayer and ceremony, this royal warrior had set off into the forest with a local woodsman, who shamefully had run away. The arquebusier emerged, several days later, empty-handed. He had returned to Paris, and the Beast had returned to its foraging. And now, they said, the dragons were coming, from the north, the north.

It was from the north, twenty years before, when Pierre Chaigne, carpenter, widower, had been a boy of thirteen, that the Commissioners had come. They had arrived, the two of them, lace at the wrist and severity upon the face, escorted by ten soldiers. They examined the temple and heard evidence, from those who came forward, concerning the enlargements that had taken place. The next day, from a mounting block, the senior of the Commissioners had explained the law. The King's Edict, he said, had given protection to their religion, that was true; but such protection had been awarded only to the religion as it had been constituted at the time of the Edict. There had been no licence to enlarge their cult: the enemies of the King's religion had been granted toleration but not encouragement. Therefore all churches built by the religion since the Edict were to be torn down, and even those churches which had merely been enlarged were to be torn down as warning and instruction to those who continued to defy the King's religion. Further, to purge their crime, it was the builders of the temple themselves who were to demolish it. Pierre Chaigne remembered at this point an outcry from those assembled. The Commissioner had thereupon announced that, in order to speed the work, four children from among the enemies of the King's religion had been placed under guard by the soldiers, and would be well and safely guarded, furnished with all that they required to eat, for as long as the dismantling of the temple might take. It was at this time that a great sadness came over the family of Pierre Chaigne, and shortly afterwards his mother had died of a winter fever.

And now the dragons were coming from the north. The priests of the King's religion had decreed that in the defence of the Holy Mother Church against the heretic anything was permissible, short of killing. The dragons themselves had another saying: What matter the road provided it led to Paradise? They had come, not so many years before, to Bougouin de Chavagne, where they had cast several of the menfolk into a great ditch at the base of the castle tower. The victims, broken by their fall, lost as in the darkness of the tomb, had comforted themselves by singing the 138th Psalm. *'Though I walk in the midst of trouble, Thou wilt revive me: Thou shalt stretch forth Thine hand against the wrath of mine enemies, and Thy right hand shall save me.'* But as each night had passed, the voices from the great ditch had grown fewer, until the 138th Psalm was chanted no more.

The three soldiers placed into Pierre Chaigne's household were old men, forty years at least. Two of them had scars visible on their faces despite their great beards. On the shoulder of their leather tunics they wore the winged beast of their regiment. An additional whorl of stitching indicated to those with military knowledge that these old men belonged to the *dragons étrangers du roi*. Pierre Chaigne had no such understanding, but he had ears, and they were enough. These men did not seem to follow anything Pierre Chaigne said to them, and spoke among themselves the rough tongue of the north, the north.

They were accompanied by the secretary of the Intendant, who read a short decree to Pierre Chaigne and his assembled family. It being given that the household of Pierre Chaigne, carpenter, widower, by its wilful failure to pay the Tallage, was in odious breach of the King's law, the dragons, one officer and two men, would be quartered upon the Chaigne family, who were to supply such needs as they might have until such time as the household chose to pay the Tallage and raise the burden from themselves. When the secretary of the Intendant withdrew, one of the two common soldiers beckoned Pierre Chaigne's daughter Marthe towards him. As she advanced, he pulled from his pocket a small fighting animal which he held by the neck, and thrust it at her. Marthe, though merely thirteen years of age, had no fear of the beast; her calmness encouraged the family and surprised the soldier, who returned the creature to the long pocket stitched into the side of his trouser.

Pierre Chaigne had been accounted an enemy of the King's religion, and thereby an enemy of the King, but he did not admit to either condition. He was loyal to the King, and wished to live in peace with the King's religion; but this was not permitted. The Intendant knew that Pierre Chaigne could not pay the Tallage imposed, or that if he did pay it, the Tallage would immediately be increased. The soldiers had been placed into the household in order to collect the Tallage; but their very presence, and the cost of entertaining them, diminished still further any chance of payment. This was known and established.

The Chaigne household consisted of five souls: Anne Rouget, widow, sister of Pierre Chaigne's mother, who had come to them when her husband, a two-plough labourer, had died; after burying her husband according to the rites of the King's religion, she had accepted the cult of her sister's family. She had now passed fifty years of age, and was consequently growing feeble of mind, but still able to cook and make the house with her great-niece Marthe. Pierre Chaigne had also two sons, Henri, aged fifteen, and Daniel, aged nine. It was for Daniel that Pierre Chaigne felt the greatest alarm. The law governing the age of conversion had been twice changed. When Pierre himself had been an infant, it was established law that a child was not permitted to leave the church of his parents until he be fourteen years old, that age being considered sufficient to confirm mental capacity. Then the age had been reduced to twelve. But the new law had lowered it still further, to a mere seven years of age. The purpose of this change was clear. A child such as Daniel, not yet having that fixity of mind which comes with adult years, might be lured from the cult by the colours and scents, the finery and display, the fairground trickery of the King's religion. It was known to have happened.

The three *dragons étrangers du roi* indicated their needs with incomprehensible speech and lucid gesture. They were to occupy the bed, and the Chaigne family were to sleep where they liked. They were to eat at the table, the Chaigne family were to wait upon them and eat whatever they left. The key to the house was surrendered to the officer, as also were the knives which Pierre and his elder son naturally carried to cut their food.

The first evening, as the three soldiers sat waiting for their soup, the officer roared at Marthe as she was placing the bowls before them. His voice was loud and strange. 'My stomach will think that my throat is cut,' he shouted. The other soldiers laughed. Marthe did not understand. The officer banged on his bowl with his spoon. Then Marthe understood, and brought his food swiftly.

The secretary of the Intendant had stated that the dragons had lawfully been placed into the Chaigne household to collect the Tallage; and on the second day the three soldiers did make some attempt to discover any money or valuable property that might have been hidden. They turned out cupboards, looked beneath the bed, rooted in Pierre Chaigne's woodstacks. They searched with a kind of dutiful anger, not expecting to find anything concealed, but wishing it to be known that they had done what was formally demanded of them. Previous campaigns had taught them that the households they were first invited to occupy were never those of the rich. When their services had initially been engaged, many years ago at the end of the War, it had seemed obvious to the authorities to quarter the dragons with those who were best able to pay the Tallage. But this method proved slow; it strengthened the sense of fraternity among members of the cult, and produced some notable martyrs, the memory of whom often inspired the obstinate. Therefore it had been found more profitable to place the soldiers in the first instance into the families of the poor. This produced a useful division among the enemies of the King's religion, when the poor observed that the rich were exempt from the sufferings inflicted upon them. Swift conversions were many times thus obtained.

On the second evening, the soldier who kept the ferret in his long knee-pocket pulled Daniel on to his knee as the boy offered him some bread. He grasped Daniel so firmly by the waist that the infant immediately began to struggle. The soldier held in his free hand a knife with which he intended to cut his bread. He put the blade flat against the table, which was made from the hardest wood known to Pierre Chaigne, carpenter, widower, and with only a gentle push raised a crisp, transparent curl from the surface of the table.

"Twould shave a mouse asleep,' he said. Pierre Chaigne and his family did not understand these words; nor did they need to.

On the next day the soldiers used the ferret to slaughter a cockerel, which they ate for dinner, and finding the house cold at midday, though the sun was shining, they broke up two chairs and burnt them in the chimney, ignoring the pile of firewood beside it.

Unlike the King's religion, the cult could be celebrated anywhere that the faithful gathered, without attendance at the temple. The dragons made efforts to prevent the family of Pierre Chaigne from fulfilling their observances: the house was locked at night, and the three soldiers disposed themselves during the day so that they could spy upon the movements of the family. But they were outnumbered by five to three, and it happened sometimes that escape was possible, and thereby a visit to a house where the cult was being celebrated. Pierre Chaigne and his family openly talked of such matters in front of the dragons; and it seemed a kind of sweet revenge to do so. But the dragons in the town, who numbered around forty, had sources of intelligence, and although the members of the cult frequently changed the house in which they met, they were as frequently discovered by the soldiers. So the enemies of the King's religion chose to gather in the open air, in the forest to the north of the town. At first they met by day, and later only by night. Many feared that the Beast of Gruissan would descend upon them in the darkness, and the first prayer offered up was always a plea to be defended from the Beast. One night they were surprised by the dragons, who ran at them screaming, then beat and cut them with their swords, chasing them from the forest. The next morning, when the widow Gibault was not to be found, they returned to the forest and discovered her there, dead of the shock.

Pierre Chaigne was able to remember a time when the two populations of the town moved freely among one another, when a funeral or a marriage was celebrated by the whole community, without regard for the creed of the participants. It was true that neither the adherents of the King's religion nor the members of the cult would enter one another's place of ritual; but one group would wait patiently outside for the ceremony to be completed, and then the whole town would follow, whether to the graveyard or to the wedding feast. But shared rejoicing and shared grief had fallen equally into desuetude. Similarly, it was now rare in the town for a family to contain members of both faiths.

Though it was summer, the dragons were in need of fire. They burnt all the furniture except that which they needed for their own use. Then they began to burn the finest wood of Pierre Chaigne, carpenter, widower. Lengths of weathered oak from trees cut by his father twenty years ago, prime sections of elm and ash, all were consumed by fire. To increase Pierre Chaigne's indignity and misery, he was himself made to saw the timber into combustible lengths. When the dragons observed that this fine wood burnt more slowly than they had hoped, they ordered Pierre Chaigne and his sons to build a great bonfire beside the workshed, and instructed them to keep the fire alight until all Pierre Chaigne's wood was consumed.

As Pierre Chaigne stood looking at the mound of ashes which was all that remained of his future as a carpenter, the officer said to him, 'God's help is nearer than the door.' Pierre Chaigne did not understand these words.

Next the soldiers took all Pierre Chaigne's tools, and those of his son Henri, and sold them to members of the King's religion. At first Pierre Chaigne felt his misery lift, for having deprived him of his timber the soldiers did him no further harm depriving him of his tools; and besides, the sale of all his fine implements might even bring in money enough to pay the Tallage and so make the soldiers depart. However, the dragons sold Pierre Chaigne's tools not for their value, but for a price so low that no one could resist buying them, and then kept the money for themselves. François Danjon, miller, widower, member of the King's religion, who had bought several of the instruments, returned them to Pierre Chaigne under cover of darkness. Pierre Chaigne wrapped them in oiled cloths and buried them in the woods against a better day.

It was at this time that a pedlar, aged nineteen, passing through the town on foot from the direction of the Cherveux, was seized by several dragons and interrogated. He had the suspicious accent of the south. After being beaten, he admitted to membership of the cult; after being beaten further, he admitted that he desired to abjure. He was taken before the priest, who gave him absolution and copied his name into the register of abjuration. The pedlar made a mark beside his name, and two of the dragons, proud of their zeal and trusting that it would be recompensed, signed as witnesses. The pedlar was sent on his way without his goods. Henri Chaigne, aged fifteen, watched the beating, which was done in the public square; and as the victim was taken off to the church, a dragon whom he had not before seen said to him in the coarse language of the north, 'What matter the road provided it lead to Paradise?' Henri Chaigne did not understand what was being said, but recognized the word Paradise.

At first conversions came quickly, among the old, the feeble, the solitary, and those infants who had been forcibly beguiled by gaudy display. But after a few weeks the number of abjurations diminished. This was often the pattern, and it was known that the dragons frequently gave way to excesses in order that the conversions continue.

When the Tallage had first been announced, there were those who had sought to flee, who had heard that it was possible to reach St Nazaire and discover the promised land elsewhere. Two families had left the town in this manner, whereupon members of the cult had been instructed by the Intendant to pull down and destroy with fire the houses they had left behind, whereupon the unpaid Tallage was not forgotten but transferred to those who remained. It was always the way. When a heretic converted to the King's religion, his Tallage was divided among the community of heretics, and their tax thus became even larger as their means of payment diminished. This led some to despair; but others, having lost everything, were made the more determined not to lose that faith on whose account they had already lost everything. Thus the booted missionaries met with more resistance as their work continued. This too was known and expected.

It was not long after Pierre Chaigne's instruments had been sold that Anne Rouget, his mother's sister, fell into sickness and became the first member of the family to abjure. When the dragons saw that she was weak and feverish, they yielded the bed to her and slept upon the floor. This chivalry was deliberate, for no sooner was she positioned in the bed than the soldiers declared her sickening unto death and summoned the priest of the King's religion. It was established by royal ordinance that when a Protestant heretic was dying, the priest had the right to visit the deathbed and offer the suffering one an opportunity to return in death to the Holy Mother Church. This visit, which the family were forbidden to prevent, was to take place in the presence of a magistrate; and the priest was not allowed to use any duress when attempting to obtain a conversion. However, such terms and conditions were not always strictly followed. The magistrate being occupied elsewhere, the priest was accompanied into the Chaigne household by the officer of the dragons. The family was expelled into the day's heat, two dragons guarded the door, and at the end of six hours Anne Rouget had been received back into the church where she had spent the first thirty years of her life. The priest departed with satisfaction, and that night the soldiers reclaimed the bed as their own and returned Anne Rouget to the floor.

'Why?' asked Pierre Chaigne.

'Leave me in peace,' replied Anne Rouget.

'Why?'

'One or the other is true.'

She did not speak beyond that, and died two days later, though whether from her fever, her despair or her apostasy Pierre Chaigne was unable to determine.

The child Daniel, aged nine, was the next to abjure. He was taken to the church of the King's religion, where it was explained to him that Anne Rouget, who had done the service of a mother for him, was awaiting him in Heaven, and that he would surely see her again one day unless he clung to heresy and chose to burn in Hell. Then he was shown fine vestments and the gilt reliquary containing the little finger of Saint Boniface; he smelt the incense and examined the monsters carved between the choir stalls – monsters which he would doubtless meet in person if he freely chose to burn in Hell. And the following Sunday, during the Mass, Daniel Chaigne publicly abjured the cult of the temple. His conversion was received with great and impressive solemnity, and afterwards he was much petted by the women of the King's religion. The following Sunday Pierre Chaigne and his elder son tried to prevent the dragons taking Daniel Chaigne to the Mass; they were beaten and the boy was taken none the less. He did not return, and Pierre Chaigne was informed by the priest that he had been placed beyond the reach of treason in the Jesuit college on the other side of the Montagne Noire, and that his education there would be at the expense of the family until such time as they chose to repudiate their heresy.

Only the obstinate ones now remained among the heretics. It was at this point that the Intendant named as Collector of the Tallage the leading Protestant landowner of the region, Pierre Allonneau, sieur de Beaulieu, fermier de Coutaud. It became his legal duty instantly to pay the accumulated tax owed by all members of the cult since the Tallage was announced. This he was unable to do, but being reduced at once to ruin, was no longer able to help in secrecy the obstinate ones.

The three dragons had been within the Chaigne household for two months. All the chickens and both the pigs had been eaten; all but a little of the furniture had been burnt; Pierre

Chaigne's timber had been consumed with the exception of a rough pile of worthless lumber at the back of his shed. Others in the town who might have supported the family were now equally destitute. Each day Pierre Chaigne and his son Henri were obliged to traverse the woods and fields to obtain food. Two of the soldiers came with them, leaving the officer to guard Marthe. It was difficult to find enough food to satisfy six mouths, and the two dragons offered no assistance in the chase of a rabbit or the search for mushrooms. When there was not enough food for the soldiers to eat until they belched, the Chaigne family went hungry.

It was on their return from one of these daily expeditions that Pierre Chaigne and Henri Chaigne discovered that the officer had taken Marthe Chaigne, aged thirteen, into the bed with him. This sight caused Pierre Chaigne much anger and despair; only his religion prevented him from seeking that very same night the death of the officer.

The following day the officer chose to accompany the two heretics on the search for food, and one of the ordinary soldiers stayed behind to guard Marthe. This soldier also took her into the bed with him. No explanation was offered, and none was required. Marthe Chaigne refused to talk to her father or her brother about what had been done.

After nine days of seeing his sister taken as a whore, Henri Chaigne abjured his faith. But this action did not prevent the dragons from continuing to take his sister as a whore. Consequently, at the celebration of Mass the following Sunday, Henri Chaigne spat out of his mouth the holy wafer and the holy wine he had received from the priest. For this blasphemy against the body and blood of Our Lord, Henri Chaigne was duly tried by the bishop's court, condemned to death and handed over to the soldiers who burnt him with fire.

Afterwards, the three soldiers separated Pierre Chaigne and his daughter, not permitting them to talk to one another. Marthe kept the house and whored for the dragons; her father hunted for nourishment and cut wood in the forest, since the autumn air was now turning cold. Pierre Chaigne, who had suffered greatly, was resolved to resist apostasy even unto death. His daughter was equally certain in her faith, and underwent her daily ordeal with the fortitude of a martyr.

One morning, after the officer had taken her into the bed

49

with him but treated her less roughly for once, she received a brutal surprise. The officer had been accustomed to talk to her in the rough language of the north while he used her as a whore, to shout words and afterwards to mutter quietly. She had become familiar with this, and at times it helped her bear the suffering more easily, for she was able to imagine that the man who spoke these words from the north was himself as distant as the north.

Now, as he still lay athwart her, he said, 'You are brave, young girl.'

It took her a moment to realize that he had spoken her own language. He raised himself on an elbow and shunted off her. 'I admire that,' he went on, still in her language, 'and so I want to spare you further suffering.'

'You speak our tongue.'

'Yes.'

'So you have understood what we have said in the house since you came here?'

'Yes.'

'And the others too?'

'We have been in your country many years.'

Marthe Chaigne was silent. She remembered what her brother Henri had openly said about the dragons, and about the priest of the King's religion. Her father had revealed where the cult was to be celebrated, little suspecting the consequences. She herself had uttered words of hatred.

'And because I wish to spare you suffering,' the officer continued, 'I shall explain what will happen.'

What could happen? More pain of this kind. Worse. Torture. Death. No doubt. But then Paradise, surely.

'What will happen is that you will become with child. And then we shall testify that your father used you as a whore in our presence. And you will be taken before the court, your father and you, and there condemned. You will be burnt to death, you and your father, as also will be the child of this incestuous union within you.'

The soldier paused, and allowed the rigid girl fully to understand what he had said. 'You will abjure. You will abjure, and thereby you will save your father's life.'

'My father would rather die.'

'Your father does not have the choice. Only you have the choice whether your father dies or not. So you will abjure.'

Marthe Chaigne lay motionless in the bed. The soldier got up, adjusted his clothing roughly, and sat at the table waiting for her to agree. He was wise enough in his profession not to add unnecessary words.

Eventually the girl said, 'Where do you come from?'

The soldier laughed at the unexpectedness of the question. 'From the north.'

'Where? *Where?*'

'A country called Ireland.'

'Where is that?'

'Beyond the water. Near to England.'

'Where is that?'

'Beyond the water too. In the north.'

The girl in the bed remained with her head turned away from the soldier. 'And why do you come so far to persecute us?'

'You are heretics. Your heresy endangers the Holy Mother Church. All, everywhere, have a duty to defend Her.'

'Thirty pieces of silver.'

The officer appeared close to anger, but kept in mind the purpose of the day.

'If you have not heard of England then you have not heard of Cromwell.'

'Who is he?'

'He is dead now.'

'Is he your King? Did he recruit you? To come here and persecute us?'

'No. On the contrary.' The soldier began to remember things it did no good to remember, things which had fixed his life for ever, many years ago. Childhood, its sights, and its terrifying sounds. The harsh voices of England. 'Yes, I suppose he did. He recruited me, you could say.'

'Then I curse his name and all his family.'

The officer sighed. Where could he begin? There was so much to unravel, and he was an old man now, past forty. The child did not even know where England was. Where could he begin? 'Yes,' said the officer wearily. 'You curse his name. I curse his name too. We both curse his name. And on Sunday you will abjure.'

That Sunday, while incense stung her nostrils and her eye was assailed by the whorish colours of the King's religion, Marthe

Chaigne, aged thirteen, her heart burdened by the sorrow she was causing her father and by the knowledge that she would never be permitted to explain, abjured her faith. She made a mark on the register beside her name, and the officer of the dragons signed as witness. After he had signed, he looked up at the priest and said, in his own language, 'What matter the road provided it lead to Paradise?'

Marthe Chaigne was taken that day to the Union Chrétienne on the other side of the Montagne Noire, where she would be educated by the good sisters. The cost of her education would be added to the Tallage owed by Pierre Chaigne.

The following week the dragons left the town. The heretics had been reduced in number from 176 to eight. There were always the obstinate ones, but experience had shown that when they were greatly outnumbered they had little influence and ended their lives in bitterness and despair. The dragons were to move south and start their work in a new place.

The eight obstinate ones were burdened by the Tallage of those who had converted, with the cost of educating their own children as Catholics, and with numerous additional imposts. By ordinance they were forbidden from practising their trade or from hiring out their labour to members of the King's religion. They were also forbidden from abandoning their homes and seeking the promised land elsewhere.

Two nights after the dragons left, Pierre Chaigne, carpenter, widower, returned to his workshed. He took down the lantern he had made and slid out three of its glass panels. From the pile of discarded lumber too contemptible even to be burnt by the soldiers he uncovered the three oblongs of thin beechwood. He pushed them gently between the runners sticky with mutton fat. Then he lit the candle and set the hood back in place. Lacking three-quarters of its glass, the instrument did not illuminate universally. But it gave a brighter, purer light for the direction in which it was pointed. Pierre Chaigne, carpenter, widower, would follow that light to the end of its journey. He walked to the door of his shed, lifted the latch, and set off into the cold night. The yellow beam of his lamp reached tremblingly towards the forest, where the other obstinate ones waited for him to join them in prayer.

The Dream Lover

WILLIAM BOYD

'NONE OF THESE girls is French, right?'

'No. But they're European.'

'Not the same thing, man. French is crucial.'

'Of course . . .' I don't know what he is talking about but it seems politic to agree.

'You know any French girls?'

'Of course,' I say again. This is almost a lie, but it doesn't matter at this stage.

'But *well*? I mean well enough to ask out?'

'I don't see why not.' Now this time we are well into mendacity, but I am unconcerned. I feel good, adult, quite confident today. This lie can germinate and grow for a while.

I am standing in a pale parallelogram of March sunshine, leaning against a wall, talking to my American friend, Preston. The wall belongs to the Centre Universitaire Méditerranéan, a large stuccoed villa on the promenade at Nice. In front of us is a small cobbled courtyard bounded by a balustrade. Beyond is the Promenade des Anglais, its four lanes busy with Nice's traffic. Over the burnished roofs of the cars I can see the Mediterranean. The Baie des Anges looks grey and grimy in this season: old, tired water – ashy, cindery.

'We got to do something . . .' Preston says, a hint of petulant desperation in his voice. I like the 'we'. Preston scratches his short hard hair noisily. 'What with the new apartment, and all.'

53

'You moved out of the hotel?'

'Yeah. Want to come by tonight?' He shifts his big frame as if troubled by a fugitive itch, and pats his pockets – breast, hip, thigh – looking for his cigarettes. 'We got a bar on the roof.'

I am intrigued, but I explain that the invitation has to be turned down as it is a Monday, and every Monday night I have a dinner appointment with a French family – friends of friends of my mother.

Preston shrugs, then finds and sets fire to a cigarette. He smokes an American brand called 'Picayune' which is made in New Orleans. When he came to France he brought two thousand with him. He has never smoked anything else since he was fourteen, he insists.

We watch our fellow students saunter into the building. They are nearly all strangers to me, these bright boys and girls, as I have only been in Nice a few weeks, and, so far, Preston is the only friend I have made. Slightly envious of their easy conviviality, I watch the others chatter and mingle – Germans, Scandinavians, Italians, Tunisians, Nigerians . . . We are all foreigners, trying hard to learn French and win our diplomas . . . Except for Preston, who makes no effort at all and seems quite content to remain monoglot.

A young guy with long hair rides his motorbike into the courtyard. He is wearing no shirt. He is English and, apart from me, the only other English person in the place. He revs his motorbike unnecessarily a few times before parking it and switching it off. He takes a T-shirt out of a saddle bag and nonchalantly pulls it on. I think how I too would like to own a motorbike and do exactly what he has done . . . His name is Tim. One day, I imagine, we might be friends. We'll see.

Monsieur Cambrai welcomes me with his usual exhausting, impossible geniality. He shakes my hand fervently and shouts to his wife over his shoulder.

'Ne bouge pas. C'est l'habitué. L'habitué!'

That's what he calls me – l'habitué, l'habitué de lundi, to give the appellation in full, so called because I am invited to dinner every Monday night without fail. He almost never uses my proper name and sometimes I find this perpetual alias a little wearing, a little stressful. 'Salut, l'habitué', 'Bien mangé, l'habitué?', 'Encore du vin, l'habitué?' and so on. But I like him and the entire Cambrai family; in fact I like them so much that it makes me feel weak, insufficient, cowed.

Monsieur and Madame are small people, fit, sophisticated and nimble, with neat spry figures. Both of them are dentists, it so happens, who teach at the big medical school here in Nice. A significant portion of my affection for them owes to the fact that they have three daughters – Delphine, Stephane and Annique – all older than me and all possessed of – to my fogged and blurry eyes – an incandescent, almost supernatural beauty. Stephane and Annique still live with their parents. Delphine has a flat somewhere in the city, but she often dines at home. These are the French girls that I claimed to know, though 'know' is far too inadequate a word to sum up the complexity of my feelings for them. I come to their house on Monday nights as a supplicant and votary, both frightened and in awe of them. I sit in their luminous presence, quiet and eager, for two hours or so, unmanned by my astonishing good fortune.

I am numbed further when I consider the family's disarming, disinterested kindness. When I arrived in Nice they were the only contacts I had in the city and, on my mother's urging, I duly wrote to them citing our tenuous connection via my mother's friend. To my surprise I was promptly invited to dinner and then invited back every Monday night. What shamed me was that I knew I myself could never be so hospitable so quickly, not even to a close friend, and what was more I knew no one else who would be, either. So I cross the Cambrai threshold each Monday with a rich cocktail of emotions gurgling inside me: shame, guilt, gratitude, admiration and – it goes without saying – lust.

Preston's new address is on the Promenade des Anglais itself – the 'Résidence Les Anges'. I stand outside the building, looking up, impressed. I have passed it many times before, a distressing and vulgar edifice on this celebrated boulevard, an unadorned rectangle of coppery, smoked glass with stacked ranks of gilded aluminium balconies.

I press a buzzer in a slim, freestanding concrete post and speak into a crackling wire grille. When I mention the name 'Mr Fairfield' glass doors part softly and I am admitted to a bare granite lobby where a taciturn man in a tight suit shows me to the lift.

Preston rents a small studio apartment with a bathroom and

kitchenette. It is a neat, pastel coloured and efficient module. On the wall are a series of prints of exotic birds: a toucan, a bataleur eagle, something called a blue shrike. As I stand there looking round I think of my own temporary home, my thin room in Madame d'Amico's ancient, dim apartment, and the inefficient and bathless bathroom I have to share with her other lodgers, and a sudden hot envy rises through me. I half hear Preston enumerating the various financial consequences of his tenancy: how much this studio costs a month; the outrageous supplement he had to pay even to rent it in the first place; and how he had been obliged to cash in his return fare to the States (first class) in order to meet it. He says he has called his father for more money.

We ride up to the roof, six storeys above the Promenade. To my vague alarm there is a small swimming pool up here and a large glassed in cabaña – furnished with a bamboo bar and some rattan seats – labelled 'Club Les Anges' in neon copperplate. A barman in a short cerise jacket runs this place, a portly, pale faced fellow with a poor moustache whose name is Serge. Although Preston jokes patronisingly with him it is immediately quite clear to me both that Serge loathes Preston and that Preston is completely unaware of this powerful animus directed against him.

I order a large gin and tonic from Serge and for a shrill palpitating minute I loathe Preston too. I know there are many better examples on offer, of course, but for the time being this shiny building and its accoutrements will do nicely as an approximation of The Good Life for me. And as I sip my sour drink a sour sense of the world's huge unfairness crowds ruthlessly in. Why should this guileless, big American, barely older than me, with his two thousand Louisiana cigarettes, and his cashable first-class air tickets have all *this* . . . while I live in a narrow frowsty room in an old woman's decrepit apartment? (My straitened circumstances are caused by a seemingly interminable postal strike in Britain that means money cannot be transferred to my Nice account and I have to husband my financial resources like a neurotic peasant conscious of a hard winter lowering ahead.) Where is *my* money, I want to know, *my* exotic bird prints, *my* pool? How long will I have to wait before these artefacts become the commonplace of my life? . . . I allow this unpleasant voice to whine and whinge on in my head as we stand on the terrace and admire the view of the long bay. One habit I have already learnt, even at my age, is not to resist these fervent grudges – give them a loose rein, let them run themselves out, it is always better in the long run.

In fact I am drawn to Preston, and want him to be my friend. He is tall and powerfully built – the word 'rangy' comes to mind – affable and not particularly intelligent. To my eyes his clothes are so parodically American as to be beyond caricature: pale blue baggy shirts with button-down collars, old khaki trousers short enough to reveal his white-socked ankles and big brown loafers. He has a gold watch, a zippo lighter and an ugly ring with a red stone set in it. He told me once, in all candour, in all modesty, that he 'played tennis to Davis Cup standard'.

I always wondered what he was doing in Nice, studying at the Centre. At first I thought he might be a draftee avoiding the war in Vietnam but I now suspect – based on some hints he has dropped – that he has been sent off to France as an obscure punishment of some sort. His family don't want him at home: he has done something wrong and these months in Nice are his penance.

But hardly an onerous one, that's for sure: he has no interest in his classes – those he can be bothered to take – nor in the language and culture of France. He simply has to endure this exile and he will be allowed home where, I imagine, he will resume his soft life of casual privilege and unreflecting ease once more. He talks a good deal about his eventual return to the States where he plans to impose his own particular punishment, or extract his own special reward. He says he will force his father to buy him an Aston Martin. His father will have no say in the matter, he remarks with untypical vehemence and determination. He will have his Aston Martin, and it is the bright promise of this glossy English car that really seems to sustain him through these dog days on the Mediterranean littoral.

Soon I find I am a regular visitor at the Résidence Les Anges, where I go most afternoons after my classes are over. Preston and I sit in the club, or by the pool if it is sunny, and drink. We consume substantial amounts (it all goes on his tab) and consequently I am usually fairly drunk by sunset. Our conversation ranges far and wide but at some point in every discussion Preston reiterates his desire to meet French girls. If I do indeed know some French girls, he says, why don't I ask them to the Club? I reply that I am working on it, and coolly change the subject.

Steadily, over the days, I learn more about my American friend. He is an only child. His father (who has not responded to his requests for money) is a millionaire – real estate. His mother divorced him recently to marry another, richer millionaire. Between his two sets of millionaire parents Preston has a choice of eight homes to visit in and around the USA: in Miami, New York, Palm Springs and a ranch in Montana. Preston dropped out of college after two semesters and does not work.

'Why should I?' he argues reasonably. 'They've got more than enough money for me too. Why should I bust my ass working trying to earn more?'

'But isn't it . . . What do you do all day?'

'All kinds of shit . . . But mostly I like to play tennis a lot. And I like to fuck, of course.'

'So why did you come to Nice?'

He grins. 'I was a bad boy.' He slaps his wrist and laughs. 'Naughty, naughty Preston.'

He won't tell me what he did.

It is spring in Nice. Each day we start to enjoy a little more sunshine and whenever it appears within ten minutes there is a particular girl, lying on the plage publique in front of the Centre, sunbathing. Often I stand and watch her spread out there, still, supine on the cool pebbles – the only sunbather along the entire bay. It turns out she is well known, that this is a phenomenon that occurs every year. By early summer her tan is solidly established and she is very brown indeed. By August she is virtually black, with that kind of dense, matt tan, the life burned out of the skin, her pores brimming with melanin. Her ambition each year, they say, is to be the brownest girl on the Côte d'Azure . . .

I watch her lying there, immobile beneath the invisible rain of ultra violet. It is definitely not warm . . . even in my jacket and scarf I shiver slightly in the fresh breeze. How can she be bothered? I wonder, but at the same time I have to admit there is something admirable in such singlemindedness, such ludicrous dedication.

Eventually I take my first girl to the Club to meet Preston. Her name is Ingrid, she is in my class, a Norwegian, but with dark auburn hair. I don't know her well but she seems a friendly, uncomplicated soul. She speaks perfect English and German.

'Are you French?' Preston asks, almost immediately.

Ingrid is very amused by this. 'I'm Norwegian,' she explains. 'Is it important?'

I apologise to Preston when Ingrid goes off to change into her swimming costume, but he waves it away, not to worry he says, she's cute. Ingrid returns and we sit in the sun and order the first of our many drinks. Ingrid, after some prompting, smokes one of Preston's Picayune cigarettes. The small flaw that emerges to mar our pleasant afternoon is that, the more Ingrid drinks, so does her conversation become dominated by references to a French boy she is seeing called Jean-Jacques. Preston hides his disappointment; he is the acme of good manners.

Later, we play poker using cheese biscuits as chips. Ingrid sits opposite me in her multicoloured swimsuit. She is plumper than I had imagined, and I decide that if I had to sum her up in one word it would be 'homely'. Except for one detail: she has very hairy armpits. On one occasion she sits back in her chair, studying her cards for a full minute, her free hand idly scratching a bite on the back of her neck. Both Preston's and my eyes are drawn to the thick divot of auburn hair that is revealed by this gesture: we stare at it, fascinated, as Ingrid deliberates whether to call or raise.

After she has gone Preston confesses that he found her unshavenness quite erotic. I am not so sure.

That night we sit on in the Club long into the night, as usual the place's sole customers, with Serge unsmilingly replenishing our drinks as Preston calls for them. Ingrid's presence, the unwitting erotic charge that she has detonated in our normally tranquil, bibulous afternoons, seems to have unsettled and troubled Preston somewhat and without any serious prompting on my part he tells me why he has come to Nice. He informs me that the man his mother remarried was a widower, an older man, with four children already in their twenties. When Preston dropped out of college he went to stay with his mother and new stepfather. He exhales, he eats several olives, his face goes serious and solemn for a moment.

'This man, his name's Michael, had three daughters – and a son, who was already married – and, man, you should have seen those girls.' He grins, a stupid, gormless grin. 'I was eighteen years old and I got three beautiful girls sleeping down the corridor from me. What am I supposed to do?'

The answer, unvoiced, seemed to slip into the Club like a draught of air. I felt my spine tauten.

'You mean –?'

'Yeah, sure. All three of them. Eventually.'

I don't want to speak, so I think through this. I imagine a big silent house, night, long dark corridors, closed doors. Three bored blonde tanned stepsisters. Suddenly there's a tall young man in the house, a virtual stranger, who plays tennis to Davis Cup standard.

'What went wrong?' I manage.

'Oldest one, Janie, got pregnant, didn't she? Last year.'

'Abortion?'

'Are you kidding? She just married her fiancé real fast.'

'You mean she was engaged when –'

'He doesn't know a thing. But she told my mother.'

'The, the child was –'

'Haven't seen him yet.' He turns and calls for Serge. 'No one knows, no one suspects . . .' He grins again. 'Until the kid starts smoking Picayunes.' He reflects on his life a moment, and turns his big mild face to me. 'That's why I'm here. Keeping my head down. Not exactly flavour of the month back home.'

The next girl I take to the Club is also Scandinavian – we have eight in our class – but this time a Swede, called Danni. Danni is very attractive and vivacious, in my opinion, with straight white-blonde hair. She's a tall girl, full breasted, and she would be perfect but for the fact that she has one slightly withered leg, noticeably thinner than the other, which causes her to limp. She is admirably unselfconscious about her disability.

'Hi,' Preston says, 'are you French?'

Danni hides her incredulity. 'Mais, oui, monsieur. Bien sûr.' Like Ingrid, she finds this presumption highly amusing. Preston soon realises his mistake, and makes light of his disappointment.

Danni wears a small cobalt bikini and even swims in the pool, which is freezing. (Serge says there is something wrong with the heating mechanism but we don't believe him.) Danni's fortitude impresses Preston: I can see it in his eyes, as he watches her dry herself. He asks her what happened to her leg and she tells him she had polio as a child.

'Shit, you were lucky you don't need a caliper.'

This breaks the ice and we soon get noisily drunk, much to Serge's irritation. But there is little he can do as there is no one else in the Club who might complain. Danni produces some grass and we blatantly smoke a joint. Typically, apart from faint nausea, the drug has not the slightest effect on me, but it affords Serge a chance to be officious and as he clears away a round of empty glasses he says to Preston, 'Ça va pas, monsieur, non, non, ça va pas.'

'Fuck you, Serge,' he says amiably and Danni's unstoppable blurt of laughter sets us all off. I sense Serge's humiliation and realise the relationship with Preston is changing fast: the truculent deference has gone; the dislike is overt, almost a challenge.

After Danni has left, Preston tells me about his latest money problems. His bar bill at the Club now stands at over $400 and the management is insisting it be settled. His father won't return his calls, acknowledge telegrams and Preston has no credit cards. He is contemplating pawning his watch in order to pay something into the account and defer suspicion. I buy it off him for 500 francs.

I look around my class counting the girls I know. I know most of them by now, well enough to talk to. Both Ingrid and Danni have been back to the Club and have enthused about their afternoons there, and I realise that to my fellow students I have become an object of some curiosity as a result of my unexpected ability to dispense these small doses of luxury and decadence: the exclusive addresses, the privacy of the Club, the pool on the roof, the endless flow of free drinks . . .

Preston decided to abandon his French classes a while ago and I am now his sole link with the Centre. It is with some mixed emotions – I feel vaguely pimp-like, oddly smirched – that I realise how simple it is to attract girls to the Club Les Anges.

Annique Cambrai is the youngest of the Cambrai daughters and the closest to me in age. She is only two years older than me but seems considerably more than that. I was, I confess, oddly daunted by her mature good looks, dark with a lean, attractive face, and because of this at first I think she found me rather aloof, but now, after many Monday dinners, we have become more relaxed and friendly. She is studying law at the University of Nice and speaks good English with a marked American accent. When I comment on this she explains that most French universities now offer you a choice of accents when you study English and, like ninety per cent of students, she has chosen American.

I see my opportunity and take it immediately: would she, I diffidently enquire, like to come to the Résidence Les Anges to meet an American friend of mine and perhaps try her new accent out on him?

The next morning, on my way down the rue de France to the Centre I see Preston standing outside a pharmacy reading the *Herald Tribune*. I call his name and cross the road to tell him the excellent news about Annique.

'You won't believe this,' I say, 'but I finally got a real French girl.'

Preston's face looks odd: half a smile, half a morose grimace of disappointment.

'That's great,' he says, dully, 'wonderful.'

A tall slim girl steps out of the pharmacy and hands him a plastic bag.

'This is Lois,' he says. We shake hands.

I know who Lois is, Preston has often spoken of her: my damn-near fiancée, he calls her. It transpires that Lois has flown over spontaneously and unannounced to visit him.

'And, boy, are my Mom and Dad mad as hell,' she laughs.

Lois is a pretty girl, with a round, innocent face quite free of make-up. She is tall, even in her sneakers she is as tall as me, with a head of incredibly thick, dense brown hair which, for some reason, I associate particularly with American girls. I feel sure also, though as yet I have no evidence, that she is a very clean person – physically clean, I mean to say – someone who showers and washes regularly, redolent of soap and the lingering farinaceous odour of talcum powder.

I stroll back with them to the Résidence. Lois's arrival has temporarily solved Preston's money problems: they have cashed in her return ticket and paid off the bar bill and the next quarter's rent which had come due. Preston feels rich enough to buy back his watch from me.

Annique looks less mature and daunting in her swimsuit, I'm pleased to say, though I was disappointed that she favoured a demure apple-green one-piece. The pool's heater has been 'fixed' and for the first time we all swim in the small azure rectangle – Preston and Lois, Annique and me. It is both strange and exciting for me to see Annique so comparatively unclothed and even stranger to lie side by side, thigh by thigh, inches apart, sunbathing.

Lois obviously assumes Annique and I are a couple – a quite natural assumption under the circumstances, I suppose – she would never imagine I had brought her for Preston. I keep catching him gazing at Annique, and a mood of frustration and intense sadness seems to emanate from him – a mood of which only I am aware. And in turn a peculiar exhilaration builds inside me, not just because of Lois's innocent assumption about my relation to Annique, but also because I know now that I have succeeded. I have brought Preston the perfect French girl: Annique, by his standards, represents the paradigm, the Platonic ideal for this American male. Here she is, unclothed, lying by his pool, in his club, drinking his drinks, but he can do nothing – and what makes my own excitement grow is the realisation that for the first time in our friendship – perhaps for the first time in his life – Preston envies another person. Me.

Now that Lois has arrived I stay away from the Résidence Les Anges. It won't be the same again and, despite my secret delight, I don't want to taunt Preston with the spectre of Annique. But I find that without the spur of his envy the tender fantasy inevitably dims; for my dream life, my dream love, to flourish, I need to share it with Preston. I decide to pay a visit. Preston opens the door of his studio.

'Hi stranger,' he says, with some enthusiasm. 'Am I glad to see you.' He seems sincere. I follow him into the apartment. The small room is untidy, the bed unmade, the floor strewn with female clothes. I hear the noise of the shower from the bathroom: Lois may be a clean person but it is clear she is also something of a slut.

'How are things with Annique?' he asks, almost at once, as casually as he can manage. He has to ask, I know it.

I look at him. 'Good.' I let the pause develop, pregnant with innuendo. 'No, they're good.'

His nostrils flare and he shakes his head.

'God, you're one lucky –'

Lois comes in from the bathroom in a dressing-gown, towelling her thick hair dry.

'Hi, Edward,' she says, 'what's new?' Then she sits down on the bed and begins to weep.

We stand and look at her as she sobs quietly.

'It's nothing,' Preston says. 'She just wants to go home.' He tells me that neither of them has left the building for eight days. They are completely, literally, penniless. Lois's parents have cancelled her credit cards and collect calls home have failed to produce any response. Preston has been unable to locate his father and now his stepfather refuses to speak to him (a worrying sign) and although his mother would like to help she is powerless for the moment, given Preston's fall from grace. Preston and Lois have been living on a diet of olives, peanuts and cheese biscuits served up in the bar and, of course, copious alcohol.

'Yeah, but now we're even banned from there,' Lois says, with an unfamiliar edge to her voice.

'Last night I beat up on that fuckwit, Serge,' Preston explains with a shrug. 'Something I had to do.'

He goes on to enumerate their other problems: their bar bill stands at over $300; Serge is threatening to go to the police unless he is compensated; the management has grown hostile and suspicious.

'We got to get out of here,' Lois says miserably. 'I hate it here, I hate it.'

Preston turns to me. 'Can you help us out?' he says. I feel the laugh erupt within me.

I stand in Nice station and hand Preston two train tickets to Luxembourg and two one-way Icelandair tickets to New York. Lois reaches out to touch them as if they were sacred relics.

'You've got a six-hour wait in Reykjavik for your connection,' I tell him, 'but, believe me, there is no cheaper way to fly.'

I bask in their voluble gratitude for a while. They have no luggage with them as they could not be seen to be quitting the Résidence. Preston says his father is now in New York and assures me I will be reimbursed the day they arrive. I have spent almost everything I possess on these tickets, but I don't care – I am intoxicated with my own generosity and the strange power it has conferred on me. Lois leaves us to go in search of a toilette and Preston embraces me in a clumsy hug.

'I won't forget this, man,' he says many times. We celebrate our short but intense friendship and affirm its continuance, but all the while I am waiting for him to ask me – I can feel the question growing in his head like a tumour. Through the crowds of passengers we see Lois making her way back. He doesn't have much time left.

'Listen,' he begins, his voice low, 'did you and Annique . . .? I mean, are you –'

'We've been looking for an apartment. That's why you haven't seen much of me.'

'Jesus . . .'

Lois calls out something about the train timetable, but we are not listening. Preston seems to be trembling, he turns away, and when he turns back I see the pale fires of impotent resentment light in his eyes.

'Are you fucking her?'

'Why else would we be looking for an apartment?'

'What's going on?' Lois asks. 'The train's leaving soon.'

Preston gestures at me, as if he can't pronounce my name. 'Annique . . . They're moving in together.'

Lois squeals. She's so pleased, she really is, she really really likes Annique.

By the time I see them onto the train Preston has calmed down and our final farewells are sincere. He looks around the modest station intently as if trying to record its essence, as if now he wished to preserve something of this city he inhabited so complacently, with such absence of curiosity.

'God, it's too bad,' he says with an exquisite fervour. 'I know I could have liked Nice. I *know*. I really could.'

I back off, wordless, this is too good, this is too generous of him. This is perfect.

'Give my love to Annique,' Preston says quietly, as Lois calls loud goodbyes.

'Oh, don't worry,' I say, looking at Preston. 'I will.'

The Last Island Boy

GEORGE MACKAY BROWN

'CHRISTMAS!' SAID THE man. 'What do we want with Christmas? What's Christmas to us? All I know is, it's winter. The worst storms are still to come. Will we last through the winter? That's what I'd like to know.'

The woman said nothing. She put a few pieces of salt fish into the pot and began to peel potatoes.

Outside, it was another grey cold day. Sometimes the greyness outside would darken, as if another shadow or cloud had been mixed into it. Then sleet would blatter on the window for a while, a bleak cold sound.

'We should never have come here in the first place,' said the man. 'It hasn't worked. But if I hadn't come – if I hadn't left that office in Leeds and come, I would be tormenting myself still with the dream – the island of innocence and peace in the north, face to face with the elements. That, I thought in my ignorance, was how people should live . . .'

The boy had just been ferried across from the bigger island that had the school on it. From the few lights on the pier he had been ferried, the sole passenger, to the lamp in the solitary island croft.

'It's just that they're having a Christmas party in the school,' he said.

The woman broke another peat into the range and stirred the ribs till a new flame appeared.

'Come over and warm yourself,' she said.

*

The next day was Saturday. The boy lay warm in the nest of his bed till nine o'clock.

When he got up and went into the kitchen the lamp was still lit. The woman was baking at the table. Her face was flushed. It seemed to be a different baking from the usual Saturday morning oatcakes and floury bannocks. There were three stone jars on the table. She was intent on a cookery book. The whole stove seemed to throb with the red glow of the peat.

'There's tea in the pot,' said the woman. 'The porridge is a bit cold.'

'Where is he?' said the boy.

'He's out in the boat,' said the woman. 'There's a storm forecast. He wants to get a few fish if he can.'

It was a much better morning. The night wind had swept the sky clear of the last rag of cloud. The sky was a delicate blue, like china. The sun was low in the south-east, making silver undulations on the rise and fall of the sea.

'Goodness!' cried the woman, 'the sun's out . . .' She screwed down the wick and blew out the lamp flame with a small spurt of breath.

The boy wandered outside, among a quick welcome and dispersal of hens (because they saw he had no food for them).

He had the whole morning to himself. He wondered if it would be possible, before dinner-time, to visit every ruined croft in the island . . . No, it wouldn't be possible. The midwinter sun would be down before he had half completed his round, and he might not find his way home again.

Still, he would manage six or seven.

The first croft, Smert, wasn't far away, across two fields and a wet ditch. It was still in passable shape, Smert. An island family had lived there till two years before, then suddenly they had sold up and gone to live in the town. The croft had been advertised for sale. Nobody had wanted it. (Who would want to live and work in a dying island?)

But for his dark resolute father, there were no crofters in the island now.

The boy peered through the window of Smert. There was a table and two chairs inside, a box bed, a rusted range; a picture of the Channel Fleet on one wall. But the place breathed dampness and decay.

The boy left Smert and ran towards the next croft. It was an utter ruin. He did not know what its name was. Naked rafters showed through the few roofing flags that remained. Door and windows were vacant rectangles. Long and low the croft lay on the first slope of the hill, as if it had sailed forever on that green wave, from the foundation stone to the first sag of the roof: ten generations maybe. Beyond the living-quarters lay the remnants of byre and barn; the floor a confusion of stones.

And yet, thought the boy, there was a freshness and cleanness about it, like a bone in the wind and rain, now that the last rags and shards of life were no longer there.

The nameless place must have been deserted for half a century, at least.

From the top of the low island hill the boy could see seven or eight other islands. His own island was spread beneath him like a drab brown cloth, pitted with ruins and half-ruins, and a few mounds from the very ancient past.

The winter sun had reached its zenith and in another three hours would go, a cold bright diamond, into the Atlantic.

Ah, there was the boat, under the cliff, with the man in it! He was leaning over and looking deep into the sea, one oar upraised.

And there she was, the woman, outside the door, throwing cold porridge and breadcrumbs and oats to the hens.

(Since the time of the poor harvest, they had stopped using names. 'The man', 'the woman', 'the boy' – that's how they referred to each other.)

He drifted down, slowly, to the biggest house in the island, the laird's Hall. The tall house was stubborn in its fight against time. The great door still stood, and the shutters, though the paint had long since peeled from them and they were beginning to warp. But the stonework – it could outface centuries, so firmly the masonry had been dressed and set. The walls of the great garden, too, showed not a breach or a fissure, though the garden itself – once plotted into a formal Italian style by two gardeners from the south – was a jungle of weeds and nettles.

The tall octagonal sundial intrigued the boy. Last summer the indicator had thrown the sun's shadow on precisely the right mark. The wet autumn had corroded it, and time fell a blank on the stone's intricate angles.

Here, in the great drawing-room, there would have been winter balls a hundred years ago, rustling of silk gowns, music of violin and piano, old formal courtesies of invitation and acceptance, smells of Havana cigars, hot punch, trout, grouse.

Standing on tiptoe outside the tall window, the boy felt a desolation he had not known before. Where was it now, all that wealth and beauty? When had the roses and butterflies left the garden?

He ran, squelching through a wet field to the shore. Well, he had heard all about this ruin and its former tenant. It had been called 'Jamaica', and Captain Haraldson had lived there between his retirement from the sea until he went his last voyage to the hospital, and soon into the deeper waters of death.

The islanders said he hadn't been a skipper at all; an ordinary seaman all his career, at best maybe bosun. And the left forearm he said had been taken by a shark – that, said the last islanders, had been the result of a wild punch-up in Amsterdam in his youth. 'That shark,' the skipper had said, 'he had my arm, but I had his life – I ripped him open from fin to tail!' And the wives he had had, in the Gilbert Islands and San Francisco and St John's, and the horde of children, scattered world-wide . . . 'It's a funny thing,' old Widow Wilson had said, 'whenever he came on leave, not a lass would look at him, in this island or that.'

The ruin of the skipper's house stood right on the edge of the sea-banks. Erosion was eating so fast into this part of the shore, that a cornerstone of the house was actually overhanging the edge of the shallow cliff. It would not be very long, thought the boy, till all those stones would be mingled with the shore stones and the sea.

He wondered where the old sailor had sat and told his stories. Over there it must be, in a chair beside that black-ened stone, the hearth. He stopped and turned a stone. The sun through the broken west wall took a dull gleam from a coin! The boy picked it up. It had strange devices on either side, and foreign lettering. Was it – could it conceivably be – gold? It was yellow and untarnished. Had the skipper hidden it away for some purpose? Had it fallen out of his coin-box one night and rolled into an interstice of the flagstone floor?

Whatever had happened, it was a marvellous thing to have found! He would carry it home. Perhaps it would save them from ruin that the man said was staring them in the face . . .

The thought that next year the island might be utterly empty put a shiver of fear over him.

He stowed the coin carefully in his pocket.

Across the Sound he could see the island where he went to school five mornings a week. He looked. Yes, there it was, the big building at the back of the village, between the church and the shop. As he looked, the declining sun flashed from the school window, suddenly, intolerable brightness, as if the interior was a mass of cold silver flames.

He walked along the shore, eastwards. A few skeletons of fishing boats rotted among the stones. He could just make out the name of one boat: *Star*.

Going up the shore path to the road above, he passed the green mound with its few underground dwellings where the archaeologists from England had worked all last summer. There, in stone hollows not so very different from the crofts of recent times, had lived the first islanders of all, with their fish-oil lamps and clay pots of grain and milk. But were they really the first? The boy's mind moved back through time to a still earlier folk. Ah, how cruel it must have been for them in winter, clad in sealskin and otter skin, with only a few shreds of beach-growth to put in their mouths! And yet they had endured till the light's return. How wonderful it must have been to those shadowy folk, the sun of early summer, the springing grass, larksong, the silver legions of fish . . .

Right on the ness stood the ruins of a little medieval monastery.

The boy thought he might just get there before the sun went down. Then he could find his way home well enough in the sunset afterglow.

How tired he was! Here and there, the chapel walls were almost at ground level, but the apse and stone floor of the nave were still there, and a single arch in the south.

About a dozen monks had lived there, the teacher had told him, and the brothers had farmed, fished, kept bees, and recited or sung the 'office' that was appropriate to each season of the turning year.

As the boy sat against a grey-lichened wall near the ruined floor, he heard them singing. The separate voices, high and low, grave yet full of joy, interwove, mingled, blended. There issued from the invisible choir a texture of peace deeper than any natural silence. The hymn was in a foreign language – Norwegian? Gaelic? – and yet the boy seemed to grasp a meaning at once.

Benedictus es, qui ambulas

super pennas ventorum, super
undas maris. Et laudabilis,
et gloriosus in secula . . .

The sun was down. The first wind of night began to stir, and it shifted a thin wash of sea over the shore stones below, again and again.

The voices in the choir mingled with the wind and the sea and were lost . . .

Ah, there was the lamp in the window!

The boy ran up the last slope to the door.

A rich spicy smell met him at the threshold. The woman – his mother – had baked a large cake.

There it stood on the table, cooling on a wire tray.

The man – his father – was not long in from the sea. A basket of haddocks stood at the door. The fisherman was testing the edge of a knife on his thumb.

'I'm glad you're home,' said the woman. 'There's going to be another storm.'

The wind was beginning to make songs in the chimney.

The boy could hear, through the open door, the noise of the breakers against the stones.

The cow lowed from the byre.

Medusa's Ankles

A. S. BYATT

SHE HAD WALKED in one day because she had seen the Rosy
Nude through the plate glass. That was odd, she thought, to
have that lavish and complex creature stretched voluptuously
above the coat rack, where one might have expected the stare,
silver and supercilious or jetty and frenzied, of the model girl.
They were all girls now, not women. The Rosy Nude was pure
flat colour, but suggested mass. She had huge haunches and a
monumental knee, lazily propped high. She had round breasts,
contemplations of the circle, reflections on flesh and its fall.

She had asked cautiously for a cut and blow dry. He had
done her himself, the owner, Lucian of 'Lucian's', slender
and soft-moving, resembling a balletic Hamlet with full white
sleeves and tight black trousers. She remembered the trousers,
at first, the first few times she came, better than his face, which
she saw only in the mirror behind her own, which she felt a
middle-aged disinclination to study. A woman's relation with
her hairdresser is anatomically odd. Her face meets his belt,
his haunches skim her breathing, his face is far away, high and
behind. His face had a closed and monkish look, rather fine, she
thought, under soft straight, dark hair, bright with health, not
with added fats, or so it seemed.

'I like your Matisse,' she said, the first time.

He looked blank.

'The pink nude. I love her.'

'Oh, that. I saw it in a shop. I thought it went exactly

72

with the colour-scheme I was planning.'

Their eyes met in the mirror.

'I thought she was wonderful,' he said. 'So calm, so damn sure of herself, such a lovely colour, I do think, don't you? I fell for her, absolutely. I saw her in this shop in the Charing Cross Road and I went home, and said to my wife, I might think of placing her in the salon, and she thought nothing to it, but the next day I went back and just got her. She gives the salon a bit of class. I like things to have class.'

In those days the salon was like the interior of a rosy cloud, all pinks and creams, with creamy muslin curtains here and there, and ivory brushes and combs, and here and there – the mirror-frames, the little trollies – a kind of sky-blue, a dark sky-blue, the colour of the couch or bed on which the rosy nude spread herself. Music played – Susannah hated piped music – but this music was tinkling and tripping and dropping, quiet seraglio music, like sherbet. He gave her coffee in pink cups, with a pink and white wafer biscuit in the saucer. He soothed her middle-aged hair into a cunningly blown and natural wind-swept sweep, with escaping strands and tendrils, softening brow and chin. She remembered the hairdressing shop of her war-time childhood, with its boarded wooden cubicles, its advertise-ments for Amami shampoo, depicting ladies with blonde page-boys and red lips, in the forties bow which was wider than the thirties rosebud. Amami, she had always supposed, rhymed with smarmy and was somehow related to it. When she became a linguist, and could decline the verb to love in several languages, she saw suddenly one day that Amami was an erotic invitation, or command. Ama-mi, love me, the blondes said, under their impeccably massed rolls of hair. Her mother had gone draggled under the chipped dome of the hairdryer, bristling with metal rollers, bobby-pins and pipe-cleaners. And had come out under a rigidly bouncy 'set', like a mountain of wax fruit, that made her seem artificial and embarrassing, drawing attention somehow to the unnatural whiteness of her false teeth.

They had seemed like some kind of electrically shocking initiation into womanhood, those clamped domes descending and engulfing. She remembered her own first 'set', the heat and buzzing, and afterwards a slight torn tenderness of the scalp, a slight tindery dryness to the hair.

In the sixties and seventies she had kept a natural look, had grown her hair long and straight and heavy, a chestnut-glossy curtain, had avoided places like this. And in the years of her avoidance, the cubicles had gone, everything was open and shared and above board, blow-dryers had largely replaced the hoods, plastic spikes the bristles.

She had had to come back because her hair began to grow old. The ends split, the weight of it broke, a kind of frizzed fur replaced the gloss. Lucian said that curls and waves – following the lines of the new unevenness – would dissimulate, would render natural-looking, that was, young, what was indeed natural, the death of the cells. Short and bouncy was best, Lucian said, and proved it, tactfully. He stood above her with his fine hands cupped lightly round her new bubbles and wisps, like the hands of a priest round a Grail. She looked, quickly, quickly, it was better than before, thanked him and averted her eyes.

She came to trust him with her disintegration.

He was always late to their appointment, to all appointments. The salon was full of whisking young things, male and female, and he stopped to speak to all of them, to all the patient sitters, with their questing, mirror-bound stares. The telephone rang perpetually. She sat on a rosy foamy pouffe and read in a glossy magazine, *Her Hair*, an article at once solemnly portentous and remorselessly jokey (such tones are common) about the hairdresser as the new healer, with his cure of souls. Once, the magazine informed her, the barber had been the local surgeon, had drawn teeth, set bones and dealt with female problems. Now in the rush of modern alienated life, the hairdresser performed the all-important function of listening. He elicited the tale of your troubles and calmed you.

Lucian did not. He had another way. He created his own psychiatrist and guru from his captive hearer. Or at least, so Susannah found, who may have been specially selected because she was plump, which could be read as motherly, and because, as a university teacher, she was, as he detected, herself a professional listener. He asked her advice.

'I don't see myself shut in here for the next twenty years. I want more out of life. Life has to have a meaning. I tried Tantric Art and the School of Meditation. Do you know about that sort of thing, about the inner life?'

His fingers flicked and flicked in her hair, he compressed a ridge and scythed it.

'Not really. I'm an agnostic.'

'I'd like to know about art. You know about art. You know about that pink nude, don't you? How do I find out?'

She told him to read Lawrence Gowing, and he clamped the tress he was attending to, put down his scissors, and wrote it all down in a little dove-grey leather book. She told him where to find good extra-mural classes and who was good among the gallery lecturers.

Next time she came it was not art, it was archaeology. There was no evidence that he had gone to the galleries or read the books.

'The past pulls you,' he said. 'Bones in the ground and gold coins in a hoard, all that. I went down to the city and saw them digging up the Mithraic temples. There's a religion, all that bull's blood, dark and light, fascinating.'

She wished he would tidy her head and be quiet. She could recognise the flitting mind, she considered. It frightened her. What she knew, what she cared about, what was coherent, separate shards for him to flit over, remaining separate. You wrote books and gave lectures, and these little ribbons of fact shone briefly and vanished.

'I don't want to put the best years of my life into making suburban old dears presentable,' he said. 'I want something more.'

'What?' she said, meeting his brooding stare above the wet mat of her mop. He puffed foam into it and said:

'Beauty. I want beauty. I must have beauty. I want to sail on a yacht among the Greek isles, with beautiful people.' He caught her eye. 'And see those temples and those sculptures.'

He pressed close, he pushed at the nape of her neck, her nose was near his discreet zip.

'You've been washing it without conditioner,' he said. 'You aren't doing yourself any good. I can tell.'

She bent her head submissively, and he scraped the base of her skull.

'You could have highlights,' he said in a tone of no enthusiasm. 'Bronze or mixed autumnal.'

'No thanks. I prefer it natural.'

He sighed.

He began to tell her about his love life. She would have inclined, on the evidence before her eyes, to the view that he was homosexual. The salon was full of beautiful young men, who came, wielded the scissors briefly, giggled together in corners, and departed. Chinese, Indonesian, Glaswegian, South African. He shouted at them and giggled with them, they exchanged little gifts and paid off obscure little debts to each other. Once she came in late and found them sitting in a circle, playing poker. The girls were subordinate and brightly hopeless. None of them lasted long. They wore – in those days – pink overalls with cream silk bindings. She could tell he had a love life because of the amount of time he spent alternately pleading and blustering on the telephone, his voice a blotting-paper hiss, his words inaudible, though she could hear the peppery rattle of the other voice, or voices, in the ear-piece. Her sessions began to take a long time, what with these phone calls and with his lengthy explanations, which he would accompany with gestures, making her look at his mirrored excitement, like a boy riding a bicycle hands-off.

'Forgive me if I'm a bit distracted,' he said. 'My life is in crisis. Something I never believed could happen has happened. All my life I've been looking for something and now I've found it.'

He wiped suds casually from her wet brow and scraped her eye-corner. She blinked.

'Love,' he said. 'Total affinity. Absolute compatibility. A miracle. My other half. A perfectly beautiful girl.'

She could think of no sentence to answer this. She said, schoolmistressy, what other tone was there? 'And this has caused the crisis?'

'She loves me. I couldn't believe it but it is true. She loves me. She wants me to live with her.'

'And your wife?'

There was a wife, who had thought nothing to the purchase of the Rosy Nude.

'She told me to get out of the house. So I got out. I went to her flat – my girlfriend's. She came and fetched me back – my wife. She said I must choose, but she thinks I'll choose her. I said it would be better for the moment just to let it evolve. I told her how do I know what I want, in this state of ecstasy, how do I know it'll last, how do I know she'll go on loving me?'

'I expect that didn't please her.'

He frowned impatiently and waved the scissors dangerously near her temples.

'All she cares about is respectability. She says she loves me but all she cares about is what the neighbours say. I like my house, though. She keeps it nice, I have to say. It's not stylish, but it is in good taste.'

Over the next few months, maybe a year, the story evolved, in bumps and jerks, not, it must be said, with any satisfactory narrative shape. He was a very bad storyteller, Susannah realised slowly. None of the characters acquired any roundness. She formed no image of the nature of the beauty of the girlfriend, or of the way she spent her time when not demonstrating her total affinity for Lucian. She did not know whether the wife was a shrew or a sufferer, nervous or patient or even ironically detached. All these wraith-personae were inventions of Susannah's own. About six months through the narrative Lucian said that his daughter was very upset about it all, the way he was forced to come and go, sometimes living at home, sometimes shut out.

'You have a daughter?'

'Fifteen. No, seventeen, I always get ages wrong.'

She watched him touch his own gleaming hair in the mirror, and smile apprehensively at himself.

'We were married very young,' he said. 'Very young, before we knew what was what.'

'It's hard on young girls, when there are disputes at home.'

'It is. It's hard on everyone. She says if I sell the house she'll have nowhere to live while she takes her exams. I have to sell the house if I'm to afford to keep up my half of my girlfriend's flat. I can't keep up the mortgages on both. My wife doesn't want to move. It's understandable, I suppose, but she has to see we can't go on like this. I can't be torn apart like this, I've got to decide.'

'You seem to have decided for your girlfriend.'

He took a deep breath and put down everything, comb, scissors, hairdryer.

'Ah, but I'm scared. I'm scared stiff if I take the plunge, I'll be left with nothing. If she's got me all the time, my girlfriend, perhaps she won't go on loving me like this. And I like my house, you know, it feels sort of comfortable to me, I'm used to it, all the old chairs. I don't quite like to think of it all sold and gone.'

'Love isn't easy.'

'You can say that again.'

'Do you think I'm getting thinner on top?'

'What? Oh no, not really, I wouldn't worry. We'll just train this little bit to fall across there like that. Do you think she has a right to more than half the value of the house?'

'I'm not a lawyer. I'm a classicist.'

'We're going on that Greek holiday. Me and my girlfriend. Sailing through the Greek isles. I've bought scuba gear. The salon will be closed for a month.'

'I'm glad you told me.'

While he was away the salon was redecorated. He had not told her about this, also, as indeed, why should he have done? It was done very fashionably in the latest colours, battleship-grey and maroon. Dried blood and instruments of slaughter, Susannah thought on her return. The colour scheme was one she particularly disliked. Everything was changed. The blue trolleys had been replaced with hi-tech steely ones, the ceiling loured, the faintly aquarial plate-glass was replaced with storm-grey-one-way-see-through-no-glare which made even bright days dull ones. The music was now muted heavy metal. The young men and young women wore dark grey Japanese wrappers and what she thought of as the patients, which included herself, more identical maroon ones. Her face in the mirror was grey, had lost the deceptive rosy haze of the earlier lighting.

The Rosy Nude was taken down. In her place were photographs of girls with grey faces, coal-black eyes and spiky lashes, under bonfires of incandescent puce hair which matched their lips, rounded to suck, at microphones perhaps, or other things. The new teacups were black and hexagonal. The pink flowery biscuits were replaced by sugar-coated minty elliptical sweets, black and white like Go counters. She thought after the first shock of this, that she would go elsewhere. But she was afraid of being made, accidentally, by anyone else, to look a fool. He understood her hair, Lucian, she told herself. It needed understanding, these days, it was not much any more, its life was fading from it.

'Did you have a good holiday?'

'Oh, idyllic. Oh, yes, a dream. I wish I hadn't come back. She's been to a solicitor. Claiming the matrimonial home for all the work she's done on it, and because of my daughter. I say, what about when she grows up, she'll get a job, won't she, you can't assume she'll hang around her mummy forever, they don't.'

'I need to look particularly good this time. I've won a prize. A translator's medal. I have to make a speech. On television.'

'We'll have to make you look lovely, won't we? For the honour of the salon. How do you like our new look?'

'It's very smart.'

'It is. It is. I'm not quite satisfied with the photos, though. I thought we could get something more intriguing. It has to be photos to go with the grey.'

He worked above her head. He lifted her wet hair with his fingers and let the air run through it, as though there was twice as much as there was. He pulled a twist this way, and clamped it to her head, and screwed another way, and put his head on one side and another, contemplating her uninspiring bust. When her head involuntarily followed his he said quite nastily, 'Keep still, can you, I can't work if you keep bending from side to side like a swan.'

'I'm sorry.'

'No harm done, just keep still.'

She kept still as a mouse, her head bowed under his repressing palm. She turned up her eyes and saw him look at his watch, then, with a kind of balletic movement of wrists, scissors and finger-points above her brow, drive the sharp steel into the ball of his thumb, so that blood spurted, so that some of his blood even fell onto her scalp.

'Oh, dear. Will you excuse me? I've cut myself. Look.'

He waved the bloody member before her nose.

'I saw,' she said. 'I saw you cut yourself.'

He smiled at her in the mirror, a glittery smile, not meeting her eyes.

'It's a little trick we hairdressers have. When we've been driving ourselves and haven't had time for a bite or a breather, we get cut, and off we go, to the toilet, to take a bite of a Mars bar or something such, or a cheese roll if the receptionist's been considerate. Will you excuse me? I am faint for lack of food.'

'Of course,' she said.

He flashed his glass smile at her and slid away.

*

She waited. She waited. A little water dripped into her collar. A little more ran into her eyebrows. She looked at her poor face, under its dank cap and its two random corkscrews, aluminium-clamped. She felt a gentle protective rage towards this stolid face. She remembered, not as a girl, as a young woman under all that chestnut fall, looking at her skin, and wondering how it could grow into the crepe, the sag, the opulent soft bags. This was her face, she had thought then. And this, too, now, she wanted to accept for her face, trained in a respect for precision, and could not. What had left this greying skin, these flakes, these fragile stretches with no elasticity, was her, was her life, was herself. She had never been a beautiful woman, but she had been attractive, with the attraction of liveliness and warm energy, of the flow of quick blood and brightness of eye. No classic bones, which might endure, no fragile birdlike sharpness that might whitely go forward. Only the life of flesh, which began to die.

She was in a panic of fear about the television, which had come too late, when she had lost the desire to be seen or looked at. The cameras search jowl and eye-pocket, expose brush-stroke and cracks in shadow and gloss. So interesting are their revelations that words, mere words, go for nothing, fly by whilst the memory of a chipped tooth, a strayed red dot, an inappropriate hair, persists and persists.

If he had not left her so long to contemplate her wet face, it might not have happened.

On either side of her, mysteries were being enacted. On the left, a head was crammed into a pink nylon bag, something between a bank-robber's stocking and a monstrous Dutch cap. A young Chinese man was peacefully teasing threads of hair through the meshes of this with a tug and a flick, a tug and a flick. The effect was one of startling hideous pink baldness, tufted here and there. On her right, an anxious plump girl was rolling another girl's thick locks into shaky sausages of aluminium foil. There was a thrum of distant drums through the loudspeakers, a clash and crash of what sounded like shaken chains. It is all nonsense, she thought, I should go home, I can't, I am wet. They stared transfixed at their respective uglinesses.

He came back, and took up the scissors, listlessly enough.
'How much did you want off,' he said casually. 'You've

got a lot of broken ends. It's deteriorating, you haven't fed it while I've been away.'

'Not too much off. I want to look natural, I –'

'I've been talking to my girlfriend. I've decided. I shan't go back any more to my wife. I can't bear it.'

'She's too angry?'

'She's let herself go. It's her own fault. She's let herself go altogether. She's let her ankles get fat, they swell over her shoes, it disgusts me, it's impossible for me.'

'That happens to people. Fluid absorption –'

She did not look down at her own ankles. He had her by the short hairs at the nape of her neck.

'Lucian,' said the plump girl, plaintively, 'can you just take a look here at this perm, I can't seem to get the hang of this.'

'You'd better be careful,' said Lucian, 'or Madam'll go green and fry and you'll be in deep trouble. Why don't you just come and finish off my madam here – you don't mind, do you dear, Deirdre is very good with your sort of hair, very tactful, I'm training her myself – I'd better take a look at this perm. It's a new method we're just trying out, we've had a few problems, you see how it is –'

Deirdre was an elicitor, but Susannah would not speak. Vaguely, far away, she heard the anxious little voice. 'Do you have children, dear, have you far to go home, how formal do you like it, do you want back-combing? . . .' Susannah stared stony, thinking about Lucian's wife's ankles. Because her own ankles rubbed her shoes, her sympathies had to be with the unknown and ill-presented woman. She remembered with sudden total clarity a day when, Suzie then, not Susannah, she had made love all day to an Italian student on a course in Perugia. She remembered her own little round rosy breasts, her own long legs stretched over the side of the single bed, the hot, the wet, his shoulders, the clash of skulls as they tried to mix themselves completely. They had reached a point when neither could move, they had loved each other so much, they had tried to get up to get water, for they were dying of thirst, they were soaked with sweat and dry-mouthed, and they collapsed back upon the bed, naked skin on naked skin, unable to rise. What was this to anyone now? Rage rose in her, for the fat-ankled woman, like a red flood, up from her thighs across her chest, up her neck, it must flare like a flag in her face, but how to tell in this daft cruel grey light? Deirdre was rolling up curls, piling them up, who would have thought the old woman had so much hair on her head? Sausages and snail-shells, grape-clusters and twining coils. She could only see dimly, for the red flood was like a curtain at the back of her eyes, but she knew what she saw. The Japanese say demons of another world approach us through mirrors as fish rise through water, and bubble-eyed and trailing fins a fat demon swam towards her, turret-crowned, snake-crowned, her mother fresh from the dryer in all her embarrassing irreality.

'There,' said Deirdre. 'That's nice. I'll just get a mirror.'

'It isn't nice,' said Susannah, 'it's hideous.'

There was a hush in the salon. Deirdre turned a terrified gaze on Lucian.

'She did it better than I do, dear,' he said. 'She gave it a bit of lift. That's what they all want, these days. I think you look really nice.'

'It's horrible,' said Susannah. '*I look like a middle-aged woman with a hair-do.*'

She could see them all looking at each other, sharing the knowledge that this was exactly what she was.

'Not natural,' she said.

'I'll get Deirdre to tone it down,' said Lucian.

Susannah picked up a bottle, full of dark blue gel. She brought it down, heavily, on the grey glass shelf, which cracked.

'I don't want it toned down, I want –' she began, and stared mesmerised at the crack, which was smeared with gel.

'I want my real hair back,' Susannah cried, and thumped harder, shattering both shelf and bottle.

'Now, dear, I'm sorry,' said Lucian in a tone of sweet reason. She could see several of him, advancing on her; he was standing in a corner and was reflected from wall to wall, a cohort of slender trousered swordsmen, waving the bright scissors like weapons.

'Keep away,' she said. 'Get off. Keep back.'

'Calm yourself,' said Lucian.

Susannah seized a small cylindrical pot and threw it at one of his emanations. It burst with a satisfying crash and one whole mirror became a spider-web of cracks, from which fell, tinkling, a little heap of crystal nuggets. In front of Susannah was a whole row of such bombs or grenades. She lobbed them all around her. Some of the cracks made a kind of strained singing noise, some were explosive. She whirled a container of hairpins about her head and scattered it like a nailbomb. She tore dryers from their sockets and sprayed the puce punk with sweet-smelling foam. She broke basins with brushes and tripped the young Chinese male, who was the only one not apparently petrified, with a hissing trolley, swaying dangerously and scattering puffs of cotton wool and rattling trails of clips and tags. She silenced the blatter of the music with a well-aimed imitation alabaster pot of Juvenescence Emulsion, which dripped into the cassette which whirred more and more slowly in a thickening morass of blush-coloured cream.

When she had finished – and she went on, she kept going, until there was nothing else to hurl, for she was already afraid of what must happen when she had finished – there was complete human silence in the salon. There were strange, harshly musical sounds all round. A bowl rocking on a glass shelf. A pair of scissors, dancing on a hook, their frenzy diminishing. Uneven spasmodic falls of glass, like musical hailstones on shelves and floors. A susurration of hairpins on paper. A slow creaking of damaged panes.

Her own hands were bleeding. Lucian advanced crunching over the shining silt, and dabbed at them with a towel. He too was blooded – specks on his shirt, a fine dash on his brow, nothing substantial. It was a strange empty battlefield, full of glittering fragments and sweet-smelling rivulets and puddles of venous blue and fuchsia-red unguents, patches of crimson-streaked foam and odd intense spills of orange henna or cobalt and copper.

'I'd better go,' she said, turning blindly with her bleeding hands, still in her uncouth maroon drapery.

'Deirdre'll make you a cup of coffee,' said Lucian. 'You'd better sit down and take a breather.'

He took a neck brush and swept a chair for her. She stared, irresolute.

'Go on. We all feel like that, sometimes. Most of us don't dare. Sit down.'

They all gathered round, the young, making soothing, chir-ruping noises, putting out hands with vague patting, calming gestures.

'I'll send you a cheque.'

'The insurance'll pay. Don't worry too much. It's insured. You've done me a good turn in a way. It wasn't quite right, the colours. I might do something different. Or collect the insurance and give up. Me and my girlfriend are thinking of setting up a stall in the Antique Hypermarket. Costume jewellery. Thirties and forties kitsch. She has sources. I can collect the insurance and have a go. I've had enough of this. I'll tell you something – I've often felt like smashing it all up myself, just to get out of it – like a great glass cage it is – and go out into the real world. So you mustn't worry, dear.'

She sat at home and shook, her cheeks flushed, her eyes bright with tears. When she had pulled herself together, she would go and have a shower and soak out the fatal coils, reduce them to streaming rat-tails.

Her husband came in, unexpected – she had long given up expecting or not expecting him, his movements were unpredictable and unexplained. He came in tentatively, a large alert, ostentatiously work-wearied man. She looked up at him speechless. He saw her. (Usually he did not.)

'You look different. You've had your hair done. I like it. You look lovely. It takes twenty years off you. You should have it done more often.'

And he came over and kissed her on the shorn nape of her neck, quite as he used to.

'Tis Pity She's a Whore

ANGELA CARTER

THERE WAS A rancher who had two children, a son and then a daughter. A while after that, his wife died and was buried under two sticks nailed together to make a cross because there was not time, yet, to carve a stone.

Did she die of the loneliness of the prairies? Or was it anguish that killed her, anguish, and nostalgia for the close, warm neighbourly life she had left behind her when she came to this emptiness? Neither. She died of the pressure of that vast sky, that weighed down upon her and crushed her lungs until she could not breathe any more, as if the prairies were the bedrock of an ocean in which she drowned.

She told her boy: 'Look after your sister.' He, blond, solemn, little; he and Death sat with her in the room of logs her husband split to build. Death, with high cheek-bones, wore his hair in braids. His invisible presence in the cabin mocked the existence of the cabin. The round-eyed boy clutched his mother's dry

Note: John Ford: 1586–circa 1639. English dramatist of the Jacobean period. His tragedy, *'Tis Pity She's a Whore*, was published in 1633. 'Deep in a dump John Ford alone was got/With folded arms and melancholy hat.' (*Choice Drollery*, 1656.)

John Ford: 1895–1973. American film-maker. Filmography includes: *Stagecoach* (1939); *My Darling Clementine* (1946); *She Wore a Yellow Ribbon* (1949). 'My name is John Ford. I make Westerns.' (*John Ford*, Andrew Sinclair, New York 1979.)

hand. The girl was younger.

Then the mother lay with the prairies and all that careless sky upon her breast, and the children lived in their father's house. So they grew up. In his spare time, the rancher chiselled at a rock: 'Beloved wife of . . . mother of . . .' beneath the space at the top he had left for his own name.

America begins and ends in the cold and solitude. Up here, she pillows her head upon the Arctic snow. Down there, she dips her feet in the chilly waters of the South Atlantic, home of the perpetually restless albatross. America, with her torso of a woman at the time of this story, a woman with an hour-glass waist, a waist laced so tightly it snapped in two, and we put a belt of water there. America, with your child-bearing hips and your crotch of jungle, your swelling bosom of a nursing mother and your cold head, your cold head.

Its central paradox resides in this: that the top half doesn't know what the bottom half is doing. When I say the two children of the prairie, suckled on those green breasts, were the pure children of the continent, you know at once that they were *norteamericanos*, or I would not speak of them in the English language, which was their language, the language that silences the babble of this continent's multitude of tongues.

Blond children with broad, freckled faces, the boy in dungarees and the little girl in gingham and sun-bonnet. In the old play, one John Ford called them Giovanni and Annabella; the other John Ford, in the movie, might call them Johnny and Annie-Belle.

Annie-Belle will bake bread, tramp the linen clean and cook the beans and bacon; this lily of the West had not spare time enough to pause and consider the lilies of the field, who never do a hand's turn. No sir. A woman's work is never done and she became a woman early.

The gaunt paterfamilias would drive them into town to church on Sundays with the black Bible on his knee wherein their names and dates of birth were inscribed. In the buggy, his shy, big-boned, tow-headed son in best, dark, Sunday clothes, and Annie-Belle, at thirteen, fourteen, increasingly astonished at and rendered shy by her own lonely flowering. Fifteen. How pretty she was growing! They came to pray in God's house that, like their own, was built of split logs. Annie-Belle kept her eyes down; she was a good girl. They were good children. The widower drank, sometimes, but not much. They grew up in silence, in the enormous silence of the empty land, the silence that swallowed up the Saturday-night fiddler's tune, mocked the rare laughter at weddings and christenings, echoed, a vast margin, around the sermons of the preacher.

Silence and space and an unimaginable freedom which they dare not imagine.

Since his wife died, the rancher spoke rarely. They lived far out of town. He had no time for barn-raisings and church suppers. If she had lived, everything would have been different, but he occupied his spare moments in chiselling the gravestone. They did not celebrate Thanksgiving for he had nothing for which to give thanks. It was a hard life.

The Minister's wife made sure Annie-Belle knew a thing or two when she judged it about the time the girl's bleeding started. The Minister's wife, in a vague, pastoral way, thought about a husband for Annie-Belle, a wife for Johnny. 'Out there, in that little house on the prairie, so lonesome . . . Nobody for those young folks to talk to 'cept cows, cows, cows.'

What did the girl think? In summer, of the heat, and how to keep flies out of the butter; in winter, of the cold. I do not know what else she thought. Perhaps, as young girls do, she thought that a stranger would come to town and take her away to the city and so on, but, since her imagination began and ended with her experience, the farm, work, the seasons, I think she did not think so far, as if she knew already she was the object of her own desire for, in the bright light of the New World, nothing is obscure. But when they were children, all they knew was they loved each other just as surely a brother or a sister should.

She washed her hair in a tub. She washed her long, yellow hair. She was fifteen. It was spring. She washed her hair. It was the first time that year. She sat on the porch to dry her hair, she sat in the rocking-chair which her mother selected from the Sears Roebuck catalogue, where her father would never sit, now. She propped a bit of mirror on the porch railing. It caught the sun and flashed. She combed out her wet hair in the mirror. There seemed to be an awful lot of it, tangling up the comb. She wore only her petticoat, the men were off with the cattle, nobody to see her pale shoulders except that Johnny came back. The horse threw him, he knocked his head against a stone. Giddy, he came back to the house, leading his pony, and she was busy untangling her hair and did not see him, nor have a chance to cover herself.

'Why, Johnny, I declare –'

Imagine an orchestra behind them: the frame-house, the porch, the rocking-chair endlessly rocking, like a cradle, the white petticoat with eyelet lace, her water-darkened hair hanging on her shoulders and little trickles running down between her shallow breasts, the young man leading the limping pony, and, inexhaustible as light, around them the tender land.

The 'Love Theme' swells and rises. She jumps up to tend him. The jogged mirror falls.

'Seven years' bad luck –'

In the fragments of the mirror, they kneel to see their round, blond, innocent faces that, superimposed upon one another, would fit at every feature, their faces, all at once the same face, the face that never existed until now, the pure face of America.

EXTERIOR. PRAIRIE. DAY.

LONG SHOT: Farmhouse.

CLOSE UP: Petticoat falling on to porch of farmhouse.

Wisconsin, Ohio, Iowa, Missouri, Kansas, Minnesota, Nebraska, the Dakotas, Wyoming, Montana . . . Oh, those enormous territories! That Green vastness, in which anything is possible.

EXTERIOR. PRAIRIE. DAY.

CLOSE UP: Johnny and Annie-Belle kiss.
'Love Theme' up.
Dissolve.

No. It wasn't like that! Not in the least like that.

He put out his hand and touched her wet hair. He was giddy.

ANNABELLA: Methinks you are not well.

GIOVANNI: Here's none but you and I. I think you love

me, sister.

ANNABELLA: Yes, you know I do.

And they thought, then, that they should kill themselves, together now, before they did it; they remembered tumbling together in infancy, how their mother laughed to see their kisses, their embraces, when they were too young to know they should not do it, yet even in their loneliness on the enormous plain they knew they must not do it . . . do what? How did they know what to do? From watching the cows with the bull, the bitch with the dog, the hen with the cock. They were country children. Turning from the mirror, each saw the other's face as if it were their own.

Music plays.
GIOVANNI: Let not this music be a dream, ye gods.
   For pity's sake, I beg you!
   [*She kneels*]

ANNABELLA: On my knees,
   Brother, even by our mother's dust, I charge you
   Do not betray me to your mirth or hate.
   Love me, or kill me, brother.
   [*He kneels.*]

GIOVANNI: On my knees,
   Sister, even by our mother's dust, I charge you
   Do not betray me to your mirth or hate.
   Love me, or kill me, sister.

         EXTERIOR. FARMHOUSE PORCH. DAY.
         Upset water-tub, spilling over discarded petticoat.
         Empty rocking-chair, rocking, rocking.

It is the boy – or young man, rather – who is the most mysterious to me. The eagerness with which he embraces his fate. I imagine him mute or well-nigh mute; he is the silent type, his voice creaks with disuse. He turns the soil, he breaks the wills of the beautiful horses, he milks the cows, he works the land, he toils and sweats. His work consists of the vague, undistinguished 'work' of such folks in the movies. No cowboy, he, roaming the plains. Where the father took root, so has the son, in the soil that was never before broken until now.

And I imagine him with an intelligence nourished only by the black book of the father, and hence cruelly circumscribed, yet dense with allusion, seeing himself as a kind of Adam and she his unavoidable and irreplaceable Eve, the unique companion of the wilderness, although by their toil he knows they do not live in Eden and of the precise nature of the forbidden thing he remains in doubt.

Was it bliss for her too? Or was there more of love than pleasure in it? 'Look after your sister.' But it was she who looked after him as soon as she knew how and pleasured him in the same spirit as she fed him.

GIOVANNI: I am lost forever.

Lost in the green wastes, where the pioneers were lost. Death with his high cheek-bones and his braided hair helped Annie-Belle take off her clothes. She closed her eyes so that she could not see her own nakedness. Death showed her how to touch him and him her. There is more to it than farmyard ways.

> INTERIOR. MINISTER'S HOUSE. DAY.
> Dinner-table. Minister's wife dishing portions from a pot for her husband and her son.
>
> MINISTER'S WIFE: T'ain't right, just ain't right, those two out there, growing up like savages, never seeing nobody.
>
> MINISTER'S SON: She's terribly pretty, Mama.
>
> The Minister's wife and the Minister turn to look at the young man. He blushes slowly but comprehensively.

The rancher knew nothing. He worked. He kept the iron core of grief within him rustless. He looked forward to his solitary, once-monthly drink, alone on the porch, and on those nights they took a chance and slept together in the log cabin under the patchwork quilt made in the 'log cabin' pattern by their mother. Each time they lay down there together, as if she obeyed a voice that came out of the quilt telling her to put the light out, she would extinguish the candle-flame between her fingertips. All around them, the tactility of the dark.

She pondered the irreversibility of defloration. According to what the Minister's wife said, she had lost everything and was a lost girl. And yet this change did not seem to have changed her. She turned to the only one she loved, and the desolating space around them diminished to that of the soft grave their bodies dented in the long grass by the creek. When winter came, they made quick, dangerous love among the lowing beasts in the barn. The snow melted and all was green enough to blind you and there was a vinegarish smell from the rising of the sharp juices of spring. The birds came back.

A dusk bird went chink-chink-chink like a single blow on the stone xylophone of the Chinese classical orchestra.

> EXTERIOR. FARMHOUSE PORCH. DAY.
> Annie-Belle, in apron, comes out on homestead porch; strikes metal triangle.
>
> ANNIE-BELLE: Dinner's ready!
>
> INTERIOR. FARMHOUSE. NIGHT.
> Supper-table. Annie-Belle serves beans. None for herself.
>
> JOHNNY: Annie-Belle, you're not eating anything tonight.
>
> ANNIE-BELLE: Can't rightly fancy anything tonight.

The dusk bird went chink-chink-chink with the sound of a chisel on a gravestone.

He wanted to run away with her, west, further west, to Utah, to California where they could live as man and wife, but she said: What about father? He's lost enough already. When she said that, she put on, not his face, but that of their mother, and he knew in his bones the child inside her would part them.

The Minister's son, in his Sunday coat, came courting Annie-Belle. He is the second lead, you know in advance, from his tentative manner and mild eyes; he cannot long survive in this prairie scenario. He came courting Annie-Belle, although his mother wanted him to go to college. What will you do at college with a young wife? said his mother. But he put away his books; he took the buggy to go out and visit her. She was hanging washing out on the line.

Sound of the wind buffeting the sheets, the very sound of loneliness.

SORANZO: Have you not the will to love?

ANNABELLA: Not you.

SORANZO: Who, then?

ANNABELLA: That's as the fates infer.

She lowered her head and drew her foot back and forth in the dust. Her breasts hurt, she felt queasy.

> EXTERIOR. PRAIRIE. DAY.
> Johnny and Annie-Belle walking on the prairie.
>
> ANNIE-BELLE: I think he likes me, Johnny.
>
> Pan blue sky, with clouds. Johnny and Annie-Belle, dwarfed by the landscape, hand in hand, heads bowed. Their hands slowly part.
>
> Now they walk with gradually increasing distance between them.

The light, the unexhausted light of North America that, filtered through celluloid, will become the light by which we see America looking at itself.

Correction: will become the light by which we see *North* America looking at itself.

> EXTERIOR. FARMHOUSE PORCH. DAY.
> Row of bottles on a fence.
> Bang, bang, bang. Johnny shoots the bottles one by one.
> Annie-Belle on porch, washing dishes in a tub.
> Tears run down her face.
>
> EXTERIOR. FARMHOUSE PORCH. DAY.
> Father on porch, feet up on railing, glass and bottle to hand.
> Sun going down over prairie.
> Bang, bang, bang.

FATHER'S POINT OF VIEW: Johnny shooting bottles off the fence.

Clink of father's bottle against glass.

EXTERIOR. FARMHOUSE. DAY.
Minister's son rides along track in long shot.
Bang, bang, bang.

Annie-Belle, clean dress, tidy hair, red eyes, comes out of house on to porch. Clink of father's bottle against glass.

EXTERIOR. FARMHOUSE. DAY.
Minister's son tethers horse. He has brushed his Sunday coat. In his hand, a posy of flowers – cottage roses, sweet-briar, daisies. Annie-Belle smiles, takes posy.

ANNIE-BELLE: Oh! [*Holds up pricked forefinger; blood drops on to a daisy.*]

MINISTER'S SON: Let me . . . [*Takes her hand. Kisses the little wound.*] . . . make it better.

Bang, Bang, Bang.
Clink of bottle on glass.

CLOSE-UP: Annie-Belle, smiling, breathing in the scent from her posy.

And, perhaps, had it been possible, she would have learned to love the Minister's gentle son before she married him, but, not only was it impossible, she also carried within her the child that meant she must be married quickly.

INTERIOR. CHURCH. DAY.
Harmonium. Father and Johnny by the altar. Johnny white, strained; father stoical. Minister's wife thin-lipped, furious. Minister's son and Annie-Belle, in simple white cotton wedding-dress, join hands.

MINISTER: Do you take this woman . . .

CLOSE-UP: Minister's son's hand slipping wedding-ring on to Annie-Belle's finger.

ANGELA CARTER

> INTERIOR. BARN. NIGHT.
> Fiddle and banjo old-time music.
> Vigorous square dance going on; bride and groom lead.
>
> Father at table, glass in hand.
> Johnny, beside him, reaching for bottle.
>
> Bride and groom come together at end of dance;
> groom kisses bride's cheek. She laughs.
>
> CLOSE-UP: Annie-Belle looking shyly up at the
> Minister's son.
> The dance parts them again; as Annie-Belle is handed
> down the row of men, she staggers and faints.
>
> Consternation.
>
> Minister's son and Johnny both run towards her.
>
> Johnny lifts her up in his arms, her head on his
> shoulder. Eyes opening. Minister's son reaches out
> for her. Johnny lets him take hold of her.
>
> She gazes after Johnny beseechingly as he disappears
> among the crowd.

Silence swallowed up the music of the fiddle and the banjo;
Death with his hair in braids spread out the sheets on the
marriage bed.

> INTERIOR. MINISTER'S HOUSE. BEDROOM. NIGHT.
> Annie-Belle in bed, in a white night-gown, clutching
> the pillow, weeping. Minister's son, bare back, sitting
> on side of bed with his back to camera, head in hands.

In the morning, her new mother-in-law heard her vomiting
into the chamber-pot and, in spite of her son's protests, stripped
Annie-Belle and subjected her to a midwife's inspection. She
judged her three months gone, or more. She dragged the
girl round the room by the hair, slapped her, punched her,
kicked her, but Annie-Belle would not tell the father's name,
only promised, swore on the grave of her dead mother, that
she would be a good girl in future. The young bridegroom

was too bewildered by this turn of events to have an opinion about it; only, to his vague surprise, he knew he still loved the girl although she carried another man's child.

'Bitch! Whore!' said the Minister's wife and struck Annie-Belle a blow across the mouth that started her nose bleeding.

'Now, stop that, mother,' said the gentle son. 'Can't you see she ain't well?'

The terrible day drew to its end. The mother-in-law would have thrown Annie-Belle out on the street, but the boy pleaded for her, and the Minister, praying for guidance, found himself opening the Bible at the parable of the woman taken in adultery, and meditated well upon it. Only tell me the name of the father, her young husband said to Annie-Belle.

'Better you don't know it,' she said. Then she lied: 'He's gone now; gone out west.'

'Was it –' naming one or two.

'You never knew him. He came by the ranch on his way out west.'

Then she burst out crying, again, and he took her in his arms.

'It will be all over town,' said the mother-in-law. 'That girl made a fool of you.'

She slammed the dishes on the table and would have made the girl eat out the back door, but the young husband laid her a place at table with his own hands and led her in and sat her down in spite of his mother's black looks. They bowed their heads for grace. Surely, the Minister thought, seeing his boy cut bread for Annie-Belle and lay it on her plate, my son is a saint. He began to fear for him.

'I won't do anything unless you want,' her husband said in the dark after the candle went out.

The straw with which the mattress was stuffed rustled beneath her as she turned away from him.

INTERIOR. FARMHOUSE KITCHEN. NIGHT.
Johnny comes in from outside, looks at father asleep in rocking-chair.
Picks up some discarded garment of Annie-Belle's from the back of a chair, buries face in it.

95

> Shoulders shake.
> Opens cupboard, takes out bottle.
> Uncorks with teeth. Drinks.
> Bottle in hand, goes out on porch.

EXTERIOR. PRAIRIE. NIGHT.
JOHNNY'S POINT OF VIEW: Moon rising over prairie; the vast, the elegiac plain.
'Landscape Theme' rises.

INTERIOR. MINISTER'S SON'S ROOM. NIGHT.
Annie-Belle and Minister's son in bed. Moonlight through curtains. Both lie there, open-eyed. Rustle of mattress.

ANNIE-BELLE: You awake?

Minister's son moves away from her.

ANNIE-BELLE: Reckon I never properly knowed no young man before . . .

MINISTER'S SON: What about –

ANNIE-BELLE: [*shrugging the question off*] Oh . . .

Minister's son moves towards her.

For she did not consider her brother in this new category of 'young men'; he was herself. So she and her husband slept in one another's arms, that night, although they did nothing else for she was scared it might harm the baby and he was so full of pain and glory it was scarcely to be borne, it was already enough, or too much, holding her tight, in his terrible innocence.

It was not so much that she was pliant. Only, fearing the worst, it turned out that the worst had already happened; her sin found her out, or, rather, she found out she had sinned only when he offered his forgiveness, and, from her repentance, a new Annie-Belle sprang up, for whom the past did not exist.

She would have said to him: it did not signify, my darling; I only did it with my brother, we were alone together under the vast sky that made us scared and so we clung

96

together and what happened, happened. But she knew she must not say that, the most natural thing of all was just precisely the one she must not acknowledge. To lie down on the prairie with a passing stranger was one thing. To lie down with her father's son was another. So she kept silent. And when she looked at her husband, she saw, not herself, but someone who might, in time, grow even more precious.

The next night, in spite of the baby, they did it, and his mother wanted to murder her and refused to get the breakfast for this prostitute, but Annie-Belle served them, put on an apron, cut the ham and cooked it, then scrubbed the floor with such humility, such evidence of gratitude that the older woman kept her mouth shut, her narrow lips tight as a trap but she kept them shut for if there was one thing she feared, it was the atrocious gentleness of her menfolk. And. So.

Johnny came to the town, hungering after her; the gates of Paradise slammed shut in his face. He haunted the backyard of the Minister's house, hid in the sweet-briar, watched the candle in their room go out and still he could not imagine it, that she might do it with another man. But. She did.

At the store, all gossip ceased when she came in; all eyes turned towards her. The old men chewing tobacco spat brown streams when she walked past. The women's faces veiled with disapproval. She was so young, so unaccustomed to people. They talked, her husband and she; they would go, just go, out west, still further, west as far as the place where the ocean starts again, perhaps. With his schooling, he could get some clerking job or other. She would bear her child and he would love it. Then she would bear *their* children.

Yes, she said. We shall do that, she said.

EXTERIOR. FARMHOUSE. DAY.
Annie-Belle drives up in trap.
Johnny comes out on porch, in shirt-sleeves, bottle in hand.
Takes her reins. But she doesn't get down from the trap.

ANNIE-BELLE: Where's Daddy?

Johnny gestures towards the prairie.

ANNIE-BELLE: [*not looking at Johnny*] Got something to tell him.

CLOSE-UP: Johnny.

JOHNNY: Ain't you got nothing to tell me?

CLOSE-UP: Annie-Belle.

ANNIE-BELLE: Reckon I ain't.

CLOSE-UP: Johnny.

JOHNNY: Get down and visit a while, at least.

CLOSE-UP: Annie-Belle.

ANNIE-BELLE: Can't hardly spare the time.

CLOSE-UP: Johnny and Annie-Belle.

JOHNNY: Got to scurry back, get your husband's dinner, is that it?

ANNIE-BELLE: Johnny . . . why haven't you come to church since I got married, Johnny?

Johnny shrugs, turns away.

EXTERIOR. FARMHOUSE. DAY.
Annie-Belle gets down from trap, follows Johnny towards farmhouse.

ANNIE-BELLE: Oh, Johnny, you *knowed* we did wrong.

Johnny walks towards farmhouse.

ANNIE-BELLE: I count myself fortunate to have found forgiveness.

JOHNNY: What are you going to tell Daddy?

ANNIE-BELLE: I'm going out west.

GIOVANNI: What, chang'd so soon! hath your new sprightly lord

Found out a trick in night-games more than we
Could know in our simplicity? – Ha! is't so?
Or does the fit come on you, to prove treacherous
To your past vows and oaths?

ANNABELLA: Why should you jest
  At my calamity.

     EXTERIOR. FARMHOUSE. DAY.

     JOHNNY: Out west?

     Annie-Belle nods.

     JOHNNY: By yourself?

     Annie-Belle shakes her head.

     JOHNNY: With him?

     Annie-Belle nods.
     Johnny puts hand on porch rail, bends forward, hiding
     his face.

     ANNIE-BELLE: It is for the best.

     She puts her hand on his shoulder. He reaches out for
     her. She extricates herself. His hand, holding bottle;
     contents of bottle run out on grass.

     ANNIE-BELLE: It was wrong, what we did.

     JOHNNY: What about . . .

     ANNIE-BELLE: It shouldn't ever have been made,
       poor little thing. You won't never see it. Forget every-
       thing. You'll find yourself a woman, you'll marry.

     Johnny reaches out and clasps her roughly to him.

No, she said: never. No. And fought and bit and scratched:
never! It's wrong. It's a sin. But, worse than that, she said:
I don't want to, and she meant it, she knew she must not or
else her new life, that lay before her, now, with the radiant
simplicity of a child's drawing of a house, would be utterly
destroyed. So she got free of him and ran to the buggy and
drove back lickety-split to town, beating the pony round the
head with the whip.

ANGELA CARTER

*

Accompanied by a black trunk like a coffin, the Minister and his wife drove with them to a railhead such as you have often seen on the movies – the same telegraph office, the same water-tower, the same old man with the green eye-shade selling tickets. Autumn was coming on. Annie-Belle could no longer conceal her pregnancy, out it stuck; her mother-in-law could not speak to her directly but addressed remarks through the Minister, who compensated for his wife's contempt by showing Annie-Belle all the honour due to a repentant sinner.

She wore a yellow ribbon. Her hair was long and yellow. The repentant harlot has the surprised look of a pregnant virgin.

She is pale. The pregnancy does not go well. She vomits all morning. She bleeds a little. Her husband holds her hand tight. Her father came last night to say goodbye to her; he looks older. He does not take care of himself. That Johnny did not come set the tongues wagging; the gossip is, he refuses to set eyes on his sister in her disgrace. That seems the only thing to explain his attitude. All know he takes no interest in girls himself.

'Bless you, children,' says the Minister. With that troubling air of incipient sainthood, the young husband settles his wife down on the trunk and tucks a rug round her legs, for a snappy wind drives dust down the railroad track and the hills are October mauve and brown. In the distance, the train whistle blows, that haunting sound, blowing across endless distance, the sound that underlines the distance.

>EXTERIOR. FARMHOUSE. DAY.
>Johnny mounts horse. Slings rifle over shoulder. Kicks horse's sides.
>
>EXTERIOR. RAILROAD. DAY.
>Train whistle. Burst of smoke.
>Engine pulling train across prairie.
>
>EXTERIOR. PRAIRIE. DAY.
>Johnny galloping down track.
>
>EXTERIOR. RAILROAD. DAY.
>CLOSE-UP: Train wheels turning.
>
>EXTERIOR. PRAIRIE. DAY.
>Hooves churning dust.

100

EXTERIOR. STATION. DAY.

MINISTER'S WIFE: Now, you take care of yourself, you hear? And – [but she can't bring herself to say it].

MINISTER: Be sure to tell us about the baby as soon as it comes.

CLOSE-UP: Annie-Belle smiling gratefully. Train whistle.

And see them, now, as if posing for the photographer, the young man and the pregnant woman, sitting on a trunk, waiting to be transported onwards, away, elsewhere, she with the future in her belly.

EXTERIOR. STATION. DAY.
Station-master comes out of ticket-office.

STATION-MASTER: Here she comes!

LONG-SHOT: Engine appearing round bend.

EXTERIOR. STATION. DAY.
Johnny tethers his horse.

ANNIE-BELLE: Why, Johnny, you've come to say goodbye after all!

CLOSE-UP: Johnny, wracked with emotion.

JOHNNY: He shan't have you. He'll never have you. Here's where you belong, with me. Out here.

GIOVANNI: Thus die, and die by me, and by my hand!
   Revenge is mine; honour doth love command!

ANNABELLA: Oh, brother, by your hand!

EXTERIOR. STATION. DAY.

ANNIE-BELLE: Don't shoot – think of the baby! Don't –

MINISTER'S SON: Oh, my God –

Bang, bang, bang.

*

Thinking to protect his wife, the young husband threw his arms around her and so he died, by a split second, before the second bullet pierced her and both fell to the ground as the engine wheezed to a halt and passengers came tumbling off to see what Wild West antics were being played out while the parents stood and stared and did not believe, did not believe.

Seeing some life left in his sister, Johnny sank to his knees beside her and her eyes opened up and, perhaps, she saw him, for she said:

ANNABELLA: Brother, unkind, unkind . . .

So that Death would be well-satisfied, Johnny then put the barrel of the rifle into his mouth and pulled the trigger.

> EXTERIOR. STATION. DAY.
> Crane shot, the three bodies, the Minister comforting his wife, the passengers crowding off the train in order to look at the catastrophe.
>
> The 'Love Theme' rises over a pan of the prairie under the vast sky, the green breast of the continent, the earth, beloved, cruel, unkind.

Note: The Old World John Ford made Giovanni cut out Annabella's heart and carry it on stage; the stage direction reads: *Enter Giovanni, with a heart upon his dagger*. The New World John Ford would have no means of representing this scene on celluloid, although it is irresistibly reminiscent of the ritual tortures practised by the Indians who lived here before.

The Mermaid

DAVID CONSTANTINE

JACK WOKE, EV was snoring, but above that sound he could hear the sea, the wind had got up, there was a big sea, the sound of it made his heart beat faster. Gently, gently, he slid out from beside her, crept to the window, parted the curtains a fraction, enough for one eye: no rain, only the wind, a sliver of draught, the sash was trembling and across the street, across the field, there was the sea coming nearer and higher, the white sea. He thought: There'll be some wreck, the breakers coming in like friendly hounds with timbers in their mouths. Glancing down Jack saw that his John Thomas was out, up and out, sticking its head out of his pyjamas into the cold room, stiff as a chairleg. Always the same when a man wakes, especially in the middle of the night if he wakes then, he mentioned it to Stan one day when they were sitting in the Folly Field watching the visitors, and Stan said his was the same whenever he woke, especially if he woke in the night, like a tableleg, so that you wondered what was going on down there when you were sleeping, all night long, something must be going on, in the mind at least, but you never remembered it, worse luck. Gently, gently Jack slid in again. The sea. He might get a nice piece of wood. What time was it? Ev had the clock on her side and her teeth, in a glass of water, guarded it, she knew the time and what time to get up and when the alarm went off Jack went downstairs and made the tea, at a quarter to eight. Ev wore a mobcap in her sleep, lay on her back and snored, her sharp little fingers gripping the eiderdown. Jack did the trick he had learned from Stan (it seemed to work): lifted and let fall back his head six times onto the pillow, to wake at six and be on the beach before anyone else, after the wood. Funny how the brain works. Jack was listening to the sea and going down nicely to where the mind whatever it thinks is not to blame, when Ev hit him suddenly on the nose with her hard elbow. The shock was frightful, his eyes wept, he felt at his upper lip whether blood was coming out. Ev snored, the clock was smiling faintly. Marvellous how a woman knows, deep down, even in her sleep, she always knows what's going on in her loved ones.

Jack went out the back way, down the garden, past his shed, into the back lane and round. It was still dark, there was nobody about. A car came by very slowly. He stood on the little street like a malefactor; then crossed, entered the field, hurried to the beach. The sea had withdrawn, the waves were milky white in a dozen layers where they spilled and ended, the widening beach was empty. Jack got to the tideline and struck along it into the wind, shingle and dunes on his right hand, the lights of town far ahead of him on the bay's long curve. The sky, lightening, was enough to see by, and new wood always showed up. He soon spotted a nice length of six by four, tugged it out of the slippy deadweight of thong and wrack, dragged it into hiding in the dunes. So he went on – a fishbox, a wicker chair, a useful pole – making caches in the dunes. Nothing like it, nothing else in his life was like getting up early after a wind in the night and scouring along a mile or so for what the sea had left. Everything pleased him, even the plastic bottles and tubes, the women's things in different languages. You never know. He had found a bed once, without its bedding, of course, but a bed all the same, thick with barnacles and weed, he couldn't budge it, there it stayed, for weeks, he felt sorry for it in the daylight and was glad when a gale took it away again, a bed on the sea, all rough and slippery and stinking.

At the seawall, that would have taken him as far as the railway station, Jack turned back. Ev would be waking and wanting her cup of tea. It was light. The first masters and mistresses were coming along the wall, out of town, and along the beach, out of the village, with their dogs. Jack took up his best piece, a plank, and shouldered it. Later he would get Stan to come down with the car and fetch the rest. The wet plank under his steadying hand, its rasping sand, its smell of brine and tar, he nestled it into his neck. He would have liked to find some wood he could carve, but mostly it was cheap timber used for packing, or it had been in the water too long. Once he had found a log he thought he might do something with, four or five feet long and about nine inches thick, very smooth, he carried it home, it was surprisingly light. The worms were in it, shipworm, he split it and all the naked creatures, as squelchy as oysters, were brought to light in their honeycomb. Soon the two lengths, leaning against the wall, began to stink, and Ev made him take them back to the beach. He went to the trouble of throwing them back into the water at high tide, but by then, needless to say, the worms in their wooden cells were dead.

Stan said he would get Jack a nice piece of wood to carve. His neighbour had cut down a cherry tree, it was blocking the light. He cut it down one Sunday while it was flowering. Stan said the neighbour's wife was heartbroken. She was a very handsome woman, he visited her sometimes with little presents from the garden, her husband was away, driving around up country on financial business.

Stan and Jack met in the Folly Field and sat on a bench watching the visitors. In summer they liked to watch the girls going into the sea and coming out again. Stan had a word for the very short skirts they wore: he called them fanny-pelmets. Jack said the word to himself as he walked home and while he was doing woodwork in the shed. The next time he came into the Folly Field, Stan was already sitting there with a fat log of cherry wood between his knees. Mrs Wilberforce's compliments, he said. Most of the visitors had gone, there was nobody much to look at. Here, said Stan, take a look at this. And slid a pair of nutcrackers from his inside pocket, a carved black woman, naked, as a pair of nutcrackers. The nut goes in between her legs and when you squeeze, it cracks. Ethel won 'em at the Chapel ladies' whistdrive.

Jack came in the back way but Ev was at the kitchen window looking out. Jack had the log on his shoulder. He smiled, and pointed at it. Ev came into the garden, wiping her hands. That friend of yours, she said. He had it off a neighbour, Jack replied. They chopped it down, it was taking up too much light. Ev liked the look of the cherry wood. Make a nice something, she said. Take that filthy coat off before you come in. Jack laid the log on his workbench in the shed. Its bark was red and smooth. Such a beautiful length of tree. Jack stroked it, sniffed it, laid his cheek on it. Time you finished me that stool, said Ev when he came in. Nearly done, he said, one of the legs was wrong.

Next day Jack went out early picking mushrooms. They grew in the field across the street. Must have been horses in there years ago, he said to Stan. Funny to think of them nearly on the beach. Jack had a secretive way of picking mushrooms. He was sure he was the only one who knew they were growing in that field. He was out early, but other people might be out as well walking their dogs. He held a plastic bag under his old raincoat. He held on to it with his left hand through a big hole in the pocket. That way he could slip the mushrooms in and nobody noticed. Sometimes he had to stand over one and pretend to be looking out to sea. The Minister's wife was passing with her alsatian. She said: Good morning, Mr Little. Good morning, Mrs Blunt, said Jack. He picked a good lot and sorted out the best of them in his shed. They were for Mrs Wilberforce. The rest he took in for himself and Ev, to breakfast on. Not so many this morning, he said, I dunno why. Your eyesight's going, I shouldn't wonder, said Ev. She was partial to mushrooms with a bit of crispy bacon. When the tea was made and they sat down in the little kitchen by the fire she would become quite jovial and holding up a mouthful of mushroom on her fork would say, for a joke, that she hoped he wasn't poisoning her. How black the morsel looked when she held it up. No danger of that, said Jack, eating his own with relish. He was so fond of the feel and smell of mushrooms when he was picking them and of their taste when he was eating them that he could scarcely believe they were not forbidden him. And what a strange thing to come of horse-piss! It was a miracle you could eat one and not die.

After breakfast Jack went out into his shed. To finish that stool, I hope, said Ev. Later he slipped out to the Folly Field with the mushrooms for Mrs Wilberforce in a little wicker basket. Give her these, he said to Stan. And thank her very much. She can keep the basket too. I found it on the beach. Stan set off at once. Always glad of an excuse to call on Mrs Wilberforce, he said.

Jack came in at dinner time with the stool. It was a four-legged one, quite low. I put a bit of decoration on it, he said, to brighten it up. Yes, he had carved the seat into the likeness of a smiling face. It's the sun, he said. Uncomfortable to sit on, I should think, said Ev. Still, I can always cover it with a cushion, and it will be handy for standing on, to reach the Christmas pudding down.

*

There was not much doing in the Folly Field, most of the visitors had gone. The little fair had shut, all but the roundabout. She's having her morning, said Jack. The house is full. I can tell you what they'll be talking about, said Stan. You heard the news? Jack hadn't. Councillor Rabbit exposing himself in Chapel. Jack shook his head. There's something wrong with us, he said. They were singing 'Love divine, all loves excelling' when Betty Creeble looked across the aisle and there he was with it out. Of course, when she'd seen it he hung his hat on it. But by then she was hysterical. He'd just been round for the collection too. Jack shook his head. Whatever's wrong with us? The Minister's having a word with him, said Stan. Stan's daughter was coming across the Folly Field with her boy and girl. Down for a week or so, said Stan. She got a husband yet? Jack asked. She was eating an ice cream cornet. Seems not, said Stan, doesn't seem to want one either. The children ran to the roundabout and climbed into a fire engine together. They were the only customers. The girl began ringing the bell. Then they were off. Stan kept up with them and did the circuit several times, prancing and neighing like a little horse. Jack was glad their mother was not wearing a very short skirt, but her jacket was open on a pretty blouse. Dad'll give himself a heart attack, she said. Your ice cream's coming out the bottom, said Jack, if you don't mind my saying so. He felt for a handkerchief to wipe her blouse, but dared not bring it out. Never mind, she said, and put her mouth under the cone where it was leaking. Jack paid for the children to have another ride. Stan went on hands and knees in the opposite direction. The boy looked as dark as a southern Italian, the girl was as blonde as corn. Then the owner gave them a ride for nothing. Jack tugged his beret and said he'd better be off. Not going in, are you? said Stan. You must be mad. I'll be in my shed, said Jack, doing my carving. Tell Mrs W I'm doing a mermaid.

When he was carving Jack always thought of school. It was in the country, the boys came in from the farms. They were slow at words and figures, but it had happened every year that a boy in one or other of Jack's classes discovered he could use his hands. Never knew I had it in me, they used to say. They did some lovely work, Jack had some in the attic still, it was better than his own, and when they outdid him he was proud of them, he had shown them they could do it, that was his part and he was proud of that. They made serviceable things, he guessed there must be hundreds of useful household things still being used in that region of the country in the homes and perhaps even abroad. And if a boy ever asked him specially and they could get the wood, he let him carve whatever he liked, a bird or an animal, for a present. During the war there was a camp near the school, for prisoners of war, Italians, they were marvellously good with their hands. Jack slipped them pieces of wood whenever he dared and they gave him back what they had made of it with their clasp knives, in exchange for cigarettes. Once he had a crib given him at Christmas: an ox, an ass, the manger, the baby Jesus, Mother Mary and Joseph and a couple of shepherds, all simple, warm and true, they were lovely to feel in the hands. They must be still in the house somewhere, Ev had never liked them much, he thought every Christmas of giving them to somebody with children.

Jack knew that his own hands were not especially skilful. Mrs Wilberforce's log of cherry was too good for him. But he had an idea, he knew what he was trying to do. It was common knowledge what a mermaid looked like. She must have long hair and a fishy lower half and be carrying a comb and mirror. Jack thought he could do the fish scales pretty well, like leaves, like a low long skirt, and it was there that he had begun, below the waist, and she was taking shape. Time passed him quietly by. When Ev called him in for dinner he started like a guilty man and hid his carving under a pile of potato sacks.

I hear the illegits are down again, said Ev as they ate their cod. Jack admitted that he had seen them on the Folly Field. The man gave 'em a free ride, he said. I wonder she shows her face down here, said Ev. I wonder Ethel gives 'em house room. Seem nice enough to me, said Jack. They would to you, said Ev. But it's the mother I blame. Poor illegits, how'll they ever manage, I'd like to know. I wonder Ethel can look me in the face. Jack finished up his cod. He was thinking of the children on the roundabout, one blonde, one dark, and of the young woman's blouse and how she had stood next to him and given him a friendly smile. Then he wondered what Mrs Wilberforce would have to say about the illegits, and whether she was really interested in his carving. I see you put a cushion on my sun, he said. Looks better, said Ev. Behind her, on the wall, was a piece of marquetry he had done when they were married. It showed the church they were married in. He felt a crumpling sadness at the sight of it, and a sort of pity for them both. He rose. I'll see to these, he said, taking the plates, which were green and in the shape of obese fish. You'll want a nap after your morning with the ladies. There's pudding, said Ev. You know very well I always do a pudding. When she came in again – it was spotted dick – Jack said, wishing to smooth her: Bad business at the Chapel, so I hear. No woman's safe, said Ev, not even when she's singing hymns. Who told you anyway? That Stan, I suppose. I'll see to these, said Jack, as soon as he could. You'll be wanting a nap after your ladies.

Jack sent another gift of mushrooms to Mrs Wilberforce. Tell her she can keep the little box, he said. I found it on the beach. She says thank you very much, said Stan, and how's the mermaid coming on? Tell her she's coming on very well, said Jack. Her tail was done, he had even managed to give a flourish to the extremity. Then he dug out a little hole for her belly-button and that was it, all of the bottom half of her was done. Now for the rest. He admitted to Stan that he was going to find the upper half more difficult. I mean, he said, everyone knows what a fish looks like. He knew as soon as he came up to her hips and when he was making the hole and the little bulge (like half a cherry) for her belly-button that the rest of her was going to be difficult. The sea was quiet, the roundabout and every other amusement in the Folly Field had closed, on the beach the Minister's wife was unleashing her alsatian. No wreck, said Stan. Nothing, said Jack. What's Ethel say about you visiting Mrs W? Nothing, said Stan. I go in through the garden, behind the bonfire, she never misses me. You mean you do your visiting in your gardening coat? Doesn't bother her, said Stan. And what d'you do up there? Stan had the face of a childish devil when he grinned, and his hands, when he rubbed them together, sounded as though they felt like bark. Have a chat, he said, have a cup of tea. Nothing else besides? A saffron bun maybe, if I touch lucky. Jack did not know where Mrs Wilberforce lived exactly. Some days he might have gone that far and called on Stan, but his usual walk was along the beach as far as the seawall or along the front as far as the Folly Field. That way Ev knew where he was. What's she like? he asked. I've maybe seen her on Thursdays in the post office. Fullish, said Stan, and blonde.

The ladies Ev had when it was her turn to entertain were mostly grey, grey or white, but not an old colour, more like a frost and snow scene on a Christmas card. They came in talking and when they were in they began to shout. When it was over they shouted at the door, and went away again talking. They often wore blue, and jewellery, their mouths were done in red, and certainly one or two of them were fullish. Sometimes the noise they were making suddenly grew louder and Jack was worried in his shed that they might be coming out to visit him, to do him a serious mischief in a friendly sort of way. Mrs Blunt had a face which was massive and immensely powerful around the jaws, her tongue was like a steak. Betty Creeble (the lady whom Councillor Rabbit had offended) seemed to have fractured as a flint does, rather than to have worn as will, for example, chalk. Jack thought Ev's ladies fiercer than buffalo. Must be very nice, he said, at Mrs W's, I mean. Some conversation with a well-spoken woman must be very nice. Stan offered to take him along next time he went – Come up the ditch, he said, and meet me by the bonfire – or next time Ev had her ladies, to be on the safe side; but Jack declined. He was gazing at his hands. Using the chisels and the hammer so much had made them sore.

Half way. Jack decided to start at the top and work down to her middle. He gave her a round face, like the moon, but left it blank for the time being and did her hair which he imagined a golden blonde, he took it right down her back to where her fishy half began. She was lying face down, her front was unspoiled trunk of cherry tree, and he did her hair, spreading it so that her bare back was covered, streams of hair, plaited, in long knots, a semblance of wrack and thong, as was fitting. Then he hid her under the sacks and went in to wash his hands.

By the way, said Ev, as they ate their haddock, I've thought what you can do me with that nice piece of wood. The haddock was yellower than usual. Funny how very unlike a fish it looked. I'll have a lighthouse that lights up. That would be very unusual, don't you think? You mean with a flashing light? Jack asked. Yes, flashing, said Ev. And if we stand it in the corner no one'll see the wires. And do some waves around the bottom to make it look more real. I see what you mean, said Jack. But I think you'll need a longer piece, and not so fat. It's long enough, said Ev, and you can shave it if it's fat.

The bare lightbulb, the steam of his tea, the smells of wood and of the seashore. Jack lifted the mermaid out in her sacks and uncovered her. She was face up, a blank round face, her arms were still encased in the unquarried wood. He had decided she would be empty-handed after all. He had decided she would be hugging herself as though she were cold. The hair came down her shoulders as far as her waist like a cloak, but open, entirely open, at the front, so she was cold. Used to the sea, and cold? The air was colder. He gave her an open face, her smile was innocent and broad, but her eyes were so wide open it was shock her looks expressed. He roughed out her arms the way he wanted them. It was time to begin dividing and shaping her breasts. Happy valley, as Stan said. But the time was a quarter to eight and Ev had woken and would be expecting her cup of tea. Mushrooms, she said when he came in with the tray and wished her good morning. You haven't been out, I don't suppose. Just off, he said. But they're getting to the end, you know.

Soon there were no more mushrooms, neither for Ev nor for Mrs Wilberforce, the nights drew in, the mornings were darker. Jack walked on the beach as far as the seawall or sat with Stan in the deserted Folly Field. I'm doing her bust, he said. Get me some oil, will you, next time you're in town. And he gave him the money out of the pocket without a hole. Ev wants a lighthouse, he added, one that flashes.

Her bust, her breasts. Jack was doing them after an idea he had of a woman's breasts in perfection in his head. By her slim arms, vertical and horizontal, they were enclosed and given a lovely and entirely natural prominence. Day after day, in the early mornings as it grew light and in the late afternoons as it grew dark, Jack was working on the mermaid's breasts with a love and patience that were a wonder to him afterwards. He was glad to have finished with the necessary chisels and the knives. Now he eased the finer and finer sandpapers with oil to induce the wood to become as smooth as skin. Her hair was rough, as it should be, and all of her fishy half, and even her face he was happy to leave like a doll's with broad features, but on her huddled shoulders, her hugging arms, and on her breasts that were like young creatures in a nest or fold, he worked, in the sweet wood, for the perfect smoothness of a human and living form. He was in a trance of work, under the bare bulb, his mug of tea absentmindedly to hand, the sky outside either lightening or darkening. It put him in mind of the best work ever done by the most gifted boys (surprising themselves) in all his years at school, and of the animals reached out through the wire by the prisoners of war in exchange for a couple of Woodbines or a twist of tea. The memory – the association – filled him with pride. After such work he came into his own house like a stranger.

There was a big sea. Jack lay awake, listening. He would wake himself early, but not to go looking for wood. His time before Ev woke was for the mermaid. He lay awake in the night, thinking. The sea came nearer. Jack was thinking of the illegits, and of their mother, Stan's daughter, who had stood beside him carelessly in the Folly Field.

Next morning after breakfast Jack climbed into the loft and found the nativity carvings. They were in a shoebox wrapped in brown paper. When he unwrapped them on the dining-room table they gave him a shock, it was years since he had had them out, and when he took the animals and the human figures one by one into his sore hands he felt a joy and a grief that bewildered him. He fitted the baby into the crib, set father and mother at the head, and crowded the shepherds and the ox and the ass around as though their curiosity were greater even than their reverence. The carving was rough, but every figure had its own liveliness, its dignity and an almost comical manifest good nature. Jack was entranced, like a child, he sat at the table staring, reached now and then for the ox or for Joseph or for the mother herself, as though by pressing them in his grip he could get a little way further into the feelings that were troubling him. He felt regret, but also a sort of gladness and gratitude that he was coming nearer to the source of his regret. Then Ev's voice said: What d'you want getting them out for? She startled him, she stood facing him across the table and her face had slipped, he had never seen such a look on her before, she looked momentarily disfigured as though a stroke had halted her and set her oddly in relation to the world. Well? she said. Well? Her voice had gone strange. Jack was balancing Joseph and Mary in either hand. Thought I'd give 'em to the illegits, he said. Thought they'd look nice where there's a Christmas tree. Ev screamed, once, then again, it was a sound that seemed to have in it nothing at all of personal volition, as though she were ripped. Then she sat at the table and began to weep. Jack put the figures back into the shoebox and the brown paper around it easily resumed its folds. It was paper of a kind no longer ever seen, thick and with an oily texture. Written on it in Ev's big capitals, in purple copy pencil, was the one word NATIVITY. I'll have to get some more string, said Jack.

As he stood up with the box in his hands Ev uncovered her face. And where's my lighthouse? she asked. That would have been nice for Christmas in the corner. It was an ordinary morning in November, a Thursday. Shan't I be going to the post office? said Jack. Don't change the subject, Ev replied. I want my lighthouse. Jack set down the nativity box again, went down the garden to his shed, took up the mermaid in her sacks and carried her thus into the living room. There he unwrapped her on the table, turned on the standard lamp and set her upright on the orange floral chair. I made this instead, he said. Ev stared, said nothing, only stared at the mermaid standing on her fishy tail and smiling foolishly and hugging her breasts as though she were very cold. Ev said: So that's what you've been down there doing. Yes, said Jack. What do you think? Nice, said Ev, very nice. A mermaid will be very unusual. Her voice was quiet, Jack was beginning to smile. So you don't mind then? Stan says he'll get me another log. He tells me Mrs W's got one left. Mrs W, eh? said Ev. So that's where you get your pieces of wood from, is it? Just the one, said Jack. But she'll very likely give me another, for your lighthouse.

Very nice, Ev said again. She was standing in the lamplight next to the floral chair on which the mermaid was standing. Only one little thing, she said: her tits will have to come off. pardon me? said Jack. Cut 'em off, said Ev. I have my ladies round. They can't be expected to look at things like that. It isn't fit. You'll cut 'em off. Then she'll be very nice. Quite unusual really. Jack was looking at his hands. They were calloused and sore from the work he had done on the mermaid. Ev, he said. Her face was remarkable for its infinite creases and wrinkles, but her hair was newly permed. She was smiling, she seemed on the verge of a sort of hilarity. It wouldn't be natural, said Jack. Who ever saw a mermaid without a bust? That's not the point, said Ev. You'll do as I say. Jack got to his feet. He found that his hands were trembling. He took up the mermaid and was wrapping her safely in the potato sacks. Ev said: And don't think I'm having her down there in your shed. She belongs in my front room. I'm having her on show. Jack backed away, hugging his burden.

When he came in again the table was laid for dinner. The

nativity box was lying on the hearth empty. The fire was burning very fiercely. Ev set before him the pale-green fish-shaped
plate. I've done you a nice piece of sole, she said.

Jack sat in the Folly Field with Stan. He was cold. She wants me
to cut her bust off, he said. Hell hath no fury, said Stan. I don't
follow, said Jack. I told her it wouldn't look natural, but she's
adamant. He did not tell Stan about the nativity figures. He was
ashamed. Stan finished his cigarette and tossed it away towards
the empty beach. I'll tell you what, he said. Why don't you
give her to Mrs Wilberforce? She's always asking how you're
getting on. Jack was tempted, he was very tempted. His heart
raced at the proposal. Though he could not be certain that he
had ever seen Mrs Wilberforce, the idea of her, the idea in his
head, which came not only when he sat with Stan in the Folly
Field, was luminous and detailed. In spirit at least he often sat
alongside Stan on the comfortable sofa in her parlour drinking
tea and, on the luckiest days, eating one of her buns whilst
the winter evening drew in. She lit the lamp, but left the big
curtains open to watch the starlings hurtle past on a livid sky.
And she might ask Stan would he mind throwing another log
on the fire, and there they sat, making conversation without
any difficulty, and she was indeed, as Stan had often said, a
handsome woman. No doubt about it, the mermaid would
look very well in that room. The sea was not so far distant
(you could hear it when the wind was right), and the noise
the big trees made when there was a wind in them was very
like the sea. And didn't the mermaid belong there after all, to
make up for the flowering cherry tree which Mrs W had been
so sorry to lose? She'd murder me, he said. She'd never know,
said Stan. She would, said Jack. She finds out everything when
her ladies come. Pity, said Stan. Would have made a nice present.
Jack wondered whether his friend was deceiving him. Perhaps
Mrs Wilberforce never asked after him, perhaps she had never
heard he was making a mermaid, perhaps Stan would present
it to her one evening as the work of his own hands. Suddenly
Jack even doubted whether he had been given any credit for
the mushrooms. Stan could be very sly. Jack recalled numerous
instances of his slyness in the course of their long friendship. Jack
had become very downhearted by the time he said goodbye.

Jack switched the light on and unwrapped the mermaid. She
lay on her back, her face as round as the moon, a helpless smile,

hugging herself for cold. He was amazed at his achievement; or call it luck, a once in a lifetime abundance of good luck. The way her breasts were was exactly how the idea of them was in his head. He laid his cheek on them, closed his eyes, took into the blood of his heart her scent of oil and wood. Then he left her uncovered on the workbench, under the bare bulb.

Ev was getting the tea ready, a nice salad. Well? she said, chopping a cucumber. What if I made 'em a bit smaller? said Jack. Ev put a hardboiled egg in the egg slicer. Cut 'em off, she said.

Next day, in the afternoon, Ev had her ladies. Jack took an unusual walk, away from the Folly Field. He walked through the village to the cemetery, and sat there for an hour or so looking out to sea. When it got dark he came home again, though he knew that the ladies would only just be having their tea. He could hear them from the kitchen, they were in the front room and the door was closed, their noise seemed greater than he had ever heard it. Were they more numerous? Had every lady in the Chapel come? He went a little way into the hall. The ladies were in the highest spirits. They beat at one another with their voices. Jack went a little nearer, applied his ear. But nothing very distinct was audible. He bowed himself, he knelt, he applied his eye. He saw his mermaid. She had been brought out of the corner and was standing on her tail in an easy chair. She smiled her smile, without any hope of pleasing. It seemed to Jack that the space within her arms was cavernous. Then she was obscured by a welter of blue and silver and gold. The hairdos of the ladies fitted their heads like shining helmets, their mouths, open for an enormous hilarity, were as red as jam. Jack rose very slowly and out of habit made towards the back door and the garden – but bethought himself and turned and climbed the stairs to bed.

Jack woke in the night, there was a high wind, Ev was snoring by his side, but above that sound he could hear the sound of the sea, the sea had risen, he imagined it foaming white and slung across the bay from point to point. There'll be some wreck, he thought, and did the trick with his head he had learned from Stan. He rose secretly before first light and taking his old coat from the garden shed was soon on the beach along the high water mark. The tide had turned and was beginning to withdraw, it dragged down the shingle like a death rattle. The weed was a yard high, packed solid. The wind had scarcely lessened and there was rain on it. Jack's small exaltation left him at once. He could see no wood, nor anything else worth picking up. The lights of the railway station and the town looked infinitely beyond his strength, even the seawall was too far, he skidded and stumbled in the weed and on the pebbles. Then it was enough, and he halted. Rolled in weed there was a dead thing at his feet, a seal, and for no good reason he began to tug at the slippery stuff, to free it. He got the head clear and the flippers, then desisted. One eye had gone, the other was beaten in, the head, so shapely on a living beast in water, was monstrous. And all below was deadweight in a stinking winding sheet.

A wet light eastwards over home. Jack stood. In the narrow strip between the shingle and the surf a man and his dog were making their way. Jack moved from the cadaver as though he were guilty. The walker was Councillor Rabbit and his dog, a dachshund, trotted beside him on a lead. Meeting Jack, he cast down his eyes and halted to let him pass. But Jack addressed him. Wet, he said, I'm turning back. Councillor Rabbit was a big man in a trilby, which he had to clutch hold of or the wind would have taken it. He wore a very large herringbone overcoat and polished Oxford shoes. His face, when he allowed Jack to look into it, was as sorrowful as a bloodhound's. It had slipped, it had collapsed. Though Jack had hardly exchanged a word with him in all the years, he grasped him now almost familiarly by the elbow and turned him towards home. He did not want the dog to go sniffing at the seal.

Councillor Rabbit was easily led. There was enough room for the two men and the dachshund to walk side by side between the pebbles and the waves. You never let him off? said Jack, nodding down at the adipose dog. Safer the way he is, said the Councillor. Besides, he's going blind. From under the brim of his trilby he was glancing fearfully at Jack. They made their way, exchanging remarks about this and that. What's he called? Jack asked. Billy, said the Councillor. The little dog's belly left a trail on the wet sand. He's not much of a runner, said the Councillor. As they neared the dunes and the wider beach below the Folly Field other dogs and their masters and mistresses appeared. I generally come out early, said the Councillor. You'll maybe want to go ahead. No, no, said Jack. I'm in no hurry. And again he touched the Councillor amicably on the elbow.

First came the Minister's wife, Mrs Blunt, and her alsatian. It was bounding free, in and out of the retreating tide, and others were advancing after her, more or less frolicsome and fierce. The Councillor was inclined to halt, it seemed he might have stared into the dunes until the trade and Chapel people had all passed, but Jack with gentle touches to the elbow kept him going. So they shuffled forwards, Jack and Councillor Rabbit and between them, on a tight lead, Billy the little wheezing dog.

A Death in the Family

MICHAEL DIBDIN

THANK YOU FOR agreeing to see me at such short notice, Doctor. As a matter of fact, I had been going to consult you in any case, before I had this relapse. You were highly recommended by people I spoke to at home before leaving. Did you know that Argentina has more psychiatrists per capita than any other country? It's the only world record we still hold, our one sad distinction. However, it was out of the question for me to seek treatment there, as you will see. And then as soon as I arrived here in London, I unfortunately had one of my bad spells. Yes, I'm off the drugs now. I don't like taking them for any longer than I must. They don't cure me, they just turn me into someone else, someone who doesn't need to be cured. Perhaps that's all that *can* be done, I don't know. That's what I want you to tell me. But first I must explain the problem. It won't take long.

I am a *porteña*, a native of Buenos Aires. I had a privileged upbringing. My father was a naval officer, my mother a direct descendant of Julio Roca, the general who led the extermination of the indigenous tribes. Just when they had given up hope of being able to have a family – my mother was in her early forties by then – I appeared. But this miracle remained a unique event. As if to try and make up for this, I was denied nothing. I attended an exclusive private school, kept a horse and several dogs, had tennis tuition from an ex-Wimbledon competitor, and so on. Every winter we went skiing at Bariloche or San Martín, the summers we spent at our villa near Punta del Este in Uruguay.

Like many only children, I was imaginative and intellectually advanced for my age. I read as widely as I could, given that my parents had very conservative views on what was and was not suitable. I can still remember my father's fury on discovering the novel by Sartre I had found at the lending library at Harrods on Calle Florida. Sartre was a communist and an atheist, I was told, and his books subversive propaganda. If you want to read modern literature, he said, read our own Jorge Luis Borges, who is famous all over the world, and whose political views are perfectly sound.

It was like falling into a whirlpool. My ideas about history and personality and character, which were just beginning to form, were promptly dissolved by the power of Borges's imagination, plunged back into a dreamlike state of potentiality where anything could happen to anyone at any time. It was inevitable that I should make the pilgrimage to the bookshop where the old man was to be found most afternoons. Eventually I overcame my trepidation and asked him to sign my copy of *Ficciones*.

The huge, soft, benign face turned slowly, the eyes seemingly fixed on someone standing slightly to one side of me. I knew very well that Borges was blind, of course, but this impression was so strong that I couldn't help glancing around. Needless to say, there was no one there.

He asked me which of his stories I preferred. I mentioned one I had just read, the only title I could think of on the spur of the moment. A peculiar smile appeared on his lips, as though appreciating an irony only he was aware of. Then he wrote a few lines in the book, and signed it. I was too nervous to look at the inscription until I was outside the shop and on my way home. It was the last line of *Emma Zunz*, the story I had mentioned. 'Only the circumstances were false, the time, and one or two names.' I assumed it was the influence of these words which had led to the unfortunate mistake in the dedication. My first name, Eva, was correct, but instead of Martinez, Borges had written 'Marqués'.

I was bitterly disappointed, but I didn't have the nerve to go back and point out the mistake. That evening my father asked to see the book. The moment he saw what Borges had written, he flinched as though he had been slapped by an invisible hand. Then he ripped the page out and threw it into the fire. 'The old man's brain has gone soft,' he said. The matter was never referred to again, and when I looked at the book a few days later there was no sign of the torn flyleaf. Someone must have bought a new copy and exchanged it for the spoiled one. It was as if the whole incident had been cancelled from my life, as though it had never happened.

This disturbing and inexplicable event seemed just one more proof of the widening gulf between me and my parents. Increasingly, I felt that our home life was just a sham, a hollow façade. It never occurred to me that this was anything but the sort of adolescent alienation which my friends were all going through too. I assumed that it was just part of growing up, of breaking the parental mould. I was proud of my dark hair and swarthy skin because they seemed to mark me out as destined for a more exotic and colourful future than the pallidly correct couple I lived with. I liked to imagine that I looked Jewish, because that seemed to sum up everything my parents were not, everything they rejected and dismissed. But in reality I never questioned their explanation that my looks represented a genetic throwback to a strain of *moreno* beauty last exemplified by my great grandmother, whose oil portrait, which hung above the fireplace, was always cited whenever the topic came up.

The next episode occurred when my father and I went to Punta del Este one weekend in early summer. My mother stayed behind. She had been suffering from heart trouble for some time, and had also taken a dislike to the villa after an attempted robbery at a neighbouring property in which one of our friends had been shot and seriously injured. Since she would not come my father had invited one of his colleagues from the Navy Mechanics School to join us. Our flight left early in the morning. As usual, we took a taxi to the Aeroparque. I sat in the back, between the two men. I was in that state between sleeping and waking, when reality has not yet exerted its reassuring tyranny. The streets were almost empty. The taxi drove fast, ignoring red lights and stop signs. Darkness surged in through the open windows.

Suddenly, I was overcome by the knowledge that all this had happened before, though not to me. Although brief, the experience was intensely threatening, inducing an almost physical sense of nausea. I slumped forward, lost in the tidal currents and swirling memories of this alien self. The sensation eventually passed, but the sense of horror and panic, of utter helplessness and sickening terror, remained with me throughout the whole weekend, and indeed long after.

That summer I passed my examinations with distinction. As a reward my parents sent me to Europe to study English for a month in Oxford. I was in the centre of that town one afternoon when it suddenly started to rain. I took shelter in the doorway of a bookshop and when it became clear that the rain was going to last for some time I went inside to browse around. I normally love books, but I was feeling lonely and homesick, and the rows and rows of volumes seemed to threaten to crush me beneath the brute weight of Anglo-Saxon culture. So when a title in my own language suddenly popped out at me, I greeted it like a friend sighted amidst a crowd of strangers.

The book was called *Nunca Mas* – 'Never Again' – which reminded me of Poe's poem about the raven. Unfortunately, only the title was in Spanish, and the text was too difficult for me to read. Leafing through it, however, I found to my surprise and delight a detailed plan and description of the Navy Mechanics School where my father worked. There was also a section of photographs showing dull-looking buildings in the federal capital and various provincial cities like Tucumán and Formosa. I couldn't see why anyone would want to photograph places like that when there were so many great beauty spots in Argentina, but I bought the book anyway, as a nostalgic gesture, a token of home.

Over the next few days I spent odd moments struggling through the book with the help of a dictionary. I gradually came to realise that it was an official report by the commission set up to investigate the fate of those who had disappeared during the so-called 'dirty-war'. This was the period when my country was brought to the brink of anarchy as a result of a campaign of terror waged by foreign-trained communist subversives. It was only after a long and arduous struggle that the armed forces had finally succeeded in ensuring the survival of civilised western, Christian values.

That at least was what I had been brought up to believe. The book told a very different story. In horrific detail it described a nightmare world in which men, women and children of all ages, most of them having no connection whatever with the guerrilla movement, were dragged from their homes by armed thugs and taken to secret detention centres where they were tortured for weeks or even months before being shot and their bodies burned, buried in unmarked mass graves or dumped at sea. When women gave birth during their detention, their babies

121

were taken from them and given to the families of the military to bring up as their own, while the mothers were killed. One of the principal centres for these activities had been the Navy Mechanics School, that elegant black-and-white building on Avenida del Libertador where I had visited my father on numerous occasions.

During my last week in England I fell seriously ill. My temperature soared to a critical fever point and I was rushed into hospital for a series of tests. Unknown to me, the school contacted my father in Buenos Aires. One evening I awoke from a delirious sleep to find him standing by my bed. 'My poor Eva,' he said, wiping my brow. 'I'm afraid I have some bad news for you. Your mother . . .' He broke off, sighing deeply. It took an immense effort to meet his eyes. 'My mother is dead,' I said.

A look of amazement and fear crossed his face, and then he nodded slowly. From that moment on I had no further doubts. I knew everything that had happened as though I had been there. Indeed, I *had*. I had been there when my mother was seized early one morning and driven away in a fast car, the streets almost empty, the darkness surging in through the open windows. I had been saturated in her terror, her panic, her agony. Amniotic fluid is an excellent conductor of electricity, you know. Hooded in her womb, I had been spared nothing except her death. Torn from her labouring body, chained to the delivery bed, I was handed over to one of the officers who had supervised her torture, a man whose wife was unfortunately unable to have children.

And now she was dead too. I was told a massive heart attack had felled her, like a shot from an executioner's pistol. A few days later we flew home to attend the funeral. My friends found me a changed person, but ascribed this to the shock of my mother's death. I gave up eating meat, which in Argentina is practically a national crime. I also broke off relations with all the young men who had been competing for my attention. Ever since learning about one particularly obscene torment inflicted on women detainees I visualised every male as carrying a live rat between his legs, savage and voracious, eager to burrow its way into my inner tissue.

After several months had passed, my guardian, as I now thought of him, finally lost patience with what he took to be my exaggerated grief and tried to impose his old authority once again. Having vainly attempted to persuade, cajole or threaten, he laid hands on me, and in a way I could not regard as purely paternal. I was by now a well-developed young woman, his wife was dead, and the taboo of incest was inoperative since he knew that I was his daughter in name only. He was expecting me to submit, of course. He was expecting a victim, gagged by dutiful obedience, hooded by filial affection.

Instead, all my pent-up loathing burst out with a venom that amazed even me. I lost all my self-control. I screamed abuse at him, calling him a filthy old man, a rapist, a murderer, a devil. Shocked by this transformation of his doting darling into a ravening angel of vengeance, he backed away, muttering incoherent apologies and denials. I could have pressed on, revealing everything that I had guessed and demanding to know the rest, but I had enough sense to realise that my unexpected victory had been due to surprise, an advantage I would never have again. From now on, I would have to be as cold as ice, and plan my every move.

It was his custom to take a taxi back from work, but not all the way to the house. We lived in San Isidro, a secluded suburb of quiet, leafy streets overlooking the River Plate. My guardian used to get the taxi to drop him at the turning of the main road, claiming that during the ten-minute walk to the house all the cares of his working day dropped away, leaving him free to enjoy his family life to the full. Now that I knew how he had spent his working day, and the exact nature of those 'cares', I trembled to remember how I had rushed to be picked up and kissed when he came home, and how by tickling me he had made me laugh until I cried.

I hired the car in Avellaneda, a tough southern suburb where animals are slaughtered and packaged for human consumption. I rode the *colectivo* to the end of the line, then walked until I found the bar I was looking for. I recognised it the moment I saw it, a poky little tavern at the corner of two unremarkable streets lost in the vast, anonymous grid of the Buenos Aires suburbs. I had never seen it before, and would never be able to find it again. It was a place with no history and no future. It existed in that moment, a mocked-up frontage for the scene I was about to play.

Inside, five men were playing cards. I went up to the bar, ordered a coffee and told the proprietor that I needed the use of a car for a few hours and was prepared to pay well. I was expecting him to contact a friend, maybe one of the card players, and arrange to steal a vehicle. I expected to have all my money stolen, and perhaps be raped into the bargain. I was even expecting to have to come back another day, to another bar, and go through it all again. I was prepared for all that, and more. But the owner simply shrugged and handed me a set of keys. 'You can take mine,' he said. The car was a sixties Ford Falcon, one of those finned and winged monsters. It also happened to be the vehicle most commonly used by the snatch squads who disappeared people during the dirty war.

My guardian was crossing a side street, about halfway between the main road and our house when the accident occurred. I had parked close to where the taxi dropped him, then circled round. As he appeared I slowed to give way, and gestured him across. I was wearing a headscarf and dark glasses. He waved his thanks and stepped out into the street. I was aiming for his legs, but in the end I took rather more of him. By the time I reached the hospital, having returned the car, they had completed the radiography. Both legs were broken, one in three places as well as the left hip, the collarbone and three ribs. This however, the doctors dismissed as merely superficial. What really worried them was the hairline fracture of the spine which could lead to permanent paralysis. Only time would tell. Once the sedation wore off, it became apparent that the patient was in 'some considerable discomfort', as the nurse put it. The police had been informed of the incident, but unfortunately my guardian was unable to give them any information about the driver or the car.

Six weeks later he finally completed his trip home in a wheelchair. The doctors held out hopes of his eventually gaining at least a measure of independent mobility, but for the foreseeable future he would require full-time nursing. I took it upon myself to cater to all his needs. I fed him, bathed him, dressed and undressed him, read to him, took him to the lavatory. This selfless behaviour was praised by all our friends and relations and held up as an example to less sublimely devoted sons and daughters. The priest at our local church made me the subject of an inspirational homily, while a Peronist deputy referred to my conduct as 'stirring proof that the ideals which made this republic great, based on the traditional principles of respect for the Church, the state and the family, have not been extirpated by the excesses of libertarian democracy'.

Months passed before my guardian's condition improved sufficiently for me to suggest the possibility of our visiting the villa in Uruguay. An isolated property set on a ridge of land between a deserted sandy beach and a swampy lagoon where flamingoes swarmed, he had bought it as a refuge from the pressures of everyday life, and it had always been associated in his mind with happy memories and a relaxing, informal way of life. In Buenos Aires we had a large staff to run the house and spent much time entertaining and doing the social round, but at Punta del Este we looked after ourselves and saw no one but a few close friends. The psychological effect, I argued, would undoubtedly be beneficial. As for the practical problems, was not my ability to care lovingly for my father already a national legend?

The specialists and consultants gave their unanimous approval. As usual, we flew direct to the property in a small plane belonging to a family friend. Cattle and sheep graze on the open pampas near the villa. We passed over the *estancia* some fifteen kilometres up the dirt road, which is the nearest human habitation, made a preliminary sweep to clear the animals off the grass landing strip, then circled back to touch down. Ten minutes later the plane took off again, leaving us alone.

I knew exactly what was going to happen. I had thought about little else during the long dreary days and nights I had devoted to my patient's needs, filling one hole, cleaning the other, hauling that deadweight of flesh about the house. I had come to know it very well, and had plenty of time to consider its fate in some detail. It still wasn't easy, now the moment had come to act. That night at the villa was a veritable Gethsemane for me. But whenever I found myself wishing that this cup might pass from me, I recalled the fate of my real father and my resolve was strengthened. The whisky I drank helped too. People speak of personality as though it were a fixed attribute, like the colour of one's eyes or the pattern of a fingerprint. We all collaborate in maintaining this fiction, precisely because we know it to be one, and because that knowledge is intolerable.

When the dawn finally broke over the lonely salt flats and sand dunes around the villa, I had become another person, unrecognisable to myself, capable of anything. I entered the room where my guardian was sleeping and covered his head with a leather bag he had given me for my eleventh birthday. When he tried to remove the bag, I rolled him off the edge of the bed. His fractures were still incompletely healed and, judging by his howls, the 'discomfort' of falling to the floor was indeed quite considerable. Certainly, he made little resistance when I slipped a length of clothesline around his wrists and tied them up tightly. I then stripped off his pyjamas, had another slug of whisky, and set to work.

My techniques were all modelled on those he himself would have used on my parents. I fetched the vacuum cleaner from the store-room, unwound the lead fully and then severed it from the machine with a pair of pliers. I stripped the insulation back a few centimetres, exposing the metal wire, then plugged the other end into the wall. To improve conductivity, I poured water over the body on the floor. It was all much easier than I had supposed. I immediately appreciated the benefits of hooding the victim. Not only does this increase his sense of disorientation and helplessness, but it makes it much easier to get on with the work in hand. It is no longer a person you're dealing with, only a body, and a comically defaced one at that, a figure of fun.

As well as the live wires, I made use of two appliances I had purchased in Buenos Aires before leaving, a rotary sanding device fitted with a variety of abrasive wheels, and a butane torch intended for stripping paint. I tried to work systematically, but as time passed I became increasingly distraught. One of the effects of electrocution is to stimulate vomiting and evacuation of the bowels, and then, of course, there was the screaming. It's difficult to remain calm and lucid in such conditions, particularly with all the whisky you need to settle your stomach and keep your nerve. But, as those who worked with my guardian at the Navy Mechanics School knew, there is no need for subtlety or refinement when the victim is doomed.

Like them, I wanted names. Not the names of casual friends and acquaintances who would then be seized and tortured in turn to add to the notional network of subversives the military were supposedly eradicating, like a demonic version of a pyramid-selling scam. The name I wanted was my own, and those of my murdered mother and father. It took longer than I had supposed, longer than I would have believed possible. For hours he continued to deny everything. Then, shortly after I started a second application of the blowtorch, he broke, not only admitting that I was not his natural child, but proclaiming it in a vehement tone of voice, as though *proud* of the fact. I then put it to him that I had been born in the detention centre and adopted by him and his wife as a substitute for the child they could not have, that my real name was indeed Marqués as the sightless seer Borges had written in the book.

Unfortunately the crushing of my guardian's *macho* spirit – and by a mere girl – caused a rapid collapse into hysteria. Alternately laughing and weeping, he agreed to everything I said. This did not assuage his sufferings, any more than the affirmations or denials of his own victims had theirs. On the contrary, the knowledge that he was of no further use to me merely increased my contempt for his inarticulate shrieks and disgusting convulsions. I drank deep of the whisky, turned up the radio as loud as it would go, and pressed ahead with ever more extreme measures in an effort to bring this degrading spectacle to an end as quickly as possible.

When it was over, I showered the filth from my body and changed into clean clothes. I packed my soiled garments into a plastic sack, and all the gold and silver ornaments I could find into another. Then I fetched the jeep from the garage and loaded the two sacks into it. I drove into town by a roundabout route, dropping the weighted sacks into a drainage culvert on the way. I went to a supermarket and bought supplies for the week, then had lunch at a restaurant. On the way back to the villa I stopped off at the neighbouring farm. I explained to the inhabitants that we had not been able to visit the area for some time, firstly because of my mother's fears about the gang of burglars and then, after her death, as a result of my father's accident. We chatted for an hour or so, then I said I had better be getting back.

At the villa, nothing had changed. The house was more than just quiet; it was at peace at last. The police told me that they would be there as quickly as possible. I spent the time meditating on the fate of my real parents: the brutal irruption of armed men into their home, the looting of all items of value, the succession of questions to which they had no answers, the slow, systematic destruction of body and mind that followed. When the police arrived, I told them what had happened: intruders had entered the house during my absence. They had stolen whatever they could find, but no doubt thought that there were other concealed valuables. They had tried to make my father tell them where they were. Infuriated by his repeated protestations of ignorance, they had then murdered him. And like Borges's Emma Zunz, I was believed, because my story was substantially true. Only the circumstances were false, the time, and one or two names.

Funerals, like Christmas, bring together relations who never otherwise meet. Certainly, I never recalled seeing my Aunt Esmeralda anywhere other than the Recoleta cemetery, aside from once a year on Christmas Eve at her own gothic monstrosity of a house in the Palermo district. No doubt it was this association, together with the heavy furnishing and perpetually lowered blinds, which made me think of the place as a funeral parlour. It was there that I was summoned, a month after my father's burial, to receive my aunt's commiserations on my orphanhood. 'You poor child,' she said as I advanced towards her through the cluttered gloom of the drawing room, 'you poor, poor child!' It was on the tip of my tongue to point out that poor was one thing I certainly wasn't. On the contrary, I had just inherited a fortune, the extent of which had surprised me. Even after substantial donations to relief organisations set up to help dependants of 'the disappeared' – for much of my guardian's wealth, I suspected, was the accumulated spoils of booty from the dirty war – I was still very comfortably provided for. But Aunt Esmeralda wanted to commiserate.

'You poor child, all alone in the world! When I think of my poor sister, how happy she was when they told her she was pregnant. She had almost given up hope by then, you see. Don't look at me like that, dear. You're a woman now, we can discuss these things. And the birth was terrible. You were badly placed inside her, you see. Deep transverse arrest, they call it. They had to use forceps in the end to get you out. I was there the whole time, and I don't know which of us suffered most. Ah, but afterwards to see the joy in your father's face! That made it all worth it. How they smothered you with kisses! Oh, I'm sorry, my dear! How tactless of me to speak of such things when your grief is still fresh.'

For some weeks I tried to believe that Aunt Esmeralda was part of some monstrous conspiracy set up by my father to conceal the truth about his crimes even after his death. But a time came when I could sustain this fiction no longer. As well as my aunt's testimony, there was the material I found when I went through the family archives: documents, letters and photographs dating from the day of my birth in the city's main hospital and proving beyond all reasonable doubt that the man and woman who brought me up were indeed my father and mother.

As for the Borges inscription, I discovered from a jealous relative, disappointed by the provision made for her in my father's will, that one of his sisters, after whom I had been named, had caused a scandal by leaving her husband to take up with a famous tango singer named Marqués. The affair had been the talk of Buenos Aires in its day, said my informant, pursing her lips in disapproval, or suppressed amusement. The ageing Borges's mistake, and my father's indignant reaction, had been a final echo of that notoriety.

Concerning my father's activities at the Navy Mechanics School, I was unable to find out anything definite. No one wants to talk about those events in Argentina nowadays. It's an unhappy episode we'd rather not think about, an error of judgement that's best forgotten. Which is all *I* want to do, believe me. The problem is, I don't seem to have the knack. I can manage for weeks at a time, but sooner or later I have one of these relapses.

I don't want to go on doping myself for ever, Doctor, but what's the alternative? Can I learn to come to terms with reality? What do you think?

Forain

MAVIS GALLANT

ABOUT AN HOUR before the funeral service for Adam Tremski, snow mixed with rain began to fall, and by the time the first of the mourners arrived the stone steps of the church were dangerously wet. Blaise Forain, Tremski's French publisher, now his literary executor, was not surprised when, later, an elderly woman slipped and fell and had to be carried by ambulance to the Hôtel-Dieu hospital. Forain, in an attempt to promote Cartesian order over Slavic frenzy, sent for the ambulance, then found himself obliged to accompany the patient to the emergency section and fork over a deposit. The old lady had no social security.

Taken together, façade and steps formed an escarpment – looming, abrupt, above all unfamiliar. The friends of Tremski's last years had been Polish, Jewish, a few French. Of the French, only Forain was used to a variety of last rites. He was expected to attend the funerals not only of his authors but of their wives. He knew all the Polish churches of Paris, the Hungarian mission, the synagogues on the Rue Copernic and the Rue de la Victoire, and the mock chapel of the crematorium at Père Lachaise cemetery. For nonbelievers a few words at the graveside sufficed. Their friends said, by way of a greeting, 'Another one gone'. However, no one they knew ever had been buried from this particular church. The parish was said to be the oldest in the city, yet the edifice built on the ancient site looked forbidding and cold. Tremski for some forty years had occupied the same walkup flat on the fringe of Montparnasse.

What was he doing over here, on the wrong side of the Seine?

Four months before this, Forain had been present for the last blessing of Barbara, Tremski's wife, at the Polish church on the Rue Saint-Honoré. The church, a chapel really, was round in shape, with no fixed pews – just rows of chairs pushed together. The dome was a mistake – too imposing for the squat structure – but it had stood for centuries, and only the very nervous could consider it a threat. Here, Forain had noticed, tears came easily, not only for the lost friend but for all the broken ties and old, unwilling journeys. The tears of strangers around him, that is; grief, when it reached him, was pale and dry. He was thirty-eight, divorced, had a daughter of twelve who lived in Nice with her mother and the mother's lover. Only one or two of Forain's friends had ever met the girl. Most people, when told, found it hard to believe he had ever been married. The service for Tremski's wife had been disrupted by the late entrance of *her* daughter – child of her first husband – who had made a show of arriving late, kneeling alone in the aisle, kissing the velvet pall over the coffin, and noisily marching out. Halina was her name. She had straight, greying hair and a cross face with small features. Forain knew that some of the older mourners could remember her as a pretty, unsmiling, not too clever child. A few perhaps thought Tremski was her father and wondered if he had been unkind to his wife. Tremski, sitting with his head bowed, may not have noticed. At any rate, he had never mentioned anything.

Tremski was Jewish. His wife had been born a Catholic, though no one was certain what had come next. To be blunt, was she in or out? The fact was that she had lived in adultery – if one wanted to be specific – with Tremski until her husband had obliged the pair by dying. There had been no question of a divorce; probably she had never asked for one. For his wedding to Barbara, Tremski had bought a dark-blue suit at a good place, Creed or Lanvin Hommes, which he had on at her funeral, and in which he would be buried. He had never owned another, had shambled around Paris looking as though he slept under restaurant tables, on a bed of cigarette ashes and crumbs. It would have taken a team of devoted women, not just one wife, to keep him spruce.

Forain knew only from hearsay about the wedding ceremony in one of the town halls of Paris ('Tremski was still untranslated then, had a job in a book-store near the Jardin des Plantes, had paid back the advance for the dark-blue suit over eleven months) – the names signed in a register, the daughter's refusal to attend, the wine drunk with friends in a café on the Avenue du Maine. It was a cheerless place, but Tremski knew the owner. He had talked of throwing a party but never got round to it; his flat was too small. Any day now he would move to larger quarters and invite two hundred and fifty intimate friends to a banquet. In the mean time, he stuck to his rented flat, a standard émigré dwelling of the nineteen-fifties, almost a period piece now: two rooms on a court, windowless kitchen, splintered floors, unheatable bathroom, no elevator, intimidating landlord – a figure central to his comic anecdotes and private worries. What did his wife think? Nobody knew, though if he had sent two hundred and fifty invitations she would undoubtedly have started to borrow two hundred and fifty glasses and plates. Even after Tremski could afford to move, he remained anchored to his seedy rooms: there were all those books, and the boxes filled with unanswered mail, and the important documents he would not let anyone file. Snapshots and group portraits of novelists and poets, wearing the clothes and haircuts of the fifties and sixties, took up much of a wall. A new desire to sort out the past, put its artifacts in order, had occupied Tremski's conversation on his wedding day. His friends had soon grown bored, although his wife seemed to be listening. Tremski, married at last, was off on an oblique course, preaching the need for discipline and a thought-out future. It didn't last.

At Forain's first meeting with Barbara, they drank harsh tea from mismatched cups and appraised each other in the grey light that filtered in from the court. She asked him, gently, about his fitness to translate and publish Tremski – then still at the bookstore, selling wartime memoirs and paperbacks and addressing parcels. Did Forain have close ties with the Nobel Prize committee? How many of his authors had received important awards, gone on to international fame? She was warm and friendly and made him think of a large buttercup. He was about the age of her daughter, Halina; so Barbara said. He felt paternal, wise, rid of mistaken ideals. He would become Tremski's guide and father. He thought, This is the sort of woman I should have married – although most probably he should never have married anyone.

*

Only a few of the mourners mounting the treacherous steps can have had a thought to spare for Tremski's private affairs. His wife's flight from a brave and decent husband, dragging by the hand a child of three, belonged to the folklore, not the history, of mid-century emigration. The chronicle of two generations, displaced and dispossessed, had come to a stop. The evaluation could begin; had already started. Scholars who looked dismayingly youthful, speaking the same language, but with a new jarring vocabulary, were trekking to Western capitals – taping reminiscences, copying old letters. History turned out to be a plodding science. What most émigrés settled for now was the haphazard accuracy of a memory like Tremski's. In the end it was always a poem that ran through the mind – not a string of dates.

Some may have wondered why Tremski was entitled to a Christian service; or, to apply another kind of reasoning, why it had been thrust upon him. Given his shifting views on eternity and the afterlife, a simple get-together might have done, with remarks from admirers, a poem or two read aloud, a priest wearing a turtleneck sweater, or a young rabbi with a literary bent. Or one of each, offering prayers and tributes in turn. Tremski had nothing against prayers. He had spent half his life inventing them.

As it turned out, the steep church was not as severe as it looked from the street. It was in the hands of a small charismatic order, perhaps full of high spirits but by no means schismatic. No one had bothered to ask if Tremski was a true convert or just a writer who sometimes sounded like one. His sole relative was his stepdaughter. She had made an arrangement that suited her: she lived nearby, in a street until recently classed as a slum, now renovated and highly prized. Between her seventeenth-century flat and the venerable site was a large, comfortable, cluttered department store, where, over the years, Tremski's friends had bought their pots of paint and rollers, their sturdy plates and cups, their burglarproof door locks, their long-lasting cardigan sweaters. The store was more familiar than the church. The stepdaughter was a stranger.

She was also Tremski's heir and she did not understand Forain's role, taking executor to mean an honorary function, godfather to the dead. She had told Forain that Tremski had destroyed her father and blighted her childhood. He had enslaved her mother, spoken loud Polish in restaurants, had tried to keep Halina from achieving a French social identity. Made responsible, by his astonishing will, for organising a suitable funeral, she had chosen a French sendoff, to be followed by burial in a Polish cemetery outside Paris. Because of the weather and because there was a shortage of cars, friends were excused from attending the burial. Most of them were thankful: more than one fatal cold had been brought on by standing in the icy mud of a graveyard. When she had complained she was doing her best, that Tremski had never said what he wanted, she was probably speaking the truth. He could claim one thing and its opposite in the same sentence. Only God could keep track. If today's rite was a cosmic error, Forain decided, it was up to Him to erase Tremski's name from the ledger and enter it in the proper column. If He cared.

The mourners climbed the church steps slowly. Some were helped by younger relatives, who had taken time off from work. A few had migrated to high-rise apartments in the outer suburbs, to deeper loneliness but cheaper rents. They had set out early, as if they still believed no day could start without them, and after a long journey underground and a difficult change of direction had emerged from the Hôtel de Ville métro station. They held their umbrellas at a slant, as if countering some force of nature arriving head-on. Actually, there was not the least stir in the air, although strong winds and sleet were forecast. The snow and rain came down in thin soft strings, clung to fur or woollen hats, and became a meagre amount of slush underfoot.

Forain was just inside the doors, accepting murmured sympathy and handshakes. He was not usurping a family role but trying to make up for the absence of Halina. Perhaps she would stride in late, as at her mother's funeral, driving home some private grudge. He had on a long cashmere overcoat, the only black garment he owned. A friend had left it to him. More exactly, the friend, aware that he was to die very soon, had told Forain to collect it at the tailor's. It had been fitted, finished, paid for, never worn. Forain knew there was a mean joke abroad about his wearing dead men's clothes. It also applied to his professional life: he was supposed to have said he preferred the backlist of any dead writer to the stress and tension of trying to deal with a live one.

His hair and shoes felt damp. The hand he gave to be shaken must have chilled all those it touched. He was squarely in the path of one of those church drafts that become gales anywhere close to a door. He wondered if Halina had been put off coming because of some firm remarks of his, the day before (he had defended Tremski against the charge of shouting in restaurants), or even had decided it was undignified to pretend she cared for a second how Tremski was dispatched; but at the last minute she turned up, with her French husband – a reporter of French political affairs on a weekly – and a daughter of fourteen in jacket and jeans. These two had not been able to read a word of Tremski's until Forain had published a novel in translation about six years before. Tremski believed they had never looked at it – to be fair, the girl was only eight at the time – or any of the books that had followed; although the girl clipped and saved reviews. It was remarkable, Tremski had said, the way literate people, reasonably well travelled and educated, comfortably off, could live adequate lives without wanting to know what had gone before or happened elsewhere. Even the husband, the political journalist, was like that: a few names, a date looked up, a notion of geography satisfied him.

Forain could tell Tremski minded. He had wanted Halina to think well of him at least on one count, his life's work. She was the daughter of a former Army officer who had died – like Barbara, like Tremski – in a foreign city. She considered herself, no less than her father, the victim of a selfish adventure. She also believed she was made of better stuff than Tremski, by descent and status, and that was harder to take. In Tremski's own view, comparisons were not up for debate.

For the moment, the three were behaving well. It was as much as Forain expected from anybody. He had given up measuring social conduct, except where it ran its course in fiction. His firm made a speciality of translating and publishing work from Eastern and Central Europe; it kept him at a remove. Halina seemed tame now, even thanked him for standing in and welcoming all those strangers. She had a story to explain why she was late, but it was farfetched, and Forain forgot it immediately. The delay most likely had been caused by a knockdown argument over the jacket and jeans. Halina was a cold skirmisher, narrow in scope but heavily principled. She wore a fur-and-leather coat, a pale grey hat with a brim, and a scarf – authentic Hermès? Taiwan fake? Forain could have told by rubbing the silk between his fingers, but it was a wild idea, and he kept his distance.

The girl had about her a look of Barbara: for that reason, no other, Forain found her appealing. Blaise ought to sit with the family, she said – using his first name, the way young people did now. A front pew had been kept just for the three of them. There was plenty of room. Forain thought that Halina might begin to wrangle, in whispers, within earshot (so to speak) of the dead. He said yes, which was easier than to refuse, and decided no. He left them at the door, greeting stragglers, and found a place at the end of a pew halfway down the aisle. If Halina mentioned anything later, he would say he had been afraid he might have to leave before the end. She walked by without noticing and, once settled, did not look around.

The pale hat had belonged to Halina's mother. Forain was sure he remembered it. When his wife died, Tremski had let Halina and her husband ransack the flat. Halina made several trips while the husband waited downstairs. He had come up only to help carry a crate of papers belonging to Tremski. It contained, among other documents, some of them rubbish, a number of manuscripts not quite complete. Since 'Barbara's funeral Tremski had not bothered to shave or even put his teeth in. He sat in the room she had used, wearing a dressing gown torn at the elbows. Her wardrobe stood empty, the door wide, just a few hangers inside. He clutched Forain by the sleeve and said that Halina had taken some things of his away. As soon as she realised her error she would bring them back.

Forain would have preferred to cross the Seine on horseback, lashing at anyone who resembled Halina or her husband, but he had driven to her street by taxi, past the old, reassuring, unchanging department store. No warning, no telephone call: he walked up a curving stone staircase, newly sandblasted and scrubbed, and pressed the doorbell on a continued note until someone came running.

She let him in, just so far. 'Adam can't be trusted to look after his own affairs,' she said. 'He was always careless and dirty, but now the place smells of dirt. Did you look at the kitchen table? He must keep eating from the same plate. As for my mother's letters, if that's what you're after, he had already started to tear them up.'

'Did you save any?'

'They belong to me.'

How like a ferret she looked, just then; and she was the child of such handsome parents. A studio portrait of her father, the Polish officer, taken in London, in civilian clothes, smoking a long cigarette, stood on a table in the entrance hall. (Forain was admitted no further.) Forain took in the likeness of the man who had fought a war for nothing. Barbara had deserted that composed, distinguished, somewhat careful face for Tremski. She must have forced Tremski's hand, arrived on his doorstep, bag, baggage, and child. He had never come to a resolution about anything in his life.

Forain had retrieved every scrap of paper, of course – all but the letters. Fired by a mixture of duty and self-interest, he was unbeatable. Halina had nothing on her side but a desire to reclaim her mother, remove the Tremski influence, return her – if only her shoes and blouses and skirts – to the patient and defeated man with his frozen cigarette. Her entitlement seemed to include a portion of Tremski, too; but she had resented him, which weakened her grasp. Replaying every move, Forain saw how strong her case might have been if she had acknowledged Tremski as her mother's choice. Denying it, she became – almost became; Forain stopped her in time – the defendant in a cheap sort of litigation.

Tremski's friends sat with their shoes in puddles. They kept their gloves on and pulled their knitted scarves tight. Some had spent all these years in France without social security or health insurance, either for want of means or because they had never found their feet in the right sort of employment. Possibly they believed that a long life was in itself full payment for a safe old age. Should the end turn out to be costly and prolonged, then, please, allow us to dream and float in the thickest, deepest darkness, unaware of the inconvenience and clerical work we may cause. So, Forain guessed, ran their prayers.

Funerals came along in close ranks now, especially in bronchial winters. One of Forain's earliest recollections was the Mass in Latin, but he could not say he missed it: he associated Latin with early-morning hunger, and sitting still. The charismatic movement seemed to have replaced incomprehension and mystery with theatricals. He observed the five priests in full regalia, sitting to the right of the altar. One had a bad cold and kept taking a handkerchief from his sleeve. Another more than once glanced at his watch. A choir, concealed or on tape, sang 'Jesu, bleibet meine Freude', after which a smooth, trained voice began to recite the Twenty-fifth Psalm. The voice seemed to emanate from Tremski's coffin but was too perfectly French to be his. In the middle of Verse 7, just after 'Remember not the sins of my youth', the speaker wavered and broke off. A man seated in front of Forain got up and walked down the aisle, in a solemn and ponderous way. The coffin was on a trestle, draped in purple and white, heaped with roses, tulips, and chrysanthemums. He edged past it, picked up a black box lying on the ground, and pressed two clicking buttons. 'Jesu' started up, from the beginning. Returning, the stranger gave Forain an angry stare, as if he had created the mishap.

Forain knew that some of Tremski's friends thought he was unreliable. He had a reputation for not paying authors their due. There were writers who complained they had never received the price of a postage stamp; they could not make sense of his elegant hand-written statements. Actually, Tremski had been the exception. Forain had arranged his foreign rights, when they began to occur, on a half-and-half basis. Tremski thought of money as a useful substance that covered rent and cigarettes. His wife didn't see it that way. Her forefinger at the end of a column of figures, her quiet, seductive voice saying, 'Blaise, what's this?' called for a thought-out answer.

She had never bothered to visit Forain's office, but made him take her to tea at Angelina's, on the Rue de Rivoli. After her strawberry tart had been eaten and the plate removed, she would bring out of her handbag the folded, annotated account. Outdone, outclassed, slipping the tearoom cheque into his wallet to be dissolved in general expenses, he would look around and obtain at least one satisfaction: she was still the best-looking woman in sight, of any age. He had not been tripped up by someone of inferior appearance and quality. The more he felt harassed by larger issues, the more he made of small compensations. He ran his business with a staff of loyal, worn-out women, connected to him by a belief in what he was doing, or some lapsed personal tie, or because it was too late and they had nowhere to go. At eight o'clock this morning, the day of the funeral, his staunch Lisette, at his side from the beginning of the venture, had called to tell him she had enough social-security points for retirement. He saw the points as splashes of ink on a clean page. All he could think to answer was that she would soon get bored, having no reason to get up each day. Lisette had replied, not disagreeably, that she planned to spend the next ten years in bed. He could not even coax her to stay by improving her salary: except for the reserve of capital required by law, he had next to no money, had to scrape to pay the monthly settlement on his daughter, and was in continual debt to printers and banks.

He was often described in the trade as poor but selfless. He had performed an immeasurable service to world culture, bringing to the West voices that had been muffled for decades in the East. Well, of course, his thimble-size firm had not been able to attract the leviathan prophets, the booming novelists, the great mentors and tireless definers. Tremski had been at the very limit of Forain's financial reach – good Tremski, who had stuck to Forain even after he could have moved on. Common sense had kept Forain from approaching the next-best, second-level oracles, articulate and attractive, subsidised to the ears, chain-smoking and explaining, still wandering the universities and congresses of the West. Their travel requirements were beyond him: no grant could cover the unassuming but ruinous little hotel on the Left Bank, the long afternoons and evenings spent in bars with leather armchairs, where the visitors expected to meet clever and cultivated people in order to exchange ideas.

Forain's own little flock, by contrast, seemed to have entered the world with no expectations. Apart from the odd, rare, humble complaint, they were content to be put up on the top storey of a hotel with a steep, neglected staircase, a wealth of literary associations, and one bath to a floor. For recreation, they went to the café across the street, made a pot of hot water and a tea bag last two and a half hours, and, as Forain encouraged them to keep in mind, could watch the Market Economy saunter by. Docile, holding only a modest estimation of their own gifts, they still provided a handicap: their names, like those of their characters, all sounded alike to barbaric Western ears. It had been a triumph of perseverance on the part of Forain to get notice taken of their books. He wanted every work he published to survive in collective memory, even when the paper it was printed on had been pulped, burned in the city's vast incinerators, or lay mouldering at the bottom of the Seine.

Season after season, his stomach eaten up with anxiety, his heart pounding out hope, hope, hope, he produced a satirical novella set in Odessa; a dense, sober private journal, translated from the Romanian, best understood by the author and his friends; or another wry glance at the harebrained makers of history. (There were few women. In that particular part of Europe they seemed to figure as brusque, flirtatious mistresses

139

or uncomplaining wives.) At least once a year he committed the near-suicide of short stories and poetry. There were rewards, none financial. A few critics thought it a safe bet occasionally to mention a book he sent along for review: he was considered sound in an area no one knew much about, and too hard up to sponsor a pure disaster. Any day now some stumbling, tender, newborn calf of his could turn into a literary water ox. As a result, it was not unusual for one of his writers to receive a sheaf of tiny clippings, sometimes even illustrated by a minia- ture photograph, taken at the Place de la Bastille, with traffic whirling around. A clutch of large banknotes would have been good, too, but only Tremski's wife had held out for both.

Money! Forain's opinion was the same as that of any poet striving to be read in translation. He never said so. The name of the firm, Blaise Éditions, rang with an honest chime in spheres where trade and literature are supposed to have no connection. When the Minister of Culture had decorated him, not long before, mentioning in encouraging terms Forain's addition to the House of Europe, Forain had tried to look diffident but essential. It seemed to him at that instant that his reputation for voluntary self-denial was a stone memorial pinning him to earth. He wanted to cry out for help – to the Minister? It would look terrible. He felt honoured but con- fused. Again, summoned to the refurbished embassy of a new democracy, welcomed by an ambassador and a cultural attaché recently arrived (the working staff was unchanged), Forain had dared say to himself, 'Why don't they just give me the cheque for whatever all this is costing?' – the champagne, the exquisite catering, the medal in a velvet box – all the while hoping his thoughts would not show on his face.

The truth was that the destruction of the Wall – radiant paradigm – had all but demolished Forain. The difference was that Forain could not be hammered to still smaller pieces and sold all over the world. In much the same way Vatican II had reduced to bankruptcy more than one publisher of prayer books in Latin. A couple of them had tried to recoup by dumping the obsolete missals on congregations in Asia and Africa, but by the time the Third World began to ask for its money back the pub- lishers had gone down with all hands. Briefly, Forain pondered the possibility of unloading on readers in Senegal and Cameroon the entire edition of a subtle and allusive study of corruption in Minsk, set in 1973. Could one still get away with it – better

yet, charge it off to cultural cooperation? He answered himself:
No. Not after November, 1989. Gone were the stories in which
socialist incoherence was matched by Western irrelevance. Gone
from Forain's intention to publish, that is: his flock continued
to turn them in. He had instructed his underpaid, patient professional readers – teachers of foreign languages, for the most
part – to look only at the first three and last two pages of any
manuscript. If they promised another version of the East-West
dilemma, disguised as a fresh look at the recent past, he did not
want to see so much as a one-sentence summary.

By leaning into the aisle he could watch the last blessing.
A line of mourners, Halina and her sobbing daughter at the
head, shuffled around the coffin, each person ready to add
an individual appeal for God's mercy. Forain stayed where he
was. He neither pestered nor tried to influence imponderables;
not since the death of the friend who had owned the cashmere
coat. If the firm went into deeper decline, if it took the slide
from shaky to foundering, he would turn to writing. Why not?
At least he knew what he wanted to publish. It would get rid of
any further need of dealing with living authors: their rent, their
divorces, their abscessed teeth, not to speak of that new craze
in the East – their psychiatrists. His first novel – what would he
call it? He allowed a title to rise from his dormant unconscious
imagination. It emerged, black and strong, on the cover of a
book propped up in a store window. 'The Cherry Orchard'.
His mind accepted the challenge. What about a sly, quiet
novel, teasingly based on the play? A former property owner,
after forty-seven years of exile, returns to Karl-Marx-Stadt to
reclaim the family home. It now houses sixteen hardworking
couples and thirty-eight small children. He throws them out,
and the novel winds down with a moody description of curses
and fistfights as imported workers try to install a satellite dish
in the garden, where the children's swings used to be. It would
keep a foot in the old territory, Forain thought, but with a radical
shift of focus. He had to move sidelong: he could not all of a
sudden start to publish poems about North Sea pollution and
the threat to the herring catch.

Here was a joke he could have shared with Tremski. The
stepdaughter had disconnected the telephone while Tremski
was still in hospital, waiting to die; not that Forain wanted
to dial an extinct number and let it ring. Even in Tremski's

mortal grief over Barbara, the thought of Forain as his own author would have made him smile. He had accepted Forain, would listen to nothing said against him – just as he could not be dislodged from his fusty apartment and had remained faithful to his wife – but he had considered Forain's best efforts to be a kind of amateur, Western fiddling, and all his bright ideas to be false dawns. Forain lived a publisher's dream life, Tremski believed – head of a platoon of self-effacing, flat-broke writers who asked only to be read, believing they had something to say that was crucial to the West, that might even goad it into action. What sort of action? Forain still wondered. The intelligent fellow whose remains had just been committed to eternity was no different. He knew Forain was poor but believed he was rich. He thought a great new war would leave Central Europe untouched. The liberating missiles would sail across without ruffling the topmost leaf of a poplar tree. As for the contenders, well, perhaps their time was up.

The congregation had risen. Instead of a last prayer, diffuse and anonymous, Forain chose to offer up a firmer reminder of Tremski: the final inventory of his flat. First, the entrance, where a faint light under a blue shade revealed layers of coats on pegs but not the boots and umbrellas over which visitors tripped. Barbara had never interfered, never scolded, never tried to clean things up. It was Tremski's place. Through an archway, the room Barbara had used. In a corner, the chair piled with newspapers and journals that Tremski still intended to read. Next, unpainted shelves containing files, some empty, some spilling foolscap not to be touched until Tremski had a chance to sort everything out. Another bookcase, this time with books. Above it, the spread of photographs of his old friends. A window, and the sort of view that prisoners see. In front of the window, a drop-leaf table that had to be cleared for meals. The narrow couch, still spread with a blanket, where Halina had slept until she ran away. (To the end, Barbara had expected her to return saying, 'It was a mistake.' Tremski would have made her welcome and even bought another sofa, at the flea market, for the child.) The dark-red armchair in which Forain had sat during his first meeting with Barbara. Her own straight-backed chair and the small desk where she wrote business letters for Tremski. On the wall, a charcoal drawing of Tremski – by an amateur artist, probably – dated June, 1945. It was a face that had come through; only just.

Mourners accustomed to the ceremonial turned to a neighbour to exchange the kiss of peace. Those who were not shrank slightly, as if the touch without warmth was a new form of aggression. Forain found unfocused, symbolised love positively terrifying. He refused the universal coming-together, rammed his hands in his pockets – like a rebellious child – and joined the untidy lines shuffling out into the rain.

Two hours later, the time between amply filled by the accident, the arrival and departure of the ambulance, the long admittance procedure, and the waiting around natural to a service called Emergency, Forain left the hospital. The old lady was too stunned to have much to say for herself, but she could enunciate clearly, 'No family, no insurance.' He had left his address and, with even less inclination, a cheque he sincerely hoped was not a dud. The wind and sleet promised earlier in the day battered and drenched him. He skirted the building and, across a narrow street, caught sight of lines of immigrants standing along the north side of central police headquarters. Algerians stood in a separate queue.

There were no taxis. He was too hungry and wet to cross the bridge to the Place Saint-Michel – a three-minute walk. In a café on the Boulevard du Palais he hung his coat where he could keep an eye on it and ordered a toasted ham-and-cheese sandwich, a glass of Badoit mineral water, and a small carafe of wine, and black coffee – all at once. The waiter forgot the wine. When he finally remembered, Forain was ready to leave. He wanted to argue about the bill but saw that the waiter looked frightened. He was young, with clumsy hands, feverish red streaks under his eyes, and coarse fair hair: foreign, probably working without papers, in the shadow of the most powerful police in France. All right, Forain said to himself, but no tip. He noticed how the waiter kept glancing towards someone or something at the far end of the room: his employer, Forain guessed. He felt, as he had felt much of the day, baited, badgered, and trapped. He dropped a tin of random coins on the tray and pulled on his coat. The waiter grinned but did not thank him, put the coins in his pocket, and carried the untouched wine back to the kitchen.

Shoulders hunched, collar turned up, Forain made his way to the taxi rank at the Place Saint-Michel. Six or seven people under streaming umbrellas waited along the curb. Around the corner a cab suddenly drew up and a woman got out. Forain took her place, as if it were the most natural thing in the world. He had stopped feeling hungry, but seemed to be wearing layers of damp towels. The driver, in a heavy accent, probably Portuguese, told Forain to quit the taxi. He was not allowed to pick up a passenger at that particular spot, close to a stand. Forain pointed out that the stand was empty. He snapped the lock shut – as if that made a difference – folded his arms, and sat shivering. He wished the driver the worst fate he could think of – to stand on the north side of police headquarters and wait for nothing.

'You're lucky to be working,' he suddenly said. 'You should see all those people without jobs, without papers, just over there, across the Seine.'

'I've seen them,' the driver said. 'I could be out of a job just for picking you up. You should be waiting your turn next to that sign, around the corner.'

They sat for some seconds without speaking. Forain studied the set of the man's neck and shoulders; it was rigid, tense. An afternoon quiz show on the radio seemed to take his attention, or perhaps he was pretending to listen and trying to decide if it was a good idea to appeal to a policeman. Such an encounter could rebound against the driver, should Forain turn out to be someone important – assistant to the office manager of a Cabinet minister, say.

Forain knew he had won. It was a matter of seconds now. He heard 'What was the name of the Queen of Sheba?' 'Which one?' 'The one who paid a visit to King Solomon.' 'Can you give me a letter?' 'B.' 'Brigitte?'

The driver moved his head back and forth. His shoulders dropped slightly. Using a low, pleasant voice, Forain gave the address of his office, offering the St Vincent de Paul convent as a landmark. He had thought of going straight home and changing his shoes, but catching pneumonia was nothing to the loss of the staunch Lisette; the sooner he could talk to her, the better. She should have come to the funeral. He could start with that. He realised that he had not given a thought to Tremski for almost three hours now. He continued the inventory, his substitute for a prayer. He was not sure where he had broken off – with the telephone on Barbara's desk? Tremski would not have a telephone in the room where he worked, but at the first ring he would call through the wall, 'Who is it?' Then 'What does he want?' . . . He met me *where*? . . . When we were in high school? . . . Tell him I'm too busy. No – let me talk to him.'

The driver turned the radio up, then down. 'I could have lost my job,' he said.

Every light in the city was ablaze in the dark rain. Seen through rivulets on a window, the least promising streets showed glitter and well-being. It seemed to Forain that in Tremski's dark entry there had been a Charlie Chaplin poster, relic of some Polish film festival. There had been crates and boxes, too, that had never been unpacked. Tremski would not move out, but in a sense he had never moved in. Suddenly, although he had not really forgotten them, Forain remembered the manuscripts he had snatched back from Halina. She had said none was actually finished, but what did she know? What if there were only a little, very little, left to be composed? The first thing to do was have them read by someone competent – not his usual painstaking and very slow professional readers but a bright young Polish critic, who could tell at a glance what was required. Filling gaps was a question of style and logic, and could just as well take place after translation.

When they reached the Rue du Bac the driver drew up as closely as he could to the entrance, even tried to wedge the cab between two parked cars, so that Forain would not have to step into a gutter filled with running water. Forain could not decide what to do about the tip, whether to give the man something extra (it was true that he could have refused to take him anywhere) or make him aware he had been aggressive. 'You should be waiting your turn . . .' still rankled. In the end, he made a Tremski-like gesture, waving aside change that must have amounted to thirty-five per cent of the fare. He asked for a receipt. It was not until after the man had driven away that Forain saw he had not included the tip in the total sum. No Tremski flourish was ever likely to carry a reward. That was another lesson of the day.

More than a year later, Lisette – now working only part-time – mentioned that Halina had neglected to publish in *Le Monde* the anniversary notice of Tremski's death. Did Forain want one to appear, in the name of the firm? Yes, of course. It would be wrong to say he had forgotten the apartment and everything in it, but the inventory, the imaginary camera moving around the rooms, filled him with impatience and a sense of useless effort. His mind stopped at the narrow couch with the brown blanket,

Halina's bed, and he said to himself, What a pair those two were. The girl was right to run away. As soon as he had finished the thought he placed his hand over his mouth, as if to prevent the words from emerging. He went one further – bowed his head, like Tremski at Barbara's funeral, promising himself he would keep in mind things as they once were, not as they seemed to him now. But the apartment was vacated, and Tremski had disappeared. He had been prayed over thoroughly by a great number of people, and the only enjoyment he might have had from the present scene was to watch Forain make a fool of himself to no purpose.

There were changes in the office, too. Lisette had agreed to stay for the time it would take to train a new hand: a thin, pretty girl, part of the recent, nonpolitical immigration – wore a short leather skirt, said she did not care about money but loved literature and did not want to waste her life working on something dull. She got on with Halina and had even spared Forain the odd difficult meeting. As she began to get the hang of her new life, she lost no time spreading the story that Forain had been the lover of Barbara and would not let go a handsome and expensive coat that had belonged to Tremski. A posthumous, novel–length manuscript of Tremski's was almost ready for the printer, with a last chapter knitted up from fragments he had left trailing. The new girl, gifted in languages, compared the two versions and said he would have approved; and when Forain showed a moment of doubt and hesitation she was able to remind him of how, in the long run, Tremski had never known what he wanted.

The Book of Ands

ROBERT GROSSMITH

> In the beginning was the word and.
>
> St John 1:1

and and and and and and and and and and and and and and and and and and and and and and and and and and and and and and and and and and and and and and and and and and and and and and and . . . I quote from memory the opening words of the *Book of Ands*. In the intervals between the conjunctions lies my story, lie all stories. I'm sorry, this is not the best way to begin. Let me try again.

It is a convention of most stories these days to declare their own fictiveness. Mine, however, is true. I live alone in a top-floor flat in a small university town in a universe expanding at both ands. One more try.

Alone in my flat one afternoon a few months ago (better), I heard a ring at the door. I opened it and a stranger stood there. Dressed in a brightly coloured headband, a tie-dyed grandad vest and plastic sandals, he had an anachronistic look about him. I asked him what he wanted.

'Got some books to sell,' he said. 'Sci-fi and fantasy mainly. The guy in the bookshop round the corner said you might be interested.'

I could not restrain a smile. Whenever old Kowalski found himself beleaguered by students trying to unload their books on him for holiday money at the end of the summer term, he always gave them my address, though he knew my tastes were specialised and my funds limited. I would invariably send them on their way unrewarded after examining their wares with a pretence of interest. It was a sort of running joke between us.

'Well, you've come to the right place,' I said. 'I am something of a collector, yes.' I gestured behind me to the sagging bookshelves lining my walls. 'So what rarities do you have to offer me?'

He loosened the drawstring of the duffel bag he carried on his shoulder and emptied its contents on to the mat at my feet. In the cataract of dog-eared paperbacks with garish covers and fanciful titles disgorged for my inspection, my eye fixed on a slim hardback still sporting its glossy white jacket (although somewhat stained and darkened by age), like a dinner guest at the wrong party. The dustflap bore the title *The Book of Ands* and below it in smaller print the author's name, George Lewis Berg. 'What's this?' I said, picking out the volume from the mass grave in which it lay half-buried and opening it at random. The page was filled with regularly spaced columns of the single word 'and'. I thumbed further ahead, then back to the beginning; each page was the same. 'Seems to be some sort of joke, isn't it, a parody?' I said to hide my dismay, thinking of Hemingway and Dickens, those aficionados of the 'and'.

'Sort of, yeah. It was a present from a girl I used to go out with. It's my name, you see. Well, Andy really, but everyone calls me And. I guess she thought it was funny.'

'The flesh made word,' I said.

'Sorry?'

'Nothing.' I had been fingering the book while we spoke, stroking it, caressing it, rehearsing my proprietary rights. I admit, such curiosities excite me. With feigned indifference I enquired, 'And how much are you asking for this masterpiece, this attack of literary conjunctivitis?'

'I couldn't let it go for less than a quid. Sentimental value. You know.'

I offered him fifty pence and he accepted.

The transaction completed, I invited my visitor in for a coffee. I do not receive many callers and thought it might be agreeable to pass an idle hour or two in bookish conversation. To this end I tried to elicit from my guest his opinion of the British contribution to fantasy literature, with particular reference to Stevenson and the early Wells. Unfortunately he appeared singularly ill-informed about the whole subject – he seemed to be under the impression that Stevenson invented the rocket – and when he had dribbled the last of his coffee into his matted beard I invented an excuse about a dental appointment and saw him to the door. There are so few people these days with whom one can talk about matters that matter.

One such person, perhaps the only person among my own narrow circle of acquaintances, was my friend Kowalski the bookseller, and the following morning I paid him a visit.

'Anything to your liking?'

I didn't understand him at first.

'From that fellow I sent round yesterday?' He had a playful gleam in his eye.

'As a matter of fact I did get one interesting item from him, yes. Something of a surprise. A very odd book. Ever heard of the name George Lewis Berg?'

'Berg, Berg,' he repeated. 'Sounds familiar. So many Bergers and Burgesses these days. But Berg, no, I don't think so. Want me to look in the ELB for you?'

'The Elbe?'

'Encyclopaedia of Literary Biography. Twelve volumes, one volume slightly damaged. Offers invited.'

'Not my line, you know that. My interest is the work, not the life. But yes, look him up for me, will you? B-e-r-g, Berg. I'll keep an eye on the shop for you.'

He laughed. 'Don't worry. No one will come in. People don't buy books any more. Not the sort of books I sell, anyway.'

He wandered off through the dusty stacks crammed with high-quality art books and slim volumes of verse (poetry was his special passion), disappearing through a low arch and round a corner, where I could hear him humming tunelessly to himself as he dragged a stepladder across the wooden floor and mounted it. Some minutes later he returned bearing a weighty folio-sized tome open on his arms, crooked at the spine like a sleeping child.

'Berg, George Lewis,' he read. '1885 to 1949. Novelist and poet. Born Andorra of mixed parentage, German and English. Moved to England aged . . .'

'Where?'

'England.'

'No, where did you say he was born?'

'Andorra. Here, you can read it yourself.' He transferred

149

the volume to my arms and I took it to the window, where the light was better, to read it.

The entry consisted of a two-column biography and a list of Berg's major works – some dozen novels and collections of verse, none of which I had heard of. I learned that he had worked for most of his life as a librarian, until failing eyesight forced him to retire, and had fought against the Fascists in the Spanish Civil War. More to the point as far as I was concerned, I discovered that he had spent the last ten years of his life as a virtual recluse, apparently composing his *magnum opus*. After his death, however, the only manuscript found in his possession was that which came to be published as the *Book of Ands* (a brief description of which was included). Provision had been made in his will for his final work to be privately printed, should he die before completing it, and in the absence of any other manuscript, and out of respect for the dead man's wishes, this was done, thereby producing 'perhaps the most bizarre literary artefact in the history of English letters'. Berg was said to have suffered several bouts of mental instability in his youth, the implication appearing to be that at the end of his life his sanity must finally have deserted him.

I summarised all this for Kowalski and told him how I had purchased a copy of the *Book of Ands* from the student he had sent me the previous day.

'Sounds crazy. Why should anyone want to write a book like that for? Where's the pleasure in such a book?'

'I don't know, it's very strange.' A thought suddenly occurred to me. 'Perhaps, well, perhaps he did write his *magnum opus* and then simply began cutting it.'

'How do you mean?'

'Well, look at the facts. He worked on this novel for ten years, supposedly. How many "ands" can you write in ten years? Enough to fill a whole shelf of books. Yet after his death it seems only a small bundle of pages was found, suggesting he may have written them not long before he died. What did he do for the rest of the time?'

'Are you asking me or telling me?'

'I'm just guessing, but well, perhaps when he'd finished his novel he came to see that any conventional work of fiction – any narrative composed of nouns, verbs, adjectives of the author's choosing – any conventional prose style inevitably limits the reader's imagination, forces him to accept the writer's version of events rather than create his own. Perhaps he began by cutting the odd adjective here and there, as many writers do, and it grew into a passion, a style, or anti-style. Perhaps he cut so much of his original novel that in the end he only had one word left.'

' "And"?'

'Well, perhaps he then threw the manuscript of the novel away and just kept retyping the one word he'd saved, the only word that freed rather than limited the reader's imagination. Perhaps if he'd lived another year the book would have been a couple of thousand pages longer. How can an infinite series be terminated, and all that.'

'Wait a minute, I don't understand. You mean he wanted the reader to sort of . . .'

'Fill in the gaps between the words himself. Yes.'

'In other words . . .'

'Complete the novel himself. Exactly. Supply his own nouns, verbs and adjectives. The perfect collaborative enterprise between reader and writer. Democracy on the page.'

'Sounds crazy,' Kowalski repeated. 'Where's the pleasure in that? Would Byron have written such a book? Would Keats?'

'Perhaps Berg would have regarded Byron and Keats as tyrants. Authorial autocrats, dictators of the *dicht*, imposing their private sensibilities on the reader, stifling the reader's own.'

He shook his head with an expression of pity. 'We can't all be great poets, you know. Some of us are content to sit at the feet of the masters and enjoy the Muse at second-hand. Some of us have no wish to be writers, some of us are happy as readers.' He closed the covers of the unsaleable encyclopaedia and shuffled back with it into the gloom at the rear of the shop. 'If everyone wrote their own books,' he called over his shoulder, 'what would become of the humble bookseller?'

The principle I had hit upon to explain the curious structure of the *Book of Ands* – the reader as writer – intrigued me enormously, and I was keen to put it to the test. Returning home from Kowalski's, I made myself a cup of coffee, lit a cigarette and settled down at my desk with the *Book* opened at page one before me, intending to approach it as I would any other novel, to read each page consecutively, left to right, top to bottom, start to finish. For the first few pages my concentration wavered: the words rang emptily in my ear, an idiot's meaningless stammer echoed to infinity, a beginning never reaching a middle or end.

But as I read further I found my attention slowly drifting away from the black blocks of print and drawn instead towards the white spaces between them, as some composers tell us that the silences between the notes in a piece of music are as important as the notes themselves. I recited aloud, louder, thumping out the words with my fist on the desktop, setting up a rhythm, mantra-like, in my brain, till the symbols on the page began to grow dim and diaphanous, as though around them, between them, something else was trying to show, struggling to achieve presence. And for no obvious reason I found myself thinking back to my childhood and the day my mother died, and how I happened to find a ten-shilling note, torn and rain-sodden, in a puddle on my way home from school, and the look of pain on my father's face when I burst into the house, singing my good fortune, and the terrible tremor in his voice as he told me of the accident and how my mother had gone to heaven, and the numbness I felt, then the rage, then the grief, and the tears I shed and the nights I lay awake praying to God to take me too, take me too, and how it rained like a monsoon on the day of the funeral, and the relatives stroking my hair and doing their best to comfort me, pity disfiguring their faces, and my father all in black, biting his lip so as not to cry, and the wreath I bought with the ten-shilling note, and how it fell from my hand and dropped in a puddle when I saw the coffin being lowered into the earth, never to re-emerge. And a thousand other more trivial memories, random images from a forgotten past, joining ands, forming a ring, making sense of absence. Reading the *Book* that day, I wrote the story of my own life. I stayed up late into the night to finish it.

Over the next few weeks my obsession with the *Book* deepened. I would walk about the flat with it open in my hands, reading from it like a breviary. I would stand at the window as before a pulpit and declaim its message to the bemused passers-by looking up and exchanging comments in the street below. Each time I opened it I wrote the story of my life anew. How could one life be subject to so many different readings, I wondered. In my more sober moments I reflected on how here was the book predicted by Roland Barthes, the *scriptible* rather than *lisible* novel. I thought of developing my views on the *Book* into a scholarly article and submitting it to one of the literary quarterlies, representing it as a sort of *nouveau roman avant la lettre*, the zero degree of writing, the minimalist text *par excellence*, the literature of exhaustion and silence. I even got as far as a confused and verbose first draft before I started, inevitably, to cut. I considered destroying all my other books, of deleting all but the 'ands'.

I should have understood what was happening sooner, got rid of it sooner. By the time I did, it was too late. I was seated at my desk after a particularly enervating all-night session with the *Book* in which I had again recomposed my life. As I stood up and walked to the window to let in some air and light, I felt myself succumbing to a peculiar sense of dislocation, dispersion, of which I was unable at first to identify the cause. For some moments I stood motionless, gazing dumbly at the curtained window, trying to hold myself together, to grasp what was happening. Then it struck me. If my life could be written or read in so many different ways, if it contained so many different plots, as many plots as readings, did it not follow that it lacked any plot at all? The more I probed this thought, the more alarming it became. What was my life, after all, but a random series of disconnected events, a chaos of discrete impressions strung by memory on a necklace of conjunctions, assigned a spurious structure to create this illusion of a unitary I? Wherein did the order of my life consist but in the momentary arrangement of the fragments of time into a notional pattern of sense, a pattern as arbitrary and ephemeral as the chance constellation of glass beads in a kaleidoscope? What was that famous whimsical definition of a net: a collection of holes held together with string? What was my life, what was the universe, but such a net – a fabric of absences sewn by thought, a chain forged by fancy, the *Book of Ands* made flesh?

Had I possessed a less reverential attitude towards the written word, I might have destroyed the *Book* at once. But I am a true bibliophile: all books for me are holy, sacred texts, scriptures. And I could not bring myself to do it.

I took it instead to Kowalski. 'Here,' I said. 'It's yours. Please.'

'Ah, so this is your famous *Book of Ands*.' He fanned the pages with a practised thumb. 'No,' he said. 'I have no use for this. Who would buy such a book? Keep it.'

'Please!' I insisted. 'Hide it for me. Somewhere no one will find it. High up on a shelf where no one ever looks. Behind another book. Please!'

153

He gazed at me with curiosity and concern, then shrugged. 'OK,' he said, 'if that's what you want. Crazy, crazy,' I could hear him muttering as he shambled away, though whether he was referring to the book or to me I could not tell.

I left the shop before I could see where he shelved it. But I felt no easier when it was done. I carried the *Book* with me, I knew, and would do so forever, distributing the world between its conjunctions, fitting my thought to its syntax. I understood that the *Book* was a book that had to be written but should never perhaps be read, because once read it could never be forgotten, never be unread. Like the universe itself, infinite but bounded, it would continue, mercilessly, to expand.

People for Lunch

GEORGINA HAMMICK

'I MUST GET up,' Mrs Nightingale said, but did not move. During the night she had worked her way down the bed so that her feet were now resting on the brass rail at its end. Two years ago today it had been Edward's feet striking this same brass rail with peculiar force that had woken her. 'I don't feel well,' he'd said, and she'd replied – sleepily? sharply? – she needed to know but could not remember – 'Then you'd better not go to work today.' When he'd gone on, haltingly, to murmur: 'No. I can't,' she sat up, wide awake and afraid. For Edward was a workaholic. Nothing prevented him going to the office. She'd leant over him and seen that his face and neck were beaded with sweat. She'd touched his forehead and found it as cold and green as marble. 'I've got a pain,' he said, 'in my chest.' Each word was a single, concentrated effort. 'I can't breathe.' Stumbling to the telephone which lived on Edward's side of the bed, she'd started to panic. How could she explain to the doctor, probably still in bed and asleep, how serious it was with Edward lying beside her listening? It was then that she'd begun to shake, and her teeth to rattle in her jaw like pebbles in a bag. She'd knocked the telephone directory on to the floor and misdialled the number half a dozen times. (It was not true that anxious, panicky people proved themselves level-headed under fire.) 'Be calm, Fanny. Go at it slowly,' Edward had said, lying still, his eyes unfocused on the ceiling.

*

A shuddering sigh on Mrs Nightingale's left made her turn her head. Lying close on the adjoining pillow was the face of Bone. The dog's small body was concealed by the duvet, as was Mrs Nightingale's own. Mrs Nightingale stared at Bone's black nose, at the white whiskers that sprouted from her muzzle and chin, at her short sandy eyelashes. Bone's eyes were shut, but the left ear was open, its flap splayed on the pillow to reveal an intricacy of shiny and waxy pink coils. Mrs Nightingale leant across and blew gently in this ear. Bone opened one eye and shut it again. Mrs Nightingale put her arms round Bone and laid her head against the dog's neck. It smelt faintly of chicken soup. Bone jerked her head away and stretched her legs so that her claws lodged themselves in Mrs Nightingale's stomach. Mrs Nightingale kissed Bone on the muzzle just above the black, shiny lip. Bone opened her jaws wide in a foetid yawn and stretched again and went back to sleep. Mrs Nightingale got out of bed and left Bone, still covered to her neck by the duvet, sleeping peacefully.

Bone was not allowed in beds, only on them, and she reminded the dog of this. 'I don't like dogs,' she added untruthfully. The house was very quiet. Mrs Nightingale walked out bare-footed on the uncarpeted landing and stood for a moment listening to the inharmonious ticking of the clocks downstairs. There was no sound from her children's bedrooms and their doors were uninvitingly shut. 'I hate being a widow,' she said aloud.

The bathroom door was blocked by a wrinkled dustbin sack full to overflowing with clothes intended for a jumble sale. She dragged it out of the way. From its torn side hung the yellowing arm of a Viyella cricket shirt. From its top protruded a brown Harris tweed skirt. Liza's name was still stitched to the tiny waistband. Had she ever really been that size? Mrs Nightingale had meant, before the move, to unpick the nametape from Liza's old uniform and take it back to the school for resale, but there had never been the time. This black sack was one of many about the house. Before moving she'd labelled them as to contents, but on examination recently they all contained the same things: outgrown clothes, single football boots, curtains originally made for Georgian sash windows that would not fit in the small casements here, curtain hooks, picture hooks, bent wire coat hangers.

Lying motionless in the bath Mrs Nightingale saw Edward

on the stretcher being carried into the ambulance. He had joked with the ambulance men. She would never forgive him for that. It had been his joking, and the doctor saying on arrival, just before he'd sent her out of the room: 'If you move, Edward, you're a dead man. If you lie still and do exactly what I say, you'll be all right,' that had given her hope. She could see Edward now, calling out from the stretcher to the twins, shivering in their night things on the front door step: 'Be good, monkeys. I'll be back soon.' And she could see herself, wrapped in his dressing-gown, bending down to kiss his cold cheek before the ambulance doors closed. She'd wanted to go with him, she'd needed to go with him, but had had to wait for her mother to come and look after the twins.

The bath water was by now tepid and Mrs Nightingale's finger ends were white and shrunk. As she lay there, unable to move, the church bells began a faint tolling through the shut window and at once the image of the ambulance with its frenetic blue light turning out of the drive was replaced by a picture of dead tulips and lilac in the vase beneath the lectern. She'd seen these on Friday when she'd gone to the church to check the Flower Rota List and found her name down for this Sunday. She forced herself out of the bath and pounded down the passage to Liza's room. She shook the mound of bedclothes.

'Liza – did you remember to do the church flowers yesterday?'

Liza was gliding through a dark lake on the back of a sea-serpent. She opened blank blue eyes for a second and then shut them again.

'Did you do the church flowers?'

The eyes opened again, flickered and then closed. Waking was a trial for Liza.

'Liza –'

'No. I didn't. Sorry.'

'You're the absolute end.' Mrs Nightingale was furious. 'You asked what you could do to help and I said –'

'Sorry, Mum.'

'You're not asked to do much. And you're eighteen, not six.'

'Don't flap,' – Liza's voice sounded as though it had been dredged from the bottom of a deep lake – 'the congregation's geriatric. No one will notice if the flowers are dead.' She yawned. 'You're sopping wet,' she said incuriously to her mother.

'I need your help,' Mrs Nightingale cried. 'Get up at once,

now, before you fall asleep again.' She stood for a moment awaiting results, but as there were none, left the room banging the door behind her.

Mrs Nightingale visited the twins' room next. They were fast asleep on their backs. Lily, on the camp bed they took turns for, was snoring.

'Wake up, both of you,' Mrs Nightingale said. She trampled over their discarded clothes. 'Wake up now.' They sat up slowly, looking hurt and puzzled. 'It's late,' Mrs Nightingale said, 'nine o'clock. They'll be here by half past twelve and there's a lot to do. You must get up. Now.'

'Who'll be here?' Poppy asked.

'Nine o'clock isn't late, it's early,' Lily said. 'It's Sunday.'

'Now,' Mrs Nightingale said and left the room.

When Mrs Nightingale opened Dave's door he was propped on one elbow, reading. His hair, which had been recently cut by a fellow student using blunt nail scissors, stuck out in stiff tufts. Here and there patches of scalp were visible. They'd had a row about the hair when he arrived. Usually Mrs Nightingale cut Dave's hair, and when she did he looked very nice. This present cut, which he'd admitted he wasn't that keen on himself, was an example of the perversity her son was given to and that Mrs Nightingale found exasperating and incomprehensible. He glanced up at her as she came in.

'Hallo, Mamma. How are you, darlin'?'

The question took Mrs Nightingale off-guard. Suddenly, she wanted to tell him. She wanted to say: 'Daddy died two years ago today.' She wanted to collapse on Dave's bed and howl, perhaps all day, perhaps for ever. Instead she stayed in the middle of the room and stared at the row of hats that hung from hooks above Dave's bed and which, together with the accents – foreign, regional – he adopted, formed part of her son's disguise kit.

'If you're awake, why aren't you up?' Mrs Nightingale heard herself say.

'Stay cool,' Dave said. 'I'm just tucking into Elizabeth Bishop.' He waved a paperback in the air that his mother recognised as her own and removed from its shelf without permission.

'How do you rate her? Compared to Lowell . . . ?'

'Get up, please,' Mrs Nightingale said.

'Okay, Marlene. Tuck in.'

Marlene, the second syllable of which was pronounced to rhyme with Jean, was not Mrs Nightingale's name, which was Frances. Marlene, which sometimes became Marlena, second syllable to rhyme with Gina, was the name Dave had bestowed on his mother some years ago when she'd started regularly cutting his hair. 'I'm due for a visit to Marlene's salon,' he'd say, ringing her from Leeds. 'Is the head stylist available?'

Mrs Nightingale moved backwards to Dave's door and fell over the bicycle wheel she'd noted on her way in and taken care to avoid.

'Shit. And your room's in shit, Dave.'

'Cool it.'

'Look, it is in shit and it smells. Do you have to sleep with the window shut? Why are you wearing that T-shirt in bed?'

'I haven't any pyjamas, that's why,' Dave said reasonably.

'I know if I leave now you'll just go on reading' – Mrs Nightingale was getting desperate – 'so get out now, while I'm here.'

'I will as soon as you go. I've got nothing on below this T-shirt, and the sight of my amazing, user-friendly equipment might unsettle you for the day. Tuck in, Marlene.' He yawned, showing a white tongue and all his fillings, and stretched his huge arms above his head.

Mrs Nightingale returned to her bedroom and dressed herself in scruffy, everyday clothes. Then she pulled Bone out of the bed and swept the bottom sheet with her hands. Being white, Bone's hairs did not show up well against the sheet but Mrs Nightingale knew they were there, and sure enough they flew around the room and settled in the floorboards like snowflakes in a paperweight snowstorm. Mrs Nightingale straightened the duvet and banged the pillows while Bone sat on her haunches, sorrowfully watching. As soon as the lace cover was on Bone leapt back on the bed and made herself comfortable among the cushions. Mrs Nightingale looked at her watch. This time two years ago she had just arrived at the hospital having driven at ninety most of the way. There'd been nowhere to park so she'd parked in one of the doctors' spaces. 'You can't park there,' an old man planting out geraniums by the hospital steps had told her, having watched her manoeuvre. Three floors up, on Harnham Ward, Sister had looked up from her notes and said: 'The specialist has examined your husband and would like to see you now.' Mrs Nightingale suddenly remembered the specialist's nose, aquiline and messily freckled. She'd stared at it as they sat opposite each other, divided by a desk. 'He's on the edge of a precipice,' the specialist had said. 'It was an almost total infarct – that means the supply of blood and oxygen to the heart has been severely reduced. A large part of the heart muscle is already dead. The next forty-eight hours will be crucial. If he survives, and I can give you no assurances, the dead muscle will be replaced in time by scar tissue, which is very tough and can do the same sort of job –'

I hate doctors, Mrs Nightingale thought as she went downstairs. Hate them. She took one look at the kitchen, then shut the door and went into the drawing-room, a room too poky to deserve the title that, from the habit of a lifetime, she had given it. It smelled of soot and damp and cigarettes, and of something indefinable that might have been the previous owners. Mrs Nightingale got down on her knees in front of the fireplace and swept the wood ash and cigarette stubs she found there into a dome. She stuck a firelighter on top of this, but the log baskets were empty except for two pieces of bark and several families of woodlice, so she got up again and started to punch the sofa cushions into shape. Dave came in while she was doing this. He was still wearing the T-shirt but to his lower half he'd now added an Indian tablecloth which he'd wrapped twice round himself and tucked in at the waist.

'You left a filthy mess in the kitchen last night,' Mrs Nightingale said, remembering the slag heap of coffee grounds decorated by a rusty Brillo pad on the kitchen table. 'I thought you were going to get dressed.'

'Liza's in the bathroom.' Dave scratched his armpit, then sat down heavily on the sofa cushions and rested his head on his knees.

'Dave, I've just done that sofa. We've got people for lunch –'

'Yup. Sure thing. Sorry. What can I do?' He stayed where he was and Mrs Nightingale stared, mesmerized, at his large yellow feet. The toenails were black and torn. Black wire sprouted from his big toes. The same wire twined his calves, visible beneath the tablecloth. It stopped at the ankles, but continued, Mrs Nightingale knew, beyond his knees to his thighs, where it no longer twined, but curled. It was impossible that this huge male person had ever been inside her body. 'Well, the log baskets are empty, as you see,' Mrs Nightingale said, 'so when you're dressed –'

'Sure, sure.'

'I did ask you, you know,' Mrs Nightingale bravely continued, 'when you arrived, if you'd be responsible for getting the wood in, and you said –'

'Yeah. Yeah. Sure. Yup. Tuck in.' He sat for a moment longer and then got up, hitching the tablecloth which had slipped a little. He looked round the room. 'I like your little house, Marlene.'

'It isn't *my* house.' Mrs Nightingale was hurt by Dave's choice of possessive adjective. 'It's *our* house. It's home.'

'Yup.'

'No chance, I suppose,' she said as he padded to the door, 'of your wearing your contact lenses at lunch?' Dave stopped dead in his tracks and turned sharply. 'What's wrong with my specs?' He whipped them off and examined them myopically, close to his nose. They were bright scarlet with butterfly sides, the sort typists wore in the fifties. One arm was attached to the frame by a grubby Sellotape bandage.

'Nothing's wrong with them. It's just that you look nicer without them. You're quite nice-looking, so it seems a shame –'

'Oh Christ,' Dave said and then hit his head on the beam above the door. 'Fuck. I hit my head everywhere I go in this fucking house. Cottage. Hen coop. Hovel.'

By the time Mrs Nightingale had finished scrubbing the potatoes they were all down in the kitchen with her. The kitchen was too small for five people comfortably to be in at one time. She had once, when they were all tripping over each other, made this observation and had received a long lecture from Dave on the living conditions of the average farm-labourer and his family in the latter part of the nineteenth century. Her son was nothing if not inconsistent, Mrs Nightingale thought, remembering the hen coop remark.

'Who's finished the Shreddies?' Poppy was on her knees on the brick floor, peering in a cupboard.

'Dave had them last night – don't you remember?' Liza said, sawing at a grapefruit with the bread knife. A pool of cloudy juice and pips spread over the table, soaking an unpaid telephone bill. Mrs Nightingale snatched it up.

'Here, have this' – Liza plonked the grapefruit halves into bowls and handed one of them to Poppy. 'This is better for you. You're too fat for cereal.'

GEORGINA HAMMICK

'Speak for yourself, you great spotty oaf. At least I haven't got suppurating zits all over my face –'

'You will soon,' Dave interrupted cheerfully. 'You're into a pubescent exploding-hormone situation. Tuck in.'

'If you had, they might detract from your nose which, by the way,' – Liza glanced at it casually – 'is one big blackhead.'

There was a skirmish. Mrs Nightingale caught the milk bottle as it leapt from the table.

'Cool it, girls.' Dave had seen his mother's face. 'Marlene's trying to get organised. Aren't you Marlene?' He was propped against the Rayburn, dressed now in one of his father's city shirts and scarlet trousers, the bottoms of which were tucked into old school games stockings, one brilliantly striped, the other grey, and shovelling Weetabix into his mouth from a bowl held within an inch of his face. Each time the spoon went in it banged horribly against his teeth. 'Is the Rayburn *meant* to be off?' he asked, mock-innocently, between mouthfuls.

Mrs Nightingale was about to burst into tears.

'What? Out of my way please.' She pushed the red legs to one side, and knelt on the dog bed in front of the stove. Inside an erratic flame flickered. She turned the thermostat as high as it would go.

'Why's the heat gone down?'

'How the fuck should I know? The wind, probably –'

'Don't swear, Mummy,' Poppy said, grabbing a banana from the fruit bowl and stripping it.

'Put that banana back! It's for lunch.'

'We've got rhubarb crumble for lunch. I made it yesterday, remember.' Poppy took a bite out of the banana, folded the skin over the end and replaced it in the fruit bowl on top of a shrivelled orange.

'Look,' Mrs Nightingale said, 'we'll never be ready at this rate. Couldn't you all just –'

'Keep calm, Mamma. Sit down a moment and drink this.' Liza handed her mother a mug of coffee. 'There's nothing to do. Really. They won't be here till one at the earliest. All we've got to do is get the joint in –'

'Are we eating animals? Yuk. Unreal. Animals are people –'

'Shut up, Lily. – Do the spuds and the veg and lay the table and light the fire and pick some flowers – five minutes at the most.'

'The whole house is in chaos,' Mrs Nightingale said, 'it's

composed of nothing but tea chests and plastic bags.'

'They're not coming to see the house. They know we've only just moved. They're coming to see *you*.'

'Actually, they're coming to inspect our reduced circumstances,' Dave said in a prissy voice. He picked up a piece of toast and stretched for the marmalade. Mrs Nightingale pushed it out of his reach. 'No, you've had enough.'

'Daddy couldn't bear them,' Lily said, staring into space.

'Couldn't bear who?' Poppy paused at the door.

'The Hendersons, stupid.'

'The Hendersons? Are *they* coming to lunch? Unreal.'

'Where do you think you're going to, Poppy? You haven't cleared up your breakfast things –'

'I'm going to the lav, if you must know. I'm coming back.'

'While you're up there, Fatso, take some of the gunge off your face!' Dave shouted at her.

'Have you got the logs in?' Mrs Nightingale asked Dave, knowing that he hadn't.

'I'm just about to. We shouldn't *need* a fire in May,' he said, resentfully as though his mother were to blame for the weather. 'Right, Marlena.' He rubbed his hands. 'Here we go-o,' he added in the manner of an air hostess about to deposit a snack on the knees of a passenger. He sat down on Poppy's chair and pulled a pair of canvas boots from under the table. A lace snapped as he put them on.

'Are you going to shave before they arrive?' Mrs Nightingale asked, eyeing him.

'Dunno. Oi moigh.' – Dave rubbed his chin so that it rasped – 'an' yere agine oi moigh 'na'. Don't you like me looking manly and virile?' Mrs Nightingale said No, she didn't much. No.

'Mrs Henderson will, though. She's got a yen for me. She'll really tuck in.'

'Oh ha ha,' Liza snorted from the sink.

'Mr Henderson has too. He's always putting his arm around my shoulder. Squeezing me. Kissing –'

'I don't suppose he's that desperate to get herpes. He hasn't seen you since you were about ten –'

'Do something for me, Lil, would you,' Mrs Nightingale said, as Dave minced from the room flexing his biceps. Lily sighed. Did she know what today was? Mrs Nightingale thought perhaps she did. It was impossible to get near Lily at the moment. She resented everything her mother said and did, prefacing her argument with 'Daddy always said' or 'Daddy would have agreed with me that . . .' She'd been in a sulk since the move because the cottage was thatched i.e. spooky, witchy, bug-infested – and because her father had never been in it. 'Wake up, there,' – Mrs Nightingale waved her hand slowly up and down in front of Lily's face. Lily managed not to blink.

'Go and get Bone off my bed and put her out. She hasn't had a pee yet.' Lily went on sitting there, expressionless. Then all of a sudden she leapt up, scraping back her chair, and ran out of the room.

'Bone, Bone, my darling one, I'm coming.' They could hear her clattering up the stairs, calling 'Bone, beloved angel, Bone –'

'She's mad,' Liza said, stacking plates in the rack. 'All my family's mad. And Dave is completely off the wall.' Mrs Nightingale kissed Liza's spotty face, pink and damp with steam. 'I love you, Lize,' she said.

As Mrs Nightingale rootled in the kitchen drawer looking for enough knives to lay the dining-room table with, Dave's face appeared at the window above the sink. He flattened his nose against the pane and drummed on it with his fingers. 'Open up! Open up!' he shouted. Liza leaned across the taps and biffed the window. It opened in a rush. Dave's face disappeared for a second, and then reappeared half in the window. 'Ladies,' he said with a South London inflexion and in confidential tones, holding up what looked like a piece of string and dangling it from between his fingers and thumb, 'do your hubbies' jock-straps pass the window test? If not –' he leered and let go of the jock-strap which fell across the sill and draped itself over the hot tap, and then held up a packet of something: 'Try new Weedol! Fast-acting, rainproof and guaranteed to eradicate all biological stains for an entire season. Just one *sachette*' – he paused to consult the packet – 'treats 160 yards, or – if you ladies prefer a more up-to-date terminology – 135 square metres, of normally soiled jock-straps.' He backed away from the window, creased with laughter, and tripped over a flower pot.

'Pathetic,' Liza said, tugging at the window catch, 'quite pathetic.'

'Logs!' Mrs Nightingale shouted at him, just before the window jerked to, scattering them with raindrops, 'Logs, logs, logs!'

*

Mrs Nightingale did her best with the dining-room which, not being a room they had so far needed to use, had become a dumping ground. There were ten full tea chests stacked in one corner, her husband's golf clubs in a khaki bag, a clothes horse, innumerable lampshades and a depressed-looking cockatoo under a glass dome. Beneath the window precariously stacked books awaited the bookshelves Dave had promised to put up in the summer holidays. Everything in the room, including a dining-table much too large for it, was deep in dust. Mrs Nightingale looked at her watch. This time two years ago she'd sat beside Edward, who'd lain on his back without pillows, his chest and arms wired to a machine. Attached to the machine was a cardiograph that measured and recorded his heartbeat. The signal had gone all over the place, sometimes shooting to the top of the screen, and the bleeps, at each beat, had been similarly erratic – six, say, in succession followed by a silence which, each time it occurred, she'd felt would never be broken. 'The heroin was delicious,' Ed had murmured in a moment of consciousness, 'it took all the pain away, but they won't let me have any more in case I get hooked.' Why couldn't you have died at once, Mrs Nightingale thought, remembering her agony watching the nurse adjusting the drip, which had kept getting stuck, and checking the leads on Ed's chest which, because he rolled around a lot, were in constant danger of coming loose. This had happened once, when there'd been no nurse in the room. She'd been on the edge of her chair, her eyes alternately on Ed, and on the screen, when suddenly the bleeps had stopped and the signal had flattened into a straight, horizontal line. A red light had come on at the side of the machine and with it a whine like the unobtainable tone when you dial. He's dead, she'd thought. Sister had rushed in at once and checked Ed's pulse and then the leads and after a minute or two the crazy signal was back and the bleeps. 'Try not to worry, dear,' Sister had said. 'Worrying doesn't help.'

Mrs Nightingale forced herself out of her chair and went in search of a duster.

'The joint's in the oven,' Liza said. She had an apron on which bore the message I Hate Cooking, and was standing at the stove stirring a saucepan. 'I'm making onion sauce.' She looked up. 'Are you okay, Ma?' By way of an answer Mrs Nightingale enquired if anyone had seen the silver anywhere.

Poppy knew. She and Lily were scraping carrots and glaring at each other across the kitchen table. She got up and helped her mother drag the despatch box from under the sink in the washroom. Back in the dining-room she stood and watched her mother dust the table.

'Mum – can I have a friend to stay – Julia, I mean, in the holidays?'

'Maybe. If we're straighter by then.' Mrs Nightingale didn't like Julia. On the child's last visit Mrs Nightingale had caught her in her clothes cupboard, examining the labels and checking to see how many pairs of Gucci shoes Mrs Nightingale owned, which was none. Mrs Nightingale didn't own a Gucci watch, either, and evidently wasn't worth speaking to: Julia hadn't addressed one word to her in five days. She'd managed a few indirect hits, though, as when at breakfast one morning, having accepted without comment the plate of scrambled eggs Mrs Nightingale had handed her, she'd leaned on one elbow to enquire of Poppy: 'Presumably your mother will be racing at Goodwood next week?' Mrs Nightingale was damned if she'd have Julia to stay again.

'I get bored without a friend,' Poppy moaned on. Mrs Nightingale wasn't having any of that. 'You can't be bored,' she said, 'and you've got Lily.' She unwrapped a yellowing candlestick from a piece of yellowing newspaper. 'Here, take this.'

'We don't get on,' Poppy said. 'We've got nothing in common.' That was rubbish, Mrs Nightingale told her.

'It isn't rubbish. She's so moody. She never speaks – just sits and stares.'

Since the truth of this could not be denied, Mrs Nightingale changed tack:

'As a matter of fact you don't deserve to have a friend to stay.' Poppy put down the spoon she'd been tentatively rubbing with a duster and stared at her mother with her mouth open.

'Your half-term report is the worst yet,' Mrs Nightingale continued, 'and we ought to discuss it. Not now. I don't mean now. Later. This evening, perhaps, when they've gone.'

'Miss Ansell doesn't like me. It's not my fault.'

'It isn't just Miss Ansell,' Mrs Nightingale said, more in sorrow than in anger. 'No one, no one – apart from Miss Whatsername – you know, games mistress – had a good word to say about you. You won't get a single "O" Level at this rate. Lily, on the other hand –'

'*Don't* compare me with her. She's quite different to me.'

'Different *from* me. Yes, She knows how to work, for one thing. And she reads. You never open a book.'

'I do.'

'The *Beano* annual. And you're *thirteen*.'

Poppy grinned sheepishly at that. 'Oh, Muzkin,' she said, and sidled up to her mother and put her arms round her waist.

'Muzkin nothing,' Mrs Nightingale said, disentangling herself. For it really was worrying. Poppy never did open a book. If ever she happened by some mischance to pick one up, she'd drop it again as soon as she'd realised her mistake. As a result of this her ignorance went wide and deep. Mrs Nightingale spent sleepless nights discussing the problem with Bone.

Liza's head appeared round the dining-room door.

'Bone's eaten the Brie, I'm afraid,' Liza said, 'so there's only mousetrap for lunch.'

'Where is she? I'll kill her!' Mrs Nightingale cried preparing to do so.

'I've already beaten her,' Liza said. 'It's my business, she's my dog.'

Not when it comes to spending millions of pounds a year on Chum and Butch and Winalot and vet's bills, Mrs Nightingale thought. Not when it comes to clearing up mountains of dog sick and dog shit. Then she's my dog. She followed Liza back to the kitchen. 'Where's Dave?' she asked crossly. 'Where's the wood?'

'He's gone to get some milk and the papers,' Liza said, knowing what her mother's reaction would be.

'*What?*'

'I asked him to go because we're out of milk and you'll want the papers so that the Hendersons can read them after lunch.'

'Has he taken my car?' Mrs Nightingale was beside herself.

'Of course he's taken your car. How else would he go?'

Mrs Nightingale hated Dave taking her car. She hated him taking it because being stuck up a track with rusty bicycles the only means of escape made her feel a prisoner. She hated him taking it because he hadn't asked permission and because she didn't trust him not to drive like a racing driver – i.e. a maniac. It was her car. She hated Dave too because he ought to have remembered what the day was. There was something wrong with him that he hadn't. Something very wrong indeed.

'He has no business to take my car,' she said, 'he'll be gone for hours.'

Liza was taking glasses out of a cupboard. 'Don't be stupid,' she said briskly. 'He'll be back in a minute. He's only gone for the papers, for God's sake. He was *trying* to be helpful.' She held a glass up to the light. 'These glasses are filthy. I'd better wash them.'

'Get up, Lily,' Mrs Nightingale was now in a state of rage and panic. Lily was lying in the dog bed on top of Bone, kissing Bone's ears. 'Get up! Have you made your bed and tidied your room?'

'You can't make a camp bed.' Lily got up reluctantly, her navy jersey angora now covered with dog hairs.

'Answer that, would you, on your way,' Mrs Nightingale snapped as the telephone rang from the drawing-room. Lily returned almost at once.

'It's Granny. She wants to talk to *you*.'

'Fuck,' Mrs Nightingale said. 'Didn't you tell her we've got people for lunch?' Lily shrugged. 'Well, go back and tell her I'm frantic –'

'I'll say,' murmured Liza, putting glasses on a tray. 'These glasses are gross – did you get them from the garage?'

'– and that I'll ring her after tea. Go on. Hurry.'

'Granny sounded a bit hurt,' Lily said when she came back. 'She said to tell you she was thinking about you today.'

'What for?' Liza said.

What for, Mrs Nightingale repeated to herself, what for –? 'What can Dave be doing?' she said, 'he's been gone for hours.' She opened the oven door. The joint seemed to be sizzling satisfactorily.

'Stop flapping,' Liza said.

'Did you put garlic on the joint? And rosemary? I couldn't see any.'

'Of course. Stop flapping.'

'Poppy, you're *soaked*! Couldn't you have worn a mac?' Poppy squelched into the kitchen and dumped a collection of sodden wild flowers on the table.

'*I* was going to do the flowers,' Liza said.

'God, the gratitude you get in this place,' Poppy fingered the limp cluster. 'What are these?'

'Ladies' smocks. *Must* you do that in here?' Liza said as Poppy found an assortment of jugs and lined them up on the table. 'I'm trying to get lunch. You can't put wallflowers in with that lot,' she added in disgust.

'Why can't I?' Poppy wanted to know.

'Because they're orange, stupid.'

'Piss off. I like them. I like the *smell*.'

Mrs Nightingale left her daughters to it and took the tray of glasses into the dining-room. Perhaps Dave *had* had an accident. Perhaps, at this very moment, firemen were fighting to cut his lifeless body from the wreckage. That was all she needed. It was typical of him to put her in this position of anxiety today of all days. 'If he's alive I'll kill him,' she thought aloud, knowing that when – please God – he did walk in she'd feel nothing but relief. As she went back into the kitchen he came in by the other door, accompanied by a smell of deep frying. The Sunday papers and two cartons of long-life milk were crushed against his chest. He uncrossed his arms and unloaded their contents into the watery mess of broken stems and leaves on the kitchen table.

'Hey – mind my flowers,' Poppy said. She sniffed. 'I can smell chips.'

'Whoops. Sorry.' Dave straightened up and caught sight of his mother. 'Hi there, Marlene.' He licked his fingers, slowly and deliberately. 'Finger fuckin' good,' he said when he'd finished. There was a silence, succeeded by a snort of laughter from Liza, succeeded by another silence.

'Dave, could I have a word with you, please –' Mrs Nightingale spoke through clenched teeth. She jerked her thumb towards the door. 'Outside.'

'Righto, Marlena.' He snatched up the *Observer* and followed his mother into the hall.

'Watch out, Dave,' Poppy sang out after him. 'You're in deep trouble, Boyo.'

'What are you screwed-up about?' Dave asked when Mrs Nightingale, determined that they shouldn't be overheard, had shut the drawing-room door. Dave plonked himself into the nearest armchair.

'Get out of that chair! Put that newspaper down!' Dave got up, very slowly. 'Take that smirk off your face!' Mrs Nightingale shouted. He towered above her, shifting from one foot to the other, while his eyes examined the ceiling with interest. 'I've had you,' Mrs Nightingale went on, her

169

voice shaking. 'I wish you weren't here. You're twenty years old. You're the only so-called man in this house. I should be able to look to you for help and support. You had no business to take my car without asking –'

'Liza said we were out of milk –'

'It's not her car. It's *mine*. And I'd asked you to get the wood in. That's *all* I asked you to do. All all *all*!'

'Oh come *on* –'

'I won't come on.' Mrs Nightingale's voice rose. 'You were gone for hours while everyone else was working. Did you really eat chips, by the way?'

'I was hungry, I'm a big boy,' Dave said, perhaps hoping to appeal to that need (he supposed all women had) to mother and protect huge grown men as though they were babies.

'You didn't have breakfast till ten. And it'll be lunchtime any minute. You can't have been hungry.' Dave said nothing. He was bored with this interview and showed it by jiggling his knee. 'That finger business wasn't funny,' Mrs Nightingale said. 'It was disgusting. How could you, in front of Lily and Poppy?'

'Lily wasn't in the kitchen, actually,' Dave said. He started to pace about with his head down, a sure sign that he was losing his temper.

'Don't be pedantic with me, Dave.' Dave stopped pacing and swung round and pointed his finger at his mother in a threatening fashion.

'Fuck *you*,' he said. 'You're a complete hypocrite. No one in this house uses filthier language than you. It's "shit this" and "bugger that" all fucking day. We took the words in with your milk –' There was a pause, during which Mrs Nightingale considered reminding him that the twins, at least, had been bottle-fed, but Dave was quite capable of turning this fact to his advantage, so she said nothing. 'Well, I'm sick of your dramas and panics,' he continued, warming to his theme of self-justification. 'I can't stand the atmosphere in this place. I can't *work* here. I'm going back to Leeds. My tutor didn't want me to take time off to help you, and I've missed two important lectures already.' He made for the door.

'Typical,' Mrs Nightingale said, taking care not to say 'fucking well typical' as she would normally have done. 'You can't take any sort of criticism, ever. You just shout abuse and then walk out – it's too easy. What's more, you haven't been any help to me at all. You haven't lifted a finger –'

'Mum,' – Liza's head appeared round the door as Dave reached it. He took two steps backwards – 'Shouldn't you be putting your face on? It's after twelve.'

'Go away,' Mrs Nightingale said, 'I'm talking to Dave.'

'Sounds like it. Poor Dave.' Liza's head withdrew. The door banged shut.

Mrs Nightingale and her son stood in silence, both waiting for something. Dave stared at the floor and at the front page of the *Observer* which lay at his feet. He pushed it with the toe of one green canvas boot.

'Sorry I was rude,' he said at last without looking up.

Mrs Nightingale gave a sigh. Dave was good at apologies – much better than she was – and sometimes indulged in them for days after a particularly bloody row, castigating himself and telling anyone who'd listen what a shit he'd been. The trouble was, the apologies changed nothing, as Mrs Nightingale had learned. They never prevented his being rude and aggressive (and unfair, she thought, *unfair*) next time round. She didn't want his apologies. She wanted him to stop the behaviour that made them necessary. She watched him now get down on his knees and take off his specs and rub them on a dirty red-and-white spotted handkerchief and put them back on his nose. He picked up the *Observer* with his left hand and then struck at it with the fist of his right.

'I'm going to kill Mrs Thatcher,' he said, 'listen to this –'

Oh dear, thought Mrs Nightingale.

Dave and newspapers did not mix. Cruise missiles, violence in inner cities, child abuse, drug abuse, vivisection, famine, rape, murder, abortion, multiple births, divorce rate, pollution, terrorism, persecution of Blacks and homosexuals, sex discrimination, unemployment, pornography, police brutality, rate capping – the stuff that newspapers were made of – were a daily cross he bore alone. 'You can't take the whole burden of the world on your shoulders,' she'd tell him when he rang from a Leeds call box desperate over the destruction of South American rain forests, or the plight of the latest hijack victims. 'The world has always been a terrible place,' she'd say, 'we just know more about it now because of the media. Horror used to be more *local*.' Then – since it seemed important to end on a positive note – she'd go on to remind him of ways

171

in which the world had changed for the better, instancing the huge advances made in medicine this century (T.B. and polio virtually wiped out, infant mortality and death in childbirth negligible, etc.) and reminding him that there were salmon in the Thames these days, and that people could fall into the river and swallow whole bucketfuls of its waters and not die. 'Try and get a sense of proportion,' she'd say, something she'd never managed herself. She knew that when she lectured Dave it was herself she was trying to comfort. The world was a far nastier place than it'd been when she was a child, even though there'd been a world war going on for some of that time. Far nastier.

Thinking about all this she was spared hearing Mrs Thatcher's latest pronouncement, although it was impossible to miss the passion in Dave's recital of the same. She came to when he stopped in mid-sentence, and put the paper down.

'It's the twenty-third today,' he said. 'Did you realise?'

'I know,' Mrs Nightingale said.

'Oh, Mum, I'm sorry. Why didn't you say?'

Dave, on his knees, began to rock backwards and forwards, his arms folded across his stomach. 'Poor old Dad, poor old Dad,' he said. Then he burst into tears. Mrs Nightingale got down on her knees beside her son. She put her arm round his shoulders which reeked of wet wool and chipped potatoes. She sensed that he did not want her arms round him but did not know how to extricate himself. After several minutes he blew his nose on the red-spotted handkerchief and licked at the tears which were running down his chin.

'I must get the wood in and light the fire.' He disengaged himself and got up. 'Then I'll shave. Sorry, Mum.' He gave her a pale smile. At the door he turned, and said in a sharper tone: 'But I still don't understand why you didn't *say*. And why didn't we go to church this morning – or did you, before we were up?'

'No,' Mrs Nightingale said.

'And why are the fucking Hendersons coming to lunch? You don't like them and Pa couldn't stand them. None of it makes sense.' He shook his head, spraying the room with water like a wet dog.

'Look, Dave,' Mrs Nightingale began. She explained that she hadn't asked the Hendersons, they'd asked themselves. She couldn't put them off for ever. Also she'd thought that having people to lunch might make the day easier in some way. And as for church – well, he didn't like Rite A any more than she did. It always put them into a rage, so there was no point, was there, in going.

'True,' Dave said.

It *was* true, she told him. But what she thought they might do, once they'd got rid of the Hendersons, was drive up to the churchyard and take Poppy's flowers perhaps, and put them on Daddy's grave.

Dave's eyes started to fill again. '. . . and then go to Evensong in the Cathedral, if there's time. It'll be a proper service with proper singing and anthems and sung responses.'

'Yup. Cool.'

'All right, sweetheart?' Dave nodded and fiddled with his watchstrap, a thin piece of canvas, once red and white striped. 'I suppose you realise,' Mrs Nightingale lied, 'that when I asked you to give me a hand this week, it was just an excuse for wanting you here today, I needed you.' But perhaps it was not a lie, she thought. Perhaps, subconsciously, she had needed him.

'I'm getting the wood now,' Dave said. He peered out of a dismal mullioned window, against which a yew branch flapped in the gale. 'I think the rain's stopping.'

The kitchen when Mrs Nightingale entered it was clean and tidy, everything washed up and put away. Liza was taking off her apron.

'All done,' she said.

She was a wonder, Mrs Nightingale told her, a real star.

'Mum you must get changed, they'll be here –'

Mrs Nightingale stopped in the doorway. 'Lize – do you know what today is?'

'It's the day Daddy died,' Liza said. 'Go on, Mum, I'll come and talk to you when I've done the ice.'

The back door banged as Mrs Nightingale climbed the stairs. She could hear Dave's grunts as he humped the log baskets into the hall. It was a relief to be on her own for five minutes. She needed to be alone with Edward who – she stood on the dark landing and peered at her watch – this time two years ago had been about to leave her. Suddenly, without warning and without saying goodbye. Not even a look. Not even a pressure of the hand. She'd hated him for this, until it had dawned on her that it was inevitable. He'd been hopeless at partings. The number of times she'd driven him to Heathrow and been rewarded not with hugs and the 'I'll miss you, darlings' and 'Take care of your precious selves' other people seemed to get, but with a preoccupied peck and then his backview disappearing through the barrier. 'Turn round and wave, you bugger,' she used to will him, but he never did.

'You two ready?' she called, in hopeless competition with Madness, through the twins' bedroom door. Then she opened her own. The room looked as though burglars had visited it. The drawers of both clothes chests had been wrenched out; garments spilled from them on to the floor. A brassière, its strap looped round a wooden drawer knob, trailed greyly to the rug where two leather belts lay like coiled springs. Mrs Nightingale turned her gaze to the dressing table. Here unnumbered treasures drooped from every drawer and orifice. The surface of the table was littered with screws of cotton wool and with unstoppered scent bottles, from which all London, Paris and New York disagreeably breathed. A cylinder of moisturising lotion lay on its side oozing cucumber extract into the contents of her jewel case which sat, open and empty, on the stool. Three cotton wool buds, their ends clotted with ear wax, had been placed in the china tray which normally housed Mrs Nightingale's lipsticks. Only two lipsticks remained in the tray; the rest, which had been torn apart and abandoned with their tongues protruding, were jumbled up with beads and cotton wool. Mrs Nightingale recognised her daughter Poppy's hand in all this. She opened her mouth wide in anger and despair, but no sound came. Instead, the telephone screamed from the table by her bed. When after the eighth ring no one had answered downstairs, Mrs Nightingale picked up the receiver.

'Mrs Nightingale? Mr Selby-Willis here.'

'Oh hallo, Jerry,' Mrs Nightingale said. (Fuck fuck fuck fuck fuck). 'How are you?'

'How are *you*?' Jerry Selby-Willis asked, in his best bedroom drawl.

'Well if you must know, I'm frantic. I've got people arriving for lunch any minute.'

'One normally does on a Sunday. Grania's just gone off to the station to meet our lot. I can't imagine *you* being frantic about anything –'

'It just goes to show how little –'

'When are you going to have luncheon with me?' Jerry Selby-Willis interrupted her. 'Or dinner?'

'Jerry, I've only *just* moved house –' Mrs Nightingale began. She had accepted none of his invitations. 'Then you're in need of a nice, relaxing dinner. Tuesday. Have you got your diary there?'

'No. Look, I'm afraid I must go. I haven't got my face on –'

'I'll ring you tomorrow, from the office.'

She must remember to leave the telephone off the hook tomorrow, Mrs Nightingale thought, as she wrenched garments from hangers, tried them on, examined the result in the looking glass, and tore them off again. Or else get the children to answer the telephone and say she was out.

'I've got nothing to wear!' she wailed, as Liza came into the room.

'That looks fine,' Liza said. 'Where's your hairbrush?'

While Liza brushed her mother's hair, Mrs Nightingale perched on the dressing-table stool and searched for her blue beads.

'I can't find my blue beads,' she said, turning out another drawer.

'Poppy's wearing them,' Liza said. 'She said you said she could. Time you dyed your hair, I think, or else made with the Grecian 2000,' she said kindly, putting the brush down.

'I think I heard a car,' Mrs Nightingale said, 'do you think you could round everyone up and go down and tell the Hendersons I'm coming. Give them a drink.'

Alone, Mrs Nightingale looked at her watch. It was ten past one. Edward was dead. He'd been dead a full quarter of an hour. At five to one, no doubt when she'd been fending off Jerry Selby-Willis, the signal on the cardiograph had flattened into a straight line for real this time, and the bleeps had ceased. She had not kept vigil; she had not been with him, holding his hand. She sat on the stool, twisting her wedding ring round and round her finger, for comfort. When at last she lifted her head she caught her reflection in the glass and was dismayed to see how pinched and wary and closed her face had become. 'Things have got to get better,' she said aloud. 'I must make them better.' There was a little moisturiser left in the bottle. She squeezed some into her palm and rubbed it into her forehead and cheeks, into the slack skin under her chin, into her crêpey neck. 'I am alive,' she said, 'I am not old. I am not a young woman. I could live for another forty years yet.' She fumbled for the blusher, and worked it into her cheeks. 'I am a *person*,' she said threateningly into the glass. 'I am me, Frances.'

There was a thundering on the stairs, followed by Dave, out of breath at the door.

'Hi, folks, it's Lamborghini time,' he hissed. 'The Hendersons are in an arriving situation.' He had not shaved, after all, but on the other hand he was not wearing his red secretary spectacles either. You could not have everything, Mrs Nightingale supposed.

'Hurry up, Marlene,' he said. 'You can't leave us alone with them.' He vanished, and then immediately reappeared. 'You should know that Mrs H. is wearing a salmon two-piece, with turquoise accessories. Tuck in.'

Mrs Nightingale grabbed a lipstick from the table and stretched her mouth into the grimace that, with her, always preceded its application. At the first pressure the lipstick, which had been broken by Poppy earlier and stuck back by her into its case, toppled and fell, grazing Mrs Nightingale's chin as it did so with a long gash of *Wicked Rose*.

Five Paintings of the New Japan

STEVEN HEIGHTON

A National Gallery

I Sunflowers

I WAS THE first foreigner to wait tables in the *Yume no ato*.
Summer enrolment was down at the English school where I
taught so I needed to earn some extra money, and since I'd
been eating at the restaurant on and off for months it was the
first place I thought of applying. It was a small establishment
built just after the war in a bombed-out section of the city,
but when I saw it the area was studded with bank towers,
slick boutiques, coffee shops and flourishing bars and the
Yume no ato was one of the oldest and most venerable
places around. I was there most of the summer and I wish
I could go back. I heard the other day from Nori, the dish-
washer, who works part-time now in a camera store, that
our ex-boss Mr Onishi has just fought and lost a battle with
cancer.

'We have problems here every summer,' Mr Onishi sighed
during my interview, 'with a foreign tourist people.' He peered
up at me from behind his desk, two shadowy half-moons
drooping under his eyes. 'Especially the Americans. If I hire
you, you can deal to them.'

'With them,' I said automatically.

'You have experienced waitering?'

'A little,' I lied.

'You understand Japanese?'

'I took a course.'

'Say something to me in Japanese.'

I froze for a moment, then was ambushed by a phrase from my primer.

'*Niwa ni wa furu-ike ga arimasu.*'

'In the garden,' translated Mr Onishi, 'there is an old pond.'

I stared abjectly at his bald patch.

'You cannot say a sentence more difficult than that?'

I told Mr Onishi it was a beginner's course. He glanced up at me and ran his fingers through a greying Vandyke beard.

'How well do you know the Japanese cuisine?'

'Not so well,' I answered in a light bantering tone that I hoped would disarm him, 'but I know what I like.'

He frowned and checked his watch, then darted a glance at the bank calendar on the wall by his desk.

'Morinaga speaks a little English,' he said. 'He will be your trainer. Tomorrow at 1600 hours you start.'

'You won't be sorry, sir,' I told him.

'I shall exploit you,' he said, 'until someone more qualitied applies.'

Nori Morinaga leaned against the steam table and picked his nose with the languid, luxurious gestures of an epicure enjoying an after-dinner cigar. He was the biggest Japanese I'd ever seen and the coke-bottle glasses perched above his huge nose seemed comically small.

'Ah, *gaijin-san!*' he exclaimed as he saw me, collecting himself and inflating to his full height. 'Welcome in! Hail fellow well-hung!'

I wondered if I'd heard him correctly.

'It gives me great pressure!'

I had. I had.

Nori Morinaga offered me his hand at the same moment I tried to bow. Nervously we grinned at each other, then began to laugh. He was a full head taller than I was, burly as a line-backer but prematurely hunched as if stooping in doorways and under low ceilings had already affected his spine. He couldn't have been over twenty-five. His hair was brush-cut like a Marine's and when he spoke English his voice and manner seemed earnest and irreverent at the same time.

'Onishi-San tells me I will help *throw you the ropes*,' he chuckled. 'Ah, I like that expression. Do you know it? I study English at the University but the *gaijin-sensei* always says Japanese students must be more idiomatic so I picked up this book' – his giant hand brandished a thick paperback – 'and I study it *like a rat out of hell.*'

He grinned enigmatically, then giggled. I couldn't tell if he was serious or making fun of me.

Nori pronounced his idiomatic gleanings with savage enthusiasm, his magnified eyes widening and big shoulders bunching for emphasis as if to ensure his scholarship did not pass unseen. I took the book and examined it: a dog-eared, discount edition of UP-TO-DATE ENGLISH PHRASES FOR JAPANESE STUDENTS – in the 1955 edition.

'We open in an hour,' he said. 'We are *oppressed for time.* Come on, *I'm going to show you what's what.*'

Situated in a basement, under a popular *karaoke* bar, the *Yume na ato*'s two small rooms were dimly lit and the atmosphere under the low ceiling was damp and cool, as in an air-raid shelter or submarine. I wondered if this cramped, covert aura hadn't disturbed some of the earliest patrons, whose memories of the air-raids would still have been fresh – but I didn't ask Nori about that. The place had always been popular, he said, especially in summer, when it was one of the coolest spots in Ōsaka.

A stairway descended from street level directly into the dining room so on summer days, after the heat and bright sunshine of the city, guests would sink into a cool aquatic atmosphere of dim light and swaying shadows. The stairway was flanked on one side by a small bar and on the other by the sushi counter where I'd eaten before. An adjoining room contained a larger, more formal dining space which gave onto the kitchen through a swinging door at the back. Despite the rather western-style seating arrangements (tables and chairs instead of the traditional *zabuton* and *tatami*) the dining area was decorated in authentic Japanese fashion with hanging lanterns, calligraphic scrolls, a *tokonoma* containing an empty *maki-e* vase, *bonsai* and *noren* and several framed, original *sumi-e* prints. The only unindigenous ornament was a large reproduction of Van Gogh's 'Sunflowers' hung conspicuously on the wall behind the sushi bar.

'Onishi-San says it's for the behoof of the American tourists,' Nori explained, 'but I'd *bet my bottom* he put it there for the bankers who come *in the wee-wee hours.* It's the bankers who are really interested in that stuff.' He sniffed and gestured contemptuously towards 'Sunflowers' and towards the *sumi-e* prints as well, as if wanting me to see he considered all art frivolous and dispensible, no matter where it came from.

I didn't realise till much later the gesture meant something else.

Nori showed me around the kitchen and introduced me to the cooks, who were just arriving. Kenji Komatsu was head chef. Before returning to Japan and starting a family he'd worked for a few years in Vancouver and Montreal and his memories of that time were good, so he was delighted to hear I was Canadian. He insisted I call him Mat. 'And don't listen to anything this big whale tells you,' he warned me affably, poking Nori in the stomach. 'So much sugar and McDonald's the young ones are eating these days . . . This one should be in the *sumō* ring, not my kitchen.'

'*Sumō* is for old folk,' Nori said, tightening his gut and ironically saluting a small, aproned man who had just emerged from the walk-in fridge.

'*Time is on the march,*' Nori intoned. '*Nothing can stop it now!*'

Second chef Yukio Miyoshi glared at Nori, then at me, with frank disgust and muttered to himself in Japanese. He marched towards the back of the kitchen and began gutting a large fish. 'Doesn't like the foreigners,' Nori grinned indifferently. 'So it is. You can't pleasure everybody.'

The swinging door burst open and a small dark form hurtled into the kitchen and disappeared behind the steam table. Nori grabbed me by the arm.

'It's Oh–San, the sushi chef – come, we must hurry.'

Mr Oh was a jittery middle-aged man who scurried through the restaurant, both hands frantically embracing a mug of fresh coffee. Like all the elder folks, Nori explained, Mr Oh worked too hard . . .

We finally cornered him by the walk-in fridge and Nori introduced us. Clearly he had not heard of Mr Onishi's latest hiring decision – he flung down his mug and gawked as if I were a health inspector who'd just told him that twenty of last night's customers were in the hospital with food poisoning.

The *yukata* which Mr Oh insisted I try on looked all right, and in the changeroom I finally gave in and let him brylcreem and comb back my curly hair into the slick, shining facsimile of a typical Japanese cut. As he worked with the comb, his face close to mine, I could see the tic in his left eye and smell his breath, pungent with coffee.

'You look *marvellous*,' Nori laughed on my return, 'and you know who you are!' He winked and blew me a kiss.

Mr Onishi entered and snapped some brusque truculent command. When the others had fled to their stations he addressed me in English.

'I hope you are ready for your first shift. We will have many guests tonight. Come – you will have to serve the aliens.'

From the corner of my eye I could see Nori clowning behind the grille, two chopsticks pressed to his forehead like antennae.

As I trailed Mr Onishi into the dining room two men and a woman, all young, tall, clad smartly in *yukata*, issued from behind the bar and lined up for inspection. One of the men wore a pearl earring and his hair was unusually long for a Japanese, while the woman had a rich brown, luminous skin and plump, attractive features. Mr Onishi introduced the other man as Akiburo. He was a college student and looked the part with his regulation haircut and sly, wisecracking expression.

With patent distaste Mr Onishi billed the long-haired man as 'your bartender, who likes to be known as Johnnie Walker'. The man fingered his earring and smiled out of the side of his mouth. 'And this is Suzuki Michiko, a waitress.' She bowed awkwardly and studied her plump brown hands, the pale skin on the underside of her wrists.

My comrades, as Mr Onishi called them, had been expecting me, and now they would show me to my sector of the restaurant – three small tables in the corner of the second room. In this occidental ghetto, it seemed, Mr Onishi thought I would do the least possible damage to the restaurant's ambience and reputation. Michiko explained in simple Japanese that since my tables were right by the kitchen door I could ask Nori for help as soon as I got in trouble.

The *tokonoma*, I now saw, had been decorated with a spray of poppies.

'We open shortly,' Mr Onishi declared, striding towards us. His manner was vigorous and forceful but his eyes seemed tired, their light extinguished. 'We probably will have some American guests tonight. Your job will be to service them.'

'I'll do my best sir.'

'And coffee – you will now take over from Michiko and

bring Mr Oh his coffee. He will want a fresh supply every half-hour. Do not forget!'

For the first hour the second room remained empty, as did the tables of the front room, but the sushi bar was overrun within minutes by an army of ravenous, demanding guests. 'Coffee,' cried Mr Oh, and I brought him cup after cup while the customers gaped at me and hurled at Mr Oh questions I could not understand. The coffee yellowed his tongue and reddened his eyes, which took on a weird, narcotic glaze, while steam mixed with sweat and stood out in bold clear beads on his cheeks and upper lip. Orders were called out as more guests arrived. Mr Oh's small red hands scuttled like sand crabs over the counter, making predatory forays into the display case to seize hapless chunks of smelt or salmon or eel and then wielding above them a fish-silver knife, replacing the knife deftly, swooping down on speckled quail eggs and snapping shells between thumb and forefinger and squeezing the yolk onto bricks of rice the other hand had just formed. Then, with fingers dangling, the hands would hover above an almost-completed dish, and they would waver slightly like squid or octopuses in currents over the ocean floor, then pounce, abrupt and accurate, on an errant grain of rice or any garnish or strip of ginger imperfectly arranged, and an instant later the finished work, irreproachable and beyond time like a still-life or a great sculpture, would appear on the glass above the display case from which it was snatched within seconds by the grateful customers or attentive staff.

The process was dizzying. I was keenly aware of my ignorance and when I was not airlifting coffee to the sushi bar I was busy in my own sector studying the menu and straightening tables.

Around eight o'clock Mr Onishi entered the second room, carrying menus, followed by a man and woman who were both heavyset, tall and fair-haired. The man wore a tailored navy suit and carried a briefcase. The woman's hair was piled high in a steep bun that resembled the nose-cone of a rocket, and her lipstick, like her dress, was a pushy, persistent shade of red.

'Take good care with Mr and Mrs Cruikshank,' Onishi-San murmured as he passed me and showed them to their seats. 'Mr Cruikshank is a very important man – a diplomat, from America. Bring two dry martinis to begin.'

Mr Cruikshank's voice was genteel and collected, his manner

smooth as good brandy. 'How long have you been working in this place?' he inquired.

'Two hours,' I told him, serving the martinis.

'Surprised they'd have an American working here.' With one hand he yanked a small plastic sabre from his olive, then pinched the olive and held it aloft like a tiny globe.

'I'm not American,' I said.

There was a pause while Mr and Mrs Cruikshank processed this unlooked-for information.

'Well surely you're not Japanese?' Mrs Cruikshank asked, slurring her words a little. 'Maybe half?'

Mr Cruikshank swallowed his olive then impaled his wife's with the plastic sword. He turned to me, inadvertently aiming the harmless tip at my throat.

'*Nihongo wakaru?*' he asked in plain, masculine speech. *You understand Japanese?* I recognised his accent as outstanding.

'Only a little,' I said.

'I'll bet he's Dutch,' Mrs Cruikshank wagered. 'The Dutch speak such beautiful English – hardly any accent at all.'

'You'll find it hard here without any Japanese,' Mr Cruikshank advised me, ignoring his wife, drawing the sword from his teeth so the gleaming olive stayed clenched between them.

'*Coffee*,' Mr Oh called from the sushi bar.

'I'll only be serving the foreign customers, sir.'

Mr Cruikshank bit into his olive. 'Some of the foreign customers,' he said, 'prefer being served in Japanese.'

'Or maybe German,' said Mrs Cruikshank.

'I can speak some German,' I said. 'Would you like it if –'

'*Coffee*,' cried Mr Oh from the sushi bar.

Mrs Cruikshank was beaming. 'I was right,' she said, lifting her martini glass in a kind of toast. '*Wie geht's?*'

'We'd like some sushi,' Mr Cruikshank interrupted his wife, who was now grimacing at her drink as if trying to recall another German phrase.

I fumbled with my pad.

'An order each of *maguro, saba, hamachi*, and – why not? – some sea urchin. Hear it's full of mercury these days, but hell, we've got to eat something.'

'Yes, sir.'

'And two more martinis.' He pointed at his glass with the plastic sword.

'Got it.'

'*Danke schön*,' roared Mrs Cruikshank as I hurried from the room . . .

While waiting for Johnnie Walker to finish the martinis I noticed an older guest rise from the sushi bar and stumble towards the washrooms. As he saw me, his red eyes widened and he lost his footing and crashed into the bar, slamming a frail elbow against the cash register. He righted himself with quick slapstick dignity and stood blushing. When I moved to help him he waved me off.

Johnnie Walker smirked and muttered as he shook the martinis and for a moment the words and the rattling ice took on a primitive, mocking rhythm, like a chant. The older man began to swear at him and reached out as if to grab his earring, his long hair. *Shin jin rui*, the old man muttered – *strange inscrutable creature*! I'd heard it was a new phrase coined by the old to describe the young.

'Wake up, old man,' Johnnie snapped in plain Japanese as he poured the martinis. 'Watch out where you're going.'

The man lurched off.

'Always drunk, or fast asleep in their chairs.'

'*Coffee*,' cried Mr Oh from the sushi bar.

II The Dream

'Tell me something about the restaurant,' I said to Nori, sweeping my hand in a half-circle and nodding at the closed bar. 'How old is the place?'

Nori finished his Budweiser and balanced the empty can on a growing tower of empties. 'It was built after the war ends,' he belched – and I couldn't help noticing how casually he used the word *war*. His expression was unchanged, his voice was still firm, his eyes had not recoiled as if shamed by some unspeakable profanity. That was how my older students reacted when The War came up in a lesson. No doubt Mr Onishi would react the same way. But not Nori. For him the war was history, fiction – as unreal and insubstantial as a dimly remembered dream, a dream of jungles, the faded memory of a picture in a storybook. He wasn't much younger than me.

'What about the name,' I said, '*Yume no ato*? I mean, I can figure out the individual words, but I can't make sense of the whole thing.' *Yume*, I knew, meant 'dream', *no* signified possession, like an apostrophe and an 's', and *ato*, I thought, meant 'after'.

Nori lit a cigarette and trained a mischievous gaze on my hairline. His capacity for drink was larger than average for a Japanese but now after four tins of beer he was flushed, theatrical and giddy. He wrinkled his broad nose, as if at a whiff of something rotten, and spat out, 'It's a line from a poem we had to study in the high school. Ah, Steve-San, University is so much better, we have fun in the sun, we make whoopee, we live for the present tense and forget all our yesterdays and tomorrows – I hated high school, so much work. We had to study this famous poem.'

He stood and recited the lines with mock gravity:

'*Natsu kusa ya!*
Tsuamono domo ga
Yume no ato.'

'It's a *haiku*,' I said.

'Aye, aye, captain.' He slumped down and the tower of beer cans wobbled. 'Do you watch Star Trek?'

'I'm not sure,' I said, 'that I understand it.'

'Oh, well, it's just a TV show – about the future and the stars.'

'I mean the poem, Nori, the *haiku*.'

'Ah, the poem – naturally you don't understand. It's old Japanese – old Japanese language, old Japanese mind – not so easy for us to understand either. It's Matsuo Bashō, dead like Shakespeare over three hundred years. Tomorrow and tomorrow and tomorrow. We had to study them both in school. Full fathom five and all that.'

'But about that last line . . .'

'*Yume no ato?*'

I nodded.

'That's the name of the restaurant. You see, when Mr Onishi's uncle built the place after the war he gave it that name. It's a very strange name for a restaurant! Mr Onishi was just a boy then.'

'What does it mean?'

'I don't think Mr Onishi would have called it that, but when his uncle went over the bucket he didn't want to change the name. Out of respect.'

I finished my own beer and contributed to the tower of cans. The other staff had gone upstairs to the *karaoke* place but they'd drunk a lot of Bud and Kirin beforehand and the tower was growing high.

185

'I wonder,' I said, 'if the words mean "when the dream is over"?'

Nori took a long drag on his cigarette. 'I don't think they do,' he finally said. 'And besides, the dream had only just begun . . . The uncle was smart and he built *Yume no ato* to attract foreigners as well as Japanese and it's done really well, as you can see.' His eyes brightened. '*We're going great guns.*'

Mr Onishi's telephone began to ring from the back of the restaurant, where he was still working. We heard him answer.

'The first line,' I said, 'is "Ah! Summer grasses", right?'

Nori seemed to be weighing this, then blurted out, '*Yume no ato* means . . . it means what's left over after a dream.'

Mr Onishi's voice could be heard faintly. I surveyed the shaky tower, the ashtrays, the skeletons of fish beached on the sides of our empty plates.

'Leftovers,' I said, ironically.

'There's another word.'

'What about vestige? No? Remnant?'

Nori stubbed out his cigarette like a game-show panelist pressing a buzzer. '*Remnant!*' he cried, '*Your choice is absolutely correct, for five thousand dollars and a dream home!*' Suddenly he grew calm, thoughtful. 'So many foreign words sound alike,' he mused. 'There's a famous Dutch painter with that name.'

'Rembrandt?' I said.

'That's him. A bank here in Umeda just bought a Remnant for nine hundred million yen.'

'*Yume no ato,*' I said, 'must mean "the remnant of dreams".'

Nori furrowed his brow, then nodded.

'Funny name for a restaurant,' I said. 'You like game shows?'

As if in a fresh wind the paper *noren* in the doorway behind the sushi bar blew open and a haggard phantom came in. Mr Onishi. He seemed to look right through us. Nori suggested we clean up and leave. We began to pile the chopsticks and empty plates onto a tray. I glanced up and saw Mr Onishi beckoning Nori.

'Please go examine the guest toilet,' Nori told me.

The guest washroom was immaculate – I'd cleaned it myself two hours before – but I spent a few minutes checking it again so Nori and Mr Onishi would know I was thorough. For the second time that night I was intrigued by a notice in the stall, pencilled on the back of an old menu and taped to the door –

TO ALL FOREIGNERS:
OUR TUBES ARE IN ILL REPAIR, PLEASE
DO NOT THROW YOUR PEEPERS
IN THE TOILET.

When I came out of the washroom Mr Onishi was gone. 'The boss looks awful,' I whispered to Nori, my smile forced. 'When he was on the phone before – maybe a guest was calling to complain about the new waiter, eh?'

'Possibly,' Nori said, 'but more likely it was a banker.'

'What, at this time of night?'

Nori shrugged. 'The elder folks, I told you, they're working late. And early, too – there was a banker here first thing this morning to talk at Mr Onishi.'

'Bankers,' I scoffed, shaking my head. 'Not trouble, I hope . . .'

Nori laughed abruptly. Arm tensed karate-style he approached the tower of cans.

III   The Kermess

KAMPAI!

A month has gone past and the whole staff, *gaijin-san* included, are relaxing after a manic Saturday night in the *Yume no ato*. August in Ōsaka: with other waiters and students and salarymen we sit in a beer garden under the full moon above twenty-two storeys of department store merchandise, imported clothing and cologne and books and records, Japanese-made electronics, wedding supplies, Persian carpets and French cigarettes and aquariums full of swordfish and coral and casino–pink sand from the Arabian Sea, appliances and appliqué, blue–china chopstick-holders computers patio–furniture coffee-shops chefs and friendly clerks and full–colour reproductions of well-known Western portraits, etchings, sketches, sculptures, landscapes that Japanese banks are buying like real estate and bringing back to Ōsaka, anything, anything at all, SPEND AND IT SHALL BE GIVEN, endless armies of customers and ah, summer tourists billowing like grain through the grounds of Ōsaka's most famous department store. SURELY, quoth the televangelist from the multitudinous screens, SURELY THE PEOPLE IS GRASS.

(For a moment the tables shudder as a tremor ripples

through toxic earth under the Bargain Basement, and passes.)

KAMPAI! Western rock and roll music blasts from hidden speakers. In a few minutes the *O-bon* fireworks are due to start and we've got the best seats in the house. The plastic table sags and may soon buckle as another round of draft materialises and is swiftly distributed. A toast to this, a toast to that, *kampai*, *KAMPAI*, every time we lift our steins to take a drink, someone is proposing another toast: in a rare gesture Komatsu toasts the wait-staff (Akiburo and Johnnie and Michiko and me) because (this in English) we were really on the balls tonight and made no errors at all. *Kampai*! Akiburo toasts Komatsu and Mr Oh and second chef Miyoshi in return, presumably for turning out so much good food on such a busy night and making it all look easy. *Kampai*! Mr Oh raises his glass of ice-coffee in thanks while second chef Miyoshi, drunk and expansive, in a rare good mood, toasts Nori for not smacking his head in the storeroom when he went back for extra soy sauce, *KAMPAI*, (this translated by the delighted Nori, who immediately hefts his stein and decrees a toast to Michiko, the waitress, simply because he's mad about her and isn't it lucky she doesn't speak English?).

The blushing Michiko lifts her heavy stein with soft plump hands and meekly suggests, in Japanese, that it might be possible, perhaps, to maybe if it isn't too much trouble drink a toast to our skilful bartender, Johnnie Walker, without whom we could hardly have survived the night, it seems to me, after all, or maybe we might have? *Kampai*! *Kampai*! The flesh of Johnnie's ear lobe reddens around his pearl stud. He smirks and belts back another slug of whiskey.

'To Onishi-San,' he says in English. 'To *Yume no ato*.' And he quickly adds some other remark in harsh, staccato Japanese.

'*KAMPAI*!' I holler, hoisting my stein triumphantly so that beer froths up and sloshes over the lip of the glass. But no one else has followed suit. They are all gazing without expression at the table or into their drinks. Johnnie Walker's head hangs lowest, his features hidden.

Komatsu glances at his watch and predicts that the fireworks will start in thirty seconds.

I turn to Nori. 'Did I do something wrong?'

Miyoshi and Mr Oh both snap something at him. I can't make out a word.

'Well, not at all,' says Nori softly, 'I guess people just don't feel like talking about work after a busy night.'

I purse my lips. 'I have the feeling you're not being completely honest with me.'

'Of course I'm not!' Nori protests, and I wonder if we've understood each other.

At that moment the fireworks start. Everyone at our table looks up, relieved. 'O-bon,' Nori says to me, relaxed again. 'To-night, the ancestors return.' Flippantly he rolls his eyes, or only seems to – I can't be sure because his coke-bottle lenses reflect the moonlight and the fierce red glare of the first rockets. One after another they arc up out of the dark expanse of Nagai Park, miles to the north, then slow down and pause at their zenith and explode in corollas of violet, emerald, coral, cream, apricot and indigo. Hanabi, they call them in Japanese: fire-flowers. The steins are raised again, glasses rammed together, toasts made and spirits drawn skyward by the aerial barrage.

My flat is somewhere down there on the far side of Nagai Park and now I picture a defective missile veering off course and buzzing my neighbourhood, terrifying the old folks, plunging with a shriek like an air-raid siren through the roof of my flat . . .

Nori grabs my arm with steely fingers. 'Steve-san, listen – do you hear what I hear?' I'm still concentrating on the look and sound of the exploding flowers, but suddenly I pick it out: the bouncy unmistakable opening bars of 'Like a Virgin.'

'It's the Madonna!'

'I hear it, Nori.'

He lumbers to his feet. 'You want to dance? Hey, get up! Come off it!'

Michiko and Johnnie Walker are already up beside the table, strobe-lit by the fireworks, shaking themselves to the beat, Michiko with a timid, tentative look and Johnnie with self-conscious abandon. The older staff sit motionless and watch the exploding rockets. Nori glances at them, at Michiko, at me, and I can tell he doesn't want to lose her. As she dances her small hands seem to catch and juggle the light.

'Life is so curt,' he pleads. 'You only lived once!' He gives me a half-smile, a sly wink, and I'm no longer sure he doesn't know exactly what he's saying.

KAMPAI! Nori hauls me to my feet and heaves me from the table in a blind teetering polka, out towards Johnnie and Michiko, his big boorish feet beating a mad tattoo on my toes. Komatsu and Mr Oh, the elders in the crowd, link arms and start keening some old Japanese song. Steins raised, they sway together to a stately rhythm much slower than Madonna's, their voices rolling mournfully over the antique minors and archaic words. The rockets keep exploding. Their sound takes on a rhythm which seems to fall between the beats of the opposing songs – then as I watch, one of the rockets fails to burst. Like a falling star it streaks earthward in silence and disappears over the city.

IV   Guernica

I woke early the next morning with a headache and a burning stomach. I'd been dreaming. I dreamed Michiko had come home with me to my flat and we stood together hand-in-hand on the threshold, staring in at a gutted interior. The guilty rocket, however, had not actually exploded – it was resting in perfect condition, very comfortably, on an unburnt, freshly-made *futon* in the centre of the room.

Michiko took me by the hand and led me into the ruin. When the smoke began to drown me she covered my mouth with her own. Her breath was clean and renewing as wind off an early-morning sea and when she pulled away the smell of burning was gone. She removed her flowered kimono and stood naked before me. The nipples of her firm small breasts were now the accusing eyes of a seduced and betrayed woman – then I was naked too, and utterly absolved, and we were lying side by side amid the acrid wreckage by the futon. She climbed atop me and took me inside her, slowly, making small articulate sighs and rolling her head back and forth so her dark bangs rippled like a midnight waterfall across my nipples, and the blue-black hair was curved as space-time and full of sparks like the Milky Way, which in the Japanese tongue is called *ama no gawa*, the river of heaven.

I wanted to come, to fill the gathering space inside her, and I wanted to run my tongue down the soft pale line of hair from her breasts to her belly and on up the wooded mound of Venus and lick the nectar from her tender orchid, as the Japanese poets say, but then it came to me that Nori had meant to tell me something important – about Michiko? About a poem? Or was there something I'd asked him that he hadn't answered?

Summer grasses . . . Something left over after dreams . . .

What a stupid time to be thinking about poetry.

I woke embarrassed, but with a feeling of desperate tenderness for Michiko, to whom I'd hardly ever spoken and who had inspired, I thought, no more than a generic interest on my part. It was like missing a lover who'd slept beside me all night and had just left and gone home before I woke . . .

Well, I reflected, a dream like that was better than the waitering nightmares I'd had all the time till recently, and still woke from now and then. Usually I'd enter the restaurant and be told I was two hours late and none of the other wait-staff had shown up and the restaurant was full and we were booked solid till midnight. Other times I would realise I'd forgotten a couple or threesome who'd been seated two hours ago in the back corner of the second room and would they believe now it was just an honest mistake and I'd been really busy and meaning to get to them all along? Sometimes they were the Cruikshanks, and sometimes Mr Sato, who (Nori had told me) was a professor at the University in Kyōto but had been demoted and now taught primary kids in Nagai, and that was why he drank so much and was so cold and pedantic when he spoke to you. In fact the unrequited dream-diners could be just about anyone, because the summer had been busy and now I was serving both foreigners and Japanese alike.

It had been the busiest summer in years, Komatsu said, and we were attracting more tourists than ever before – so why the visible anxiety whenever talk after-hours came round to the restaurant? Mr Onishi did not look like a man with a flourishing business. Perhaps he was ill and everyone was worried? I'd been reading articles lately about the soaring incidence of cancer in Japan, the spread of big business and factories into the countryside, toxins in the soil, polluted water, poisonous seafood . . .

'I think you'd better level with me,' I told Nori the night of my dream.

Miyoshi was standing by the walk-in, reading the *Sangyo Keizai*, and Komatsu was behind the steam table chopping onion. But I had the feeling they were listening to us, and so did Nori.

'*Not here,*' he whispered.

'Ah, such good news,' growled Miyoshi, lowering his paper with an unpleasant smile. Since he hardly ever spoke English I knew the remark was meant for me. 'Such good news about the yen!'

Nori shook his head. 'For some the war has never ended.'

'*Nihon ichiban!*' Miyoshi cried. 'Japan is number one!'

'And he wasn't even born till after,' Nori grumbled. 'I don't understand.'

'Maybe we should talk somewhere else,' I said.

Nori nodded, but Komatsu set down his knife and said quickly 'No. It's all right. Steve-san is part of the restaurant now – we should tell him the truth.' Eyes pink and glistening, he walked out from behind the steam table and pulled the newspaper from Miyoshi's hands.

Miyoshi scowled, did an about-face and marched into the fridge.

'Look at this,' Komatsu sniffled, handing me the paper.

'You know I can't read Japanese.'

'Of course. Don't read, just look – the pictures.'

In the lower right-hand corner of the front page several well-known pieces of European art were reproduced in hazy black and white. One was a Rousseau, the second a Gauguin, the third a Brueghel. I couldn't read the caption beneath but I could make out the name of a prominent Ōsaka bank, written in *romaji*.

'And Van Gogh,' Komatsu said, frowning. 'I hear they just bought another costly painting by Van Gogh – so many paintings they are buying and bringing to Japan.'

We could hear Miyoshi in the fridge, muttering to himself, furiously shifting things around.

'They're buying everything in their sights,' Nori said, his usual gusto tangibly absent.

I told them I knew a bit about these purchases, but didn't see what they had to do with us.

'Well,' Komatsu started, 'they need some place to put these paintings . . .' His voice tapered off on the last words. I sensed I was being counted on, in customary Japanese fashion, to finish the sentence mentally so that everyone would be spared embarrassment.

'Chagall, too,' Komatsu resumed, 'and Rembrandt and Picasso.' *Bigasshole*, it sounded like, but I knew who he meant. 'Costly things . . . they need to find a place to put them all . . .'

'Like an art gallery,' I said.

Komatsu rubbed his eyes with a corner of his apron. 'I'm afraid so.'

It had been just like Dallas, Nori groaned, describing how the bank had first made polite offers to the dozen businesses operating in the block where they meant to build, and most were politely accepted. But several proprietors (including Mr Onishi and the owner of the Idaho Caffeine Palace, a large coffee shop dating to the late forties) had refused to consider them. Secretly the bank made more attractive offers, then a final offer which the firm's representative begged Mr Onishi to accept, because if a negotiated settlement proved necessary then payment would revert to the level of the initial sum – or, conceivably, somewhat less.

Mr Onishi had ignored the bank's covert threats and a negotiated settlement proved necessary. Unfortunately it did not involve negotiation. The bank produced lawyers who showed that actual title to the land had belonged to the bank till the end of the war and they argued that the transfer of deeds had been improperly handled by the over-worked civil authorities of the time.

The young lawyers (I could just hear them) moved further that since the art gallery would be a public facility of great benefit to all citizens of the prefecture and would attract hundreds of thousands of foreigners to Ōsaka, it was in effect a civic institution, albeit privately owned, and the city should urge Mr Onishi to come to terms.

'The court is asking Mr Onishi to accept,' Nori said, 'but he just says no.'

Nihon ichiban, we heard faintly from the fridge.

Komatsu took the newspaper from me and walked back around the steam table. He began to giggle, like a bad comedian setting up a punchline. 'They're going to tear us down,' he said, laughing openly. 'Soon!'

Nori was chuckling, too, as the Japanese often will when speaking of their own misfortunes. Komatsu was laughing harder than I'd ever seen him, so I knew he must really be upset.

I paused respectfully. 'Listen, I'm really sorry to hear this.'

Komatsu roared with laughter. Nori continued to cackle. I asked them if they knew when these things were going to happen.

'There's no time like presently,' Nori said, slapping me on the shoulder a bit harder than he needed to. 'Come on, it's a busy night tonight, we'd better get happening.'

'Please take coffee now to Mr Oh-San,' Komatsu giggled.
Miyoshi was still marching around in the fridge.

V   The Starry Night

September in Ōsaka is just as hot as July or August and this
year it was worse. Though many of the tourists were gone,
the *Yume no ato* was busier than ever: Mr Onishi's struggle
with the bank was now common knowledge, so old customers
came often to show their support and the sushi bar was crowded
with curious locals. Meanwhile enrolment was picking up at the
school and I had to cut back on my hours as a waiter.

Mr Onishi was upset when I told him, but since I knew
now of the epic struggle he was waging each day in the courts
(Nori got the details from Komatsu and passed them on to me)
I found it hard to feel angry in return. The boss, after all, was
showing tremendous pluck. Sure, he was of another generation,
a hardy breed of industrious survivors, and as a child he would
have absorbed with his mother's milk the bracing formula of
bushidō, but this was valour way beyond the call of duty. He
was giving Japan's second biggest bank the fight of its life.
Already the original date for demolition was three weeks in
arrears . . .

I heard that after receiving the court's final decision, Mr
Onishi sighed and said '*Yappari nah*. It is as I expected. They
will build a museum and a new country and fill both with
foreign things.'

The demolition was set for the end of September and
the *Yume no ato* was to close a week before.

On the last night, a Saturday, the dining room was booked
solid from five till closing with regular customers, both Japanese
and foreign. We assembled by the bar a few minutes before five
to wait for Mr Onishi and at five sharp he emerged from his
office. He marched up to us, a menu tucked under one arm like
a swagger stick, then briefed us in a formal and highly nuanced
Japanese that I could not follow, though the general tenor of
his speech was easy enough to guess. Or was it? Sometimes
I wondered if I'd ever done more than misimagine what these
people felt and believed.

A current of laughter rippled through the staff and Nori
nudged me appreciatively, forgetting for a moment I did not
understand.

Mr Onishi dismissed us and we hurried off to complete our preparations as he climbed the stairs and opened the door. A long shaft of dirty sunlight pierced the cool gloom, and a few seconds later our guests began to descend, bringing with them the hot muggy air of the street.

'Meet me in the back,' I told Nori.

We stood in the kitchen on either side of the open rice machine, slowly filling it with the contents of two clay cooking pots. Thick billows of steam rose between us and Nori's face was intermittently clouded, his eyes nacreous, indistinct, like a man under a foot of water.

'So what did Onishi-San say,' I asked, scooping the soft, sweet-smelling grains into the machine.

'He was apologising.'

'Apologising,' I said.

'Sure. He was apologising for letting the bank close the *Yume no ato*. He says it's all on his shoulders. He feels responsible for the jobs we will lose. He says he is sorry because he has felled us.'

The steam was thinning and I could see Nori clearly. His big face was pink and sweating.

'He says his uncle was a soldier in the old navy and after the war he built this restaurant with his own two hands. So he says that by losing the restaurant he has felled his uncle, too.'

'But isn't his uncle dead?'

Nori put down his pot and gave me a faintly disappointed look.

'For many years. But so the old people believe – they can fell the dead as well as the breathing. Like being caught *between the devil and the deep blue sea, neh*?'

I nodded and stared into the rice cooker, its churning steam spectral and hypnotic.

'I feel sorry for him,' I said.

'So it is, all the while. The big fish eat the little.'

There was a harsh grating sound as he scraped rice from the bottom of his pot.

It was the busiest night of the summer but the customers were gentle and undemanding and the atmosphere, as at a funeral reception, was chastened and sadly festive and thick with solidarity. The foreigners left huge tips and Mr Oh grunted graciously whenever I freshened his coffee. It fell to Michiko to serve the disagreeable Mr Sato for the last time and though he usually deplored the grammar and fashions of her generation, he was tolerant tonight and even remarked at one point on her resemblance to his own daughter. The Cruikshanks were among the last to arrive. When they left, just before closing, Mrs Cruikshank said she trusted I wouldn't have to go home to Germany just yet and surely with my good English I could land another job . . .

The last guests, our oldest customers, intoxicated and teary-eyed, staggered up the stairs around midnight and we dragged together a few tables and sank down for a last meal. Mat and Nori and second chef Miyoshi filed from the kitchen bearing platters of steaming rice and salmon teriyaki; at Mr Onishi's behest Johnnie Walker opened the bar to all staff. And now, though I'd felt more and more a part of things over the last months, I sensed my saddened colleagues closing ranks, retreating into dialect, resorting to nuance, idiom and silence, a semaphore of glances and tics and nods. Nori loomed on the far side of the table with Michiko beside him. They were talking quietly. In the shadows by their chair-legs I could see two hands linked, like sinuous sea-creatures, twined and mating in the deep.

Johnnie had finished the last of the Johnnie Walker Red and was now working on a bottle of Old Granddad. Mr Oh was not drinking. He sat mutely, his agile hands wrapped around one beer tin after another, crushing them and laying them to rest among the plates and ashtrays. Komatsu and second chef Miyoshi were smoking side by side, eyes half-closed, meditating on the fumes that rose and spread outward over their heads.

Mr Onishi, I suppose, was in his office. At one-thirty he came out and told everyone it was time to leave. There were some last half-hearted toasts and deep bowing and then we all stumbled upstairs and outside. The night air was cool and fresh. We looked, I thought, like a beaten rabble. As if wounded, Nori tottered over and proffered a scrap of paper the size of a cheque or a phone bill. 'Here,' he said, his speech slurred, 'I almost forgot. That poem they called the restaurant for . . . Remember?'

He and Michiko swayed before me, their features painted a smooth flawless amber by the gentle light of the doorway. Behind them the brooding profiles of bank and office towers and beyond those in long swirling ranks the constellations of early autumn.

I took the slip of paper and held it to the light:

Ah! summer grass/this group of warriors'/remnant of
   dream
(this poem by Matsuo Bashō, lived same time as
   Shakespeare)
   So long and take care of yourself. Nori.

He shrugged when I thanked him. 'We had to study it
back then. A real pin in the ass.'

'Drop by the school sometime,' I said. 'Please, both of
you . . .'

I knew they wouldn't come.

Gradually the rest straggled off alone or in pairs and I
headed for the station. Waves of heat rising from sewers,
smokestacks and vacant pavement set the stars quivering,
like the scales of small fish in dark water. In the late-summer
heat of 1945, after the surrender, Japanese armies trudged back
through the remains of Ōsaka and there was little where these
buildings now stood but rubble, refuse, dust and blowing ash.
A stubble of fireweed and wildflowers bloomed on the ruins,
rippled in the hot wind. There was nothing for the children to
eat. I heard these things from a neighbour, a toothless old man
who had been a soldier at that time, and I heard other things as
well: how faceless Japan had been, how for a while it had been
a different place – beaten, levelled and overrun, unable to rise –
waiting for the first touch of a foreign hand. For a sea change,
into something rich, and strange.

On the train to Nagai I had a half-hour to experiment with
the words on Nori's farewell card. By the time I got home I
had the translation done, though the line 'yume no ato' was
still troublesome and I found it hard to focus on the page.

Ah, summer grass!
   All that survives
      Of the warrior's dream . . .

I keep thinking I should send a copy to Nori.

Maundy

CHRISTOPHER HOPE

A FEW DAYS before Easter, Maggie's father found a man in a sanitary lane, and took him home. All through Badminton, our housing estate, sandy, stony sanitary lanes ran between the houses on Edward Avenue and Henry Street and Elizabeth Crescent. They had been built so that the night-soil men, coming like ghosts after dark, could remove the black rubber buckets without being seen.

Our fathers returned home from the desert war in Egypt and Libya and began battling the bare veldt. Every weekend they wrestled the hard, red earth into gardens. Badminton was a new housing estate, built outside Johannesburg for returning soldiers. Its streets were named after English kings and queens, because we were English South Africans. The boxy new houses, with their corrugated-iron roofs, ran down a slope to a small stream and a copse of giant blue gums. Seven years after the war ended, soldiers who had gone to fight against Germans had turned into gardeners in uniform. My father worked in his Army boots. Gus Trupshaw wore a sailor's blue shirt. Nathan Swirsky put on his leather flying helmet when he took out his motorbike.

Our fathers looked up from their zinnias, mopped their brows, and said, 'It's hotter down south than it was up north, make no mistake.' They cursed the African heat. They cursed the stubborn shale that had to be broken up with picks, forked over, sieved, spread and sweetened with rich brown earth, delivered by Errol the topsoil man.

They cursed the burglars. My mother said that there were swarms of burglars hiding among the blue gum trees. They ran down the sanitary lanes at night and slipped into the houses like greased lightning. As I lay in bed at night, I saw the sanitary lanes teeming with burglars and night-soil men, coming and going. Nobody talked about the night-soil men. They came and went in our sleep, though in the morning we caught the scent of something we wished to forget.

Nobody talked about Maggie, either. She lived next door and took off all her clothes from time to time and ran around her house. And we all pretended not to notice. She was the fastest ten-year-old on the estate.

My mother was next door in a flash when she saw the man working in Maggie's garden. He wore old khaki shorts. His legs ended in stumps, inches below the shorts, and the stumps were tied up in sacking. He pulled himself everywhere in a red tin wagon, hauling himself along with strong arms. His muscles were huge. The legless man sat upon a paper bag that he had spread in the bottom of his wagon. It read 'Buy Your Brand-New Zephyr at Dominion Motors.'

'Hell's bells! What could I do? He just followed me home,' said Maggie's father. 'He tells me his name's Salisbury.'

'I don't care if he's the King of Siam,' my mother said to my father a little while later. 'It's bad enough when that little girl tears about the place in the you-know-what, for all the world and his wife to stare. Now they have a cripple in their garden!'

My father was studying the annual report of the South African Sugar Association. 'Figures for 1952 show exports up.'

'Some of us cannot lose ourselves in sugar reports,' my mother said. 'Some of us have to look life in the eye.'

'For heaven's sake, Monica,' my father said. 'The poor sod's lost his legs. I'm sure he doesn't like it any more than you do. But he's still human. Well, more or less.'

Then Maggie appeared, running around the side of her house. 'Speak of the devil!' my mother said. Maggie was skinny and very brown. Her bare legs flashing, round and round the house she ran. Her dog, a Dobermann called Tamburlaine, ran after her, barking loudly.

'Martin,' said my mother, 'come away from the window. It only encourages her if you stare.'

Maggie's father was chasing her with a blanket. He caught up, and threw it over her. Like a big grey butterfly net.

'You'd hardly think this was Easter,' said my mother. 'I don't know where to put my face.'

Salisbury sat in his red wagon, doing some weeding. 'What on earth do you think is going through his head?' my mother demanded. 'That little girl might be less keen to parade in the altogether if she knew what was going through his head.'

'I see that Henry's been planting out beardless irises,' said my father. 'The beardless iris loves a sunny spot and a good bit of wall.'

'Heavens above, where will it all end?' my mother asked. 'Our neighbours have a cripple in their garden. Easter is almost on us. There are burglars in the blue gums. Soon the streets will be full of servants. Did you know that they've taken to asking for Easter boxes? First Christmas boxes, now Easter boxes. I suppose they'll be asking for Michaelmas boxes next. Dressed to the nines, some of them. And worse for wear.'

I went to bed that night and thought about the burglars down among the blue gums that grew thickly across the road from the big houses in Edward Avenue. All over Badminton our fathers, home from the war, slept with their Army-issue pistols in their sock drawers, ready at any moment to rush naked into the African night, blasting away. The burglars were said to creep up on the houses and cast fishing lines through the burglar bars to hook wallets and handbags from our bedrooms.

We all believed in the burglars. Everyone except for Ruthie Swirsky, the chemist's new wife. But she was English, from Wimbledon. Swirsky had travelled to Europe and brought her home with him. 'Burglars with fishing rods,' Ruthie Swirsky said to my father just after she moved to the estate. 'I've never heard of anything so absurd. Pull the other one, Gordon.'

'Pull the other what?' my mother wanted to know later.

'How would I know, Monica?' said my father. 'Leg, I suppose.'

'Whatever she had in mind, it wasn't a leg,' said my mother.

'Whatever she had in mind, it wasn't a leg!' sang my friends Tony, Sally, and Eric, and I as we rolled down the steep, grassy banks in Tony's garden that Eastertime in Badminton.

For the rest of the holiday, nothing much seemed likely to happen. The days looming ahead were too hot somehow, even though we were well into autumn. Our fathers worked in their gardens tending to their petunias and phlox and chrysanthemums. They sprayed their rosebushes against black spot, moving in the thick clouds of lime sulphur like refugees from a gas attack in the trenches.

Ernest Langbein had fallen in love with Maggie. Ernest was an altar server at the Church of the Resurrection in Cyrildene, and he told Eric that if only Maggie would stop taking off her clothes, their love might be possible. Maggie was not easy to get on with. When she had no clothes on, she wasn't really there. And when she was dressed she was inclined to make savage remarks. I met her in Swirsky's Pharmacy on Maundy Thursday. She wore a blue dress with thick black stockings. Her brown, pixie face was shaded by a big white panama hat, tied beneath her chin with thick elastic. I was wearing shorts. I'd never seen her look so covered up. She looked at my bare feet and said, 'You have hammer toes, Martin.' It seemed very unfair.

We were standing behind the wall of blue magnesia bottles which Swirsky built across his shop on festive occasions, like Christmas and Easter. We heard Ruthie Swirsky say to Mrs Raubenheimer of the Jewish Old Age Home across the road, 'I'm collecting Maundy money. It's an Easter custom we have in England. The Royal Mint makes its own money, and the Queen gives it to pensioners and suchlike. The deserving poor. In a special purse.'

Mrs Raubenheimer said that those who could afford it could afford it. Swirsky came around the magnesia wall and grinned at us. He crackled in his starched white coat. His moustache was full and yet feathery beneath his nose. Black feathers, it was. 'Well, kiddies,' he said. 'Can I count on you? Pocket money is welcome for Ruthie's Maundy box. What Ruthie wants she usually gets.' He rattled a black wooden collection box.

My mother said, 'It's appalling. The Swirskys aren't even Easter people. The Queen of England does not live on an estate infested with burglars. Have you seen the collection box Ruthie Swirsky's using? I happen to know that it belongs to St John's Ambulance. She simply turned it around so you can't see the badge.'

'If you're going to divide the world into those who are and those who are not Easter people,' said my father, 'you may as well go and join the government. They do it all the time.'

'I have no intention,' said my mother, 'of joining the government.'

All the kids gave to Ruthie Swirsky's Maundy-money box. We collected empty soft-drink bottles and got back a penny deposit down at the Greek Tea Rom. Swirsky shook the box until our pennies rattled. 'Give till it hurts,' he said. 'Baby needs new booties.'

A deputation arrived at the pharmacy. Gus Trupshaw had been elected to speak for the estate. He wore his demob suit and brown Army boots with well-polished toes. He said that everyone objected to the idea of Ruthie's giving away money to the servants. What would they expect next Easter? It might be difficult for an English person to understand. But the cleaners, cooks, and gardeners of Badminton got board and lodging and wages. 'They might be poor,' Gus Trupshaw explained, 'but they're not deserving.'

'Are you telling me I may not give my Maundy money to whomsoever I choose?' Ruthie asked, her face white beneath her red hair. 'This is outrageous.'

'This isn't Wimbledon,' said Gus Trupshaw. 'When in Rome, do as the Romans do.'

Swirsky leaned over to us and whispered. 'When you're next in Rome, I can recommend the Trevi Fountain. But watch out for pickpockets.'

Ruthie Swirsky tapped the black collection box with her finger after Gus Trupshaw left. She told Swirsky she was so mad she could spit. She asked him to find Errol the topsoil man. 'Tell him I have a job for his wheelbarrow.'

Later, it was my mother who spotted Errol wheeling his barrow into the yard next door. 'There appears to be some movement at the neighbours'. I think I'll go and lie down,' she said.

Errol stopped beside Salisbury with his wheelbarrow. He laid the paper bag from Dominion Motors on the floor of the barrow and lifted Salisbury out of his wagon. Then he set off up Henry Street, wheeling Salisbury, with my friend Sally, her brother Tony, Eric and me tagging along behind them.

We heard the iron wheels scattering gravel in Henry Street.

'Where are we going?' Salisbury asked Errol in a deep, growling voice.

'Boss Swirsky's place. Sit still and don't make trouble.' Errol manoeuvred the barrow right up to the front door of Swirsky's

Pharmacy. Papas, the owner of the Greek Tea Room, and Mr Benjamin, the Rug Doctor, came out of their shops to stare. A couple of ladies from the Jewish Old Age Home also stopped to watch. Ruthie Swirsky came out of the pharmacy. Nathan was next to her. There was sun on his moustache, and it looked as if it had been dipped in oil. Swirsky carried the collection box. He held it carefully, as if it were a baby, and his face when he looked at Ruthie was soft and loving. A crowd of cleaners, cooks, and gardeners gathered across the road. They looked angry.

'I hear you're a poor man, Salisbury,' said Ruthie. 'So I've decided to help you.'

'Yes, Madam,' said Salisbury.

'I hope you're not going to leave him there all day, Mrs Swirsky,' said Mrs Raubenheimer.

Ruthie ignored everyone. 'This box is yours. Take it home with you. Take it back to your family. Take it with my blessings.'

'Yes, Madam,' said Salisbury.

Errol wheeled him home quickly. Salisbury held the box tight to his chest. All over the estate there were servants watching. You could tell the servants were angry because they weren't allowed to have any of the Maundy money. Some of them shouted at Errol as he wheeled Salisbury down Henry Street.

'That's what you get from Africans and Asians,' said my mother. 'That's exactly the sort of thing that led to the Cato Manor Riots. We could be facing more of them. Mark my words.'

Later that night, we were woken by people shouting next door. Tamburlaine the Dobermann began barking. Someone was crying. My father got up and put on his brown woollen dressing-gown. 'Take your hockey stick, Gordon,' said my mother. To me she said, 'Martin, you take the torch. I'm going to call the police.'

We found Maggie and her father trying to lift Salisbury into his red wagon. He was crying and swearing and waving his strong arms about.

'He's as strong as a lion, Gordon,' said Maggie's father. 'Help me. I think Tamburlaine's taken a nip out of him.'

Then Gus Trupshaw arrived and fired several shots. He thought he was using his starting pistol, but it was a flare gun and the sky was like noon for minutes. I could see Salisbury's tears.

'He says somebody has stolen his money,' said Maggie's father. 'People came and robbed him. I let him sleep here last night. I gave him the toolshed to doss down in. In the morning, Errol was going to wheel him to the bus stop. He was going home.'

Salisbury sat in the red tin wagon, rubbing his eyes and crying.

'Lock him in the toolshed,' my father suggested. 'Anything to keep him away from that dog. We'll sort this out in the morning.'

'It's very hard,' said Gus Trupshaw. 'We'll have to replace the money. We'll have a whip round. I just hope Ruthie Swirsky knows what she's done. You can't mess around with Africa.'

But they had reckoned without Salisbury's strong arms.

When they went to the toolshed in the morning, Salisbury was gone. He had torn the door off its hinges. He had levered himself into his little red wagon, and he had vanished.

'Thank heavens for small mercies,' said my mother.

On Good Friday afternoon, Errol found the little tin wagon down by the blue gums. Then a party of men found Salisbury. He was hanging from a branch by his belt. The men made a kind of tent of blankets around him, so that the children shouldn't see.

Ruthie Swirsky waited for the police to come and take Salisbury away. She asked the constable if she might send a little something to his next of kin. The constable laughed at her and said, 'People like Salisbury have no next of kin.' Ruthie Swirsky asked the constable for his number. And he threatened to arrest her.

The police took Salisbury away, and it might have ended there. Except that Ruthie Swirsky found out that he had a brother and a sister in a village sixty miles away. 'This is ridiculous!' said Gus Trupshaw. 'If we had to take responsibility for every soul that dies, where would we be?'

On Easter Saturday, the coffin turned up on the back of Errol the topsoil man's truck. 'Mrs Swirsky, she arranged it,' said Errol.

'She actually believes she's still in Wimbledon,' said my father. But he and Gus Trupshaw offered to drive the coffin back to Salisbury's home village. We all watched as they loaded the coffin on to the back of Gus Trupshaw's new Ford truck. 'If you don't hear from us in a week, send a search party,' said Gus Trupshaw.

'For heaven's sake,' said my mother. 'You're only driving to the other side of Rustenburg. Just explain that you're very sorry about what happened, and don't tell them where you live.'

The men got home at sunset. 'We would've been back earlier,' my father said, grinning. 'But we had a feast with the family. It's tradition. They wanted to thank us for bringing him home.'

'Chicken and rice,' said Gus Trupshaw.

'Quite normal, really,' said my father.

'Normal? My godfathers, Gordon,' said my mother. 'It may be normal to you. But I was worried sick. And there are Easter eggs to be hidden in our garden tonight. The children have waited up while you've been eating chicken and rice.'

You could tell that the men were pleased with themselves. It was as if they had been through some huge adventure at the other end of the world.

'Yes,' said Gus Trupshaw, as though they did such things every day. 'First chicken and rice, and then peaches.'

They came into the kitchen and my mother said to me, 'Your father's been eating chicken, with strangers.'

'Quite normal, really,' said my father again.

My mother held up a hand. 'Please. Not another word. It gives me the heebie-jeebies just thinking about it.'

We were sitting around the house waiting to be sent to bed as soon as our fathers were ready to hide the Easter eggs. They always hid them the night before. On Easter morning, we would go searching for them before the sun was high enough to melt the chocolate. Maggie was saying that dogs always bit black people, because they had different blood.

Sally said, 'But I saw blood on the ground after Tamburlaine bit Salisbury. And it was red. Just like mine.'

'Then why do dogs only bite black people?' Tony asked.

'They don't. Last year, our Aunt Mary got bitten – didn't she? And she's from Kenya,' said Sally. 'Do you know anyone not black who has been bitten, Martin?' Sally wore a dress the colour of apricots. Her shiny yellow hair was held tightly in a blue Alice band. Her brown legs were bare. She had this way of feeding the toes of one foot into the other.

I said, 'I remember Strydom's dog, Attila, bit the postman once.'

'Martin will say anything. Just to please you,' Tony loudly

snapped the elastic in the waistband of his brown boxer shorts. 'Because Martin adores you.'

'Rubbish!' said Sally. 'You don't really adore me, do you, Mart?'

'I don't adore anyone,' I said.

'Oh, yes, Mart. Then why are you blushing?' Maggie asked.

Swirsky arrived on his motorbike with Papas sitting in the sidecar. Papas carried a big cardboard box with 'Sundowner Brandy' written on it. We knew that the box held our Easter eggs, which Papas got wholesale from his cousin in Orange Grove. One Easter, Gus Trupshaw had said he could get eggs much cheaper through a connection in Fordsburg. But my father said Papas would not stand for that. The Greeks were very big on Easter.

Other fathers began arriving. They made a barbecue and stood around the fire, watching the meat sizzling on the old garden sieve my father used for a grill. They drank beer. By about eight o'clock, Papas was singing 'She'll be comin' round the mountain when she comes.' My mother stuck her head out the kitchen window and said, 'Excuse me! May I remind you that there are still children present.'

Gus Trupshaw called back, 'Aye, aye, Captain.'

'Right, that's the last straw,' my mother said, and sent us to bed.

Later, for what seemed like hours, I lay in my dark bedroom listening to the men calling to each other. I heard my father saying, 'Go left, Gus, further left! Dead on target now. That's beautiful.' Then Papas would call out, 'Am I on course, Gordon?' And my father would shout back, 'You're at two o'clock, George. Beautiful. Just hold that position.'

Much later, I grew sleepy and it seemed to me that the men in the garden were not men at all. They were planes and tanks moving across the sand in the desert war in North Africa. While, in the yard next door, Tamburlaine keened and whimpered. His long chain, which had been tied to the steel pole that held the washing line, clashed like the waves of a metal sea.

On Easter morning, we were out in the garden soon after breakfast. Our fathers stood blinking in the early-morning sunshine, rubbing their eyes and yawning. They had not had time to shave. Mr Swirsky brought Ruthie to watch her very first African Easter-egg hunt. She told my mother she would never get used to Easter in autumn. South Africa was all upside down. My mother told her to hang on to her hat. *She'd* been living in South Africa all her life, and there was lots she still was not used to. Swirsky smoothed his moustache with a small, soft white hand. He seemed to be stroking the wings of a special bird. Ruthie wore sunglasses. With her red hair and pale skin, she looked very mysterious. None of us had ever seen anyone in sunglasses.

'Ruthie has sensitive eyes,' Swirsky said proudly. 'Those glasses were specially shipped all the way from England. I kid you not.'

One by one, we set off to find our eggs while the men gave us clues. 'You're ice-cold, Martin! Your right foot's a bit warmer now. Which one is your right foot? Now your knee is getting rather warm. Oh, Martin, your knee is on fire. Can't you feel the heat, boy?'

Swirsky got carried away and tried to take over from my father. He kept shouting out, 'Two o'clock, Martin. Angels at two o'clock!'

When we had all found our chocolate eggs, it was Nicodemus' turn. Nicodemus was our cook and gardener. My father found him in the garage when we moved to Badminton after the war and so we kept him.

'We treat Nicodemus as one of the family,' my mother told Ruth Swirsky. 'At Christmas and Easter, Nicodemus is always included. We don't have to do it. We choose to do it.'

Nicodemus fell on his knees and clapped his hands when my father called him from the kitchen. 'No, no, Nicodemus.' My mother clicked her tongue. 'That's only for Christmas. You have to find your egg in the garden now. Stand up, Nicodemus, and go into the garden.' She explained quietly to Ruthie Swirsky, 'He's a bit touched in the head. Easter must be a real puzzle. Their customs are very different from ours. But I suppose that's something you well understand.'

'You mean, being British?' Ruthie asked.

'Well, that, too,' said my mother.

Nicodemus did not understand the 'hot' and 'cold' directions. He walked about the garden as if he were hunting game. His ears were pricked; his hands were held in little paws in front of his chest. He was very springy on his feet, making little leaps this way and that. He danced across to the rockery. The men shouted, 'You're cold, cold, Nicodemus!' Then he went the other way, and they shouted, 'You're warm, warmer, Nicodemus!' But Nicodemus didn't listen to them. He went back to the rockery and fell on his knees, and my father said, 'Oh God, not another praying session.'

And my ·mother called out, 'Language, Gordon. This is Easter Sunday.'

When Nicodemus got to his feet, he had found something. But it wasn't wrapped in silver paper like the other eggs. It was square and black. Gus Trupshaw said, 'Now, what the hell have you got there, boy?'

'That's my Maundy-money box,' Ruthie said. 'Give it to me, Nicodemus.' She reached her hands for it. But Nicodemus fell on his knees again, smiling hugely and happily, and hugged the black wooden box to his chest.

'Happy, happy,' said Nicodemus.

'Hell's bells!' I heard my father say. 'This could be tricky.'

Ruthie said, in her clear English voice, 'But this is absurd! Someone make him give me my box.'

'He thinks it's finders keepers,' Gus Trupshaw said. 'Nicodemus thinks he was meant to find it.'

'But it doesn't belong to him,' Ruthie said. 'Somebody stole that box from Salisbury. They must have hidden it in your garden. Salisbury did away with himself because he thought he'd never see that money again. And all the time it was a few feet away.' And she began crying.

Swirsky said, 'Don't, sweetie. I'll fix it.' But from the sound of his voice we knew that there was nothing much to be done.

'Strictly speaking,' my mother said when the Swirskys had left, 'that box belongs to St John's Ambulance. It wasn't hers to give away in the first place.'

Nicodemus took the black wooden box to his room. He put it on his table with a photograph cut from a newspaper which showed Mussolini in full-dress uniform. 'Nicodemus is happy,' he told me.

Nobody else was happy. The cooks and cleaners and gardeners from Badminton Estate took to stopping outside our fence and staring. Someone shouted. A stone was thrown. Nicodemus would rush inside when he saw them and hide under his bed.

Then Gus Trupshaw announced that his maid and several other women who had been washing clothes down by the blue gums had been frightened by a vision of Salisbury. Salisbury wore the belt that he'd used to hang himself. He had come back to haunt them, floating above the ground, skimming along the gravel, belt flying from his neck. He had chased the women all the way up Edward Avenue.

'Flying ghosts at Easter!' my mother said. 'What will they think of next? I only hope Ruth Swirsky realises what she's done. Once they get an idea into their heads like this, they don't let go. We'll have the police here. Mark my words.'

In the afternoon, Swirsky arrived and asked to see Nicodemus. Swirsky was wearing a stethoscope and his wife's dark glasses. His chemist's coat was as smooth as an envelope. His moustache was looking oiled again. My mother told him that Nicodemus had locked himself in his room because people were threatening to kill him.

'I intend to fight fire with fire,' said Swirsky. Then he went out to Nicodemus' room and knocked on the door.

When he came back, a long time later, Nicodemus was with him. Swirsky looked pale. His moustache was so black it might have been drawn with charcoal. Somehow, he looked undressed. Nicodemus wore Swirsky's white chemist's coat. He wore Ruthie Swirsky's dark glasses and he had Swirsky's stethoscope around his neck. Nicodemus put the stethoscope to his chest and listened proudly to his heart. 'Boum, boum, boum,' he said.

Swirsky carried the St John's Ambulance box. 'Fair exchange, no robbery,' said Swirsky. 'But he drives a hard bargain, your Nicodemus. If he had a proper chance, he could run the country.'

'Would you please keep your voice down?' my mother asked, smiling, and speaking without moving her lips.

Later that afternoon, Sally came round to my place and said that there was a religious meeting in the blue gums. We ran down the hill to the little frothing river in the thick bank of enormous trees. Errol the topsoil man was there. Gus Trupshaw stopped in his new truck. 'Is this a church parade?' he asked. 'Where's the bally sky pilot?' A crowd of servants waited under the blue gums. Swirsky and his wife arrived in his blue A40. From the back of the car stepped a tall black woman in a red skirt. She was barefoot. She wore great bracelets of beads around her wrists. There were chicken bladders in her hair, like little yellow balloons. There were rows of beads crossed over her chest.

CHRISTOPHER HOPE

Ruthie Swirsky held up her hand for silence. 'This is Ethel,' she pointed to the tall woman. 'Ethel is a *sangoma*. A witch doctor.'

Ethel knelt on the ground. She untied a leather bag that was hanging from her waist. She opened the bag and put it on the ground in front of her. Then she closed her eyes and seemed to go to sleep. With her eyes still closed, she tipped some bones from the bag into her palms and blew on them – a long, loud breath. She threw them in the dirt as if she were throwing dice. Then she opened her eyes and studied the bones. Next she took from under her arm the wooden St John's Ambulance box. Swirsky stepped forward, pulling Salisbury's red wagon. The crowd groaned and shivered when they saw that it still carried the brown paper with which Salisbury had lined the bottom: 'Buy Your Brand-New Zephyr at Dominion Motors.' Ethel shook the collection box. We heard our pennies and sixpences rattling inside. People began clapping softly. Ethel produced a bottle of petrol and a box of matches. In a moment, the box was blazing in the red wagon. No one said a word. We watched until nothing was left but a smell of paint from the red wagon, ashes, and a pile of glowing, smoking coins.

Ethel leaned over and stirred the money to cool it. Everybody was given a piece of money, black from the fire. I got a sixpence. Sally received a shilling. Even Errol the topsoil man got a florin. Examining the scorched money, Swirsky said, 'King George doesn't look too pleased – he's got a black eye.'

Sally said, 'It's like getting coins out of a Christmas pudding.'

Then Ethel, the witch doctor, stepped back into the A40.

'I was very moved,' Ruthie Swirsky told her.

Ethel lit a Mills cigarette and blew smoke at the roof of the car. 'You're welcome,' said Ethel.

'Will Salisbury be happy, Mr Swirsky?' Eric asked.

'We had to make contact,' Swirsky said. 'That's Ethel's real forte. Making contact. Apparently, the wandering spirit needs some form of direction. This way or that? It's a bit like looking for Easter eggs. Colder? Or warmer? We made a special fire so the spirit of Salisbury could warm itself.'

'And the Maundy money I collected was given to the deserving poor. If I'd been allowed to do that in the first place, none of this would have happened,' said Ruthie Swirsky.

210

My mother said, when I showed her my blackened sixpence, 'Don't try and spend it, Martin. Scorched coins are not legal tender. Ask your father.'

Unperformed Experiments Have No Results

JANETTE TURNER HOSPITAL

YOU COULD SAY it began with the man in the canoe rather than with the dream, though I can no longer be certain of the sequence of events. It is possible, after all, that the letter arrived before either the dream or that frail and curious vessel, though I do not think so. I used to be without doubts on this matter. Chronology used not to be even a question. But since the disappearances, trying to catch hold of any kind of certainty has been like catching hold of water.

Sometimes, when a tradesman or a parcel delivery man comes to the door, I have to restrain myself, by a fierce act of the will, from grabbing him by the lapels or by the denim coverall straps and demanding: 'What do accidents mean, do you think? Do you have an opinion? Are you a gambling man? Have you ever been spooked by coincidence?' The truth is, I have become obsessed with the patterns of chance – the neatness of them, the provocation such neatness gives – but chance is a subject that very much resists scrutiny, and the more I ponder random conjunctions of events, the more intensely I try to focus my memory, the hazier things become. You cannot, as the physicists keep telling us, engage in the act of close observation without changing the thing observed. Of course I resort to such analogies because it is Brian who is dying.

Nevertheless, though it may or may not be the first cause, I will start with that afternoon on my dock and with the man

212

in the canoe. It was a late summer afternoon and very humid, and the forecast – for thunderstorms – was sufficient to keep most boats in marinas. There were whitecaps on the lake and the river. When I looked east, I could see the pines on the tip of Howe Island bending like crippled old men in the wind. Westward, past the Spectacles, past Milton Island, I thought I could just see one of the ferries, veiled in great fans of spray, crossing the neck of the lake. Wolfe Island, directly opposite, was invisible, or almost so, behind a billowing indigo cloud that threw the whole head of the river into twilight, although it was only about four o'clock in the afternoon.

I was right at the end of my dock, and I had a book propped on my knees, but the wind kept buffeting my light aluminium deck-chair to such an extent that I began to wonder if it was aerodynamically possible to be lifted up on a gust and dumped into the water. I kept looking up over the page, partly to assess my chances of staying dry, but mostly to enjoy the extravagant theatre of wind and water. And then, startled, I thought I saw a canoe emerging from the bateau channel between Howe Island and the shore.

I'm imagining things, I decided, rubbing my eyes. Who would be so foolhardy on such a day? Or so strong, for that matter. Here, the currents are swift and ruthless. Every summer, bits and pieces of our ageing dock disappear, and end up, no doubt, somewhere round Montreal; every winter the pack-ice brings us splintered paddles and fragments of boats bearing registration marks from Toronto, Niagara, and even, once, from Thunder Bay. I shaded my eyes and squinted. Nothing there.

Wait . . . Yes, there it was again, a canoe, definitely, with a solitary paddler, heading upriver against all this mad seaward-running energy.

It is by no means impossible to paddle upriver – I have done it myself – but even without a headwind it is very hard work and is rarely tried solo. Astonished, I kept my eyes on the paddler. He must have muscles like steel ropes, I thought. His chances of capsizing seemed extraordinarily high. Clearly, he was someone who liked danger, someone who was excited by risk, perhaps even someone who got a certain kick out of pain, or at any rate, out of enduring it. But for how long, I wondered, could his arms take such punishment?

*

Do not undertake anything unless you desire to continue it; for example, do not begin to paddle unless you are inclined to continue paddling. Take from the start the place in the canoe that you wish to keep.

Old advice, three centuries old, but still as sound as when Jean de Brébeuf sent his letter home to Paris full of tips 'for the Fathers of our society who shall be sent to the Hurons'. I always think of them, those French Jesuits, *voyageurs*, when I see a canoe pitching itself against the current. I think of them often, as a matter of fact, since I moved out here on to the river. I keep their *Relations* on my bedside table, I frequently browse through those lively, detailed, sometimes despairing reports to their superiors. Paris, Rome: it must have seemed as uncertain as prayer, dispatching words by ship.

The Relation for 1649 to the General of the Society of Jesus at Rome: I have received, very Reverend Paternity, your letter dated January 20, 1647. If you wrote to us last year, 1648, we have not yet received that letter . . .

With canoes, they had more reliable, more intimate relations.

The Relation for 1637: You must be prompt in embarking and disembarking; and tuck up your gowns so that they will not get wet, and so that you will not carry either water or sand into the canoe. To be properly dressed, you must have your feet and legs bare; while crossing the rapids, you can wear your shoes, and, in the long portages, even your leggings.

I imagine them with their blistered European hands and their cassocks hoisted up around their thighs, paddling full pelt up their *Great River St Lawrence* (they wrote of it with such affectionate possessiveness, with such respect for its stern powers), dipping their paddles toward their deaths, skimming past these very rocks that buttress (and will eventually smash) my dock, heading west with their mad cargo of idealism, dedication, and wrong-headedness.

You must try and eat at daybreak unless you can take your meal with you in the canoe; for the day is very long, if you have to pass it without eating. The Barbarians eat only at Sunrise and Sunset, when they are on their journeys.

*

I could see the flash of the paddle now, knifing into the water, keeping to the right side, pulling closer to shore. His arms are giving out, I thought. He is going to try to beach on this stretch. Now that the canoe was close enough, I could see that it was neither fibre-glass nor aluminium, but birchbark. It wasn't until the next day that I was struck by the oddness of this, and by the fact that I had never seen a bark canoe before, except in photographs and museums. At the time it seemed quite unsurprising, or at least, not significant. I merely noted it, wondering exactly where the canoeist would reach shore, and if he would manage this before capsizing.

And then, gradually, it became clear to me that the paddler had no intention of trying to land. He's crazy, I thought. Shoulders hunched forward, head slightly down, eyes on the prow of his craft, he was bent on defying the current and continuing upriver, parallel to shore and now only about thirty feet out. It seemed incredible. He was all manic energy and obstinacy, and I fancied I could hear the pure high humming note of his will above the general bluster of the wind. His strength, which seemed supernatural, was oddly infectious. It was as though infusions of energy were pumping themselves into my body, as though the paddler's adrenalin was an atmosphere that I inhaled. I couldn't take my eyes off him. *Go, go, go*, I urged, weirdly excited.

It is odd how certain body shapes, certain ways of moving the body, are retained like templates on the memory. So we recognise a voice, a face – we take this as unremarkable – but so also a gesture or a way of walking can be recalled. I could still see only the outline of the figure (though I'd assumed from the start the paddler was male), and he was wearing a hooded windbreaker so that he (or even she) could have been anyone. And yet, watching the way the shoulders lunged forward, the way the arms dug into the water, the sharp thought came to me: *This reminds me of someone. Who is it? Who? Who?*

It was maddening. It was like meeting someone at a party and *knowing* you have met that person before somewhere, but being unable to summon up a name or a context. This sort of incomplete recollection can drive you crazy. The canoe was drawing level with my dock now, and I wished I'd brought my binoculars down. The plunge and lift and dip of the shoulder blades, oh, it was at the tip of my mind, who did that movement remind me of? Now the canoe was level with the end of my dock, but the hooded head kept its eyes resolutely on the prow and the water, the paddle flashed.

Oh please look up, I willed.

And he did.

'Good God!' I cried out, thunderstruck. 'Brian!'

Brian – no, of course, not Brian, I was aware almost instantaneously that it couldn't possibly be Brian, who was either in Australia or Japan – not Brian, then, but the man in the canoe simply sat there, resting his paddle and staring at me, startled, which naturally meant that he scudded back downstream very swiftly. He dug the paddle furiously into the water, dip, dip, dip, until he drew level again, closer this time. He rested his paddle and stared. I felt, as the current again bucked him backwards, that I had to do something potent and instant to stop time unwinding itself, but I could neither speak nor move, the resemblance to Brian was so eerie. I was experiencing something like vertigo, and a pain like angina in my chest.

I was dimly aware that my book had fallen into the water and that I was on my hands and knees on the dock. I watched the canoe draw level a third time, and the paddler and I stared at each other (he was very pale, and there seemed, now, to be no expression at all on his face), and then he, Brian, I mean the man in the birchbark canoe, turned away and lowered his head, and resumed paddling more fiercely than ever.

I watched until he disappeared from sight, which seemed to take hours. I have no idea how long I stayed on my hands and knees. I know that when I tried to climb the steep steps up our cliff, my legs felt like jelly and kept shaking so badly I had to stop and rest several times.

People climbing mountains and cliffs hyper-ventilate, this is common knowledge. They see things. Visitations alight on them.

Between the fiftieth step and the fifty-first, the past distends itself like a balloon, and I climb into it. I can feel its soft sealed walls. *Trapped*, I think. And simultaneously, pleasurably: *home*. I can smell the rainforest, smell Queensland, feel the moist air of the rich sub-tropics again.

Brian is a few feet ahead of me, both of us drenched, both feeling for handholds and footholds, both of us (I realise it now) equally scared, but too proud to admit it.

(This would have been our last year in high school, and this was something we did every year, spend a day in our own bit of rainforest – we thought of it that way – on the outskirts of Brisbane, climbing the waterfall. But our last year in high school was the year of the floods. I think we both gulped a little when we saw the falls, but neither would ever have been the first to back out. We were both given to constant high anxiety, and both temperamentally incapable of backing away from our fears.)

So. Every handhold slips, every foothold is algae-slick. My fingers keep giving way. My heart thumps – thud, thud, thud – against its cage. Delirium, the salt flavour of panic: I can taste them. Just inches above my eyes, I see the tendon in Brian's ankle. If I were to touch it, it would snap. I tilt my head back and see his shoulder blades, corded tight, lift like wings, pause, settle, lift again. He reaches and pulls, reaches and pulls, he is a machine of bodily will. The energy field of his determination – pulses of it, like a kind of white light, bouncing off him – brush against me, charging the air. This keeps me going.

At the top of the falls, we collapse. We lie on the flat wet rocks. We do not speak. Our clothes give off curls of steam that drift up into the canopy, and creepers trail down to meet them. We float into sleep, or perhaps it is merely a long sensuous silence that is sweeter than sleep. I dream of flying. I have languid wings. I can feel updrafts of warm air, like pillows, against my breast feathers.

'Mmm,' I murmur drowsily at last, 'I love this heat. I could lie here for ever. How come the water's so cold, when it's so hot here on the rocks?'

'I'm not even going to answer that, Philippa,' Brian says lazily. 'It's such a dumb question.'

'Piss off,' I say. I inch forward on my stomach and peer over the lip of the falls. I can't believe we have climbed them. I watch the solid column of water smash itself on the rocks below. I feel queasy. I can see four years of high school shredding themselves, all the particles parting, nothing ever the same again. 'Where do you reckon we'll be five years from now?' I ask him. I have to shout. My voice falls down into the rift and loses itself in spray.

Brian crawls across and joins me. Side by side, we stare down ravines and years, high school, adolescence, childhood, we've climbed out of them all. There is just university ahead, and then the unmapped future.

'Where will we end up, d'you reckon?'

217

'Not here,' Brian shouts. 'We won't be in Brisbane.'

'Bet we will. And even if we aren't, we'll come back. Let's do this every year for the rest of our lives.'

'Not me,' Brian says. 'After uni, I'm never coming back.'

The shouting takes too much energy, and we crawl back to the relative hush of the flat rocks ringed with ferns.

'So where will you be?'

'I don't know. Cambridge. Japan, maybe. There's some interesting stuff coming out of Tokyo. Wherever's best for the kind of physics I'm interested in.'

'What if you don't get into Cambridge?' I ask, although I know it's another dumb question. It's like asking: what if you don't get to the top of the falls?

Brian doesn't bother to answer.

'I'll probably still be here,' I say.

'No you won't.'

'You're such a bloody know-it-all, Brian.'

'I know you and me.'

'You think you do.'

'Philippa,' he says irritably, with finality, 'I know us well enough to know we won't stay in Brisbane. You'll end up somewhere extreme, Africa, Canada, somewhere crazy.'

'You're nuts,' I say. 'Anyway, wise guy, wherever I am, you can bet I'm going to stay close to water.'

'Yes,' he says. 'You win that one. We'll both be near water.'

In the dream, I am at the end of my dock, reading, when I notice the most curious light over Wolfe Island. The whole island seems burnished with gold leaf, and there is an extraordinary clarity to things, to individual trees, for instance, as though each detail has been out-lined with a fine-tipped black brush. I can see vines, orchids, staghorn ferns against the tree-trunks. I can see that Wolfe Island has gone tropical, that it is thick with rainforest, that lorikeets and kingfishers are flashing their colours on the St Lawrence banks.

Then I note that there is a suspension bridge, the catwalk kind, with wooden planks and rope sides, the kind sometimes strung a hundred and fifty feet up in the rainforest canopy to allow tourists to see the aerial garden running riot up there. This bridge starts at the end of my dock and crosses the river to Wolfe Island, but it is submerged.

What catches my eye first are the ropes tied to the end of

my dock, just below water level. I lie flat on my stomach and peer down. I can see the arc of the bridge, little seaweed gardens swaying on its planks, curving down and away from me.

There is someone lying on his back on the bridge, or rather floating with it, just above the planks, just below the rope siderails. It is Brian. His eyes are open but unseeing, his skin has the pallor of a drowned man, algae spreads up from his ankles, tiny shell colonies are crusting themselves at all his joints. Seaweed ferns move with him and around him. He looks like Ophelia. *There with fantastic garlands did she come . . .*

'Alas, then,' I say to him, 'are you drowned?'

'Drowned, drowned,' he says.

No one would be too surprised by the fact of my dream. First I see a man in a canoe who reminds me of someone I know, and that very night I dream of Brian. A canoeist in a storm is at risk; I dream of death. There is a simple logic to this sequence of events; anyone would subscribe to it.

Nevertheless, I woke in a state of panic. I woke with the certainty that something was wrong. I hadn't seen Brian for, I had to count back . . . well over a year, it must have been. It was always hit or miss with Brian. Luckily, childhood friends had a slightly better chance of making contact with him than ex-lovers or his ex-wife, but no one alive could compete with the sharp scent of a new hypothesis. I used to picture him literally *living* in his research lab, Melbourne or Tokyo, either city it was the same. I used to imagine a rollaway bed tucked under the computer desk. The last time we met for dinner in Melbourne he said, sometime after midnight:

'My God, the time! I've got to get back to the lab.'

'You sleep there?' I asked sardonically.

'Quite often,' he said.

On principle, Brian never answered his phone, He kept it unplugged (both in his lab, and at the home address he rarely used) except for when he was calling out. I knew this. Nevertheless I called, Melbourne and Tokyo, both, and of course got no answer.

I sent faxes and got no response.

I called the secretary at his research institute in Melbourne. 'Professor Leckie is in Tokyo,' she said, 'but no one has seen him for weeks. We still get his e-mail though, so he's all right.'

E-mail! I never remembered to check mine, I used it so

rarely. I plugged in the modem on my computer, keyed in my password, got into the system, and opened my 'mailbox' on screen.

There was only one message, undated.

Philippa: I'm going away and wanted to say goodbye. Remember the falls? Those were the good old days, weren't they, when nothing could stop us? I often think of you. Of us back then. Pity we can't go backwards. Take care. Brian.

I sent a message back instantly.

Brian, I typed on to my screen. *Had a disturbing dream about you last night. Are you okay? I miss you. Take care. Philippa.*

Back then, on the day of the message on my screen, the order was still beyond question for me. First the man in the canoe, then the dream, then the message. I began to be less confident of this sequence after the letter from my mother in Brisbane. Not immediately, of course. But a few weeks after the letter, I had to make a point of reminding myself that the terrible thunderstorm weather had begun in late August, that my mother's letter was postmarked September, and that I could not anchor (by any external proof) either my dream or my e-mail to a date.

I bumped into Brian's mother in the city last week, my mother wrote. *She says something's the matter with Brian, some nervous system disorder, I think she said, something quite dreadful, there was a Latin-sounding word but I can't remember. She said she flew down to visit him in the Royal Melbourne, and he looked like a skeleton, he'd lost so much weight. He's not taking it well, she said. He's never been able to tolerate any kind of interference with his work, not even his marriage, as you know. She's terribly worried. He refused treatment and checked himself out and flew to Tokyo, can you believe that? You know he used to phone her once a week from wherever he was? Well, he's stopped doing it. She's quite depressed and quite frightened. I thought maybe you could get him to phone her, poor dear. Or maybe you'd like to write to her yourself? She must be awfully lonely since Mr Leckie died. We thought perhaps we should invite her for Christmas, but it's hard to tell whether she'd enjoy this or not. Maybe you should write to her, Philippa. You know her much better than we do.*

Every day I would begin a letter in my mind.

Dear Mrs Leckie: Remember when Brian and I used to go on rainforest treks and get home hours later than we planned? You used to worry yourself sick, and my parents too. But we always did show

up, remember? Brian's just off on another trek, he's lost track of time,
that's all . . .

No. Begin again.

Dear Mrs Leckie: Brian's gone on a journey, as we always knew
he would, from which (both you and I have a hunch about this) he
might not return. He carries everything he needs inside his head, and
always has. In his own way, he misses us. I promise I'll visit when
I'm in Brisbane next year. How is your frangipani tree? Remember
when Brian and I . . . ?

I never sent these unwritten letters.

I began to ask myself whether I'd imagined the man in the
canoe. Or whether I'd dreamed him. Or whether I'd dreamed
the e-mail message which had vanished into electronic ether
without a trace.

For my night-time reading, I followed records of lost trails.
The Relation of 1673, for example, written by Father Claude
Dablon:

> *He had long premeditated this undertaking, influenced by a most*
> *ardent desire to extend the kingdom of knowledge . . . he has the*
> *Courage to dread nothing where everything is to be Feared . . . and*
> *if, having passed through a thousand dangers, he had not unfortunately*
> *been wrecked in the very harbour, his Canoe having been upset below*
> *sault St Louys, near Montreal . . .*

In Brisbane (two years ago? three?), on the verandah of the
Regatta Hotel, a mere stone's throw from the university, a jug
of beer between us, Brian said: 'D'you ever get panic attacks
that you'll burn up all your energy before you get there?'

'Get where?' I asked.

'I shouldn't even answer that, Philippa. God, you can be
annoying,' Brian said. 'Get to where you wanted to go.'

I couldn't concentrate. I stared across Coronation Drive at
the Brisbane River. I could never quite believe that the present
had inched forward from the past. 'Look at those barges,' I
said. 'I bet they haven't replaced them since we were students.
They're decrepit, it's a miracle they're still afloat. I could swear
even the graffiti hasn't changed.'

'It hasn't,' Brian said. 'We come back younger because
we're in orbit, that's all. Brisbane gets older, we get younger.
A clock on a spaceship moves slower than clocks on earth,
don't you know that, Philippa? If we went on a journey to

Canopus, a few light-years out, a few back, we'd come back younger than our great-great-grandchildren. Got that? And we've moved light-years from Brisbane, haven't we? So it figures. The trouble with you arty types is you don't know your relativity ABCs.'

Dear Mrs Leckie, I could write. *Brian's in orbit. He's simply on a different timetrack, it's all relative. We could go backwards, and swing on your front gate again. We could unclimb the waterfall. We could go back through the looking-glass and watch the future before it came.*

I sent out daily e-mail messages to Brian's number. *Past calling the future,* I signalled. *Brisbane calling Far Traveller. Please send back bulletins. I miss you. P.*

I tried to goad him into verbal duelling: *Which clocktime are you travelling on? Please report light-year deviation from Greenwich Mean.*

Every day I checked my 'box'. There was nothing.

I called Brian's secretary in Melbourne again. 'When you said you were still getting his e-mail,' I asked, 'how often did you mean? And where is it coming from?'

'You never know where e-mail is coming from,' his secretary said. 'Actually, we haven't had any for several weeks, but that's not so unusual for him. Once he went silent for months. When he gets obsessed with a new theory . . .'

'How long has he been ill?' I ask.

'I didn't know he was ill,' she said. 'But it doesn't surprise me. We're always half expecting all our researchers to drop dead from heart attacks. They're all so driven.'

I think of the last time I saw him, in Melbourne. 'Why don't you slow down a bit?' I asked. 'How many more prizes do you have to win, for God's sake?'

'Prizes!' He was full of contempt. 'It's got nothing to do with prizes. Honestly, Philippa, you exasperate me sometimes.'

'What's it got to do with then?'

'It's got to do with getting where I want to go.' I could hear our beer glasses rattling a little on the table. I think it was his heartbeat bumping things. He couldn't keep still. His fingers drummed a tattoo, his feet tapped to a manic tune. 'I'm running out of time,' he said. I would have to describe the expression on his face at that moment as one of anguish.

'You frighten me sometimes, Brian. Sometimes, it's exhausting just being with you.'

Brian laughed. 'Look who's talking.'

'Compared to you, I'm a drifter. Wouldn't it be, you know, more *efficient*, if you just, even just a little, slowed down?'

'When I slow down,' he said, 'you'll know I'm dead.'

Between the soup and the main course of a dinner party, my mind elsewhere, I heard these words: *that birchbark canoe that washed up* . . . and *police inquiries* . . .

I had a peppermill in my hand at the time, and I ground it slowly over my salad. I took careful note of the sharp pleasing contrast made by cracked peppercorn against green leaf. I looked discreetly around the table. Who had spoken the words? *Had* they been spoken?

I could hear Brian say irritably: 'Honestly, Philippa, you never *verify* things. You live inside this vague world of your mind, you make things up, and then you believe they're real.'

'But so do you. You make up a theory, and then you set out to prove it's real.'

'*There*'s the crucial difference,' he says. 'My hypotheses are verifiable, one way or the other. I chase details, I nail them down. I won't stop until my theory is either proved or *dis*proved. If I can't do either, I have to discard it.'

'Same with me,' I say. 'I put riddles on one side, and come back to them. I do realise the birchbark canoe could have been a figment of my mind and my bedtime reading. I'm checking around. What's the difference?'

'I'm not even going to answer that question,' Brian says.

'But don't you ever come back to your discards?'

'Of course I do. Some problem-sets have been passed on for generations. The trick is, you have to approach from a new angle every time. Half the battle is how you frame the question. Unperformed experiments have no results.'

'Exactly,' I say.

And over the candles on a dinner table at the other end of the world, I hazarded cautiously, flippantly: 'Did someone just say something about a birchbark canoe, or did I imagine it?'

Seven pairs of eyes stared at me.

'Sometimes, Philippa,' my husband joked, 'I swear you put one part of your mind on automatic pilot, and the other part is God knows where.'

'It's true,' I said disarmingly. 'So did I hear something about a birchbark canoe, or didn't I?'

'The one washed up on the ferry dock,' one of the guests said. She waved a ringed hand and smiled, courteously tolerant. ('Bit of a flake, isn't she?' I could imagine her saying to someone later. 'Where *does* she get to, between the crackers and the cheese?') 'The one the police are making enquiries about. I was just telling everyone that I'd had to go down to the station and make a statement. And John did too, didn't you, John? Didn't you see him? Yes, I thought so, I was talking to Milly on the phone. So that makes two of us. I mean, who saw the canoe when there was someone in it. Paddling.'

'I saw him several times, as a matter of fact,' John said. 'Came within ten feet of my boat once, when I was fishing. I waved – well, it's customary – but he didn't wave back. Funny, I only ever saw him paddling upriver. Beautiful canoe.'

'The Burketts,' someone else said, 'the ones who live on Howe Island, you know? – they said there was a hunter camped there most of July and August. No one knew where he was from, and no one was very happy about it, but that's who it must have been. I mean, they said he had a birchbark canoe and it's not as though you see them every day. And then he just up and disappeared. The Burketts gave the police a full description and they're putting out a trace, you know, for next of kin.'

'I expect they'll find the body eventually,' John said. 'I wouldn't mind buying the canoe, she was a real beauty. I suppose she'll go up on police auction sooner or later.'

'Won't they have to hang on to it as evidence until the body is found?' someone asked.

'I expect so,' John said. 'Yes, I expect so. Still, sooner or later. The police boats are out dragging every day.'

'I hope they don't find him,' I said.

Everyone looked at me.

Sooner or later, I think, evidence of one kind or another will cast itself up: a dream, a letter, an item in the newspaper. Every day, I read the 'Police and Fire Watch' column in the local paper. Every day, I am relieved that no body has been found. Of course this is ridiculous, and I know it. There's a name for it: *sympathetic magic*.

And there's that other matter too, for which Brian had a word: *synchronicities*.

*

What do they mean? I ask myself. What do they *mean*? In the evenings, I read of doomed voyages.

> *The Relation of Christophe Regnaut concerning the martyrdom and blessed death of Father de Brébeuf . . . captured on the 16th day of March, in the morning, with Father Lalemant, in the year 1649. Father de Brébeuf died the same day as his capture, about 4 o'clock in the afternoon . . . I saw and touched the top of his scalped head . . .*

> *The Relation of 1702: Father Bineteau died there from exhaustion; but if he had had a few drops of Spanish wine, for which he asked us during his last illness . . . or had we been able to procure some fresh food for him, he would perhaps be still alive. Father Pinet and Father Marest are wearing out their strength; and they are two saints, who take pleasure in being deprived of everything . . . For my part I am in good health, but I have no cassock . . . I am in a sorry plight, and the others are hardly less so . . .*

I read also of survival against all odds.

> *The Relation of the First Voyage made by Father Marquette toward New Mexico in 1673: . . . his Canoe having been upset below the sault, where he lost both his men and his papers, and whence he escaped only by a sort of Miracle . . .*

I check my e-mail every day, I send out messages, I wait. I spin theories and discard them. I shuffle sequences as I might shuffle a pack of cards.

The joker comes up every time. Any riddles for recycling? he grins. Any letters for uncertain destinations? Any unperformed experiments to go?

I'm not even going to answer, I say.

Sisters

COLUM McCANN

I HAVE COME to think of our lives as the colours of that place – hers a piece of bog cotton, mine as black as the water found when men slash too deep in the soil with a shovel.

I remember, when I was fifteen, cycling across those bogs in the early evenings, on my way to the dance-hall in my clean, yellow socks. My sister stayed at home. I tried to avoid puddles but there would always be a splash or two on the back of my dress. Boys at the dance-hall wore blue anoraks and watched me when I danced. Outside they leaned against my bike and smoked shared cigarettes in the night. I gave myself. One of them, once, left an Easter lily in the basket. Later it was men in granite-grey suits who would lean into me, heads cocked sideways like hawks, eyes closed. Sometimes I would hold my hands out beyond their shoulders and pretend that I could shape or carve something out of my hand, something that had eyes and a face, someone very little, within my hand, whose job it was to somehow understand.

A man with a walrus moustache gone grey at the tips took me down to the public lavatories in Castlebar. He was a sailor. He smelled of ropes and disuse and seaport harridans. There were bays and coverts, hillsides and heather in that place. Between a statue of Our Lady and a Celtic cross commemorating the dead of Ireland, my hand made out the shape of a question mark as a farm boy furrowed his way inside me. My promiscuity was my autograph. I was hourglassy, had turf-coloured hair and eyes green as wine bottles. Someone once bought me an ice-cream cone in Achill Island, then we chipped some amethyst out of the rockbanks, and we climbed the radio tower, then woke up, late, at the edge of a cliff, with the waves lashing in from the Atlantic. There was a moon of white in that water. The next day my father, at the dinner table, told us that John F. Kennedy had landed a man on the moon. It was a shame, he said looking at me, that it had turned out to be heap of ash. My legs were stronger and I strolled to the dance-hall now, aware, the bogs around me wet and dark. The boy with Easter lilies tried it again, this time with nasturtiums stolen from outside the police station. My body continued to go out and around in all the right places. My father waited up late and smoked Woodbines down to the quick. He told me once that he had overheard a man at his printing shop call me 'a wee whore' and I heard him weeping as I tuned in Radio Luxemburg in my room.

My older sister, Brigid, succeeded with a spectacular anorexia. After classes she would sidle off into the bog, to a large rock where nobody could see her, her school sandwiches in her skirt, her Bible in her hand. There she would perch on her feet like a raked robin, and bit by bit she would tear up the bread, like a sacrament, and throw it all around her. The rock had a history – in penal times it had been used as meeting place for mass. I sometimes watched her from a distance. She was a house of bones, my sister throwing her bread away. Once, out on the rock, I saw her take my father's pliers to her fingers and slowly pluck out the nail from the middle of her left hand. She did it because she heard that it was what the Cromwellians had done to the harpists in the seventeenth century, so they could no longer pluck the cat-gut to make music. She wanted to know how it felt. Her finger bled for days. She told our father that she had caught her hand in a school door. He stayed unaware of Brigid's condition, still caught in the oblivion caused, many years before, by the death of our mother – lifted from a cliff by a light wind while out strolling. Since that day Brigid had lived a strange sort of martyrdom. People loved her frail whiteness, but never really knew what was going on under all those sweaters. She never went to the dance-hall. She, naturally, wore the brown school socks that the nuns made obligatory. Her legs within them were thin as twigs. We seldom talked. I never tried. I envied her that unused body that needed so little, yet I also loved her with a bitterness that only sisters can have.

Now, two decades later, in the boot of a car, huddled, squashed, under a blanket, I ask myself why I am smuggling myself across the Canadian border to go into a country that never allowed me to stay, to see a sister I never really knew in the first place?

It is dark and cramped and hollow and black in here. My knees are up against my breasts. Exhaust fumes cough on up. A cold wind whistles in. We are probably still in the province of Quebec. At every traffic light I have hoped that this is the border station, leading into Maine. Perhaps when we're finally across we will stop by a frozen lake, and skim and slide for a long time, out there on the ice, Michael and I. Or maybe not.

When I asked Michael to help smuggle me across the border from Canada he didn't hesitate. He liked the idea of being what the Mexicans call a 'coyote'. It goes, he said, somewhat with his Navajo blood, his forefathers believing that coyotes were the songdogs that howled in the beginning of the universe. Knowing the reputation of my youth, he joked that I could never have believed in that legend, that I must go in for the Big Bang. In the rear of the car I laugh and shudder in the cold. I wear a blue wool hat pulled down over my ears. My body does not sandwich up the way it used to.

I met Michael on a Greyhound bus in the early Seventies not long after leaving the bogs. I had left Brigid at home with her platefuls of food. My father had hugged and cradled me like his last cigarette at Shannon Airport. On the plane I realised that I was gone forever to a new country – I was tired of the knowing way that women back home had nodded their heads at me. I was on my way to San Francisco, wearing a string of beads. In the bus station at Port Authority I noticed Michael first for his menacing darkness, the way his skin looked like it had been dipped into hot molasses. And then I noticed the necklace of teeth that hung over his chest. I learned later that they were mountain-lion teeth. He had found the lion one afternoon on the outskirts of a wilderness area in Idaho, the victim of a road kill. He came and sat beside me, saying nothing, smelling faintly of woodsmoke. His face was aquiline, acned. His wrists were thick. He wore a leather waistcoat, jeans, boots. Later I leaned my head on his shoulder, feigning sleep, and my hand reached over and played with the necklace of teeth. He laughed when I blew on them and I said they sounded like wind chimes, rattling together, though they didn't sound anything faintly like that.

We rattled across a huge America. I lived with him for many years on Delores Street, near the Mission, the foghorn of the Golden Gate keening a lament, up until the raid. And after the raid, in 1978, when I was gone and home in Ireland, I would never again sleep with another man.

Once more the car shudders to a halt. My head lolls against the lid of the boot. I would rather hack through a pillar of stone with a pin than ever go through this again. This is dangerous. There is a huge illegal trade going on with cigarettes and alcohol between these two borders. We could be caught. Michael wanted to take me across by floating canoes down the Kennebec River. Something in his eyes had coffined downwards when I had said I would rather just do it in the boot of a car. Now I wish different. 'Up a lazy river with a robin song, it's a lazy lazy river we can float along, blue skies up above everyone's in love . . .' My father had sung that when Brigid and I were very young.

The car pitched forward slowly. I wonder if we are finally there, or if this is just another traffic light in a town along the way. We stay stopped and then we inch up. I wonder what plays in Michael's head. I was shocked when I saw him first, just three days ago, because he still looked much the same after thirteen years. I was ashamed of myself. I felt dowdy and grey. When I went to sleep on his sofa bed, alone, I remembered the new creases on the back of my thighs. Now I feel more his equal. He has cut his hair and put on a suit to lessen the risk of interrogation – giving him some of the time that I have found, or lost, I don't know which.

A muffle of voices. I curl my self deeper into a ball and press my face against cold metal. If the border patrol asks to examine his luggage I am gone once again, I am history come the full circle. But I hear the sound of a hand slapping twice on the roof of the car, a grind of gears, a jolt forward, and we are within moments, in America, the country, as someone once said, that God gave to Cain. A few moments down the road I hear Michael whoop and roar and laugh.

'Greetings,' he shouts, 'from the sebaceous glands. I'll have you out of there in a few minutes, Sheona.'

His voice is muffled and my toes are frozen.

On an August night in 1978 I clocked off my job as a singing waitress in a bar down on Geary Street. Wearing an old wedding dress I had bought in a pawn shop, hair let loose, yellow socks on – they were always my trademark – I got into our old Ford pick-up with the purple hubcaps and drove up the coast. Michael was up, for a weekend, in a cabin somewhere north of Mendicino, helping bring in a crop of California's best. Across the bridge where the hell–divers swooped, into Sausalito, around by Mount Tamalpais, where I flung a few cigarette butts in the wind to the ghosts of Jack Kerouac and John Muir, up along the coast, the sun rising like a dirty red aspirin over the sea, I kept steady to the white lines, those on the dashboard and those on the road. The morning had cracked well when I turned up the Russian River and followed the directions Michael had written on the back of a dollar bill.

The cabin was up a drunken mountain road, parts of old motorbikes perched on by cats, straggles of orange crates, pieces of a windmill, tatters of wild berries and sunlight streaming in shafts through sequoias. Michael and his friends met me with guns slung down by their waists. There had been no guns on Mayo, just schoolgirl rumours of an IRA man who lived in a boghole about a mile from Brigid's rock. They scared me, the guns. I asked Michael to tuck his away. Late that evening, when all the others had gone with a truckload of dope, I asked him if we could spend a moment together. I wanted to get away from the guns. I got them, though. Four hours later, naked on the side of a creek, I was quoting Kavanagh for some reason, 'leafy with love-banks, the green waters of the canal . . .' when I looked up beyond his shoulder at four cops, guns cocked, laughing. They forced Michael to bend over and shoved a branch of tree up his anus. They tried to take me, these new hawks, eyes open, and eventually they did. Four in a row. This time my eyes closed, arms and hands to the ground, nothing to watch me from my fingerhouse.

Five days later, taking the simple way out – a lean, young lawyer in a white fedora had begun to take an interest in my case – they deported me for not having a green card. Past the Beniano Bufano 'Peace' statue – the mosaic face of all races – at San Francisco International, handcuffed, they escorted me to JFK on to an Aer Lingus Boeing 747. I flung my beads down into the toilet.

Michael is lifting me from the boot. He swirls me around in his arms, in the middle of a Maine dirt road. It is pitch black, but I can almost smell, in the swirl, the lakes and the fir trees, the clean snow that nestles upon branches. A winter Orion thrusts his sword after Taurus in the sky. 'That might be a ghost,' I whisper to Michael, and he stops his dance, questioning. 'I mean, the light hitting our eyes from those stars left millions of years ago. It just might be that the thing is a ghost, already imploded. A supernova.'

'The only thing I know about the stars is that they come out at night,' he says. 'My grandfather sometimes sat in a chair outside our house and compared them to my grandmother's teeth.'

I laugh and lean into him. He looks around at the sky.

'Teach me some more scientific wonders,' he says.

I babble about the notion that if we could travel faster than the speed of light we would get to a place we never really wanted to go before we even left. He looks at me quizzically, puts his finger on my lips, walks me to the car and lays me down gently into the front seat, saying: 'Your sister.'

He takes off his tie, wraps it around his head like a bandanna, feels for a moment for his gone ponytail, turns up the stereo, and we drive towards New York.

I had seen my sister one day in Dublin, outside the Dawson Lounge. I suppose her new convent clothes suited her well. Black to hide the thinness. Muttering prayers as she walked. The hair had grown thick on her hands and her cheekbones were sculleried away in her head. I followed behind her, up around St Stephen's Green, and on down toward the Dáil. She shuffled her shoes meticulously, never lifting them very high off the ground. She stopped at the gate of the Dáil where a group of homeless families sat protesting their destitution, flapping their arms like hummingbirds to keep themselves warm. It was Christmas Eve. She talked with a few of them for a moment, then took out a blanket and sat down among them. It shocked me, from the other side of the street, to see her laugh and to watch a small girl leap into her lap. I walked away, bought a loaf of bread, and threw it to the ducks in the Green. A boy in Doc Martens didn't smile at me and I thought of a dance-hall.

'None of these coins have our birthdates on them any more,' I say as I search in my handbag for some money for a toll booth.

'I enjoyed that back there,' he says. 'The danger. Hell of a lot better than hanging from a scaffold. Hey, you should have seen the face of the border patrol guy. Waved me through without a flinch.'

'You think we just get older and then we . . .?'

'Look, Sheona, you know the saying.'

'What saying?'

'A woman is as old as she feels.' Then he chuckles. 'And a man is as old as the woman he feels.'

'Very funny.'

'I'm only kidding,' he says.

'I'm sorry, Mike. I'm just nervous.'

I lean back in the seat and watch him. In his six years of prison notes there is one I remember now the most. 'I wouldn't mind dying in the desert with you, Sheona,' he had written. 'We could both lick the dew off of rocks, then lie in the sun, watch it, let it blind us. Dig two holes and piss in them. Put a tin can in the bottom. Cover the hole with a piece of plastic and weigh down the centre with a rock. The sun'll purify it, let it gather in droplets on the plastic, where it'll run towards the centre, then drop in the tin can, making water. After a day we can drink from each other's bodies. Then let the buzzards come down from the thermals. I hate being away from you. I am dead already.'

The day I received that letter I thought of quitting my secretarial job in a glass tower down by Kavanagh's canals. I thought of going back to Mayo and striking a shovel into a boghole, seeping down into the water, breathing out the rest of my life through a hollow piece of reed grass. But I never quit my job and I never wrote back to him. The thought of that sort of death was way too beautiful.

Days in Dublin were derelict and ordinary. A flat on Appian Way near enough to Raglan Road, where my own dark hair weaved a snare. Thirteen years somehow slipped away, like they do, not even autumn foliage now, but manured delicately into my skin. I watched, unseen as a road sweeper in Temple Bar whistled like he had a bird in his throat. I began to notice cranes leapfrogging across the sky-line. Dublin was cosmopolitan now. A drug addict in a doorway on Leeson Street shocked me when I saw him ferret in his bowels for a small bag of cocaine. The canals carried fabulously coloured litter. The postman asked me if I was lonely. I went to Torremolinos in 1985 and watched girls, whose age I should have been, get knocked up in alleyways.

But I didn't miss the men. I bought saucepans, cooked beautiful food, wrote poems by a single-bar electric heater. Once I even went out with a policeman from Donegal, but when he lifted my skirt I knocked his glasses off. At work, in a ribboned blouse, I was so fabulously unhappy that I didn't switch jobs, always breaking my fingernails on the phone slots. I watched a harpist in the Concert Hall, playing beautifully on nylon strings. In a fit of daring I tried to find my sister exactly two years to the day that I had seen her, huddled with the homeless in a Foxford blanket. 'Sister Brigid,' I was told, 'is spreading the word of God in Central America.' I didn't have the nerve to ask for the address. All I knew of Central America was dogs leaner then her.

We are off the highway now, the darkness being bled into by the sun in the east, looking for a New Hampshire petrol station. Michael refuses to go to the ones that lick the big interstate. He prefers a smaller town. That is still him. That is still the man who now has a necklace of mountain-lion teeth hanging over an open-necked Oxford. Because I trust him now, because he still believes in simpler, more honest things, I tell him about why I think Brigid is sick. I am very simple in my ideas of Central America. My philosophy comes from newspapers. She is sick, I tell him, because she was heartbroken amongst maguey. She is sick because there are soldiers on the outskirts of town who carry either Kalashnikovs or Ak–47s, hammering the barrels through the brick kilns that make the dough rise. She is sick because she saw things that she thought belonged only to Irish history. She is sick because there is a girl with a bony hand who wanted to be like her and there was no such thing as a miracle to be found. She is sick, she is in an infirmary convent on Long Island for nuns who have, or have not, done their jobs. Though really, honestly, she is sick, I think because she knew I was watching when she flung her bread from a rock, and I flung mine into a pond, shamed by a boy in red boots, and I never said a word.

'You're too hard on yourself,' says Michael.

'I've been hacking through a stone with a pin.'

'What does that mean?'

'Oh come on, Michael, it's not as if we're twenty-one any more. All those years spat away.'

'It doesn't help to be bitter,' he says.

'Oh, and you're not bitter?'

'I've learned not to think about it.'

'That's worse than being bitter, Michael.'

'Come on,' he says, reaching across to take my hand. 'You can't change the past.'

'No, we can't,' I say. My hand is limp. 'We can't, can we?'

Embarrassed at my anger I tell him once again, for the umpteenth time over the last three days, about how I found out where she was. I decided, only a week ago, to go back and see my father and bring him a carton of Major, because I couldn't find Woodbines. I have no idea what stirred me to see him, except that one of the other secretaries in Dublin had talked all morning long about her pet collie dog throwing up all over her favourite rug and she was actually weeping over it, more for the rug, I imagined, than for the dog. I walked out to the canals and sat watching boys diving in, breaking up the oily slime. Their bravery astounded me. I went to Heuston Station and took a train west.

He was dead, of course. The couple who had bought our old bungalow had three babies now. They said that they had been with my father in a hospital in Galway where, in an oxygen tent, he asked for a nip of Bushmill's and a smoke. The doctors had told him that he would explode and he had said, 'That's grand, give me a smoke, so.' The husband who asked who I was knew exactly who I was, even though I didn't want him to bring out nasturtiums or Easter lilies. I told him, in front of his wife, that I was a distant cousin. In a whisper, at the gate, he told me that he had heard that Brigid was sick and was living now in a convent in the Big Apple. He said the words as if he had just peeled the skin off, then he stole a furtive kiss on my cheek. I wiped it off in disgust, went home to Dublin and made phone calls until I found Michael, a building-site foreman, living in Quebec.

'Michael, I need to get back in. I can get a flight from London into Canada, no hassle.'

'I'll pick you up at the airport in Montreal.'

'Are you married?' I asked.

'Are you kidding?' Are you?'

'Are you kidding?' I laughed. 'Will you take me there?'

'Yeah.'

It's one highway, 95, all the way, a torrent of petrol stations, neon, motels, fast-food spires. Michael talks of a different world, beyond this, where the sun fell and rose and fell again. San Quentin had taught him of windows within walls. The day he got out, in a suit two sizes too big, he learned how to cartwheel again and ended up tearing the polyester knees. He took a bus to Yosemite and got a job as a guide. When my letters stopped coming he had taken a motorbike, a 'riceburner' he called it, from California to Gallup, New Mexico, where his mother and father pissed away a monthly government cheque into a dry creekbed at the back of their house. Michael slept in a shed full of Thunderbird bottles, a hole in the corrugated ceiling where he watched the stars, bitterly following their roll across the sky. He followed the roll. He walked scaffolds to build New York City high-rises. Indian climbers were in big demand for that type of job and the money was good.

Then there was a girl. She brought him to Quebec. They climbed frozen waterfalls in a northern forest. The girl was long gone, but the waterfalls weren't. Maybe, he says, when we get back to Quebec he'll put me in a harness and spiked boots and we'll climb. I finger my thighs and say perhaps.

Floods of neon rushing by.

We stop in a diner and a trucker offers Michael ten dollars for the lion-tooth necklace. Michael tells him that it's a family heirloom and, trying to make sure that I don't hear – me, in my red-crocheted cardigan and grey skirt – the trucker offers him a bag full of pills. Michael still has that sort of face. It's been years since I've been wired and I have a faint urge to drop some pills. But Michael thanks the trucker, says he hasn't done speed in years and we drive away.

By late evening, the next day, we snarl into the New York city traffic and head down towards the Village. Michael's eyes are creased and tired. The car is littered with coffee cups and the smell of cigarettes lingers in our clothes. The city is much like any other to me now, a clog of people and cars. It seems appropriate that there is no room for us in the Chelsea Hotel, no more Dylan, no more Behan, no more Cohen remembering us well when we were famous and our hearts were legends. We stay with an old friend of Michael's on Bleeker Street. I have brought two nightdresses in my suitcase. My greatest daring is that I don't wear either of them. Michael and his friend curl on the ends of the sofa. I sleep in a bed, scared of the sheets. Four hawks in badges grunting down from the thermals, red-beaked, by a gentle creek in sequoia sunlight. A bouquet of boys shimmy in from the bogs and glare in brown tweed hats and pants tucked with silver bicycle clips. My father lights a carton of cigarettes and burns in a plastic tent, watching. A nun runs around with dough rising up in her belly. My wrists pinned to pine needles, no light wind to carry me away. Blood running down the backs of his thighs. The talons of a robin carrying flowers off, I toss

235

and turn in sweat that gathers in folds and it is not until Michael finally comes over and kisses my eyelids that I find sleep.

On the drive out to Long Island I buy a bunch of daffodils from a street-corner vendor. He tells me that daffodils mean marriage. I tell him that they're for a nun. He tugs at his hat. 'You never know, hon,' he says. 'You never know these days.'

Michael still gropes for the back of his hair as he drives and every now and then squeezes my forearm and says it'll be all right. The expressway is a vomit of cars but gradually, as we move, the traffic thins out and the pace slows. Occasional flecks of snow get flicked away by the windscreen wipers. I curl into a shell and listen to the sound of what might be waves, remembering a man who perhaps sucked on a reed in a boghole, there to claim his own. I am older now. I have no right to be afraid. I think about plucking the petals from the flowers, one by one. We drive towards the ocean. Far off I can see gulls arguing over the waves. Perhaps they have come from where I have.

The convent, at Bluepoint, looks like a school. There seems little holy about the place except for the statue of Our Lady on the front lawn, a coat of snow on her shoulders. We park the car and I ask Michael to wait. Under his shirt collar I flick out the necklace of teeth and, for the first time since I've seen him, kiss him flush on the lips. 'Go on,' he says, 'don't be getting soppy on me now. And don't stay too long. Those waterfalls in Quebec melt very easily.'

He turns the stereo up full blast on a classical music station and I walk towards the front entrance. Hold. Buckle. Swallow. The words of a poet who should have known: 'What I do is me. For that I came.' I rasp my fingers along the wood but it takes a long time for the heavy door to swing open.

'Yes dear?' says the old nun. She is Irish too, her face creased into dun and purple lines.

'I'd like to see Brigid O'Dwyer.'

She looks at me, scans my face. 'No visitors, I'm sorry,' she says. 'Sister Brigid needs just a wee bit of peace and quiet.' She begins to close the door, smiling gently at me.

'*Is mise a dhreifeur*,' I stutter. The door opens again and she looks at me, askance.

'*Bhfuil tu cinnte*.'

'*Sea*.' I laugh. '*Taim cinnte*.'

'*Cad a bhfuil uait?*' she asks.

'I want to see her, *Se do thoil e*.'

She stares at me for a long time. '*Tar isteach*. Come on, girl.' She takes the daffodils and touches my cheek. 'You have her eyes.'

I move into the corridor where some other old nuns gather like moss, asking questions. 'She's very sick,' says one. 'She won't be seeing anyone.' The nun who met me at the door shuffles away. There are flowers by the doorway, paintings on the walls, a smell of potpourri, a quality of whiteness flooding all the colours. I sit in a steel chair with my knees nailed together, my hands in my lap, watching their faces, hearing the sombre chatter, not responding. A statue of the madonna stares at me. I am a teenager now in a brown school skirt. These are the women amongst whom I flagrantly rode my bicycle to the dance-hall. After *camogie*, in the showers, one or two of them would stand around and watch us. They had seen bruises on my inner thigh and told me about Magdalene. I run now from the school gates. I see her there, on the rock, sucking her finger, making a cross of reeds, the emblem of the saint for whom she was named. Michael walks, sucking the dew off desert rocks. My father puts some peat on the fire. That's grand, give me a smoke, so.

'Will you join us for a cup? She's sleeping now.' It's the old nun who had answered the door.

'Thank you, sister.'

'You look white, dear.'

'I've been travelling a long time.'

Over tea and scones they begin to melt, these women. They surprise me with their cackle and their smiles. They become carragheen, asking of the gone place. Brigid, they say. What a character. Was she always like that? The holy spirit up to the ears?

Two nuns there had spent the last few years with her. They tell me that she has been living in El Salvador in a convent outside a coffee plantation. One day recently three other nuns in the convent were shot, one of them almost fatally, so Brigid slipped out to a mountain for a few hours to pray for their health. She was found three days later, pinned to a rock. They look at me curiously when I ask about her fingernails. No, they say, her fingernails were fine. It was the lack of food that did it to her. Five campesinos had carried her down from the mountain. She was a favourite among the locals. She had always taken her food to the women of the adobe houses, and the men had respected her for the way she had hidden it under her clothes, so that they wouldn't be shamed by charity. She'd spent a couple of weeks in a hospital in San Salvador, on an intravenous drip, then they transported her to Long Island to recover. She had never talked of any brothers or sisters, though she had got letters from Ireland. She did some of the strangest things in Central America, however. She carried a pebble in her mouth. It was all the way from the Saragossa Sea. She had learned how to dance. She reared four piglets behind the sacristy in the local church. She had shown people how to skin rabbits. The pebble had made little chips in her teeth. She had taken to wearing some very strange colours of socks.

I start to laugh.

'Everyone,' says one of the nuns in a Spanish accent, 'is allowed a little bit of madness, even if you're a nun. I don't see what's wrong with that.'

'No, no, no, there's nothing wrong with it, I'm just thinking.'

'It does get cold down there, you know,' she replies.

Someone wheezes about the time she burnt the pinto beans. The time the pigs got loose from the pen. The time the rabbit ran away from her. Another says she once dropped a piece of cake from her dress when she knelt at the altar and one of the priests, from Wales, said that God gave his only begotten bun. But the priest was forgiven for the joke since he was not a blasphemer, just a bit of a clown. The gardener comes in, a man from Sligo, and says: 'I've seen more fat on a butcher's knife than I have on your sister.' I leave the raisins on the side of the saucer. I am still laughing.

'Can I see her?' I say, turning to the nun who opened the door for me. 'I really need to see her. I have a friend waiting for me outside and I must go soon.'

The nun shuffles off to the kitchen. I wait. I think of a piece of turf and the way it has held so much history inside. I should have brought my sister a sod of soil. Or a rock. Or something.

An old nun, with an African accent, singing a hymn, comes out of the kitchen carrying a piece of toast and a glass of water. She has put a dollop of jam on the side of the white plate, 'for a special occasion'. She winks at me and tells me to follow her. I feel eyes on my back, then a hum of voices as we leave the dining area. She leads me up the stairs, past a statue, eerie and white, down a long clean corridor, towards a room with a picture of

Archbishop Romero on the door. We stop. I hold my breath. A piece of turf. A rock. Anything.

'Go in, child.' The nun squeezes my hand. 'You're shaking.'

'Thank you,' I say. I stand at the door and open it slowly. 'Brigid?' There is a crumple in the bed, as if it has just been tossed. 'Brigid. It's me. Sheona.'

There's no sound, just a tiny hint of movement in the bedsheets. I walk over. Her eyes are open, but she's not there within them. Her hair is netted and grey. The lines on her face cut inwards. Age has abseiled her cheekbones. I feel angry. I take down the picture of the Sacred Heart that is spraying red light out into the room and place it face down on the floor. She murmurs and a little spittle comes out from the side of her mouth. So she is there, after all, I look in her eyes again. This is the first time I have seen her since we were still that age. A bitterness in there now, perhaps, borne deep. 'I just want some neutral ground,' I say. Then I realise that I don't know who I'm talking to and I put the picture back on the wall.

I sit on the bed and touch her ashtrayed hair. 'Talk to me,' I say. She turns slightly. The toast is growing cold on a plate on the floor. I have no idea if she knows who I am as I feed her, but I have a feeling she does. I'm afraid to lay my hand on her for fear of snapping bones. She doesn't want to be fed. She hisses and spits the bread out of dehydrated lips. She closes her mouth on my fingers, but it takes no effort to pry it open. Her teeth are as brittle as chalk. I lay the toast on her tongue again. Each time it gets moister and eventually it dissolves. I wash it down with some water. I try to say something but I can't, so I sing a Hoagy Carmichael tune, but she doesn't recognise it. If I try to lift her I think I would find a heap of dust in my hand, my own hand, which is speaking to me again, carving out a shape that is in a flux.

I want to find out who is under the bedsheets. 'Talk to me.' She rolls away and turns her back. I stand and look around the room. It all crumples down to a lump in the bed. An empty chamberpot. Some full-bloom chrysanthemums by the window. A white plate with a smear of jam. A dead archbishop on the outside, looking in.

'Just a single word' I say. 'Just give me a single word.'

Some voices float in from down the white corridor. Frantic, I move to a set of drawers and a cupboard to look at the bits and pieces that go to make her up now. I pull the drawers out and dump the contents on the floor. I cannot understand the mosaic. A bible. Some neatly folded blouses. Long underwear. A bundle of letters in an elastic band. Lots of hairpins. Stamps gleaned from the Book of Kells. Letters. I do not want to read them. A painting of a man sowing seeds, by a child's hand. A photograph of our mother and father, from a long time ago, standing together by Nelson's Pillar, him with a cigar, her with netting hanging down from her hat. A copy of a newspaper from a recent election. A Mayan doll. Lotus-legged on the floor, I am disappointed amongst somebody else's life. I haven't found what I'm looking for.

I shuffle to the end of the bed and lift the sheets. Her feet are blue and very cold to the touch. I rub them slowly at first. I remember when we were children, very young, before all that, and we had held buttercups to each other's chins on the edges of brown fields. I want her feet to tell me about butter. As I massage I think I see her lean her head sideways and smile, though I'm not sure. I don't know why, but I want to take her feet in my mouth. It seems obscene, but I want to and I don't. 'Up a lazy river with the robin song, it's a lazy river, we can float along blue skies up above, everyone's in love, up a lazy river with me.' She mumbles when I lean over her face and kiss her. There is spittle on her chin and she is horribly ruined.

I walk to the window. Far off, in the parking lot, I can see Michael, head slumped forward on the steering wheel, sleeping. Two nuns look in the passenger window at him, curious, a cup of tea and some scones in their hands. I am aware of myself now. I watch him, wondering about the last few days. An old feeling, new now. There is an ocean I know of that laps between here and there, washing. I watch him. Teeth around his neck. I want a bicycle. Sequoia seedlings in the basket. A flurry of puddles to ride through to a place where water is suspended. I will stay here now I know that. When she recovers I will go to Quebec and climb. But there is something I need first.

I smile, go away from the window, lean towards Brigid, and whisper: 'Where, Sister, did you put those yellow socks of mine anyway?'

The Wrong Vocation

MOY McCRORY

'WHEN GOD CALLS you, he is never denied,' Sister Mercy told us with a finality which struck terror into our hearts.

She stood at the front of the room with the window behind her, so we were blinded and could not see her features but we knew she smiled.

'He waits patiently until we hear his voice. When that happens, you are never the same.'

It terrified me when this thing called a vocation might come; any day out of nowhere to drop into my mind and wedge there like a piece of grit.

'God is looking now, seeing who is pure of heart and ready to be offered up.'

Every girl shifted uncomfortably. Sister looked at our up-turned faces and seemed pleased with the effect she was having. By way of illustration she told us about a young woman from a rich home who was always laughing, with young men waiting to escort her here, there and everywhere, and a big family house with chandeliers in the rooms and a lake in the garden.

'I've seen it. It was on the telly the other night,' Nancy Lyons whispered to me.

'With all these good things in life, she was spoiled. Her wealthy father indulged his daughter's every wish. And do you think she was happy?'

'She damned well ought to be,' Nancy hissed while around us the more pious members of the form shook their heads.

241

Sister placed her bony hands across her chest and stood up on her tiptoes as if reaching with her ribcage for something that would constantly evade it.

'Her heart was empty.'

Sister went on to tell us how the young woman resisted the call, but eventually realised she would never be happy until she devoted her life to Christ. Going out beside the lake, she asked him to enter her life.

'She is one of our very own nuns, right here in this convent. Of course I cannot tell you which sister she is, but when you imagine that we were all born as nuns, remember that we were once young girls like yourselves, without a thought in our heads that we should devote our lives to God.'

There was a silence. We all stared out past her head.

'Oh Sister, it's beautiful,' said a voice. Nancy rolled her eyes to heaven. Lumpy, boring Beatrice, who always sat at the front, would like it. She was so slow-witted and so good. She was one of the least popular girls in the class, a reporter of bad news and always the first to give homework in. With mini-skirts *de rigueur*, her uniform remained stoically unadapted. She must have been the only girl in the school that did not need to have her hemline checked at the end of the day. While we struggled to turn over our waistbands Beatrice always wore her skirt a good two inches below her plump knees and looked like one of the early photographs, all sepia and foggy, of the old girls in their heyday.

Nancy pulled her face.

'But wasn't her rich father angry?' someone asked, and Sister Mercy nodded.

'Mine would sodding kill me. They don't even want me to stay on at school. Me mother's always reminding me how much money they're losing because I'm not bringing any wages home.'

'Do you have something to say, Nancy Lyons?' Sister's stern voice rapped.

'No Sister, I was just saying what a great sacrifice it was to make.'

'Ah yes, a great sacrifice indeed.'

But the sacrifice was not just on the nun's part. Everyone else was made to suffer. There was a woman in our street who never recovered after her eldest daughter joined the Carmelites. Mrs Roddy's daughter was a teacher in the order. It was not so much that she would never give her mother grandchildren that caused the greatest upset, but the economics of it where all a nun's earnings go straight back into the convent. Mrs Roddy used to wring her hands.

'That money's mine,' she would shout, 'for feeding and clothing her all those years. The church has no right to it!'

Then her daughter went peculiar. We only noticed because they sent her home for a week on holiday, and we thought that was unusual, but it was around the time they were relaxing the rule. Nuns were appearing on the streets with skirts that let them walk easily, skimming their calves instead of the pavement.

During that week she got her cousin to perm her hair, on account of the new headdress. She assured her that it was all right because even nuns had to look groomed now their hair showed at the front, and every night she continued to lead the family in the joyful mysteries.

'I'll tell you Mrs Mac, I'm worn out with all the praying since our Delcia's been back,' her mother would confide to mine as they passed quickly in the street, while her daughter muttered 'God bless you' to no one in particular and with a vague smile into the air.

But indoors, she borrowed her mother's lipstick, deep red because Mrs Roddy still had the same one from before the war. That was when they thought she was going a bit far, when they saw her outmoded, crimson mouth chanting the rosary. She drove her family mad. She had tantrums and kept slamming doors. Then they saw her out in the street asking to be taken for rides on Nessie Moran's motorbike. Everyone said she had taken her vows too young. She crammed all those teenage things she never did into that week. By the end of it they were relieved to send her back.

Her mother hated nuns. She did not mind priests half as much.

'At least they're human,' she would say. 'Well, half human. Nuns aren't people; they're not proper women. They don't know what it is to be a mother and they'll never be high up in the church. They'll never be the next Pope. They can't even say Mass. What good are they? They're stuck in the middle, not one thing or the other. Brides of Christ! They make me sick. Let them try cooking, cleaning and running a home on nothing. It would be a damned easier life I'd have if I'd married Christ, instead of that lazy bugger inside.'

But she was fond of the young priest at her church, a

good-looking, fresh-faced man from Antrim who would sit and have a drink with them at the parish club.

'At least you can have a laugh with him,' she'd say, 'but that stuck-up lot, they're all po-faced up at Saint Ursula's. They're no better than any of us. I'm a woman, don't I know what their minds are like. We're no different. Gossipy, unnatural creatures, those ones are. Look what's happened to our poor Delcia after being with them.'

And then the convent sent Delcia home to be looked after by her family. An extended family, they called it, on account of her stress and exhaustion.

'They've used her up, now they don't want what's left over, so I've got her again. What good is she to anyone now? She can't look after herself. She can't even make a bloody cup of tea. How will she fend for herself if the order won't have her back? I'm dying, Mrs Mac, I can't be doing with her.'

My mother would tut and nod and shut the door.

'It's a shame. What sort of life has that poor girl had?' she would say indoors, shaking her head at the tragedy.

'I know she's gone soft now, but she was good at school. Her mam and dad thought she'd be something and now she's fit for nothing if the church can't keep her.'

In the evening we would hear Mrs Roddy shouting, 'Get in off the street!'

Finally they took her into a hospice and we heard no more about it, but Mrs Roddy always crossed the road to avoid nuns. Once outside Lewis's a Poor Clare thrust a collection box at her and asked for a donation. Mrs Roddy tried to take it from her and the box was pulled back and forth like a bird tugging at a worm. It was not the nun's iron grip, but the bit of elastic which wrapped itself around her wrist that foiled Mrs Roddy's attempt to redistribute the church's wealth.

'They're just like vultures,' she would say, 'waiting to see what they can tear from your limbs. They're only happy when they've picked you clean. Better hide your purse!'

At the collection on Sundays she sat tight-lipped and the servers knew better than to pass the collecting plate her way.

'A vocation gone wrong' was what my father called Delcia Roddy. He would shake his head from side to side and murmur things like 'the shame' or 'the waste'. He had a great deal of sympathy for her tortured soul. It was about this time that I became tortured. He had no sympathy for me.

Sister Mercy's words had stung like gravel in a grazed knee. At night I could hear them as her voice insisted, 'You cannot fight God's plan,' and I would pray that God keep his plans to himself.

'You must pray for a vocation,' she told us.

I gritted my teeth and begged his blessed mother to intervene.

'I'll be worse than the Roddy girl,' I threatened, 'and look what a disgrace she was.' Then, echoing the epitaph of W. B. Yeats, I would point in the darkness and urge 'Horseman; Pass by!'

It was rather the reverse of the chosen people who daubed their doorposts and let the angel of death pass over, in order to survive and play out God's plan. I wanted God's plan to pass over.

'We are instruments in God's will,' Sister Mercy told us and I did not want to be an instrument.

I knew if God had any sense he would not want me, but Sister Mercy frightened us. Beatrice was the one headed for a convent. She had made plain her intentions at the last retreat when she stood up and announced to the study group that she was thinking of devoting her life to Christ.

'She may as well, there's nothing else down for her,' Nancy commented.

Yet Sister Mercy told us that it was the ones we did not suspect who had vocations, and she had looked around the room like a mind reader scrutinising the audience before pulling out likely candidates.

The convent terrified me; the vocation stalked my shadow like a store detective. One day it would pounce and I would be deadlocked into a religious life, my will subsumed by one greater than I. Up there was a rapacious appetite which consumed whole lives, like chicken legs. I dreaded that I should end up in a place where every day promised the same, the gates locked behind me and all other escape sealed off. It wasn't that I had any ambitions for what I might do, but I could not happily reconcile myself to an existence where the main attraction was death. I dreaded hearing God's call.

'He can spend years. He can wait. God is patient.'

I decided that I would have to exasperate him, and fast.

Down at the Pier Head, pigeons gathered in thousands.

The Liver Buildings were obscured by their flight when they all rose in unison like a blanket of grey and down. I never knew where my fear came from, but I was terrified of those birds. Harmless seagulls twice their size flew about me, followed the ferry out across the water to Birkenhead and landed flapping and breathless on the landing plank. Their screech was piercing, and they never disturbed me. Yet when I stepped out into Hamilton Square and saw the tiny cluster of city birds waiting, my heart would beat in panic. City birds who left slime where they went, their excrement the colour of the new granite buildings springing up. They nodded their heads and watched you out of the sides of their eyes. They knocked smaller birds out of the way and I had seen them taking bread away from each other. They were a fighting, quarrelsome brood, an untidy shambling army, with nothing to do all day but walk around the Pier Head or follow me through Princess Park and make my life a misery.

Once I was crossing for a bus just a streak of them flew up into the air. I put my hands over my head, the worst fear being that one should touch my face, and I could think of nothing more sickening than the feel of one of these ragged creatures, bloated with disease; the flying vermin which flocked around the Life Assurance building, to remind us we were mortal.

A nightmare I had at the time was of being buried alive under thousands of these birds. They would make that strange cooing noise as they slowly suffocated me. Their fat greasy bodies would pulsate and swell as, satiated, they nestled down on to me for the heat my body could provide. Under this sweltering, stinking mass I would be unable to scream. Each time I opened my mouth it filled with dusty feathers.

Then my nightmare changed. Another element crept into my dreams. Alongside the pigeons crept the awful shape that was a vocation. It came in all colours, brown and white, black and white, beige, mottled, grey and sandy, as the different robes of each order clustered around me, knocking pigeons out of the way. They muttered snatches of Latin, bits of psalms, and rubbed their claw-like hands together like bank tellers. The big change in the dream was that they, unlike the pigeons, did not suffocate me, but slowly drew away, leaving me alone in a great empty space, that at first I thought was the bus terminal, but which Nancy Lyons assured me was the image of my life to be.

Her older sister read tea leaves and was very interested in dreams. Nancy borrowed a book from her.

'It says here that dreaming about water means a birth.'

'I was dreaming about pigeons, and then nuns.'

'Yeah, but you said you were down at the Pier Head, didn't you, and that's water.'

'I don't know if I was at the Pier Head.'

'Oh you must have been. Where else would you get all them pigeons?' Nancy was a realist. 'Water means birth,' she repeated firmly. 'I bet your mam gets pregnant.'

I knew she was wrong, I was the last my mother would ever have, she told me often enough. But Nancy would not be put off. The book was lacking on nuns, so she held out for the water and maintained that the big empty space was my future.

'There's nothing down for you unless you go with the sisters,' she said.

It was not because I lacked faith that I dreaded the vocation. I suffered from its excesses; it hung around me, watching every move, and passing judgement. I was a failed miserable sinner and I knew it, but I did not want to atone. I did not want the empty future I was sure it offered. Our interpretation of the dream differed.

Around this time I had a Saturday job in a delicatessen in town. I was on the cold-meat counter. None of the girls were allowed to touch the bacon slicer. Only Mr Calderbraith could do that. He wore a white coat and must have fancied himself as an engineer the way he carried on about the gauge of the blades. He would spend hours unscrewing the metal plates and cleaning out the bolts and screws with a look of extreme concentration upon his face.

His balding head put out a few dark strands of hair which he grew to a ludicrous length and wore combined across his scalp to give the impression of growth. Some of the girls said he wore a toupée after work, and that if we were to meet him on a Sunday we would not know him.

He used to pretend he was the manager. He would come over and ask customers solicitously if everything was all right and remark that if the service was slow, it was because he was breaking in new staff.

'Who does he think he's kidding!' Elsie said after he had leaned across the counter one morning. 'He couldn't break in his shoes.'

Shoes were a problem. I was on my feet all day, and they would ache by the time we came to cash up. I used to catch the bus from the Pier Head at around five-thirty, if I could get the glass of the counter wiped down and the till cashed. The managers and seniors were obsessed with dishonesty. Cashing-up had to be done in strict military formations. None of us were allowed to move until we heard a bell and the assistant manager would take the cash floats from us in silence.

Inside his glass office the manager sat on a high stool with mirrors all around him, surveying us. If any of the girls sneezed, or moved out of synch, another bell would sound and we would all have to instantly shut our tills while the manager shouted over the loudspeaker system, 'Disturbance at counter number four,' or wherever it was. Sometimes it took ages.

They never failed to inform us that staff were all dishonest. Not the manager, Calderbraith nor the senior staff, but the floor workers, and especially the temporary staff, the Saturday workers, because as they told us, we had the least to lose, and we were 'fly by nights' according to the manager, who grinned as he told us that.

I could not imagine anything there worth stealing. It was all continental meats and strange cheese that smelt strongly, the mouldier the better.

'Have you seen that bread they're selling?' Elsie said to me one Saturday.

'The stuff that looks like it's got mouse droppings on top?'

But people came from all over the city and placed orders.

One Saturday evening I was waiting for the next bus, having missed the five-thirty. My feet ached. The managers would not let you sit down. Even when there was not a customer in sight you were supposed to stand to attention. I took it in turns with Elsie to duck beneath the wooden counter supports and sit on the floor when business was slack. Whenever Mr Calderbraith was about, we both stood rigidly. He loathed serving customers.

'See to that Lady,' he would say, if anyone asked him for a quarter of liver sausage.

I had worn the wrong shoes, they had heels. Throughout the week I wore comfortable brown lace-ups, but at the weekend I wanted to wear things that did not scream 'schoolgirl'. But my mother had been right. I was crippled.

After a few minutes I leant back on the rail and kicked

one shoe off. My toes looked puffy and red. I put that one back and kicked off the other. It shot into the gutter. Before I had a chance to hop after it, a pigeon the size of a cat flopped down and stood between it and me. It looked at me, then slowly began to walk around the shoe. I was rigid, gripping the rail and keeping my foot off the pavement. Then the bird hopped up inside the shoe and seemed to settle as a hen might in a nest. It began to coo. I was perspiring. I would never be able to take the shoe from it, and even if I managed to I would not be able to put my foot inside it after that vile creature had sat in it. I was desperate. Suddenly, as if it sensed my fright, it flew up in the air towards me almost brushing my face with its wings, then it circled and landed squarely back inside the shoe. I did not wait. It could have it. I hopped away from the bus stop and limped towards the taxi stand. I reckoned I had just enough money to get a cab home. It would be all my pay for the Saturday, and I would not be able to go out that night, but I did not care. It would take me, shoeless, right to the front door and away from the pigeon.

Then, I thought it was my mind playing tricks, but I saw three shapes blowing in the breeze, veils flapping behind them. The Pier Head was so windy, I thought they might become airborne. They got bigger. I was certain that they flew. Soon they would be right on top of me. God was giving me a sign. The Vocation had decided to swoop after so long pecking into my dreams. Three silent figures, as mysterious as the Trinity, crossed the tarmac of the bus terminal. I could not take my eyes from them. They seemed to swell the way a pigeon puffs out its chest to make itself important. They were getting fatter and rounder like brown and cream balloons. Carmelites. I could not stay where I was, I had to escape. Some people moved to one side as I hobbled to a grass verge. I tripped on the concrete rim of the grassy area and caught my ankle. As I put my hand down to catch myself, several birds pecking on rubbish rose into the air just in front of me, and I thought for one deluded second that I was flying with them as the white sky span and I tumbled over. Only when my head came level with a brown paper carrier bag did I smell the grossly familiar scent of cold meats.

'Young lady, are you in some sort of difficulty?'

The voice of Mr Calderbraith pulled me out of my terrified stupor. I lifted my head and came eye to quizzical eye.

'Whatever is wrong with you? Can't you walk properly? Good heavens, what has happened to your shoe? Have you been in some sort of accident?' He straightened up and looked around desperately.

'Tell me who did it,' he insisted, 'check that you still have your front door keys.'

I raised myself up on one knee and obediently opened my bag. Everything was intact. Mr Calderbraith's eyes opened wide.

'I really don't understand . . .' he began.

Behind him I could see a triangle formation moving against the empty sky. The three sisters seemed to glide inside its rigid outline like characters in the medals people brought back from Fatima. Behind them flapped wings, veils, patches of brown, and feathers. Dark against the white sky they enveloped me, just as my dream had forewarned. I could not speak. My hands shook.

'What is it? Have you seen the culprit?'

I nodded, still struggling to rise.

'They often work in a gang, these hoodlums,' Mr Calderbraith continued. 'Oh, yes. I've watched enough detective programmes to know how they operate.' He glanced from side to side furtively.

'They've probably left their look-out nearby. Acting casual.' He glowered menacingly at any passers-by.

They were closing in behind Mr Calderbraith. They peered over his shoulder. Inhuman, they cheeped and shrieked. I could not understand a thing. Mr Calderbraith was nodding at me, his head pecked up and down. I reached out and pointed and a dreadful magnetic force pulled me towards them. I was on my feet in seconds.

Mr Calderbraith turned round and saw the three. He shrank away from them.

'You don't mean these, surely?' he said. 'That is stretching it. Have you been drinking? Tell me, were you on relief at the spirit counter?'

'She's had a bit of a fall,' a passer-by said.

'I think she fell on her head,' Mr Calderbraith nodded.

Then turning to the spectators who had crossed from the bus shelter, he reassured them that everything was all right.

'She is one of my staff members, it's all under control, I know this young lady. Let me deal with it.'

The smallest nun, a tiny frail sparrow, hopped lightly towards me, concern marked by the way she held her head on one side. Her scrawny hand scratched at the ground and she caught up a carrier bag that lay askew on the grass verge. The others clucked solicitously. Then there was a stillness. All fluttering seemed to stop. She handed the bag to me and I took it as my voice returned to tumble out in hopeless apologies while my face burned. Hugging the carrier bag to me, I stumbled towards a taxi which pulled up. I fell inside and slammed the door. I breathed deeply, thinking that I was going to cry from embarrassment. Out of the back window I could see the nuns standing with Mr Calderbraith who was looking about as if he had lost something.

'Where to, love?' the driver asked.

My voice was thin and weary as I told him. I put my head back and sighed. Only when we were half-way along the Dock Road did I realise that I was still hugging the bag. I peered inside. It was stuffed with pieces of meat, slivers of pork and the ends of joints, all wrapped up in Mr Calderbraith's sandwich papers. There was a great big knuckle of honey roast ham. It would be a sin to waste it.

Then I started to laugh. I couldn't stop. Tears ran down my face. Sister Mercy had told us that we had to be spotless, our souls bleached in God's grace. We had to repent our past and ask Him to take up residence in our hearts. I put my hand into the bag and drew out a piece of meat. I crammed it into my mouth. I swallowed my guilt, ate it whole and let it fill my body. As I chewed I wondered at how I still felt the same. I was no different, only I had become the receiver of stolen goods. I wondered if Mr Calderbraith would be nicer to me? I would not be surprised if he let me have a go on the bacon slicer next weekend.

'Are you all right love?' the driver asked.

I was choking on a piece of meat.

'I'm fine,' I coughed, scarcely waiting long enough before I stuffed another bit into my mouth. I ate with frenzied gulping sounds. When I looked up I saw the driver watching me in his mirror.

'God but you must be starving,' he said.

I nodded.

'Well you're a growing girl. You don't know how lucky you are to have all your life in front of you.'

'I do, I really do,' I told him as I pulled another bit of meat off a bone with my teeth. Between mouthfuls I laughed. My one regret was that it wasn't a Friday – I could have doubled my sin without any effort. Then I realised that I had subverted three nuns into being accomplices. What more did I need?

I slapped my knees and howled. God would have to be desperate to want me now.

As the taxi pulled up outside the house I saw the curtains twitch. I did not know how I was going to explain losing my shoe, but nothing could lower my spirits, not even hiccups.

Creatures of the Earth

JOHN McGAHERN

IN WILD, WET January weather, two months after Mr Waldron's death, Mrs Waldron and her daughter, Eileen, closed their big house outside Castlebar and moved to their summer cottage on Achill.

The whole family – two other daughters, their husbands, two sons, their wives and three grandchildren – had gathered in the big house that Christmas. They would have preferred it to be kept open until at least the summer, but their mother was determined to move, even on her own. The Waldrons were an unusual family, all of them secure in good professions, and they had little interest in their inheritance other than for it to be settled according to their parents' wishes. Their chief inheritance, a good education, had already been given. Michael Flynn was to be kept on two days a week to look after the gardens and grounds, and Eileen, a solicitor, who worked in Castlebar, might sometimes use the house in bad weather or whenever there were late court sittings. With some reluctance it was agreed that the horses and the few cattle that had been their father's main diversion would be sold. In a year's time they could look at the situation again. With relief and some nervous laughter it was settled that nothing more had to be done or said. They could start opening the wines they would have with the Christmas dinner.

Eileen would have been as happy to stay as to move. There was a man her own age in Castlebar who interested her.

It was she who had been the closest to her father. She did not like the idea at first of his horses being sold, but had to admit that keeping them made little sense. Secretly she was glad of the hour-long drive from Achill to Castlebar: it might help shake off the listlessness and sense of emptiness she had begun to feel once her initial anger at the death had passed. And she had come to that unnerving time when youth is rapidly disappearing into early middle age.

The wind rocked the heavy, white Mercedes as they crossed the Sound to the island the January Saturday they moved, the sea and sky rain-sodden and wild. They had taken very little with them from Castlebar. The only precious thing they took was an old, trusting black cat they were all very attached to. The black cat had four white paws and a white star on her forehead and was called Fats.

In the evenings the cat used to wait for the surgeon's car to come from the hospital. Often Mr Waldron carried her indoors on his shoulder, and when he went over the fields to look at the cattle or horses the cat went with him, racing ahead and crying to be lifted on to his shoulder whenever the grass was wet. All through his final illness the cat slept at the foot of his bed. Whenever Mrs Waldron attempted to remove her from the folded quilt, he woke instantly. 'No. Leave her be. *She* has not deserted us' – a humorous reference to the apparent avoidance of them early in the illness, especially by many of the people who had worked for years with him at the hospital. All through their long life together it had been agreed that it was vanity, a waste, to consider how they appeared in the eyes of others.

In merriment they had often recalled walking behind the professor of philosophy on a clear winter's morning when they were undergraduates on their way to the Saturday market and hearing him demand after each person passed, 'Did they *snub* us or did they *not* see us?' Over the years it had become one of the playful catch-phrases of the house: 'Did they not see us or did they *snub* us?'

At first Mrs Waldron did not believe that his colleagues were avoiding him, thought indeed it was all in his imagination: 'You'll be as paranoiac as old Professor Ryan soon if you're not careful.'

'I don't think so. In fact, I'm glad they're avoiding us. Most of the time I'm too tired to receive them if they did want to visit.'

Then, when it was clear he would not recover, she noticed the wives melt away to another part of the supermarket, the husbands disappear down side-streets in the middle of the town.

'We are no longer useful. It is as simple as that.'

'It can't be that simple.'

'Not complicated, then, either. They work with sick people but they are not ill. They are outside and above all that. They have to be. They loom like gods in the eyes of most of these poor creatures. Now that I am sick I simply am no longer part of the necessary lie that works. I have to be shut out. Gods can never appear ill or wounded.'

'*You* never behaved that way.'

'I like to think I was a little different, but maybe not all that different either. Anyhow . . .'

The day before he died, he woke briefly, recognised her and said, 'I think we were a good pair,' and almost at once the heavy, monotonous breathing resumed. They were the last words he spoke, and broke her heart, but they were a deep source of solace in the days ahead. She lifted the cat from the foot of the bed, burying her face in the fur, and left the darkened room to the nurse who came behind her and closed the door softly.

'What do you think of all this?' Mrs Waldron said as she stroked the cat stretched like a lion on the dashboard of the car. The black cat suddenly yawned, rose to her feet and looked gravely down on the surging water of the Sound.

The cottage was by a stream beyond the village, well below the road, which gave some protection against the storms. At high tide the ocean covered the rocks on the other side of the raised road. When the tide was out, there was a long, bright strand between two curving headlands. The cottage was whitewashed in the traditional way, with a blue stone slate roof and a small porch in front. A garage had been added to the side that faced the stream, and a large living room and bathroom were hidden at the back. Mrs Waldron loved the slow, crunching sound the car tyres made as they rolled down to the porch.

Each morning, before Eileen left for work in Castlebar, the two women rose and had breakfast together. 'I know there's no need for me to get up so early, but it helps give shape to the day.' After Eileen left, Mrs Waldron tidied the house, fed the cat in the shelter of the porch, watching her with an amusement that was pure affection as she performed her toilet, with ceremony and great gravity, in the black earth beneath the escallonias. Then Mrs Waldron read. Even during the busiest times of her young life in the town, if she had not managed to set at least an hour aside for reading she felt that the day had lacked concentration, had somehow been dissipated and lost.

Now her only interruptions were rare telephone calls – and when her reading brought her face to face with some affection or sharp memory. 'She had done more than she wanted to, less than she ought.' She found herself repeating the sentence long after she had closed the book, seeing elements of her own life and people she knew reflected in it, elements of that life seen and given a moral sweetness that was close to smiling.

'Smith told me he's given up reading!' her husband informed her boisterously one evening years ago after he came home from the hospital.

'What's so funny about that?'

'He told me it's too passive. He's going to concentrate on hill and mountain climbing!'

'Then he'll be happier climbing.'

'Oh, love, don't be so serious.' He tried to waltz her away from whatever she was preparing for dinner.

'Are you sure you've not been drinking?'

'Not a drop. But I intend to have a stiff drink before dinner. We have to examine Smith's momentous decision. Will you join me?'

Without reading, she would feel her whole life now to be spiritually idle. All through their marriage she and her husband had talked to one another about the good things that they'd happened upon, that lightened and deepened life, gave recognition and pleasure.

After a light lunch she rested and then set out on her walk. In all but the worst weather she walked, and never varied it unless the wind forced her in another direction, but these walks were never as enjoyable as the ones she and her husband took together in the last years when they were alone.

She went by the harbour. It was empty now of boats except for four old curraghs resting upside down on concrete blocks, roped down against the storms. There were a few wooden crayfish creels along the short pier wall and these were also weighted down, as was some torn and tangled netting. Passing the harbour she could choose between several sheep paths through the heather, but generally she went by the path closest to the ocean. The only person she met on her walks that February was a fat little old man in green oilskins with a pair of binoculars. Always he was in the same place, resting in the shelter of a big boulder and looking out to sea. Only after she'd passed him several times did he look at her and nod. Then, sometimes, she was the first to smile and nod. He seemed pleased, but still they did not speak. She thought he might be a relict, like herself, who had taken up bird-watching, or someone just fascinated by the power and beauty of the ocean, ever changing. What did *he* see there?

A school fife-and-drum band marching past the cottage to early Mass woke both mother and daughter to St Patrick's Day. The weather was warmer. People suddenly seemed to be in better spirits. Along all the cottages on the road to the harbour, people were digging their kitchen gardens, spreading manure and seaweed, shovelling the rich, black earth. Some waved to her with their spades or shovels as she passed.

'God bless the work.'

'And you, too, Missus, when you're at it.'

At the harbour they were scraping and tarring the boats. A man was lovingly measuring a square of calico over weakened timbers before covering it with a boiling mixture of tar and pitch from a tin jug. She loved the smell of the boiling tar in the sea air. There was a crazy doctor by the name of Doorley she remembered from her childhood who believed in the healing properties of tar, and each summer he tarred his ten children from head to toe. All of them were disturbed in later life. One became a beggar on the roads. Two committed suicide. Though her father, who was also a medical doctor, and others complained about his behaviour, nobody was able or willing to bring it to a stop. Everybody was too afraid. Authority could not be questioned then, especially when vested in a priest or doctor. How rapidly all that had changed. Sometimes she could hardly believe it had all taken place in the brief space of a lifetime.

As soon as the weather turned, the man with binoculars discarded his green oilskins for a thick jersey of unwashed grey wool with a worn black suit and a cloth cap. One day she stopped to talk to him, and the stop became almost mandatory. He had worked all his life in England, near Didcot, on buildings and line maintenance. Tommy McHugh was his name. He had five children, all grown. When they were growing up he saw them at Christmas and a few weeks each summer. During the war he didn't see his family for four years. A child conceived during one visit was three years old when he next returned. Dog-tired after the boat and train journey, he woke in the morning to see a small boy standing at the foot of the bed, saying to all who'd listen, 'That's my Daddy!' His wife and he had never lived together until he returned for good. She thought it must have been hard for them to come together after such absences, but she noticed he never talked about his wife unless she reflected a part of his own life.

'Is it the colours you watch or the sea birds or just the ocean itself?'

'I'd not be stupid enough to be watching anything like that,' he replied slowly, a sly smile in his eyes. He looked at her with approval, as if she had laid a clever trap and he had danced clear. 'I'd have no taste for watching anything like that. I'd be watching those sheep over there.' He gestured towards the Head and handed her the binoculars. What were white specks beforehand grew into clear shapes.

'Sheep are very stupid animals,' he confided. 'Hardly a week goes by but one of them doesn't fall off.'

'What do you do then?'

'Sometimes you can get them back on their feet. More times they're finished.'

'Are you not too far off here?'

'You can see better from here than on the Head, and it's a cruel climb. The trouble is that it's a very tasty bit of land.'

From that day on he always handed her the binoculars to look at the sheep. Over and over he told her about his hard life in England, the monies he sent home out of every pay-packet, how difficult it was to pass the time after work, but fortunately there was everlasting overtime.

One day he had with him a beautiful black-and-white collie pup on a long line of binder twine, timid and anxious to please, its coat woolly still, and before long she found herself looking forward to seeing it each day. At first, the man was enamoured: he was going to train it into the best working dog on the island. But during the weeks that followed, as the pup grew into a young, eager dog, and the training proceeded, complaints replaced the early in-loveness and praise.

Sometimes the collie was 'as stupid as the sheep' he rushed and scattered. She observed how self-absorbed the man was, how impatient. Increasingly, she disliked that the young dog was in his control. She found herself wondering what his wife was like and how had she coped with his return? Thinking of the man and his life, and the dog and sheep, without warning, a buried memory of her father scattered the day. It was summer. She was home from college. Her father was late returning from a round of sick calls. Lunch was already on the table, and she was standing with her mother in the open bay window, when her father's car came up the laurelled avenue and turned on the big square of gravel. Instead of coming straight into the house, he went around the car and took a whole side of lamb from the boot, placing a towel on his shoulder to carry it proudly in. The lamb was probably some payment in kind.

She saw no significance in the memory other than it had displaced this actual day of her life and the disturbance her observations of Tommy McHugh had caused. Her life with her father and mother had passed. Her life with her husband had now passed. Was her whole life, then, all nothing? Was it just what happened and the memory of those happenings, like the old classmate she had once chanced upon in the ship's restaurant during a Holyhead–Dublin crossing? The classmate had grown old, was only dimly recognisable, as she herself had grown old, having to be asked, if, indeed, she was the girl at Earlsfort Terrace who played hockey and married one of the medical students. The memory of her father, though, had not grown old, had come to her out of all those dead years with more freshness and vividness than the actual sea thistle and heather between the rocks at her feet high above the pounding ocean. It could not all be nothing. 'A mind lively and at ease with itself is content to look at nothing,' she recalled a favourite passage from Jane Austen, 'and that nothing will always answer back;' and suddenly the recollection itself gave heart and belief to her walk. That was what always answered back, all that we had loved, all that we had cared for. Love is never tired or dispirited. Love is ever watchful and lively and at ease.

The black cat was waiting for her return to the cottage. She lifted her on to her shoulder and carried her into the house just as her husband used to do on his return from work. The cat, at least, seemed to have taken on a new lease of life since the move to Achill. She had started to hunt again and had brought mice and small birds, even a frog, into the bedroom through the partially open window as she had done in Castlebar when she was young. Other times she sat out on dry stones in the middle of the stream, gazing down studiously at the small trout streaking about or lying still in the pools. Mrs Waldron didn't like the offerings of the mice or small birds in the bedroom. She hadn't liked it in Castlebar, but her husband had said, 'What harm is it anyhow? It's her nature,' and as he had sanctioned it, she did not want to be the one to end it now. After meticulous crunching of small bones, she heard a vigorous licking, then loud purring as the cat curled into the eiderdown, declaring to all her own approval of the good, providing cat she knew herself to be.

In the evenings Mrs Waldron prepared dinner for herself and Eileen. Mostly they talked of Eileen's day, of practical things that concerned the house and gardens in Castlebar and of Michael Flynn. They never talked other than glancingly of the dead man, and when they did the conversation was quick to move.

Hotels and restaurants on the island began to reopen for Easter, and the Waldrons returned to Castlebar for two weeks of the holiday. Nearly all the family came back over Easter, but for no more than a day or two, and all of them arrived and left separately. After they left, Mrs Waldron was more eager than ever to get back to Achill. For the time being. Eileen still didn't mind the hour-long drive on and off the island. 'It fills a space where loss can't get in.'

The summer was unusual, dry and hot, with hardly any of the usual soft rain. The island became crowded. Motor bikes roared past. People carrying blaring transistors walked or cycled by the cottage. Wild music came through open windows of passing cars and into fields sloping down to the harbour where whole families were saving hay. There was much broken glass along the roads. Eileen had taken holidays and gone to France for two weeks. Then her sister and brother and their families came to the house in Castlebar, and there was much to-ing and fro-ing between the house and the island, so much so that Mrs Waldron was seldom alone. She was fond of all of them and glad to have them, but glad too to have two whole days to herself before Eileen came back.

The morning Eileen was due she felt too excited to concentrate on anything, and after feeding the black cat she cleaned the entire cottage. Then she went to buy some staples that were running low. Close to the shops she came on a van selling fresh fish and bought a sea trout for dinner. She thought it a lucky or happy omen for Eileen's return: though this place was surrounded by the ocean, it was difficult to obtain fresh fish. With all the preparations for the homecoming, she was later than usual setting out on her walk. Tommy McHugh kept her talking for a long time, and he was full of complaint about the young collie who cowered now more than ever when approached. This changed her mood so much that she took a different route back to the cottage to avoid them. There was a lack of feeling, of sensitivity, in the man that disturbed her, and she was beginning to regret ever having come to know him.

While Mrs Waldron was talking to Tommy McHugh, Murphy and Heslin came up the road to the cottage. They wore jeans and sneakers, and because of the heat they had taken off their shirts and knotted the sleeves around their throats so that the light cotton floated out behind them in the ocean breeze, leaving their torsos bare. Murphy carried a loud-playing transistor. Heslin had a large, canvas bag slung from his shoulder in which there was a pair of collapsible stools, swimming-trunks, three six-packs of lager and a deck of cards. They were both in their twenties, sold encyclopaedias for a living and had come to the island because they'd heard it attracted working-class girls from Scotland and Northern Ireland who were reputedly free with their favours. Heslin was the better-looking and more forceful of the two and was admired by Murphy. Three nights they had been on the island, and so far had had no luck with girls, even though they drank each night into the hopeful hours in several bars and discos. They never rose before midday.

The black cat was waiting between the gate and escallonias for Mrs Waldron, and when Murphy and Heslin paused she went towards them and rubbed her fur against the bars of the gate. As she had known nothing but kindness, she did not flee when Heslin stooped to lift her into the crook of his arm. She continued to purr as she was carried the first few yards from the house, but when she tried to get away he held her tight. Once she began to claw and cry he took her in his strong hands and thrust her into the canvas bag. The cat alternately tore and struggled, or cried plaintively, but every ploy she tried was ineffective.

They passed Gielty's Bar and the whitewashed cottage where Tommy McHugh lived with his wife beside another small stream at its entrance.

'You wouldn't be interested in a pint before heading for the bay?' Murphy suggested as they passed the bar.

'Not with the bloody cat.'

'What'll you do with it?'

'I'm not sure. We'll see.'

Cars passed them as they began to climb the Head. A gang of bikers roared past aggressively in red helmets and black leather, a blue insignia painted on the back of the jackets. Below them a solitary old woman was threading her way back through the sheep and rabbit paths. They kept their heads low as they climbed, but as soon as they reached the summit they could see the bright strand in the two arms of the bay, the high, dark cliffs rising on the far side. There were no boats on the ocean. They descended quickly, the cat crying and struggling in the bag. An ugly, flat-roofed concrete hut or storeroom stood on the road above the bay. The bikers had turned around, revving the engines before roaring back. There were a few cars parked in a lay-by past the concrete hut. A couple of families were picnicking on the rocks between the cars and the strand. The sand was as white and unspoiled as it had looked from the summit and was completely empty. The tide was about to turn, and they walked far out to the water's edge, a white froth marking the tideline, a gentle, dirty backwash of water and sand curling back underneath the froth. A single man followed them out and searched along the froth until he found a green plastic oil can which marked a set line. He then began to lift the hooks, freshly baiting each one with sand eels taken from a red plastic bucket. His catch was small, three little plaice, a dogfish, the white head of a sea trout. Before removing the head and rebaiting the hook, he paused in obvious disappointment: by the size of the head the trout must have been two or three pounds, a prize catch but for the seals. Murphy and Heslin were afraid he'd be attracted by the cries from the canvas bag, but he didn't appear to notice. Throwing a metal weight on the end of the line far out into the tide when he finished, he disappeared up the strand with his bucket and the few fish he'd caught.

As he disappeared, Heslin handed the canvas bag to Murphy.

He took a ball of fishing-line from his jeans, made a running noose on the end of it and cut off five or six feet with a penknife. Then he found a long, flat piece of rock and knotted the cut end of the line round its centre. Gingerly he inserted his arm into the bag Murphy still held. The cat cried, then went still, and he searched about until he could grip the fur on the back of the neck. Quickly he slipped the noose over her head before she could claw herself free. The cat shot away but was held by the line and rock. More strain and she would strangle herself. She tried to claw the noose free but it was too tight.

The two men fixed the collapsible stools on the sand, opened beer bottles, placed a towel between the stools, and Murphy cut the pack of cards and dealt two hands face down on the towel. Heslin turned the transistor high and drank the first of the bottles of beer. Behind them the black cat struggled against the incoming tide. An oldish, wiry man with a white terrier came on to the strand and seemed to notice the struggling cat. As he approached, Murphy and Heslin turned their stools to face him directly, lifted their beer bottles and put the transistor up to its full volume. The man paused and then, very reluctantly, turned away. A few times he looked back before leaving the beach. By then the black cat, through drowning or struggling or pure terror, floated about like any lifeless thing on the end of the line. The tide now washed around the stools, and the two moved further in as they continued playing cards and drinking. As they did so, they looked back for a long time at the incoming tide, but they weren't able to pick out the cat being tossed about on any of the low waves.

Murphy and Heslin kept moving in, letting the tide take their empties. When the strand was half-filled, two curraghs were taken by a group of men from the concrete hut and carried upside down to the water. There were four men to each curragh. The men's heads and shoulders were covered by the black canvas so that the curragh looked like an enormous insect with eight legs advancing into the water. There they floated the boats and fixed the oars in their pins, and a white nylon net was passed between them before they rowed apart. After they'd stretched the net, a man in each boat waved what looked like a crudely made spear to a watcher on the high cliffs, who blew a shrill whistle by way of recognition. Heslin and Murphy stopped playing cards to watch.

The crude spears were made from the leaves of old car springs, sharpened to a blade and attached to the long poles. The men were fishing for basking sharks. The watcher, high on the cliff, was able to see the shadow on the bright sand as soon as the shark entered the bay, and through a series of whistles was able to tell the men in the boats where the shark was moving. Obeying the whistles, they rowed in a wide arc until they had encircled the shark with the pale net, and then they drew the net tight. They killed the shark with the homemade spears. What they had to be most careful of as they thrust the spear into the flesh was the shark's tail: a single flick would make matchwood of the boats. They could sit out there in the boats without anything happening for days on end, and then two or three sharks could come in during the course of a single evening.

Murphy and Heslin watched the boats for some time as they bobbed listlessly on the water, the men resting on their oars with occasional strokes to keep their position, but as nothing appeared to be happening they went back to playing cards. They kept moving in ahead of the tide, playing for small stakes, till they had the six-packs drunk. The tide was three-quarters full, but still the men rested on the oars in the boats out on the bay without anything happening. It was easier now to make out the watcher high on the cliff.

'I wonder what the fuck they're waiting about there in the boats for,' Murphy said.

'I don't know and I couldn't care less,' Heslin said fiercely as he slapped down a winning card.

The two men then decided to have a last game. Whoever lost would buy the drinks in Gielty's on the way back. Then they folded the stools and towel and put them into the canvas bag. Several cars passed them as they climbed the hill up to the main road. As there was an evening chill in the breeze, they put on and buttoned up their shirts. It was very dark in Gielty's after the sealight. They ordered pints of stout, and Heslin paid.

'Would you fancy a second?' Murphy offered as they rose to leave.

'No. We have the whole night to get through yet,' Heslin said. 'And if we hit fish we better be able to reel them in.'

They rose and left the bar and walked back down to the village. A white Mercedes stood in front of the cottage. Further up the small stream a boy was dabbling a worm in one of the larger pools.

'They must be rich,' Heslin said as they walked nonchalantly past the cottage.

'Wouldn't you just love to send them a video of what happened to the fukken cat?' Murphy replied.

Mrs Waldron missed the cat as soon as she came through the gate, so constant was her wait by the escallonias. She looked at the stone in the stream and saw the boy fishing, and then about the house, and thought no more about it. Perhaps she had caught a mouse or a bird and was sleeping somewhere. In the excitement of Eileen's return, the cat was forgotten. The presents she brought – a silk scarf, soft leather gloves and different kinds of mushrooms and herbs from a market in Rennes – had to be examined and admired. Readily, Eileen answered her mother's questions about the towns she'd stopped in, the hotels, the restaurants, the markets, the shops, châteaux, museums, cathedrals, but there was a slowness in the responses, as if something weighed on her mind. Seeing this, her mother concentrated on the preparations for dinner, content to wait. Over the sea trout, mushrooms and the bottle of dry white wine she'd brought back from Nantes, Eileen spoke about what had been on her mind since her return.

'I didn't like to tell you till I saw how it went . . . I was in France with someone I've been seeing for months.'

'I can hardly pretend to be surprised. Did it go well?'

'I think so. I'm afraid though that Father might not have approved of him.'

'What makes you say that?'

'He's not a professional man. In fact, he manages a super-market. His name is John Quinn.'

'If he's decent and hard-working and kind, I don't think your father would have minded what he was. I hope you'll be happy.'

'Did anything happen to Fats while I was away?' Eileen asked suddenly, missing the cat for the first time and anxious to change the subject. 'It's not like her to miss fish of this quality.'

'She was here all morning, but I missed her when I got back. I am worried but I didn't want to bring it up. She always waited for me by the gate.'

'Why don't we look for her while there's still light?'

They searched the road on both sides of the cottage. The ocean pounded relentlessly on the strand.

'She might come yet through the window during the night.'

'That would be happiness.'

Two days later, Mrs Waldron said, 'Fats won't come back now. Something has happened to her.' The sense of loss was palpable. It was as if the dull ache of the surgeon's death had been sharpened to a blade. He was gone, and now the whole irrelevant playful heart of that time had gone too. They counted back the years that the cat had been part of their lives. She had been with them almost thirteen.

'I sensed it at the time and now I know it. Fats marked thirteen years of intense happiness . . . years of amazing luck . . . and they could not last. Yet we had all that . . . It's hard to imagine now. All that.'

Eileen returned to her work in Castlebar. Several times Mrs Waldron set out to walk, but each time found herself without heart to go further than the small harbour. She was ashamed of her own grief, the continual sense of absence instead of presence, glancing down at the stream and seeing only the bare stones by the pools.

Then one morning she woke up determined to walk the whole way out along the cliffs. The previous evening Eileen told her that she wanted to invite John Quinn to lunch the following Sunday. She looked forward with an excitement that was as much apprehension as curiosity, and knew that most of the weekend would go into planning the lunch.

She read all morning, made a light lunch and set out. 'A mind lively and at ease can look out on nothing, and that nothing will always answer back.' Was her mind at ease? Love was ever watchful. But was there a final going out of the light, a turning of the face to the earth? The light would belong to others then. They would watch. They would walk in the light.

She climbed away from the harbour, at once meeting the stiff breeze from the ocean, and was so intent on her path that before she noticed him she was beside Tommy McHugh. His face glowed with pleasure, and he came forward with an outstretched hand.

'You're welcome back. I was beginning to be afraid something had happened to you. There's not many of our kind left now.'

'My daughter came back from France. And we've had many visitors,' she said almost by way of apology.

'You're welcome back anyhow.'

'Where's Shep today?' she asked after a pause.

'It got so bad he'd do nothing I'd tell him. He was driving those sheep mad. So I took him . . . I took him and threw him – and threw him over the cliff, and I have peace ever since.'

She heard and didn't hear. She could see the petrified black-and-white shape blur in the air as it was flung out over the water. She had to get away quickly.

'Well. I'm glad to see you too,' she said as she started to move away.

There was something about the abruptness of her leaving, her distracted air, that displeased Tommy McHugh. He followed her disappearing figure for a long time, then said in the sing-song, confiding voice he had often used with the young collie when the two of them were sitting alone together above the ocean: 'I don't believe any of that stuff about the daughter coming from France, or the visitors. I wouldn't entertain it for even one holy, eternal minute. Let me tell you something for nothing, lad. Let me tell it to you for now and for ever and for world without end, Amen, deliver us, lad, that yon old bird is on her sweet effing way out,' he declared to the absent collie in a voice that sang out that they alone among all the creatures of the earth would never have to go that way.

A Pair of Spoons

SHENA MACKAY

VILLAGERS PASSING THE Old Post Office were stopped in their tracks by a naked woman dancing in the window. Not quite naked, for she wore a black straw hat dripping cherries and a string of red glass beads which made her white nudity more shocking. When they perceived that the figure behind the dusty glass was a dummy, a mannequin or shop-front model, they quickened their steps, clucking, peevish and alarmed like the pheasants that scurried down the lane and disappeared through the hedge. After a while only visitors to the village hidden in a fold of the Herefordshire hills, those who had parked their cars outside Minimarket and, seduced by the stream with its yellow irises and dragonflies, had wandered along the grassy bank that ran down one side of the lane, were struck by the nude with cherry hat and beads, frozen in mid-dance by their scandalised stares.

The Old Post Office, which had done business from the double-fronted room jutting out into the lane, had stood empty for several years following the death of the retired postmaster. Posters advertising National Savings, warning against the invasion of the Colorado beetle, and depicting heroic postmen struggling to the outposts of Empire still hung on the walls, curled and faded to the disappointing pinks, yellows, greens and blues of a magic painting book, while stamps and pensions were dispensed and bureaucratic rituals were enacted now through a grille of reinforced plastic at the back of Minimarket.

268

In that shop window was a notice board and prominent among the advertisements for puppies, firewood, machine-knitted garments and sponsored fun-runs, walks, swims and bake-ins, was a card which read in antiqued scrolly script: We buy Old Gold, Silver, Pewter, Brass and Broken Jewellery, any condition. China, Clocks, Furniture, Books, Comics, Tin Toys, Dinkies, Matchbox etc., Farm Animals, Clothes, Victoriana, Edwardiana, Bijouterie. Houses Cleared. Best Prices. Friendly Old-Established Firm. Ring us on 64 and we will call with No Obligation.

Parts of the Old Post Office house predated the fourteenth-century church whose clock and mossy graves could be seen from the kitchen window through a tangle of leggy basil plants on the sill above the stone sink. Anybody peeping in on a summer evening would have seen the old-established firm, Vivien and Bonnie, sharp-featured and straight-backed, tearing bread, keeping an eye on each other's plates, taking quick mouthfuls with a predatory air as if they had poached the pasta under the gamekeeper's eye; two stoats sitting up to table. Their neat hindquarters, in narrow jeans, rested on grubby embroidered cushions set with bits of broken mirror and sequins which overlapped the seats of the Sheraton-style fruitwood chairs; they rested their elbows on a wormy Jacobean table whose wonky leg was stabilised by a copy of *Antique Dealer's Guide*. It was Vivien, with her art-school training, who had calligraphed the notice in the village shop: after meeting Bonnie, she had taken a crash course in English porcelain and glass. Bonnie relied on the instinct which had brought her from assistant on a stall in the Portobello Road, where she had become expert in rubbing dust into the rough little flowers and fleeces and faked crazed-glaze of reproduction shepherdesses, goatherds, cupidons, lambs and spaniels, to co-owner of this ever-appreciated pile of bricks and beams. Vivien and Bonnie moved through Antiques Fayres like weasels in a hen house. To their fellow dealers they were known, inevitably, as Bonnie and Clyde or the Terrible Twins.

At night they slept curved into each other in their blue sheets like a pair of spoons in a box lined with dusty blue velvet or stained pink silk in summer: two spoons, silver-gilt a little tarnished by time, stems a little bent, which would realise less than half of their value sold singly rather than as a pair.

They had grown more alike through the years since they had been married in a simple ceremony at the now-defunct and much-lamented Gateways club. How to tell them apart? Vivien bore a tiny scar like a spider-crack on glass on her left cheekbone, the almost invisible legacy of the party that followed their nuptials, where Bonnie's former lover had thrown a glass of wine in her face. Or had it been Vivien's rejected girlfriend? Nobody could remember now, least of all the person who had flung the wine.

'Vivien is more vivid, and Bonnie's bonnier,' suggested a friend when the topic of their similarity was raised.

'No, it's the other way round,' another objected.

'A bit like dog owners turning into their dogs . . .'

'But who is the dog, and who the owner?'

'Now you're being bitchy.'

That conversation, which took place in London, would have struck an uneasy chord of recognition in Vivien had it been transmitted over the miles. She had become aware of an invisible lead attached to her collar and held kindly but firmly in Bonnie's hand. There were days when she seemed as insubstantial as Bonnie's shadow; she became aware that she mirrored Bonnie's every action. Bonnie took off her sweater, Vivien took off hers; Bonnie reached for her green and gold tobacco tin; Vivien took out her own cigarette papers; Bonnie felt like a coffee, so did Vivien; they sipped in unison; Bonnie ground pepper on to her food, Vivien held out her hand for the mill; when Bonnie, at the wheel of the van, pulled down her sun visor, Vivien's automatic hand reached up and she confronted her worried face in the vanity mirror. At night when they read in bed the pages of their books rasped in synchronicity until Bonnie's light clicked off and then Vivien's pillow was blacked out as suddenly as a tropical sky at sunset.

'You go on reading, love, if you want to. It won't disturb me.'

'No, I'm shattered,' replied Vivien catching Bonnie's yawn, and swallowing it as the choke-chain tightened round her throat. In the morning, after noticing her Marmite soldiers had lined up in the precise formation of Bonnie's troop, she pushed her plate away.

'Do you think you could manage on your own today? I don't feel so good.'

'You do look a bit green round the gills. I hope you're not coming down with something.'

Bonnie laid one hand on Vivien's brow and with the other appropriated her toast.

'You haven't got a temperature.'

'Well I feel funny.'

'We're supposed to be going to pick up that grandmother clock from that old boy, and there's that car-boot sale – oh well, I suppose I *can* go on my own . . . hope to Christ he hasn't done anything stupid like having it valued, you can't trust those old buzzards, dead crafty, some of them . . .'

Their two egg shells lay on her polished plate, hardly damaged, sucked clean by a nifty rodent.

Vivien guided the van out into the lane; Bonnie had taken off one of the gates on the rearside wing once when she was cross. Vivien waved her off and watched the dust settle. She felt an immediate surge of energy and fuelled it with a doorstep of toast spread with honey found in the cupboard of a house they had cleared, crunching on the cells of a comb rifled from the hive by the fingers of a dead woman. The bees had all buzzed off by the time Bonnie and Vivien had hacked their way through the tangled garden, and the empty hives of wood, weathered to grey silk, stood now in their cobbled yard.

Vivien left her sticky plate and knife in the sink and, sucking sweetness from her teeth, locked the door and set off down the lane with a wave to the woman dancing in the window. The vicar, passing by on the other side, ducked his head in the cold nod that was the most, in charity, that he need vouchsafe the Londoners since Bonnie had made him an offer for the paten and chalice.

'Morning, vicar. Lovely morning, isn't it? Makes you feel good to be alive,' Vivien called out uncharacteristically, surprising them both.

The incumbent was forced to look at her across the lane, a skinny lumberjack, cramming into her mouth a spray of the redcurrants which hung like cheap glass beads among the fuchsias in her red and purple raggedy hedge, and caught a glitter of glass crimson fire on plastic flesh, and a dangle of cherries.

'Hedge could do with a trim,' he said.

'Oh, we like it like that,' reminding him that she was half of that dubious duo. She was sucking the end of a honeysuckle trumpet. At this rate she wouldn't need the hedge trimmer he had been about to offer. She would soon have eaten the whole hedge.

'Ah well,' he concluded.

His skirt departed to the east and Vivien's jeans loped westward. She was trying to suppress the little maggot of anxiety whose mealy mouth warned that Bonnie might telephone to find out how she was. As she passed the call-box she had such a vivid image of Bonnie impotently misting up the glass panes of an identical construction standing among moon daisies on a grassy verge, while the phone rang and rang in their empty kitchen that she could only assume that telepathy was at work. She thought, and walked on, stopping outside a garden at a box of wormeaten windfalls with 'Please help yourselves' scrawled on a piece of cardboard. Vivien filled her pockets. She came to a gate, placed one hand on the topmost bar, and vaulted into a field of corn. She followed a natural track through the furrows, now spitting husks and crunching sweet kernels, now negotiating an apple, until she was faced with barbed wire and a ditch of nettles. She stood wavering wildly on the wire and hurled herself forward landing, with only the softest malevolent graze of leaves on her bare ankles, in a field whose hay had been harvested leaving its scent in the air. The field was bordered on three sides by massive trees, oak, sycamore, ash, sweet chestnut, and although it was only July, recent rain had brought down a scattering of tiny green conkers. 'Like medieval fairies' weapons,' thought Vivien, whose fancy, when not stamped on by Bonnie, flew on such flights, 'those spiked balls on chains.' Aluminium animal troughs rusted in a heap. At the far end of the field was a gate set in a high hedge and Vivien walked towards it dreamily with the sun freckling her face and her arms beneath her rolled-up sleeves.

The latch lifted but she had to force the gate against hanks of long grass, and squeezed herself through the gap. She was at the edge of a garden and now she saw a house which was not visible from the field. Old glass in the windows glittered like insects' wings. No dog barked. The house exuded emptiness, shimmering in the heat haze while housemartins flew in and out of their shells of honeycombed mud under the eaves. As she walked over the lawn she realised that the grass here had been cut not very long ago: it was springy beneath her feet, studded with purple milkwort and daisies and buttercups that seemed to acknowledge the futility of growing too tall. Somebody, therefore, cared for the garden. The roses needed to be deadheaded, the petals were falling from the irises and peonies revealing shiny seed cases, but apart from the soggy roses and a faint mist here and there of lesser willowherb and an occasional intrusive cow parsley and weedy seedling brought up by the rain, the flowerbeds were orderly. She meant only to peep through the windows.

It was strange, she thought, as she walked on rose petals round the back ground-floor windows, pressing her face against the old dark glass, how she did not feel like a trespasser, but as though she had inadvertently locked herself out of those rooms hung with faded velvet curtains and had the right to walk on the pale carpets and curl up in that yellow velvet chair with a blond dog at her feet. She stared at old wooden kitchen cupboards holding china and utensils behind their half-open sliding doors, the mottled enamel gas cooker, the pyramidal iron saucepan stand, the fossilised pink soap and rusty brillo pad on the draining board, the clean tea towels, bleached and brittle as ancient flags. A movement by her foot made her look down. A toad regarded her with amber eyes. She crouched before it and reached out to pick it up. The toad leaped for the dank shadow under a flat scratchy plant. Vivien thrust her fingers after it and scrabbled in dead leaves and needles. Instead of pulsating skin, she struck metal. She drew out a key. It came as no surprise that the key fitted the lock on the scullery door, and turned, through cobwebs and flakes of rust, to admit her to the stone-flagged floor. The mangle, the stone sink, the disconnected twin-tub, had been waiting for her.

Vivien moved through the rooms, acknowledging the pile of enamel dogs' dishes in the kitchen, the Chinese umbrella stand holding walking sticks, knobkerries, a brace of Union Jacks, the wellies sealed with cobwebs, the waterproof coats and jackets on the pegs, the polished tallboys, chests of drawers, the empty vases, the glass-fronted cabinets holding miniatures and enamelled boxes, scent bottles and figurines, the groves of books, the quiet beds, the framed photographs, the high dry baths, the box spilling shoes. Everywhere she saw herself reflected, framed in elaborate gilt on the walls, elongated in tilted cheval glasses, in triplicate and thence to infinity above dressing tables, dimly in the glass of pictures. She touched nothing. At last she let herself out again, locked the scullery door, and put the key in her pocket.

'The state of you!' Bonnie scolded. 'Where've you *been*? I've been back for an hour. I rang to see how you were but there was no reply . . .'

'Just for a walk. I needed some air.'

'You could have got that in the garden.' Bonnie waved an arm at the sofa spewing horsehair onto the cobbles.

'It's damp and smelly,' Vivien protested. 'Did you get the clock?'

'No. I didn't.' Bonnie brushed grimly at grass seeds and burrs clinging to Vivien's clothes. 'You look as if you've been rolling in the hay. Have you?'

'Chance would be a fine thing. Ouch.' The village maidens had a tendency to obesity and anoraks and, this summer, fluorescent shorts. Bonnie slapped at Vivien's jeans, reactivating the nettle stings. Stung into memory of her first sights of the house, and walking again in its peaceful rooms, Vivien half-heard Bonnie's voice.

'. . . decided not to part with it for sentimental reasons, lying old toad, then he let slip that he'd heard the Antiques Roadshow might be coming round next year . . . thought I'd really cracked it . . . who did he think he was kidding, you could practically see him rehearsing the greedy smile of wonderment that would light up his toothless old chops when they told him his crappy clock was worth a small fortune . . . I'd like to tear up his bus pass, he practically promised me . . . sell their own grandmothers, these people . . .'

'I thought that was precisely what he wouldn't do?' Vivien returned to the present.

'What?'

'Sell his grandmother. Clock.'

'*Don't* try to be clever, it doesn't suit you.'

I am clever, thought Vivien, and it might suit me very well.

'Shall we go to the pub later?' she said.

'No. What do you want to go there for? I thought we agreed that the ambiente was nonsimpatico?'

'Well, yes. I just thought you might fancy going out for a change.'

Vivien ripped the ring-pulls from two cold beers from the fridge and handed one to Bonnie. It was true that the pub was uncongenial. The locals were a cliquey lot. Bonnie could take off their accent brilliantly. 'Oooh-arr' she had riposted to those guys' offer to buy them a drink, and suddenly she and Vivien were on the outside of a circle of broad backs. No sense of humour. And boring – most of their conversation was limited to the agricultural; there were so many overheard references to filling in dykes that the girls could not but feel uneasy, especially as those ditches were not a feature of the local landscape. Aggression flared in wet patches in the armpits and on the bulging bellies scarcely contained in T-shirts that bobbed like balloons along the bar. The landlord, who was in the early stages of vegetabliasis – so far his nose had turned into an aubergine – snarled at them, as if he thought they would turn the beer.

'Let's go and sit in the garden,' said Vivien, leading the way. 'How was the car-boot sale?'

'Like a car boot-sale.'

They ate outside, sucking little bones and tossing them against the rising moon, straining their eyes in the dusk to pick out their autumn wardrobe from the L.L. Bean catalogue, and going into the house only when it grew too dark to read even by moonlight and starlight, and it was time to luxuriate with a nightcap in the pleasures of *Prisoner Cell-Block H*, propped up in bed by pillows, in front of the television. Long after Bonnie had fallen asleep, whimpering slightly as if dreaming of chasing rabbits, Vivien lay awake with a glass-fronted cabinet glowing in the dark before her eyes. A slight flaw or bend in the glass gave a mocking, flirtatious twist to the rosy lips of the porcelain boy in a yellow jacket and pink breeches, ruffled in a gentle breeze the green feather in his red hat, lifted the wings of the bird in his hands, and raised an eyebrow at the little girl clutching a wriggling piglet against her low-cut laced bodice over a skirt striped with flowers. A black and gold spotted leopard with a pretty face and gold-tipped paws lounged benignly between them, and putti, half-decorously wreathed, offered baskets of flowers.

Vivien, falling into sleep, put her hand out in the moonlight and found that the cabinet had no key. The moon hung between the open curtains like a huge battered gold coin almost within grasp.

A week passed before Vivien could return to her house. At the wheel of the van, at the kitchen cooker, in dusty halls where people haggled over trinkets and dead people's clothes and crazed enamel hairbrushes and three-tiered cake stands, she cherished her secret. Had she asked herself why, she might have replied that it was because it was the only secret she had ever had from Bonnie; or she might have said that for the first time she wanted to look at and touch beautiful objects without putting a price on them, or even that there was something in the air of the house that stayed her hand from desecration, but she was careful not to ask herself any questions. Once or twice she caught Bonnie giving her a look. They slept uneasily, with bad dreams of each other.

It happened that Bonnie had to attend a surprise family party for her parents' Golden Wedding. The anticipation of the celebration, where she would stand as a barren fig tree among the Laura Ashley floribunda and fecundity, put her in such a black mood that Vivien expired a long sigh of relief, as if anxiety had been expelled from her by the despairing farewell toot as the van lurched like a tumbrel into the lane. The golden present, exquisitely encased in a gold foil with much gold ribbon twirled to curlicues round a pencil to disguise its essential tackiness, had been wrapped by Vivien but her name did not appear on the gold gift tag. Bonnie's Russian wedding ring and the true lover's knot, the twin of that which circled Vivien's little finger would dissolve into invisibility when she crossed the family threshold. An uncle would prod her stomach and tell her she ought to get some meat on her bones, a man likes something he can get hold of; a sister-in-law, made bold by Malibu and cake, might enquire after Bonnie's flatmate while rearranging by a fraction of an inch her own present of a pair of gilded ovals framing studio portraits of gap-toothed grandchildren. Much later, she would offer on a stained paper plate the stale and indigestible news that she had once been disconcerted by a desire to kiss a schoolfriend, and on the homeward journey the memory of her confession would jolt into her stomach and the motorway verge would receive a shower of shame and disgust for the unnatural recipient of her secret. Meanwhile, however, Bonnie was being introduced to the fiancé of a niece, who was omitting her name from his mental list of wedding guests even as they shook hands.

'You might have made the effort to put on a skirt for once,' her mother told her. In fact, Bonnie and Vivien occasionally outraged their friends by wearing skirts. The last time had been when they turned up at the Treacle Pudding in a heat wave in their batiks and had been refused entry, but she didn't tell her mother this. Bonnie went into the garden and made herself a roll-up.

'You'll die if you smoke,' said a small boy in a red waistcoat with matching bow-tie on elastic.

'Want a drag?' Bonnie held out the cigarette.

He shook his head so hard that his eyes rolled like blue doll's eyes, as if they would fall out, and ran in to report the death threat, and shot her with a plastic machine gun from an upstairs window. Bonnie looked at her watch, reflecting with relief that the late-night, half-hearted discussions with Vivien about adoption early in their marriage, had fizzled away with the morning Alka-Seltzer. If they *had* been allowed to adopt one, they would have to have had it adopted. She went in to the telephone on the public shelf above the hall radiator and dialled home, clamping the receiver to her ear to keep out the sounds of merrymaking, the mouthpiece poised to muffle her low desperate 'Hi babe, it's me. Just needed to hear your voice'; words that she was to be deprived of muttering. No comfort came from the shrilling 1940s' handset in the Old Post Office kitchen and, blinded by a paper hat which someone had slipped over her head, she went back to join the party.

'I rang. You weren't there,' she said as she slammed the van door and strode past Vivien who had run to meet her, into the house.

'Is that my doggie bag?' Vivien pulled at the purple Liberty carrier in Bonnie's hand. 'What have you brought me?'

'Nothing. You didn't deserve anything. I ate it in the van. Where were you, when I needed you?'

Vivien might have replied, 'I was in my house, perfectly happy. I was reading, grazing among the books, and walking in the garden, and suddenly I thought of the hard little face, the mean mouth that I fell in love with, and I came running home.'

'I went for a walk, babe. I was very lonesome all by my little self, without you.'

Bonnie, half-placated, dropped the bag onto the table.

'There's a bit of cake left.'

Vivien drew it out.

'You've eaten off the icing. You pig.'

'Yes,' said Bonnie sternly.

'What's this?' Vivien scrabbled in Bonnie's bag and pulled out by the leg a mothy-looking toy.

'My old teddy. It's so threadbare I thought we could pass it off as Victorian. They're fetching a good price now.'

'Oh Bonnie, you can't sell him, he's cute. Look at his little beady eyes.'

'Give it here. I'll pull one off, make it even cuter – nothing more poignant than a sad teddy, is there?'

'No! I won't let you. How could you be so cruel? I'm going to keep him. He's probably your oldest friend . . .'

. . . A tiny Bonnie, rosy from her bath, toddled up the wooden hill to Bedfordshire, holding a sleepy teddy by the paw . . .

'Actually she's a girl. Tedina. I used to smack her with my hairbrush.'

Vivien thought a flicker of fear passed over Tedina's tiny black eyes. She rooted in a box and found a Victorian christening robe.

'Perfect,' said Bonnie. 'Fifty quid at least.'

'There's a fatal flaw in your plan,' Vivien told her. 'Teddy bears weren't invented in Victorian times.'

'Don't be stupid. Of course they were. Albert brought one back from Germany or something one Christmas. They're called after him.' Sensing a flaw in her argument, if not in her plan, Bonnie let the subject drop. Tedina, in her white pintucked robe was carried upstairs to their bed by Vivien, and the hairbrush, a section of the carapace of a dead tortoise set in silver, was put tactfully in a drawer.

It was when she picked up the local paper that she saw an unmistakable photograph, the notice that read 'House for Sale By Auction with contents'. She stuffed the paper under a pile of back numbers of *Forum* and *Men Only* that, with a plastic *Thomas the Tank Engine*, had been purchased as a job lot, with a Clarice Cliff bowl thrown in, for a tenner. 'They're not quite the sort of old comics and toys we had in mind,' she was explaining, backing towards the door, when her eye fell on the bowl, holding a dead busy lizzie.

The owner, a desperate-looking woman hung about with small children, intercepted her quick appraisal.

'What about the bowl, then? That's antique, it belonged to my grandma.'

'There's no call for that sort of Budgie-Ware,' said Bonnie, her tongue flicking over dry lips, her nose quivering. 'We've got two or three we can't shift, taking up space, gathering dust,' as she flicked the bright feathers of the two birds in relief on a branch of ivy that curved round the pale grey bowl patterned with darker grey leaves.

'They used to give them as prizes at fairgrounds,' Vivien added, lifting the bowl to read the signature on its base. 'They were known as fairings.'

'I thought those were biscuits,' said the woman dully. 'Cornish Fairings?'

'Of course, *some* of them *were* biscuits,' Vivien conceded. 'In Cornwall.'

The deal having been struck the woman was so grateful she made them a cup of pale tea by dunking the same tea bag in two mugs. There were no biscuits. She stroked the birds surreptitiously as she wrapped them in a piece of newspaper. One of the children started to wail 'I don't want those ladies to take our budgies.'

There was the sound of a slap as the door closed. Vivien and Bonnie went whistling to the van.

Six wooden chairs stood in a row in the back yard. Bonnie and Vivien were hard at work in the morning sun, removing the chipped white gloss paint from two of them.

'We'll need some more stripper,' Bonnie said, straightening her back painfully. 'God, how I hate this job.'

'You go and get some and I'll carry on with what's left,' Vivien suggested and Bonnie was only too willing to agree. Fifteen minutes later, satisfied that Bonnie was too far on the road to turn back for anything she might have forgotten, Vivien stripped off the Cornish fisherman's smock she wore for working, pulled on a sweatshirt and, walking as quickly as possible without attracting attention, made for the house.

'This may be the last time I shall come here,' she told it as she stood inside the scullery door, which she left unlocked in case she had to make a quick getaway. The rooks she had startled into raucous proclamation of her guilt lapsed into spasms of complaint in the copper beech. Nobody had rallied to their alarm. Vivien went from room to room, resisting the desire to stroke the dust from satiny fruitwood, walnut, maple, mahogany, to lift the plates from the dresser to read the maker's name, and the marks on the dulling silver in the kitchen, to dust the dead flies from the window ledges and to light the candles in their porcelain sticks. There, on the shelves and in the faded, painted bookcases were all the books she would never read. She longed to take one and curl up in her yellow velvet chair and read the morning away until the yellow dog prevailed upon her to follow him into the garden where a straw hat with lattices broken by time, and a trug awaited her. She admired for the last time the spilled jewels of the crystal doorknob, and stood in front of the glass cabinet committing to memory the figures therein: the man and woman riding on mild goats to meet each other, he with kids' heads peeping from his panniers, and she with hers filled with flowers and a basket of babies on her back, riding homewards in the evening in the cawing of rooks, the . . .

'Is this a private party, or can anybody join in?'

Vivien screamed, whirling round. There, filling the doorway, just like Bea in the latest episode of *Prisoner Cell-Block H*, stood Bonnie, with a knobkerrie in her hand.

'So this is your little game. I've known you were up to something for days.'

'Bea, Bonnie, I can explain.'

'You'd better, You've got a lot of explaining to do – my God, are those what I think they are?'

She advanced on the cabinet.

'Don't touch!'

'Why not? You must've left your dabs all over everything. So this is what you were up to. Planned to sell the stuff behind my back and make yourself a juicy little profit, didn't you?'

Bonnie slumped into the yellow chair. 'You were going to leave me, weren't you? Run off and set up on your own.'

Her words were thick and bitter like the tears which rolled from her eyes.

'I'll kill you first.' She leaped up, brandishing the knobkerrie.

'How can you think, I don't believe I'm hearing this –'

Vivien caught her raised arm, they fought for the weapon, Bonnie trying frantically to bring it down on Vivien's head, Vivien struggling to hold the murderous arm aloft. A kick in the shins brought howling Bonnie to her knees and Vivien dragged the knobkerrie from her hand. Vivien twisted one of her arms behind her back and pushed her face downwards to the carpet.

'Babe, I love you,' she explained, punctuating her words with light blows from the knobkerrie. 'I swear I wasn't planning to run out on you. I haven't touched anything here, and I'm not going to. Understand?'

'Ouch, you bitch, get off me.' Bonnie spat out carpet fibres.

'If I let you get up, do you promise to sit quietly and listen?'

'Ouch. Thuk.' She spat.

'Very well. Go and sit over there.'

Bonnie slunk, snarling like a dog to the sofa at which her master pointed the club. A resurgence of rage brought her half to her feet.

'Sit!'

Vivien could see, even after ten minutes of explanation that Bonnie would never quite believe her. 'It was like being under a spell. As if I were meant to be here. It's so beautiful. So peaceful. I just wanted to be here. It was like being in another world for a little while.'

'Another world from which you excluded me.'

'I was going to tell you. I was going to bring you here later today. I swear.'

'A likely story. Are you sure there's no one else involved? You've been meeting someone here haven't you? Where is she, hiding under the bed? Or is it a he?'

'Don't be so bloody stupid! Look, I'll show you all over the house, you can look under every bed if you like. Can't you get it into your thick skull that I just liked being alone here?'

'No I can't. I never want to be alone without you. I just don't believe you.'

Vivien led Bonnie from room to room. They found no brawny limbs in fluorescent shorts under the beds – nothing but dust, a pair of silver shoes, and hanks of horsehair from a torn mattress. Dresses and suits hung empty in the cupboards, linen lay innocently in chests and clean towels were in the airing cupboard, if the spiders in the baths should want them. They pulled their sleeves over their hands to touch knobs and handles. In a chest of drawers they found dozens of pairs of kid gloves with pearl buttons never unfastened, in a millefeuille of virginal tissue.

'Satisfied?' They were back in the drawing room.

'Bonnie?'

Bonnie was standing in the centre of the room with a rapt expression on her face.

'Bonnie? It's getting to you, isn't it? The magic of the place. You understand now?'

'What I simply cannot understand, or believe, is how someone who has been in the business as long as you have could be so incredibly stupid as to let such an opportunity pass.'

'You don't understand at all . . . I hoped. Oh forget it. Let's go.'

'How could you be so SELFISH? Not telling me. Those wonderful pieces. Just sitting there. Shows how much you value our relationship.'

'It's not like that . . .'

'Isn't it?'

'No it isn't.'

Vivien knew she could not defend herself against the charge of wanting to keep the house a secret, or wanting to be alone there. She did not know if that, or her lack of professional loyalty or acumen, was the more hurtful.

'Anyway,' she said, 'this is the last time I'll be coming here. The house goes up for auction next week.'

'Does it? That doesn't give us much time then.'

'No, Bonnie. We're not taking anything.'

Vivien looked from the miniatures and figurines to Bonnie, tear-stained and tense as a whippet, poised on the edge of their marriage.

'Come on then,' she said.

They raced for the stairs. They plundered the glove drawer, forcing their fingers into the unstretched kid; a pearl button hit the floor and rolled away.

'There's a pile of plastic carriers in the kitchen. Where's the van?'

'At home. I watched you leave the house, parked the van and followed you on foot.'

'Good. Thank goodness you didn't bring it here. I should have known someone was there when the rooks started squawking,' Vivien panted as they worked, each knowing instinctively what to take. A team. Although Bonnie would need kid-glove treatment for a while.

'How did you find the key?'

'A toad showed me the way.'

'A toad? Sure you don't mean a robin, like in *The Secret Garden*? I know how you love poring over those mildewed kids' books.'

As Bonnie spoke she jiggled a hairpin, found in a dressing-table tray, in the lock of a china cabinet.

'Brilliant,' Vivien said but she walked over to the window and looked out into the garden as Bonnie lifted out the first cupid and the pretty spotted leopard with gold-tipped paws. They left no mess, no trace of their presence. Vivien locked the door and replaced the wiped key under the plant. As they passed the drawing-room windows she saw the person she might have been, watching them go from the velvet yellow chair in the room defiled by their fight.

They met nobody on the way home but if they had it would have been apparent that those two weirdos from the Old Post Office had been doing their shopping, and not stinting themselves from the look of their bulging bags.

At home Vivien said, 'We must be mad. We'll be the obvious suspects when the stuff's missed. The only dealers for miles around . . . We could put it back . . .'

'And risk getting caught in the act, apart from the fact that this is the biggest coup of our career? No way, José. By the way, how did you know the house is going up for auction?'

'It was in the local paper.'

'Oh well, the plan is we'll drive up to London first thing tomorrow. We can stay with Frankie and Flossie for a few days while we unload the stuff. And I think I know somebody who will be *very* interested . . .'

'But . . .'

'Those frigging freeloaders owe us. Think of the times they've pitched up here without so much as a bottle of Sainsbury's plonk. Besides, they're our best friends!'

The kid gloves shrivelled and blackened on the barbie, giving a peculiar taste to the burgers and green peppers that had sweated and spat on the grid above them. The tiny pearl buttons glimmered among discs of bone, horn, glass and plastic in the tall jar of assorted buttons.

'Shampoo?'

'Shampoo!'

Bonnie and Vivien had returned in high spirits from their successful stay in London. They had taken in a sale of the stock of a bankrupt theatrical costumiers on the way back. It was nine o'clock in the evening. The man on the doorstep heard music and caught a glimpse of two figures, beyond the nude in her hat and necklace, locked together in a slow dance once known as the Gateways grind, out of sync with the jaunty song.

'Good evening, ladies. Filth,' he smiled, flashing his ID

at the wolf in a lime-green beaded dress who answered the door.

'Who is it?' came the bark of the fox behind her.

'It's the Filth – mean the police,' came the slightly muffled reply. For a moment they stood, the wolf in green and the fox in a scarlet sheath fringed with black, staring at him with glassy eyes, then simultaneously pulled off their heads, and he felt that they had removed their sharp, sly masks to reveal features identical to the heads they held in their hands, so that he still faced a fox and wolf, but with fear in their eyes.

He touched delicately one of the tubular beads on Bonnie's dress, standing in his linen suit crumpled from a day's policing. 'Nice,' he said. 'Bugle beads, aren't they? That's Blossom Dearie, isn't it?' He sang 'There ought to be a moonlight-saving time, so I could love that man of mine . . .' glancing towards the uniformed constable at the wheel of the police car.

'You'd better come in,' said Vivien the Fox. The animals, on high heels, led him into the front room. He saw a bottle of champagne and two glasses.

'I don't suppose you'd like a drink? You can't when you're on duty, can you?'

'You've been watching too much television,' he replied, picking up a dusty green glass from a sideboard. 'Regular Aladdin's cave you've here, haven't you? Cheers.' He raised his glass to the model and looked round at the piles and rails of clothes, the jumble of china and glass, silver, brass and pewter, the old books, the trivia, the ephemera that refused to die, the worthless and the valuable bits of furniture, the glass jar that held the tiny pearl buttons snipped from two pairs of burned skin gloves.

'I caught one of her shows at the Pizza on the Park,' he said. 'Blossom Dearie.'

'Oh, so did we. Perhaps –'

'How can we help you,' Bonnie broke in.

'There's been a break-in. At an empty house down the road, the old Emerson place. Some valuable pieces taken. I've got the list here. We thought you might come across some of them in your travels, or someone might try to pass them off on you, you being the most local and obvious outlet – if our perpetrators are the bunch of amateurs we suspect they are. If that should happen, we'd be very grateful if you would let us know.'

'Of course.' Vivien took the photocopied list he held out. It shook in her hand although there was no draught that humid evening.

'Let's see.' Bonnie read aloud over Vivien's shoulder. 'Meissen Shepherdess with birdcage. Harlequin and Columbine, cupids representing four seasons. Leopard. Man and woman, riding goats, Staffordshire. Chelsea, Derby, Bow . . . pair of berry spoons, circa 1820 . . .'

She whistled. 'There's some nice stuff here, priceless. Any idea who could have done the job?'

'We're working on it. Whoever it was did a pretty good demolition job on the drawing room and kindly left us a few genetic fingerprints. Shouldn't be too difficult.'

The fox went as red as the cherries on the dummy's hat, as if she had been responsible for the violation.

'But those lovely things – the shepherdess, the leopard, the porcelain – what were they doing in an empty house? Wasn't there a burglar alarm at least to protect them?'

'The house and contents were due to be auctioned the following day. It was just bad luck. Old Mrs Emerson's godson, she left it to him, has no interest in the place apart from the proceedings from the sale – serves him right, really. Nasty piece of work – greedy and careless – a dangerous combination. More money than sense already. There's an old local couple who kept an eye on the place – he did a bit in the garden, kept the grass down, and she kept the dust down. It seems likely that one of them forgot to reset the alarm the last time they were there, but that's academic really. They're both in deep shock. Aged ten years overnight. Heartbroken. Keep saying they've betrayed old Mrs Emerson's trust. From the look of them they'll be apologising to her in person soon . . . Well, thank you for your co-operation. Sorry to intrude on your evening.'

'We were just pricing some new stock,' Bonnie felt obliged to explain, waving a hand at the fox and wolf heads staring at them from the floor, as he rose to leave.

'Phew!! What an incredible stroke of luck! That someone should actually break in while we were away! I can't believe it! Somebody up there must like us . . .' Bonnie sank into a chair kicking off her high-heeled shoes.

'And us prancing around like a couple of drag queens in animal heads,' she went on, 'I thought I would die. I could hear those prison gates clanging, couldn't you? Cell-block H, here we come! Let's have a look at that list again. "Silver salt spoon convolvulus design handle"? How come we missed that?'

'I don't know.'

Vivien crossed her fingers behind her back and hoped that Tedina, who had watched her unscrew the brass knob of the bedpost and drop in a silver spoon, would keep her mouth shut. Then the spoon with its convolvulus wreathed stem would lie safely and inaccessibly locked in the bedpost, a tiny silver secret salvaged from her house, as long as the marriage lasted. She pulled the chenille bedspread that served as a curtain across the window, refilled their glasses and turned over the record.

'Where were we, before we were so rudely interrupted?'

She held out both her hands and they resumed the dance, the Friendly Old-Established Firm back in business.

Alas for the Egg

HILARY MANTEL

ON SUNDAY, THEY went to Nicosia. On their right as they drove, but far in the distance, was the faint blue line of the sea. Nearer at hand, pylons were slung across the landscape between the outcrops of white chalk; knolls and tumuli arose from flat green fields. The road began to climb. Sage-coloured trees of perfect form stood against the skyline.

The sun – it was now midday – gilded June's bare arm, and glinted on her nail polish; a shade called Frosted Peach, which she had applied freshly at the hotel that morning. An army lorry, its canvas top flapping, ate up the road before them. Beside the asphalt, anemones burned in shocking scarlet. When they stopped to admire the view, Gregory looked in the guidebook. The flowers, it said, were the tears of Venus, shed for the murdered Adonis and transformed as they fell to blood. It was a piece of information he decided to keep to himself.

They sat for five minutes or so, while Gregory read, and June, her face empty of expression, gazed inland. Gesturing vaguely, Gregory said, 'There's a neolithic site up there. Burial mounds.' June gave an affected shudder. 'It wouldn't take long,' he said.

June consulted her watch. 'We'll miss the first race.'

'That doesn't matter.'

'Oh, why bother then?' she snapped. 'Why go at all?'

A moment later she was climbing out so that he could photograph her, posed by their hired car. Her bad temper, even on holiday, never lasted long. She was a quick passionate woman, but inclined to overlook his failings. She knew he could not help them. He focused carefully; the motorway was just on his right, and he wanted to keep it out of the picture. June stood with her feet planted sturdily, calf-high in yellow flowers. Ever since they arrived, he had been photographing her. She wanted something she could show her neighbours; something she could show her grandchildren, when Kerry and Dennis got round to it. He felt, as he looked through the camera's eye, that he had never really seen her before.

Every morning so far they had taken breakfast on the hotel terrace, overlooking the sea. It was warm, even at 7 o'clock, and the hotel staff were affable and wide-eyed, bustling between the tables with their cheese omelettes to order and their straw baskets of the coarse undersalted local bread. He made do with cornflakes; he'd had indigestion for days. June said, 'You'd think they liked being waiters.' She sounded rather sour, but what she was doing, Gregory knew, was weighing them up as potential employees. You needed, in hairdressing, any amount of public pleasantness; but at the same time, you had to be able to stand up to the customers. Ever since they left home she had been worrying about Maison Sonya, and whether Kerry was coping.

'If we were in Abersoch,' she said, 'I could be at home in two hours, if necessary.' Abersoch, a caravan site there, was their usual holiday choice; but this was their dream holiday. Gregory had retired, and they felt they should do something to mark it; the pension fund had paid out.

If there was one thing that had pleased June about Cyprus, it was the flourishing state of the hairdressing trade. Every *taverna*, every burger bar, seemed buttressed by unisex salons; Seville Hair Fashions, Youlia Crimpers, Maros Style International. It seemed that a whole people, if not engaged in chopping salad or building holiday flats, were employed in doing each other's hair. On their third day they made for Paphos, over to the west, and June counted the salons through the Limassol outskirts. She was silent for most of the journey. Gregory didn't make conversation. His eyes were for the seascapes afforded by each bend in the road. 'Careful,' June said, once or twice. At Paphos they saw the mosaics. He was moved, far more than he had expected, by the faces of the gods; by the ageless tiger, feral breath cast in stone; by the single pomegranate, two millennia in ripeness of flesh. June nudged him, to look at a young woman going around with a touring party. 'That's a good feather-cut,' she said. 'Look at her fringe, that's what you call hairdressing.' At the Baths of Aphrodite she saw a blow-wave that really pleased her.

He looked, when she pointed; obediently at the young men, but with a certain furtive interest, which he tried to suppress, at the young girls. Sleek, shapely, they were shedding their winter layers; it was almost April, after all. But why not look, he asked himself. I am old now, it is my prerogative. I am retired, and must have hobbies. Buntings decked the roadsides, and wreaths of spring flowers. It was carnival week. *Carne vale*: farewell to flesh.

June had set out the pattern of their days, with attention to what she called Value for Money. Breakfast; an excursion, then an hour by the hotel pool; a bath, some titivation, then the descent to the cocktail bar. A drink or two; then dinner. 'We have to try and cram it all in,' she said. Some mornings, on a whim, they had their sunbathing before their outing. It amused him to see the patrons in the same places at the pool, day after day. Their habits overrode their need for sun or shade. 'They're territorial,' he said to June. 'The territorial imperative.' June said nothing; went on reading her magazine. When Kerry was a little girl, she used to pay threepence at the sweet shop on the corner for something called a Lucky Bag. You didn't know what you might get; you might pull out a lollipop, then an aniseed ball, or some sort of humbug. His mind, June said, was something like that.

He was not used to the sun. It made him sleepy. He would lie back, the guide book propped open on his chest, ostensibly planning tomorrow's excursion, but really just day-dreaming. June asked him 'What are you thinking about?' and he said, 'The future.'

'Oh yes,' June said. She thought in terms of the summer ahead. In July it would be Abersoch again, but this time they would be buying their caravan, not renting. After all, this holiday was a one-off. They would not be able to afford it every year. They had tried other places – Anglesey, for example – but they had always come back to Abersoch.

When he thought of the future, it was the next twenty years he had in mind. June had the business. She was a lot younger than he was; they both, thank God, had their health. The shop had been nothing when June bought it; grubby nets at the window, fading photographs of rigidly permed starlets flapping on the walls. Who were those starlets now? Grandmothers. When June took over she had the shop refitted in the latest glass and chrome and canework. She stood on her feet for eight hours a day. She ate her lunch standing up; or didn't bother. There was a girl, at hairdressing college two days a week, ripping up the beauty magazines with a big pair of scissors, seeking out the latest trends. On Fridays and Saturdays they had late openings. 'Mum's a phenomenon,' Kerry said. She couldn't keep up with her, although she was half her age. June would never retire. She once said she'd run the salon from a wheelchair if she had to. But why should she have to? Something in her transcended ordinary health.

Gregory's own job had never absorbed him in quite the same way. It had not used him up; left him free to cultivate his mind. He had not been sorry to retire, and yet there was something, a kind of weight on his chest, that he had not bargained for. It is a life-crisis, he told himself, it is a rite of passage. After this indolent summer I will find things to do. Trifles; pastimes. June would not reproach him with inactivity. Her energy level had always been higher than his; it was a fact of life. Her earning power would keep them cosy. He had much to be grateful for. That, he supposed, was the weight he bore.

Tired of bearing it, he turned his head, for diversion; stretched his body along the sunlounger. He turned back, read his guide book a little; but deliberately, sideways from half-closed eyes, he watched Nell. Nell across the pool; Nell somnolent, in her blue bikini. What age would she be? He remembered her pleasant low voice, greeting him on the breakfast terrace; greeting June too, but when June turned to interrogate the waiter she had given him a smile. The first time he had seen Nell sunbathing, he had thought she was topless. Sucking his lip, he had read furiously of the ruins at Salamis, until the moment came when he allowed himself to glance up again, his pulse quickening. But she was not topless, it was an illusion; the half-cups of her bikini clung to the undershadow of heavy full breasts. She looked up, across the pool, and saw him watching her.

On their first morning, the two couples had only exchanged a greeting, but on the second day it had progressed. Ted, Nell's husband, had asked him if he knew the cricket score. 'Care for a look at *The Times*?' he'd said and passed it across the table. 'It's yesterday's.' They introduced themselves. They seemed a close couple. Childless, I'll bet, June said later. Nell had this sleepy, warm smile.

June had warned him, when they were up in their room. 'Leave them alone, Gregory, they're not our sort. You don't want to be palling up with them, and getting towed off somewhere expensive for the evening.' June despised people from the south of England, as much as she feared them. Nevertheless, he heard her telling Nell in the bar that night about the latest perming techniques, and confiding her fear that Kerry would not cope.

'Never mind,' Nell said soothingly, 'you're on holiday. You must try to relax.'

'Relaxing never built up a hairdressing business,' June said. She was afraid that Kerry would be conned by some customer, that some woman would come in and say her hair was falling out, and Kerry, without the wit to say she wasn't liable, would put her hand in the till and pay the old bag off. 'I could make your blood run cold,' June told Nell, 'with tales of what the public get up to.'

Nell seemed amused, but she held back her smile. He wished she would not hold it back; already by the second day he loved to see it, and as she turned up the corners of her mouth an adolescent heat touched his body, a feeling he thought he had forgotten. It was as if he had met some former self in the dank back alleys of the Old Town: halt, who goes there? Tentatively Nell patted her own soft brown hair. June said she pitied her; it had no body.

On the third evening of their holiday, they met by chance in the bar. June would choose cocktails from the bar list, and challenge the barman to mix them for her; he would do it with a flourish, humming while he plied his shaker, making a business of it. June stood at the bar counter watching him with a broad smile. It was the second thing she had enjoyed about Cyprus, and although Gregory found the showmanship embarrassing he couldn't bear to spoil her pleasure. Stavros would deck out the frothy little glasses with sticky cherries, sprigs of mint, coloured sunshades of pleated paper. 'You're only young once,' June said; and laughed, and winked extravagantly, to show that she knew she had made a joke.

It seemed – he was relieved – that Nell quite liked June's

company. There was a lively, admiring glint in Nell's hazel eyes. Perhaps she was too calm, too kind, to pick holes in people. Pettiness would not be in her. 'You must come and see us,' she said, 'if you're ever in Horsham.'

Ted did not have much to say. 'Enjoying yourself?' Gregory asked.

'We always do. Hotel seems a good sort of place.'

'You've been here before then?'

'Never away. Nell enjoys it. Friendly people. Stayed at the Churchill last year. Churchill's a good sort of place.' He paused. 'Like a change though.'

'Oh yes,' Gregory said warmly. 'We all like a change.'

Nell did not have cocktails. She had a small, pale glass of Cyprus sherry, on which her neat pale fingers closed; in holiday mood, and yet discreet. When she was inside her clothes, indoors, Nell seemed a different person; trim, rather grey. You would never guess she had such a front; her silk blouse did not show it. He must, Gregory knew, put some name to his feelings about her. I have my feelings, like other men, he thought: gallantries, cravings, sudden despairs. Advance, friend, and be recognised.

The days passed too quickly now. The hotel held a Cyprus night; there was dancing and bouzouki music. Stavros, the barman, showed unsuspected talents. He ran between the tables, bouncing and beaming, with ten glass tumblers balanced on his head. It seemed impossible; people threw money at him. At first June seemed to be enjoying it, but when she saw Nell clapping and laughing, she withdrew into herself, putting it down as Horsham entertainment. Often now, when he was drowsing by the pool, or just driving somewhere, June's proprietorial voice would carve into his thoughts. Now he had retired, he thought, he would be at her mercy. At her beck and call. He went out on the balcony in the evenings, before they went down to the bar, and watched the girls passing in the street. His appetite was a smooth easy flow; not all in Nell's direction. Who would have thought that sun and idleness would work on him in this way? He could not have predicted it. He had taken a whole reel of pictures of June now, and when he looked at her, it was as if he always looked through his camera, and she was there, indelible, the firm jaw-line, the discontented mouth, the outline of sturdy thighs under her dress. He had heard of holidays having this purpose; that couples got to know each other better.

After the Cyprus night, with its charcoal grills and sticky puddings, his indigestion seemed worse than ever. June was not sympathetic. He should have less of the local cuisine, she told him, less garlic; have what I have, a nice plain piece of fish. It's an island, isn't it, so you know it's going to be fresh.

Ted and Nell spent most of the first week by the pool. They would hire a car at the weekend, they said, and go somewhere, but meanwhile they were glad to be lazy. 'You're always on the go,' Nell said, expostulating. 'Dashing hither and thither.'

But June said they were bent on getting their money's worth; otherwise they might as well have stayed at home, where she would have had less anxiety. 'Besides,' she said, 'Gregory is fond of culture. He likes these icons, etcetera, don't you? He finds the rock formations very interesting, too.'

Ted and Nell nodded gravely. There was no irony in June's tone. She was proud of him; they understood this. 'I'm just off upstairs to see if I can pick up the World Service,' Ted said. He leapt up from his lounger and flapped off in his sandals. Gregory's eyes snatched at Nell's. I saw you half-naked, his gaze said. I thought I did; I know more of you than other people know. Her glance was gentle; but without complicity.

On Friday they drove into the mountains. They climbed; five thousand feet, six thousand feet. Drifts of snow, rather yellow now, still lay in the hollows, but the ground was carpeted with flowers. 'I wish I'd brought my flower book,' Gregory said. Then 'Do you know, June, what we're standing on? We're standing on the ocean floor.'

'What?' she said. 'Up here? What do you mean?'

'You see,' he said, and made his hands the landmasses of the world: 'Africa, you see, is crashing into Europe, like this; the continents are sliding together. The Mediterranean used to be an immense ocean. And this mountain range is really a bit of the sea-bed, cast up.'

June stared at him. 'What happened to the water?' she said.

He was at a loss. 'I expect it drained away.'

'Well, how can they make that out? How can they make that out, that it was the sea-bed?'

'By the fossil evidence. By the microscopic fossils. And by the composition of the rocks.'

'So Africa's crashing into Europe, is it?' She sounded not so much alarmed, as affronted. 'Does it mean there'll be an earthquake? Is it happening now?'

'Yes, it's happening now,' he said. 'But it's happening very slowly.' He closed his eyes. Suddenly he felt very tired. 'I'm talking about millions of years, June, tens of millions of years. No disaster is imminent, I can assure you. I'm sorry the drift of the continents can't be held up, because we are on holiday. But we'll be on that plane on Tuesday, don't you fret.'

On Mount Olympus the air was damp, but sharp and resinous. A single bird called, on a high insistent note, and beyond that there was silence, except for the click of June's heels on the tarred road. Hearing them, she said, 'These have been a good pair of shoes.'

By the time we leave for home, he thought, the snow here will have melted. The sun blazed fiercely over the radar station. 'Don't think I'm not enjoying myself,' June said, 'but I half-wish we were going back on Sunday, then I could get into the salon for Monday afternoon. It's the pensioners' half-price on a Monday, you know, and some of them are devils. I don't know that Kerry can cope. They don't respect her. They treat her like a bit of a kid.'

'I'm sure she can stand up to them.'

'No, she can't stand up to anybody,' June said. Her voice was matter-of-fact. 'She's susceptible to people. She gets it from you.'

'Just stop a minute,' he said. He put his hand on her arm. That niggle of pain again; like the tip of a knitting needle, worked between the ribs.

'All right, are you?'

'Yes, I'm fine.' He stared down at the ground. The golden pine-cones and shards of stripped bark were alive with tiny ladybirds. A cloud passed over the sun. He looked down, down into the abyss, to the villages, the monasteries, the vineyards. He felt, for a moment, the presence of the gods; then June's hand on his sleeve. The gods don't interfere in our lives nowadays, he thought; more's the pity.

When they went down to the bar that evening they found Ted and Nell there already. June perused the bar list, held Stavros in conversation, then ordered a White Lady. She seemed oblivious of Nell, waiting to launch out on a story.

'Our first day out, and we were hijacked,' Nell said.

'Oh, yes?' Gregory cocked an eyebrow at her. 'Hijacked, how?'

'We took a turning, off the Nicosia road, and there was an old chap thumbing a lift –'

'Ancient,' Ted put in. 'Decrepit.'

'So we stopped, and he begged us, positively begged us, to take him to the top of the hill.' Nell moved forward a little in her seat, holding them in suspense. 'And when we got there, it was one of these tiny villages –'

'Poor sort of place,' Ted said.

'– and he asked us, well, insisted really, that we should go to his home and meet his family and take coffee. We were quite overwhelmed, but then –'

'He wanted to sell you something,' June said. She nodded. It was her experience of human life.

'Yes, table linen.' Nell raised her glass of sherry to her lips. 'They embroider it. It's terribly expensive.'

'Couldn't get away,' Ted said. 'Brought in coffee, preserved fruit, you name it – whole family crowding round – talk about the hard sell.'

'I hope you sent them packing,' June said. 'That's unscrupulous. Putting you under an obligation. Or trying to.'

Ted and Nell looked at each other, smiling slightly.

'They're very poor people,' Nell said.

'You mean you bought?' June was shocked. 'You let them prevail on you?'

'I'm afraid we did, and the great joke is –' they exchanged another glance, enjoying it, 'they foisted off on us eight napkins and this enormous round table-cloth –'

'And we haven't got a round table,' Ted said. 'Never have had. Never shall.' He popped a potato crisp into his mouth and crunched it happily. 'Most useless purchase we ever made.'

Gregory and June did not look at each other. If this had happened to them, the mutual embarrassment, the recriminations, would have soured their whole holiday.

'I was foolish,' Nell said, more soberly. Her eyes flickered over June's face. 'Ted tried to tow me off, but after I'd eaten all these little pots of jam – and by the way they were quite delicious –'

'You were too soft,' June said crushingly. She swept a glance over her husband, as if to say, where would you be with a creature like this, thank your lucky stars you have me.

'Mm.' Nell looked into the depth of her glass. 'You're

probably right, June. It certainly set us back a few pounds.'
She raised her face. 'But it was fun.'

Ted leaned forward. 'It may be useless to us,' he said, 'but it
seems a very good kind of table-cloth.' Fleetingly, he touched
Nell's white hand as it lay on the table; Nell smiled. Gregory
turned his face away. Two tears, unprecedented, sharp as flint,
stood in his eyes. He rose from the table. 'Call of nature,' he
said. 'Excuse.' He blundered out of the bar, and stood blinking
in the marble lobby, by the door of the Coffee Shop. June was
crushing him, he thought, crushing him utterly. The process
was imperceptible, merciless; it was the worst kind of destruction, the one to which not even its victim bears witness. Until
this week. The air in the lobby seemed close, stifling. Stavros
the barman, lean and curly-headed, came out bearing a tray.
He paused.

'You feeling okay, Sir?'

'Yes, thanks, I'm okay.' The moment had passed. June
would have explained it to him; to be crushed was in his
nature. There was a Cypriot proverb, translated in his guide
book, which seemed to fit his situation. Alas for the egg when
the stone falls on it; alas for the egg when it falls on the stone.

Sunday came. 'What do you do on a Sunday?' June asked.
He'd said he wouldn't mind driving into Limassol and going
to an Orthodox service, just out of curiosity.

'Church?' June said. 'But you've never been a church-goer.'

'No . . . all right then. Why don't we go to the races?'

'Races? Where?'

'Nicosia. It's a proper track. I've been reading about it.
It would make a change.'

It was true that it would make a change. They had never been
racegoers either, but June did not find the idea so revolutionary
as that of divine service. She even warmed to it; did her nails.
'You usually just want to do cultural things,' she said happily,
'I could have a flutter. Just for once.'

They took the old road to Nicosia, but even with a pause for
photographs they were there in an hour. He pulled up near the
city walls and spread out the rather inadequate map provided
by the car-hire company. It was no use asking June to read it;
she could not tell left from right, and navigation provoked the
worst excesses of her temper. When she made errors she claimed
that signposts had been turned around, as if in a country at war.

He set off cautiously, through the shuttered Sunday streets.

Here was the Museum of Antiquities; here the Municipal Gardens. He wound down his window, letting in the sun and the light breeze; 'Lovely day,' he said to June. He propped one elbow on the window ledge, careless, his other hand loose on the wheel. Homer Avenue, Gladstone Street.

June said, 'We're lost, aren't we?'

'We do seem to be running out of town. There should have been a roundabout.'

'Here, give me the map.' June unflapped it confidently.

'You ought to head back for the city. Go at it again.' She looked at her watch. 'The first race starts at one-thirty,' she said.

He did as she told him, reversing, heading back. All the routes from the middle of the town seemed to look alike. It was one-thirty already when he found the roundabout. 'Right, here we go,' he said. June gave him advice. She also said, why do we always get lost, Gregory? He thought, but did not say, because we are too proud and stubborn to ask the way.

It was five minutes before his doubts set in; ten, before they hardened. 'This can't be it, can it? I'll have to go back on myself. Back to the roundabout, then find another road off.'

Now June was growing exasperated. 'We'll miss it, we'll miss it,' she cried.

'Heavens, woman,' he said, 'they go on till half-past five.'

June said, 'Don't you woman me.'

It seemed a low point. The whole week had been coming to this: the frank quarrel. Soon, if he did not find the right road, she would accuse him of getting lost deliberately, to spoil her pleasure. He felt he could hardly stand it; a week of her hairdresser's conversation, the nagging ache in his side, his sudden insight in the lobby. He stopped, reversed sharply into a drive-way, and swung the car around.

The narrow roads running out of town were lined with small bungalows, recently built, their walls washed with orange and blue. Chickens ran in the road; the householders, with their families and dogs, were taking lunch on the verandahs. Beyond a small row of shops – fruit and veg, video rental – the road ran out on them, a wire fence strung across their path. 'I thought this was the way,' Gregory said. He turned left; the car crawled along. In a moment he had to stop again. A barrier confronted him, and a wooden sentry hut; a young man in camouflage gear, with a sub-machine gun.

'What's going on?' June demanded.

Gregory said, 'It's the border.'

'But we want to go up there,' June said, outraged.

'That's a Turk,' he said patiently. 'That's a Turk, June. We can't.'

The border guard watched him. He did a three-point turn. The young man's expression was curious, even amiable. How would it be, Gregory wondered, if I pushed her out into the road? Would he shoot her? Would he shoot her dead? His own rage shocked him. His hands tightened on the wheel. There had been a time when he had thought his wife's stupidity a misfortune; now he knew that it was a vice. Yet what to do? He had heard of worms turning, but eggs have not that capacity.

As it happened, the programme was running late and they had only missed two races. They had trouble parking, but they squeezed in, and they hurried through the Tote Hall, through the weekend crowds. The breeze got up. 'Button your jacket, Gregory,' June ordered him. Yes, anything. He hurried to obey. What can an egg do, but most treacherously crack, before you can consume it? The twenty-foot-high figure of a Marlboro cowboy dominated the sky beyond the winning post; behind him, the mountains of Kyrenia.

It was all new to him, all fresh; the horses dancing in their stalls, the roaring glee of the crowd as they pressed against the rails, the flurry and speed with which the action was over. Between the races, he had plenty of time to look about. The spectators were mostly young Cypriot men, with a sprinkling of the black grannies, in their headscarves and wrinkled stockings, who were already familiar to him from pictures of Greece. And there were the girls in the crowd, always in pairs it seemed, arms entwined, turning their avid faces on each other, not the horses; chattering, dressed alike, mouths splashed with vivid lipstick; then looking about them, faces raised to the sun and wind, long hair blowing, tiny waists, hands like temple dancers; their smiles scattered towards him down the track, bowled towards him in the dust kicked up by the horses' hooves. He thought of Nell. The crowd surged down from the stand as the seven runners in the three o'clock rounded the final bend: Super Nova, Wild Boy, Touch Me Not.

When the race was over and the winner was led off, the crowd drifted away in search of refreshments. 'Sporting afternoon, eh?' a voice said.

'It's Ted.' June jogged his elbow. 'He's on his own.'

Gregory was glad to see him. It seemed an age since they had met at breakfast; a geological age. Ted appeared and disappeared, bobbing in the crowd, as if he were at sea. 'I say,' he said, 'I've got a radio in my hire car, I can get the Test score.'

'Where's Nell?'

'She's gone on a picnic. Some of the staff asked her. The hotel staff. Splendid day for it. Her little whim. Get to know the locals.'

'Oh yes?' June said, half to herself; breathing hard, in Gregory's shadow. He turned away from Ted, as the crowd bore him off again, looked into June's face. He saw contempt. June gave a low, merciless chuckle. 'Some picnic,' she said.

'What do you mean?' he demanded.

June said, 'I can read her like a book.'

A group of British servicemen jostled by them, young faces, pink, faintly porcine, each one under shorn fair hair. The general good-humour seemed to have entered into them as they crammed together on the stand, for they were laughing, and swigging from beer bottles, and showing each other their tattoos. The sight of them pleased June; it made her feel patriotic. She gripped his upper arm. 'Gregory, go and put me some money on that one.' She pointed to a lively bay with a jockey of minuscule proportions. 'He's only a little lad,' she said fondly.

'He's probably a grandfather.'

'Put me a pound on.'

He looked over at the bay. It seemed what Ted would call a good kind of horse. 'To win or for a place, June? A Cyprus pound, or an English pound? Anything, June.'

'What?' She looked up at him, and then her toothy grin invaded her face. 'What, anything?' she said lewdly. She has no idea, he thought, how much in these last few hours I have decided to hate her.

'Speak now,' he said, 'or forever hold your peace.'

'You must have been drinking,' she said.

By four o'clock the novelty had worn off, for June at least. The wind was keener; her horse had lost, she was cold, she wanted to go. She said she was looking forward to her bath, and to putting her blue frock on, and to getting down to the hotel bar. 'We'll be on our own tonight,' she said. 'They won't be in.'

'Perhaps Stavros won't be there either,' he said. 'Perhaps it's his day off.'

'No doubt it is,' she said, with a kind of saved-up bitterness. 'No doubt it is. But I suppose somebody else can mix my drinks.'

They pushed their way out through the turnstiles. The wind had struck russet into June's cheeks; her skin seemed roughened, frangible, like the skin of a pear. 'Oh, bloody hell,' she said. 'We're blocked in.'

He walked around the car; around the van that was parked slantwise across the space where he had hoped to reverse out. He looked at his watch. It was four-thirty, and it would be more than an hour before the last race began; more than an hour and a half, perhaps, before the van's owner, having collected his winnings and perhaps enjoyed a drink, decided to turn up and free him. It was one of those things that happen. June's small blue eyes blazed at once with frustration. Home, she'd said, bath, bar; she didn't expect to be thwarted.

'Don't blame me,' he said meekly.

'I'm not blaming you.' She aimed a great kick at the van's tyre. 'I'm not holding you responsible.'

He shivered. What else can an egg do, but get left on your face? 'I think I could back out,' he said. 'Just about. But you'll have to guide me.'

'Okay.' She glowered. Rubbed her hands together. He edged forward, edged back. Wrenched the wheel over, once, twice, three times forward and back, creeping out by inches, tensed for the clank and scrape. In the end 'You've got it this time,' she shouted.

Yes, he was out; an inch to spare. She strode around to the passenger door. He leaned across, as if to open it for her; then, instead, snapped the lock down. He saw her cardigan, flapping in the breeze; her fingers, wrapped around the door handle, wrenching at it. Her face was up in the sky somewhere, in the scudding clouds. She banged on the roof; once, like a thunderbolt.

And then he was off; bouncing over the loose white stones, swerving at a reckless speed out of the carpark and into the narrow white lanes of the suburb of Ayios Dhometrios. The verandahs were deserted now. Lunch guests were leaving for home. He had to slow up, by the video rentals shop, he had to wait at a cross-roads by a Coca-Cola sign, and he half-expected her to appear, sprinting along the road in her Clark's sandals, banging on the roof again, swearing at him, smashing him up. His heart raced. He had acted on impulse, like an animal, he thought, like some dim vegetable creature; an egg has no forethought, it has no sense of responsibility. He drove on; he did not turn back. He remembered the moment when the car had shot forward; his sudden and last glimpse, in the rear-view mirror, of June's face. She had no need to chase him. She could wait.

Through Nicosia he took the old road again, heading back towards Limassol. Although the late afternoon had grown so chilly, a fine mist of perspiration covered his neck and face. He fumbled his handkerchief out and wiped it away. Was it so terrible, what he had done? Ted would find her, and bring her back to the hotel. He would be home before them; he would sit on his twin bed, waiting, and hear the clatter of the lift doors, and June's hand rattling the doorknob, and June in the corridor, clearing her throat. It would be a new era in their relationship; a new era, and a worse.

And then later, after he had locked himself in the bathroom to recover himself, and a temporary repair had been effected to June's face, they would have to take up their lives again. They would have to go down to the bar, and face Ted and Nell. What would Ted have told her? He imagined June, crammed into the passenger seat of Ted's hired car, restrained by seat-belt at Ted's insistence; June smouldering in her furious embarrassment, while Ted fiddled around with his radio, trying to get Sports Round-Up on the World Service. Ted would not say much. But he had stumbled by accident on Gregory's private life; and being British, he would recoil when next they met, as if from a poisonous snake.

Gregory stopped the car. His indigestion was making itself felt again. Ever since he had left the suburbs, the pressure behind his ribs had seemed to build up. Below, to his left, the ground fell away, small hollows screened by trees. He released his seat-belt, opened his door. Breath of air, he thought. He sat half out of the car, legs dangling. Are you sorry? he asked himself. It was evening now, and long purple shadows slid like fingers into the valleys. He saw, first, the litter left behind by a picnic; the fierce glow of dropped orange peel, luminous in the half-light. Then the white table-cloth, like a perfect circle cut out of the dimness, sailing before the wind. It twisted and knotted as it

301

blew up the hillside; like a fleeing human form, or a ghost, skimmed across the road. Nell followed it; climbing, breathless, laughing, her face flushed, and a blanket clutched about her. Her bare legs were blue with cold. Stavros waited below in the hollow; naked, a minor deity, among the rocks. Nell saw Gregory. She stopped dead by the roadside. She seemed to peer at him, her head jutting forward on her neck. For a second her face showed fear. But then she smiled, and advanced on him; a warm, slow, forgive-me smile. She held the blanket up, over her breasts. 'Get in, Nell,' he said. Her feet, he thought, must be bleeding. He opened the passenger door.

She hesitated, then eased herself in beside him. For a moment neither of them spoke, but each appraised the other. Then, 'What have you done with June?' she asked.

He didn't answer. 'I'd better drive you back to the hotel. Don't you think so?'

'But my clothes . . .'

'I could always retrieve the table-cloth.'

It had come to rest in a hollow at the other side of the road; a swag of it billowed in the half-light, and then subsided.

'Look,' she said, 'Ted understands.'

'But I don't. I don't understand.'

As he spoke, panic gripped him; he choked. His mouth opened, gasping for air. Pain moved deeper into his chest, slow, silent, implosive. He put a hand to his rib cage, an almost casual movement; but he thought he was dying. How can dying go on, he thought, and on and on, so that half a lifetime is dragging by? He struggled. There was a scraping intake of air, an alien sound, too far away to issue from his chest. For a second it seemed to him that he had been jerked out of his own body, and that he looked down on a stranger; but what he saw was not a dying man, but a man laughing, and nightfall, and an empty road.

Nell's face loomed over him. Her eyes were huge. 'Are you ill?' she demanded. 'Gregory?' Her cold fingertips brushed at his face and neck. He exhaled, a noisy shudder.

Almost at once, and perceptibly, moment by moment, the pain began to ebb. His breathing slowed, and became steadier. He repossessed himself; here you are half-dead, half dying, in your hire car, and yet still alive, and in the evening, seven o'clock, night coming down; nothing predictable now. The attack, he realised, could only have lasted for a second. There was a sensation of emptiness in his chest; and in his mind a chilly incredulity, that he was surviving any of this. He cast an eye into the rear-view mirror, to see his own face; he touched the synthetic tweed of the seat beside him, and the tacky vinyl trim, and put his hand against the glass. He heard the breathing of the woman beside him, and noted the mottled, loose flesh of her upper arm, marbled by the blood beneath; and he remembered the gods at Paphos with their amber hair, and their chipped garlands, and their curving mouths. He felt a moment's lightness, as if he were new born. He glanced up, away from the sea and towards the hills. The space the pain had occupied filled up, creepingly, with relish.

He thought, if we sit here long enough, Ted and June will come along. 'I'm all right,' he said. 'I had a turn.' His voice sounded hollow, malicious, remote. 'I can't drive yet. Let's just sit a while.' He tried, hedgingly, a deep breath. 'June's with Ted at the racecourse,' he said. 'Funny what holidays do to people.'

She pulled away from him, diving for the door handle, but he stopped her with a hand around her wrist. 'I'm not fit to be left,' he said. 'Let's just stay here and sit still.'

Nell collapsed back into the passenger seat. Her face looked pinched, but the features were growing indistinct; in the nacreous twilight, sea and mountain merged, earth and air. Nell, silent, stared at the dashboard. He moved his hand heavily and dropped it on her thigh. From the ditch across the road, a corner of the table-cloth lifted in the wind and flapped at him slowly, like the wave of a seaside tripper from the water to the land. He imagined June, left gaping in the parking-lot; and, death, left gaping on the road. Soon they will be here, he thought; and then, as June would say, the fat will be in the fire. Let others fry, and I'll roll on. He put his arm around Nell's bare shoulders, feeling her flinch at the contact, then sigh, then close her eyes. Stavros climbs shivering up the hillside; headlights creep through the gloom. Details vanish, colours fade, the eggshell of the old life is chipping away; out hatches the surprising future.

Remission

ADAM MARS-JONES

Yoghurt. YOGHURT TAUGHT me something yesterday. I was
eating a yoghurt, not one I'd bought, something one of the
lovers picked up for me, a really creamy one with a crust
of fat, not at all my usual style of yoghurt. Maybe it was
the creaminess, or maybe it was the absurd clashing of the
fruits (apricot and mango, of all combinations), but I could
really taste it; first thing I've really tasted in months. The fruit
was only there in shreds, but there was enough juice in those
shreds, juice or sugar or something, electricity for all I know,
to give my mouth the feel of something vivid. And I thought
– first thinking I've done in months, too, I dare say – I thought,
illness is a failure, that's obvious. You don't have to be well to
know that. But what is it a failure of? And at that moment, the
answer seemed to be: imagination. It seemed to me then, reeling
as I was from the impact of the fruit in the yoghurt, that with
a little effort, with a little imagination, I could taste anything,
take pleasure in anything.

The yoghurt didn't stay down, of course; it wasn't such a
new beginning as all that. But what it had to teach me it taught
me on the way down; on the way up it had nothing to say. And
even that was a lesson of sorts. It was no more unpleasant to
vomit that yoghurt than it was to throw up my usual watery
potlet. Its curds were no viler as they rose in my throat. I
suppose I've been following a policy of appeasement with my
stomach, and that's always a mistake. I've been behaving as if

my insides were just being temperamental, and if I could find some perfectly inoffensive food for them, they would do the decent thing and hang on to it. And it just isn't so. I might as well eat what has a chance of giving me pleasure. My stomach will lob it up indifferently.

At the end of all that, after I had vomited, I was – I imagine – just fractionally weaker than when I had started. I had used some energy (vomiting is hard physical work) and I hadn't managed to get any nourishment. Trying to break down the yoghurt had been, as it turned out, a costly waste of gastric juice. But in spite of that, I had had three distinct phases of pleasure – one, the taste of the yoghurt itself; two, the long, incredulous moment when it seemed that it would stay down; three, the euphoria, after it came up, of having expelled poison, of knowing it wouldn't be fizzing in my guts for the rest of the day – and only one phase of unpleasantness when it was actually coming up. In some strange way it seemed that I was ahead on the day's transactions. That's when I thought of making this tape.

It's only a cheap little secretarial Sony, this machine, but it's got everything I need. The controls are very simple; you don't even have to look at them. When things get bad, I can curl up with it under the bedclothes, a muttering foetus that can't get comfortable. [   ] If I get a coughing fit, I can edit it out, like that, by using the pause button. I've just got the two tapes, so I can change them over very easily, with the minimum of fumbling around.

There's the shits–and–vomits tape, which I'll use when I'm making the same old complaints, when I'm sicking up the same old record of bodily disasters. I'm never going to play it back. I'll just record on top of it, same old rant anyway. It's not for listening to, just for getting out of my system.

This tape is different. I've written the word *remission* on the spine of the cassette, and that's what I mean to concentrate on, every little quantum of forgiveness I can find in my body or my circumstances. I'll play it back eventually, but I'll wait as long as I can, so that I have a real hoard of positive moments to refresh myself with.

It's a bit odd, using the same channel to get rid of some experiences and intensify others. But I don't have to look further than my underpants to remember a similar arrangement.

And if there's a medical breakthrough soon, very soon –

in the next twenty minutes, say – then I may not have to go back to the shits-and-vomits tape at all, just steam on with my remission. But I'll still go on thinking *remission*, however long it lasts: I'll never say *cure*. I can't be doing with that word. It makes everything impossible. It's a real obstacle to getting on with things.

What else fits the requirements for the remission tape? *The video*. Sleep is sweeter than it ever was, and I resent time wasted on anything else. But my video has taken all the angst out of insomnia. I sleep quite a lot in the day, so I'm likely to wake up in the middle of the night, quite suddenly, as if there was someone flashing a torch an inch from my eyes. Television will have packed up hours before, the sleepy-head announcer yawning after the late film (it's past midnight, imagine!), wishing all the other sleepy-heads out there good-night. There's a programme on before close-down that has the nerve to call itself *Night Thoughts*. It's on at different times depending on the schedule, but always before one. *Night Thoughts* indeed! Can you beat it? The tube trains are hardly tucked up in their sheds for the night, and there's a lot of thinking to be done before morning, unless you have a video.

I bought the video quite a while ago, and it was one of those bits of self-indulgence that turn out to be good resolutions in disguise (having said that, I can't think of any others). I thought I'd turn into an addict, and I certainly taped a lot of programmes, but I never got round to watching them. I'd just buy more tapes as they got filled up. I never got into the habit of labelling the cassettes, so now I never know what I'm watching. I watch episodes of *Hill Street Blues* from two different series, and the only way I can tell them apart is by seeing whether Henry Goldbloom has a moustache or not. Promotions and romances don't help me much with the chronology, but with Henry's moustache I know where I am. I always did like moustaches. On top of that, Henry Goldbloom is always talking suicides down from their high places, reasoning with them through his megaphone of good intentions, and I suppose that's bound to strike some sort of chord.

The great thing about the video, of course, is that I can play things as fast or as slowly as I want. The other night I watched an old episode of *The Avengers*, in which John Steed was meant to dispose of a bomb by lobbing it into the bell of a euphonium. The detonation made the euphonium uncoil, like one of those irritating party-blowers. Except that the actor was too clumsy, or too drunk, to throw the bomb properly, and it rolled under a chair. The euphonium blew up all the same, of course, but if you rewind the video and play the sequence again you can see that it had no reason to. I found the whole thing extravagantly amusing, the other night, and I played it again and again, perhaps because it was one of the few things I'd come across in some time that was in no way a metaphor of my present condition.

That can't be right. Surely I can do better than that. With the explosion, all the instrument's brass knitting unravels. What remains on the carpet is revealed as an intestine, tarnished and smoking. Good. Do better. What *The Avengers* was telling me, in an episode made around the time of my puberty, is that euphoniums end up unrolled and in ruins, even if they don't take a bomb in the bell. That's just what happens, with euphoniums. Good thought. Hang on to that.

Change the subject. *The lovers.* I have two lovers at the moment. *Lovers* is the wrong word, but then it always is. All I can say is, these two do everything for me a lover could do, and that's pretty amazing. We treat each other as if we had a history of sex, but that isn't the intimacy that binds us. I've had half-lovers before, even three-quarters lovers, once or twice, but these two are somehow fully loving towards me, and that's worth putting down on this privileged spool of tape (chrome dioxide for a longer life).

Dead parents. Anyone whose doctors are not cheerful should try as a first step not to have parents alive. I'm not being unduly oriental here; it's not that I think it's disrespectful in some way to turn in while your parents are still around and about. But I'm sure it confuses things. There's a touch of the bailiff about parents, I've always thought, as if they were waiting for you to fall behind with the payments on your life, so they could repossess it. What a terrible thing to say.

I'm not always so cynical, but I try. Anyway, I'm sure it makes it worse, having your parents around. Not my problem. Having your parents die is unpleasant in its own right of course, and not only in the expected ways. Example: my father had this terrible rightness about him. From his hospital bed he corrected the doctors' pronunciation and finished their sentences for them. I always hated that. It makes me think, now, how robust he was in his dying, how reliable his vitality was right up to the moment that it fell away from him. But the point is that while he was alive, I didn't realise that I have a scarcely less terrible rightness myself, though everyone I've known must have noticed it. I finish people's sentences for them too – I just interrupt them later on in their flow – so I've always fooled myself I'm a good listener. And compared to my Dad, I *am* a good listener, but the people I've shut up over the years didn't know that.

The lovers are going to get a bit of a shock, when I get some strength back and start bossing them about. I think they deserve an entry of their own, while their patience has yet to be tested, while my character is still blurred by my powerlessness.

The lovers. I had a lover, of a sort, when I was diagnosed, but I soon got rid of him. I'd already placed a small ad which defined me as a Lonely Heart, which was my way of serving notice to myself that I was going to serve notice on him, and then I was diagnosed. I thought at once, that settles it (that was my first thought), I've got to get rid of him, and I did. He thought his health made him necessary to me, and I had hell's own job convincing him it made him even more of a nuisance than he was before, more of a menace, more of a pest. I couldn't carry him and illness too.

So when the magazine forwarded the replies to my ad, everything had changed, and they were replying to someone who didn't exist any more. There were only two replies, perhaps because I was never the world's most beautiful man, and my advert wasn't exactly raging with self-esteem. But I thought they deserved an explanation, and I arranged to meet them, both of them together so I didn't need to repeat myself.

By treating these strangers well after behaving so badly to someone who thought he was close to me, I think I was exercising in some final way the prerogatives of vigour. That's how I've worked it out since then. It was a choosing spree, and now my choices are made.

All the same: it wasn't as easy as I thought. I felt a terrible lurch when I started talking, and I had something like an anxiety attack. Perhaps it was simply grief for the person who had placed the ad and wasn't around any more. It's hard to be sure what it is you're having when you know your body is scheduled to fail you piecemeal – and your mind doesn't have a lot to look forward to, come to that – and you experience a sensation of intense heat and horror. Whether it was only an anxiety attack or what, I wasn't able to stay as long as I'd meant to, and I stumbled out while their drinks were still half finished. And a couple of hours later they phoned, the two of them, to ask how I was, and to say they'd like to help me in any way they could, if I'd let them.

If I try, knowing them as well as I do now, I can probably reconstruct the conversation that led up to their phone call. But I don't care to analyse something that has become so necessary to me. I answered. They offered. I accepted. We've developed some useful routines.

Diagnosis broke me up, the way a plough breaks earth, and all the recent growth, rooted so lightly, was pulled right up. But I was left all ready for seeding. When they phoned – it was Rory actually holding the phone and doing the talking – I remember I said, 'Let's get one thing straight. I have never depended on the kindness of strangers.' Then I had to break it to them that what I was saying was Yes.

The lovers. Leo and Rory, my lovers, my lions. They pay their visits separately; I know they meet up at least once a week to arrange their timetables. They used to visit in the day, but now they know that day isn't really the time they're most useful. They used to be great soup-merchants, the pair of them, but they soon got sick of eating their own soups. Now Rory helps me pay my bills on time, which is much more important. Leo has a car, and Rory doesn't, so it's Leo who stays the night, assuming he's free, when I have a clinic appointment in the morning. If it's Rory keeping me company, we take a taxi.

The taxi costs money, of course, but I prefer Rory's company at the clinic. Leo gets very tense, and I more or less have to look after him. Rory is different. I've been particularly unwell for a few weeks, and the hospital wanted a stool sample. That's not easy when your stools move at a hundred miles an hour, like mine do at the moment. With a straight face they gave me a little pot with a screw top, as if what they wanted collecting was a butterfly and not a bowel movement. Rory wasn't with me that day. Anyway, I tried. Day after day I'd go to the lavatory with my little pot, but I was never quick enough. It was as frustrating as my train-spotting days as a boy, when I would stand by the main line in the early morning mist as the express thundered by, trying to read the number on the engine. Anyway, I got my sample at last, and took it along. After a week, I went back for the results, and they told me the sample had leaked and couldn't be used for analysis. They hadn't phoned me, of course, to say so. Didn't want to depress me. I dare say. So they gave me another pot and sent me back home again, to wait for the express.

These grumbles shouldn't be on this tape at all – they're classic shits-and-vomits stuff – but it all leads to Rory and why he's good to have around. When I'd got my second sample to the hospital and they'd analysed it at last, the doctor prescribed Dioralyte, which she said I have to take every time I have a loose bowel motion. She added, 'It comes in three flavours, avoid the pineapple,' and I could catch Rory's eye and know that he was feeling the same tickle of amusement at her phrasing. The doctor pinched the skin of my arm to see how dehydrated I was, and we both watched the little swag of raised flesh she left, which took a good long time to fade. If they'd told me about Dioralyte earlier on, of course, I wouldn't be dehydrated in the first place, but you can get it from the chemist even without a prescription, so it's not the sort of thing that holds a highly trained person's attention.

Or she can be explaining about *cryptospiridion*, the guest in my gut, and be saying, 'It produces nausea in the upper tract and diarrhoea in the lower, you see, because the whole intestine is implicated.' I can look at Rory and know he's thinking what I'm thinking: *Implicated? It's up to its bloody neck.* Leo would just sit there squirming, willing her to change the subject and talk about something nice.

I wish I'd had Rory with me when the doctor – the first doctor – asked me his three little questions. Did I receive anal intercourse? On occasion I did. He made a note. Had I visited Central Africa? On occasion I had. He made another note. Had I received blood there, by any chance? I seemed to remember something of the sort, when I was weak and confused from hepatitis. As I came out with the last of my answers, I could see the doctor's lips framing a word that looked like 'Bingo', and it would have been handy having Rory's eyes there for mine to meet.

Not that Rory's perfect. When we first heard about *crypto*, he and I, when she first mentioned the name, he blurted out, 'Oh dear, that's a stubborn one, isn't it?' I couldn't resist saying, 'Thanks a bunch, that's all I need,' just to see him flinch, though it really doesn't make any difference to me. In fact I'm glad he knows what he's about, if he does, so I don't have to worry about him the way I worry about Leo.

It's at night that Leo comes into his own, and not because he sleeps in the buff. He has a beguiling little body and all that, hairless and pale-skinned, but it's really only memory that tells me so. I let him sleep on the side of the bed away from the window, otherwise he thinks he won't sleep. It doesn't bother me which side of the bed I'm on, but with Rory I pretend I have a preference for lying away from the window. That way I know who it is that's staying over, even when I'm half asleep, just by our positions, just by feeling which side the warmth's coming from.

I couldn't really be in any doubt, anyway. Leo may wear no night-clothes, but he keeps to his side of the bed, and he turns his back on me – slowly, quietly, as if I'll be offended – when he's going to sleep. Rory sleeps in a night-shirt, but all the same he hugs me and holds me to him, which is all very nice. Just as he's dropping off to sleep, he's been known to stroke my nipple absent-mindedly with his thumb, but my nipple, quite unlike itself, inverts instead of stiffening.

There can't be much doubt in their minds about who they're sleeping with, that's for sure. The guest in my gut, the gate-crasher in my gut, sends out smells beneath the duvet. And when I have my sweats, I can't think it's pleasant for them. The sheets spread my wetness pretty widely.

I cheat them both, I suppose, by sleeping so much in the day. But it makes such a difference having a lover installed and snoring if I'm not doing much sleeping at night. And Leo is perfect, regularly breathing, just the minimal presence I need. Leo's snoring is my night-light. Sleep works on him like a humane killer, stunning him before it bleeds the consciousness out of him. If he stays up too late, he slurs his words, and then starts to doze with his eyes open, and I expect he's replying to my conversation in his head, and doesn't realise he's making no sound.

In the morning it works the other way round. He opens his eyes when I bring him a cup of tea, but it's a minute or two before he can properly hold the cup. Till then he blinks, yawns, changes position, groans and scrabbles at his hair. I know he's embarrassed that I bring him tea in the morning, but I'm solidly grateful that he sleeps so soundly, and I'll reward him in any way I can, even if it involves effort.

Rory is a much more partial sleeper, and when I get up he often joins me in front of the video. Or he'll go to the kitchen and mix up some Complan, with bananas and honey, the way I 'like' it, the way I can sometimes even tolerate it.

As he pads in, Rory asks me which series we're in, that is, are we escaping to 1982 or 1984? Does Henry Goldbloom have a moustache?

I tell him what year it is in the violently reassuring world of *Hill Street Blues*. Sometimes Rory seems to be doing a Henry Goldbloom himself, but all it means is that he's skipping shaving for a day or two. He gets rid of the growth before it has a real prospect of changing the balance of his face. It's a shame, he's got a great thick growth of hair right up his neck – what we used to call a poor man's cravat – so he actually looks a little odd clean-shaven.

It's wonderful of him to keep me company, I know, but I wish he'd go back to bed. Sometimes I put on a yawning routine, and we both go back to bed again, then I sneak out and go back to the video. It's not him I mind, it's the company he brings with him. If I can slide out of bed without waking him, I can get half an hour uninterrupted in front of the video. But when he gets up, and especially when he starts moving with a sort of muffled purposefulness round the kitchen, a gnawing and a churning wake up too. The gnawing is hunger and the churning is nausea, and wouldn't you know it, the gnawing is exactly in the middle of the churning, so there's no way I can get to it. So what with Rory and the Complan and the gnawing and the churning, it gets to be too much of a huddle round the video, and my view of the screen gets blocked off.

Lower levels of illness. I'm supposed to have mellowed: that seems to be the general verdict. I don't believe a word of it, myself. What really happens is different. There's an awkward interval, when you're ill but not yet conditioned by illness. You're far enough down to be spending all your time below ground, but every now and then you come across shafts of something very like daylight. That makes you impatient and hard to deal with. Things get easier, for other people at least, when you don't have moments of real vitality to show up the false. By now it's second nature for me to follow the cues I get from Leo and from Rory, and not to hang around waiting for my own spontaneity. Only if that draining away of impulse is mellowing can I take credit for it.

The new, eroded me – but for form's sake we'll say *mellow* – the new mellow me has learned to put up with a lot of goodness from people lately. I had to get Rory to pay for this tape recorder, for one thing, and for everything I needed for quite a while. I could have given him cheques, of course; all it would have cost was a little embarrassment if I'd needed help writing them. But he didn't mind waiting for his money. I have this memory thing, you see. I have trouble remembering how to spell, particularly the last part of words for some reason. The words are all there, but I can't seem to spell them. That's what makes this recorder such a good idea. But it also means I can't remember the code number for my cashcard. I hadn't written it down, so I couldn't tell it to Rory. If I'd been up to it, I would have gone to the cashpoint myself, just to see if there was still some memory in my fingertips when I stood in front of the machine. As it was, Rory went for me. I told him he could take his revenge for every time the machine has been out of money on a Saturday night, or swallowed his card without provocation. I told him to mash the keys just as hard as he liked, all three times the machine gave him a chance of getting the number right. Then the card was swallowed up, and my bank sent me a replacement, and by the next post the new number for it. This time I gave the number to Rory to look after.

He's earned my patience. He tries to get me to lie down when I eat, as if that was going to help me hang on to my food, when all it means is more trouble being tidy when I throw up, but I forgive him for that. I know he means well even when he mixes me up some Dioralyte the moment I've had my *loose motion*, though I'm quite capable of throwing up the Dioralyte on the spot, before it's even properly gone down, just to make it clear that my system discriminates against digestion impartially, from both ends of the process.

These days I keep my mouth shut when Rory talks about diabetes. His dad is diabetic, but so what? When Rory talks about it I get rather too clearly the feeling he's trying to teach me something. He tells me diabetes used to be a fatal illness, and that insulin is the crudest sort of treatment you could imagine: just a matter of smashing up bits of animals and injecting them into you, but that's enough to change everything. I want to say, wasn't there a film about the heartbreak of diabetes in that season they had on the box, just recently, of socially concerned American dramas (made for TV, naturally)? I'm sure I taped some of those. Instead I listen to what Rory has to say about his father. Before too long I'll ask Rory if he thinks there might be something of the same sort coming my way, some sort of vinegar-and-brown-paper job, some way of jury-rigging the body, just to show him I've been listening.

Eroded as I am into mellowness, I've even learned to have mercy on Leo. We were in bed the other night, but for once he wasn't sleeping, for the very good reason that every time I lay down in bed I was having an attack of coughing. I tried sitting up in bed for a while, and then gradually sliding down to horizontal, but you can't fool a cough that way. I was trying it one more time just the same, when there was a knock on the door. It was very late, and we were both surprised. Leo put on a shirt and went to answer it. When he came back, he took off the shirt and got back into bed without explaining. I asked him who it was, and he said it was someone delivering pizza who'd got the wrong address.

'At this time of night?' I asked him.

'Yes.'

I didn't even know you could have pizza delivered around here.

'What address was he looking for?'

'Don't know.'

'Did he find where it was?'

'Don't know.' We lay for a moment, and Leo turned slowly over in bed, away from me.

Suddenly I had the idea that what I wanted most in the world was pizza. A sudden flow of saliva even soothed my cough for a moment. I suppose it was partly because it was so late, my nausea was deeply asleep, and for a moment I had a clear view of my hunger. And then the pizza seemed so near, so ready on the other side of a door. So I said, 'Leo, this may sound silly, but could you go out and see if that pizza man is still around? If he is, tell him I'll take it off his hands. I'm not fussy about toppings. I'll even pay full whack.'

Leo dragged himself slowly out of bed, put on the shirt again, some trousers and some shoes, and stumbled across the room towards the door. Then he came back and sat on the bed. He told me then that he'd made it up about the pizza. When he'd opened the front door there was a man there in dressing-gown and slippers, holding out a bottle of Benylin, that heavy-duty cough stuff, and saying, without a lot of warmth, 'Try this.' Leo hadn't wanted to tell me. He put the Benylin somewhere

where he was going to pick it up the next morning and take it away with him. He hadn't known what else to do.

Nor did I for a moment, and then I asked him to fetch me the bottle, I'd have a swig anyway, just to be friendly. The nausea was wide awake by then, so it didn't cost me a lot to be generous, just a little. Leo undressed again and fell asleep soon after that, and so did I, I think, though I woke up towards morning for a little practice hacking, which Leo slept through, and I hope everybody in the street did too.

Salmon sperm! What's the word? Milt. It's unbelievable! They just told me today. It turns out that milt is clever stuff. It has a Suppressing Effect. What it Suppresses is Replication. It's such clever stuff. And what that means is, salmon sperm is on my side. Milt loves me! And I love milt.

They're very dour about it. They say, don't build up your hopes too high. They never said that about fears. They never said don't build up your fears too high. And I'm not getting carried away. All I say is, milt loves me and I love milt! I don't even need to fellate the fish to get at it, though God knows I'd do it if I had to. They've synthesised it for me. They say, warning me, that it'll taste like metal. I say, you're wrong, it'll taste like Life. And they say, warning me, that I'll have to take it every four hours at first, day and night. And I say, nursing mothers have to put up with a lot more than that. I'll set the alarm for the middle of the night, and when it goes off I'll know what makes it worth while waking, there's no sleep so deep that I won't know. I'll know it's my Life waking me for its four o'clock feed.

They tell me it isn't a cure, as if I didn't know that. I tell them I know it could only be a poison, that's all doctors can ever give you, poison; you just have to hope that it hates you less than it hates what you've got. They tell me salmon sperm can attack your red cells, and your white cells come to that, so it might help to take some iron and vitamin B. I tell them I've always liked spinach. Oh, I've got all the answers. I just want to be able to put off the questions a bit.

Remission. Maybe I'll be able to move over to this tape for good. Shut away the shits-and-vomits tape in its little case and never need to pull it out again.[

]Remission. I had my remission.[

]I had my remission, and I didn't record it. I didn't even write anything down.[

315

]When I listen back to this tape, I hear myself explaining what I'm going to use it for, but I never do. I never do.[

]Some things I don't need help remembering. I remember getting the first prescription for my salmon sperm, and going along with it to the hospital pharmacy. Rory was with me that day, but he was shutting up for once. The new twist my case was taking seemed to have robbed him of his small talk. The Aussie I've always hated was on duty in the pharmacy, with his usual tan, only more so, and the stupid bleach-streaked hair, only more so. And of course that awful voice! When you're waiting your turn, eyes down or looking at the warnings on the walls for innocent things like whooping-cough, and he's bellowing instructions to the customers before you in the line, you can think he must have picked up an old copy of *Punch* from the table, and rolled it up to make his voice so deafening. Then when it's your turn you find it's even worse. He *roars* at me as he passes over the box of Dioralyte, 'Make up a sachet after every loose bowel movement,' and then tells me how many times a day I need to take my antibiotics, as if it wasn't written on the container. He seems to have a heroic notion of his job, as if he was still a life-guard back in Australia – though I think you need broad shoulders for that – striding across toasted sand and warning red-heads not to sun-bathe. Then he pushes across the salmon sperm. I'd expected it to be a liquid, somehow, a heavy metallic liquid, what with its being so new and precious and rationed. I must have been thinking, too, of cod-liver oil. So I was disappointed for a moment when it was just ordinary capsules, like the timed-release symptom-suppressors you take for a cold, except with a different paint-job, white with a thin blue belt at the middle. Then I was impressed all over again by the size of the bottle, it wasn't really big, but bigger than I'm used to, so it looked like a sweetie-jar in an old-fashioned corner shop. For a moment I thought, almost tearful with gratitude, *All that, for me?* £250 for a fortnight's treatment isn't peanuts, but why should I have been so surprised to be worth it? Then the Aussie booms out, 'You have to take these every four hours, day and night, do you understand? The best thing is to take 'em at four, and eight, and twelve. That way you only need to get up once in the night.'

And I thought, this idiot knows *nothing*; if I was sleeping eight hours a stretch I wouldn't be needing the salmon sperm, would I? I'd be holding down a job, wouldn't I, the way a paper-weight holds down a pile of prescription forms, the way you hold down yours. The week before, I'd just have let it wash over me, but this time it was as if the salmon sperm was giving me strength already, just by sitting there on the counter, so I said, 'Oh, I think I'll miss the four o'clock dose, get a full night's sleep.' I tried to make my voice campy. 'I'm not really an early morning person.' I could see Rory out of the corner of my eye, trying not to giggle.

But of course the Pharmacist From Bondi Beach looked really concerned, and he even lowered his voice, and he said, 'You really should, sir, it's important.'

If I'd had more than just the sight of the salmon sperm to give me strength, perhaps I'd have said something really crushing. But I couldn't think of anything anyway, so I just lowered my voice, all the way down to a whisper, and said, 'Just to please you, then.'

There was no holding me. I nipped into the waiting room on my way out, flashed the nurse a big smile and asked, 'Would it be possible, do you think, to trace the kind person who brings along all those back numbers of opera magazines?' Then, just as she got launched on the sort of smile that says you've made someone's day, I said, 'Because I'd really like to push him off a small cliff. That would make my day.'

I remember that day because I had only had a premonition of health. I was still outside the world of the well, that world which I understand so little of now.

I have to reconstruct those weeks, those (admit it) months, from what they left behind, like a pathologist reconstructing a dead person's last meal. I remember looking at my first capsule, with a tiny animal printed on it in blue, like the little lions that used to be stamped on eggs, and what I took to be the word WELCOME in tiny letters. I remember thinking with real fervour, *Welcome yourself*, before I saw that the L in the word was double.

I know I became impatient with Leo and Rory almost instantly. They seemed so petty and nannyish, so ignorant of the real business of life. They nagged me to take my salmon sperm, as if it was something I'd forget just to be annoying. In fact I became very good at waking up seconds before the alarm went off for the three o'clock and seven o'clock feeds – I just had to be different, didn't I? – as if there really was a baby in the room, screaming. It should have struck me as funny when

Leo struggled out of sleep at ten past seven one morning and started shaking me, convinced that I'd missed the seven o'clock feed and probably the three o'clock too, which of course he'd also snored through. It should have seemed funny, but it didn't. I suppose it was hard for them. They had suited themselves to me by an effort of will: it must have seemed ungrateful on my part to discharge myself – and so suddenly – from the intensive care I had demanded from them. But that didn't stop me from thinking what my mother used to say, poor bitch, of a piece of furniture that no longer pleased her: I'd rather have your space than your company.

Something peculiar must have happened. I stopped being feverish all the time, in that low-level way that becomes your new normal after a few months. But I entered another kind of fever; I was in a fever of health. That must be the explanation. I know I took a lot of trouble to repeat, in my new health, experiences that I'd had in sickness. That must be a very sophisticated pleasure.

I know, for instance, that in my sickness I had made a trip to Highgate Ponds. I needed to be driven, by Leo of course, and I needed to take a little rest at the unofficial gay sun-bathing area before I tottered down to the nudists' compound.

Leo and I laid out our towels on the concrete. I'd brought along a blanket and a pillow (which Leo was carrying, of course) for a little extra padding, but at least I laid the towel on top. I wasn't ashamed to strip off, though of course I was worried in case I had to run for the dingy lavatory, under the eyes of the ghastly crew by the weight-bench. But shame didn't get a look in. As far as I was concerned, this was strictly between me and the sun. I wasn't going to be done out of our date just because I could hardly walk.

I was surprised to see that Leo was shy, and kept a pair of swimming trunks on. I wanted to tempt him out of them, so I could at least look at the label and see whether they were bought from C&A or the British Home Stores.

After a while I struggled into a swimsuit myself, and walked weakly through to the pond. I was hoping that I would feel strong enough for a dip at least, which was a pretty bizarre hope. Perhaps I thought that, all other sources of energy having failed, I would turn out to be solar-powered. I lay down on the diving-board. I had been there about ten seconds, feeling the wind on me almost warm, and watching the people sprawled on the raft in the middle of the pond, when a man came out of a hut and shouted at me that sun-bathing was not allowed in the swimming area.

The trip I made in my health, I seem to think, was very different. I took bus after bus to get there, by myself. I strode past the sun-bathing area, and straight into the compound, though this time I was reluctant to take off my underwear. By then I had a little roll of tummy fat which I was very proud of, and which showed to best effect above the waistline of a pair of underpants, and I wasn't in any hurry to have it vanish the moment I took my briefs off and lay down. I expect I was waiting for someone to call out, 'Wonderful! I can't see your ribs. Well done!'

Before the sun had properly got to work I was standing up again and pulling my swimming trunks up. I went out into the swimming area, but I wasn't quite brave enough for the diving-board. The water looked cloudy, but I knew it was supposed to be pure and clean, equally free of pollution and disinfectant. I let myself down an iron ladder that had a lot of weed attached to it. The ladder wasn't full-length, as I had assumed, it stopped only a little below the surface, so I slipped into the coldest water I have ever touched. My body gasped and went on gasping. The water was unexpectedly deep, too, considering it was so near the edge of the pond. I set out to swim to the raft, which supported what looked like the same group of sun-worshippers, but I found myself swimming instead in a tight circle back to where I started. I wanted to strike out for that floating island of health, but my body wasn't having it. My feet had no memory of the ladder, and scrabbled for purchase where the rungs were imaginary. Then I remembered, and felt for the actual bottom of the actual ladder, and managed to pull myself out.

I slumped on the jetty to recover. Not even the most officious attendant, seeing me there flat out and wheezing, could imagine I was having a sun-bathe on the sly, but the men on the raft set up a round of ironic applause that I could hear even through the numbness of my ears.

I wasn't going to give up. I didn't hang around until my skin had dried off and my trunks felt cold and clammy. I went back down the ladder and swam out through the cold. The water got warmer after a while, or else it stayed cold and I got used to it. The raft was only fifty feet or so away, but that was quite far enough. I could feel the special uneasiness of swimming in water of unknown depth. As I got near the raft, all I could see above the edge of it was the soles of someone's feet, those odd sort of feet with the second toe longer than the big one.

The ladder by the raft was even shorter than the one on the jetty. In my memory, it has only two rungs. I know I had to pull myself up with what felt like the last of my strength. But when I looked at the raft, which rocked under my weight and wasn't as securely tethered as I'd expected, it was covered with shit. I don't mean that the men there were lying in it; they were too fastidious for that, with their uniform tans, as if they'd all chosen the same shade from a paint card. But there were sub-stantial little turds scattered all over the raft. They were bigger than anything I've known a bird do, but I couldn't imagine what beast could have got there to lay them. I was tired out from my swim, but lying in shit was too recent a memory – from nights when I improvised a pair of incontinence pants out of an old Marks and Sparks bag – for me to be able to stay on the raft. I climbed down the rusty ladder, losing my footing one more time, and swam back to the jetty. It may be that my strength was failing towards the end, but I think the water near the jetty was the coldest of all.

I know I did all that. I even remember it all, in the sense that I still bear traces of those thoughts and sensations. I remember what my body felt in its health, what it touched, how it reacted. But I have no sense of how my body felt to itself. Health was just one more thing that happened to me, and I have kept nothing from it. The tape is blank for all those weeks and months.

And now I am back in my siege of fevers. What it feels like, as always, is shame, as if this raised temperature was nothing more than a hideous extended blush, which I could get rid of if I just did the right thing. I find myself wondering what it was I did wrong, what crime my body remembers with this heat of shame. They didn't lie to me about the salmon sperm. I knew it could nibble away at my cells. I knew there was a price to be paid for the job it did. I knew it wasn't a medicine so much as a protection racket; I just hoped we could get along. I took vitamins, I took iron, I took supplements. Was there one night when I passed up a dish of green vegetables, in my feverish health, snubbing all those B vitamins, and went out instead? There must have been. I know there were times when I was too bound up in the play I was watching to remember my feed.

I'd glared in the dark at people whose watch alarms went off in the theatre for too many years to commit that crime myself. And there was the terrible day I lost my bottle of capsules. I had to dash across London, whimpering, for replacements. I'd lost six expensive days' worth. To make myself feel better I asked if anyone had lost their salmon sperm before me. But I was the first.

How can I put it, to make myself feel I have made heroic choices? Health for me is more than being not-yet-dead. It's not something you patrol; it's something you must forget to patrol or it's not any sort of health at all. That should do it. That sounds right. That must be why I didn't use this tape to hoard up bits of my health, so I could live off them at a later date.

And here I am with a body that's ashamed of itself, that's burning with remorse for something it did or didn't do, and with the word *surge* beating at my ears. They warned me what would happen when I came off the salmon sperm. A surge of virus. Virus replicating uninhibited. *Surge* is a word that sounds overwhelming even on the smallest scale, down on the cellular level. What chance do I have, against a *surge*?

Every time I went to hospital for some more salmon sperm, and they took blood, I must have known they were monitoring my levels. Fourteen. Twelve and a half. Eleven. Nine. It was more than a pit stop. And when I went below nine, and they started to give me transfusions, I knew what they were about. But I tried to think, closing my eyes when the prick came in my arm, and then the slowly growing ache in it, that I was giving blood rather than getting it, that from my overflowing health I was giving freely of my surplus. Nine and a half. Nine. Eight. I tried to think I was paying my taxes, when all the time my bloodstream was being heavily subsidised. On long car journeys as a child, I remember, to stop from feeling sick – from motion, from too many boiled sweets, from my father's Senior Service and my mother's Piccadilly – I would close my eyes and try to interpret the sensations in terms of movement backward, though I don't quite know why that was comforting. I could produce a surprisingly strong and consistent illusion until I opened my eyes at a bump in the road, or when my mother asked if I was asleep, and the world came crashing back at me.[

]The lovers are back. They can deal with me again. And I suppose that really means that I can deal with them. Rory has that handsome look in the face that means he's certain to shave in the morning, and Leo smells so strongly of soap he must wear a bar around his neck.[

]They've done something very tactful with the key. I'm not very steady on my feet just at the moment, and my neighbour has a spare set of keys. She's always been a hypochondriac, can't bear to be in the room with anyone who has a cold, so I suppose it's something of a miracle that she's not returned them, or that they don't reek of disinfectant. This I noticed today, and it qualifies for inclusion on this tape. That's what this tape is supposed to be for, isn't it? Sometimes my neighbour even leaves groceries outside the door. Anyway, when Rory last came by he let himself in, and explained that he had happened to run into my neighbour outside the house. Then *Leo* let himself in next time he paid a visit, and he looked all tense and startled, as if at any moment he might be called upon to lie. So my guess is they've made a policy decision not to make me walk any more than I have to. They must knock on my neighbour's door every time they come round. For all I know, they get her to leave the key under the mat when she goes out. I think they're waiting for me to twig and get angry, but they'll have to wait a little while longer. I'll either keep it to myself or let it hitch a ride on a real grievance. 'And another thing,' I'll say, 'about the keys . . .'[

]We've started taking baths together, the lovers and I. Rory lifts me into the tub very competently, which is so reassuring it's sinister, but at least he climbs right in with me, like no nurse in the world who wants to remain in employment. Suddenly I wonder if he answered my ad – poor idiot – to get his life moving again after grief, and has to keep his teeth clenched on his knowledge. So I'm more than usually grateful that he gets into the bath with me. He sits behind me with his knees bent, so I can rest my head on his chest, and he strokes me a little awkwardly with a sponge. It's a posture I like anyway, and now in particular I'm glad of it because it's not a position that encourages talking. We can't really see each other's faces. I think he closes his eyes in the steam, and from time to time he seems to drift off. He doesn't seem to mind that the water gets cold; perhaps he doesn't even feel it.

If there was just a little more water in the bath I'd be floating. As it is my head bumps softly against Rory's chest. Here and only here, in this limbo inside another, I remember my lover, the lover I disposed of so efficiently, dumping his body in an acid bath of resentment. What I remember isn't the friendship, which I resisted, or even the sex, which I wanted only when I wanted it, but the game we used to play when we were out together, the game he taught me and that he may even have invented, the sweetly innocent game he called *compelled*-to-fuck. One or other of us would say, 'If you were *compelled* to fuck a set number of people – under pain of death, mind . . .' (or later just, 'If you were *compelled* . . .'). Then the other would say, 'How many?' And the answer would be, 'One on this bus,' or 'Two before we leave the Food Hall,' or 'Three before the next traffic light.' Then he would say, 'Three? You'll be lucky. That one, at a pinch. Another one? No chance. All right, the thinner of these two bobbies, the less fat I mean. That's the lot. That's my last offer. One more? Do I really have to? Let it be the one with the tie, then. Cancel that. The other bobby. If I have to.' What I remember best is the grudging lust in all its variety that he could call up on his face, as he made his protesting selections.

Sooner or later I have to tell Rory that it's time for me to get out. I start shivering, even in the water, even against his skin. He doesn't risk trying to lift me out while he's wet and slippery, so he dries himself as quickly as he can and comes back for me with a hot towel. By now I'm really shivering. He helps me stand up and pulls the plug out. He wraps the towel round me and rubs away until at last a tingle passes to me from the towel. By then I'm likely to be exhausted, and once he even had a shot at carrying me to the bed. He was staggering by the time we got there, and he didn't so much lay me down as fall with me down on to the mattress.

Leo is different, of course. He has a hard time lifting me into the bath, so I hang on to the towel rail just in case – though I'm not sure I could support my weight for more than a second or two, if he lost his grip. He puts stuff in the bath so that it's full of nutty-smelling bubbles by the time I arrive in it, which relaxes me and relaxes him too, because he doesn't have to see me naked for more than a few moments. I'd rather he joined me in the bath – the edge of the tub is hard against my shoulders – but he likes to stay where he is. Still, he's become something of a pro as a back-scrubber, and that's something. At first he used a nail-brush, but one day he couldn't find it so he used my toothbrush instead, and we've never gone back to the nail-brush. He's even brought along a toothbrush which is specifically for scrubbing my back.

He starts on my left shoulder, pressing hard with the bristles, moving his wrist in tiny circles. It's extraordinary how – even the first time he did it, and much more so now – my skin anticipates the sideways progress of the brush as he moves it across my back, so that I develop a roving itch that is always just a fraction ahead of the scrubbing. When he has reached the outside edge of my right shoulderblade, he drops his hand an inch or so and scrubs steadily back to the left again. I try to concentrate all my attention on the itch, which moves ahead of the toothbrush all the way. It's as if there was a poem written on my back that I learnt by heart in childhood. I have wholly forgotten it, but each word that I am prompted to remember sparks the memory of the next. I close my eyes. The travelling itch holds still, for once, at the extremity of my back, until the brush comes to scrub it out.[

I lose the ability to talk. My voice unravels, and speech drops away from me like the mouthpiece of an instrument I am suddenly unable to play, a medieval instrument that I don't even recognise as a possible source of music.

When I open my eyes again, they are both there, both the lovers. Leo and Rory. Imagination is the last thing to fail me. I see them lying side by side on their fronts, their arms around each other, their faces pushed into the pillows. They turn slowly to each other, and I see Rory trace a line with his finger down Leo's cheek. I can see a tear on Leo's skin by the tip of Rory's finger, but from my point of view I can't make out whether Rory is following its progress as it trickles, or drawing it out of Leo's eye with the gesture he makes. Rory leans over and kisses the tear where it has come to rest, and I flinch in spite of myself. Leo turns away from the kiss, so they are both on their sides now, facing the same way.

Rory sets up a gentle motion of the hips, which Leo's hips take up. A terrible rattle of protest and warning bursts from me, behind clenched teeth. Their hips are in rhythm now, and Rory's face is pressed against Leo's neck, just as it was against the pillow a few moments ago.

I turn my head away, and see the cardboard box that contains all my medicines in their varied containers. I see also the little piles of Leo's and Rory's clothes. Their two pairs of trousers have fallen in an oddly symmetrical pattern, forming a sort of star, and I can see among the keys attached to one belt-loop a new pale-silver copy of a familiar shape. I glance at the keys on the other trousers, to locate the twin of it. But I forgive my lovers their ability to comfort themselves and each other, and I forgive myself for bringing them together, as I cross the room as quietly as I can and open the door, as quietly as I can. Then I close the door after all, walk back across the room, not worrying any more about whether I make any noise, and sit back down on the edge of the bed.

A Real Life

ALICE MUNRO

A MAN CAME along and fell in love with Dorrie Beck. At least, he wanted to marry her. It was true.

'If her brother were alive she would never have needed to get married,' Millicent said. What did she mean? Not something shameful. And she didn't mean money, either. She meant that love had existed, kindness had created comfort, and in the poor, somewhat feckless life Dorrie and Albert Beck had lived together, loneliness had not been a threat. Millicent, who was shrewd and practical in some ways, was stubbornly sentimental in others. She believed always in the sweetness of affection that was untainted by sex.

She thought it was the way Dorrie used her knife and fork that had captivated the man. Indeed, it was the same way he used his. Dorrie kept her fork in her left hand and used the right only for cutting. That was because she had been to Whitby Ladies' College when she was young. A last spurt of the Becks' money. Another thing she had learned there was a beautiful handwriting, and that might have been a factor as well, because after the first meeting the entire courtship appeared to have been conducted by letter. Millicent loved the sound of Whitby Ladies' College, and it was her plan – not shared with anybody – that her own daughter would go there someday.

Millicent was not an uneducated person herself. She had taught school, she hadn't married early. She had rejected two serious boyfriends – one because she couldn't stand his mother, one because he tried putting his tongue in her mouth – before she agreed to marry Porter, who was nineteen years older than she was. He owned three farms, and he promised her a bathroom within a year, and a dining-room suite and a chesterfield and chairs. On their wedding night he said, 'Now you've got to take what's coming to you,' but she knew it was not unkindly meant.

That was in 1933.

She had three children, fairly quickly, and after the third baby she developed some problems. Porter was decent – mostly, after that, he let her alone.

The Beck house was on Porter's land, but he wasn't the one who had bought them out. He bought Albert and Dorrie's place from the man who had bought it from them. So, technically, they were renting their old house back from Porter. But money did not enter the picture. When Albert was alive he would show up and work for a day when important jobs were undertaken – when they were pouring the cement floor in the barn or putting the hay in the mow. Dorrie had come along on those occasions, and also when Millicent had a new baby or was house-cleaning. Dorrie had remarkable strength for lugging furniture about, and could do a man's work, like putting up the storm windows. At the start of a hard job – such as ripping the wallpaper off a whole room – she would settle back her shoulders and draw a deep, happy breath. She glowed with resolution. She was a big, firm woman with heavy legs, chestnut-brown hair, a broad, bashful face and dark freckles like dots of velvet. A man in the area had named a horse after her.

In spite of her enjoyment of house-cleaning, she did not do a lot of it at home. The house that she and Albert had lived in – that she lived in alone after his death – was large and handsomely laid out but practically without furniture. Furniture would come up in Dorrie's conversation – the oak sideboard, Mother's wardrobe, the spool bed – but tacked on to this mention was always the phrase 'that went at the Auction'. The Auction sounded like a natural disaster, something like a flood and windstorm together, about which it would be pointless to complain. No carpets remained, either, and no pictures. There was just the calendar from Nunn's Grocery, which Albert used to work for. Absences of customary things – and the presence of others, such as Dorrie's traps and guns and the boards for stretching rabbit and muskrat skins – had made the rooms lose their designations, made the notion of cleaning them frivolous. Once in the summer, Millicent saw a pile of dog dirt at the head of the stairs. She didn't see it while it was fresh, but it was fresh enough to seem an offence. Through the summer it changed, from brown to grey. It became stony, dignified, and stable, and, strangely, Millicent herself found less and less need to see it as anything but something that had a right to be there.

Delilah was the dog responsible. She was black, part Labrador. She chased cars, and eventually this was how she got herself killed. After Albert's death, both she and Dorrie may have become a little unhinged. But this was not something anybody could spot right away. At first, it was just that there was no man coming home, and so no set time to get supper. There were no men's clothes to wash – cutting out the idea of regular washing. Nobody to talk to, so Dorrie talked more to Millicent or to both Millicent and Porter. She talked about Albert and his job, which had been driving Nunn's Grocery Wagon, and later their truck, all over the countryside. He had gone to college, he was no dunce, but when he came home from the Great War he was not very well, and he thought it best to be out-of-doors, so he got the job driving for Nunn's and kept it until he died. He was a man of inexhaustible sociability and did more than simply deliver groceries. He gave people a lift to town. He brought patients home from the hospital. He had a crazy woman on his route, and once when he was getting her groceries out of the truck had a compulsion to look around. There she stood with a hatchet, about to brain him. In fact, her swing had already begun, and when he slipped out of range she had to continue, chopping neatly into the box of groceries and cleaving a pound of butter. He kept on making deliveries to her, not having the heart to turn her over to the authorities, who would take her to the asylum. She never took up the hatchet again but gave him cupcakes sprinkled with evil-looking seeds, which he threw into the grass at the end of the lane. Other women, more than one, had shown themselves to him naked. One of them arose out of a tub of bath water in the middle of the kitchen floor, and Albert bowed low and set the groceries at her feet. 'Aren't some people amazing?' said Dorrie. And she also told about a bachelor whose house was overrun by rats, so that he had to keep his food slung in a sack from the kitchen beams. But the rats ran out along the beams and leaped upon the sack and clawed it apart, and eventually the fellow was obliged to take all his food into bed with him.

'Albert always said people living alone are to be pitied,' said Dorrie – as if she did not understand that she was now one of them. Albert's heart had given out – he had only had time to pull to the side of the road and stop the truck. He died in a lovely spot, where black oaks grew in a bottom-land, and a sweet, clear creek ran beside the road.

Dorrie mentioned other things Albert had told her, concerning the Becks in the early days. How they came up the river in a raft, two brothers, and started a mill at the Big Bend, where there was nothing but the wildwoods. And nothing now, either, but the ruins of their mill and dam. The farm was never a livelihood but a hobby, when they built the big house and brought out the furniture from Edinburgh. The bedsteads, the chairs, the carved chests that went in the Auction. They brought it round the Horn, Dorrie said, and up Lake Huron and so up the river. Oh, Dorrie, said Millicent, that is not possible, and she brought a school geography book she had kept, to point out the error. It must have been a canal, then, said Dorrie. I recall a canal. The Panama Canal? More likely it was the Erie Canal, said Millicent.

'Yes,' said Dorrie. 'Round the Horn and into the Erie Canal.'

'Dorrie is a true lady, no matter what anybody says,' said Millicent to Porter, who did not argue. He was used to her absolute, personal judgements. 'She is a hundred times more a lady than Muriel Snow,' said Millicent, naming the person who might be called her best friend. 'I say that, and I love Muriel Snow dearly.'

Porter was used to hearing that, too: 'I love Muriel Snow dearly, and I would stick up for her no matter what.' 'I love Muriel Snow, but that does not mean I approve of everything she does.'

The smoking. And saying hot damn, Chrissakes, poop. *I nearly pooped my pants.*

Muriel Snow had not been Millicent's first choice for best friend. In the early days of her marriage she had set her sights high. Mrs Lawyer Nesbitt. Mrs Doctor Finnegan. Mrs Doud. They let her take on a donkey's load of work in the Women's Auxiliary at the church, but they never asked her to their tea parties. She was never inside their houses, unless it was to a meeting. Porter was a farmer. No matter how many farms. She should have known.

She met Muriel when she decided that her daughter, Betty Jean, would take piano lessons. Muriel was the music teacher. She taught in the schools as well as privately. Times being what they were, she charged only twenty cents a lesson. She played the organ at the church and directed various choirs, but some of that was for nothing. She and Millicent got on so well that soon she was in Millicent's house as often as Dorrie was, though on a rather different footing.

Muriel was over thirty and had never been married. Getting married was something she talked about openly, jokingly, and plaintively, particularly when Porter was around. 'Don't you know any men, Porter?' she would say. 'Can't you dig up just one decent man for me?' Porter would say maybe he could, but maybe she wouldn't think they were so decent. In the summers Muriel went to visit a sister in Montreal, and once she went to stay with some cousins she had never met, only written to, in Philadelphia. The first thing she reported on, when she got back, was the man situation.

'Terrible. They all get married young, they're Catholics, and the wives never die – they're too busy having babies.'

'Oh, they had somebody lined up for me, but I saw right away he would never pan out. He was one of those ones with the mothers.'

'I did meet one, but he had an awful failing. He didn't cut his toenails. Big yellow toenails. Well? Aren't you going to ask me how I found out?'

Muriel was always dressed in some shade of blue. A woman should pick a colour that really suits her and wear it all the time, she said. Like your perfume. It should be your signature. Blue was widely thought to be a colour for blondes, but that was incorrect. Blue often made a blonde look more washed-out than she was to start with. It suited best a warm-looking skin, like Muriel's – skin that took a good tan and never entirely lost it. It suited brown hair and brown eyes, which were hers as well. She never skimped on her clothes – it was a mistake to. Her fingernails were always painted – a rich and distracting colour, apricot or blood ruby or even gold. She was small and round; she did exercises to keep her tidy waistline. She had a dark mole on the front of her neck, like a jewel on an invisible chain, and another, like a tear, at the corner of one eye.

'The word for you is not "pretty",' Millicent said one day, surprising herself. 'It's "*bewitching*".' Then she flushed at her own tribute, knowing she sounded childish and excessive.

Muriel flushed a little too, but with pleasure. She drank in admiration, frankly courted it. Once she dropped in on her way to a concert in Walley, which she hoped would yield rewards. She had on an ice-blue dress that shimmered.

'And that isn't all,' she said. 'Everything I have on is new, and everything is *silk*.'

It wasn't true that she never found a man. She found one fairly often but hardly ever one that she could bring to supper. She found them in other towns, where she took her choirs to massed concerts, in Toronto at piano recitals to which she might take a promising student. Sometimes she found them in the students' own homes. They were the uncles, the fathers, the grandfathers, and the reason that they would not come into Millicent's house but only wave – sometimes curtly, sometimes with bravado – from a waiting car was that they were married. A bedridden wife, a drinking wife, a vicious shrew of a wife? Perhaps. Sometimes no mention at all – a ghost of a wife. They escorted Muriel to musical events, an interest in music being the ready excuse. Sometimes there was even a performing child, to act as chaperon. They took her to dinners in restaurants in distant towns. They were referred to as friends. Millicent defended her. How could there be any harm when it was all so out in the open? But it wasn't, quite, and it would all end in misunderstandings, harsh words, unkindness. A wife on the phone. Miss Snow, I am sorry we are cancelling – Or simply silence. A date not kept, a note not answered, a name never to be mentioned again.

'I don't expect so much,' Muriel said. 'I expect a friend to be a friend. Then they hightail it off at the first whiff of trouble, after saying they would always stand up for me. Why is that?'

'Well, you know, Muriel,' Millicent said once, 'a wife is a wife. It's all well and good to have friends, but a marriage is a marriage.'

Muriel blew up at that – she said that Millicent thought the worst of her, like everybody else, and was she never to be permitted to have a good time, an innocent good time? She banged the door and ran her car over the calla lilies, surely on purpose. For a day Millicent's face was blotchy from weeping. But enmity did not last and Muriel was back, tearful as well, and taking blame on herself.

'I was a fool from the start,' she said, and went into the front room to play the piano. Millicent got to know the pattern. When Muriel was happy and had a new friend she played mournful, tender songs, like 'The Flowers of the Forest'. Or:

> She dressed herself in male attire,
> And gaily she was dressed –

Then, when she was disappointed, she came down hard and fast on the keys, and she sang scornfully some such song as 'Bonnie Dundee'.

> To the Lords of Convention
> 'Twas Claverhouse spoke,
> Ere the King's head go down
> There are heads to be broke!

Sometimes Millicent asked people to supper (though not the Finnegans or the Nesbitts or the Douds), and then she liked to ask Dorrie and Muriel as well. Dorrie was a help in washing up the pots and pans afterwards, and Muriel could entertain on the piano.

A couple of years after Albert died, Millicent asked the Anglican minister to come on Sunday, after Evensong, and bring the friend she had heard was staying with him. The Anglican minister was a bachelor, but Muriel had given up on him early. Neither fish nor fowl, she said. Too bad. Millicent liked him, chiefly for his voice. She had been brought up an Anglican, and though she'd switched to United, which was what Porter said he was (so was everybody else, so were all the important and substantial people in the town), she still favoured Anglican customs. Evensong, the church bell, the choir coming up the aisle in meagre state, singing – instead of just all clumping in together and sitting down. Best of all, the words. *But thou, O Lord, have mercy upon us, miserable offenders. Spare thou them, O God, which confess their faults. Restore thou them that are penitent; According to thy promises . . .*

Porter went with her once and hated it.

Preparations for this evening's supper were considerable. The damask was brought out, the silver serving spoon, the black dessert plates painted by hand with pansies. The cloth had to be pressed and all the silverware polished, and then there was the apprehension that a tiny smear of polish might remain, a grey gum on the tines of a fork or among the grapes round the rim of the wedding teapot. All day Sunday Millicent was torn between pleasure and agony, hope and suspense. The things that could go wrong multiplied. The Bavarian cream might not set (they had no refrigerator yet and had to chill things in summer by setting them on the cellar floor). The angel-food cake might not rise to its full glory. If it did rise, it might be dry. The biscuits might taste of tainted flour or a beetle might crawl out of the salad. By five o'clock she was in such a state of tension and misgiving that nobody could stay in the kitchen with her. Muriel had arrived early, to help out, but she had not chopped the potatoes finely enough, and had managed to scrape her knuckles while grating carrots, so she was told off for being useless and sent to play the piano.

Muriel was dressed up in turquoise crêpe and smelled of her Spanish perfume. She might have written off the minister but she had not seen his visitor yet. A bachelor, perhaps, or a widower, since he was travelling alone. Rich, or he would not be travelling at all, not so far. He came from England, people said. Someone said no, Australia.

She was trying to get up the 'Polovtsian Dances.'

Dorrie was late. It threw a crimp in things. The jellied salad had to be taken down cellar again, lest it should soften. The biscuits put to warm in the oven had to be taken out, for fear of their getting too hard. The three men sat on the veranda – the meal was to be eaten there, buffet style – and drank fizzy lemonade. Millicent had seen what drink did in her own family – her father had died of it when she was ten – and she had required a promise from Porter, before they married, that he would never touch it again. Of course he did – he kept a bottle in the granary – but when he drank he kept his distance, and she truly believed the promise had been kept. This was a fairly common pattern, at that time, at least among farmers – drinking in the barn, abstinence in the house. Most men would have felt there was something the matter with a woman who didn't lay down such a law.

But Muriel, when she came out on the veranda in her high heels and slinky crêpe, cried out at once, 'Oh, my favourite drink! Gin and lemon!' She took a sip and pouted at Porter. 'You did it again. You forgot the gin again!' Then she teased the minister, asking if he didn't have a flask in his pocket. The minister was gallant, or perhaps made reckless by boredom. He said he wished he had.

The visitor who rose to be introduced was tall and thin and sallow, with a face that seemed to hang in pleats, precise and melancholy. Muriel did not give way to disappointment. She sat down beside him and tried in a most spirited way to get him into conversation. She told him about her music teaching and was scathing about the local choirs and musicians. She did not spare the Anglicans, telling about the Sunday-school concert when the master of ceremonies announced that she would play a piece by Chopin, pronouncing it 'Choppin'.

Porter had done the chores early and washed and changed into his suit, but he kept looking uneasily towards the barnyard, as if recalling something that was left undone. One of the cows was bawling loudly in the field, and at last he excused himself to go and see what was wrong with her. He found that her calf had got caught in the wire fence and managed to strangle itself. He did not speak of this loss when he came back with newly washed hands. 'Calf caught up in the fence,' was all he said. But he connected the mishap somehow with this entertainment, with dressing up and having to eat off your knees. It was not natural.

'Those cows are as bad as children,' Millicent said. 'Always wanting your attention at the wrong time!' Her own children, fed earlier, peered from between the banisters to watch the food being carried to the veranda. 'I think we will have to commence without Dorrie. You men must be starving. This is just a simple little buffet. We sometimes enjoy eating outside on a Sunday evening.'

'Commence, commence!' cried Muriel, who had helped to carry out the various dishes – the potato salad, carrot salad, jellied salad, cabbage salad, the devilled eggs and cold roast chicken, the salmon loaf and warm biscuits, and the relishes. Just when they had everything set out, Dorrie came around the side of the house, looking warm from her walk across the field, or from excitement. She was wearing her good summer dress, a navy-blue organdie with white dots and white collar, suitable for a little girl or an old lady. Threads showed where she had pulled the torn lace off the collar instead of mending it, and in spite of the hot day a rim of undershirt was hanging out of one sleeve. Her shoes had been so recently and sloppily cleaned that they left traces of whitener on the grass.

'I would have been on time,' Dorrie said, 'but I had to shoot a feral cat. She was prowling around my house and carrying on so, I was convinced she was rabid.'

Dorrie had wet her hair and crimped it into place with bobby pins. With that, and her pink, shiny face, she looked like a doll with a china head and limbs attached to a cloth body firmly stuffed with straw.

'I thought at first she might have been in heat, but she didn't really behave that way. She didn't do any of the rubbing along on her stomach such as I'm used to seeing. And I noticed some spitting. So I thought the only thing to do was to shoot her. Then I put her in a sack and called up Fred Nunn to see if he would run her over to Walley, to the vet. I want to know if she really was rabid, and Fred always likes the excuse to get out in his car. I told him to leave the sack on the step if the vet wasn't home on a Sunday night.'

'I wonder what he'll think it is?' said Muriel. 'A present?'

'No. I pinned on a note, in case. There was definite spitting and dribbling.' Dorrie touched her own face to show where the dribbling had been. 'Are you enjoying your visit here?' she said to the minister, who had been in town for three years and had been the one to bury her brother.

'It is Mr Speirs who is the visitor, Dorrie,' said Millicent. Dorrie acknowledged the introduction and seemed unembarrassed by her mistake. She said that the reason she took the animal for a feral cat was that its coat was all matted and hideous, and she thought that a feral cat would never come near the house unless it was rabid.

'But I will put an explanation in the paper, just in case. I will be sorry if it is anybody's pet. I lost my own pet three months ago – my dog, Delilah. She was struck down by a car.'

It was strange to hear that dog called a pet, that big black Delilah who used to lollop along with Dorrie all over the countryside, who tore across the fields in such savage glee to attack cars. Dorrie had been distraught at the death; indeed, she had said she had expected it some day. But now, to hear her say 'pet', Millicent thought there might have been grief she didn't show.

'Come and fill up your plate or we'll all have to starve,' Muriel said to Mr Speirs. 'You're the guest, you have to go first. If the egg yolks look dark, it's just what the hens have been eating – they won't poison you. I grated the carrots for that salad myself, so if you notice some blood it's just where I got a little too enthusiastic and grated in some skin off my knuckles. I had better shut up now or Millicent will kill me.'

And Millicent was laughing angrily, saying, 'Oh, they are not! Oh, you did *not*!'

Mr Speirs had paid close attention to everything Dorrie said. Maybe that was what had made Muriel so saucy. Millicent thought that perhaps he saw Dorrie as a novelty, a Canadian wild woman who went around shooting things. He might be studying her so that he could go home and describe her to his friends in England.

Dorrie kept quiet while eating, and she ate quite a lot. Mr Speirs ate a lot, too – Millicent was happy to see that – and he appeared to be a silent person at all times. The minister kept the conversation going by describing a book he was reading. It was called *The Oregon Trail*.

'Terrible, the hardships,' he said.

Millicent said she had heard of it. 'I have some cousins living out in Oregon, but I cannot remember the name of the town,' she said. 'I wonder if they went on that trail.'

The minister said that if they went out a hundred years ago it was most probable.

'Oh, I wouldn't think it was that long,' Millicent said. 'Their name was Rafferty.'

'Man the name of Rafferty used to race pigeons,' said Porter, with sudden energy. 'This was way back, when there was more of that kind of thing. There was money going on it, too. Well, he said the problem with the pigeons' house, they don't go in right away, and that means they don't trip the wire and don't get counted in. So he took an egg one of his pigeons was on, and he blew it clear, and he put a beetle inside. And the beetle inside made such a racket the pigeon naturally thought she had an egg getting ready to hatch. And she flew a beeline home and tripped the wire, and all the ones that bet on her made a lot of money. Him, too, of course. In fact, this was over in Ireland, and this man that told the story, that was how he got the money to come out to Canada.'

Millicent didn't believe that the man's name had been Rafferty at all. That had just been an excuse.

'So you keep a gun in the house?' said the minister to Dorrie. 'Does that mean you are worried about tramps and suchlike?'

Dorrie put down her knife and fork, chewed something up carefully, and swallowed. 'I keep it for shooting,' she said.

After a pause she said that she shot groundhogs and rabbits. She took the groundhogs over to the other side of town and sold them to the mink farm. She skinned the rabbits and stretched the skins, then sold them to a place in Walley which did a big trade with the tourists. She enjoyed fried or boiled rabbit meat but could not possibly eat it all herself, so she often took a rabbit carcass, cleaned and skinned, around to some family that was on relief. Many times her offering was refused. People thought it was as bad as eating a dog or a cat. Though even that, she believed, was not considered out of the way in China.

'That is true,' said Mr Speirs. 'I have eaten them both.'

'Well, then, you know,' said Dorrie. 'People are prejudiced.'

He asked about the skins, saying they must have to be removed very carefully, and Dorrie said that was true, and you needed a knife you could trust. She described with pleasure the first clean slit down the belly. 'Even more difficult with the muskrats, because you have to be more careful with the fur, it is more valuable,' she said. 'It is a denser fur. Waterproof.'

'You do not shoot the muskrats?' said Mr Speirs.

No, no, said Dorrie. She trapped them. Trapped them, yes, said Mr Speirs, and Dorrie described her favourite trap, on which she had made little improvements of her own. She had thought of taking out a patent but had never got around to it. She spoke about the spring watercourses, the system of creeks she followed, tramping for miles day after day, after the snow was mostly melted but before the leaves came out, when the muskrats' fur was prime. Millicent knew that Dorrie did these things, but she had thought she did them to get a little money. To hear her talk now, it would seem she loved that life. The blackflies out already, the cold water over her boot tops, the drowned rats. And Mr Speirs listened like an old dog, perhaps a hunting dog, that has been sitting with his eyes half shut, just prevented, by his own good opinion of himself, from falling into an unmannerly stupor. Now he has got a whiff of something – his eyes open all the way and his nose quivers as he remembers some day of recklessness and dedication. How many miles did she cover in a day, Mr Speirs asked, and how high is the water, how much do the muskrats weigh and how many could you count on in a day and for muskrats is it still the same sort of knife?

Muriel asked the minister for a cigarette and got one, smoked for a few moments, and stubbed it out in the middle of her dish of the Bavarian cream. 'So I won't eat it and get fat,' she said. She got up and started to help clear the dishes, but soon ended up at the piano, back at the 'Polovtsian Dances'.

Millicent was pleased that there was conversation with the guest, though its attraction mystified her. Also, the food had been good and there had not been any humiliation – no queer taste or sticky cup handle.

'I had thought the trappers were all up north,' said Mr Speirs. 'I thought that they were beyond the Arctic Circle or at least on the Precambrian shield.'

'I used to have an idea of going there,' Dorrie said. Her voice thickened for the first time, with embarrassment – or excitement. 'I thought I could live in a cabin and trap all winter. But I had my brother. I couldn't leave my brother. And I know it here.'

Late in the winter Dorrie arrived at Millicent's house with a large piece of white satin. She said that she intended to make a wedding dress. That was the first anybody had heard of a wedding – she said it would be in May – or learned the first name of Mr Speirs. It was Wilkinson. Wilkie.

When and where had Dorrie seen him, since that supper on the veranda?

Nowhere. He had gone off to Australia, where he had property. Letters had gone back and forth between them.

Millicent's questions drew out a little more information. Wilkie had been born in England but was now an Australian. He had travelled all over the world, climbed mountains, and gone up a river into the jungle. In Africa, or South America – Dorrie was not sure which.

'He thinks I am adventurous,' said Dorrie, as if to answer an unspoken question about as to what he saw in her.

'And is he in love with you?' said Millicent. It was she who blushed then, not Dorrie. But Dorrie, unblushing, unfidgeting, was like a column of heat, bare and concentrated. Millicent had an awful thought of her naked, so that she hardly heard what Dorrie said. She amended the question to what she believed she had meant: 'Will he be good to you?'

'Oh – yes,' said Dorrie, rather carelessly.

Sheets were laid down on the dining-room floor, with the

dining table pushed against the wall. The satin was spread out over them. Its broad, bright extent, its shining vulnerability, cast a hush over the whole house. The children came, only to stare at it, and Millicent shouted to them to clear off. She was afraid to cut into it. And Dorrie, who could so easily slit the skin of an animal, laid the scissors down. She confessed to shaking hands.

A call was put in to Muriel, to drop by after school. She clapped her hand to her heart when she heard the news, and called Dorrie a slyboots, a Cleopatra who had fascinated a millionaire.

'I bet he's a millionaire,' Muriel said. 'Property in Australia – what does that mean? I bet it's not a pig farm! All I can hope is maybe he'll have a brother. Oh, Dorrie, am I so mean I didn't even say congratulations?'

She gave Dorrie lavish, loud kisses – Dorrie standing still for them, as if she were five years old.

Dorrie said that she and Mr Speirs planned to go through 'a form of marriage'. What do you mean, said Millicent, do you mean a marriage ceremony, is that what you mean? – and Dorrie said yes.

Muriel made the first cut into the satin, saying that somebody had to do it, though maybe if she were doing it again it wouldn't be in quite that place.

Soon they got used to mistakes. Mistakes and rectifications. Late every afternoon, when Muriel got there, they tackled a new stage – the cutting, the pinning, the basting, the sewing – with clenched teeth and grim rallying cries. They had to alter the pattern as they went along, to allow for problems unforeseen, such as the tight set of a sleeve, the bunching of the heavy satin at the waist, the eccentricities of Dorrie's figure. Dorrie was a menace at the job, so they set her to sweeping up scraps and filling the bobbin. Whenever she sat at the sewing machine she clamped her tongue between her teeth. Sometimes she had nothing to do, and she walked from room to room in Millicent's house, stopping to stare out the windows at the snow and sleet, the long-drawn-out end of winter. Or she stood like a docile beast in her woollen underwear, which smelled quite frankly of her flesh, while they pulled and tugged the material around her.

Muriel had taken charge of the clothes. She knew what there had to be. There had to be more than a wedding dress. There had to be a going-away outfit, and a wedding nightgown and a matching dressing gown, and of course an entire new supply of underwear. Silk stockings, and a brassiere – the first that Dorrie had ever worn.

Dorrie had not known about any of that. 'I considered the wedding dress as the major hurdle,' she said. 'I could not think beyond it.'

The snow melted, the creeks filled up, the muskrats would be swimming in the cold water, sleek and sporty, with their treasure on their backs. If Dorrie thought of her traps she did not say so. The only walk she took these days was across the field from her house to Millicent's.

Made bold by experience, Muriel cut out a dressmaker suit of fine russet wool, and a lining. She was letting her choir rehearsals go all to pot.

Millicent had to think about the wedding luncheon. It was to be held in the Brunswick Hotel. But who was there to invite, except the minister? Lots of people knew Dorrie, but they knew her as the lady who left skinned rabbits on doorsteps, who went through the fields and the woods with her dog and gun and waded along the flooded creeks in her high rubber boots. Few people knew anything about the old Becks, though all remembered Albert and had liked him. Dorrie was not quite a joke – something protected her from that, either Albert's popularity or her own gruffness and dignity – but the news of her wedding had roused a lot of interest, not exactly of a sympathetic nature. Her marriage was being spoken of as a freakish event, mildly scandalous, possibly a hoax. Porter said that bets were being laid on whether the man would show up.

Finally, Millicent recalled some cousins, who had come to Albert's funeral. Ordinary, respectable people. Dorrie had their addresses, invitations were sent. Then the Nunn brothers from the grocery, whom Albert had worked for, and their wives. A couple of Albert's lawn-bowling friends and their wives. The people who owned the mink farm where Dorrie sold her groundhogs? The woman from the bake-shop who was going to ice the cake?

The cake was being made at home, then taken to the shop to be iced by the woman who had got a diploma in cake decorating from a place in Chicago. It would be covered with white roses, lacy scallops, hearts and garlands and silver leaves and those tiny silver candies you can break your tooth on. Meanwhile it had to be mixed and baked, and this was where Dorrie's strong arms could come into play, stirring and stirring a mixture so stiff it appeared to be all candied fruit and raisins and currants with a little gingery batter holding everything together like glue. When Dorrie got the big bowl against her stomach and took up the beating spoon, Millicent heard the first satisfied sigh to come out of her in a long while.

Muriel decided that there had to be a maid of honour. Or a matron of honour. It could not be her, because she would be playing the organ. 'O Perfect Love'. And the Mendelssohn.

It would have to be Millicent. Muriel would not take no for an answer. She brought over an evening dress of her own, a long sky-blue dress, which she ripped open at the waist – how confident and cavalier she was by now, about dressmaking! – and she proposed a lace midriff, of darker blue, with a matching lace bolero. It will look like new and suit you to a T, she said.

Millicent laughed when she first tried it on, and she said, 'There's a sight to scare the pigeons!' But she was pleased. She and Porter had not had much of a wedding – they had just gone to the rectory, deciding to put the money saved into furniture. 'I suppose I'll need some kind of thingamajig,' she said. 'Something on my head.'

'Her veil!' cried Muriel. 'What about Dorrie's veil? We've been concentrating so much on wedding dresses, we've forgotten all about a veil!'

Dorrie spoke up unexpectedly and said that she would never wear a veil. She could not stand to have one draped over her, it would feel like cobwebs. Her use of the word 'cobwebs' gave Muriel and Millicent a start, because there were jokes being made about cobwebs in other places.

'She's right,' said Muriel. 'A veil would be too much.' She considered what else. A wreath of flowers? No, too much again. A picture hat? Yes, get an old summer hat and cover it with white satin. Then get another and cover it with the dark-blue lace.

'Here is the menu,' said Millicent dubiously. 'Creamed chicken in pastry shells, little round biscuits, moulded jellies, that salad with the apples and the walnuts, pink and white ice-cream with the cake –'

Thinking of the cake, Muriel said, 'Does he by any chance have a sword, Dorrie?'

Dorrie said, 'Who?'

'Wilkie. Your Wilkie. Does he have a sword?'

'What would he have a sword for?' Millicent said.

'I just thought he might,' said Muriel.

'I cannot enlighten you,' said Dorrie.

Then there was a moment in which they all fell silent, because they had to think of the bridegroom. They had to admit him to the room and set him down in the midst of all this. Picture hats. Creamed chicken. Silver leaves. They were stricken with doubts. At least Millicent was, and Muriel. They hardly dared to look at each other.

'I just thought since he was English, or whatever he is,' said Muriel.

Millicent said, 'He is a fine man, anyway.'

The wedding was set for the second Saturday in May. Mr Speirs was to arrive on the Wednesday and stay with the minister. The Sunday before, Dorrie was supposed to come over to have supper with Millicent and Porter. Muriel was there too. Dorrie didn't arrive, and they went ahead and started without her.

Millicent stood up in the middle of the meal. 'I'm going over there,' she said. 'She'd better be sharper than this getting to her wedding.'

'I can keep you company,' said Muriel.

Millicent said no thanks. Two might make it worse.

Make what worse?

She didn't know.

She went across the field by herself. It was a warm evening, and the back door of Dorrie's house was standing open. Between the house and where the barn used to be there was a grove of walnut trees, whose branches were still bare, since walnut trees are among the very latest to get their leaves. The hot sunlight pouring through bare branches seemed unnatural. Her feet did not make any sound on the grass.

And there on the back platform was Albert's old armchair, never taken in all winter.

What was in her mind was that Dorrie might have had an accident. Something to do with a gun. Maybe while cleaning her gun. That happened to people. Or she might be lying out in a field somewhere, lying in the woods among the old, dead leaves and the new leeks and bloodroot. Tripped while getting over a fence. Had to go out one last time. And then, after all the safe times, the gun had gone off. Millicent had never had any such fears for Dorrie before, and she knew that in some ways Dorrie was very careful and competent. It must be that what had happened this year made anything seem possible. The proposed marriage, such wild luck, could make you believe in calamity also.

But it was not an accident that was on Millicent's mind. Not really. Under this busy, fearful imagining of accidents, she hid what she really feared.

She called Dorrie's name at the open door. And so prepared was she for an answering silence, the evil silence and indifference of a house lately vacated by somebody who had met with disaster (or not vacated, yet, by the body of the person who had met with, who had *brought about*, that disaster) – so prepared was she for the worst that she was shocked, she went watery in the knees, at the sight of Dorrie herself in her old field pants and shirt.

'We were waiting for you,' Millicent said. 'We were waiting for you to come to supper.'

Dorrie said, 'I must've lost track of the time.'

'Oh, have all your clocks stopped?' said Millicent, recovering her nerve as she was led through the back hall with its familiar, mysterious debris. She could smell cooking.

The kitchen was dark because of the big, unruly lilac pressing against the window. Dorrie used the house's original wood-burning cookstove, and she had one of those old kitchen tables with drawers for the knives and forks. It was a relief to see that the calendar on the wall was for this year.

Yes – Dorrie was cooking some supper. She was in the middle of chopping up a purple onion, to add to the bits of bacon and sliced potatoes she had frying up in the pan. So much for losing track of the time.

'You go ahead,' said Millicent. 'Go ahead and make your meal. I did get something to eat before I took it into my head to go and look for you.'

'I made tea,' said Dorrie. It was keeping warm on the back of the stove, and when she poured it out it was like ink.

'I can't leave,' she said, prying up some of the bacon that was sputtering in the pan. 'I can't leave here.'

Millicent decided to treat this as she would a child's announcement that she could not go to school.

'Well, that'll be a nice piece of news for Mr Speirs,' she said. 'When he has come all this way.'

343

Dorrie leaned back as the grease became fractious.

'Better move that off the heat a bit,' Millicent said.

'I can't leave.'

'I heard that before.'

Dorrie finished her cooking and scooped the results on to a plate. She added ketchup and a couple of thick slices of bread soaked in the grease that was left in the pan. She sat down to eat, and did not speak.

Millicent was sitting, too, waiting her out. Finally she said, 'Give a reason.'

Dorrie shrugged and chewed.

'Maybe you know something I don't,' Millicent said. 'What have you found out? Is he poor?'

Dorrie shook her head. 'Rich,' she said.

So, Muriel was right.

'A lot of women would give their eye teeth.'

'I don't care about that,' Dorrie said. She chewed and swallowed and repeated, 'I don't care.'

Millicent had to take a chance, though it embarrassed her. 'If you are thinking about what I think you may be thinking about, then it could be that you are worried over nothing. A lot of the time when they get older they don't even want to bother.'

'Oh, it isn't that! I know all about that.'

Oh, do you, thought Millicent, and if so, how? Dorrie might imagine she knew, from animals. Millicent had sometimes thought that no woman would get married, if she really knew.

Nevertheless, she said, 'Marriage takes you out of yourself and gives you a real life.'

'I have a life,' Dorrie said. 'Perhaps I am not adventurous,' she added.

'All right, then,' said Millicent, as if she had given up arguing. She sat and drank her poison tea. She was getting an inspiration. She let time pass and then she said, 'It's up to you, it certainly is. But there is a problem about where you will live. You can't live here. When Porter and I found out you were getting married we put this place on the market, and we sold it.'

Dorrie said instantly, 'You're lying.'

'We didn't want it standing empty to make a haven for tramps. We went ahead and sold it.'

'You would never do such a trick on me.'

'What kind of a trick would it be when you were getting married?'

Millicent was already believing what she said. Soon it could come true. They could offer the place at a low enough price, and somebody would buy it. It could still be fixed up. Or it could be torn down, for the bricks and the woodwork. Porter would be glad to be rid of it.

Dorrie said, 'You would not put me out of my house.'

Millicent kept quiet.

'You are lying, aren't you?' said Dorrie.

'Give me your Bible,' Millicent said. 'I will swear on it.'

Dorrie actually looked around. She said, 'I don't know where it is.'

'Dorrie, listen. All of this is for your own good. It may seem like I am pushing you out, but all it is is making you do what you are not quite up to doing on your own.'

'Oh,' said Dorrie. 'Why?'

Because the wedding cake is made, thought Millicent, and the satin dress is made, and the luncheon has been ordered and the invitations have been sent. All this trouble that has been gone to. People might say that was a silly reason, but those who said that would not be the people who had gone to the trouble. It was not fair, to have your best efforts squandered.

But it was more than that, for she believed what she had said, telling Dorrie that this was how she could have a life. And what did Dorrie mean by 'here'? If she meant that she would be homesick, let her be! Homesickness was never anything you couldn't get over. Millicent was not going to pay any attention to that 'here'. Nobody had any business living a life out 'here' if they had been offered what Dorrie had. It was a kind of sin, to refuse such an offer. Out of stubbornness, out of fearfulness, and idiocy.

She had begun to get the feeling that Dorrie was cornered. Dorrie might be giving up, or letting the idea of giving up seep through her. Perhaps. She sat as still as a stump, but there was a chance such a stump might be pulpy within.

But it was Millicent who began suddenly to weep. 'Oh, Dorrie,' she said. 'Don't be stupid!' They both got up and grabbed hold of each other, and then Dorrie had to do the comforting, patting and soothing in a magisterial way, while

Millicent wept, and repeated some words that did not hang together. *Happy. Help. Ridiculous.*

'I will look after Albert,' she said, when she had calmed down somewhat. 'I'll put flowers. And I won't mention this to Muriel Snow. Or to Porter. Nobody needs to know.'

Dorrie said nothing. She seemed a little lost, absent-minded, as if she was busy turning something over and over, resigning herself to the weight and strangeness of it.

'That tea is awful,' said Millicent. 'Can't we make some that's fit to drink?' She went to throw the contents of her cup into the slop pail.

There stood Dorrie in the dim window light – mulish, obedient, childish, female – a most mysterious and maddening person, whom Millicent seemed now to have conquered, to be sending away. At greater cost to herself, Millicent was thinking – greater cost than she had understood. She tried to engage Dorrie in a sombre but encouraging look, cancelling her fit of tears. She said, 'The die is cast.'

Dorrie walked to her wedding. Nobody had known that she intended to do that. When Porter and Millicent stopped the car in front of her house, to pick her up, Millicent was still anxious. 'Honk the horn,' she said. 'She better be ready now.'

Porter said, 'Isn't that her down ahead?'

It was. She was wearing a light-grey coat of Albert's over her satin dress and was carrying her picture hat in one hand, a bunch of lilacs in the other. They stopped the car and she said, 'No. I want the exercise. It will clear out my head.'

They had no choice but to drive on and wait at the church and see her approaching down the street, people coming out of shops to look, a few cars honking sportively, people waving and calling out, 'Here comes the bride!' As she got closer to the church she stopped and removed Albert's coat, and then she was gleaming, miraculous, like the pillar of salt in the Bible.

Muriel was inside the church, playing the organ, so she did not have to realise, at this last moment, that they had forgotten all about gloves and that Dorrie clutched the woody stems of the lilac in her bare hands. Mr Speirs had been in the church, too, but he had come out, breaking all rules, leaving the minister to stand there on his own. He was as lean and yellow and wolfish as Millicent remembered, but when he saw Dorrie fling the old coat into the back of Porter's car and settle the hat on her head – Millicent had to run up and fix it right – he appeared nobly satisfied. Millicent had a picture of him and Dorrie mounted high, mounted on elephants, panoplied, borne cumbrously forward, adventuring. A vision. She was filled with optimism and relief and she whispered to Dorrie, 'He'll take you everywhere! He'll make you a queen!'

'I have grown as fat as the Queen of Tonga,' wrote Dorrie from Australia, some years on. A photograph showed that she was not exaggerating. Her hair was white, her skin brown, as if all her freckles had got loose and run together. She wore a vast garment, coloured like tropical flowers. The war had come and put an end to any idea of travelling, and then when it was over Wilkie was dying. Dorrie stayed on, in Queensland, on a great property where she grew sugar cane and pineapples, cotton, peanuts, tobacco. She rode horses, in spite of her size, and had learned to fly an airplane. She took up some travels of her own in that part of the world. She had shot crocodiles. She died in the Fifties, in New Zealand, climbing up to look at a volcano.

Millicent told everybody what she had said she would not mention. She took credit, naturally. She recalled her inspiration, her stratagem, with no apologies. 'Somebody had to take the bull by the horns,' she said. She felt that she was the creator of a life – more effectively, in Dorrie's case, than in the case of her own children. She had created happiness, or something close. She forgot the way she had wept without knowing why.

The wedding had its effect on Muriel. She handed in her resignation, she went off to Alberta. 'I'll give it a year,' she said. And within a year she had found a husband – not the sort of man she had ever had anything to do with in the past. A widower with two small children. A Christian minister. Millicent wondered at Muriel's describing him that way. Weren't all ministers Christian? When they came back for a visit – by this time there were two more children, their own – she saw the point of the description. Smoking and drinking and swearing were out, and so was wearing make-up, and the kind of music that Muriel used to play. She played hymns now – the sort she had once made fun of. She wore any colour at all and had a bad permanent – her hair, going grey, stood up from her forehead in frizzy bunches. 'A lot of my former life turns my stomach – just to think about it,' she said, and Millicent got the impression that she and Porter were seen mostly as belonging to those stomach-turning times.

The house was not sold or rented. It was not torn down, either, and its construction was so sound that it did not readily give way. It was capable of standing for years and years and presenting a plausible appearance. A tree of cracks can branch out among the bricks, but the wall does not fall down. Window sashes settle, at an angle, but the window does not fall out. The doors were locked, but it was probable that children got in and wrote things on the walls and broke up the crockery that Dorrie had left behind. Millicent never went in to see.

There was a thing that Dorrie and Albert used to do, and then Dorrie did alone. It must have started when they were children. Every year, in the fall, they – and then, she – collected up all the walnuts that had fallen off the trees. They kept going, collecting fewer and fewer walnuts every day, until they were fairly sure that they had got the last, or the next-to-last, one. Then they counted them, and they wrote the total on the cellar wall. The date, the year, the total. The walnuts were not used for anything once they were collected. They were just dumped along the edge of the field and allowed to rot.

Millicent did not continue this useless chore. She had plenty of other chores to do, and plenty for her children to do. But at the time of year when the walnuts were lying in the long grass she would think of that custom, and how Dorrie must have expected to keep it up until she died. A life of customs, of seasons. The walnuts drop, the muskrats swim in the creek. Dorrie must have believed that she was meant to live so, in her reasonable eccentricity, her manageable loneliness. Probably she would have got another dog.

But I would not allow that, thinks Millicent. She would not allow it, and surely she was right. She had lived to be an old lady, she is living yet, though Porter has been dead for decades. She doesn't often notice the house. It is just there. But once in a while she does see its cracked face and the blank, slanted windows. The walnut trees behind, losing again, again, their delicate canopy of leaves.

I ought to knock that down and sell the bricks, she says, and seems puzzled that she has not already done so.

Wilderness

EDNA O'BRIEN

YES, DEATH STALKED the city that night, stalked the city like a great water wolf. The river – sheer, ruffled, grey, brown, black and khaki – took them into her inhospitable bosom. Why? Why did the river want them, and for what?

All her life Nell had believed that she would have a presentiment if a mishap should befall either of her children. Her bones would tell it. Her bloodstream would tell it. Every hair would stand on end. Often she had half imagined such a thing – indeed, on occasion, went with the delirium of it upon hearing of an accident in this street or that, on a motorway or a leafy lane – and had waited, and the wait had seemed both necessary and ludicrous. She knew the ropes. A policeman, or rather two policemen, came and knocked on one's door. She had heard that somewhere. Yet, as the taxi-driver rattled on about an accident, young people, partying, she had no intimation of anything, just felt glad to be going home to sleep. It was a Saturday. Party night. A pleasure boat had collided with a barge on the Thames, and many were drowned or drowning. She felt a flash of dismay, a mockery of the sadness to come.

When a mother sees two policemen at her front door, she knows. She thought it was her younger son, Tristan, was certain that a truck had gone off the road in Turkey, where he and his friends were spending the summer doing relief work. It was Paddy. He was one of the crowd of young people on the pleasure boat and, as he was still missing, they had to inform her. Missing. Missing is not dead. When a mother knows, she does everything to unknow. She goes to her bedroom to dress. She discards the old stockings that she had been wearing in the daytime for a new pair. God knows why. She says that this is not true, this is a false alarm testing her last reservoir of strength. She puts on powder, hurriedly, then returns and, as on any normal occasion, offers brandy or tea. The policemen say it is better for them to get moving, to get back to the scene, since all the force is needed. She sits in a black van with them and slowly and solemnly recites, as her own chant, the words of Christ in the Garden of Gethsemane: 'O, Father, if it be possible, let this chalice pass from me.' Missing is not dead. She says that aloud to the policemen and adds how providential the night is, since it is so still, since there is scarcely a wind. They recognise that undertow of hope and look at each other with eyes in which she believes there are recesses of non-hope. She cannot see their eyes but she can see them fidget. They have already been there; they have already seen people crawling out of the water, senseless, unable to grasp their whereabouts, asking, 'What's happened? . . . What's happened?' They have heard the screaming, the disbelief, the shouts of crazed, incensed people, and they are not in the business of doling out niceties. She has not seen these things yet. Now she does. Ambulances bursting from the hospital's steps, their lights whirling round and round, but no siren sounding. Ghost machines. Inside, commotion, delirium. People who had been inches from death asking, asking. Everyone asking; voices charging each other across the waiting room. Has Alex been found? 'Found'. The word both urgent and wan. A girlfriend has lost her boyfriend. She calls his name, shouts it. He does not materialise. She runs, the double glass doors almost swallowing her. A man has lost his wife. He stands, a sodden picture of despair, with a blanket slipping off, saying quietly, 'My wife . . . My beautiful wife.' A younger man weeps for the woman he swam with. Where is she, where is she? He describes how they held hands – tight, tight – until in the end she slipped away from him, eluded his grasp. Was she dead? Was she still struggling?

Nell is sitting quietly, sitting by herself. She is afraid of these people. They pace, then are still, then give reign to some outburst. This night has dislodged their reserves of sanity. Nurses, who go about with forms and thermometers and blankets, are told to piss off. It has the insubstantiality of a dream but it is not a dream. It is a raw, raucous, unashamed confrontation with life or non-life. The names are shouted incessantly. Samantha and Sue and Paul and Jeff. No one says 'Paddy,' as if no one knew him but her. Outside, the sirens now screech with animal intonations. Inside, coffee, cups of coffee, a voice asking for someone to put another spoon of sugar in, sloshing. Paddy, where are you? She has been told to sit and wait. She will be informed the moment there is news. Rumours bob up the way she imagines, cannot stop herself from imagining, the faces appearing on the water. His face. His alone. A body has been found eight miles upriver at Hammersmith. A woman's. Not a man's. Not him. Should she go to Hammersmith? Did drowned bodies follow one another like shoals of fish? She must go somewhere. Paddy, where are you? She is told again to sit and wait. They know her name and her son's name. It is on a document. Many of the saved are at the hospital. They are weeping, claiming that they do not want to live if their comrades are dead. Their teeth are chattering, they shiver, their features slavered in black mud and ooze.

'Where's my mates? Where's my fucking mates?' a young man shouts as he enters the hospital. His head is gashed, and the blood streaming down his face has black rivulets in it. He is telling everyone how cold it is, how cold and how stupid. She runs from the building and down a narrow footpath to the riverbank, where people are milling and shouting around a posse of police. It is dark and deathlike, everything spectral. The police and the rescue workers are like shadows giving and taking orders, their voices terse. The river is calm but black, a black pit that everyone dreads. Calm, black swishings of water. Looking at it for the first time, looking at it steadily, she thinks it cannot be. He is not in there. He has swum ashore, he is somewhere, he is one of the dazed people in blankets, covered in mud. He is asking someone to telephone her. He is. He is. She hears the tide, its slipslap against the lifeboats, and she thinks, you have not got him. The chains, however, which go clank-clank, tell a different story – a death knell. And the line comes, how could it not: 'A current under sea picked his bones in whispers.' A young policeman loses control, says how the hell does he know what one boat was doing crashing into another. Sirens fill the streets and she thinks that if Paddy is still in the water, which she now thinks he must be, those sirens will be a clarion to him, a reminder that everyone is on the alert, everything is being done.

'Oh, Paddy, we are coming to you, we are coming,' she says, and going over to an officer, she asks if there is any way they could light up the water more, give hope to those who were still struggling in it. For some reason he thinks she is a journalist and tells her to shut her trap. She screams back, screams that she is a mother.

'Why isn't the water lit, the way it's lit for a jubilee or a coronation?' she says, and he looks at her with a kind of murderousness and says that those who are still in there have had it by now. She lets out half a cry – a short, unearthly, broken cry. This shadow, this totem of authority, wishes them dead. A senior officer tries to calm her, says that they are doing everything they possibly can, that any bodies still in the water will be found. 'Found'. There is that word again. She asks him if by any chance she can go to the morgue at Southwark in the police van, since others are going. He looks at her with the candour of a man who has to refuse, and says no, that it would be better for her to go back into the hospital and stay put.

In the hospital, a group of young people is silently weeping, holding one another and rocking back and forth in grief, like children in a play-pen. A boy and two girls. They have lost their mate, their mate. The boy had jumped in the water to search and had to be hauled out. They rock back and forth, like women in labour, giving birth to their grief. Each time they smoke they give Nell a cigarette too. Some time later one of them, a girl, looks up and screams. A man is coming towards them. She is afraid it is not true. It can't be true. She looks down, she covers her eyes and ask them, Jesus, to look up. It is him. It is Justin. He has been found. Or has he? Is he a spirit? He walks towards them, in his slather of wet clothes, with a strange dazedness. He is holding half a rubber life ring. They get up. They all embrace, four friends, lost for words, unable to speak. They don't believe it. A miracle. Then they do believe it. They cry. They kiss. He cannot speak. He cannot say how he swam ashore. He holds up the bit of black rubber, refuses to let it go. It saved him. It. Then one of them speaks, one of them says that they are going to get out of this hellhole and get in his little banger and drive somewhere and get booze and get fish and chips, and they are going to ring everyone they know and have ever known and give the party of their lives, a party that means welcome home, Justin, welcome home.

Nell shrinks away from them, and they know why. She is still one of the waiting ones. There is nothing to be said. They cannot swap with her. Were she the lucky one she would not swap, either. It is as primal as that.

What she must do is give Paddy strength, send messages to him, urge him, tell him to kick, to kick, not to give in. Her breathing quickens, and it is as if she, too, has dared the water. Then she pauses and says, 'Turn over on your back, love and float.' She does this unendingly, because there is one thing that she cannot unknow: some are trapped in their sunken vessel, were caught in a downstairs suite – corpses side by side, or cleaving to furniture. The vessel cannot be brought up till daylight, when the toll will be taken. He is not among them. She is certain of that. He got out – crawled out and swam and is making his way, is holding on to a raft, is on a little bit of beach, waiting to be picked up. He is that seagull he loves to read about, who flew higher than all the other seagulls, up into the lonely altitudes; hearing herself say 'seagull', she shrieks, glimpsing the maelstroms ahead.

Waiting. Another day. Parents. Relatives. Police. Waiting at the hospital for names to be called out, now for people to go into the morgue in the back and identify their own. Bodies in glass cubicles under sheets – bloated, puffed, disfigured, all prey to the same lunatic fate.

The policeman lifts a sheet, and what she sees is not a face with features but something grey, prehistoric. A purple cowl hides the hair and the body. She does not know if it is a boy or a girl. The hairline is black and eerie, an eerie streak like a charcoal line. Although her name has not been called, she creeps into the morgue furtively, to mettle herself. But now she turns away. Paddy has not been found – he and six others. She goes back to the morgue's anteroom, the chapel of rest where mourners sit silently, too silent by far, praying to a bare altar, a bare God. A mother and a father sit fingering one black rosary. Not long after, a man comes and speaks in a whisper to them, saying yes, it is Jason, their Jason, he recognises the two back fillings he had done the Easter before. In his hand an envelope with the X-ray of the teeth. They confer. The father goes in while the mother stays in the chapel, praying, a tower of strength. Suddenly the silence is shattered – a woman's cry. A different mother insists that the girl they have shown her is not her daughter, Fiona, is not the white maiden, and that no one can tell her so. Fiona is not that lump of disfigurement in there. The policeman tries to reason with the woman, says she had been warned, advised not to go in alone. 'I got to, hadn't I?' the woman says, lashing out at all and sundry, saying it was clear that they were all drunk on the boat except for her Fiona, who had never touched a drop in her life, and was sacrificed, sacrificed for what – scoundrels, brigands, drunks. Looking across at Nell, who is looking at her aghast, she screams and says, 'Who do you think you're looking at?' and Nell shrinks into the corner, hoping the whitewashed wall will absorb her. The woman, while discussing her Fiona, is holding her daughter's jewellery – bracelets, a jingle of them, bone and silver, bracelets and rings. How unfair that these could escape the ravages of the water.

He had no ornaments but an indigo tattoo, and she wonders if this would discolour. 'Oh, please, God, let him be found,' Nell keeps saying over and over again to herself, so she does not break down. Words replace the terror in her mouth and in her windpipe. For him to be found is now all that she asks. She is beginning to lose hope of his being alive.

In the morgue's makeshift refreshment room things are heated, embattled. A small group have already started to rally, to press about fighting for their rights, for compensation, for lolly. She cannot join in. She cannot even be righteous. She says, 'Who can tell what happened in the water in the dark?'

'Now you listen,' a woman says to her, but cannot think what to say next. Rage and grief are battling in her, and her eyes are like wounds from crying. 'I am listening,' Nell says, and the woman throws back her head in a hateful grimace and says she knows exactly the lawyer she'll go to, exactly the shark who will fight her cause. A friend encourages her. Cites shipowners with untold wealth and villas in Spain. The talk seems odd, inappropriate, considering how close they are to the morgue, how the depths of their feelings are just waiting to be met, in there.

At midnight, a detective came to the morgue and asked her to go home and get some sleep. 'I'd rather stay here,' she said.

'It's orders, Ma'am,' he said, and she knew that he hated saying it, because it meant that they had more or less given up. Paddy would not be found. The tears that had been lying in wait came then, unheralded, unannounced, in a burst. She was sobbing. A desecration. Before that she had merely cried like the others, into her sleeve or into her handkerchief, but this was torrents. The few mourners left were stunned into silence. She had allowed the truth to seep into her. The truth was that she would not see him again. That was worse than death. It seemed to be above and beyond death. A rigmarole then of how he would not walk through the door or ride his bicycle or run a comb through his hair again was more significant than death. She was telling them that.

'Squeeze my hand, just squeeze my hand,' a detective kept saying, while the tears poured out of her – baths, basins, buckets, reservoirs of tears that seemed hot and life-giving as blood. Why her? Why her? Why him? Why them? The words flew out of her like bits of old food. Telling them how Paddy believed that seagulls on the river were the souls of dead lightermen. Seagulls. She thought she saw a little brace of them whizzing about, beating the air, then vanishing. She had gone that far. 'You're all right now,' the detective said.

'Yes, I'm all right now,' she said, and remembered that during her outburst he had told her there was a pamphlet by a famous specialist which described death by drowning – how beautiful it was, not a painful death, happy, a kind of ecstasy once the body submitted and allowed the water in.

'Could you find it?' she said.

'I'll try,' he said, and helped her towards the swinging door.

Outside, everyone gone. Her banshee tears had sent them scarpering. Nothing but statues and the shadows they cast. Iron men. Iron women, iron horses, and an iron Boadicea. Fawn clock tower and fawn buildings insubstantial inside these self-same cages.

'Where are my friends now? . . . Where are my friends?' she yelled, hand and arm going up wildly to hail a taxi, missing this one and that, crossing a road, recrossing, waving an overnight bag – Paddy's bag with a few of his childhood effects in it, to put beside him to keep him company, a little tobacco tin and a fob watch which her father had given him, but which never worked.

'You look as if you want the airport,' the driver said.

'No. I want home.' She told him the address.

'So why did I think you wanted the airport?' he said grumpily.

'I want home,' she said weakly.

Home. Once she was there, the doorbell or the phone would ring to say he had been found. He would be found, and the kiss or the clinch or whatever it was would be exchanged between them. She would not quake at the cruel metamorphosis of death, oh no – her son was her son, a little image locked inside her, inviolate, as when he had roamed and sallied inside her womb. And to keep that image company she gave him the voice and the recitation that he had had when he was four or five, his voice like a toy xylophone saying:

> Pam pam pipe
> Plum jam
> Ten bob
> Tip-tip, Peter all the way.

She would bury him. She would bury him as best she could. His friends would come and there would be flowers, lots of flowers – it was summer, after all, high summer, the time of the hollyhocks and the Canterbury bells – and she would have a little party, and then what? Then was a blank in her thoughts, a wall, so to speak, against which memories would be placed end to end, increasing and multiplying like stacks of books. But first he must be found and then he must be buried, because that was fundamental, because earth and not water was the kindest, meetest resting place. Why did she so fear water – water, from whence he came, the waters of herself and of her own mother, womb of waters, known and unknown, nourishing and leaching, giving and taking back. She kept picturing earth, little slants of earth, little mounds, graveyards with things growing out of them, anything, daisies, moss, anything.

The driver was not going fast enough and not going the most direct route and was determined that she suffer the indignities inflicted by his previous fare. Foreigners. Zulus. Couldn't breathe with the four of them in the cab. Under her breath she kept upbraiding him, but she did not want a contretemps. Even one vexed exchange would break her down.

She believed that the moment they could not reach her would be the moment they rang to say he had been found, so she confined herself to her own house, to the pier at Westminster, to the morgue at Southwark – policemen turning away from her in embarrassment. She was understanding, overunderstanding, so as not to rattle them. They had to go on to other things, after all. She felt so alone. No husband, no Tristan. The husband, Walter, long gone, in the West Country, and Tristan travelling in Turkey and as yet not reached. After five days, no word, so she ran to another venue, to her office, where everyone offered to do something for her that was of no use just then. Though she insisted to herself that he would be found, she had a scraping fear, all the time, that he wouldn't, and that this would be the deepest, the most unfinished hurt of all – a hurt incapable of death, of dying, a hole inside her that would grow bigger and sturdier and uglier each day – so that she cursed the God whom hitherto she had implored so passionately.

That night: that drive, that dawn, that mouthful of toast at the pier, the blonde girl at the pier who screamed at her because of the way she described Paddy, every detail, his eyes so very mixed between blue and grey, like gravel, only softer, and his few freckles and his beautiful hands, like a pianist's, and the girl telling her for fuck's sake to belt up, because her boyfriend had had beautiful hands, too, and they were to have been married in September. That night or the next, and that dawn – raw, bleached, drained of light as dawns are – and her own house for an hour or two, then a dash to Paddy's flat, where she should have gone sooner but couldn't, going up the stairs, becoming petrified because Penny might be there. Penny, Paddy's girlfriend and, as she said, soul mate. Penny was not there. Penny was in Spain, working in a pottery. Paddy had moved to a flat to sort himself out, as he put it. Climbing the last bit of steep stairs, Nell remembers how he would have opened the door by then and found her puffing and admitted that he puffed too, when he hadn't been to the gym and – oh, madness of madness – she thinks, He has not died; the policemen are mistaken, askew; he is here; he is here, either asleep or awake, and the door will open from the inside. Lucky that he has given her a key. They exchanged keys. A sure sign of their reconciliation. Paddy's dog, Charlie, comes toward her with an abject look, a frightened look, and all she can say as she pats him is, 'Charlie, you haven't done number two,' and, saying it, she thinks of her children's youth and of Dixie the dog, years before, years that now seem blithe compared to this inferno. Charlie licks her a lick of thanks, relief, and imprecation. He is hungry. He is desperate to go out. In the front garden, she stands a few yards away from him, disowning him, in case a landlady or a caretaker taps a window and shakes a fist. He takes his time as he squats under a lilac tree. He is nervous, overnervous. His tail and his hind legs shake uncontrollably, but nothing comes; his eyes are fixed on her in case she stirs. Three whole days he has been abandoned. The lilac tree is withered. Dead blossoms like used lavatory brushes. Some rotting smell. What happens to a body in the river? She must look it up in a book. No, she mustn't. Charlie staggers from one spot to another for dribbles, then gives up.

Upstairs, she begins to go through Paddy's things. A diary with entries and little mottoes he copied to better himself. What would he have been? A teacher, she thinks. Yes, a teacher of man, his conscience always smiting him and his pity, pity for those who had not. A teacher of man. There are birthdays. Her birthday is among them. She is not left out. A motto written on a card: 'The lapwing cries loudest when far from its nest.' Why that? Beside the diary are his three pipes and a stack of pipe cleaners, then a photograph of Penny in a pair of shorts, looking so young, so vulnerable, not the needly Penny she knows. The pregnancy that had been mentioned was not. Was not. What happened? Nell would never know. The curtains she gave him are drawn. He drew them before he went out that night. Yes, they are there, and the wooden armchair that he got off a rubbish heap, and a beautiful lapis bowl, the one beautiful thing in the room. She must get some of his clothes, because he will be cold, shivering – madness was taking root, because clothes are for the living. A shroud is for the dead – brown, grey, or off-white. Going shyly to the bedroom she tiptoes, knocks as if he were there with Penny. Traces of them are there and, opening the wardrobe door, she cries at not having given him more money, because his clothes are so spare and so pitiful. There are some secondhand suits, a stack of sweaters, and three gaudy ties, probably birthday presents from friends. His sanctum. She does not touch a thing, or rather touches all of them with a little glide of the fingers, and then she goes out.

It is a mad dash to a shop to get Charlie some sliced ham, which he eats on the street, in a twinkling, and then he tries to eat the greaseproof paper that she is still holding.

Different people at the morgue than the times before, and fewer – new recruits, hopeful, despairing. The others have all gone home, are in their houses now, facing it, resentments piling up in them. She tells a woman she has never seen before that yes, she has another son and that he is in Turkey, that he has gone there with his friends to do relief work but that she has not had him alerted, not yet, not until his brother is found. That will be the time to tell him and have him brought home. She does not mention her husband, the man to whom she has not spoken in over a decade.

Yes, Charlie knew, because the next night he started up his own incantation, his own wake, his own subhuman howl. First it was from the kitchen. She was wakened from a clotted sleep. She took half a sleeping tablet, cut it carefully down the centre, not wanting to be blurry on the morrow yet wanting sleep, even ten minutes of sleep, wanting her mind to be borne somewhere else, even to a different nightmare. The phone would ring, and she must not be so asleep that she could not hear it. The nice detective had promised her that the moment the body was found they would summon her, no matter what the hour. He was Welsh, friendlier than the others. He had not yet found the pamphlet, but he assured her that he remembered the line written by the neurosurgeon, the line that said the sensation was ecstatic once the water entered the lungs and the body gave up the fight. Nell was wakened instead by Charlie, with a howl that had a human plaint in it. Her own hysteria speaking back to her, but animalised. Charlie knew. He missed his master. He went around smelling shoes to find the smell of his master. He smelled shoes and Wellingtons; he did not give up. Down to the kitchen to give Charlie a telling off, whereupon he skulked, becoming silent until she went back to her room and the howling started up again. This time she thumped the floor with a broom, the two ends of the broom – the worn, wiry twigs and then the handle as a parting shot. She put her winter coat under the door to shut out all sound. If she did not sleep she would be in danger of going mad. No use. He started again. She dragged him into the garden, thinking it was that, but it was not that, then in the kitchen coaxed him with a sodden ginger biscuit. He spat it out. He was not taking this. She left him again but the howl that started up bit into her brain, and, hurrying back and full of vengeance now, she simply said, as if he could comprehend, 'Charlie, I've had it. I've had it.' His teeth marks on the rungs of the chair told her what she already knew: Charlie was wild, Charlie was unmanageable. The teeth marks on the chair, her bitten coat, the ravelled, grey-white threads, all too much.

She barely saw the streets she drove through with Charlie – the traffic lights, a slice of river as it sauntered upstream to disgorge its prey, or maybe downstream to do the identical thing. How can one plead with water? It is never still, always moving, scheming, eluding. How well she knew its colours. She had lived by it. She had loved it once, claimed to have been moved, oh, so moved by its sheers, its ruffles, its greys, its currents, its debris, and so on. Paddy had loved the water too, had made a little logbook of the river. She didn't look at Charlie once. Barely seeing the streets, skimming, the dainty lacelike girders of a bridge an affront.

The building was a smearish colour, mud brown. A man going by with his dog on a leash shouted: no animal of his would set foot there. Inside, baying. A great swell of it that rose and dipped and rerose like the swell of a foaming sea. Multiple bayings. Then individual barks, individual cries saying, 'Find me! Come along down to my little cubby and find me!' She shouldn't be doing it to Charlie. It was to Paddy she was doing it. Passing the cages was the worst. Some of the animals yapped. Others stared in silence. Some dozed in aluminium basins, and everywhere there was fresh and not so fresh shit. Charlie's temperament, Charlie's teeth, and Charlie's hair were all subjects for discussion. Then Nell was by herself, while Charlie was taken off to be examined and vaccinated. Did it hurt? Of course it hurt. Everything hurt. In a little room that adjoined an empty café, she struggled with a form. Where was her heart? It was gone. It was murdered. It was with her son on the bed of the river, trying to find him, two hearts missing each other the way people miss one another in dreams. It was in a sack, like a dead animal – bleeding, the blood oozing out of it. The questions were routine: her name, her occupation, how long she had known Charlie, and could he be trusted with children. Staring at her from the wall, a newsletter about a dog called Patch, who had been badly treated, abandoned twice, and twice brought here, where he made a miraculous recovery. In the end Patch had found a good home, and it was the owners of the good home who wrote this eulogy after his death. Why was she doing this? Only because Charlie howled, a raw howl that cut notches in her.

Back to the chapel of rest that adjoined the hospital, glad to be with others for a moment, or a fraction of a moment, escaping her own stew. Lives that had thought they were booking a holiday, or going to learn to drive, or to plant sweet peas were heading for a voyage of permanent mourning. Everything slashed, every plan and half plan and every dream. The others gave her strength. While she was with them she did not think of how she would tell Tristan, how she would break it to him. She thought only, You do not know yet, sweetheart; you can laugh; you can joke that little bit longer. Had she had her way, he would never know; he would live in ignorance of it.

'She was my morning's light and my evening's lamp.' A mother who stood in the pulpit of the Cathedral kept saying it, her voice dramatic, measured, calling her daughter in various intonations. Services and cremations, in the city, in the suburbs, all over the country. Young people having stabs at gaiety – short skirts, blouses and shirts like those worn in a bullring. The draped and decked coffins a far cry from the cold consignments of flesh in the morgue.

A vicar praised those who had come to mourn and those who had died. Talked of the necessity of fun and how no one must fault these young people, stressed the fact that they were not to blame and the skippers were not to blame either – all were blameless. Then a psalm, then 'Lucy in the Sky with Diamonds' and a short reading from 'The Little Prince'. A man had given her that book once. A lover. Finnish. It came to her that if she were to make love the frostbite of death might be taken away, even momentarily. She had heard that somewhere.

The plots in the cremation grounds were so minuscule. Midget slab-stones as in a doggy's grave, and wan messages, a single yellow iris in a Lucozade bottle. Oh, the paucity of it all. They had to queue for the cremation ceremony. Mourners treated like cattle. A mother in jeans, grumbling because of this. The fact that she was in jeans seemed wrong, seemed inappropriate, worse when she tightened her belt to show how dishy she was. A young man, a thin, sepulchral-looking young man, stepped aside as if to pray. Had the look of Hamlet. Seemed stunned.

Everywhere shock and those outbursts and now the woman taking the white belt of her jeans off and using it to hit, to hit out.

Hated going home. Into her dark house. Into sleep and into dreams: searchlights in her innards and men shouting – shouting what? Then a cold, white ship, a liner on to which guests were coming, la-di-da people, oodles of them, with parasols and handbags. Famishing. 'Hold on till I plug in the fire,' she called, not wanting them to shiver, not wanting to be inhospitable. The electric plug going soft in her hand, soft and warmish, turning into a wet tea bag.

Not long after, the people higher up at her office clubbed together to send her to a health farm. Thought it might help. As soon as she crossed the threshold she knew she must leave. It was all too bright and hygienic – that, and a smell of grapefruit. She fled. She went to Paddy's flat so she could not be traced. She slept in Paddy's bed and thought he might appear to her. In a way, he did. A dream, a salve. He came alive in it. It was a strange place, a square flooded in warm golden light, a southern town, yellowish walls, turreted, sun pouring down, white tables. A beautiful girl stood in waiting in leopardskin trousers and high leopardskin boots. Penny waved to the girl. Had an errand for her. The errand was to go to Paddy with a message, to search him out in the monk's room, where he burrowed and where he was praying for guidance. He was to come to the square, the golden square, where he would receive instruction. He agreed. In the dream he looked thin, emaciated, but he smiled at the news of his release. Then it was next day – morning, with the white chairs stacked on the round, white tables, their legs ungainly. He arrived clean-shaven, in praying robes and a white shirt that was threadbare at the cuffs. He looked around to meet his messenger, the woman in leopardskin. Instead, Penny appeared and moved towards him, radiant, then laughing because she had played a joke on him. They danced in the square. The pink stone of the cobbles was dark where it had just been splashed with water, and the music came not in a night-time spasm but in a trickle, like a flute heard across distances of mountains. They danced between the tables and chairs, danced beautifully towards a sign that read 'Tivoli Gardens'. Nell wakened almost happy. She would write to Penny. Nell would write to tell her this dream and, by telling it, say, 'It means we must be friends.' She posted it to Penny's pottery in Spain. They could bury the hatchet. There was no child, the child was a blind, and there was no Paddy, Paddy was among the perch and the slippery eel, but, as Nell had to keep saying, free of them now, free of all predatoriness, adrift among the algae and the slapping vegetation.

On her kitchen windowpane, a sign – galling, galling. Its appearance brought on by the steam. In a blur of grey, in a fog of steam came his initial, 'P' for Paddy. Pasta boiling over in a saucepan. Long strips of it, a dyed green. A great splutter on the stove, spitting and hopping, beads of water jumping about like translucent insects, the kitchen all foggy, fogbound like a river late at night. In his handwriting, his particular little squiggle. Jesus Christ. She crossed over to it. It was a 'P'. He must have written it once with a crayon while she was cooking dinner, one of the evenings that was either amicable or testy, written it where it lay in hiding, needing only a bit of steam to show up again, apparition-like. She ran her finger along it, tracing it slowly, not wanting to blot it out, and thought that if anything could invoke the dead, it must be this. An afterbirth of hope. Then she rang someone. The bereaved were told to ring each other at moments like this, for counselling, co-counselling. The woman she reached was livid, calling all journalists scum and newspaper proprietors worse scum, millionaires – making packets out of tragedy. There had been an article claiming that her son was gay, that he had lived with a young man, that they had had wedding vows, a wedding ceremony, that they were going to adopt a baby. Lies. Total lies. Garbage. She was going to the editor on the morrow. The next woman Nell rang told her to go to a spiritualist centre. It was the only thing. It did wonders for people, it brought peace of mind. There was a place in Belgravia. This woman would find out the hours, and they would go together. The pasta Nell had made tasted like glue, or like porridge that she had had in Scotland. How long ago was that? Too long ago. 'They're peeing on us from a great height,' the first woman on the phone had said, and suddenly Nell laughed a mad laugh, remembering Paddy and Tristan, two brothers peeing on each other from apple trees and shouting 'Bang, bang, you're dead, I'm not dead,' brothers vying with each other as to who could pee longest and say the most warring things.

She had found it easily in Paddy's address book, under 'F' for 'Father.' Walter was in a home, but she hadn't known where. Lost his marbles, or some of them. She'd lost hers too, but not the ones that enabled her to remember. Memory weevilling into her every minute, a fresh issue of pain, memory picking, like the hook of a crochet needle, drawing blood. Awful journey. Monotonous. Fields, more fields. Cows. Cattle. Lines of washing. Towns with their miserable little chimney pots. Signs for life insurance. Paddy had made a will and left her everything. Big houses with gates. More fields. Like going across the steppes of Russia. She had brought a book to read; *Light in August*. Sad, stubborn book. The deep, kind of animal sad. Arriving at a neat little railway station, which had won a prize. Hanging baskets and things. Out in the street, affable, smiling faces. Away from the rat race. Recognised her as a stranger in the town. Tea shops. White scones and clotted cream, and barley sugar in twists. Big geranium in the conservatory of the nursing home. Gigantic, clawlike. Bright orange. Flaming orange. The colour of life. Of fire. White is the colour of death. Paddy's friend Baxter had said that. Had written her a beautiful letter. The names of all those missing had been in the paper. Baxter had tried to be manly. Said life had changed a bit since he last met Nell. Paddy and he had done so many things – gone down a pit in Yorkshire, went about half a mile underground and then into a coal tunnel forty-two inches high, just the two of them. In a PS he mentioned Aphrodite coming out of the sea, then apologised for being a bit stoned.

Nell would do anything not to go up those stairs and meet her husband, anything. Slight hitch. He was in the toilet. She must wait. She'd made a bolt for it. Ran down a passage, through a door, into another narrow passage, and found a white door that slid like a trapdoor. Near-naked woman by the lavatory bowl, looking in at it laughing, roaring with laughter. In her shift. Legs like candles, spent candles, white. Age and death. Youth and death. Nurse saying, 'You can come now. Your husband is ready.' Worst would be over in an hour. Stand up to him, fight back if he should say, 'You left me,' or 'You destroyed them,' or 'It's your fault that he went there.' Needn't have worried. Man in pyjamas, vacant, vacant, sitting upright on bed. Shadow of tyrant who had once been, who had exchanged a 'love, honour, and obey' rigmarole. More metamorphoses. Breathing lightly and staring. Staring. She had to sit. A waiting white chair said to her to sit, and she said back to it, with the little gumption that remained in her, 'I am not here . . . I am not here . . . I am not sitting down . . . I was never married to this man . . . And I do not intend to apologise.' Geranium downstairs bursting with life and rage, brushing the old-fashioned glass of the skylight. A waiting taxi. Freedom only two staircases away. His mouth was moving to say something, the something not coming, the sympathy for his son – for surely he must have read the telegram that she had sent; he must know. Lips squashing, unsquashing, then stretching out like rubber bands, a sound of sorts, but no meaning to it. Lips pursing, nearly saying it, but not. Man in the bed across showing no such rectitude. Roaring like a jackass. A roar she well knew – fathers, husbands, mothers all mingling in. Better take the bull by the horns, but not yet. His lips like mauve, trodden-upon fruits. Eyes very sharp, angry eyes, like nails that dig in. His son dead and his not grasping it. She had said it clearly, very clearly. On the bed, beside him, a pen and pad. Maybe she should write it down. No, that was too drastic. His eyes looking daggers at her. He knew. He was about to pontificate. 'Do you sleep?' she asked. 'I slee . . . eee . . . eee . . . ppppppp,' the words like mince. Getting out the gifts she'd brought. Shades of love, or would-be love. Flowers from the station. Red carnations sunk in a white haze of gypsophila. Red and white. She would give the things Paddy left her to Tristan. Tristan would save her, as he had before. His birth had saved her when she was in the dumps – his little kisses, the teeth he cut, the teeth he lost, and the sixpences she put in eggcups as rewards. She had brought flowers and a bottle of pink champagne.

Impossible to think she and Walter were once married. He was unrecognisable, and yet recognisable by that sneer, that disdain. Otherwise a stranger, a stranger with parchment skin. No trace of his other self, his gallant self, his dash. They had stood together, proud to be married, a ceremony in the sacristy of a church where a priest grudgingly tied the knot. Workmen as witnesses. Paddy kicking away like blazes, saying, Let me out, let me out of here. Her firstborn. She was too afraid, afraid of his fragility, the little well in the crown of his bare head giving her the shivers. Two lines of bone, opening and closing like a mouth, saying something. Still, she tried. Got the pepper the day he put pebbles up his nose. He was crawling then. Thought the stones were boiled sweets. She ran and got pepper so that he sneezed like billy-o and then she hugged him and then delivered a bit of a scolding, which he was impervious to. Rascals. They were Walter's, too, his and hers. Sitting upright now, he was telling her slowly but determinedly that he refused hospital food because it was poison. She should have brought baby food. Each word, each bit of word, taking an eternity to get out. Had to be wrenched out.

'Paddy got drowned,' is what she heard herself say, calmly but bluntly.

'You got drowned,' was what she heard back. A smile. Vengeance even in dementia.

'You . . . got . . . drow . . . ned.' A smile within a smile, in the recesses of blur. The eyes, both tortured and torturing, wished to nail her. Man opposite deciding to shout louder and louder for the nurse. The worst was uttered.

'No – Paddy, not me.'

'You got drowned,' he said, triumphant. The speech quite quick, quite clear, and the meaning. The hate he had for her was like a pilot light, waiting not for extinction but to be relit. She hated him, too, remembered a whole nest of wrongs, yet more than anything she wished that they could throw a crumb to each other, they who never had. Why did they mate? What stars had caused such a strange conjunction? What, now, was the fresh bafflement in his eyes? Hearing others go down to tea, she rose to fetch him some, but once outside she knew that she would not cross that threshold again.

At first it seemed to her that Tristan was breaking, spilling in her arms, his sobs punctuating the little things he was saying so as not to seem so broken. He had gained some hours on the flight from Istanbul, he said. The difference in time between Turkey and home was a difference of hours. At moments she thought he was going to retch. She held him. He held on. It was a clumsy embrace. He would have come sooner, the very instant it happened. She should not have borne it alone. She should not have had to bear it alone. Did she know the people who had given the party? Of course not. Sorry. Sorry. He should not have asked that. He would not ask anything else. Questions were cruel. Everything was said to comfort, to show solidarity. He had gained three hours and that was something. He had brought gifts. He did not say for whom, apart from her. It was a goatskin, dappled, luxurious, a brown that had suffered the scorching heat of the animal's life, so it was almost black. She laid it on the stairs where she and Tristan sat making plans. Plans of a sort. He would go to Paddy's flat and move the things, give them for a jumble sale. Paddy had a little insurance policy, which she said Tristan could have. He didn't want it. He didn't want anything. 'You could live there if you wanted, my pet.'

'No. I'll stay with you, stay with my mother.' In every syllable, in every thought, in every fresh bout of grief he grew closer to her, snatching with one hand at the fringing of the rug for comfort, his other arm shielding his eyes from the light. A window smothered in creeper looked in on them, each leaf of it smarting in the heat. He inquired about the summer. It had been warm, though not as warm as where he had been. He had eaten a lot of yogurt – grown fond of it, to his surprise. Been invited into houses that were out in the wilds, dogs following the truck, big dogs with muzzles, leaping up; the women in the houses were veiled, veiled and spinning. Got drunk with his friend Andy on his last night in Istanbul. Met many carpet merchants, in one tavern after another; got back to his lodgings somehow, his pockets full of business cards, replete with the names and addresses of numerous carpet dealers.

'Where's Charlie?' he said, looking around, ready to whistle.

'Charlie . . .' she said, flustered, knowing that he had known before she even started to speak. Charlie's crying had got to her, 'bitten into' her, as she said, using the word 'banshee' more than once. He did not say 'How could you?' but, as he suddenly stood, a brute determination seemed to rise in him, and he trembled with hate.

'I couldn't sleep, I was going mad,' she said, and tried to make him imagine the house empty, the hoping, the ebbing of hope, and then Charlie, and then Charlie. It seemed a long pause, too long, as Tristan's tongue sought words to annul the spleen that had just entered him, but finally he said he would go straight to the Dogs' Home and find Charlie, no matter what.

Find him he did, so there was a truce of a kind as Charlie pattered around, much quieter now, much more subdued, almost speaking to them – so happy was he to be back, so abjectly happy, licking even her who had consigned him to exile. A tick under Charlie's ear had to be removed. She fetched her tweezers and watched Tristan filch it out, deftly and with love; he showed her the fat, squat belly of blood, Charlie's blood, which had supplied the tick's homestead for the week. Charlie mewled with excitement, relief; he showed not a trace of venom as she held him. Then he was ensconced in the bath, a thing she would normally have objected to. They took turns soaping him. She thought, Tristan doesn't hate me now – it was a passing thing. Later, he poured boiling water on to a soup plate, dunking the tweezers into it to sterilise them. Tristan and she were near now. They would hold each other up, be props for each other. She did not know then that he, too, would go. She did not know the change that would take place in him once the death had sunk in, how dark and troubled he would become. She did not know that he would not shave for weeks, or eat, and that he would not talk or be talked to.

Penny had still not appeared. After Nell had sent her the account of her dream about the Tivoli Gardens, and appropriate condolences, she got a letter back with somewhat similar sentiments except that it ended with 'I knew him better than anyone in the world and yet I didn't know him.' Ending with that. Others had written such beautiful things, heartfelt things. A girl who had done group therapy with him had written a poem for Nell, a poem that said, 'It was only a dream that I had a son.' A cleaner from Paddy's school, saying he had visited her after she had an operation. Tributes from his teachers. Getting to know him through his friends. Baxter asked if he could have his pipe as a keepsake – his awful, smelly old pipe.

In the two weeks that followed Tristan's arrival, the two of them tried to be buoyant, tried to make jokes, had suppers in front of the television. He made a point of talking about Paddy – of plays he had directed at school and leading ladies he had fallen in love with. He had been sent home once for drink, she said, he and a friend called Norrie, and she described the two boys going to a Turkish bath to sweat out their guilt. She kept urging Tristan to see friends, his own and Paddy's. Tristan left notes, such as 'Gone to mow a meadow.' Charlie followed him like his shadow, lay in wait behind the front door. Charlie knew his footstep two streets away. Charlie was bounced in his arms, flung up to the ceiling, caught on the way down, and then tossed up again like a pancake. Tristan had arranged with his university for permission to bring Charlie and put him in a kennel nearby. He had not discussed it with her. That was the first wedge in their nearness. She thought, To the outside world we seem near, but something has happened; he is disappointed in me, he thinks I am wallowing in my grief, but he doesn't know what it is to be older and to be a mother. She bought him gifts, bribes. She thought about a time long ago, in the country, when she had crossed a meadow to pick a few rhododendrons that took her fancy, the deep-red ones. From afar they looked massed, each flower brushing against its neighbouring cluster of petals, but close up that was not the case at all; each flower was on its own little stalk - separate, surviving, the way it is with every living thing.

The memorial service was to be a grand event, which many dignitaries were to attend. She had her ticket, a yellow ticket ornamented with the crest of the Cathedral. The mourners were invited to gather in the Glaziers' Hall afterward. She shrank from the pomp and stoicism of it: 'The Lord is my shepherd, I shall not want.' Untruer words never spoken. Tristan decided at the last minute that he would not come up from university, though he did not say why. His grief had become darker, and he was having quarrels with people. He and another boy had had a fistfight in chambers. 'Please do not write to me for the time being,' Tristan had written. Her tribulations were getting to him. He didn't shave. He didn't eat. The proctor believed Tristan's grief would run its course. Tristan kept Charlie in his room – was allowed to, in clemency.

On the steps of the chapel she saw the relatives, whom she had last seen so squashed and numb, now loquacious, rallying. They wore hats or head scarves in bright colours. Few were in black. Why hadn't she come to the meetings? Why had she gone into the woodwork? Why? She must know that it was important that everyone fight the fight, that it was not the time for wallflowers.

'I wasn't able,' she said, pleading ill health. Ill health! Men on drink, women on tranquillisers, families wrecked beyond redemption, and she couldn't give her support. As she turned to escape, a young man approached, touched her sleeve, and at that touch she felt a premonition. He was thin, wore a threadbare gabardine coat, and had the bluest eyes she had ever seen. They reminded her of school ink. His hair – soft brown and closely cropped – was like the bristles of a shaving brush upon his meek skull. Everything about him was crushed, shorn.

'I was the last person with your son. We met on that boat.'

'Don't,' she said. It pierced. A quite different stab from when the news was first broken to her.

'I have wanted to talk to you. I have phoned but I didn't have the guts to speak.'

'So it's you,' she said, inflamed. At first she had thought the hang-ups were journalists; later she believed it was Tristan, wanting to give her a pasting, a piece of his mind.

'How could you?' she said.

'Nerves,' he said, and laughed skittishly. How she disliked him. How she took that laugh for insolence and hated his little blackheads.

People were passing on either side, and she wanted to join them, to go inside, to suffer the sermons, the fugues, and the hymns, to get it over with because a rage engulfed her, a rage at this young man who had just told her he met her son on the boat, had hit it off with him because of their interest in the theatre. He was an actor – yes, an actor, he stressed. He was determined that she should listen. He had to tell her. Like it or lump it. For six weeks he had been preparing his confession, and here it was: he and Paddy had gone down to the loo together, both dying for a leak, so they decided to toss for it.

'A leak,' she said, affronted.

'Yes, a leak, and we tossed for the loo, and he went in, and next thing I know it's happening. I see black, blackness. I am being sucked into it and all I hear is screaming – somebody saying, "Elsa can't swim! Elsa can't swim!" and I don't know if I'm swimming, but I must be, because I'm moving through this black hellhole. I bump into something; it thumps me and – would you believe? it's a barrel – so I cling to it, or it clings to me . . . This barrel and myself in the wilderness, and "Elsa can't swim" in my bloody head . . . Then a bridge, a fucking bridge, the stone base; I touch it, my tombstone, and I'm so fucking wet and winded that I am thankful to be about to die, thankful to give it all up.'

'Except that you didn't,' she said, her eyes now on the wobble of his Adam's apple, which looks like a goitre.

'No, I didn't,' he said sadly, and withdrew for a second into some corner of his thinking before describing the mercy ship that was lit up like a bus, the arms – several arms – hauling him through, though he didn't want to go, he wanted to be dead. Once on board, a bloody sight, shivering and shaking.

He needed a brandy, but the barman said, 'if he needs a brandy, someone's got to pay for it,' and at first no one did. Then a girl called them all shits, throwing her biker's jacket on the counter, saying she'll pay for the drink. He can still see the studs on her jacket, blinking at him.

'Why in Christ's name did you tell me all this?' Nell said and ran, ran past the people, down the steps, and into a taxi that has just disgorged some smartly dressed mourners. She asked to be taken to the river.

November again, the holy souls, the rain. She would pray that she might pray in earnest. The rain beat slantwise down the long office window and soaked into the woodwork. Soaked into the bricks of the houses, too, altering the shades of colour, so they were like abortive frescoes. She had promised herself that she would go back to Italy, she hoped with Tristan. Something about seeing frescoes. She dreamed one night that Tristan had written her a letter of forgiveness, on parchment, and that it was headed by a Leonardo da Vinci painting. She dreaded Christmas, breaking-down time. There were invitations, oodles of invitations, including one from a family in Guildford, one from an author whose book she had worked on, and one from her boss and mistress, Miss Flite. Yes, he had made the break – rather, had made it three times, and each time before had gone back to his wife, each time taking a holiday with her – a 'second honeymoon', as it was called – and the last time, in the Lake District, they had almost frozen to death and had not had the heart left to warm each other. Miss Flite had won. A bitter divorce and smears in the newspapers and his getting suddenly older, much older-looking – the shame of it all being too much, too wounding. They were welcome, she and her son, to stay overnight. The one thing that could not happen was for them to be alone. When you are empty and depleted, being alone with someone you love is quite the worst, most ghastly thing. When she asked Tristan on the phone, he said, 'We'll see, we'll see.' He seemed not to want to go. Probably a girl. Normally, he talked about the girls – their beauty or their prettiness, their little ways, such as who was shy, or who loved horseback riding – but this girl, whoever she was, was an enigma.

It was a manor house, with open fires and plenty to drink. Neighbours called throughout the day. A big tin of caviar was

opened after Mass. People were so nice to her; even Miss Flite
had taken special trouble with her gifts. Miss Flite had given
her a woolly, but a very special woolly, a grey shawl that was
half cashmere. Tristan was a success with them all. He carried
in logs, he mended the record-player, he put on the records that
Miss Flite loved – the jazz records she danced to so beautifully
that people looked and thought, What carriage, what carriage!
Nell kept having to disappear in order to cry. Secret crying,
like secret drinking. Someone or other called her, called her
name, because they knew. Christmas was not a time to brood.
At midnight Mass she had prayed both for Paddy and to him,
but went awry. Luckily, Nell and Tristan had got there late
and had to squash in anywhere they could, so that she was
with strangers; it was strangers' hands that she shook and
wished peace upon, though she was in torment. The turkey
was delicious, the stuffing a triumph. Stuffing from a recipe in
a French magazine, with unusual things in it – smoked oysters
and angelica. She drank champagne, glugged it. Tristan watched
her drinking and gave a little cautionary wag of a finger. Upstairs
she cornered him to give him his present – mistake; it meant that
she was recalling to him her asylum of woe. What she gave him
was a leather briefcase with his initials and, inside, a little photo
album of Paddy and himself from infancy on. There were too
many words on her card, endearments. He was edging from the
room towards the door, down to the others, down to Charlie,
and the pheasants for tomorrow that he was to help Miss Flite
with, to pluck.

'Are you cold, love?'

'I think they want us downstairs.' Dancing attendance on
Miss Flite, helping with the fire, the Christmas crackers, carrying the box of truffles around. When he kissed her good-night
and she asked if there was anything wrong, he said, 'Tush.'
'Tush' was his word now, both a propitiation and to ward
her off. She heard him on the phone to the railway station,
making an inquiry about trains to Exeter. In a way she was
relieved. They must each grapple with it alone. Each in his
dripping cell.

Easter. Soon the Easter bells would be ringing out, masculine
and feminine, pewter and lead, bongs of resurrection. Oh, to
meet the risen! She and Tristan were going to a Russian Mass.
She had asked him on the phone. He lost no time with her as

he came in, with only a small bag. He was saying something as he came through the kitchen door, his jacket slung over his shoulder. It was warm as summer, with gnats in little swarms outside.

'I think you had better know –' he began, his eyes fixed firmly on her, saying, by their expression, 'Don't interrupt and don't try to make it easy.' She was thinking that he had come home to say that, in fact, he would rather spend Easter with friends, and that she would retaliate by saying what a good thing that would be, and how it was not healthy to be hatching indoors with her, and how she understood, understood.

'Penny and I are going to live together.'

'Penny,' she said, and although she had not shrieked, it seemed as if she had. 'Have you been seeing Penny?' she asked, with as much composure as she could muster. Her heart was beating against her blouse, beating wildly.

'Yes,' he said quietly.

'How did you run into her?' she asked, trying to hide the scalding curiosity that gripped her. Why hadn't she known? Why hadn't she been told? In deference or distractedness, she was also offering a plate of hot cross buns.

'She wrote to me after Paddy died,' he said, and then blurted out that Penny was having a baby, his voice a little shy and a little solicitous and, above all, concerned.

'His,' Nell said, unable to say Paddy's name, unable to join them together.

'Maybe his,' he said, and looked away.

'Maybe his, but maybe not his – what does that mean?'

'She's not sure,' he said, his face still turned away, obviously wishing that she would not make it as brutal as this.

'She's a slut,' she said. The word had tumbled out of her.

'She's not a slut,' he said, with a cold look.

She gripped his arm, deciding that somehow she must reach him, she must reason with him, point out that he was young, at university, and that he did not have to take on this legacy, this lie. Then, in a terrible instant, she saw his resemblance to Paddy, the transmitted resemblance of his face when he hated her.

'We can always have the bloods tested,' she said, waspishly, her voice octaves high.

'What would be the point?' he said, gall in his voice.

'So you're going to live with her?' Nell said – her turn now to walk away, to swallow the curd of banishment. He said yes, that for now Penny could not be alone – she had nightmares, she was racked with guilt, she was frightened and going to have a child.

'Do you love her?' she asked, each word cutting him like a hacksaw. He didn't answer. He had taken on his brother's mantle and, possibly, his brother's love. Or was it sacrifice, needless sacrifice?

'Is it pity you feel?' she asked, unable to hold her tongue.

'It's not pity, Nell,' he said, and the tart way he pronounced her name made her feel that he was finished with her. In desperation, she heard herself reverting to Penny's previous pregnancy – the 'high on poetry, short on prams' scenario, as Nell put it. Would that she had not voiced it. Would that she had not.

'If you saw her you'd believe her,' he said, then shouted, in case she needed to know, the lyrical name of the maternity ward where Penny was to be admitted, and the name of her obstetrician, who was a woman. Nothing more. When he left the kitchen, it was obvious that he was going to his room, to pack some of the things he had left at home, and obvious, too, that this was the final breach.

She walks now with a vengeance, with the malice of the destinationless and the pounding of someone who will not concede that she has nowhere to go. She believes it to be her last walk. She cannot go on. She might as well never have had children or a husband or parents – phantoms all. She thinks that no one will ever know or should know the spleen within her. This walk is her last. In the shop-windows she knows so well are the things she knows too well. A necklace from Africa, each pendant a golden acorn, the gold dun-coloured like that of icons. Then the wedding dresses in the dry cleaner's, the same batch or an identical batch, dispatched by the newly wed. Successions of them each week. Lifelike, ghostlike. Hanging from the ceiling – cream and ivory and white, creations stuffed with tissue, ready to float. The tissue gives the arms and the chest a sturdiness, so they seem to breathe. The little white arms are asking to be picked up.

Walking, racing, her glance on the ground mostly, seeing cigarette butts, swirls of dust, and, here and there, carbuncles in the pavement where the cement had bulged up. In a restaurant window little meringue cases, not quite sallow and not quite white. A tiny dish of raspberries catches her eye, each one like a rosebud, moist. Only nature can touch her now, a fleeting touch at that. Was he going to Penny for the sake of his brother, or was he going for the sake of himself? Passing a half-finished block of buildings, she reads a sign chalked on hardboard: 'Lads, no work today, go to yard.' Cruelty. Lashings of it. A sudden brain wave, a ruse. She will buy a bottle of champagne and bring it to Tristan's and Penny's flat, a bribe to patch things up.

'You see,' she says to herself, 'you are even prepared to lie, simply to cling to him, to cling; you have become as craven as that.'

'But I am doing my best,' she answers, and in an oblong of mirror at the side of a shut shoe shop, she sees a face that bears no resemblance to the face of even half a year ago. A wounded face, eyes stark, upbraiding, all traces of beauty gone. The shoe shop has closed for good, but there are shoes left in the window. They stand, like solitary props, on glass plinths, with a little tag in front of each one of them. Circulars and letters cram the passage inside.

'You don't remember me,' a voice says. She is in the wine shop now, having decided to go the whole hog of hypocrisy. She does not recognise the face or the very blue eyes or the short, brown, upthrust hair, like the hairs of a shaving brush. She should. The man repeats himself and gives his little laugh, his laugh of insolence. Suddenly she does remember and gasps at the sheer galling coincidence of it. He is working here. The actor Paddy met on the fatal night. Why is she here? Why did she cross the road at that point? Only because the other light was green, and she wanted to walk as fast as she could, and she saw a glut of bottles crammed into wooden barrels, plus, as she sees, now, lore about wine and wine tasting, which gives her the pip.

'I thought you were an actor,' she says, tartly.

'Not at the moment,' he says, and she detects the same little mendacious sneer from which she retreated on the oratory steps. She inquires about wine. He is fluent with description – adjectives rolling off his tongue, false confidence in his narrow, hurt eyes as he says, in a blasé voice, 'South African, Bulgarian, Italian, Californian, Lebanese.' As if she didn't know. As if she couldn't read. He points to the barrels, and she knows why. A barrel saved him. She remembers that. The iron hoop of the barrel cutting his neck. Part of her – indeed, an almost vanished part of her – wishes to throw the gauntlet down and tell him her latest bombshell and weep. Ridiculous. Feelings have died. Not so – feelings are alive and bucking in her, vicious feelings, growing, like a child that swells but does not come out, an alien battering the walls of her mind.

'I'll have the Mâcon,' she says, to which he asks officiously if she wants the Villages or the Lugny. 'Whichever is cheaper,' she says, and detests the remark, as if she were asking him to take pity on her straits. He pounced on it. He has the advantage. He will give her the better one at the lesser price. She doesn't want that. She does not want charity, especially not his. When they tossed the coin, did he choose heads or tails? His eyes are more cavernous than when they last met. The blue is all fear, droplets of fear. She feels that if she and he were opened up liquid would spill out, gurglings of it; his would be this vitiated blue and hers a viscous black-red. She vows to smash the bottle on the way home and carry the jagged neck like a weapon, a weapon she is no longer afraid to brandish. He wraps it and hands her warm coins, coins so warm that they are perspiring. They disgust her.

'So you don't act any more?' is her parting shot.

'No. I don't act any more. The thing is, I just don't sleep,' he says, and he says it softly, and if there were a moment in this world for a person to forgive another or to initiate a gesture of reconciliation it is this moment, except that she can't – she is all balk, blunder, stammer, umbrage, woundedness and hate – so she flees.

In the luxury and hush of a chapel, she moves among blues and golds, among pews and escutcheons, around the myriad altars, holding the bottle, skulking. She sees the guttering candle flame heaving this way and that, teetering, recovering, swelling, like air being pumped into a bellows; sees the brown oak of the confessionals, the dropsical expressions of martyrs overlooked by sages with sage hands and sage, punitive eyes; she sees virgins like queens, like whores, and in recesses angels, naked, determined to frisk. In the blue dome of the rotunda a vapourish light, the smell and smokiness of the quenched altar candles still linger. A barricade of flowers to one side on an iron rest. Mass has finished. The smell of incense a floating presence. Oddments have been forgotten – gloves, rosary beads, a baby's knitted boot. Candles have been lit, to beam and intercede for those who have fled to their lunches or their copulations or their tennis courts or their gymnasiums.

Plumes of light, spiring, aspiring as in a theatre. She kneels by St Anthony, he who once brought gleanings of hope. The bottom of the infant Jesus fits snugly, fleshily into the hollow of St Anthony's outstretched palm. Comical. Both man and child are smiling, as if they shared a joke. She cannot pray and yet she waits, the way someone waiting to be sick waits. There are two black boxes on metal stands. One for alms and one in His honour. She cannot give. That is the truth of it. That is her plight. Her sin. She cannot give. Too much has been taken away from her, everything, her sons, first one and now the other. Galling to see necklaces and lockets and trinkets in the oblong case next to St Anthony, offerings from those who can give – mothers such as herself, wives such as herself, daughters such as herself. Hers not the only tragedy, except to her. She cannot give. She will not give. She would steal the barricade of flowers from the altar, but they seem so vulgar, so secular, so vast, so overblown. To think that she thought she might pray. What does one do with grief? What does one do with hate? She thinks of refuse dumps. They are everywhere, only a mile or two from your stately manor or your green-grow-the-rushes lake. A phantasmagoria of ashes, plastic, paper, food, condoms, flowers, mush – the afterbirth of all hope, toil and aspiration merged into a grotesqueness that cannot be destroyed. She thinks that she is like that, and calls out to her dead mother – the pity, the raw pity that they had never known that milky oneness, each alone in her slough of dark.

How could the actor have known? At any rate, he is there, chaining his bicycle to the church's black railing. The blue of the chain transparent, the metal inside like a series of snakes, each coil snug in its socket.

'Mass is finished,' she says, harshly, harshly.

'I've just come to say my little prayers.'

'Oh, you're religious.'

'Let me tell you,' he says, and he moves towards her, his hackles out now, his moment for retribution. She may think he killed her son. She may think he cadged a ticket to life. She has another guess coming. He would gladly have died. Yes, lady, to relive the moment before the toss of the coin, the heave-ho, the black, watery hole that he squirmed in is worse. He has been there. Knowing that everyone else has forgotten it, the shemozzle has died down, and that you're alone and that you've lost your three lifelong friends isn't a picnic. He laughs, a strange, metallic laugh, and says evidently it was his fate, his karma. His outburst does not frighten her, merely makes her pause for a moment to think.

'Your three lifelong friends?'

He nods. He fears that he has said too much, babbled.

'Say anything, say anything,' she whispers.

'Well, we have dinner sometimes,' and he looks to see if this is too fantastic, but it isn't. 'Jim loved soup, so I make soup, tomato or lentil. We have it in mugs, brown pottery mugs. Pasco and I go swimming – he was a great swimmer, the best swimmer of us all – he's teaching me to dive. Then Hugo, the ringleader, the king, wants diversion. He was going to be a rock star, he had all the makings. He left a song. Well, a bit of a song – "Love Is Gonna Cut You Down". We put different lines to it, different beginnings, different ends. "Love Is Gonna Cut You Down". I make him an omelette, and he throws it back in my face, and he says "Jeeves, it's runny – it's not the way I like it," so I add this and that to it, a bit of grated cheese, herbs, then I whisk it, put it back in the pan, and I brown it and toss it and say, "Is that the way you like it, Hugo?" He loves it. He tells me he loves it. I put a few flowers in a pot on the window-sill, and I say, "They're for you, and they're for you, and they're for you."'

Suddenly he stops, and she sees that he is about to cry and that he does not want her to see him. She shrinks from pity. She thinks, How childlike and how beautiful. So this is what he does with his pain. He regards the dead friends as living, or at least living in the spot inside him that matters. Most likely Hugo and he were lovers – yes, they were lovers, because he now singles him out and says that Hugo did not want to go to the party, that he woke up and said he'd had a dream in which his boots were too clumsy for swimming. They had gone to bed, they had made love, then Hugo's dream, then Hugo ignoring his dream, then down to the pier and meeting others, being introduced to Paddy.

'So that's how you manage,' she says quietly.

'Sometimes. Some days are worse. I haven't been to the bottom yet, the very bottom,' he says. But she already knows.

Then she asks his name. He is called Mitch, short for Mitchell.

'Maybe you'll visit me sometime, Mitch,' she says, and gives her address in a voice that falters.

'Or if I'm in a show you'll come and we'll have supper.' Supper, symbol of another world, a world so far behind both of them, suave and light-hearted.

'So you will be acting.'

'I hope to. The thing is . . . at the moment, I just don't sleep.'

Their bodies more or less collide into each other in a sudden embrace. He is all vertebrae, so it is like holding a musical instrument that is about to break yet won't. He will keep faith with something within – innocence, perhaps.

At home there was no barking. Tristan and Charlie had both left. What met her on the hallway floor were the gifts that she had left for him – 'necessities', as she called them. A radio, a blender, a coffeepot, and a packet of fresh coffee beans. Seeing them as he had put them, in a heap, she thought, He has not even acknowledged them; he has left them there to show his anger and confirm his separateness. The note had slipped down behind. She read it many times. She read, 'Ta for these things but I don't need them yet. I am never far from you and always at the other end of the telephone. Thanks too for everything.' He had signed it with love and a little flourish of hasty kisses. It was the PS that touched her most of all: 'Do you remember one summer we all went to Arezzo?' A stab of memory. A wash of words, baptism. They were not like words at all, they were like something animate, touching her, a hand, a voice, a presence from long, long ago, a presence within absence and, yes, within pain, within death. Everything radiant for a moment, as if she reached or was reached beyond the boundaries of herself, as if she had known him, and he her, before – a friendship that transcended time and place and even those little ruses by which we lay claim on one another.

'I can bear it,' she said, and looked around at the air, so harmless, so flaccid, and so still – a stillness such as she had not known since it had happened, or maybe ever. In the stillness there was a silence, but there was no word for that yet, because it was so new, a pale sanctuary devoid at last of all consolation.

'You can bear it,' the silence said, because this is all there is – this now that then, this present that past, this life this death, and the involuntary shudder that keeps reminding us we are alive.

Oranges from Spain

DAVID PARK

IT'S NOT A fruit shop any more. Afterwards, his wife sold it and
someone opened up a fast food business. You wouldn't recognise
it now – it's all flashing neon, girls in identical uniforms and the
type of food that has no taste. Even Gerry Breen wouldn't recognise it. Either consciously or unconsciously, I don't seem to pass
that way very often, but when I do I always stop and look at it.
The neon brightness burns the senses and sears the memories like
a wound being cauterised; but then it all comes back and out flows
a flood of memory that nothing can stem.

I was sixteen years old and very young when I went to
work for Mr Breen in his fruit shop. It was that summer
when it seemed to rain every day and a good day stood out
like something special. I got the job through patronage. My
father and Gerry Breen went back a long way – that always
struck me as strange, because they were so unlike as men.
Apparently, they were both born in the same street and grew
up together, and even when my father's career as a solicitor
took him upmarket, they still got together occasionally. My
father collected an order of fruit every Friday night on his way
home from work, and as children we always talked about 'Gerry
Breen's apples'. It's funny the things you remember, and I can
recall very clearly my mother and father having an argument
about it one day. She wanted to start getting fruit from the
supermarket for some reason, but my father wouldn't hear of
it. He got quite agitated about it and almost ended up shouting,

which was very unlike him. Maybe he acted out of loyalty, or maybe he owed him some kind of favour, but whatever the reason, the arrangement continued.

If his name is mentioned now they never do it in front of me. It's almost as if he never existed. At first it angered me – it was almost as if they thought I would disintegrate at its sound – but gradually I came to be grateful for it. I didn't even go to the funeral, and from that moment it was obvious my family sought to draw a curtain over the whole event. My mother had taken me away for a week's holiday. We stayed with one of her sisters who lives in Donegal, and I've never had a more miserable time. Inevitably, it rained every day and there was nothing to do but mope around and remember, trapped in a house full of women, where the only sounds were the clink of china cups and the click of knitting needles. It was then the dreams started. The intervening years have lessened their frequency but not their horror. When I woke up screaming for about the tenth time, they took me to a special doctor who reassured them with all the usual platitudes – I'd grow out of it, time was a great healer, and so on. In one sense I did grow out of it – I stopped telling anyone about the nightmares and kept them strictly private. They don't come very often now, but when they do only my wife knows. Sometimes she cradles me in her arms like a child until I fall asleep again.

I hadn't even really wanted a job in the first place. It was all my father's idea. He remembered the long weeks of boredom I had complained about the summer before and probably the nuisance I had been as I lazed about the house. I walked right into his trap. He knew I'd been working up to ask if I could have a motorbike for my next birthday. The signs weren't good, and my mother's instinctive caution would have been as difficult a barrier to surmount as the expense, so it came as a surprise when my father casually enquired if I'd be interested in starting to save for one. I took the bait, and before I knew what was happening, I'd been fixed up with a summer job, working in Gerry Breen's fruit shop.

I didn't like the man much at first. He was rough and ready and he would've walked ten miles on his knees to save a penny. I don't think he liked me much either. The first day he saw me he looked me up and down with unconcealed disappointment, with the expression of someone who'd just bought a horse that wasn't strong enough to do the work he had envisaged for it.

381

He stopped short of feeling my arm muscles, but passed some comment about me needing to fill out a bit. Although he wasn't tall himself, he was squat and had a kind of stocky strength about him that carried him through every physical situation. You knew that when he put his shoulder to the wheel, the chances were the wheel would spin. He wore this green coat as if it was some sort of uniform, and I never saw him in the shop without it. It was shiny at the elbows and collar, but it always looked clean. He had sandy-coloured hair that was slicked back and oiled down in a style that suggested he had once had an affinity with the Teddy boys. The first time I met him I noticed his hands, which were flat and square, and his chisel-shaped fingers. He had this little red pen-knife, and at regular intervals he used it to clean them. The other habit he had was a continual hitching-up of his trousers, even though there was no apparent prospect of them falling down. He was a man who seemed to be in perpetual motion. Even when he was standing talking to someone, there was always some part of him that was moving, whether it was transferring his pencil from one ear to the other, or hoisting up the trousers. It was as if there was some kind of mechanism inside him. Sometimes I saw him shuffle his feet through three hundred and sixty degrees like some kind of clockwork toy. For him sitting still would have been like wearing a straitjacket, and I don't think any chair, no matter how comfortable, ever held him for more than a few minutes.

On my first morning, after his initial disappointment had worn off and he had obviously resolved to make the best of a bad job, he handed me a green coat, similar to his own but even older. It had a musty smell about it that suggested it had been hanging in a dark cupboard for some considerable time, and although I took it home that first weekend for my mother to wash, I don't think the smell ever left it. The sleeves were too long, so all summer I wore it with the cuffs turned up. My first job was chopping sticks. As well as fruit and vegetables, he sold various other things, including bundles of firewood. Out in the back yard was a mountain of wood, mostly old fruit boxes, and for the rest of that morning I chopped them into sticks and put them in polythene bags. At regular intervals he came out to supervise the work and caution me with monotonous regularity to be careful with the hatchet. It was obvious I wasn't doing it to his satisfaction; his dissatisfaction was communicated by a narrowing of his eyes and a snakelike hiss. As far as I was concerned, there weren't too many ways you could chop sticks, but I was wrong. Unable to restrain his frustration any longer, he took the hatchet and proceeded to instruct me in the correct technique. This involved gently inserting it into the end of the piece of wood and then tapping the other end lightly on the ground so that it split gently along the grain. When he was assured I had mastered the method, he watched critically over my first efforts.

'Too thick, son, too thick. Did your da never teach you how to chop sticks?'

It was only when I had produced a series of the thinnest slivers that he seemed content. I suppose it meant he got more bundles of firewood, but you wouldn't have got much of a fire out of them. It made me feel guilty somehow, like I was an accessory to his stinginess. 'Did your da never teach you how to?' was a phrase I heard repeatedly that summer, and it inevitably prefaced a period of instruction in the correct technique and subsequent supervision.

The rest of my time that first morning was divided between sweeping up and humping bags of spuds from the yard into the store-room. No matter how often I brushed that shop floor, it always seemed to need to be done again. I must have filled a whole dump with cauliflower leaves, and I never stopped hating that smell. Perhaps, if I'm honest, I felt the job was a little beneath me. By the time the day was over, my back was aching and I was still trying to extract splinters from my hands. The prospect of a summer spent working like that filled me with despondency, and the attraction of a motorbike lost some of its appeal. I thought of telling my father I didn't want to go back, but was stopped by the knowledge that I would have to listen to eternal speeches about how soft young people were, and how they wanted everything on a plate. That I didn't need, and so I resolved to grit my teeth and stick it out.

The shop was situated at the bottom of the Antrim Road, and while it wasn't that big, every bit of space was used, either for display or storage. It started outside on the pavement where each morning, after carrying out wooden trestles and resting planks on them, we set out trays of fruit, carefully arranged and hand-picked, designed to attract and entice the passer-by. Above all this stretched a green canvas canopy which was supported by ancient iron stanchions, black with age. When it rained it would drip on to the front displays of fruit and so all that summer I had to carry them in and out of the shop. Inside was a long counter with old-fashioned scales and a till that rang as loudly as church bells. Under the counter were paper bags of every size, miles of string, metal hooks, bamboo canes, withered yellow rubber gloves, weights, elastic bands and a paraphernalia of utensils of unfathomable purpose. On the wall behind the counter was an assortment of glass-fronted shelving, sagging under the weight of fruit and vegetables. Above head height, the walls were covered in advertising posters that had obviously arrived free with consignments of fruit and looked like they had been there since the shop opened. On the customer side was more shelving and below it a clutter of wooden and cardboard boxes that seemed designed to ladder tights or catch the wheels of shopping trolleys. If there was any kind of logical system in the layout, I never managed to work it out. I got the impression it had evolved into a sprawling disorder and that so long as everything was close at hand, the owner saw no reason to change it.

In the back of the shop was a store-room where among merchandise and debris stood a wooden table, two chairs, a gas cooker and a sink. The only other room was a small washroom. Beyond this was a small cobbled yard, enclosed by a brick wall topped with broken glass. Over everything hung the sweet, ripe smell of a fruit shop, but in Mr Breen's shop it was mixed with a mildewed mustiness, a strange hybrid that stayed in my senses long after I had left the scene.

I worked my butt off that first day and it was obvious he intended getting value for money out of me. Maybe my father had told him it was what I needed – I don't know. It was nearly time to close and the shop was empty. He was working out some calculations on the back of a brown paper bag and I was moving fruit into the store-room, when he glanced up at me with a kind of puzzled look, as if he was trying to work out what I was thinking.

'Sure, son, it's money for old rope. Isn't that right?'

I gave a non-committal nod of my head and kept on working. Then he told me I could go, and I could tell he was wondering whether he would see me the next day. Returning to his calculations again, he licked the stub of the pencil he was using and hitched up his trousers. I said goodbye and just as I was going out the door he called me back.

'Do you want to know something, son?'

I looked at him, unsure of what response he expected. Then, signalling me closer, he whispered loudly, 'My best friends are bananas.' I forced a smile at his joke, then walked out into the street and took a deep breath of fresh air.

The fruit shop did steady business. Most of the trade came from the housewives who lived in the neighbourhood, but there was also a regular source of custom from people who arrived outside the shop in cars, and by their appearance didn't live locally – the type who bought garlic. He knew them all by name and sometimes even had their order already made up, always making a fuss over them and getting me to carry it out to their car. They were obviously long-standing customers, and I suppose they must have stayed loyal to him because they were assured of good quality fruit. He had a way with him – I had to admit that. He called every woman 'madam' for a start, even those who obviously weren't, but when he said it, it didn't sound like flattery, or like he was patronising them. It just sounded polite in an old-fashioned way. He had a great line in chat as well. If he didn't know them it was usually some remark about the weather, but if he did, he would ask about their families or make jokes, always cutting his cloth according to his audience. When a gaggle of local women were in, it was all 'Now, come on, ladies, get your grapes. Sweetest you can taste. Just the thing for putting passion into your marriage', or 'Best bananas – good enough to eat sideways'. They all loved it, and I'm sure it was good for business. Whatever their bills came to, he always gave them back the few odd pence, and I'm sure they thought he was very generous. As far as I was concerned, I thought he was one of the meanest men I'd ever met. For a start, he never threw anything away – that was one of the things that was wrong with the shop. Whether it was a bit of string or a piece of wood, he stored it carefully, and if he saw me about to throw something away, he'd stop me with a 'Never know when it might come in useful, son'. Most of the produce he collected himself from the market early in the morning, but whenever deliveries were made, he inspected each consignment rigorously, with an energy that frequently exasperated the deliverer. If he found a damaged piece of fruit, he would hold it up for mutual observation and, wrestling up his trousers with the other hand, would say something like, 'Now come on George, are you trying to put me out of business?' and he'd haggle anew over already arranged prices. Watching

385

him sniffing out flawed produce would have made you think he'd an in-built radar system. And he was always looking for something for nothing. Sometimes it was embarrassing. If the Antrim Road had still had horses going up and down it, he'd have been out collecting the droppings and selling them for manure.

One day Father Hennessy came into the shop. Mr Breen's face dropped noticeably and about half a dozen parts of his body seemed to fidget all at once.

'Hello, Father. What can I do for you?'

'Hello, Gerry. How's business?'

'Slow, Father, very slow.'

The priest smiled and, lifting an apple, rubbed it on his sleeve, the red bright against the black.

'I'm popping over to the Mater to visit some parishioners. I thought a nice parcel of fruit would cheer them up. Help them to get better.'

He started to eat the apple and his eyes were smiling.

'Of course, Father. A very good idea.'

With well-disguised misery, he parcelled up a variety of fruit and handed it over the counter.

'God bless you, Gerry. Treasure in heaven, treasure in heaven.'

With the package tucked under his arm, and still eating the apple, the priest sauntered out to his car. If he had looked back, he would have seen Mr Breen slumped on the counter, his head resting on both hands.

'The church'll be the ruin of me. He does that about three times a month. Thinks my name's Mr Del Monte, not Gerry Breen. Treasure in heaven's no use to me when I go to pay the bills at the end of the month.'

The frustration poured out of him and I listened in silence, knowing he wasn't really talking to me.

'Does he go up to Michael Devlin in the bank and ask him for some money because he's going to visit the poor? Since when did it become part of my purpose in life to subsidise the National Health system? I pay my taxes like anyone else.'

I think he'd have gone on indefinitely in a similar vein, but for the arrival of a customer, and then it was all smiles and jokes about the rain.

'Do you know, Mrs Caskey, what I and my assistant are building out in the yard?'

Mrs Caskey didn't know but her aroused curiosity was impatient for an answer.

'We're building an ark! And whenever it's finished we're going to load up two of every type of fruit and float away up the road.'

'Get away with you, Gerry. You're a desperate man.'

And then he sold her tomatoes and a lettuce which he described as 'the best lettuce in the shop'. I'd almost have believed him myself, but for the fact that I'd already heard the same phrase on about three previous occasions that day.

Gerry Breen was very proud of his shop, but he took a special pride in his displays outside, and he did this expert printing with whitening on the front window. Not only did he fancy himself a bit of an artist, but also as a kind of poet laureate among fruiterers. He had all these bits of cardboard – I think they were backing cards out of shirts – and on them he printed, not only the names and prices of the fruit, but also descriptive phrases meant to stimulate the taste buds of the reader. Grapes might be described as 'deliciously sweet' or strawberries as 'the sweet taste of summer' while Comber spuds were always 'balls of flour'. The front window always looked well. Bedded on a gentle slope of simulated grass rested the various sections of produce, complete with printed labels. Each morning when he had arranged it he would go out on the pavement and stand with his hands on his hips, studying it like an art critic viewing a painting. Inside he had other signs saying things like 'Reach for a peach', 'Iceberg lettuce – just a tip of the selection' or 'Fancy an apple – why not eat a pear?'

After the first week or so we started to get on a little better. I think he realised that I was trustworthy and prepared to pull my weight. He probably thought of me as being a bit snobbish, but tolerated it so long as he got good value for his money. I in turn became less critical of what I considered his defects. Gradually, he began to employ more of my time on less menial jobs. After three weeks I had progressed to serving customers and weighing their fruit, and then a week later I was allowed to enter the holy of holies and put my hand in the till. I still had to chop sticks and brush up of course, but whenever the shop was busy I served behind the counter. I almost began to feel part of the business. The continual wet weather stopped me from missing out on the usual activities of summer and I was increasingly optimistic that my father would reward my industry with a motorbike. Mr Breen didn't much like the rain – he was always complaining how bad it was for business. According to him, it discouraged passing trade, and people didn't buy as much as they did in warm weather. He was probably right. Sometimes, when a lull in trade created boredom, I tried to wind him up a little.

'Mr Breen, do you not think it's wrong to sell South African fruit?'

'Aw, don't be daft, son.'

'But do you not think that by selling their fruit you're supporting apartheid?'

He swopped his pencil from ear to ear and did what looked a bit like a tap dance.

'I'm only supporting myself and the wife. Sure wouldn't the blacks be the first to suffer if I stopped selling it? They'd all end up starving and how would that help them?'

I was about to provoke him further when a customer appeared and I let him have the last word.

'God knows, son, they have my sympathy – don't I work like a black myself?'

The customer turned out to be Mr Breen's wife. She was all dressed up in a blue and white suit and was on her way to some social function. She had one of those golden charm bracelets that clunked so many heavy charms I wondered how her wrist bore the strain, and while she hardly looked sideways at him, she made an embarrassing fuss over me, asking about my parents and school, and gushing on in a slightly artificial way. When she finished whatever business she had, she said goodbye to me and warned Gerald not to work me too hard. I smiled at the name Gerald, and I could see him squirming behind the counter. A heavy shower came on and we both stood in the doorway watching it bounce off the road. He was unusually silent and I glanced at him a few times to see if he was all right. When he spoke, his voice was strangely colourless.

'Never get married, son – it's the end of your happiness.'

I didn't know whether he was joking or not, so I just went on staring at the rain.

'My wife's ashamed of me,' he said in the same lifeless voice.

I uttered some vague and unconvincing disagreement and then turned away in embarrassment. I started to brush the floor, glancing up from time to time as he stood motionless in the doorway. In a minute or so the rain eased and it seemed to break the spell, but for the rest of that afternoon he was subdued and functioned in a mechanical way. He even closed the shop half an hour early – something he'd never done before.

Nothing like that ever happened again, my first experience of work slipped into an uneventful routine. One day, though, comes clearly to mind. One afternoon when business was slack he asked me to deliver fruit round to a Mrs McCausland. The address was a couple of streets away and I felt a little self-conscious as I set off in my green coat. It wasn't a big order – just a few apples and oranges and things. I followed the directions I had been given and arrived at a terraced house. Unlike most of its neighbours, the front door was closed, and the net curtain in the window offered no glimpse of the interior. At first, it seemed as if no one was in, and I was just about to turn and leave, when there was the slow undrawing of a bolt and the rattle of a chain. The door opened wide enough to allow an old woman's face to peer out at me, suspicion speckling her eyes. I identified myself and showed the fruit to reassure her. Then there was another pause before the door gradually opened to reveal an old woman leaning heavily on a walking stick. Inviting me in, she hobbled off slowly and painfully down the hall and into her tiny living room. She made me sit down and, despite my polite protests, proceeded to make me a cup of tea. The room resembled a kind of grotto, adorned with religious objects and pictures. Her rosary beads hung from the fireplace clock and a black cat slept on the rug-covered sofa. She talked to me from the kitchen as she worked.

'Isn't the weather terrible?'

'Desperate – you'd never think it was the summer,' I replied, smiling as I listened to myself. I had started to sound like Gerry Breen's apprentice.

'Summers never used to be like this. I can remember summers when the streets were baked hot as an oven and everyone used to sit on their doorsteps for you could hardly get a breath. If you sat on your doorstep these past few days you'd get pneumonia.'

She brought me a cup of tea in a china cup, and a slice of fruit cake, but nothing for herself. She sat down and scrutinised me intently.

'So you're working for Gerry for the summer. I'm sure that's good fun for you. You work hard and maybe he'll keep you on permanent.'

389

I didn't correct her misunderstanding, but I laughed silently inside.

'He says if it keeps on raining he's going to start building an ark.'

She smiled and rearranged the cushion supporting her back.

'Gerry's the salt of the earth. Do you see that fruit you brought? He's been doing that for the best part of fifteen years and nobody knows but him and me.'

She paused to pour more tea into my cup and I listened with curiosity as she continued, her words making me feel as if I was looking at a familiar object from a new and unexpected perspective.

'I gave him a wee bit of help a long time ago and he's never forgotten it, not through all these years. I don't get out much now, but sometimes I take a walk round to the shop, just to see how he's getting on. He's a great man for the crack, isn't he?'

I smiled in agreement and she shuffled forward in her seat, leaning confidentially towards me.

'Have you met Lady Muck yet? Thon woman's more airs and graces then royalty. She was born and bred a stone's throw from here and to listen to her now you'd think she came from the Malone Road. I knew her family and they didn't have two pennies to rub together between the lot of them. Now she traipses round the town like she was a duchess. You'll never catch her serving behind the counter.'

It was obvious that the woman wanted to talk – she was probably starved of company – and no matter how often I attempted a polite exit, she insisted on my staying a little longer, assuring me that Gerry wouldn't mind. I wasn't so sure, but there was no easy escape, as she produced a photograph album and talked me through a maze of memories and mementoes.

Parts of it were interesting and when she told me about the Belfast blitz I learned things I hadn't known before. Before I finally got up to go, she returned to the subject of the weather, her voice serious and solemn.

'This weather's a sign. I've been reading about it in a tract that was sent to me. It's by this holy scholar, very high up in the church, and he says we're living in the last days. All these wars and famines – they're all signs. All this rain – it's a sign too. I believe it.'

When she opened the front door it was still raining and I almost started to believe it too. I ran back quickly, partly to get out of the rain and partly because I anticipated a rebuke about the length of my absence.

There were no customers in the shop when I entered and he merely lifted his head from what he was reading, asked if everything was all right with Mrs McCausland, and returned to his study. It surprised me a little that he said nothing about the time. He was filling in his pools coupon and concentrating on winning a fortune, so perhaps he was distracted by the complexities of the Australian leagues. He had been doing them all summer and his approach never varied. He did two columns every week, the first by studying the form and this forced him to ponder such probabilities as whether Inala City would draw with Slacks Creek, or Altona with Bulleen. For the second column, he selected random numbers, his eyes screwed up and an expression on his face as if he was waiting for some kind of celestial message. On this particular afternoon, reception must have been bad, because he asked me to shout them out. Out of genuine curiosity, I asked him what he would do if he did win a fortune. He looked at me to see if I was winding him up, but must have sensed that I wasn't, because, on a wet and miserable Belfast afternoon, he told me his dream.

'It's all worked out in here,' he said, tapping the side of his head with a chisel-shaped finger. 'I've it all planned out. Thinking about it keeps you going – makes you feel better on days like this.'

He paused to check if I was laughing at him, then took a hand out of his coat pocket and gestured slowly round the shop.

'Look around you, son. What do you see?'

A still, grey light seemed to have filtered into the shop. The lights were off and it was quiet in an almost eerie way. Nothing rustled or stirred, and the only sound was the soft fall of the rain. In the gloom the bright colours smouldered like embers; rhubarb like long tongues of flame; red sparks of apples; peaches, perfect in their velvety softness, yellows and oranges flickering gently.

'Fruit,' I answered. 'Different kinds of fruit.'

'Now, do you know what I see?'

I shook my head.

'I see places. A hundred different places. Look again.' And as

391

he spoke he began to point with his finger. 'Oranges from Spain, apples from New Zealand, cabbages from Holland, peaches from Italy, grapes from the Cape, bananas from Ecuador – fruit from all over the world. Crops grown and harvested by hands I never see, packed and transported by other hands in a chain that brings them here to me. It's a miracle if you think about it. When we're sleeping in our beds, hands all over the world are packing and picking so that Gerry Breen can sell it here in this shop.'

We both stood and looked, absorbing the magnitude of the miracle.

'You asked me what I'd do if I won the jackpot – well, I've it all thought out. I'd go to every country whose fruit I sell, go and see it grow, right there in the fields and the groves, in the orchards and the vineyards. All over the world!'

He looked at me out of the corner of his eye to see if I thought he was crazy, then turned away and began to tidy the counter. I didn't say anything, but in that moment, if he'd asked me, I would have gone with him. All these years later, I still regret that I didn't tell him that. Told him while there was still time.

Four days later, Gerry Breen was dead. A man walked into the shop and shot him twice. He became another bystander, another nobody, sucked into the vortex by a random and malignant fate that marked him out. They needed a Catholic to balance the score – he became a casualty of convenience, a victim of retribution, propitiation of a different god. No one even claimed it. Just one more sectarian murder – unclaimed, unsolved, soon unremembered but by a few. A name lost in the anonymity of a long list. I would forget too, but I can't.

I remember it all. There were no customers when a motorbike stopped outside with two men on it. The engine was still running as the passenger came towards the shop. I was behind the counter looking out. He had one hand inside his black motorcycle tunic and wore a blue crash helmet – the type that encloses the whole head. A green scarf covered the bottom half of his face, so only his eyes were visible. Only his eyes – that's all I ever saw of him. Mr Breen was standing holding a tray of oranges he had just brought from the back.

Suddenly, the man pulled a gun out of his tunic and I thought we were going to be robbed, but he never spoke, and as he raised the gun and pointed at Mr Breen, his hand was shaking so much he had to support it with the other one. It was then I knew he hadn't come for money. The first shot hit Gerry Breen in the chest, spinning him round, and as he slumped to the floor the oranges scattered and rolled in all directions. He lay there, face down, and his body was still moving. Then, as I screamed an appeal for mercy, the man walked forward and, kneeling over the body, shot him in the back of the head. His body kicked and shuddered, and then was suddenly and unnaturally still. I screamed again in fear and anger and then, pointing the gun at me, the man walked slowly backwards to the door of the shop, ran to the waiting bike and was gone. Shaking uncontrollably and stomach heaving with vomit, I tried to turn Mr Breen over on to his back, but he was too heavy for me. Blood splashed his green coat, and flowed from the dark gaping wound, streaming across the floor, mixing with the oranges that were strewn all around us. Oranges from Spain.

They say help arrived almost immediately. I don't know. All I can remember is thinking of the old woman's words and hoping it really was the end of the world, and being glad and asking God to drown the world, wanting it to rain for a thousand years, rain and rain and never stop until all the blood was washed away and every street was washed clean. There were voices then and helping hands trying to lift me away, but no one could move me as I knelt beside him, clutching frantically at his green coat, begging God not to let him die, praying he'd let Gerry Breen live to build his ark and bring aboard the fruit of the world. All the fruit of the world safely stored. Oranges from Spain, apples from the Cape – the sweet taste of summer preserved for ever, eternal and incorruptible.

A Fairly Regular Four

FREDERIC RAPHAEL

IT BEGAN, LIKE modern history, in the mid-1960s. At first I used only to observe them enviously. Ronnie Trafford and his friends were often next on court after I had finished my lesson with old Ralph. Ralph had been a Davis Cup player, for England. Immediately after his doubles match, he'd been given the elbow. By the time I became his pupil at Abacus Road, on one of the few covered courts then available in London, he was bent at the waist like some antique butler, warped by deference. On the high-roofed court, he called you 'sir' in a tone which promised no further concessions.

After I had done my stint of properly constructed forehand drives, he would propose that I advance to the net. The volley, Ralph insisted, was the simplest of shots: 'You are a carpenter,' he would remind me, 'tapping in a nail.'

If my volleying happened to induce a measure of complacency, Ralph had a trick to trump my vanity. He could, it seemed, procure a net-cord pretty well at will. The ball, delivered from the baseline, would strike the tape and hop over my outstretched 'wand', as Ralph termed the plunderous wooden weapon. 'Pity!' Ralph said. 'Pity!' was my cue to thank him for my helpful humiliation.

There was a spectators' gallery along one side of Ralph's court, high under the wired glass roof. At the end of my hour, Ronnie Trafford would appear, doubly-sweatered like a fast bowler in the deep field. He watched the clock jerk towards the end of my lease. Ronnie detested being kept waiting by any of those who made up what he called his 'syndicate'.

One day, as Ralph allowed one of my smashes to be too good for him and muttered, 'On that note, I think we should stop,' Ronnie Trafford called down that he had a problem. 'Franco's mother appears to be poorly. We're one class-player short. Ralph, would you make us up?'

Ralph was nudging several dozen balls towards the corner where he caged them in a plastic waste-paper basket. 'Short notice,' he said.

'Come on, Ralph. You can relive past glories.'

'Doubt it. What about my partner here?'

'He's tired,' Ronnie said, with brutal consideration.

'He's young,' Ralph replied.

Ronnie Trafford looked at me as if he doubted it. I doubted it myself. 'I've got a programme to write,' I said.

'I say,' Ronnie said, with a little more warmth, 'I've seen you on the television, haven't I?'

As I went to the dressing room, Ronnie was on his way down from the gallery, hand outstretched. 'Just a friendly four,' he said. 'Do make us up.'

During the next few weeks, as I progressed from raw recruit to not infrequent participant, I learned that daggers were regularly drawn. Hostilities began with the twiddling ritual of rackets to decide who should partner whom. Normally, smooth played with smooth, rough with rough, but if there was one outstanding competent guest, Ronnie would pre-empt the honour. After all, it was he who had secured the privileged hour of our session. It was his secretary, the invaluable Miss Pomfret, who circularised the syndicate for their availability, before informing them in terse style who had been chosen by Ronnie's one-man selection committee for the following month. Anyone late on parade tended to find himself relegated to stand-by.

Ronnie had begun in modest circumstances, but he was determined to rise above them. The Jag was already in the driveway and the driveway was in Ealing, like the estate agency founded by his late father. It had been a small local firm when Ronnie returned from decorated services in the Kosbies. The army had been his travel scholarship, the officers' mess his university. The M. C. was his unarguable ace of trumps. And he played it as often as it was needed.

Good form, I soon discovered, was important to him. He

glared at Milstein's terrible socks (black, with red lozenges) when he had to wear them on court. He was appalled when Milstein then went on to his office in the same sweaty pair. Ronnie carried his business suit into the changing room in a plastic sack. His toiletries were arranged on the cracked glass shelf in the showers. He didn't snap the regimental cuff-links until he was as powdered as Turkish Delight. Having been an officer, he had every intention of being a gentleman.

If Ronnie had a fault, it was that he very much liked to win. I should confess, before others accuse me, that I myself can get quite sulky over tiddlywinks. Ronnie showed none of my sullen signs of bad breeding, but he did take an elastic view of the baseline. When Oliver Randell and I were deemed to have lost a crucial point, after my partner's smash had clearly whitened the tape at Ronnie's end, it required something between a shrug and a smirk from Oliver to ensure that my congratulations were effusive enough to keep me in the syndicate.

As the sixties swung by, I became more and more of a fixture. Some people dropped out; new ones dropped in. A film star, courting Ronnie's ravishing daughter, aced us handsomely before decamping to shoot it out on a TV series in Arizona leaving Flora briefly flat. Juan-Carlos O'Higgins, from the Chilean embassy, was rather too good for us, especially after being appropriated as a C.D.-plated partner by Ronnie. When Jolyon Taggart and I had gone down 6-0, 6-0, 6-0, it was hard to sustain the illusion of a close-run thing.

The syndicate soldiered on, in good fours and in bad. Ronnie prospered in all political climates. His son married well; the resuscitated Flora even better. Ronnie and his wife moved from Ealing to Chiswick Mall. His West End office effaced Acton and the Jaguar yielded to a new Roller.

The quartet celebrated anniversaries with what seemed like accelerating regularity. Waistlines thickened; hair thinned; teeth lengthened. The game went on. Did friendships ripen? We saw each other only on court. Under those freezing or scalding Abacus Road showers, we discussed public scandal, but rarely personal matters. One startling morning, however, Jolyon Taggart's soapy back was seen to be covered with a scrawl of red lacerations, the raw advertisement of an improbable passion.

Ronnie and I looked at each other simultaneously, with amused straight faces. It was a strange, inconsequential bond between us.

Jolyon dried himself, oblivious of the script we read on his back. Shortly afterwards, he announced that he had got married. We wished him luck, but only Ronnie was surprised not to have been invited to add a little class to the occasion. For the rest of us, tennis was tennis. Life was on another court.

By the early 1970s, Ronnie had the country place (Wiltshire) and the Riviera hideaway, which – he promised me – more than paid for itself. He took the family to Gstaad immediately after Christmas and in summer they sailed out of Bodrum under the canny captaincy of good old Osman. During these absences, the syndicate discovered what *Hamlet* was like without the player-king. Fewer balls that landed plumb on the line were called out; fewer aces were deemed just to have nicked the net. On the down-side, Milstein was not so punctual as when Ronnie was time-keeping. If there was less bull, there was also less fun. When Ronnie returned from the slopes or the beaches, we smiled at his tanned shoulders and suet-pudding behind, but we rejoiced to have our winners called out and punctuality re-imposed by our manifest president.

It was against all precedent when, one winter morning, Jolyon Taggart failed to turn up. 'He'll be here,' Oliver said, as ten o'clock came and went, but he was wrong. At twenty past, the telephone rang in Ralph's back room, where he sipped Scotch Broth direct from a tin which, we guessed, often contained more scotch than broth. Jolyon was terribly sorry, but he had a crisis. He couldn't make it that week. Ronnie tried to cajole Ralph into the arena, but he pleaded age, convincingly. We played one of those unsatisfactory threesomes which everyone always pretends to have been surprisingly good fun.

Ronnie had a word with Jolyon, who swore that everything was now under control. The following week, Oliver was there ahead of time, and so was I. Ronnie's clothes preceded him into the dressing room in the hands of Trump, the chauffeur. Exit Trump to polish RBT 1, the eponymous Roller. The hour struck and we were still only three. 'Really!' Ronnie said. 'Parade's parade!' Jolyon arrived, on the double, ten minutes after we began a protracted knock-up. I greeted him affably from the far end, where Oliver and I were giving Ronnie the honour of hitting every ball, as he had assumed we would. 'You may as well play with me, young man,' Ronnie said, as Jolyon shucked his track-suit.

'You're the boss,' Jolyon said.

He was usually a resourceful and steady partner. You would not have guessed it that day. Even Ronnie's creative lines-manship could not stop Oliver and me from winning one game after another. Ronnie grew baleful. We trooped into the showers without any of the usual *badinage*. All might have been well, or at least endurable, if Ronnie had not said, 'I hope this isn't going to be a regular occurrence, young Jolyon, you keeping us waiting on the start-line.'

Jolyon had always struck me as phlegmatic. If he was capable of passion, one could never imagine him bursting into tears. That is exactly what he now did. Naked, he cried like a baby. No, worse, he cried like a man: pain convulsed him. She'd left him. Taken the kid. What was he going to do? Did we have any idea what she meant to him?

We sighed. We bit our lips. We were truly very sorry. Ronnie powdered and anointed himself and tied his kipper-tie with chin-up concentration. Jolyon stumbled into his clothes, scarcely dry from the shower, snorting his way to self-control. Ronnie took the trees from his hand-stitched shoes, adjusted his sock-suspenders, and cleared his throat. 'May I ask whether there is likely to be a repeat performance?'

'My wife's walked out on me, you bastard.'

'And is that likely to have permanent consequences on your punctuality?'

'Who exactly do you think you are?'

'Call me Muggins, if you must,' Ronnie said. 'Otherwise known as him what makes the arrangements. Who did you think I was?'

'Has anyone ever told you . . .'

'*Jolyon* . . .' I tried to blow the whistle before the foul.

'. . . what a ludicrous old cheat you are? What a stupid, pretentious, flagrant old oik you bloody well are?'

Ronnie put his shoe-trees into the pouch of his Florentine leather sack. He filed his Pour Homme toiletries in their plasti-cated sheathes. 'Do I take it,' he said, 'that Master Taggart will not be here next week?'

'If you only knew how enjoyable it is when *you're* not here to call the ball out when it's miles in – '

'Or *any* week?' Ronnie said.

'You may have been an officer, but you'll never be a gentle-man, never mind what bankrupt aristocrat your precious Flora-dora has managed to marry. You're a jumped-up poop. And why would anyone ever want to play tennis with you anyway?'

Ronnie took his belongings and his combination-locked brief-case and looked at me. I was ashamed. How often we had laughed at the Sultan behind his back! I waited for him to draw his snicker-snee and strike the infidel dead. His brave blue eyes were brimming with tears he willed himself not to shed. I realised that he could not trust himself to speak. He walked out of the dressing room.

The month ended without the usual roneoed form arriving from Miss Pomfret. I telephoned Ronnie's office to curse the Post Office and check that I was on the team-sheet. Miss Pomfret's voice was December itself. 'Mr Trafford is not in the office,' she said, 'and we're not expecting him. There are no plans for further tennis in the foreseeable future.'

I telephoned Ralph, in the hope of a keep-fit session. There was no reply. I drove to Abacus Road a day later. The place was locked. A board announced that the premises were 'Under Offer'. Ronald B. Trafford and Associates were handling the sale.

I discovered Jolyon's number and, when the daffodils pushed through, we played a few times, with Milstein and Oliver Randell, on a common-or-garden court by the Royal Hospital. No one called the ball out when it was in; no ace was retrospectively demoted to a net-cord. Milstein's scarlet socks hardly seemed to matter. We were spared advice on property investment and no famous names were dropped. No one glared if you missed an easy one or took it for granted that you preferred serving into the sun. Yet somehow the game lacked magic.

Ronnie made a bomb out of the Abacus Road site, so a satirical magazine reported. I suspected that Jolyon had passed the word. Certainly Ronnie could afford a whacking contribution to Tory Party funds just as the new broom swept into Number Ten. Might a peerage be his eventual reward? I can imagine how he will have his racket covers emblazoned with his coat-of-arms. Jolyon was quite right about him, of course, in a way, but I look back with nostalgia on the covered court in Abacus Road, where the eighteen-storey headquarters of International Pharmaceuticals is now said to appal the Prince of Wales. When I drive past, I seem to hear the ghost of Ralph, now gone, as Ronnie would say, to join the Great Umpire in the Sky, as it murmurs, 'Pity!'

Burning End

A crime story

RUTH RENDELL

AFTER SHE HAD been doing it for a year, it occurred to Linda that looking after Betty fell to her lot because she was a woman. Betty was Brian's mother, not hers, and Betty had two other children, both sons, both unmarried men. No one had ever suggested that either of them should take a hand in looking after their mother. Betty had never much liked Linda, had sometimes hinted that Brian had married beneath him, and once, in the heat of temper, said that Linda was 'not good enough' for her son, but still it was Linda who cared for her now. Linda felt a fool for not having thought of it in these terms before.

She knew she would not get very far talking about it to Brian. Brian would say – and did say – that this was women's work. A man couldn't perform intimate tasks for an old woman; it wasn't fitting. When Linda asked why not, he told her not to be silly, everyone knew why not.

'Suppose it had been your dad that was left, suppose he'd been bedridden, would I have looked after him?'

Brian looked over the top of his evening paper. He was holding the remote in his hand but he didn't turn down the sound. 'He wasn't left, was he?'

'No, but if he had been?'

'I reckon you would have. There isn't anyone else, is there? It's not as if the boys were married.'

Every morning after Brian had gone out into the farmyard

and before she went to work, Linda drove down the road, turned left at the church into the lane, and after a mile came to the small cottage on the large piece of land where Betty had lived since the death of her husband twelve years before. Betty slept downstairs in the room at the back. She was always awake when Linda got there, although that was invariably before seven thirty, and she always said she had been awake since five.

Linda got her up and changed the incontinence pad. Most mornings she had to change the sheets as well. She washed Betty, put her into a clean nightdress and clean bedjacket, socks and slippers and, while Betty shouted and moaned, lifted and shoved her as best she could into the armchair she would remain in all day. Then it was breakfast. Sweet milky tea and bread and butter and jam. Betty wouldn't use the feeding cup with the spout. What did Linda think she was, a baby? She drank from a cup and, unless Linda had remembered to cover her up with the muslin squares that had indeed once had their use for babies, the tea would go all down the clean nightdress and Betty would have to be changed again.

After Linda had left her, the district nurse would come, though not every day. The meals-on-wheels lady would come and give Betty her midday dinner, bits and pieces in foil containers, all labelled with the names of their contents. At some point Brian would come. Brian would 'look in'. Not to *do* anything, not to clear anything away or make his mother a cup of tea or run the vacuum-cleaner around but to sit in Betty's bedroom for ten minutes, smoking a cigarette and watching television. Perhaps once a month, the brother who lived two miles away would come for ten minutes and watch television with Brian. The other brother, the one who lived ten miles away, never came at all except at Christmas.

Linda knew if Brian had been there by the smell of smoke and the cigarette-end stubbed out in the ashtray. But even if there had been no smell and no stub she would have known, because Betty always told her. Betty thought Brian was a saint to spare a moment away from the farm to visit his old mother. She could no longer speak distinctly but she was articulate on the subject of Brian, the most perfect son any woman ever had.

It was about five when Linda got back there. Usually the incontinence pad needed changing again and often the nightdress too. Considering how ill she was and partially paralysed, Betty ate a great deal. Linda made her scrambled egg or sardines on toast. She brought pastries with her from the cake shop or, in the summer, strawberries and cream. She made more tea for Betty, and, when the meal was over, somehow heaved her back into that bed.

The bedroom window was never opened. Betty wouldn't have it. The room smelt of urine and lavender, camphor and meals-on-wheels, so every day on her way to work Linda opened the window in the front room and left the doors open. It didn't make much difference but she went on doing it. When she had got Betty to bed, she washed the dishes and teacups and put all the soiled linen into a plastic bag to take home. The question she asked Betty before she left had become meaningless because Betty always said no, and she hadn't asked it once since talking to Brian about whose job it was to look after his mother, but she asked it now.

'Wouldn't it be better if we moved you in with us, Mum?'

Betty's hearing was erratic. This was one of her deaf days.

'What?'

'Wouldn't you be better-off coming to live with us?'

'I'm not leaving my home till they carry me out feet first. How many times do I have to tell you?'

Linda said she would see her in the morning. Looking rather pleased at the prospect, Betty said she would be dead by the morning.

'Not you,' said Linda, which was what she always said, and so far she had always been right.

She went into the front room and closed the window. The room was furnished in a way which must have been old-fashioned even when Betty was young. In the centre of it was a square dining table, around which stood six chairs with seats of faded green silk. There was a large sideboard but no armchairs, no small tables, no books and no lamps but the central light which, enveloped in a shade of parchment panels stitched together with leather thongs, was suspended directly over the glass vase that stood on a lace mat in the absolute centre of the table.

For some reason, ever since the second stroke had incapacitated Betty, all the post, all the junk mail and every freebie news-sheet that was delivered to the cottage ended up on this table. Every few months it was cleared away, but this hadn't been done for some time, and Linda noticed that only about four inches of the glass vase now showed above the sea of paper.

The lace mat was not visible at all. She noticed something else as well.

It had been a warm sunny day, very warm for April. The cottage faced south and all afternoon the sunshine had poured through the window, was still pouring through the window, striking the neck of the vase so that the glass was too bright to look at. Where the sun-struck glass touched a sheet of paper a burning had begun. The burning glass was making a dark charred channel through the sheet of thin printed paper.

Linda screwed up her eyes. They had not deceived her. That was smoke she could see. And now she could smell burning paper. For a moment she stood there, marvelling at this phenomenon which she had heard of but had never believed in. A magnifying glass used to make boy scouts' fires, she thought, and somewhere she had read of a forest burnt down through a piece of glass left in a sunlit glade.

There was nowhere to put the piles of paper, so she found another plastic bag and filled that. Betty called out something but it was only to know why she was still there. Linda dusted the table, replaced the lace mat and the glass vase and, with a bag of soiled linen in one hand and a bag of waste paper in the other, went home to do the washing and get an evening meal for Brian and herself and the children.

The incident of the glass vase, the sun and the burning paper had been so interesting that Linda meant to tell Brian and Andrew and Gemma all about it while they were eating. But they were also watching the finals of a quiz game on television and hushed her when she started to speak. The opportunity went by and somehow there was no other until the next day. But by that time the sun and the glass setting the paper on fire no longer seemed so remarkable, and Linda decided not to mention it.

Several times in the weeks that followed Brian asked his mother to come and live with them at the farm. Betty responded very differently from when Linda asked her. Brian and his children, Betty said, shouldn't have to have a useless old woman under their roof; age and youth were not meant to live together, though nobody appreciated her son's generosity in asking her more than she did. Meanwhile Linda went on going to the cottage and looking after Betty, and cleaning the place on Saturdays and doing Betty's washing.

One afternoon while Brian was sitting with his mother

and smoking a cigarette, the doctor dropped in to pay his twice-yearly visit. He beamed at Betty, said how nice it was for her to have her family around her, and on his way out told Brian it was best for the old folks to end their days at home whenever possible. He made no comment on the cigarette. Brian must have picked up a pile of junk mail from the doormat and the new phone book from outside the door, for all this was lying on the table in the front room when Linda arrived at ten to five. The paper had accumulated during the past weeks, but when she went to look for a plastic bag she saw that the stock had been used up. She made a mental note to buy some more and, in the meantime, had to put the soiled sheets and Betty's two wet nightdresses into a pillowcase to take home. The sun wasn't shining, it had been a dull day and the forecast was for rain, so there was no danger from the conjunction of the glass vase with the piles of paper. It could safely remain where it was.

On her way home it occurred to Linda that the simplest solution was to remove not the paper but the vase. Yet, when she went back next day, she didn't remove the vase. It was a strange feeling she had that, if she moved the vase on to the mantelpiece, say, or the sideboard, she would somehow have closed a door or missed a chance. Once she had moved it, she would never be able to move it back again, for, though she could easily have explained to anyone why she had moved it from the table, she would never be able to say why she had put it back. These thoughts made her feel uneasy and she put them from her mind.

Linda bought a pack of fifty black plastic sacks. Betty said it was a wicked waste of money. In the days when she had been up and about she had been in the habit of burning waste paper. All leftover food and cans and bottles got mixed up together and went out for the dustman. Betty had never heard of the environment. When Linda insisted, one hot day in July, on opening the bedroom windows, Betty said she was freezing and Linda was trying to kill her. Linda took the curtains home and washed them but she didn't open the bedroom window again: it wasn't worth it, it caused too much trouble.

But when Brian's brother Michael got engaged, she did ask if Suzanne would take her turn looking after Betty once they were back from their honeymoon.

'You couldn't expect it of a young girl like her,' Brian said.

'She's twenty-eight,' said Linda.

'She doesn't look it.' Brian switched on the television. 'Did I tell you Geoff's been made redundant?'

'Then maybe he could help out with Betty if he hasn't got a job to go to.'

Brian looked at her and shook his head gently. 'He's feeling low enough as it is. It's a blow to a man's pride, that is, going on the dole. I couldn't ask him.'

Why does he have to be asked? Linda thought. It's his mother. The sun was already high in the sky when she got to the cottage at seven thirty next morning, already edging round the house to penetrate the front-room window by ten. Linda put the junk mail on the table and took the letter and the postcard into the bedroom. Betty wouldn't look at them. She was wet through and the bed was wet. Linda got her up and stripped off the wet clothes, wrapping Betty in a clean blanket because she said she was freezing. When she was washed and in her clean nightdress, she wanted to talk about Michael's fiancée. It was one of her articulate days.

'Dirty little trollop,' said Betty. 'I remember her when she was fifteen. Go with anyone, she would. There's no knowing how many abortions she's had; messed all her insides up, I shouldn't wonder.'

'She's very pretty, in my opinion,' said Linda, 'and a nice nature.'

'Handsome is as handsome does. It's all that make-up and hair dye as has entrapped my poor boy. One thing, she won't set foot in this house while I'm alive.'

Linda opened the window in the front room. It was going to be a hot day, but breezy. The house could do with a good draught of air blowing through to freshen it. She thought, I wonder why no one ever put flowers in that vase, there's no point in a vase without flowers. The letters and envelopes and newsprint surrounded it so that it no longer looked like a vase but like a glass tube inexplicably poking out between a stack of paper and a telephone directory.

Brian didn't visit that day. He had started harvesting. When Linda came back at five, Betty told her Michael had been in. She showed Linda the gift of chocolates that were his way of 'soft-soaping' her, Betty said. Not that a few violet creams had stopped her speaking her mind on the subject of that trollop.

The chocolates had gone soft and sticky in the heat. Linda said she would put them in the fridge, but Betty clutched the box to her chest, saying she knew Linda, she knew her sweet tooth, if she let that box out of her sight she'd never see it again. Linda washed Betty and changed her. While she was doing Betty's feet, rubbing cream round her toes and powdering them, Betty struck her on the head with the bedside clock, the only weapon she had to hand.

'You hurt my toe,' said Betty. 'You hurt me on purpose.'

'No, I didn't, Mum. I think you've broken that clock.'

'You hurt me on purpose because I wouldn't give you my chocolates my son brought me.'

Brian said he was going to cut the field behind the cottage next day. Fifty acres of barley and he'd be done by mid-afternoon, if the heat didn't kill him. He could have seen to his mother's needs, he'd be practically on the spot, but he didn't offer. Linda wouldn't have believed her ears if she'd heard him offer.

It was hotter than ever. It was even hot at seven thirty in the morning. Linda washed Betty and changed the sheets. She gave her cereal for breakfast and a boiled egg and toast. From her bed, Betty could see Brian going round the barley field on the combine and this seemed to bring her enormous pleasure, though her enjoyment was tempered with pity.

'He knows what hard work is,' Betty said, 'he doesn't spare himself when there's a job to be done,' as if Brian was cutting the fifty acres with a scythe instead of sitting up there in a cabin with twenty kingsize and a can of Coke and the Walkman on his head playing Beatles' songs from his youth.

Linda opened the window in the front room very wide. The sun would be round in a couple of hours to stream through that window. She adjusted an envelope on the top of the pile, moving the torn edge of its flap to brush against the glass vase. Then she moved it away again. She stood, looking at the table and the papers and the vase. A brisk draught of air made the thinner sheets of paper flutter a little. From the bedroom she heard Betty call out, through closed windows, to a man on a combine a quarter of a mile away, 'Hello, Brian, you all right then, are you? You keep at it, son. That's right, you got the weather on your side.'

One finger stretched out, Linda lightly poked at the torn edge of the envelope flap. She didn't really move it at all. She turned her back quickly. She marched out of the room, out of the house, to the car.

The fire must have started somewhere around four in the afternoon, the hottest part of that hot day. Brian had been in to see his mother when he had finished cutting the field at two. He had watched television with her and then she said she wanted to have a sleep. Those who know about these things said she had very likely died from suffocation without ever waking. That was why she hadn't phoned for help, though the phone was by her bed.

A farm-worker driving down the lane called the fire brigade. They were volunteers whose headquarters was five miles away and they took twenty minutes to get to the fire. By then Betty was dead and half the cottage destroyed. Nobody told Linda, there was hardly time: when she got to Betty's at five it was all over and Brian and the firemen were standing about, poking at the wet black ashes with sticks.

The will was a surprise. Betty had lived in that cottage for years without a washing machine or a freezer and her television set was rented by Brian. The bed she slept in was her marriage bed, new in 1947; the cottage hadn't been painted since she moved there and the kitchen had last been refitted just after the war. But she left what seemed an enormous sum of money. Linda could hardly believe it. A third was for Geoff, a third for Michael and the remaining third as well as the cottage, or what was left of it, for Brian.

The insurance company paid up. It was impossible to discover the cause of the fire. Something to do with the great heat, no doubt, and the thatched roof and the ancient electrical wiring. Linda, of course, knew better, but she said nothing. She kept what she knew and let it fester inside her, giving her sleepless nights and taking away her appetite.

Brian cried noisily at the funeral. All the brothers showed excessive grief and no one told Brian to pull himself together or be a man, but put their arms round his shoulders and said what a marvellous son he'd been and how he'd nothing to reproach himself with. Linda didn't cry, but soon after went into a depression from which nothing could rouse her, not the doctor's tranquillisers, nor Brian's promise of a slap-up holiday somewhere, even abroad if she liked, nor people telling her Betty hadn't felt any pain but had just slipped away in her smoky sleep.

An application to build a new house on the site of the cottage was favourably received by the planning authority and permission was granted. Why shouldn't they live in it,

Brian said, he and Linda and the children? The farmhouse
was ancient and awkward, difficult to keep clean, just the
sort of place Londoners would like for a second home. How
about a modern house, he said, with everything you want, two
bathrooms, say, and a laundry room and a sun-lounge? Design
it yourself and don't worry about the cost, he said, for he was
concerned for his wife who had always been so practical and
efficient, as well as easy-going and persuadable, but was now
a miserable, silent woman.

Linda refused to move. She didn't want a new house, especially a new house on the site of that cottage. She didn't want
a holiday or money to buy clothes. She refused to touch
Betty's money. Depression had forced her to give up her
job but, although she was at home all day and there was no
old woman to look after every morning and every evening,
she did nothing in the house, and Brian was obliged to get a
woman in to clean.

'She must have been a lot fonder of Mum than I thought,'
Brian said to his brother Michael. 'She's always been one to
keep her feelings bottled up, but that's the only explanation.
Mum must have meant a lot more to her than I ever knew.'

'Or else it's guilt,' said Michael, whose fiancée's sister was
married to a man whose brother was a psychotherapist.

'Guilt? You have to be joking. What's she got to be guilty
about? She couldn't have done more if she'd been Mum's own
daughter.'

'Yeah, but folks feel guilt over nothing when someone
dies, it's a well-known fact.'

'It is, is it? Is that what it is, Doctor? Well, let me tell
you something. If anyone ought to feel guilt it's me. I've
never said a word about this to a soul. Well, I couldn't, could
I, not if I wanted to collect the insurance, but the fact is it was
me set that place on fire.'

'You what?' said Michael.

'I don't mean on purpose. Come on, what do you take me
for, my own brother? And I don't feel guilty, I can tell you. I
don't feel a scrap of guilt; accidents will happen and there's not
a thing you can do about it. But when I went in to see Mum
that afternoon I left my cigarette burning on the side of the
chest of drawers. You know how you put them down, with
the burning end stuck out. Linda'd taken away the damned
ashtray and washed it or something. When I saw Mum was

asleep, I just crept out and left that fag-end burning. Without a backward glance.'

Awed, Michael asked in a small voice, 'When did you realise?'

'Soon as I saw the smoke, soon as I saw the fire brigade. Too late then, wasn't it? I'd crept out of there without a backward glance.'

Notes of a
Copernican Biographer

PATRICK ROGERS

A NEW BEGINNING, then. A new life.

All this week I have hired a boat to take me up the river, a slow, evil-smelling launch that forces its way down the Thames. My pilot – Ray – knows every nut and bolt of this waterfront. We charged into the grey chop and passed the entrance of West India Dock picking up speed. I never knew this part of town very well but I would never have guessed how riddled with waterways it was here, openings and gangways and catwalks. A lesser Venice.

So, a beginning of new notes. A new life. All else, all that old baggage has been thrown out, and it was left to me to break the mould. Traditional biography has had its day. Truths such as this should perhaps come to us in hallowed places, at the font of the tradition, somewhere like the Bodleian, but no such cinematic setting was granted to me for my revelation.

I was driving back through the brown, smudged Cairo squalor of east London – having wasted all morning with an ancient creature who was supposed to have been a lover of Max Anders, whose biography I was commissioned to write. I had been negotiating my way through the Byzantine clutter of her lies and half-recollected myths. Anders, you ask? He hardly matters now – the painter, deserter who spent the years of the Blitz working on his famous expressionistic canvases. The nudes in the Tate. Death by drowning. I had read eleven thousand letters written by this man, and had been pursuing any minor soul he might have spoken to forty years ago . . . Such are the pointless labours of the biographer.

The mould of biography is broken. We construct our elaborate edifice but it remains nothing but a skeleton through which we see only the sky. Now I'm finished with it, that same old obfuscation.

Amongst the drab Victorian edifices, those abandoned wharves and neglected warehouses, the acres of bulldozed rubbish, the council estates and attempted renovations, *there* I have found my new subject. He lives amongst the stink and mud and fish, and centuries-old water, congealed oil, waterlogged timber.

At the helm Ray stood like a dancer with the tiller held between his legs. That high bravado. Late October mornings, and the air at that hour is like ice.

All this I tell Lisbet. I can't remember who referred me to Lisbet, but I went to see her in one of those buildings more suited to merchant bankers or commodity scroungers than a publisher, and with a sense of elation proposed to her nothing short of a revolution in the science of biography. Biography is ready for its Copernicus. She prepared her editorial face and said: 'You don't know who this man is? The man you saw by the docks?'

'Serendipity?'

'That's his name?'

'That's what I call him,' I told her. 'I don't have to know who he is.'

That foxed her; only those in tune with the essential radicalism of my approach could follow me. She wanted to know the other biographies I had written. I told her: Castlereagh, Christopher Marlowe, Marat.

'And what about Anders? Isn't that why you have come to see me – I understood that you'd reached an impasse.'

It was finished, I told her. Abandoned. The line of that tradition had petered out into . . . lies, fictions. You have to hector these publishers. She said that she would read my biographies, but I couldn't see why she should bother. She had a biro at her mercy between crimson-painted nails and was driving the point of it against her note-pad. A nervous gesture. I told her that her office looked across to Serendip's domain, and I could see the sprawl beneath us through the autumn haze; from the floor-to-ceiling windows I could just make out a bend of the river.

Each morning I make my way down the river, past the renovated Isle of Dogs, past the turquoise gas tanks of the north bank, Greenwich, and then we enter silence, a narrow scum-filled canal, that leads to the set of three dull clinker-brick frontages and I am sure that Serendipity lives in one of them. The central one has an open loft and a rust-coloured crane fixed on the landing. Below the central pediment the name HAAG & MENDELSSOHN can be made out in faded white relief.

'Nothing lives round here,' Ray tells me, his motor idling in the channel, kicking up a yellow froth.

On both sides of the warehouses there are clearings behind wire fences, in parts concreted, scattered with bricks, which have been used as a local tip and, contrary to Ray's pronouncement, gangs of birds collected there.

None of the frantic redevelopment has reached this far up the river yet. The canal is a cul-de-sac and a few ditches at the end contribute a sulphurous discharge to the motionless water.

'We're still learning to be his contemporaries,' I told Lisbet. She always waits for me to offer more and rarely passes comment. I can no longer gaze at the panorama beyond the window behind her without feeling a rush of vertigo.

She has read my early biographies. 'They all met violent deaths. And Max Anders, too. Do you feel that this is significant?'

They perplex me, these editors. I had to explain to her again how, coming away from a morning with one of Anders' wartime creatures, I felt it, my revolution, the truth, as clear as day, as I drove down East India Dock Road, and how I turned off and stopped by the river. I was out of breath, panting with the realisation of what I had felt. Do I believe in fate, providence? That wet morning I did. I spotted Serendipity. How I had followed him, watching as he delved into an old paper bag and drew out a chicken leg, and how I lost him near a school. How well he knew his terrain.

'It struck you then?'

'That I had found my subject. Yes. Just as you say: it *struck* me. Now I had the material with which to prove my ideas. The perfect subject! No present, no future, no letters – do you realise how many letters I have read during my career?' Here was the perfect subject. At last that wraith, that fictional enigma that lay at the heart of all conventional biography, of all lives, could be erased. I could tell that she had not completely followed my reasoning. 'I might delve into his past,' I went on, 'scrape up a few anecdotes, an estranged sister, discover his war records, but what would I have uncovered?'

'Nothing,' she conceded. I liked it when she became tractable. 'So you've given up the Anders biography?' She was making notes again. Then she asked me if I understood the concept of *projection*. They never fail to amaze me now, those still rooted to the conventional ways of knowing. 'Don't you feel that your problems might derive from a lack of confidence? In your material? In who you are?' She looked at me as though she had delivered the *coup de grâce* of some monstrous modish therapy, but so as not to hurt her feelings I said nothing.

Ray, I feel, has started to enjoy our morning trips.

'What will you do when you find this bloke?'

Invariably now it rains, or a soft windless haze descends, and late in the morning a decaying greenish light covers the docklands. It is always silent amongst the buildings. The occasional seagull, or a loose piece of metal banging somewhere. So many strange things abandoned here. Here you could let go of a past. A purpose no longer understood has fallen into eclipse. Some hung on, others thankfully let go.

'Can I see the notebooks?'

'No.' Lisbet looks almost pleased when I refuse her. I have told her about Serendip's notebooks and she immediately wants to see them.

'Where did you find them?'

'That's unimportant. What is important is the existence of his true voice. These books are the stroke of luck that I've been waiting for – so that I can prove the revolutionary nature of my thesis. You see, everyone else would fall into that old trap – selected quotes, devious extractions. *I don't intend to quote a single word from them!*'

Lisbet waits and scribbles something down. Have I gone too far? Will she refuse to publish?

Instead she says: 'You are separated from your wife. You live . . . in a service flat in Paddington? For the last two years you have been reading the correspondence of this painter, and then suddenly you . . . you feel you've come out into clear air.'

'I'm going bald too!' I laugh. 'What does this have to do with anything?' Does she have a checklist? Must all her authors submit to this inane procedure? With a shot of panic I thought that she had completely failed to appreciate what I am proposing.

Suddenly something moving catches the corner of my eye, something in the bookcase.

'You're recording this!' There is a reel-to-reel tape spool very slowly rotating on a machine.

'Of course.' She is quite calm. 'I told you at the start that I will be recording all our meetings. It's general practice.'

It seemed over-thorough to me, but I said no more.

'You are continuing with your boat trips? But you haven't spotted him yet?'

'It's only a matter of time.'

She taps her biro again, summing something up. She says: 'Freud says somewhere that biographers select their subjects according to a need to enrol them in a list of infantile heroes. What do you say about that?'

'It's – it's a theory.'

'A revivification of the infant's idealised father.' She is doodling now, looking down. 'That as a consequence the biographer blurs and suppresses anything that doesn't fit the image.'

'It sounds like he was describing the biographies written about himself!'

She smiles and changes the subject. For a while we talked about my earlier writings as though they were relevant; it seems that she has quite assiduously consumed them, and then, glancing at her watch, she abruptly announces that the meeting is over.

Of course I'd be a fool to release the notebooks, especially to Lisbet. The temptation to use them in a conventional mode would be too much for the marketing side of any publisher. The mark of a person is what he or she makes of such acts of providence, and the true voice of Serendipity is not a gift that comes every day. *Tuesday. If I start getting some wood up in the loft for winter I can stay there permanent. Dug up a few more potatoes with their bodies like old turds and boiled them up. Scrumptious.* Unmistakably his, the demotic verve. The same vitality that he must invest in his distinctive life. *Down along the gantry and down to the dispatch floor. Thank God I don't have to lug the Dog any more. Buried near the potatoes, the bitch has a purpose now. Maybe that's why they're the shape they are.* These will remain my guide ropes, these old school exercise books with widely spaced lines and a pink margin, their tattered violet blotting-paper covers, and not a word shall appear in my life.

Does she understand that?

Awash these past few years on other people's detritus – and in the modern age these people *live their lives* according to the rules of biography – I had been certain at least of my own biography. Except that it was constructed according to someone else's programme! Important dates, formative experiences, key figures, recurring motifs – all fictions! That's how *I* wrote them. But now the clean slate. My own existence still wore the accretions of that old fiction, which to my amazement Lisbet continued to investigate – the separation from my wife; the noise that comes at night when the refrigerator next door sets up a trembling in the thin wall; when the tall Sikh from downstairs sets out each evening for his temple behind the garage . . . Lisbet wants me to sweep up these elements in the delusion that they have an importance, when I am trying to make it clear to her that the exact opposite is the case: they must be abraded from consciousness. Why speak of me, anyway? I insist. Here we have the first Adam of a new knowledge, an epistemological revolution.

For weeks we'd been cruising past those dead buildings, keeping to the far side on the return leg, but we had spotted nothing. Then, today, Ray suddenly pointed out the stone steps opposite. A man, my size, in an old knee-length Army trench coat.

'Quick!' I shouted. Ray swerved the tiller and accelerated, but the shadow disappeared. We cut the motor and listened. Should I have called out? Called what? It was black in the open loft of the centre building but I was certain that he was in there, watching us. Ray started the motor and as it idled the propeller blades were slowly throwing up bubbles through the murk.

But it was him. The man I had first seen by Limehouse Pier selecting morsels from his paper bag. Faith in my intuition has paid off.

Why get up just because my body wakes? What's a body, anyway?

Nights of bliss. With that mattress I got behind the printers in the Tiptree Road.

A week since I spotted Serendipity and nothing since.

'What else can you tell me about him?' Lisbet wants to know. She does not understand how fleeting his appearance had been. 'What clothes was he wearing? Did he look in your direction?' She is almost abnormally fascinated with my impressions of him, yet at times I feel that she does not believe that he exists. Today the sun is a glossy yellow in the haze that covers London. I told her that she must not fall into the old biographer's trap of interpreting appearance as important; that she must accept the contingent. I enjoy lecturing my editors. There are a thousand voices calling you, I tell her. 'Yes – I have that problem,' she says and obviously I have betrayed my surprise. 'It's true,' she went on. 'A myriad theories, a thousand voices. They blow this way and that and I only hear a snatch of one conversation before the wind changes and another drowns it out. I strain to listen. Which one is real?'

I agree with her. 'In my career I have lost count of the lies I have heard.'

'But the lies,' she smiles, 'don't you feel that they sometimes tell you more than the truth?'

Oh yes. As long as you know. That they are lies.

'You're used to biographers, I see,' I laugh.

'Biographers?' She considers this seriously. 'Yes, I suppose you could call them that. *Self*-biographers – *auto*biographers.' She is enjoying some private allusion, I suspect. 'And you are right – they all come to me with their own private programmes.'

Once people used to see me, then just that old cow at the off-licence. Then they did her in and left her in a ditch. To get her house. But no one ever said anything I wanted to hear.

Then Ray surprised me by saying after weeks of these morning trips that he knew of a back waterway. An old bricked canal behind Haag & Mendelssohn's.

The next morning we went past our usual entrance, our small launch kicking up into the brown wake of a tug whose master Ray waved to, and we pushed on through the litter of seagulls. Wharves on the waterfront there had succumbed to rabid redevelopment; others were being razed. Along Greenwich Reach in the falling damp. We approached the entrance to a narrow channel hidden by a row of high metal tanks and once there the landscape changed; a few blank rows of terraces, council blocks, and a pair of inert barge hulks were lashed up to capstans. The waterway split up and empty allotments, building sites, appeared on both sides behind wire fences or black brick walls. There was no sign of activity however. There were two or three odd bits of surviving architecture, a stranded brick chimney or a concrete arch – alien figments, Babylonian or Roman, standing under a North Sea sky – and then Ray entered a channel barely wider than his vessel and we slid along, my head level with the ground. Bald tyres were roped along the sides of the canal.

The waterway came to an end against the weir-gate where all manner of detritus floated on a scummy froth: a Wellington boot, orange peel and flaps of cardboard, skeins of fishing line, a pair of dungarees.

But ahead of us: Serendip's residence. The front, here, was in a much worse state: the concrete yard had given up to weeds and bramble, and an old curve-shouldered refrigerator lay on the remains of a bonfire, its cream sides showing streaks of soot.

We stepped around this rubbish through the open archways. Anarchy: timbers, girders, piles of weed, what looked like shards of smashed toilet bowls. In one place bags of plaster had been ripped open or tossed against the walls: petrified white explosions. I left Ray downstairs and ascended the wide steps to the perilous chapel of Serendip's loft.

With my heart pounding I *knew* I was right.

Looking out from the glassless opening I looked across the canal – and there it was, unnoticed before now: another warehouse, set back, derelict, looking across at this one.

'Find what you're looking for?' Ray shouts from below. Oh yes. I have found that all right.

Roaches here. Encroaching, Serendip puts down in his notebook, scrawling with that broad carpenter's pencil, his words often straying below the line. *You can smell them, smell their noses poking into your business. The Englishman's last privilege, his room, his mattress, turned over. Here I sleep, bastards. Here I try and shut out those dreams. Thin times, poor pickings. Rain. Remember the boots I found near Dagenham Marsh. The girl you foiled in the corner at The Sow's Ear. Remember the half-eaten chicken in the paper bag – how you scoffed it down on Limehouse Pier. Scoured those bones.*

As Christmas approaches and the weather deteriorates I am convinced that my plan makes sense.

'Facts only deepen my incomprehension,' I told Lisbet. 'The less we know the more room there is for self truth.'

She fixed me with that uncommunicative smile of hers.

'I intend to burst through into a new realm of understanding.'

'You make it sound like . . . Zen Biography.'

'Exactly!' I clap my hands so loudly that she starts. 'The beginning of all knowledge is ignorance.'

She touches the glass globule that she uses as a paperweight.

'The only way is to rid ourselves of others' misunderstandings.'

I go home from these meetings with Lisbet in an apprehensive mood these days. Now that I have made my decision I feel like a racer poised on starting blocks. I think of Serendipity in his lair, enjoying the secure knowledge that no one knows of his continued existence, and I sympathise with the anxiousness about being discovered that he has expressed in his notebooks. My own life these last few years has been approaching his state, I see: a downward spiral. Downstairs a door slams and someone turns on a radio. I have thought of my painter, my last subject, who spent his last few years close to where Serendip lives, and wondered if he too had been trying to attain this blessed state.

I remember a day when I must have been only eleven or twelve years old, standing on a grassy knoll with the sun streaking through a broken fence, and all of my playmates must have been called home and I was alone, a warm evening, and with a fit of originality that afflicts you at that age I decided: Yes, that's who I will be. I would not dream of telling Lisbet this. Who was I before deciding that?

'I advise you against pursuing this . . . new subject of yours,' she warned me. She had divined what I had in mind. 'Your boat trips are over. You're not planning anything else?'

I do not answer her.

'You need, we all need, a society that . . . that takes note of you.'

From my kitchenette window I see a city, a world, populated by people whom no one sees. The solitary Sikh wheels his bicycle out of the coal shed, but no one sees him; even at the temple his prayers are unacknowledged. The old woman next door, who digs over the narrow trench of clay to plant her vegetables, sits outside in a deckchair whenever there is any sunlight and shows her knees to the sun, certain that no one sees her, no one visits, no one conceives of her existence. The streets, the tube, the buses, are filled with these shadows.

'Sometimes,' Lisbet goes on, 'being ourselves can be a burden, but it's a weight that must be borne. To follow this tramp by the river you can't hope to discover anything.'

'Except myself.'

She paused, sighed. 'Isn't that why you came to me? Why have we had these sessions? After all, Mr Brownlow, you came to me for help.' Her mouth is pursed, tense. She starts again with her usual trickery: 'In opposition to Freud, you know, Jung maintained that we search out our opposites in the other – to complete ourselves. I realise that he was speaking about spouses, but is there much difference between courtship and biographical research?'

I can hardly keep a straight face. I ask you: What have editors ever understood of psychology?

Equipped with sleeping-bag and primus stove I got off the bus on the East India Dock Road and bought a few provisions, some rice and tinned beans, powdered milk, coffee, and made my way to the 'hide'. By walking I had hoped to become acclimatised to the new surroundings, but within minutes I was lost. There were hardly any road names, and the long high wire fences of the docks and building sites prevented any short cuts.

And yet this was the exact state of benighted perplexity I was in search of. I could hear Lisbet: You can't hope to discover anything.

And Serendip in those notebooks that she so greedily wanted to get her hands on: *Day shall come when I will not see myself in the mirror, in the water.*

I skirted around a deserted petrol station and thought I was getting my bearings. By mid-morning, long after I had hoped to be in position, I found a canal I recognised and ran down a lane to the end and clambered over a pile of broken bricks to reach my warehouse opposite Serendipity's.

Although the ground floor was still used for storage – pallet after pallet spread in all directions in the dark – upstairs had all the hallmarks of neglect. In the room at the top I could look across the canal directly into his loft. I used a bit of an old shutter to sweep aside the muck, the bird and rat droppings, then unpacked my rucksack and unrolled my brand-new sleeping-bag. I had thought of bringing a camera, but at the last minute had decided against it: such paraphernalia, along with first drafts, had had their day.

I was soon rewarded.

Early on the second day, stretched out on my stomach and idly watching a storm approach from Holland, I noticed a figure in a greatcoat appear in the doorway opposite; he looked down at the water, sniffed the air, then withdrew into the shadow.

If I could live less then I would eat less. Move less. Come down to this.

I might have written this myself. *See no one for days*, he writes. Or is it *years?* – the writing is unclear. *Feel POSSESSED. That feeling from when I was young centuries ago. Go down to the sea. Go down to the sea for sex. Cockles and mussels. Alive alive-oh.*

I have started a journal of my days here and am loath to leave the loft for long.

Day Four. Now I know how scientists felt when the first coelacanth was netted. Another sighting. He actually came out on the narrow ledge by the channel. It was high tide and the grey water slopped up the steps. He looked towards the river. It has occurred to me that he must be looking out for Ray's boat.

Day Six. About two in the afternoon. Miserable weather. He dangles his feet over the edge of the door opening, eats a pear and tosses the stripped core into the water. How I admire such luxuriousness.

Day Seven. Before it is light in the morning I hear him coughing. Some nights I see the flickering of an open flame against a wall. He must be feeling the cold as well.

Day Eight. Difficult to find clean water. The powdered milk floats like undissolved soap flakes.

And my guess was right. Serendipity has written: *Scraping for firewood. Spend the evening in reverie around the campfire dreaming back. The old boys are here again . . . Tunis, Sicily, Cannae. And that snooping boat hasn't been this way for ten days.*

I have to resist a temptation to shout across the narrow gap that separates us: I am *here*. Over *here*.

When my provisions are low I make a rush to the nearest shop. I know the habitat well now and take a route along the towpath and over a metal footbridge, past a stretch of redevelopment until I reach a pair of stranded bungalows, one alive with Christmas decorations, the other roofless. Most days it rains or turns to sleet. The stout, red-faced woman at the corner shop knows me now, as she knows all her children.

'But you're not from here.'

I'm prepared for this. 'I'm doing some work on the barrier. Tidal variants, that kind of thing.'

She's not interested, though. 'Is that your Christmas dinner?'

A tin of ham. Baked beans. Bread and cheese. I am running out of money.

'Quite a feast, eh?'

She shook her head, but when she thought I wasn't looking she threw in a bar of chocolate.

Back in position I slowly unwrapped the chocolate, peeled back the gold foil and learned to acquire some of Serendip's voluptuousness.

Sometimes he shows himself as if he wants to be seen, looking across the gap that separates us to where I am hidden in the dark. He fixes me with the gaze of a gorilla in a zoo, standing in his Army coat and boots, with woollen mittens and mangy fur cap.

He *has* seen me.

Watching, being watched. Facing each other we crouch squatting like lice over our hoard of memories. Which dwindle.

Day Ten. Very cold. Sleety rain. The only sound: Serendipity's coughing fits. As though he has custard in his lungs.

Lisbet was warning me against abnegation. But she never understood. From the start we were shouting at each other from opposing banks. The beginning of everything will only be when all that dead wood is gone from me, when I no longer wait for the fridge next door to stop its quaking, when my wife's face will mean nothing to me and Lisbet is forgotten – a cell before conception conceiving an undrawn face, an erased past.

Day Twelve. I've calculated that it must be Boxing Day. I meant to phone Lisbet and my wife on Christmas, but anyway I have no money for the phone. Low on fuel. Serendip throws a pot of tea leaves into the canal, to add to the swill. Spent the morning contemplating the cycle the tea must have made from India to the docks, etc. Do the tides here stretch to India?

. . . I glimpse him more and more. His guard down. Can hear him pumping his primus.

I only quote these references as last vestiges of attempts to affirm my existence.

. . . A fire last night. Must be out of fuel for his bloody machine . . .

I must learn to conserve, like him. Must learn to extract blood from the stone.

Lost track of the days. Snow falls. I think it is the new year already – last night I heard shouting miles away and hooting from over the river, Greenwich way. A heavy snowfall in the night, filling all the ledges.

I shovel the bloody stuff off, crack the surface of my bucket with a stick. Cold dark. Once I found a champagne bottle in the gutter. New Year's morning, and the champagne was frozen solid. Remember those trapped bubbles. Dark green glass, the sea.

Went down to the Thames this morning. The first clear day for weeks – but *bitter*. The water still kicks against the canal sides and at high tide the tyres rub down and up endlessly. By the bank I found a fruit bun in a paper bag. The cold and staleness had made it rock hard, but in my mouth it begins to thaw. Rolled those scrumptious currants over the tongue. Eyeing the tide and my threadbare mittens. Can't describe the luxury of freedom these chill, emptied mornings.

Lisbet would say that to abandon oneself to subjectivity neutralises judgement.

I no longer can tell. I barely know who I am. That rare starting point. Only where I am.

Good Advice is Rarer than Rubies

SALMAN RUSHDIE

ON THE LAST Tuesday of the month, the dawn bus brought Miss Rehana to the gates of the British Embassy. It arrived pushing a cloud of dust, veiling her beauty from the eyes of strangers until she descended. The bus was brightly painted in multicoloured arabesques, and on the front it said 'MOVE OVER DARLING' in green and gold letters; on the back it added 'TATA-BATA' and also 'OK. GOOD-LIFE.' Miss Rehana told the driver it was a beautiful bus, and he jumped down and held the door open for her.

Miss Rehana's eyes were large and black and shiny enough not to need the help of antimony, and when the advice expert Muhammad Ali saw them he felt himself becoming young again. He watched her approach the embassy gates and heard her ask the lala who guarded them when they would open. The lala usually enjoyed insulting the embassy's Tuesday-women, but he spoke to Miss Rehana with something approaching courtesy. 'Half an hour,' he said gruffly. 'Maybe two hours. Who knows? The sahibs are eating their breakfast.'

The dusty compound between the bus stop and the embassy was already full of Tuesday-women, some veiled, a few barefaced like Miss Rehana. They all looked frightened, and leaned heavily on the arms of uncles or brothers, who were trying to look confident. But Miss Rehana had come on her own, and did not seem at all alarmed. Muhammad Ali, who specialised in advising the most vulnerable-looking of these weekly supplicants, found his feet leading him towards the strange, big-eyed, independent girl.

'Miss,' he began. 'You have come for permit to London, I think so?' She was standing at a hot-snack stall in the little shantytown by the edge of the compound munching chili-pakoras contentedly. She turned to look at him, and at close range those eyes did bad things to his digestive tract.

'Yes, I have.'

'Then please, you allow me to give some advice? Small cost only.'

Miss Rehana smiled. 'Good advice is rarer than rubies,' she said. 'But I cannot pay. I am an orphan, not one of your wealthy ladies.'

'Trust my grey hairs,' Muhammad Ali told her. 'My advice is well tempered by experience. You will certainly find it good.'

She shook her head. 'I tell you I am poor. There are women here with male relatives, all earning good wages. Go to them. Good advice should find good money.'

I am going crazy, Muhammad Ali thought, because he heard his voice telling her of its own volition, 'Miss, I have been drawn to you. This is fated. I too am a poor man only, but for you my advice comes free.'

She smiled again. 'Then I must surely listen. When fate sends a gift, one receives good fortune.'

He led her to the low wooden desk in his own special corner of the shantytown. She followed, still smiling, eating pakoras from a little newspaper packet. She did not offer him any. He put a cushion on the dusty ground. 'Please to sit.' She did as he asked. He sat cross-legged across the desk from her, conscious that two or three dozen male eyes were watching him enviously, that all the other shantytown men were ogling the latest young lovely to be charmed by the old greyhair Muhammad Ali. He took a deep breath to settle himself.

'Name, please.'

'Miss Rehana,' she told him. 'Fiancée of Mustafa Dar of Bradford, London.'

'Bradford, England,' he corrected her gently. 'London is a city only, like Multan or Bahawalpur. England is a great nation full of the coldest fish in the world.'

'I see,' she responded gravely, so that he was unsure if she was making fun of him.

'You have filled application form? Then let me see, please.'

She passed him a neatly folded document in a brown envelope.

'Is it OK?' For the first time there was a note of anxiety in her voice.

He patted the desk quite near the place where her hand rested. 'I am certain,' he said. 'Wait on and I will check.'

She finished her pakoras while he scanned her papers.

'Tip-top,' he pronounced finally. 'All in order.'

'Thank you for your advice,' she said. 'I'll go now and wait by the gate.'

'What are you thinking?' he cried loudly, smiting his forehead. 'You consider this is easy business? Just give the form and poof, with a big smile they hand over the permit? Miss Rehana, I tell you you are entering a worse place than any police station.'

'Is it so, truly?' His oratory had done the trick. She was a captive audience now, and he would be able to look at her for a few moments longer. Drawing another calming breath, he launched into his speech. He told her that the sahibs thought all the women who came on Tuesdays, claiming to be dependants of bus drivers in Luton or chartered accountants in Manchester, were crooks and liars and thieves.

She protested, 'But then I will simply tell them that I, for one, am no such thing!'

Her innocence made him shiver with fear for her. She was a sparrow, he told her, and they were men with hooded eyes, like eagles. He explained that they would ask her questions, personal questions, questions such as a lady's own brother would be shy to ask. They would ask if she was a virgin, and, if not, what her fiancé's lovemaking habits were, and what secret nicknames they had invented for one another. Muhammad Ali spoke brutally, on purpose, to lessen the shock she would feel when it actually happened. Her eyes remained steady, but her hands began to flutter at the edges of the desk.

He went on. 'They will ask you how many rooms in your family home, and what colour are the walls, and what days do you empty the rubbish; they will ask your man's mother's third cousin's aunt's stepdaughter's middle name. And all these things they have already asked your Mustafa Dar in his Bradford. And if you make one mistake, you are finished.'

'Yes,' she said, and he could hear her disciplining her voice. 'And what is your advice, wise old man?'

It was at this point that Muhammad Ali usually began to

whisper, to mention that he knew a man, a very good type, who worked in the embassy, and for a fee all the necessary papers could be delivered, with all the proper authentic seals. It was a good business, because the women would often pay him five hundred rupees or give him a gold bracelet for his pains and go away happy. They came from hundreds of miles away – he always checked this before he tricked them – so even when they discovered how they had been swindled they were very unlikely to return. They went away to Sargodha or Lalu Khet and began to pack, and who knows at what point they found out they had been gulled, but it was at a too late point anyway. Life is hard, and an old man must live by his wits. It was not up to Muhammad Ali to have compassion for these Tuesday-women.

But once again his voice betrayed him, and instead of starting his customary speech it began to reveal to her his greatest secret. 'Miss Rehana,' his voice said, and he listened to it in amazement, 'you are a rare person, a jewel, and for you I will do what I would not do for my own daughter, perhaps. One document has come into my possession that can solve your worries at a stroke.'

'And what is this sorcerer's paper?' she asked, her eyes unquestionably laughing at him now.

His voice fell low-as-low. 'Miss Rehana, it is a British passport. Completely genuine and pukka goods. I have a good friend who will put your name into it and then, hey-presto, England there you come!'

He had said it! Anything was possible now, on this day of his insanity. Probably he would give her the thing free-gratis, and then kick himself for a year afterwards. Old fool, he told himself, the oldest fools are bewitched by the youngest girls.

'Let me understand you,' she was saying. 'You are proposing I should commit a crime, and go to Bradford, London, illegally, and so justify the low opinion the embassy sahibs have of us all. Old babuji, this is not good advice.'

'Bradford, *England*,' he corrected her mournfully. 'You should not take my gift in such a spirit. I am a poor fellow and I have offered this prize because you are so beautiful. Do not spit on my generosity. Take the thing. Or else don't take, go home, forget England, only do not go in that building and lose your dignity.'

But she was on her feet, turning, walking away towards

the gates, where the women had begun to cluster and the lala was swearing at them to be patient or none of them would be admitted.

'Be a fool,' Muhammad Ali shouted after her. 'It is the curse of our people. We are poor, we are ignorant, and we refuse completely to learn.'

'Hey, Muhammad Ali,' the woman at the betel-nut stall shouted to him. 'Too bad, she likes them young.'

That day Muhammad Ali did nothing but stand around the embassy gates. Many times he told himself, Go from here, fool, the lady does not wish to speak with you any further. But when she came out she found him waiting.

She seemed calm, and at peace with him again, and he thought, My God, she has pulled it off. The British sahibs have also been drowning in her eyes, and she has got her passage to England. He smiled at her; she smiled back with no trouble at all.

'Miss Rehana Begum,' he said, 'felicitations, daughter, on what is obviously your hour of triumph.'

Impulsively, she took his forearm in her hand. 'Come,' she said. 'Let me buy you a pakora to thank you for your advice and to apologise for my rudeness, too.'

They stood in the dust of the afternoon compound near the bus, which was getting ready to leave. Coolies were tying bedding rolls to the roof. A hawker shouted at the passengers, trying to sell them love stories and green medicines. Miss Rehana and happy Muhammad Ali ate their pakoras sitting on the front bumper.

'It was an arranged engagement,' Miss Rehana said suddenly. 'I was nine years old when my parents fixed it. Mustafa Dar was already thirty then, but my parents knew they were dying and wanted someone who could look after me. Then two months after they died he went to England and said he would send for me. That was many years ago. I have his photo, but I do not know what his voice sounds like. He is like a stranger to me.'

The confession took Muhammad Ali by surprise, but he nodded with what he hoped looked like wisdom. 'Still and all,' he said, 'one's parents act in one's best interests. They found you a good honest man who has kept his word and sent for you. And now you have a lifetime to get to know him, and to love.'

427

He was puzzled, now, by the bitterness that had infected her smile.

'But, old man,' she asked him, 'why have you already packed me and posted me off to England?'

He stood up, shocked. 'You looked happy, so I just assumed . . . They turned you down?'

'I got all their questions wrong,' she replied. 'Distinguishing marks, bathroom décor, all. Now I will go back to Lahore and my job. I work in a great house, as ayah to three good boys. They would be sad to see me leave.'

'But this is tragedy!' Muhammad Ali lamented. 'Oh, how I pray that you had taken up my offer! Now it is not possible. They have your form on file, cross-check can be made, even the passport will not suffice. It is spoilt, all spoilt, and it could have been so easy.'

'I do not think,' she told him as she climbed aboard the bus and gave a wave to the driver, 'I truly do not think you should be sad.'

Her last smile, which he watched from the compound until the bus concealed it in a dust cloud, was the happiest thing he had ever seen in his long, hot, hard, unloving life.

Good Friday, 1663

HELEN SIMPSON

We have a winding sheet in our mother's womb, which grows with us from our conception, and we come into the world, wound up in that winding sheet, for we come to seek a grave.

MY RUSTIC HUSBAND, preferring to be fifty years behind the times in church matters as in all else, has ordered Parson Snakepeace to preach only sermons from the old dead Divines, and to read them aloud without comment. This being Good Friday, he has chosen the horridest sermon he could find, all to do with death and earthworms.

Lord, I'm sure I am grown quite melancholy at that old barbarous tale of the thorn crown and the sponge in vinegar. Ha, ha, ha!

This church is as cold as the grave. You would not know the air was so gentle outside, all the daffodils kissing the air and the apple trees like brides.

Here, by my pew, lies my husband's mother, Myrtilla Fanshawe, twenty-six years old, d. 1634, boxed up in fine Carrara:

> God's goodness made her wise and well-beseeming
> Her wifely virtues won her much esteeming,
> Earth would not yield more pleasing earthly bliss
> Blest w'two babes, though Death brought her to this.

That shallow space over there, beneath the window showing

St Catherine, is reserved for *my* tomb. I insist on a chaste design. None of your beastly seraphim, mind; I never could endure your marble flittermice.

Myrtilla died in childbed, bearing that blockhead my husband. He sits beside me now pretending to listen to the sermon, his mouth catching flies, a pure clown, mere elementary earth, without the least spark of soul in him. That he should have claimed *me* for his wife! He would be more fitly mated with some silly, simple, peeking, sneaking country girl, one that goes with her toes in, and can't say boo to a goose.

I cannot endure him near me, with his sweating, snoring, scratching, snap-finger ways. He'll sit and yawn, and stretch like a greyhound by the fireside, till he does some nasty thing or other and so gives me an excuse to leave the room. When he has blown his nose into his handkerchief, he looks into it as if there were a diamond dropped out of his head.

There in the womb we are fitted for works of darkness, all the while deprived of light: and there in the womb we are taught cruelty, by being fed with blood, and may be damned, though we be never born.

To confine a woman just at her rambling age! take away her liberty at the very time she should use it! O barbarous aunt! O unnatural father!

My aunt Champflower is a very violent lady. She will fall into a fit or fly at you for the least piddling insignificant thing. In her day she was a beauty, but now she washes her face and hands in lead varnish to hide the dismal hollows of eight and thirty years.

The patches on her white lead face, some big, some little, look like so many raisins and currants floating in a porringer of rice-milk.

Lord, what a difference there is between me and her. How I should despise such a thing if I were a man. What a nose she has! what a chin! what a neck! She desired my ruin with all her little heart. She danced for pure joy at my wedding.

My father never would have heard Scandal's buzz had she only kept it from him. He would have let me look where I pleased for a husband. I have a tidy fortune. But no, I must be thrown away in haste to this clodpole squire.

My aunt calls me to her room and talks of Honour and Reputation with a long face like the beast of the Nile.

'Aye, aye,' says I. 'But what has such talk to do with me?'

'What indeed!' cries she in a passion.

She pauses. She trifles with a lace some time before she speaks next, making play with a certain letter, reading it to herself with a careless dropping lip and an erected brow, humming it hastily over.

I recognise the hand. It is from my Celadon.

'Well, niece, this galloping abroad and allowing young fellows to fool with you has given your reputation no very good complexion.'

'Madam, I seek only to follow your example. Besides, I have heard it said often and often when I was with you in London, that a lady's reputation ought to be a sort of brunette; then it has an attraction in it, like amber. A white reputation is as disagreeable to men, I am sure I have heard you say twenty times or more, as white eyebrows or white eyelashes.'

'Pooh pooh,' says she with a sort of snarling smile. 'You can talk in that airy impertinent way until Domesday but it will not save you. I have other letters. Your fop delights in nothing but rapes and riots, as all the world well knows. I have heard certain tales. I have ocular proof.'

'Madam,' says I, though I start to feel a little uneasy now, 'there are some persons who make it their business to tell stories, and say this and that of one and t'other, and everything in the world; and,' says I . . .

'And your father shall know all,' she finishes.

Our birth dies in infancy, and our infancy dies in youth, and youth and the rest die in age, and age also dies, and determines all. O, huzza, Parson Snakepeace; cheerful matter for an April morning! Our youth is hungry and thirsty, after those sins, which our infancy knew not; and our age is sorry and angry, that it cannot pursue those sins which our youth did.

I shall never more see the playhouse, nor go to Ponchinello nor Paradise, nor take a ramble to the Park nor Mulberry Garden. I could as soon persuade my husband to share a sillybub in New Spring Garden or to drink a pint of wine with friends at the Prince in the Sun as I could fly.

My aunt Champflower took me with her to London last

year for a spring holiday. We lodged near by St James's, and I never was so happy in all my life.

I dote upon assemblies, adore masquerades, my heart bounds at a ball; I love a play to distraction, cards enchant me, and dice put me out of my little wits.

On our third evening, then, we saunter to the pleasure gardens at Ranelagh for the sake of the Chinese lanterns and to taste a dish of oysters.

There we happen to meet again with a certain merry sharking fellow about the town, who has pursued us diligently from chocolate house to milliner to the Haymarket since our arrival. He has with him a friend; and this friend is Celadon.

'I came up, Sir, as we country-gentlewomen use, at an Easter Term,' explains my aunt demurely, 'to the destruction of tarts and cheesecakes, to see a new play, buy a new gown, take a turn in the Park, and so down again to sleep with my forefathers.'

'We see you have brought your sister with you in kindness,' says Celadon, giving me a mighty wink.

The two fine gallants pay her gross and lavish compliments, ogling and glancing and watching any occasion to do forty officious things. They have all the appearance of gentlemen about them. I notice that Celadon's eyes look sideways on me like an Egyptian drawing. He wears a fine long periwig tied up in a bag.

My aunt curtseys at last. Down goes her diving body to the ground, as if she were sinking under the conscious load of her own attractions; then launches into a flood of fine language, still playing her chest forward in fifty falls and risings, like a swan upon waving water.

Hang me if she has not conceived a violent passion for the fellow.

. . . when my mouth shall be filled with dust, and the worm shall feed, and feed sweetly upon me, when the ambitious man shall have no satisfaction, if the poorest alive tread upon him, nor the poorest receive any contentment in being made equal to Princes, for they shall be equal but in dust.

I look down now at my arms and see the fine eggshell skin with a pretty sparkle from the sun, and the violet-coloured veins at my wrist. I cannot think I am dust and worms' meat.

The carnation dew, the pouting ripeness of my honeycomb mouth, he said; and that my face was a swarm of cupids.

I do love Love. I would have all the Love in the world. What should I mind else, while I have any share of youth and beauty? When I went to Court all eyes were upon me, all tongues were whispering that's my Lord Spatchcock's fine daughter; all pressed towards me and bowed, only to get half a glance from me. When I went to the playhouse, some stood gazing on me, with their arms across their heads languishing as oppressed by beauty. The brisker fellows combed their wigs and prepared their eyes to tilt with mine. Ah, flattery was my daily bread.

Celadon is so agreeable a man, so eloquent, so unaffected, so particular, so easy, so free. All his finery is from the best in Paris – his shoes from Piccar and his gloves from Orangerie. He wears his clothes with so becoming a negligence that I can barely wish him out of them. He even soaks his handkerchief in rose water.

He had the greatest skill in arranging assignations that ever I saw; and all the while he flattered my aunt with a thousand honeyed words and promises, until I was ready to burst with laughing.

My hair was dressed in flaunting little ringlets and crimped serpentaux puffs. I wore my new under-petticoats of white dimity, embroidered like a turkey-work chair with red, green, blue and yellow, with a pin-up coat of Scotch plaid adorned with bugle lace and my gown of printed calico.

I carried my claret-coloured velvet coat with gold fringes to protect me from the dangers of the night air. Even in spring, jaunting abroad at four in the morning strikes a chill into the bones.

Parson Snakepeace has conceived the pretty notion of keeping a skull upon his desk.

I can never persuade myself that religion consists in scurvy out-of-fashion clothes and sour countenances, and when one walks abroad, not to turn one's head to the right or left, but hold it straight forward like an old blind mare.

'O that I were your lover for a month or two,' he murmured in my ear like a bumble bee.

'What then?'

'I would make that pretty heart's blood of yours ache in a fortnight.'

433

*That God, this Lord, the Lord of life could die, is a strange
contemplation; that the red sea could be dry, that the sun could
stand still, that an oven could be seven times heat and not burn, that
lions could be hungry and not bite, is strange, miraculously strange,
but supermiraculous that God could die.*

The most unnatural spectacle to be seen in Somerset since
the Flood was surely my union with Squire Clodpole here.
A dainty girl of seventeen yoked to a greasy, untoward, ill-
natured, slovenly wretch! We were the laughing stock of five
counties.

Now it is five months since our wedding, which I should
rather call a show of Merry-Andrews, with nothing pleasant
about it at all but the foolery of a farce.

The nuptial banquet was crammed with baskets of plum-
cake, Dutch gingerbread, Cheshire cheese, Naples biscuits,
macaroons, neats' tongues and cold boiled beef.

My new husband had drunk heartily. The guests cried out
for a speech. He staggered to his feet.

'My head aches consumedly,' said he; 'I am not well.'

'Good-lack!' said I, 'if those fellows in France don't press
all the grapes with their filthy naked feet. No wonder we are
poisoned with their wine.'

He raised his glass to me, then toppled over behind the table.

There was such a laughing, they roared out again. The
ladies teehee'd under their napkins. The teehee took a reverend
old gentlewoman as she was drinking, and she squirted the beer
out of her nose, as an Indian does tobacco.

By the time the bashful bride, meaning myself, was brought
to bed, this numbskull had in some wise recovered his wits.

He called for a mouthful of something to stay his stomach,
a tankard of usquebaugh with nutmeg and sugar, if you please,
and also a toast and some cheese.

Faugh, the filthy brute.

'Supper, sir!' said I. 'Why, your dinner is not out of
your mouth yet; at least 'tis all about the brims of it.'

That sharp comment confounded him, so that he cursed,
and rolled about the bedchamber like a sick passenger in a
storm; then he comes flounce into bed, dead as a salmon in a
fishmonger's basket, his feet cold as ice and his breath hot as a
furnace.

His head is a fool's egg which lies hid in a nest of hair. He hangs his nose in my neck and talks to me whether I will or no. What a poor sordid slavery there is in the state of marriage.

During our brief courtship, he wailed out some songs of love.

> 'I have a mistress that is fair
> And as sweet as sugar candy,
> Had I ten thousand pounds a year
> I'd give her half a pint of brandy.'

And all the while he gazes on me like a sick monster, with languishing eyes.

I burst into laughter: 'Lord, sir, you have such a way with you, ha, ha, ha!'

At night He went into the garden to pray, and He spent much time in prayer. I dare scarce ask thee whither thou wentest, or how thou disposedst of thy self, when it grew dark and after last night. That has set my husband a-tittering. Now he nudges me with his elbow, the filthy fellow. I have no stomach for him. *About midnight He was taken and bound with a kiss, art thou not too conformable to Him in that? Is not that too literally, too exactly thy case? at midnight to have been taken and bound with a kiss?*

Yes, yes, Parson Snakepeace, I was taken captive in a garden, at my lady Wildsapte's last summer *fête champestre*, though I cannot see why you should make a sermon of it, for it had nothing to do with you or your talk of the grave.

We went chasing off by the light of torches down an alley of trees, shamming to fight each other with long hazel twigs.

My lady's grounds are full of little pagan temples and other fancies, and at last we fell down breathless at the foot of a pretty Egyptian obelisk brought back by her son from his late stay in Rome. Screened by the friendly shade of some low bushes, we fell breathless upon the ground together; the leaves around us were of the crimson flowering currant for I can still recall the sharp smell when we bruised 'em by lying upon 'em.

'Cherubimical lass,' he called me, and gazed on me devouringly. Our eye beams were in that moment tangled beyond redemption, and I could not bring myself to draw away when he caught me by the hand, wringing and squeezing at it as if he were mad.

He offered me no other rudeness at first, but we only gazed on each other with half smiles; and our breathing grew laboured when we twisted and knotted our fingers together as if in combat. Then indeed my bounding blood beat quick and high alarms.

He swore that he would come down from London in a fortnight, and marry me.

And so we progressed until, with broken murmurs and heart-fetched sighs, he so mousled and tousled me that I cried, 'Sweetheart!' and he clapped a hand over my mouth to save us from discovery.

Good gods! What a pleasure there is in doing what we should not do.

Then were we animated by the strongest powers of love, and every vein of my body circulated liquid fires; until we came at last to that tumultuous momentary rage of which so much has been whispered since the world began.

O Jesu, when I think back to the heat of his sweet mouth and the smell of his skin, I could weep for weeks together.

Hang him, let him alone. He's gone.

Hast thou gone about to redeem thy sin, by fasting, by Alms, by disciplines and mortifications, in the way of satisfaction to the Justice of God? that will not serve, that's not the right way, we press an utter crucifying of that sin that governs thee; and that conforms thee to Christ.

Well, I am eight months gone with child. I may follow Mrs Myrtilla's example more speedily than expected. That would indeed be a convenient conclusion, to be dispatched by my own sin. That would provide matter enough for a month of fine long thundering sermons.

This husband sits beside me like a ball and chain. A pack of squalling infants will do the rest, forging my bonds link by link, and soon I shall inhabit as heavy a carcass as my sister Sarah's. Then will I keep company with the mid-wife, dry-nurse, wet-nurse, and all the rest of their accomplices, with cradle, baby-clouts and bearing clothes, possets, caudles, broth, jellies and gravies. Pish, I grow nauseous when I think of them.

I may build castles in the air, and fume and fret, and grow pale and ugly, if I please; but nothing will bring back my free and airy time.

Outside this church it is almost summer; see how the sun struggles through these coloured glass saints to fall in jewels onto my gown.

I will not die of the pip, so I will not.

O merciful God, who hast made all men, and hatest nothing that thou hast made, nor wouldest the death of a sinner, but rather that he should be converted and live; have mercy upon all Jews, Turks, infidels, and Hereticks, and take from them all ignorance, hardness of heart, and contempt of thy Word; and so fetch them home, blessed Lord, to thy flock, that they may be saved among the remnant of the true Israelites, and be made one fold under one shepherd, Jesus Christ our Lord, who liveth and reigneth with thee and the Holy Spirit, one God, world without end. Amen.

Stalin, Stalin, and Stalin

JONATHAN TREITEL

THE FIRST ANNUAL meeting of the Stalin's Doubles (Ret.) Association took place in the banquet chamber of the Great Hall of the Union, Moscow, in the autumn of 1953. An historic occasion. Columns of porphyry and marble flanked the dining space. An electric chandelier bestowed its myriad lights. The long, burnished table was set with gilt-rimmed crystal glasses, stiff napkins monogrammed with the hammer and sickle, and silver caviar dishes. And, of course, occupying one entire wall, looming over us, a larger-than-life full-length portrait of Him.

Since He had passed away only a few months earlier, this was the first opportunity we had to meet one another in a social setting. Some of us, who had worked in the more isolated regions of the country, had never encountered another Stalin before, and indeed it was not rare for an individual to believe he was the unique specimen in existence (apart from the original, that is).

It should be stressed that we were not literally identical in appearance. After all, His image was known only through idealised portraits and touched-up photographs, plus the occasional blurry news film, so no one expected a Stalin in person to resemble the iconic version too exactly. Besides, several of us had already shaved off the moustache and restyled the hair. To take an extreme example, the lone woman present (Stalin XXVII; real name Olga Kirov, from Vladivostok) would scarcely have been recognisable as a former look-alike at all, now that she had ungummed her moustache and gone in for a blonde perm, were it not for a certain squareness about the jaw and coldness in the eyes.

General conversation, first. We mingled. We did our best to work out who was who, and what aspect of His life (military, agricultural, penological, etc.) we had each been involved in. Fortunately a course in mnemonic techniques had been an integral part of our training – it is vital for a double to know whom to shake hands with, whom to salute, whom to kiss on both cheeks, whom to stride by without a glance – so we were able to link names to faces without too much difficulty. Amazing little coincidences kept coming to light: for example, Stalin XI had addressed a conference of five-year-plan-surpassing peasants in Tselinograd at precisely the same moment as Stalin III had favoured a similar gathering with his presence in Semipalatinsk!

Time to take our places around the long mahogany table. The organiser of the event, Stalin IV (real name Moshe Segal, from Vitebsk), gave a short speech. He was, it turned out, the only one among us still employed in the old profession. He assured us he was kept busy posing for deathbed scenes, and what with the motherland being perpetually threatened by imperialists and traitors, and given that the succession was disputed between Malenkov and Khrushchev, he had every expectation that the demand for busts, dioramas, and so forth would remain strong for some years to come. While his present work (he conceded) could scarcely be compared with the thrill of standing in for the live Leader, he felt honoured to have been and to continue to be cf service, and he was confident we all shared in this emotion. (*Applause.*) It was the logic of history that had brought Stalin to the forefront and it was the logic of history that demanded Stalin should have doubles. (*Loud cheers and unanimous cries of affirmation.*)

We rose to our feet. Vodka was distributed; the carafes were passed always to the left. Glasses were raised. 'Comrades. To Him!' The toast was drunk; then, as one man, we hurled the crystal over our shoulders, and it smashed against the walls and the pillars and littered the floor with iridescent shards.

Now we were more at ease. Each of us in turn narrated: My Most Memorable Experience. The Stalin voice (a raspy Georgian accent) was employed by some, while others preferred to use their everyday voices. And in any case certain doubles had been purely visual, such as Stalin XVI (real name Rahim Muhamadov, from Baku), a simple soul, who knew just a few words of Russian: *Hello. Comrade. Thank you.* In many cases the reminiscences were touching. Stalin V had visited a military hospital in the aftermath of the siege of Leningrad: wounded soldiers had cheered him to high heaven; there had been tears in his eyes. Others partook of the comic. Stalin XXI had been patting a baby in a collective-farm kindergarten near Krasnoyarsk when the baby had turned and bit him on the webby part of his hand between index finger and thumb. He had had to restrain himself from crying out, lest an overzealous bodyguard dispose of the baby and its family. Still others shed a novel light on Him. Few people know, for instance, that throughout the Potsdam Conference He suffered from a painful boil on His back (so Stalin IX informed us), or that (according to Stalin XXII) He sometimes chewed His toothbrush. A handful of Stalins seemed to misunderstand the point of sharing these testimonies. Stalin XV sang a little song about the beauties of the birch forest. Stalin XXX told us how much he loved his wife.

Then the organiser recited: 'Ode to Iosif Vissarionovich Dzhugashvili.' More toasts were drunk: 'To the Party!' 'To Malenkov!' 'To Khrushchev!' 'To History!' The caviar was eaten. Georgian champagne fizzed eloquently. A simple but satisfying meal appeared on the table and was consumed.

And at the end the organiser stood up and declared that though originally this meeting had been planned as a one-time event, since it had been such a roaring success, why should we not come back the following year, and the year after that, and so on *ad infinitum*? (*Resounding applause.*) 'His spirit lives on!'

Some of the Stalins who hailed from the more distant republics suggested that the next session should convene outside Moscow. The point was well taken. Where, then? Stalingrad was mooted, as symbolically appropriate. Also proposed were Stalinsk and Stalino. However, the three locations that seemed to command the widest support were the cities known subsequently as Brasov, Varna, and Donetsk, but named at that time, respectively, Stalin, Stalin, and Stalin. After much discussion, it was agreed that we should reconvene the following year in Stalin.

The 1954 meeting was on a smaller and in some ways more

intimate scale than the previous year's. The table was round. A plaster bust of Him was arranged as a centrepiece on a bed of dried ferns and thorny foliage. Hardly so many doubles showed up, since the travel distance was prohibitive for some, and others had more pressing engagements. As for those who did come, their resemblance to the original had decreased, partly owing to the ageing process (Stalin XIV had developed alarming jowls, and Stalin XIX was halfway bald) and partly to changes in masculine fashions. But such things are only to be expected: if Stalin Himself were alive today, He would not be so very much like Stalin.

The usual toasts were drunk: 'To the Party!' 'To Khrushchev!' 'To Malenkov!' 'To Stalin!' 'To History!' The lumpfish caviar was much appreciated. The white wine was poured into elegant, slender glasses. For all the air of bonhomie, however, the meeting was not going with quite the swing of the previous year's – it is always a mistake, arguably, to try to repeat past successes – until Stalin XII (real name Sergei Balin, from Moscow), currently employed as a telephonist at the Institute for Agronomical Development, revealed the outcome of his researches. He explained he had been working on a hunch that Stalin surely could not have been the only statesman to have possessed doubles: he had been undertaking an investigation to contact the stand-ins for other world leaders.

We held our breath. We glanced toward the swinging doors: two butlers stood on duty with grenades in hand. At any moment, we fantasised, a score of Churchills and Roosevelts could march in, re-creating the Yalta Conference many times over. Or might there still be some surviving Lenins – even a handful of mock Trotskys hiking in from Siberia?

Balin held up his hand. He regretted that, for all his diligence, he had been unable to find evidence of visual doubles, but – and here he switched on a loudspeaker system connected to the international switchboard – he had on the line a certain Norman Jones from London. Jones came over loud and clear for the most part – just a little crackly sometimes, and accompanied by a strange, watery echo. He greeted us in Russian and then announced that he had been a Churchill in his time. Nothing too grand, mind you – he just used to read speeches on the wireless, and record orations previously given by the real Prime Minister, for subsequent retransmission to the United States and the colonies. He delighted us with a medley of his all-time favourites: 'Blood, toil, tears, and sweat,' 'Some chicken. Some neck,' 'We shall fight on the beaches,' and so forth. His 'An iron curtain has descended across the Continent' was perhaps not altogether in the best of taste . . . But even those of us who could not understand English were duly impressed by Jones's immaculate growl and lisp, and his virtuoso imitation of the sucking of saliva through false teeth.

And what about the American? Surely Roosevelt, that poor invalid, must have sent in stuntmen to cope with his more pressing engagements? But apparently not. At least no deutero-Roosevelt had so far come to light. Besides, as Stalin VIII (real name Boris Backev, from Kiev) pointed out, if Roosevelt had possessed a double, the President would never have been permitted to 'die' at such an inconvenient moment in 1945 – the double would have stood in until the conclusion of the war, at least.

At this suggestion, the same thought ran through all our heads: why did *He* have to die? Surely any one of us in this room could have done a passable job as Chairman of the Party and Leader of the State. We could have carried on the torch. Why, indeed, need He ever die? New generations of doubles could be selected and trained – rendering Him virtually immortal.

The connection from England had been cut, and the wine had run out. It was time for us all to go home.

The third meeting took place in a back room in the regional Party headquarters at Stalin (not the same Stalin as the previous year's location) in October of 1955. Perhaps it had been poorly advertised, or there were difficulties with the hotel reservations, for only a dozen or fifteen doubles showed up. A colour reproduction of Stalin was framed on the wall above the samovar. In some ways, you could say, this was a more friendly, a more confidential occasion. The toasts were repeated several times ('To the Party!' 'To Krushchev!' 'To Stalin!' 'To History!'). Caviar was not available this year, but the bortsch was exceptional. Some of the more jovial, not to say rowdy, Stalins participated in an informal competition to imitate His facial expressions – the generous smile, the air of concern at the fate of His people, the jolly-worker-just-like-you chuckle, the grim glare. The prize, supplied by Stalin XIII, was a cut-throat razor still clotted with soap and a few bristles from His chin. It was won by Stalin XV, largely on the strength of the almost frightening verisimilitude of his stern stare-into-the-middle-distance.

Stalin XXII (real name Iosif Zaharudov, from Ulan Bator) stood up and cleared his throat. He declared he felt called upon to say a few words lamenting the comparative lack of interest in Stalin among the youth of today. For instance, the heroic acts He performed in His childhood (combating the hoarder, foiling the incipient capitalist, denouncing the spy) are no longer taught to schoolchildren as paradigms of socialist behaviour. Although the spirit of this contribution was in accord with our general thinking, it was felt by many of us that it was perhaps too serious, too melancholy even, for what was, after all, supposed to be a festive occasion.

We departed early.

The 1956 session was the last. We all knew that. Originally, it had been scheduled for September in a police barracks in one of the cities called Stalin, but the city had changed its name the previous month – a bad omen, surely – and, besides, the prospective attendance was down.

So on a wintry October evening we came, less than ten of us, up the three flights of stairs and along the narrow corridor into the cramped living room of Stalin IV's apartment in a Moscow suburb. We sat on the acid-green sofa and on rickety kitchen chairs; a few latecomers had to slump on the rug. A black-and-white photograph of Stalin was stapled to the side of the bookcase.

What had happened was that in February Khrushchev had denounced Stalin's 'crimes' in the course of a long, fiery speech at a closed session of the Twentieth Party Congress. To be sure, this speech had officially remained secret, but everybody knew.

No one wanted to be the first to break the silence. Eventually Stalin IV, who had arranged the first triumphal meeting of our association three years earlier, mumbled, 'I never said He was perfect.' And we all agreed that everybody is human, and mistakes will happen, and no doubt even He made the occasional error of judgement.

Stalin XII recalled that he had delivered a fiery speech in court denouncing Sirin as a Trotskyite agent, and probably Sirin was innocent after all. Well, it is easy to be wise in retrospect.

And each of us had similar anecdotes. Stalin VI had played

his part in several show trials of officers in the vicinity of Vladivostok in 1937–38, knowing full well they could not *all* have been Japanese spies, monarchists, sodomites, and so forth.

Stalin XXX, who had told us three years before how much he loved his wife, had had to denounce his father-in-law.

Stalin XVII had even been responsible for the arrest of another double (Stalin XVIII [deceased]) as a Zinovievite deviationist.

In fact, not one of us could claim to have doubled for only the better side of Stalin's personality. We all were tainted. But it is not as if (we argued) we were individually responsible. Doubtless, had we been acting *in propriis personis*, we would not have dreamed of behaving so brutally, but we had simply been doing what Stalin Himself would have done, had He been able to spare the time.

But was that really the whole story? Stalin VI recalled how several times, when he had been given only the vaguest instructions – for example, to attend a show trial and give the usual kind of testimony – he had fulminated viciously against the defendant, whereas, in fact, a milder reproof might well have been acceptable. And each of us could think of similar instances from his own experience. Indeed, looking back, we realised we had been given quite a free hand in the construction of the role, and possibly we had exaggerated the bloodthirstiness.

In fact, on reflection, we doubles had been responsible for a number of the more tragic aspects of that sorry era. It might have been that Stalin Himself was reasonably gentle. If only we had not misunderstood!

The bottle of vodka had rolled under the sofa, so it had to be kicked into the open. Shots were poured into glasses and cups and tooth mugs and bowls. Nobody felt like toasting Stalin or Khrushchev or the Party. Finally somebody blurted, 'To History!' and we all drank to that.

Two of Them

ROSE TREMAIN

WE USED TO be a family of three: my mother, Jane, my father, Hugh and me, Lewis. We lived in a house in Wiltshire with a view of the Downs. At the back of the house was an old grey orchard.

Then we became a family of two and three-quarters. I was fourteen when this happened. The quarter we lost was my father's mind. He had been a divorce solicitor for twenty years. He said to me: 'Lewis, human life should be symmetrical, but it never is.' He said: 'The only hope for the whole bang thing lies in space.' He said: 'I was informed definitively in a dream that on Mars there are no trinities.'

My mother searched for the missing bit of my father's mind in peculiar places. She looked for it in cereal packets, in the fridge, in the photographs of houses in *Country Life*. She became distracted with all this searching. One winter day, she cried into a bag of chestnuts. She said: 'Lewis, do you know what your father's doing now?'

She sent me out to find him. He was on our front lawn, measuring out two circles. When he saw me he said: 'Capital. You're good at geometry. Hold this tape.'

The circles were enormous – thirty feet in diameter. There were two of them. 'Luckily,' said my father, 'this is a damn large lawn.' He held a mallet. He marked out the circles by driving kindling sticks into the grass. When he'd finished, he said: 'All right. That's it. That's a good start.'

445

I was a weekly boarder at my school. In the weekdays, I didn't mention the fact that my father had gone crazy. I tried to keep my mind on mathematics. At night, in the dormitory, I lay very still, not talking. My bed was beside a window. I kept my glasses on in the darkness and looked at the moon.

My mother wrote to me once a week. Before we'd lost a quarter of one third of our family, she'd only written every second week because my father wrote in the weeks in between. Now, he refused to write any words anywhere on anything. He said: 'Words destroy. Enough is enough.'

My mother's letters were full of abbreviations and French phrases. I think this was how she'd been taught to express herself in the days when she'd been a débutante and had to write formal notes of acceptance or refusal or thanks. 'Darling Lewis,' she'd put, 'How goes yr maths and alg? Bien, j'espère. Drove yr f. into Sibury yest. Insisted buying tin of white gloss paint and paint gear, inc roller. Pourquoi? On verra bientôt, sans doute. What a b. mess it all is. You my only consol. and hope now.'

The year was 1955. I wished that everything would go back to how it had been.

In mathematics, there is nothing that cannot be returned to where it has been.

I started to have embarrassing dreams about being a baby again – a baby with flawless eyesight, lying in a pram and watching the sky. The bit of sky that I watched was composed of particles of wartime air.

I didn't want to be someone's only consolation and hope. I thought the burden of this would probably make me go blind. I wished I had a sister, someone who could dance for my parents and mime to their favourite songs.

When I got home one weekend, there were two painted crosses inside the circles on the lawn. They were white.

My father had taken some of the pills that were supposed to give him back the missing part of his mind and he was asleep in a chair, wearing his gardening hat.

'Look at him!' said my mother. 'I simply don't know what else is to be done.'

My mother and I went out and stood on the white crosses. I measured them with my feet. 'They're landing pads,' said my mother, 'for the supposed spaceship from Mars.'

I said: 'They're exactly sixteen by sixteen – half the diameter of the circles.'

We sat down on them. It was a spring afternoon and the air smelled of blossom and of rain. My mother was smoking a Senior Service. She said: 'The doctors tell me it might help if we went away.'

'Where to?' I asked.

'I don't know where to. I don't suppose that matters. Just away somewhere.'

I said: 'Do you mean France?'

'No,' she said. 'I think he might be worse abroad. Don't you? And the English are better about this kind of thing; they just look the other way.'

'Where, when?'

I was thinking of all the weekends I was going to have to spend alone in the empty school, if my parents left home without me. Sometimes, boys were stuck there with nothing to do for two days. A friend of mine called Pevers once told me he'd spent a total of seventeen hours throwing a tennis ball against a wall and catching it.

'What about the sea?' said my mother. 'You'd like that, wouldn't you?'

'You mean, in the summer?'

'Yes, darling,' she said. 'I couldn't manage anything like that without you.'

So then it was strange. What I thought next was that it might be better to throw a ball against a wall for seventeen hours than to be by the sea with my father watching the horizon for Martians and my mother reminding me that I was her only hope and consolation.

I got up and measured the crosses again. I said: 'They're absolutely symmetrical. That means he can still do simple calculations.'

'What about Devon or Cornwall?' said my mother. 'They get the Gulf Stream there. Something might blow in. One can never tell.'

My father woke up. The pills he was taking made his legs tremble, so he sat in his chair, calling my name: 'Lewis! Lewis! Boy!'

I went in and kissed his cheek, which was one quarter unshaved, as if the razor had a bit of itself missing. He said: 'Seen the landing sites, old chap?'

'Yes,' I said. 'They're brilliant.'

'*Two*,' he said triumphantly.

'How did you know how big to make them?'

'I didn't. I'm guessing. I think there'll be two craft with four fellas in each, making eight. So I doubled this and came up with sixteen. Seems about right. Everything with them is paired, perfectly weighted. No triangles. No discord. No argy–bargy.'

I waited. I thought my father was going to tell me how the Martians could set about saving the world after they'd landed on our front lawn, but he didn't.

'What do they eat?' I asked.

My father took off his gardening hat and stared at it. 'I don't know,' he said. 'I overlooked that.' And he began to cry.

'It won't matter,' I said. 'We can drive into Salisbury and buy masses of whatever it turns out to be. It's not as though we're poor, is it?'

'No,' he said. He put his hat back on and wiped his eyes with his fists.

My mother found a summer holiday house for us in north Cornwall. It was out on a promontory on a wild hill of gorse. From the front of it, all you could see was the beach and the ocean and the sky, but from the back – the way my bedroom faced – you could see one other house, much larger than ours. It was made of stone, like a castle. It had seven chimneys.

On our first day, I found that a narrow path led up from our house directly to it. I climbed it. I could hear people laughing in the garden. I thought, if I was a Martian, I would land on this castle roof and not on our lawn in Wiltshire; I would go and join the laughing people; I would say, 'I see you have a badminton net suspended between two conveniently situated trees.'

My parents didn't seem to have noticed this other house. Wherever they were, they behaved as though that spot was the centre of the universe.

On our first evening, they stood, hand in hand at the french windows, looking out at the sunset. I sat on a chair behind them, watching them and hearing the sea far below them. My mother said to my father: 'Do you like it here, Hugh?'

My father said: 'Beach is ideal. Just the place. Better than the bloody lawn.'

That night, when I was almost asleep, he came into my room and said: 'I'm counting on you, Lewis. There's work to be done in the morning.'

'What work?' I said.

'I'm counting on you,' he repeated. 'You're not going to let me down, are you?'

'No,' I said. 'I'm not going to let anybody down.'

But then I couldn't sleep. I tried throwing an imaginary tennis ball against an imaginary wall until the morning came.

We made circles in the sand. I was supposed to calculate the exact spot where the sun would go down, as though we were building Stonehenge. My father wanted the sun to set between the two circles.

My mother sat in a deckchair, wearing a cotton dress and sunglasses with white frames. My father took some of his pills and went wandering back to the house. My mother went with him, carrying the deckchair, and I was left alone with the work of the circles. They had to have sculpted walls, exactly two feet high. All that I had to work with was a child's spade.

I went swimming and then I lay down in the first half-made circle and floated into one of my dreams of previous time. I was woken by a sound I recognised: it was the sound of the castle laughter.

I opened my eyes. Two girls were standing in my circle. They wore identical blue bathing costumes and identical smiles. They had the kind of hair my mother referred to as 'difficult' – wild and frizzy. I lay there, staring up at them. They were of identical height.

'Hello,' I said.

One of them said: 'You're exhausted. We were watching you. Shall we come and help you?'

I stood up. My back and arms were coated with sand. I said: 'That's very kind of you.' Neither of them had a spade.

'What's your name?' they said in unison.

I was about to say 'Lewis.' I took my glasses off and pretended to clean them on my bathing trunks while I thought of a more castle-sounding name. 'Sebastian,' I said.

'I'm Fran,' said one of them.

'I'm Isabel,' said the other.

'We're twins,' said Fran, 'as if you hadn't guessed.' And they laughed.

They were taller than me. Their legs were brown. I put my glasses back on, to see whether they had a bust. It was difficult to tell, because their swimming costumes were ruched and lumpy all over.

'We're fourteen,' said Fran. 'We're actresses and playwrights. What are you, Sebastian?'

'Oh,' I said, 'nothing yet. I might be a mathematician later on. What are your plays about?'

'You can be in one with us, if you like,' said Isabel. 'Do you want to be in one?'

'I don't know,' I said.

'We only do it for fun,' said Fran. 'We just do them and forget them.'

'I don't expect I've got time,' I said. 'I've got to get these circles finished.'

'Why?' said Isabel. 'What are they for?'

'Oh,' I said, 'for my father. He's doing a kind of scientific experiment.'

'We've never met any scientists,' said Isabel. 'Have we, Fran?'

'We know tons of sculptors, though,' said Fran. 'Do you like sculpture?'

'I don't know,' I said. 'I've never thought about it.'

'We'll go and get our spades,' said Isabel, 'shall we?'

'Thanks,' I said. 'That's jolly kind.'

They ran off. Their difficult hair blew crazily about in the breeze. I watched them till my eyesight let them vanish. I felt out of breath – almost faint – as though I'd run with them into the distance and disappeared.

That night, my mother got drunk on Gin and It. She had never explained to me what 'It' was. She expected me to know thousands of things without ever being told them. She said: 'Listen Lewis, the tragedy of your father is a tragedy of *imagination*. N'est-ce pas? You see what I mean, darling? If he'd just concentrated on the Consent Orders and the Decrees and so on, this would never have happened. But he didn't. He started to imagine the *feelings*. You see?'

She was scratching her thigh through her cotton dress. Some of the Gin and It had spilled on to her knee. 'So, listen,' she said. 'In your coming life as a great mathematical person, just stick to your *numbers*. Okay? Promise me? You're my only hope now, darling, my only one. I've told you that, haven't I? So don't *start*. Promise me?'

'Start what?'

'What I'm saying is, stick to your own life. *Yours*. Just stay inside that. All right? Your mathematical life. Promise?'

'Yes,' I said. 'What does "It" stand for, Mummy?'

'What does what?'

' "It". What does it stand for?'

' "It"? It's just a *name*, sweetheart. A name for a thing. And names can make Mummy so happy, or so, you know . . . the other thing. Like your father, Hugh. Darling Hughie. Mostly the other thing now. All the time. So promise and that's it. Understood.'

'I promise,' I said.

The next day my father came to inspect the circles. Only one was finished. Just beyond the finished one was a sand sculpture of a bird. Fran and Isabel and I had stayed on the beach for hours and hours, creating it. They had made its body and wings and I had made its feet.

The bird was huge. It had a stone for an eye. My father didn't notice it. He was admiring the circle. 'Good,' he said. 'Now the other one. I'll give you a hand. Because the time's coming. I can feel it. I've been watching the sky.'

I worked with the child's spade and my father worked with his hands. The sight of his red hands scooping and moulding the sand made me feel lonely.

I waited all day for Fran and Isabel to come. At tea time, it began to rain and I knew they'd be up in the castle, doing a play to pass the time. The rain fell on the bird and speckled it.

It rained for two days. My parents tried to remember the rules of Ludo. I walked in the rain up the path as far as the castle shrubbery, where I sat and waited. I stared at the droopy badminton net. I counted its holes. And then I walked back down the path and went into the room where my mother and father sat and closed the door. They'd abandoned the Ludo game. They were just sitting there, waiting for me to return.

That night, I wrote a note to Isabel and Fran:

Dear Isabel and Fran,
When is your next play? I would like to be in it, if you
still want me to be.
Yours sincerely,
  Sebastian

I set my alarm for four o'clock and delivered the note as
the sky got light and the larks in the gorse began singing.

When the good weather came back, my father and I mended
the circle walls beaten down by the rain. My mother watched
us from her deckchair, wearing shorts. Her legs looked very
pale. Sometimes, she went to sleep, behind her glasses.

My father seemed very restless and excited. He said: 'It's
going to be soon, Lewis. And at night. I'm going to peg
down two sheets in each of the circles, I've checked the moon.
Visibility should be fair.'

'Good,' I said.

'I'm as prepared as I can be, thanks to you. Bar the food
question. But your mother will cope with that. And there's
always fish. Fish is a universal; it must be. But there's one
other important thing.'

'What?' I said.

'You've got to be there. Your mother thinks this is a lot of
drivel, so she won't come. So I'm counting on you. They want
to see two of us. I'm as certain of that as I can be of anything. If
there's only me, they'll take off again and go back to Mars.'

'Right,' I said.

But I wasn't really listening to him. My mind was on
Isabel and Fran who had sent me an answer to my note:

Dear Sebastian,
The first rehearsal for our next play is going to be in a tent
we've pitched between our house and yours. Friday evening.
Ten o'clock. Bring a glass.
Yours faithfully,
  Isabel and Fran

Ten o'clock was the bedtime of our family of two and three
quarters. When we'd been three, it had been later. Now, my
parents preferred sleep to life. In a dream, you can be transported
back in time.

I tried to imagine saying: 'Goodnight, Mummy. Good night, Dad. I'm going to a play rehearsal now,' but I couldn't. If you are the hope and consolation of anyone alive, you can't go to play rehearsals without warning.

So, I knew what I would have to do. I would have to wait until the house was silent and then creep out of it without being heard and find my way to the tent in the moonlight, remembering first to go into the kitchen and find a glass. The thought of this made me feel very hot and weak. I sat down on the sand, with my arms on my knees.

'What are you doing, boy?' said my father.

'Resting,' I said. 'Only for a moment.'

I stood at my bedroom window. There was a thin moon. Bright but thin.

It was 10.18 by my watch.

I could hear my mother coughing. She said the cough came from the sea air.

At ten thirty exactly, I let myself out of my room and closed my door. I stood on the landing, listening. There was no coughing, no sound of anything.

I went downstairs, holding my shoes. I tried to glide soundlessly, like filmstars glide into rooms.

I got a glass from the kitchen and unlocked the back door and went out into the night. I was wearing a grey shirt and grey flannel trousers and the thing I could imagine most easily was all my grey veins going into my heart.

I moved up the path. I couldn't see the tent, but I could hear laughing – castle laughter. My mind seemed to be in holes, like a badminton net.

The tent was small. I'd imagined a kind of marquee. This tent was low and tiny. It was pitched on a little clearing in the gorse.

I bent down and called softly: 'Isabel? Fran?'

The laughter stopped. I could hear them whispering. 'I've come for the rehearsal,' I said.

There was silence. Then they giggled. Then Fran stuck her frizzy head out. 'You're late,' she said.

I began to explain and apologise.

'Ssh,' said Fran. 'Sound carries. Come inside.'

She opened the little flap of the tent and took hold of my hand and pulled me in.

It was pitch dark in the tent and very hot. I felt blind.
Fran said: 'Did you bring a glass?' Isabel said: 'Can you see
us, Sebastian?'

There was a familiar smell in the little bit of air left in
me to breathe in; it was the smell of gin.

'You like gin, don't you?' said Isabel.

'I don't know,' I said. 'My mother drinks Gin and It.'

They began giggling again. Now, I could see two soft white
shapes, one either side of me. One was Fran and one was Isabel.
They were wearing identical white nightdresses. Isabel handed
me a glass of gin. She said: 'It's quite comfortable, don't you
think? We stole masses of cushions. Try the gin.'

'And lie down,' said Fran. 'Relax.'

I took a sip of the gin. I felt it go into my veins.

I lay down, holding my glass in the air. I felt a hand on my
face. I didn't know whether it was Fran's or Isabel's. The hand
removed my spectacles.

'Don't,' I said.

'We've got to,' said Isabel.

'Why?' I said.

'That's the rehearsal,' said Fran.

'What do you mean?'

'Well,' said Fran, 'don't you want to rehearse?'

'You mean the play?'

'Yes. It's a kind of play, isn't it, Isabel?'

'Yes,' said Isabel.

'Except that there are two of us and only one of you and
in the real future, when it's no longer a play, it won't be like
that. But it's okay, because we're so alike that in the dark you
won't be able to tell which of us is which.'

'What do you mean?' I said. I let my glass tilt deliberately,
splashing gin on to my face. The taste of it was beautiful.

They giggled. I felt the skirts of their nightdresses cover my
legs, like feathers. Then I saw both their faces above mine and
their crazy hair touched my forehead and my cheek.

'Come on, Sebastian,' they whispered. 'There's nothing difficult about it.'

I walked back to our house just as it was getting light.

From high up, I could see my parents on the little front
lawn, wearing their dressing gowns and clinging together.

When they saw me, they stared at me in horror. Then my

father broke away from my mother and came roaring at me. My mother followed, trying to catch him and hold him back.

'Hughie!' she screamed. 'Don't! Don't!'

But she couldn't catch him. He hit me on the jaw and I fell to earth.

I woke up in hospital, with a wire like a dog's muzzle round my face. I couldn't utter a word.

My mother was sitting by me. She looked pale and tired.

Later, she said: 'It wasn't only that we were worried, Lewis. There was the Martian business. He told me he saw them land. He saw them from his window. And he went running to find you and you weren't there, and then, as soon as he arrived on the beach, they took off again. He thought it was because there was only one of him. And then he was in despair. He felt you'd let him down and let the world down.'

I went back to school. I could move my jaw. Autumn came.

My head had emptied itself of equations and filled up with the faces and bodies of Isabel and Fran.

My father went away. My mother wrote: 'They say it's just for a while, until all's well. But I know that the only *all's well* is you.'

The night after I got this letter, I had a dream. I was at home in Wiltshire, standing in the old, grey orchard.

I saw something come out of the sky and land on the lawn. It was a shadowy thing, without shape or measurable angle, and I knew what it was: it was my life and it was a thing of no hope and no consolation. I wanted to send it into the clouds, but it stayed there, just where it was, blotting out all the further hills.

Cocktails at Doney's

WILLIAM TREVOR

'YOU'VE FORGOTTEN ME,' were the first words Mrs Faraday spoke to him in the Albergo San Lorenzo. She was a tall, black-haired woman, wearing a rust-red suede coat cut in an Italian style. She smiled. She had white, even teeth, and the shade of her lipstick appeared subtly to match the colour of her coat. Her accent was American, her voice soft, with a trace of huskiness. She was thirty-five, perhaps thirty-seven, certainly not older. 'We met a long time ago,' she said, smiling a little more. 'I don't know why I never forget a face.'

She was married to a man who owned a paper mill near some town in America he'd never heard of. She was a beautiful woman, but he could remember neither her nor her husband. Her name meant nothing to him and when she prompted him with the information about her husband's business he could not remember any better. Her eyes were brown, dominating her classic features.

'Of course,' he lied politely.

She laughed, clearly guessing it was a lie. 'Well, anyway,' she said, 'hullo to you.'

It was after dinner, almost ten o'clock. They had a drink in the bar since it seemed the natural thing to do. She had to do with fashion; she was in Florence for the Pitti Donna; she always came in February.

'It's nice to see you again. The people at these trade shows can be tacky.'

'Don't you go to the museums as well? The churches?'

'Of course.'

When he asked if her husband accompanied her on her excursions to Florence she explained that the museums, the churches, and the Pitti Donna would tire her husband immensely. He was not a man for Europe, preferring local race-tracks.

'And your wife? Is she here with you?'

'I'm actually not married.'

He wished he had not met Mrs Faraday. He didn't care for being approached in this manner, and her condemnation of the people at the trade exhibitions she spoke of seemed out of place since they were, after all, the people of her business world. And that she was married to a man who preferred race-tracks to culture was hardly of interest to a stranger. Before their conversation ended he was certain they had not ever met before.

'I have to say good-night,' he said, rising when she finished her drink. 'I tend to get up early.'

'Why, so do I!'

'Good-night, Mrs Faraday.'

In his bedroom he sat on the edge of his bed, thinking about nothing in particular. Then he undressed and brushed his teeth. He examined his face in the slightly tarnished looking-glass above the wash-basin. He was fifty-seven, but according to this reflection older. His face would seem younger if he put on a bit of weight; chubbiness could be made to cover a multitude of sins. But he didn't want that; he liked being thought of as beyond things.

He turned the looking-glass light out and got into bed. He read *Our Mutual Friend* and then lay for a moment in the darkness. He thought of Daphne and of Lucy – dark-haired, tiny Lucy who had said at first it didn't matter, Daphne with her pale-blue, trusting eyes. He had blamed Daphne, not himself, and then had taken that back and asked to be forgiven; they were both of them to blame for the awful mistake of a marriage that should never have taken place, although later he had said that neither of them was, for how could they have guessed they were not suited in that way? It was with Lucy he had begun to know the truth; poor Lucy had suffered more.

He slept, and dreamed he was in Padua with a friend of another time, walking in the Botanical Gardens and explaining to his friend that the tourist guides he composed were

457

short-lived in their usefulness because each reflected a city
ephemerally caught. 'You're ashamed of your tourist guides,'
his friend of that time interrupted, Jeremy it was. 'Why *are* the
impotent so full of shame, my dear? Why *is* it?' Then Rosie was
in the dream and Jeremy was laughing, playfully, saying he'd
been most amusingly led up the garden path. 'He led me up it
too, my God,' Rosie cried out furiously. 'All he could do was
weep.'

*Linger over the Giambologna birds in the Bargello, and the marble
reliefs of Mino da Fiesole. But that's enough for one day; you must
return tomorrow.*

He liked to lay down the law. He liked to take chances with
the facts, and wait for letters of contradiction. *At the height of the
season there are twelve times as many strangers as natives in this dusty,
littered city. Cascades of graffiti welcome them – the male sexual organ
stylised to a Florentine simplicity, belligerent swastikas, hammers and
sickles in the streets of gentle Fra Angelico . . .*

At lunchtime on the day after he had met her Mrs Faraday
was in Doney's with some other Americans. Seeing her in
that smart setting, he was surprised that she stayed in the
Albergo San Lorenzo rather than the Savoy or the Excelsior.
The San Lorenzo's grandeur all belonged to the past: the old
hotel was threadbare now, its curtains creased, its telephones
unresponsive. Not many Americans liked it.

'Hi!' she called across the restaurant, and smiled and waved
a menu.

He nodded at her, not wishing to seem stand-offish. The
people she was with were talking about the merchandise they
had been inspecting at the Pitti Donna. Wisps of their conversation drifted from their table, references to profit margins and
catching the imagination.

He ordered tagliatelle and the chef's salad, and then looked
through the *Nazione*. The body of the missing schoolgirl,
Gabriella, had been found in a park in Florence. Youths who'd
been terrorising the neighbourhood of Santa Croce had been
identified and arrested. Two German girls, hitchhiking in the
south, had been made drunk and raped in a village shed. The
Nazione suggested that Gabriella – a quiet girl – had by chance
been a witness to drug-trafficking in the park.

'I envy you your job,' Mrs Faraday said, pausing at his table
as he was finishing his tagliatelle. Her companions had gone on

ahead of her. She smiled, as at an old friend, and then sat down. 'I guess I want to lose those two.'

He offered her a glass of wine. She shook her head. 'I'd love another cappuccino.'

The coffee was ordered. He folded the newspaper and placed it on the empty chair beside him. Mrs Faraday, as though she intended to stay a while, had hung her red suede coat over the back of the chair.

'I envy you your job,' she said again. 'I'd love to travel all over.'

She was wearing pearls at her throat, above a black dress. Rings clustered her fingers, earrings made a jangling sound. Her nails were shaped and painted, her face as meticulously made up as it had been the night before.

'Did you mind,' she asked when the waiter had brought their coffee, 'my wondering if you were married?'

He said he hadn't minded.

'Marriage is no great shakes.'

She lit a cigarette. She had only ever been married to the man who owned the paper mill. She had had one child, a daughter who had died after a week. She had not been able to have other children.

'I'm sorry,' he said.

She looked at him closely, cigarette smoke curling between them. The tip of her tongue picked a shred of tobacco from the corner of her mouth. She said again that marriage was no great shakes. She added, as if to lend greater weight to this:

'I lay awake last night thinking I'd like this city to devour me.'

He did not comment, not knowing what she meant. But quite without wishing to he couldn't help thinking of this beautiful woman lying awake in her bedroom in the Albergo San Lorenzo. He imagined her staring into the darkness, the glow of her cigarette, the sound of her inhaling. She was looking for an affair, he supposed, and hoped she realised he wasn't the man for that.

'I wouldn't mind living the balance of my life here. I like it better every year.'

'Yes, it's a remarkable city.'

'There's a place called the Palazzo Ricasoli where you can hire apartments. I'd settle there.'

'I see.'

'I could tell you a secret about the Palazzo Ricasoli.'

459

'Mrs Faraday –'

'I spent a week there once.'

He drank some coffee in order to avoid speaking. He sighed without making a sound.

'With a guy I met at the Pitti Donna. A countryman of yours. He came from somewhere called Horsham.'

'I've never been to Horsham.'

'Oh, my God, I'm embarrassing you!'

'No, not at all.'

'Gosh, I'm sorry! I really am! Please say it's all right.'

'I assure you, Mrs Faraday, I'm not easily shocked.'

'I'm an awful shady lady embarrassing a nice Englishman! Please say you forgive me.'

'There is absolutely nothing to forgive.'

'It was a flop, if you want to know.' She paused. 'Say, what do you plan to write in your guidebook about Florence?'

'Banalities mostly.'

'Oh, come *on*!'

He shrugged.

'I'll tell you a nicer kind of secret. You have the cleverest face I've seen in years!'

Still he did not respond. She stubbed her cigarette out and immediately lit another. She took a map out of her handbag and unfolded it. She said:

'Can you show me where Santo Spirito is?'

He pointed out the church and directed her to it, warning her against the motorists' signs which pursued a roundabout one-way route.

'You're very kind.' She smiled at him, lavishly exposing her dazzling, even teeth as if offering a reward for his help. 'You're a kind person,' she said. 'I can tell.'

He walked around the perimeter of the vast Cascine Park, past the fun-fair and the zoo and the race-track. It was pleasant in the February sunshine, the first green of spring colouring the twiggy hedges, birches delicate by the river. Lovers sprawled on the seats or in motor-cars, children carried balloons. Stalls sold meat and nuts, and Coca-Cola and 7-Up. Runners in training-suits jogged along the bicycle track. *Ho fame* a fat young man had scrawled on a piece of cardboard propped up in front of him, and slept while he waited for charity.

Rosie, when she'd been his friend, had said he wrote about

Italian cities so that he could always be a stranger. Well, it was true, he thought in the Cascine Park, and in order to rid himself of a contemplation of his failed relationship with Rosie he allowed the beauty of Mrs Faraday to become vivid in his mind. Her beauty would have delighted him if her lipstick-stained cigarettes and her silly, repetitious chattering didn't endlessly disfigure it. Her husband was a good man, she had explained, but a good man was not always what a woman wanted. And it had come to seem all of a piece that her daughter had lived for only a week, and all of a piece also that no other children had been born, since her marriage was not worthy of children. It was the Annunciations in Santo Spirito she wanted to see, she had explained, because she loved Annunciations.

'Would it be wrong of me to invite you to dinner?' She rose from a sofa in the hall of the Albergo San Lorenzo as soon as she saw him, making no effort to disguise the fact that she'd been waiting for him. 'I'd really appreciate it if you'd accept.'

He wanted to reply that he would prefer to be left alone. He wanted to state firmly, once and for all, that he had never met her in the past, that she had no claims on him.

'You choose somewhere,' she commanded, with the arrogance of the beautiful.

In the restaurant she ate pasta without ceasing to talk, explaining to him that her boutique had been bought for her by her husband to keep her occupied and happy. It hadn't worked, she said, implying that although her fashion shop had kept her busy it hadn't brought her contentment. Her face, drained of all expression, was lovelier than he had so far seen it, so sad and fragile that it seemed not to belong to the voice that rattled on.

He looked away. The restaurant was decorated with modern paintings and was not completely full. A squat, elderly man sat on his own, conversing occasionally with waiters. A German couple spoke in whispers. Two men and a woman, talking rapidly in Italian, deplored the death of the schoolgirl, Gabriella.

'It must have been extraordinary for the Virgin Mary,' Mrs Faraday was saying. 'One moment she's reading a book and the next there's a figure with wings swooping in on her.' That only made sense, she suggested, when you thought of it as the Virgin's dream. The angel was not really there, the Virgin herself was not really reading in such plush surroundings. 'Later I

461

WILLIAM TREVOR

guess she dreamed another angel came,' Mrs Faraday continued,
'to warn her of her death.'

He didn't listen. The waiter brought them grilled salmon
and salad. Mrs Faraday lit a cigarette. She said:

'The guy I shacked up with in the Palazzo Ricasoli was
no better than a gigolo. I guess I don't know why I did that.'

He did not reply. She stubbed her cigarette out, appearing
at last to notice that food had been placed in front of her. She
asked him about the painters of the Florentine Renaissance, and
the city's aristocrats and patrons. She asked him why Savonarola
had been burnt and he said Savonarola had made people feel
afraid. She was silent for a moment, then leaned forward and
put a hand on his arm.

'Tell me more about yourself. Please.'

Her voice, eagerly insistent, irritated him more than before.
He told her superficial things, about the other Italian cities for
which he'd written guidebooks, about the hill towns of Tuscany,
and the Cinque Terre. Because of his reticence she said when he
ceased to speak:

'I don't entirely make you out.' She added that he was nicer
to talk to than anyone she could think of. She might be drunk;
it was impossible to say.

'My husband's never heard of the Medicis nor any stuff
like this. He's never even heard of Masaccio, you appreciate
that?'

'Yes, you've made it clear the kind of man your husband is.'

'I've ruined it, haven't I, telling you about the Palazzo
Ricasoli?'

'Ruined what, Mrs Faraday?'

'Oh, I don't know.'

They sat for some time longer, finishing the wine and having
coffee. Once she reached across the table and put her hand on
one of his. She repeated what she had said before, that he was
kind.

'It's late,' he said.

'I know, honey, I know. And you get up early.'

He paid the bill, although she protested that it was she
who had invited him. She would insist on their having dinner
together again so that she might have her turn. She took his
arm on the street.

'Will you come with me to Maiano one day?'

'Maiano?'

462

'It isn't far. They say it's lovely to walk at Maiano.'

'I'm really rather occupied, you know.'

'Oh, God. I'm bothering you! I'm being a nuisance! Forget Maiano. I'm sorry.'

'I'm just trying to say, Mrs Faraday, that I don't think I can be much use to you.'

He was aware, to his embarrassment, that she was holding his hand. Her arm was entwined with his and the palms of their hands had somehow come together. Her fingers, playing with his now, kept time with her flattery.

'You've got the politest voice I ever heard! Say you'll meet me just once again? Just once? Cocktails tomorrow? Please.'

'Look, Mrs Faraday –'

'Say Doney's at six. I'll promise to say nothing if you like. We'll listen to the music.'

Her palm was cool. A finger made a circular motion on one of his. Rosie had said he limped through life. In the end Jeremy had been sorry for him. Both of them were right; others had said worse. He was a crippled object of pity.

'Well, all right.'

She thanked him in the Albergo San Lorenzo for listening to her, and for the dinner and the wine. 'Every year I hope to meet someone nice in Florence,' she said on the landing outside her bedroom, seeming to mean it. 'This is the first time it has happened.'

She leaned forward and kissed him on the cheek, then closed her door. In his looking-glass he examined the faint smear of lipstick and didn't wipe it off. He woke in the night and lay there thinking about her, wondering if her lipstick was still on his cheek.

Waiting in Doney's, he ordered a glass of chilled Orvieto wine. Someone on a tape, not Judy Garland, sang *Over the Rainbow*; later there was lightly played Strauss and some rhythms of the thirties. By seven o'clock Mrs Faraday had not arrived. He left at a quarter to eight.

The next day he wandered through the cloisters of Santa Maria Novella, thinking again about the beauty of Mrs Faraday. He had received no message from her, no note to explain or apologise for her absence in Doney's. Had she simply forgotten? Or had someone better materialised? Some younger man she again hadn't been able to resist, some guy who didn't know any more about Masaccio than her good husband did? She was a woman who was always falling in love, which was what she called it, confusing love with sensuality. Was she, he wondered, what people referred to as a nymphomaniac? Was that what made her unhappy?

He imagined her with some man she'd picked up. He imagined her, satisfied because of the man's attentions, tramping the halls of a gift market, noting which shade of green was to be the new season's excitement. She would be different after her lovemaking, preoccupied with her business, no time for silliness and Annunciations. Yet it still was odd that she hadn't left a message for him. She had not for a moment seemed as rude as that, or incapable of making up an excuse.

He left the cloisters and walked slowly across the piazza of Santa Maria Novella. In spite of what she'd said and the compliments she'd paid, had she guessed that he hadn't listened properly to her, that he'd been fascinated by her appearance but not by her? Or had she simply guessed the truth about him?

That evening she was not in the bar of the hotel. He looked in at Doney's, thinking he might have misunderstood about the day. He waited for a while, and then ate alone in the restaurant with the modern paintings.

'We pack the clothes, *signore*. Is the carabinieri which can promote the enquiries for *la signora*. *Mi dispiace, signore*.'

He nodded at the heavily moustached receptionist and made his way to the bar. If she was with some lover she would have surfaced again by now: it was hard to believe that she would so messily leave a hotel bill unpaid, especially since sooner or later she would have to return for her clothes. When she had so dramatically spoken of wishing Florence to devour her she surely hadn't meant something like this? He went back to the receptionist.

'Did Mrs Faraday have her passport?'

'*Si, signore. La signora* have the passport.'

He couldn't sleep that night. Her smile and her brown, languorous eyes invaded the blur he attempted to induce. She crossed and re-crossed her legs. She lifted another glass. Her ringed fingers stubbed another cigarette. Her earrings lightly jangled.

In the morning he asked again at the reception desk. The

hotel bill wasn't important, a different receptionist generously allowed. If someone had to leave Italy in a hurry, because maybe there was sickness, even a deathbed, then a hotel bill might be overlooked for just a little while.

'*La signora* will post to us a cheque from the United States. This the carabinieri say.'

'Yes, I should imagine so.'

He looked up in the telephone directory the flats she had mentioned. The Palazzo Ricasoli was in Via Mantellate. He walked to it, up Borgo San Lorenzo and Via San Gallo. '*No*,' a porter in a glass kiosk said and directed him to the office. '*No*,' a pretty girl in the office said, shaking her head. She turned and asked another girl. '*No*,' this girl repeated.

He walked back through the city, to the American Consulate on the Lungarno Amerigo. He sat in the office of a tall, lean man called Humber, who listened with a detached air and then telephoned the police. After nearly twenty minutes he replaced the receiver. He was dressed entirely in brown, suit, shirt, tie, shoes, handkerchief. He was evenly tanned, another shade of the colour. He drawled when he spoke; he had an old-world manner.

'They suggest she's gone somewhere,' he said. 'On some kind of jaunt.' He paused in order to allow a flicker of amusement to develop in his lean features. 'They think maybe she ran up her hotel bill and skipped it.'

'She's a respectable proprietor of a fashion shop.'

'The carabinieri say the respectable are always surprising them.'

'Can you try to find out if she went back to the States? According to the hotel people, that was another theory of the carabinieri.'

Mr Humber shrugged. 'Since you have told your tale I must try, of course, sir. Would six-thirty be an agreeable hour for you to return?'

He sat outside the Piazza della Repubblica, eating tortellini and listening to the conversations. A deranged man had gone berserk in a school in Rome, taking children as hostages and killing a janitor; the mayor of Rome had intervened and the madman had given himself up. It was a terrible thing to have happened, the Italians were saying, as bad as the murder of Gabriella.

He paid for his tortellini and went away. He climbed up

465

to the Belvedere, filling in time. Once he thought he saw her, but it was someone else in the same kind of red coat.

'She's not back home,' Mr Humber said with his old-world lack of concern. 'You've started something, sir. Faraday's flying out.'

In a room in a police station he explained that Mrs Faraday had simply been a fellow guest at the Albergo San Lorenzo. They had had dinner one evening, and Mrs Faraday had not appeared to be dispirited. She knew other people who had come from America, for the same trade exhibitions. He had seen her with them in a restaurant.

'These people, sir, return already to the United States. They answer the American police at this time.'

He was five hours in the room at the police station and the next day he was summoned there again and asked the same questions. On his way out on this occasion he noticed a man who he thought might be her husband, a big blond-haired man, too worried even to glance at him. He was certain he had never met him, or even seen him before, as he'd been certain he'd never met Mrs Faraday before she'd come up to him in the hotel.

The police did not again seek to question him. His passport, which they had held for fifty-six hours, was returned to him. By the end of that week the newspaper references to a missing American woman ceased. He did not see Mr Faraday again.

'The Italian view,' said Mr Humber almost a month later, 'is that she went off on a sexual excursion and found it so much to her liking that she stayed where she was.'

'I thought the Italian view was that she skipped the hotel. Or that someone had fallen ill.'

'They revised their thinking somewhat. In the light of various matters.'

'What matters?'

'From what you said, Mrs Faraday was a gallivanting lady. Our Italian friends find some significance in that.' Mr Humber silently drummed the surface of his desk. 'You don't agree, sir?'

He shook his head. 'There was more to Mrs Faraday than that,' he said.

'Well, of course there was. The carabinieri are educated men, but they don't go in for subtleties, you know.'

'She's not a vulgar woman. From what I said to the police

they may imagine she was. Of course she's in a vulgar business. They may have jumped too easily to conclusions.'

Mr Humber said he did not understand. 'Vulgar?' he repeated.

'Like me, she deals in surface dross.'

'You're into fashion yourself, sir?'

'No, I'm not. I write tourist guides.'

'Well, that's most interesting.'

Mr Humber flicked at the surface of his desk with a forefinger. It was clear that he wished his visitor would go. He turned a sheet of paper over.

'I remind sightseers that pictures like Pietro Perugino's *Agony in the Garden* are worth a second glance. I send them to the Boboli Gardens. That kind of thing.'

Mr Humber's bland face twitched with simulated interest. Tourists were a nuisance to him. They lost their passports, they locked their ignition keys into their hired cars, they were stolen from and made a fuss. The city lived off them, but resented them as well. These thoughts were for a moment openly reflected in Mr Humber's pale brown eyes and then were gone. Flicking at his desk again, he said:

'I'm puzzled about one detail in all this. May I ask you, please?'

'Yes, of course.'

'Were you, you know, ah, seeing Mrs Faraday?'

'Was I having an affair, you mean? No, I wasn't.'

'She was a beautiful woman. By all accounts, by yours, I mean, sir, she'd been most friendly.'

'Yes, she was friendly.'

She was naive for an American, and she was careless. She wasn't fearful of strangers and foolishly she let her riches show. Vulnerability was an enticement.

'I did not mean to pry, sir,' Mr Humber apologised. 'It's simply that Mr Faraday's detectives arrived a while ago and the more they can be told the better.'

'They haven't approached me.'

'No doubt they conclude you cannot help them. Mr Faraday himself has returned to the States: a ransom note would be more likely sent to him there.'

'So Mr Faraday doesn't believe his wife went off on a sexual excursion?'

'No one can ignore the facts, sir. There is indiscriminate kidnapping in Italy.'

'Italians would have known her husband owned a paper mill?'

467

'I guess it's surprising what can be ferreted out.' Mr Humber examined the neat tips of his fingers. He re-arranged tranquillity in his face. No matter how the facts he spoke of changed there was not going to be panic in the American Consulate. 'There has been no demand, sir, but we have to bear in mind that kidnap attempts do often nowadays go wrong. In Italy as elsewhere.'

'Does Mr Faraday think it has gone wrong?'

'Faraday is naturally confused. And, of course, troubled.'

'Of course.' He nodded to emphasise his agreement. Her husband was the kind who would be troubled and confused, even though unhappiness had developed in the marriage. Clearly she'd given up on the marriage; more than anything, it was desperation that made her forthright. Without it, she might have been a different woman – and in that case, of course, there would not have been this passing relationship between them: her tiresomeness had cultivated that. 'Tell me more about yourself,' her voice echoed huskily, hungry for friendship. He had told her nothing – nothing of the shattered, destroyed relationships, and the regret and shame; nothing of the pathetic hope in hired rooms, or the anguish turning into bitterness. She had been given beauty, and he a lameness that people laughed at when they knew. Would her tiresomeness have dropped from her at once, like the shedding of a garment she had thought to be attractive, if he'd told her in the restaurant with the modern paintings? Would she, too, have angrily said he'd led her up the garden path?

'There is our own investigation also,' Mr Humber said, 'besides that of Faraday's detectives. Faraday, I assure you, has spared no expense; the carabinieri file is by no means closed. With such a concentration we'll find what there is to find, sir.'

'I'm sure you'll do your best, Mr Humber.'

'Yes, *sir*.'

He rose and Mr Humber rose also, holding out a brown, lean hand. He was glad they had met, Mr Humber said, even in such unhappy circumstances. Diplomacy was like oil in Mr Humber. It eased his movements and his words; his detachment floated in it, perfectly in place.

'Goodbye, Mr Humber.'

Ignoring the lift, he walked down the stairs of the Consulate. He knew that she was dead. He imagined her lying naked in a wood, her even teeth ugly in a rictus, her white flesh as lifeless as the virgin modesty of the schoolgirl in the park. She hadn't been like a nymphomaniac, or even a sophisticated woman, when she'd kissed his cheek good-night. Like a schoolgirl herself, she'd still been blind to the icy coldness that answered her naivety. Inept and academic, words he had written about the city which had claimed her slipped through his mind. *In the church of Santa Croce you walk on tombs, searching for Giotto's Life of St Francis. In Savonarola's own piazza the grey stone features do not forgive the tumbling hair of pretty police girls or the tourists' easy ways.* Injustice and harsh ambition had made her city what it was, the violence of greed for centuries had been its bloodstream; beneath its tinsel skin there was an iron heart. *The Florentines, like true provincials, put work and money first. In the Piazza Signoria the pigeons breakfast off the excrement of the hackney horses: in Florence nothing is wasted.*

He left the American Consulate and slowly walked along the quay. The sun was hot, the traffic noisy. He crossed the street and looked down into the green water of the Arno, wondering if the dark shroud of Mrs Faraday's life had floated away through a night. In the galleries of the Uffizi he would move from Annunciation to Annunciation, Simone Martini's, Baldovinetti's, Lorenzo di Credi's, and all the others. He would catch a glimpse of her red coat in Santa Trinità, but the face would again be someone else's. She would call out from a gelateria, but the voice would be an echo in his memory.

He turned away from the river and at the same slow pace walked into the heart of the city. He sat outside a café in the Piazza della Repubblica, imagining her thoughts as she had lain in bed on that last night, smoking her cigarettes in the darkness. She had arrived at the happiest moment of love, when nothing was yet destroyed, when anticipation was a richness in itself. She'd thought about their walk in Maiano, how she'd bring the subject up again, how this time he'd say he'd be delighted. She'd thought about their being together in an apartment in the Palazzo Ricasoli, how this time it would be different. Already she had made up her mind: she would not ever return to the town where her husband owned a paper mill. 'I have never loved anyone like this,' she whispered in the darkness.

In his hotel bedroom he shaved and had a bath and put on a suit that had just been pressed. In a way that had become a ceremony for him since the evening he had first waited for

469

her there, he went at six o'clock to Doney's. He watched the
Americans drinking cocktails, knowing it was safe to be there
because she would not suddenly arrive. He listened to the music
she'd said she liked, and mourned her as a lover might.

Ind Aff –
or Out of Love in Sarajevo

FAY WELDON

THIS IS A sad story. It has to be. It rained in Sarajevo, and we had expected fine weather.

The rain filled up Sarajevo's pride, two footprints set into a pavement which mark the spot where the young assassin Princip stood to shoot the Archduke Franz Ferdinand and his wife. (Don't forget his wife: everyone forgets his wife, the archduchess.) That was in the summer of 1914. Sarajevo is a pretty town, Balkan style, mountain-rimmed. A broad, swift, shallow river runs through its centre, carrying the mountain snow away, arched by many bridges. The one nearest the two footprints has been named the Princip Bridge. The young man is a hero in these parts. Not only does he bring in the tourists – look, look, the spot, the very spot! – but by his action, as everyone knows, he lit a spark which fired the timber which caused World War 1 which crumbled the Austro-Hungarian Empire, the crumbling of which made modern Yugoslavia possible. Forty million dead (or was it thirty?) but who cares? So long as he loved his country.

The river, they say, can run so shallow in the summer it's known derisively as 'the wet road'. Today, from what I could see through the sheets of falling rain, it seemed full enough. Yugoslavian streets are always busy – no one stays home if they can help it (thus can an indecent shortage of housing space create a sociable nation) and it seemed as if by common consent a shield of bobbing umbrellas had been erected two metres high to keep the rain off the streets. It just hadn't worked around Princip's corner.

'Come all this way,' said Peter, who was a professor of classical history, 'and you can't even see the footprints properly, just two undistinguished puddles.' Ah, but I loved him. I shivered for his disappointment. He was supervising my thesis on varying concepts of morality and duty in the early Greek States as evidenced in their poetry and drama. I was dependent upon him for my academic future. He said I had a good mind but not a first-class mind and somehow I didn't take it as an insult. I had a feeling first-class minds weren't all that good in bed.

Sarajevo is in Bosnia, in the centre of Yugoslavia, that grouping of unlikely states, that distillation of languages into the phonetic reasonableness of Serbo-Croatian. We'd sheltered from the rain in an ancient mosque in Serbian Belgrade; done the same in a monastery in Croatia; now we spent a wet couple of days in Sarajevo beneath other people's umbrellas. We planned to go on to Montenegro, on the coast, where the fish and the artists come from, to swim and lie in the sun, and recover from the exhaustion caused by the sexual and moral torments of the last year. It couldn't possibly go on raining for ever. Could it? Satellite pictures showed black clouds swishing gently all over Europe, over the Balkans, into Asia – practically all the way from Moscow to London, in fact. It wasn't that Peter and myself were being singled out. No. It was raining on his wife, too, back in Cambridge.

Peter was trying to decide, as he had been for the past year, between his wife and myself as his permanent life partner. To this end we had gone away, off the beaten track, for a holiday; if not with his wife's blessing, at least with her knowledge. Were we really, truly suited? We had to be sure, you see, that this was more than just any old professor-student romance; that it was the Real Thing, because the longer the indecision went on the longer Mrs Piper would be left dangling in uncertainty and distress. They had been married for twenty-four years; they had stopped loving each other a long time ago, of course – but there would be a fearful personal and practical upheaval entailed if he decided to leave permanently and shack up, as he put it, with me. Which I certainly wanted him to do. I loved him. And so far I was winning hands down. It didn't seem much of a contest at all, in fact. I'd been cool and thin and informed on the seat next to him in a Zagreb theatre (Mrs Piper was sweaty and only liked telly); was now eager and anxious for social and political instruction in Sarajevo (Mrs Piper spat in the face of knowledge, he'd once told me); and planned to be lissom (and I thought topless but I hadn't quite decided: this might be the area where the age difference showed) while I splashed and shrieked like a bathing belle in the shallows of the Montenegrin coast. (Mrs Piper was a swimming coach: I imagined she smelt permanently of chlorine.)

In fact so far as I could see, it was no contest at all between his wife and myself. But Peter liked to luxuriate in guilt and indecision. And I loved him with an inordinate affection.

Princip's prints are a metre apart, placed as a modern cop on a training shoot-out would place his feet – the left in front at a slight outward angle, the right behind, facing forward. There seemed great energy focused here. Both hands on the gun, run, stop, plant the feet, aim, fire! I could see the footprints well enough, in spite of Peter's complaint. They were clear enough to me.

We went to a restaurant for lunch, since it was too wet to do what we loved to do: that is, buy bread, cheese, sausage, wine, and go off somewhere in our hired car, into the woods or the hills, and picnic and make love. It was a private restaurant – Yugoslavia went over to a mixed capitalist-communist economy years back, so you get either the best or worst of both systems, depending on your mood – that is to say, we knew we would pay more but be given a choice. We chose the wild boar.

'Probably ordinary pork soaked in red cabbage water to darken it,' said Peter. He was not in a good mood.

Cucumber salad was served first.

'Everything in this country comes with cucumber salad,' complained Peter. I noticed I had become used to his complaining. I supposed that when you had been married a little you simply wouldn't hear it. He was forty-six and I was twenty-five.

'They grow a lot of cucumber,' I said.

'If they can grow cucumbers,' Peter then asked, 'why can't they grow *mange-tout*?' It seemed a why-can't-they-eat-cake sort of argument to me, but not knowing enough about horticulture not to be outflanked if I debated the point, I moved the subject on to safer ground.

'I suppose Princip's action couldn't really have started World War 1,' I remarked. 'Otherwise, what a thing to have on your conscience! One little shot and the deaths of thirty million.'

'Forty,' he corrected me. Though how they reckon these things and get them right I can't imagine. 'Of course he didn't start the war. That's just a simple tale to keep the children quiet. It takes more than an assassination to start a war. What happened was that the build-up of political and economic tensions in the Balkans was such that it had to find some release.'

'So it was merely the shot that lit the spark that fired the timber that started the war, etcetera?'

'Quite,' he said. 'World War 1 would have had to have started sooner or later.'

'A bit later or a bit sooner,' I said, 'might have made the difference of a million or so; if it was you on the battlefield in the mud and the rain you'd notice; exactly when they fired the starting-pistol; exactly when they blew the final whistle. Is that what they do when a war ends; blow a whistle? So that everyone just comes in from the trenches.'

But he wasn't listening. He was parting the flesh of the soft collapsed orangey-red pepper which sat in the middle of his cucumber salad; he was carefully extracting the pips. His nan had once told him they could never be digested, would stick inside and do terrible damage. I loved him for his dexterity and patience with his knife and fork. I'd finished my salad yonks ago, pips and all. I was hungry. I wanted my wild boar.

Peter might be forty-six, but he was six foot two and grizzled and muscled with it, in a dark-eyed, intelligent, broad-jawed kind of way. I adored him. I loved to be seen with him. 'Muscular academic, not weedy academic' as my younger sister Clare once said. 'Muscular academic is just a generally superior human being: everything works well from the brain to the toes. Weedy academic is when there isn't enough vital energy in the person, and the brain drains all the strength from the other parts.' Well, Clare should know. Clare is only twenty-three, but of the superior human variety kind herself, vividly pretty, bright and competent – somewhere behind a heavy curtain of vibrant red hair, which she only parts for effect. She had her first degree at twenty. Now she's married to a Harvard professor of economics seconded to the United Nations. She can even cook. I gave up competing yonks ago. Though she too is capable of self-deception. I would say her husband was definitely of the weedy academic rather than the muscular academic type. And they have to live in Brussels.

The archduke's chauffeur had lost his way, and was parked on the corner trying to recover his nerve when Princip came running out of a café, planted his feet, aimed, and fired. Princip was nineteen – too young to hang. But they sent him to prison for life and, since he had TB to begin with, he only lasted three years. He died in 1918, in an Austrian prison. Or perhaps it was more than TB: perhaps they gave him a hard time, not learning till later, when the Austro-Hungarian Empire collapsed, that he was a hero. Poor Princip, too young to die – like so many other millions. Dying for love of a country.

'I love you,' I said to Peter, my living man, progenitor already of three children by his chlorinated, swimming-coach wife.

'How much do you love me?'

'Inordinately! I love you with inordinate affection.' It was a joke between us. Ind Aff!

'Inordinate affection is a sin,' he'd told me. 'According to the Wesleyans. John Wesley himself worried about it to such a degree he ended up abbreviating it in his diaries. Ind Aff. He maintained that what he felt for young Sophy, the eighteen-year-old in his congregation, was not Ind Aff, which bears the spirit away from God towards the flesh: he insisted that what he felt was a pure and spiritual, if passionate, concern for her soul.'

Peter said now, as we waited for our wild boar, and he picked over his pepper, 'Your Ind Aff is my wife's sorrow, that's the trouble.' He wanted, I knew, one of the long half-wrangles, half soul-sharings that we could keep going for hours, and led to piercing pains in the heart which could only be made better in bed. But our bedroom at the Hotel Europa was small and dark and looked out into the well of the building – a punishment room if ever there was one. (Reception staff did sometimes take against us.) When Peter had tried to change it in his quasi-Serbo-Croatian, they'd shrugged their Bosnian shoulders and pretended not to understand, so we'd decided to put up with it. I did not fancy pushing hard single beds together – it seemed easier not to have the pain in the heart in the first place. 'Look,' I said, 'this holiday is supposed to be just the two of us, not Mrs Piper as well. Shall we talk about something else?'

★

Do not think that the archduke's chauffeur was merely careless, an inefficient chauffeur, when he took the wrong turning. He was, I imagine, in a state of shock, fright, and confusion. There had been two previous attempts on the archduke's life since the cavalcade had entered town. The first was a bomb which got the car in front and killed its driver. The second was a shot fired by none other than young Princip, which had missed. Princip had vanished into the crowd and gone to sit down in a corner café and ordered coffee to calm his nerves. I expect his hand trembled at the best of times – he did have TB. (Not the best choice of assassin, but no doubt those who arrange these things have to make do with what they can get.) The archduke's chauffeur panicked, took the wrong road, realised what he'd done, and stopped to await rescue and instructions just outside the café where Princip sat drinking his coffee.

'What shall we talk about?' asked Peter, in even less of a good mood.

'The collapse of the Austro–Hungarian Empire?' I suggested. 'How does an empire collapse? Is there no money to pay the military or the police, so everyone goes home? Or what?' He liked to be asked questions.

'The Hungro–Austrarian,' said Peter to me, 'didn't so much collapse as fail to exist any more. War destroys social organisations. The same thing happened after World War 2. There being no organised bodies left between Moscow and London – and for London read Washington, then as now – it was left to these two to put in their own puppet governments. Yalta, 1944. It's taken the best part of forty-five years for nations of West and East Europe to remember who they are.'

'Austro–Hungarian,' I said, 'not Hungro–Austrarian.'

'I didn't say Hungro–Austrarian,' he said.

'You did,' I said.

'Didn't,' he said. 'What the hell are they doing about our wild boar? Are they out in the hills shooting it?'

My sister Clare had been surprisingly understanding about Peter. When I worried about him being older, she pooh-poohed it; when I worried about him being married, she said, 'Just go for it, sister. If you can unhinge a marriage, it's ripe for unhinging, it would happen sooner or later, it might as well be you. See a catch, go ahead and catch! Go for it!'

Princip saw the archduke's car parked outside, and went

476

for it. Second chances are rare in life: they must be responded to. Except perhaps his second chance was missing in the first place? Should he have taken his cue from fate, and just sat and finished his coffee, and gone home to his mother? But what's a man to do when he loves his country? Fate delivered the archduke into his hands: how could he resist it? A parked car, a uniformed and medalled chest, the persecutor of his country – how could Princip not, believing God to be on his side, but see this as His intervention, push his coffee aside and leap to his feet?

Two waiters stood idly by and watched us waiting for our wild boar. One was young and handsome in a mountainous Bosnian way – flashing eyes, hooked nose, luxuriant black hair, sensuous mouth. He was about my age. He smiled. His teeth were even and white. I smiled back, and instead of the pain in the heart I'd become accustomed to as an erotic sensation, now felt, quite violently, an associated yet different pang which got my lower stomach. The true, the real pain of Ind Aff!

'Fancy him?' asked Peter.

'No,' I said. 'I just thought if I smiled the wild boar might come quicker.'

The other waiter was older and gentler: his eyes were soft and kind. I thought he looked at me reproachfully. I could see why. In a world which for once, after centuries of savagery, was finally full of young men, unslaughtered, what was I doing with this man with thinning hair?

'What are you thinking of?' Professor Piper asked me. He liked to be in my head.

'How much I love you,' I said automatically, and was finally aware how much I lied. 'And about the archduke's assassination,' I went on, to cover the kind of tremble in my head as I came to my senses, 'and let's not forget his wife, she died too – how can you say World War 1 would have happened anyway? If Princip hadn't shot the archduke, something else, some undisclosed, unsuspected variable, might have come along and defused the whole political/military situation, and neither World War 1 nor 2 ever happened. We'll just never know, will we?'

I had my passport and my travellers' cheques with me. (Peter felt it was less confusing if we each paid our own way.) I stood up, and took my raincoat from the peg.

'Where are you going?' he asked, startled.

'Home,' I said. I kissed the top of his head, where it was balding. It smelt gently of chlorine, which may have come from thinking about his wife so much, but might merely have been that he'd taken a shower that morning. ('The water all over Yugoslavia, though safe to drink, is unusually chlorinated': Guide Book.) As I left to catch a taxi to the airport the younger of the two waiters emerged from the kitchen with two piled plates of roasted wild boar, potatoes duchesse, and stewed peppers. ('Yugoslavian diet is unusually rich in proteins and fats': Guide Book.) I could tell from the glisten of oil that the food was no longer hot, and I was not tempted to stay, hungry though I was. Thus fate – or was it Bosnian wilfulness? – confirmed the wisdom of my intent.

And that was how I fell out of love with my professor, in Sarajevo, a city to which I am grateful to this day, though I never got to see very much of it, because of the rain.

It was a silly sad thing to do, in the first place, to confuse mere passing academic ambition with love: to try to outdo my sister Clare. (Professor Piper was spiteful, as it happened, and did his best to have my thesis refused, but I went to appeal, which he never thought I'd dare, and won. I had a first-class mind after all.) A silly sad episode, which I regret. As silly and sad as Princip, poor young man, with his feverish mind, his bright tubercular cheeks, and his inordinate affection for his country, pushing aside his cup of coffee, leaping to his feet, taking his gun in both hands, planting his feet, aiming, and firing – one, two, three shots – and starting World War 1. The first one missed, the second got the wife (never forget the wife), and the third got the archduke and a whole generation, and their children, and their children's children, and on and on for ever. If he'd just hung on a bit, there in Sarajevo, that June day, he might have come to his senses. People do, sometimes quite quickly.

Bank Holiday

JONATHAN WILSON

WE TAKE THE 226 bus from Dollis Hill to Golders Green Station. Along the way the houses expand and beautify. Then we hop on the single-decker 210 to Hampstead Heath. Dennis asks me, 'How many ears has Davy Crockett got?' I shake my head. 'Three,' he says. 'His left ear, his right ear, and his wild front ear.' As soon as we're off the bus we cross the no man's land near the Whitestone Pond and enter the wild frontier of the Heath. No fooling around with the coconut shy, the penny roll, or even the bumper cars. We head straight for the Rat Woman. It is August, 1967, and you can still catch a freak show at the funfair.

The entrance to the tent stands a throwback to the previous decade, a pointy-faced, vicious spiv, hair slicked back, Teddy-boy jacket, black drainpipe jeans, winkle-picker Chelsea boots covered in mud. He wants half a crown from each of us. Dennis says, 'Who are you – the Rat *Man*?' El Spivo doesn't like this. He mentions something about slicing our fucking noses off. Dennis is extremely tough, so it's OK to laugh in his face and enter the tent.

It's very hot under the canvas, and there's a pungent odour coming from the cage. At first we can't see her, because there's a whole crowd of men (and a few women) standing in front of us, trying to get a look. OK, here she is, lying stretched out in this brown wire thing that looks as though it's been put together from old fire guards. 'What? Not even tits?' says an old geezer next to us, to no one in particular. 'Shut your *fucking* mouth,' the Rat Woman replies from her supine position.

She's in a full-body leotard: the top half is sheer, with tufts of brown hair glued over her nipples. The bottom is fake rat skin with a long tail attached. She has narrow, sharp-looking, protruding front teeth, which may have got her the job in the first place. It's not the tail that gets me, or the brown and white rats crawling all over her, as if she were in a sewer – it's her long, brown, varnished, witchy nails. 'Imagine being scratched by those,' I say to Dennis, nudging him and pointing.

'Nasty,' Dennis replies.

We're up close now, with our faces almost pressed against the wire. I feel some bastard trying to pick my back pocket, but as there's nothing in it, he's going to be out of luck. 'Can I *do* something for you gentlemen?' asks the Rat Woman, giving a heavy stare and daring us to linger.

'Bite their balls off,' yells some loud-mouth from the back of the crowd.

I say to the Rat Woman, 'Want some cheese?'

'I'll give you cheese,' she screams. 'I'll give you fucking cheese.'

Before I can get out of the way she scoops up a handful of rat shit and sawdust and throws it through the cage at my face. I try to duck but get caught behind the ear. I can feel little pellets in my hair.

We get down on our hands and knees and crawl to the side of the tent. Some kid is lying there, trying to saw through one of the guy ropes with a tiny penknife. 'What are you doing?' Dennis asks him, stupidly.

The kid jabs the knife at us. 'Watch it,' I say. (He's very small.)

We roll out of the fetid tent and into some muddy caravan ruts. Behind our heads the generator for the merry-go-round is giving off a high-pitched whine, as if it's going to explode. '*Fun*fair – they call this a *fun* fair,' says Dennis.

'Well,' I reply, 'aren't you having fun?'

We scramble down the Heath to the lower part of the fair. Outside the Big Wheel, we bump into beautiful Pat McNally from our school, and her new boyfriend. 'This is Lemberg,' she says in her Wembley whine. 'He's an artist.'

Dennis looks at me. I know what he's thinking. Pat's last boyfriend, Slim, was a consummate mod: scooter, parka, big Who fan, the whole thing. But he's dead. Done in by the

Chinese heroin that blew through our school last year like a fat death wind. This guy, Lemberg, looks like a poor substitute for Slim. 'Wanna see his studio?' Pat asks us. She doesn't bother to tell him our names.

We stand in front of this huge canvas that is a portrait of naked Lemberg, giant size, thick brushes in his hand, long thick tube of a penis hanging down. A black scrawl in the bottom-right-hand corner of the painting reads 'Drive your cart and your plough over the bones of the dead'. Lemberg sits at a table in the middle of his studio, rolling a joint. He's about thirty, maybe thirty-five. 'What's this, then?' says Dennis, pointing at the penis. 'You've been using your imagination a little, haven't you?'

'Oh no,' says Pat, matter-of-factly, 'he does have a big one. Don't you?' Lemberg doesn't respond. He keeps sorting through his bag of grass. He's humming a little song to himself, like Winnie-the-Pooh:

> What you don't need
> stalks and seeds.

We respect almost anything Pat says (1) because of her recent bereavement, and (2) because she knows Twiggy. I have a third reason for respecting her. For some months she has been the object of all my fantasies, in most of which she is naked and hard at work.

Dennis starts to wander around the studio, picking up tubes of paint and squeezing blobs of colour onto his hands. Then he wipes them on his jeans. 'Look,' he says, pointing at his trousers. 'Art.'

It seems all right to be thirty-five and an artist in trendy Hampstead. You get a big bed in the middle of an open space (it's rumpled, and a not-so-small patch of dry brown blood is on the undersheet), and this gorgeous sixteen-year-old girl whom we're all, me especially, dying for, and you get to paint yourself naked. 'Leave the paint alone,' says Lemberg. Ah, he speaks. And what do you know? He's one of us. He's from our part of town. So there's not a lot we can do now, because he knows who we are, and we know who he is. That's all it takes in London, really – someone opening his mouth.

We smoke the dope. 'This is home-grown,' says Lemberg.

'You should see his set-up,' Pat adds. 'There's a whole little room covered in tinfoil, with studio lights he got from a closed-down theatre.'

'Ever try hash oil?' asks Lemberg. 'This is coated in hash oil. Makes for a trippy experience.'

'What?' Dennis asks. 'Are you telling me we can expect to hallucinate?'

'What you expect and what you get may turn out to be two different things entirely.'

'Very meaningful,' Dennis replies.

After about ten minutes Dennis says to me, 'It's big-socks time.' He's referring to that moment when the dope effects start to creep into your knees, then down towards your calves, where they irritate the area just above where the sock line would be if you were wearing big socks. Lemberg has moved over to Pat and is trying to kiss her. She keeps pushing his face away, but only in a kind of 'Just wait until they've gone' way. We go.

Outside, I look at the normally invisible hairs on the back of my hand and see a waving cornfield. 'That's a hash-oil magnification you're experiencing,' says Dennis when I describe what's going on. 'Your powers of perception have been heightened.'

Soon after, I have this idea about running up an Israeli flag on our school flagpole. I use my sharpened powers to imagine a huge blue-on-white Star of David whipping in the wind over Brondesbury, and Queens Park and Paddington. Last week, Owen (Religious Instruction) beat me badly with the 'kosher cosh' for talking in class. I have a deeper grudge against Beaglehole for humiliating me during gym. I was wearing red shorts instead of regulation black. 'Wolfson,' he said, 'this isn't a Jewish fashion show.' This kind of thing ('Cohen, stand in the wastepaper bin – you're rubbish') goes on all the time in our school, which mingles semi-intelligent socio-paths from Kilburn with recidivist Jewish kids from Willesden and Wembley.

The question is: Where to get the flag? Dennis, who has an agile but generally impractical mind, immediately suggests that we steal one. But where from? We stand outside a house with a blue plaque, where John Keats lived two hundred years ago. Dennis says, 'When was the last time you saw an Israeli flag? I mean one within graspable distance.'

I totter around on some blurry edge in my mind. I know where I'm going, but I don't quite want to get there. Eventually, I say, 'In synagogue, when your cousin Norman was bar mitzvahed. Don't you remember? They unfurled it behind him when he got his J.N.F. trees.'

'What's the problem?' Dennis yells up, in what he thinks is a whisper. I'm lying, like a fish on a platter, on one half of a huge hexagonal stained-glass window that we have managed to push open with a pole. I've scaled the concrete wall, and the friable paint job is all over my hands and clothes. My face is up against the mane of a tawny Lion of Judah. The glass, bonded in metal, feels like it's going to shatter at any minute. Meanwhile, I'm tipping forward but can't slide through. I'm thinking about the fulcrum, and how poorly I did in Physics – '26% (Highest in Form 97%); Diligence C; Comments: Lazy and incompetent' – when suddenly I'm head first on the padded seats of the temple.

Someone has been here before us. The whole place is a mess. There are prayer books with pages torn out and strewn all over the place, and ripped prayer shawls on the floor. One of the red velvet curtains in front of the ark has been slashed, as have the puffy seats where the synagogue wardens sit in their shiny top hats and tails.

I let Dennis in through the side door. He looks around. 'Someone's been enjoying themselves,' he says. 'Any sign of the flag?'

Even I am appalled by his insouciance. 'This is a serious thing,' I say.

We take a quick tour. It's mostly slashing and ripping. There is one piece of nasty art work – a black swastika on one of the side walls – but it looks as if they ran out of paint. It occurs to us both, at about the same time, that if anyone were to come in now we would have a lot of explaining to do.

We're on our way out (sans flag) when we hear the noise. It seems to be coming from the pipes in the organ loft. It's a tenebrous, adult-male groaning. When we get up there, we find the janitor. His face is blotchy and bruised; there's a crescent of half-dried blood under each of his nostrils. 'I tried to stop 'em,' he says. 'Those bastards. They come in out of the park. What do they want to do a thing like this for?'

Dennis looks around – he's developing a volcanic glow in his eyes. I've seen it before; it merges anger and impatience, and is sometimes a prelude to violence.

'Do you know where the flag is?' he asks.

'Who cares about the fucking flag?' I say, and for a moment

483

it looks as if the two of us might get into a fight (not good for me).

For a while, the janitor and I try to clear up the mess. Dennis goes into the back office to look for the flag. I stuff a lot of the torn pages under someone's seat. Then I get fed up, and I sit down and start reading. 'Lust not after her beauty in thine heart; neither let her take thee with her eyelids. For by means of a whorish woman a man is brought to a piece of bread.' What piece of bread? I try to think about Pat McNally's eyelids, but they're impossible to visualise. Eyebrows, yes – average thickness, blonde. A guide to her pubic hair? Could be.

The janitor says he's going to phone the police. Dennis appears with the flag (not quite as big as I'd hoped). He's already attached it to its staff. I ask the janitor, 'Mind if we borrow this for a while?'

He shrugs, as if to say 'Makes no difference now.'

Beyond the synagogue are the open fields of Gladstone Park. We unfurl the flag and run with it streaming behind us like a medieval banner. A couple of stray dogs chase us for a while. Dennis sends them off by aiming kicks towards their faces. Kids are on the swings, and forming lines up by the stone fountain. In the distance, past the muddy duck pond, a rainbow arches over the weeping willows and the high, thin branches of the silver birches. It must have rained while we were inside. A small girl comes up to us. She says, 'I know how doggies talk.' She gives a few yelps, then a growl, followed by a heavy bark.

Outside Electric House, on Willesden Lane, we wait a long time for a bus. Then they don't want to let us on with the flag. There's an inspector on board. 'Suppose we stop suddenly,' he says. 'You could lance that right through someone's lungs.'

The conductor adds, 'More like driving a stake through a person's heart.'

Dennis says, 'Or sticking a javelin up your arse.'

We walk.

On the way I try to get Dennis to talk about something that matters. What I want to get at is this: Why would an attractive sixteen-year-old girl give herself over – body and possibly soul – to someone like Lemberg? Now, from Lemberg's point of view it's all very clear – he wants to crush her bones. But from Pat's?

Of course, I have this special interest. In the immediate post-Slim mourning period ('Drive your cart and your plough over the bones of the dead') I had one slow dance with Pat at the Starlite Ballroom, Greenford. She wore a black miniskirt with a semi-transparent pink blouse that revealed something she told me was called a 'no-bra bra'. Her body's imprint lasted all night, as if I were sand.

When I broach the subject with Dennis I quickly discover that he has no interest in the whys and wherefores of anything. He is all business and to the point. The solid rope of dailiness is what he likes to climb. If I were to say now, as I feel like saying, 'I'm losing my enthusiasm for this flag adventure, because the day has already served up more than I can digest,' he would turn on me.

Once, Dennis brought an axe to school. During lunch break he chopped up his desk. At first, I thought this was a familiar, if extreme, assault upon the seat of learning. Then I realised he was trying to break the frozen sea within him. We stuffed the splintered wood in our gym bags and took the afternoon off to ride the tube. As we came to the semi-deserted stations at the northern end of the old Bakerloo line, Kingsbury, Queensbury, and Canons Park, we waited until the doors were about to close, then threw the wood onto the rails.

But is this what I really want? Vandalism and adventure? All summer I have been carrying around the possibilities for change, for shifting my allegiances. They rise and fall, like unexpected adolescent erections, and, appropriately, converge on issues of hardness and softness. I am awed by the former, embodied in Dennis, but generally inclined by temperament and character, towards the latter. Somewhere inside I want to surround a girl – well, Pat McNally – with the most insipid and conventional accoutrements of love.

Now, don't get me wrong – I had seen the brown-red stain on Lemberg's bed, and I knew all about the body's betrayals. What is more, almost my entire education in the sex area derived from dirty jokes, poorly photographed barbershop magazines, and badly drawn graffiti. The previous year, in order to counter-balance my developing vulgarity, my father had dragged me, one Friday night, to a small Sephardic synagogue in London's East End. He wanted me to hear a group of old men chant the Song of Songs – or Canticle of Canticles, as it was called in the prayer book. (I read this, of course, as 'Testicle of Testicles'.) But even though I had listened and learned about the little foxes, the breasts like young roes feeding among the lilies, and

485

the importance of eating the honeycomb with the honey, the notion of a higher love had not really sunk in. It is not until now, walking down Salisbury Road with this stupid flag, that the weak sun of consideration and love, hidden all season long, begins to penetrate the thick clouds of boorishness and lust that are gathered around me.

What I want, I now realise, is more Pat Woman than Rat Woman. Lemberg's bed has been a reminder that you can't have one without the other, but I have reached a decision to approach the hybrid with poetry rather than teenage aggression. I begin this excursion into 'softness' by saying to Dennis, 'Do you know whose house we were outside back in Hampstead?'

'No.'

'Keats's.'

'So fucking what?'

This is no more than I expect, but the fact that I have raised the subject is, in itself, a significant beginning.

We arrive at the school. It is late afternoon. The turbulent sun is sending a bright glare to heat things up. Dennis has red hair, and because, at this moment, it matches the colour of the sun, I start to feel oppressed by Dennis's head. I say, 'Why don't you go and raise the flag yourself?'

'What?' he replies. 'After coming all this way?' He tries to fire me up by reminding me of some heinous teacher acts. 'Do you remember when Fanny wouldn't let Sless go home early on Friday nights? How about when Fogwell threw you against the wall after your father wrote that bar-mitzvah-lesson note?' But this is second-division stuff, and Dennis knows it. He hadn't cared himself that Sless walked five miles to his Orthodox home instead of catching the bus. He had laughed, along with all the others, when I had my encounter with the wall.

'No,' I say. 'You go up there. I've had it.'

Dennis starts to move very fast. For a moment I feel as if I'm a part of observed Nature. Offscreen, someone is whispering, 'The alpha male, by displaying resolution and a sense of urgency, wishes to indicate that his companion is a coward.' Dennis throws the flag over the fence and climbs after it. I figure he'll have to get up on the gym roof, which may take him a while, and then make his way along to the crenellated turret that houses the flagpole. I've got at least twenty minutes.

I head into Queens Park and start walking towards the

bandstand. I think I'll find some shade, stretch out, meditate. Considering it's a holiday, the place is oddly deserted. Then I see why. About twenty teenagers are standing near the Pitch and Putt. They're carrying bicycle chains, golf clubs that they have stolen out of the shed, and some long sticks. They're on me before I can even think about running. I recognise a couple of them from the school for psychopaths a hundred yards down the road from our own.

First, it seems, they want to play. One of them, *Homo Kilburnus stupidus*, says, 'I didn't know Jews were allowed in this park.' His chief mate, a boy with a deceivingly innocent-looking outbreak of summer freckles on his face and a peacock tattooed on his bare chest, says, 'They're not.'

'So, what are you doing here?' the first says. 'Because you are a Jew. You are a *fucking* Jew, aren't you?'

I say, 'Yes.' This isn't bravery or defiance, because it absolutely doesn't matter what I say. 'A thing of beauty is a joy forever' or 'Fuck you, I'm Episcopalian.' – the consequences are going to be the same.

In case you think I'm taking all this with an air of cool detachment, I'm not. I shake and sweat and wait to get hit. There's a short interval while Freckles chivalrously challenges me to fight. I say, 'No, thanks.' Then he belts me in the face with a set of brass knuckles. I make myself fall down, and cover my head with my hands. I can feel the kicks coming in: nasty, sharp ones in the kidneys, and one to the head that feels as if it has broken my fingers. I'm praying that they lay off with the driving irons. I cry, choke, and bleed. For a moment I think they've stopped. I cough, and each breath brings a dragging, boiling, bubbling sound. But they're not done. Two of them pull out my arms while a third presses something into my back. A knife! I scream. They laugh. The bastards are all laughing. Someone says, 'Fuck off out of here.' I run, dribbling blood and mucus from my nose. Obviously, I haven't been stabbed. I feel my back – nothing. I reach a water fountain, sip, spit, and sip again. It is only when I take off my T-shirt to wipe my face that I see what they've done. Where once there was a blank, white space, the word 'Joo' is now inscribed; the two 'o's – jocularity or ignorance? I pull the stained, soaking T-shirt back on. It's hot enough to walk bare-chested, but I've been exposed, and I want to cover myself.

In the shade of a grey slate roof my bodyguard is asleep. The

Israeli flag which I had imagined rippling in waves of triumph, a shiny point of resistance in a constellation of hostility, droops in the windless early dusk. I can't blame Dennis for what has happened to me, although I sort of want to. We are thrown unprotected on the free, spinning world, and we have to take the blows when they come. They do come.

I try to think my beating through, and, on the way to the bus stop, I half manage it. I feel angry and impotent, no doubt about that. For a while, though, I affect a wounded-soldier aspect towards what I have been through. I say to myself, 'This is not all that unpleasant' – it's like the bruised fatigue that follows a hard soccer game. Then my kidneys start to ache, and I touch my swollen lips. Suddenly, I find myself in tears. There is nothing redeeming about my pain. It is hurt and humiliation, pure and simple, with its own vectors and swoops.

By the time I get back to Lemberg's, which takes a while, because I have trouble remembering where he lives, it's dark. There are iron clouds stamped in a blue-black sky, and all the warmth of the day has gone down with the sun. When she opens the door Pat looks at me, fails to register any shock, and says, 'Been fightin'?' 'Sort of,' I reply. Over her shoulder I see Lemberg at work. He's directing a nude model, a skinny girl with long black hair, and conical breasts like saltshakers. I suppose he's going to sketch her. As I move in through the door the girl takes up a pose, and Lemberg moves close and adjusts her limbs.

Pat leads me past the artist at work. 'You'd better come into the bathroom,' she says. 'I'll wash your face.' There's a bright, naked light bulb hanging over the sink. She touches a cold sponge to my lips and washes the caked blood from my face. I think I might lie and tell her that Dennis and I vanquished a bunch of hard nuts, but instead, I submit to her ministrations. I look in the mirror and review the copper bruises on my jaw and around my cheekbones. The door of the bathroom is open and behind me I can see Lemberg leaning forward to kiss the model. Pat says, 'Wanna go to the pictures?'

In the Hampstead Everyman I think, for about an hour and a half, that I might take hold of her hand, but in the end I don't.

Biographical Notes on the Authors

MARTIN AMIS's novels include *The Rachel Papers, Money, London Fields, Time's Arrow* and *The Information*. He is also the author of two collections of essays, *The Moronic Inferno* and *Visiting Mrs Nabokov*. He lives in London.

MARGARET ATWOOD was born in Ottawa in 1939, and grew up in northern Quebec and Ontario, and in Toronto. She has lived in many other cities, including Boston, Vancouver, Edmonton, Montreal, Berlin and London, and has travelled extensively. She has published over twenty books, including novels, poetry and literary criticism.

J. G. BALLARD was born in Shanghai, China. After the attack on Pearl Harbor, Ballard and his family were interned by the Japanese in a civilian prison camp. They returned to England in 1946. In 1956 his first story was published in *New Worlds*. His first novel, *The Drowned World*, was published in 1962. *Empire of the Sun*, a novel based on his experiences in China, was published in 1984 and won several prizes and was filmed by Steven Spielberg. In 1991 *The Kindness of Women*, sequel to *Empire of the Sun*, was published. His most recent novel is the highly acclaimed *Rushing To Paradise*.

JULIAN BARNES is the author of seven novels, which have been translated into more than twenty languages. In France he is the only writer to have been awarded both the Prix Médicis (for *Flaubert's Parrot*) and the Prix Fémina (for *Talking It Over*). In 1993 he was awarded the Shakespeare Prize by the FVS Foundation in Hamburg, and in 1995 he was made an Officier de l'Ordre des Arts et Lettres.

BIOGRAPHICAL NOTES

WILLIAM BOYD has published six novels, including *Brazzaville Beach*, which won the James Tait Black Memorial Prize, and *The Blue Afternoon*, which won the 1993 *Sunday Express* Book of the Year Award. Eight of his screenplays have been filmed, recently *A Good Man in Africa*, based on his novel, which won the 1981 Whitbread Literary Award for the best first novel and a 1982 Somerset Maugham Award. His most recent book is a collection of short stories, *The Destiny of Nathalie X*.

GEORGE MACKAY BROWN has always lived in the Orkney Islands and all his novels, stories, and poems have island themes. He has long been 'a senior citizen' but still writes every morning. His latest novel is *Beside the Ocean of Time*.

A. S. BYATT's fiction includes *Sugar and Other Stories* and *The Matisse Stories* as well as the novels *The Game, Shadow of a Sun, The Virgin in the Garden, Still Life, Possession* and *Angels and Insects*.

ANGELA CARTER was born in Sussex in 1940 and read English at Bristol University. Her novels include *Shadow Dance, The Magic Toyshop, Heroes and Villains, Love, The Infernal Desire Machines of Dr Hoffman, The Passion of the New Eve, Nights at the Circus,* and *Wise Children*. She also published three collections of short stories, *The Bloody Chamber, Fireworks,* and *Black Venus,* and two works of non-fiction, *The Sadeian Women* and *Nothing Sacred*. She died in 1992. Chatto & Windus will publish her collected stories *Burning Your Boats* later this year.

DAVID CONSTANTINE, born 4 March 1944 in Salford, Lancs., has published five volumes of poetry and a novel, all with Bloodaxe Books. His collected short stories, including 'The Mermaid', were published in 1994 by Ryburn Publishing, in a volume entitled *Back at the Spike*.

MICHAEL DIBDIN was born in 1947, grew up in Northern Ireland and attended universities in England and then Canada, remaining there until 1975. He later spent four years in Italy. He now lives in the United States where his latest novel, *Dark Spectre*, is set.

MAVIS GALLANT, English-Canadian from Montreal, was educated in French and English. Worked at the National Film Board of Canada and was for six years features writer and columnist at *The Standard*, Montreal. Left for Europe in 1950, with the intention of writing fiction. Settled in Paris, 1960. Stories in the *New Yorker* from 1951 to the present. Ten collections of stories, two novels, a volume of essays and criticism and a play. Most recent publication: *Across the Bridge* (1993).

490

ROBERT GROSSMITH was born in Dagenham in 1954. He has a PhD in the fiction of Vladimir Nabokov and currently lives in Glasgow, where he works as a lexicographer. His first novel, *The Empire of Lights*, was published in 1990. His second novel, *Somebody's Life*, is nearing completion.

GEORGINA HAMMICK's stories have appeared widely in magazines and anthologies, and have been broadcast on BBC radio. She is the author of two collections of stories, *People For Lunch* and *Spoilt*, and the editor of *The Virago Book of Love and Loss*. She lives in Wiltshire and is currently at work on a novel.

STEVEN HEIGHTON was born in Toronto in 1961. His work has appeared in many magazines and anthologies in Canada, Britain, Europe and the United States and has been translated into French, German and Spanish. He has published three collections of poetry, most recently *The Ecstasy of Skeptics* (House of Anansi, 1994), and two collections of stories, *Flight Paths of the Emperor* (The Porcupine's Quill, 1992) and *On earth as it is* (The Porcupine's Quill, 1995).

CHRISTOPHER HOPE was born in Johannesburg. He has published five novels including *A Separate Development*, *The Hottentot Room*, and the Booker Prize shortlisted *Serenity House*. His sixth, *Darkest England*, will be published by Macmillan early next year. The story 'Maundy' is collected in *The Love Songs of Nathan J. Swirsky*.

JANETTE TURNER HOSPITAL is an Australian who now divides her time between Australia and North America. In 1994, she was writer-in-residence at the International Study Centre at Herstmonceux Castle in Sussex, where she has been working on her sixth novel. She has published five novels and two collections of short stories, and won a number of international literary awards. Her most recent novel, *The Last Magician* (1992) was shortlisted for Australia's Miles Franklin Award, Canada's Trillium Award, and the Commonwealth Writers' Prize.

COLUM McCANN was born in Dublin in 1965. His collection of short stories, *Fishing the Sloe-Black River*, won the Rooney Prize for Irish Literature in 1994. His first novel, *Songdogs*, was published in 1995. He has travelled extensively around North America, Europe and Asia. He presently lives in New York, where he teaches English.

MOY McCRORY was born in Liverpool to Irish-Catholic parents. She took a degree in art at Liverpool and Belfast, and is married with one child. She has published two collections of stories, *The Water's Edge* and *Bleeding Sinners*, and a novel, *The Fading Shrine*.

JOHN MCGAHERN was born in Dublin in 1934 and brought up in the west of Ireland. He is a graduate of University College, Dublin. He is the author of three collections of short stories and five highly acclaimed novels, *The Barracks* (1962), *The Dark* (1965), *The Leavetaking* (1974), *The Pornographer* (1979) and *Amongst Women* (1990). John McGahern lives in Co. Leitrim.

SHENA MACKAY was born in Edinburgh in 1944 and grew up in Kent and London, where she now lives. Her work includes the novellas *Toddler on the Run* and *Dust Falls on Eugene Schlumberger*, published when she was twenty, *Music Upstairs, Old Crow, An Advent Calendar, A Bowl of Cherries* (1984), *Redhill Rococo* (1986) – which won the Fawcett Prize – and *Dunedin* (1992). Her stories have been collected in one volume published by Penguin.

HILARY MANTEL was born in Derbyshire, and lived for some years in Africa and the Middle East. She is the author of seven novels, of which the latest is *An Experiment In Love* (1995).

ADAM MARS-JONES was born in London in 1954. Books: *Lantern Lecture* (1981), *Monopolies of Loss* (1992), *The Waters of Thirst* (1993), *Hypo Vanilla* (in preparation).

ALICE MUNRO was born in Canada. She is the author of *The Beggar Maid* (shortlisted for the Booker Prize), one other novel, and seven collections of short stories, most recently *Open Secrets* which won the W. H. Smith Literary Award. She has twice won the Governor General's Award, and her work appears regularly in the *New Yorker*. She lives in Ontario and British Columbia.

EDNA O'BRIEN is the author of several books, her most recent being *House of Splendid Isolation*. She divides her time between Ireland, London and New York. Her forthcoming book to be published in 1996 is called *Blood*.

DAVID PARK was born into a working-class Protestant family in Belfast and has spent most of his life living and working there. He is married and currently teaches in a small grammar school between Belfast and Downpatrick.

FREDERIC RAPHAEL has published numerous novels and collections of stories. He won the Royal Television Society's Writer of the Year Award for his series of plays, *The Glittering Prizes*, and an Oscar for the screenplay of *Darling*. Married, he lives in France and London.

RUTH RENDELL has won many awards since her first novel, *From Doon with Death*, published in 1964, including the Crime Writers' Association Gold Dagger for 1976's best crime novel, *A Demon in my View*, and the Arts Council National Book Awards – genre fiction – for *Lake of Darkness* in 1980.

In 1984 Ruth Rendell won her second Edgar from the Mystery Writers of America for best short story with 'The New Girl Friend', and in 1985 received the Silver Dagger for *The Tree of Hands*. In 1987, as Barbara Vine, she won the Gold Dagger for *A Fatal Inversion*.

Ruth Rendell won the *Sunday Times* Literary Award in 1990, and in 1991 she was awarded the Crime Writers' Association Cartier Diamond Dagger Award for outstanding contribution to the genre.

Her books have been translated into twenty-two languages and are also published to great acclaim in the United States.

Ruth Rendell is married and lives in a sixteenth-century farmhouse in Suffolk.

PATRICK ROGERS was born in 1955 in the United Kingdom, emigrated to Australia at the age of ten, and has alternated between the two countries since he was twenty. He writes radio and television drama as well as fiction. He now lives in Victoria, Australia.

SALMAN RUSHDIE, born in Bombay in 1947, is the author of *Grimus, Midnight's Children* (which won the Booker Prize), *Shame, The Satanic Verses, Haroun and the Sea of Stories* and *East, West*. He lives in London.

HELEN SIMPSON's first collection of short stories, *Four Bare Legs in a Bed*, won the *Sunday Times* Young Writer of the Year and the Somerset Maugham awards. Her suspense novella, *Flesh and Grass*, appeared with Ruth Rendell's *The Strawberry Tree* under the general title *Unguarded Hours*. In 1993 she was chosen as one of *Granta*'s Best of Young British Novelists. Her second volume of stories, *Dear George*, was published this spring.

JONATHAN TREITEL was born in London in 1959 and trained as a physicist and philosopher. He has lived in San Francisco, New York, Paris, Jerusalem and Tokyo and has travelled in seventy countries. His stories have appeared in the *New Yorker*, on BBC Radio and in numerous British magazines and anthologies. He is currently writing a collection of poems, a screenplay about Freud and angels, and a non-fiction book on the subject of time.

BIOGRAPHICAL NOTES

ROSE TREMAIN is a graduate of the University of East Anglia, and has taught a creative writing course at the University of Essex. She lives in Norwich with her husband, daughter and two stepchildren. In 1983 she was chosen as one of the Best British Young Novelists. She received the Dylan Thomas Award for the best story in 1984. She has published two children's books, four novels and two collections of stories. She writes for television and radio, and in ten years has had sixteen plays performed.

WILLIAM TREVOR was born in Mitchelstown, Co. Cork in 1928, and spent his childhood in provincial Ireland. He attended a number of Irish schools and later Trinity College, Dublin. He is a member of the Irish Academy of Letters.

Among his books are *The Old Boys* (1964), winner of the Hawthornden Prize, *The Children of Dynmouth* (1976), winner of the Whitbread Award, *Fools of Fortune* (1983), winner of the Whitbread Award, *The News from Ireland* (1986), *The Silence in the Garden* (1989), winner of the *Yorkshire Post* Book of the Year Award, and *Felicia's Journey* (1944), winner of the Whitbread and the *Sunday Express* Book of the Year Prizes. His seven volumes of previously published stories together with four new stories were published together as *The Collected Stories* (1992). He has also written plays for the stage, and for radio and television. In 1977 William Trevor was awarded an honorary CBE in recognition of his services to literature.

FAY WELDON was born and brought up in New Zealand and went to St Andrew's University, where she graduated in Economics and Psychology. After a decade of odd jobs and hard times, she started writing and now, though primarily a novelist (*Praxis, Puffball, The Life and Loves of a She-Devil, The Shrapnel Academy, Leader of the Band* and *The Cloning of Joanna May*), she has also had two collections of short stories published (*Polarid* and *Watching Me, Watching You*) and writes radio and television plays.

JONATHAN WILSON was born in London in 1950 and educated at the University of Essex, Oxford and the Hebrew University of Jerusalem. He is the author of *Schoom*, a collection of short stories, and *The Hiding Room*, a novel to be published by Secker & Warburg in October. His short fiction, articles and essays appear frequently in the New Yorker. He is an Associate Professor in the English Department at Tufts University. He lives in Newton, Mass., with his wife and two sons.

Acknowledgements

'Career Move', copyright © Martin Amis 1992, was first published in the *New Yorker*, 29 June 1992, and is reprinted by permission of the author and Peters, Fraser & Dunlop, 503/4 The Chambers, Chelsea Harbour, London SW10 0XF.

'The Age of Lead', copyright © O. W. Toad Ltd 1991, was first published in *New Statesman & Society*, 20 July 1990, and also appears in Margaret Atwood's collection of short stories *Wilderness Tips*. It is reprinted by permission of the author, Curtis Brown, 28–29 Haymarket, London SW1Y 4SP and Phoebe Larmore, 228 Main Street, Venice, California 90291.

'Answers to a Questionnaire', copyright © J. G. Ballard 1985, was first published in *Ambit* 100 in 1985. It is contained in the collection *War Fever* published by HarperCollins/Flamingo, London and Farrar Straus, New York. The story is reproduced by permission of the author care of Margaret Hanbury, 27 Walcot Square, London SE11 4UB.

'Dragons', copyright © Julian Barnes 1990, was first published in *Granta* 34, autumn 1990, and is reprinted by permission of the author and Peters, Fraser & Dunlop, 503/4 The Chambers, Chelsea Harbour, London SW10 0XF.

'The Dream Lover', copyright © William Boyd 1993, was first published in *London Magazine*, February/March 1993, and is reprinted by permission of the author and Lemon, Unna & Durbridge, 24 Pottery Lane, Holland Park, London W11 4LZ.

ACKNOWLEDGEMENTS

'The Last Island Boy', copyright © George Mackay Brown 1985, was first published in the *Scotsman*, 24 December 1985, and is reprinted by permission of the author.

'Medusa's Ankles', copyright © A. S. Byatt 1990, was first published in *Woman's Journal*, September 1990, and is reprinted by permission of the author and Peters, Fraser & Dunlop, 503/4 The Chambers, Chelsea Harbour, London SE10 0XF.

''Tis Pity She's a Whore', copyright © Angela Carter 1988, was first published in *Granta* 25, autumn 1988, and is reprinted by permission of the estate of Angela Carter c/o author and Rogers, Coleridge & White, 20 Powis Mews, London W11 1JN.

'The Mermaid', copyright © David Constantine 1991, was first published in *Critical Quarterly* volume 33, number 3, autumn 1991, and is reprinted by permission of the author.

'A Death in the Family', copyright © Michael Dibdin 1990, was first published in *GQ*, December 1990, and is reprinted by permission of the author and Peters, Fraser & Dunlop, 503/4 The Chambers, Chelsea Harbour, London SW10 0XF.

'Forain', copyright © Mavis Gallant 1991, was first published in the *New Yorker*, 24 June 1991, and is reprinted by permission of the author and David Higham Assocs, 5–8 Lower John Street, Golden Square, London W1R 4HA.

'The Book of Ands', copyright © Robert Grossmith 1988, was first published in the *Critical Quarterly*, autumn 1988, and is reprinted by permission of the author.

'People for Lunch', copyright © Georgina Hammick 1986, was first published in *Stand* magazine, winter 1985–86, reprinted in *People for Lunch* (Methuen London) and reproduced by permission of the author and her publishers.

'Five Paintings of the New Japan', copyright © Steven Heighton 1991, was first published in *Stand* magazine and also appears in Steven Heighton's collection of short stories *Flight Paths of the Emperor*. It is reprinted by permission of the author and The Porcupine's Quill Inc., 68 Main St, Erin, Ontario N0B 1T0.

'Maundy', copyright © Christopher Hope 1992, was first published in the *New Yorker*, 1 June 1992, and is reprinted by permission of the author and Rogers Coleridge & White Ltd, 20 Powis Mews, London W11 1JN.

'Unperformed Experiments Have No Results', copyright © Janette Turner Hospital 1994, was first published in *Queen's Quarterly* (Canada), Volume 100 Number 4, winter 1994, and is reprinted by permission of the author and Mic Cheetham Associates, 138 Buckingham Palace Road, London SW1W 9SA.

'Sisters', copyright © Colum McCann 1992, was first published in *Analecta*, the Student Literary Journal of the University of Texas, and is reprinted by permission of the author and Sheil Land Associates Ltd, 43 Doughty Street, London WC1N 2LF.

'The Wrong Vocation', copyright © Moy McCrory 1989, was first published in *Critical Quarterly* vol. 31 no 1, and is reprinted by permission of the author and Anthony Sheil Associates Ltd, 43 Doughty Street, London WC1N 2LF.

'Creatures of the Earth', copyright © John McGahern 1994, was first published in *Granta* 49, winter 1994, and is reprinted by permission of the author and A. M. Heath, 79 St Martin's Lane, London WC2N 4AA.

'A Pair of Spoons', copyright © Shena Mackay 1990, was first published in *Critical Quarterly*, volume 32, number 1, spring 1990, and is reprinted by permission of the author and Rogers, Coleridge & White, 20 Powis Mews, London W11 1JN.

'Alas for the Egg', copyright © Hilary Mantel 1986, was first published in the *London Magazine*, December 1986/January 1987, and is reprinted by permission of the author and A. M. Heath & Co Ltd, 79 St Martin's Lane, London WC2N 4AA.

'Remission', copyright © Adam Mars-Jones 1987, was first published in *Ambit* 107, 1987, and is reprinted by permission of the author and Peters, Fraser & Dunlop, 503/4 The Chambers, Chelsea Harbour, London SW10 0XF.

'A Real Life', copyright © Alice Munro 1992, was first published in the *New Yorker*, 10 February 1992, and is reprinted by permission of the author, Virginia Barber Literary Agency, 101 Fifth Avenue, New York, NY 10003, USA, and Abner Stein, 10 Roland Gardens, London SW7 3PH.

497

ACKNOWLEDGEMENTS

'Wilderness', copyright © Edna O'Brien 1992, was first published in the *New Yorker*, 16 March 1992, and is reprinted by permission of the author and Aitken & Stone Ltd, 29 Fernshaw Road, London SW10 0TG.

'Oranges from Spain', copyright © David Park 1989, was first published in *Critical Quarterly*, vol. 31, number 2, and is reprinted by permission of the author and Anthony Sheil Associates Ltd, 43 Doughty Street, London WC1 NLF.

'A Fairly Regular Four', copyright © Volatic Ltd was first broadcast on BBC Radio 4 'Morning Story', 26 November 1990, and is reprinted here for the first time by permission of the author and Rogers, Coleridge & White, 20 Powis Mews, London W11 1JN.

'Burning End', copyright © Kingsmarkham Enterprises Ltd 1994, was first published in the *Spectator*, 17/24 December 1994, and is reprinted by permission of the author and Peters, Fraser & Dunlop, 503/4 The Chambers, Chelsea Harbour, London SW10 0XF.

'Notes of a Copernican Biographer', copyright © Patrick Rogers 1988, was first published in *Panurge* 8, April 1988, and is reprinted by permission of the author.

'Good Advice is Rarer than Rubies', copyright © Salman Rushdie 1987, was first published in the *New Yorker*, 22 June 1987, and is reprinted by permission of the author and Aitken & Stone Ltd, 29 Fernshaw Road, London SW10 0TG.

'Good Friday, 1663', copyright © Helen Simpson 1987, was first published in the *Listener*, 3 September 1987, and is reprinted by permission of the author and Peters, Fraser & Dunlop, 503/4 The Chambers, Chelsea Harbour, London SW10 0XF.

'Stalin, Stalin, and Stalin', copyright © Jonathan Treitel 1992, was first published in the *New Yorker*, 21 September 1992, and is reprinted by permission of the author.

'Two of Them', copyright © Rose Tremain 1992, was first published in *Marie Claire*, August 1992, and is reprinted by permission of the author and Richard Scott Simon Ltd, 43 Doughty Street, London WC1N 2LF.

'Cocktails at Doney's', copyright © William Trevor 1985, was first published in the *New Yorker*, 8 April 1985, and is reprinted by

ACKNOWLEDGEMENTS

permission of the author care of Peters, Fraser & Dunlop, 503/4 The Chambers, Chelsea Harbour, London SW10 0XF.

'Ind Aff – *or* Out of Love in Sarajevo', copyright © Fay Weldon 1988, was first published in the *Observer* magazine, 7 August 1988, and is reprinted by permission of the author and Ed Victor Ltd, 6 Bayley Street, Bedford Square, London WC1B 3HB.

'Bank Holiday', copyright © Jonathan Wilson 1993, was first published in the *New Yorker*, 11 January 1993, and is reprinted by permission of the author.

We are grateful to the editors of the publications in which the stories first appeared for permission to reproduce them in this volume.

Anyone wishing to reprint any of the stories elsewhere or in translation should approach the individual authors through their literary agents as indicated above or care of William Heinemann Ltd.

Index to *Best Short Stories* 1986–1995

INDEX TO *BEST SHORT STORIES* 1986–1995

502

INDEX TO *BEST SHORT STORIES* 1986–1995